THE MARKED DRAGON PRINCE

COMPLETE SERIES

JEN L. GREY

JEN L. GREY

RUTHLESS MATE

THE MARKED DRAGON PRINCE TRILOGY 1

THE LUMP in my throat was so bulky, I couldn't swallow. I placed one hand on the back of the black leather sofa and ran the other down my stomach, where it hit the black belt of my short polka-dotted dress. I couldn't fathom what might be so urgent that Drake Hale, heir to a billion-dollar company, would show up *here* at eight on a Friday night.

I'd arrived home in Asheville, North Carolina, just an hour ago to stay for a few weeks before starting med school at UNC this summer, and he'd come knocking about fifteen minutes ago. I'd let him in and pointed to the door that led to the finished basement where my stepdad's office was.

My twin half siblings didn't even glance up from whatever video game they were playing. I hadn't gotten more than a *hi* from them since getting back, which...wasn't abnormal.

Eva punched the buttons on her controller harder than necessary, a victorious grin spreading across her face. A lock of dark brown hair fell over the back of her white strapless shirt, and her steel blue eyes narrowed. "I told you I'd learned some things since the last time we played."

"I see that." Elliott scowled. The only difference between them appearance-wise was that he was male and a little taller. Also, his hair was shorter, but it still hung in his eyes. Everything else about them was like looking into a mirror. "How the hell is that possible? We just played a few nights ago."

"Where there's a will, there's a way," she sang as she continued to press the buttons on the controller.

If I left, I was certain neither of them would notice. "Aren't you at all curious why a certain visitor is here?" I asked.

"Not at all." Elliott leaned forward on the sofa, focusing on the flat-screen TV hanging on the dark gray wall. "The few times I saw him at Dad's office, he made me uncomfortable, so my motto is 'stay the fuck away.'"

"Elliott," I hissed. "Language." Before Mom passed away six years ago, she'd asked me to watch over the twins. She'd said she hated putting the burden on me, but she had no one else to ask since my stepdad had begun acting strangely. So here I was, trying to make her proud.

However, I couldn't stop wondering why the owner of the largest rental property company, whose assets my stepfather managed as part of his realty business, was visiting this late on a Friday night.

"Oh, please, Ev." Eva rolled her eyes but kept her attention glued to the game. "We're eighteen. We can totally cuss."

My heart panged. They were growing up quickly, and every passing year was another reminder of how long Mom had been gone. God, I missed her. She'd wanted me to change the world with my love of painting and art, but when cancer had stolen the only parent I'd ever known, I'd decided to change the world in a different way—through medicine. I didn't want another kid to lose a parent to this horrible disease. It had left me an orphan and my half siblings with only one parent.

Something boomed from downstairs, and the walls shook all the way up to the living room.

My lungs seized. That was *definitely* something. But the twins kept playing their game as if they hadn't noticed a thing.

Figures. This was another thing I'd have to deal with on my own.

I marched toward the white-framed door in the middle of the wall behind me. My black strappy heels clacked on the white oak floors as I walked past the sizable kitchen on the right.

As I put a hand on the doorknob, a deep, angry voice stopped me in my tracks. "Did you really think we wouldn't find out about what *you* did, Peter?" It was Drake. The man emanated power even when he wasn't speaking.

Peter had been Mom's husband, and he'd allowed me to live under this roof after she'd died. I couldn't stand idly by while Drake attacked him.

I inhaled deeply, straightened my shoulders, and cracked open the oak door. As quietly as possible, I slipped down a few of the dark gray carpeted steps and peeked into the basement.

My world tilted.

Drake stood behind my stepdad's cherrywood desk, leaning his more than seven-foot-tall frame over my stepdad in his leather desk chair, which had crashed into the white wall behind him. Drake's formidable muscles were evident through his black suit, and his onyx eyes narrowed as he grasped the black armrests. Despite the turmoil, his brown-black hair remained perfectly in place, styled upward in small spikes, and his olive complexion glowed. He was the most handsome man I'd ever seen, but even when he wasn't furious, something about him unsettled me.

My stepdad's bottom lip quivered, and the crow's feet lining his chestnut eyes deepened. I could've sworn more gray had appeared at the temples of his light brown hair. I hadn't seen him since Christmas, when I'd come home to visit.

"I...I'm sorry." My stepdad's voice quivered. "I wasn't thinking."

"Clearly," Drake rasped, and his hand flinched like he wanted to hit my stepdad.

Two men in suits stood behind Drake with their arms crossed.

They were slightly shorter than their boss but still taller than most men I'd encountered.

They were ganging up on my stepdad, and someone had to interfere.

Without thinking it through, I continued to the bottom of the stairs and cleared my throat loudly. "What's going on here?"

Drake's head spun toward me, and for a second, I swore his pupils elongated like a lizard's.

I gasped and shook my head. I had to be seeing things. His eyes were dark; it had to be a trick of the light.

"Dammit, Everly," my stepdad snapped. "You're always sticking your nose in places it doesn't belong."

My head jerked back like he'd slapped me. Here I was, trying to *help* him, and he was scolding me. Obviously, I'd messed up and needed to fix it.

"Sorry." I grimaced. I hated how weak I sounded. I'd always hoped he'd be like the dad I never had. "I thought I heard something, and I—"

"No, it's fine." A casual smile slipped over Drake's face as he straightened. He adjusted his black tie, which hadn't been out of place, and winked. "We are disagreeing over a business matter. I didn't mean to alarm you."

With his easygoing persona in place, I almost doubted what I'd walked in on, but I'd seen the conflict with my own eyes. I wasn't stupid. However, after Mom had died, I'd learned how to act myself, so I smiled back. "Well, misunderstandings happen. Don't they?"

He smirked and scanned me from head to toe before turning back to my stepdad. "Peter, you have three days to fix this in one of the two ways of which I've informed you. That's more than generous, based on the amount of time you've already had to remedy the situation. If you can't deliver, you know what will become rightfully mine."

My stepdad's Adam's apple bobbed, and he blanched.

The hairs on the nape of my neck rose. One thing was clear: the "situation" was bad, and it didn't take my perfect GPA to pick up on that.

Drake's gaze landed on me again, and he slightly bowed his head. "We'll leave now."

I nodded back. I needed to know what was going on, pronto, so I could fix it. Drake's family was the most powerful in our city. They owned most of downtown and so much more than I could even fathom, so I had to play nice.

I managed to spit out the one word I could say. "Goodbye."

My voice sounded rough, as if I hadn't drunk water in days.

"Don't worry. We're going." Drake strode around the desk, then passed me and went up the stairs, each step steady and confident. I shrank back. He oozed dominance, and his aura struck me as unbalanced.

His men followed. The thicker guard, who resembled an MMA fighter, glared at me as he went by. His cobalt irises would have been mesmerizing if it hadn't been for the scowl on his face.

I listened carefully once all three of them were upstairs. When their footsteps didn't pause and the front door opened and closed, I let out a breath I hadn't realized I was holding.

Now that we were alone, I turned back to my stepdad. "What was that all about?"

He yanked on his button-down shirt, trying to smooth out the wrinkles, but I noted the dark blue spots where sweat had pooled under his arms. He scoffed. "It's none of your concern, Everly. Why are you even here?"

I flinched. I'd come downstairs to check on him, and that was the thanks I got? "I took my last exam at UNC and drove straight here. Thought I'd stay for the couple of weeks between now and the summer semester. I wanted to see my brother and sister." I kicked at the concrete floor, hating the way I explained myself to him all the time.

"You could've called them." He stood and rolled his chair back to the desk.

I called at least once a week, and half the time, they didn't answer. But I didn't want to get into that with him. I'd made a promise to Mom, and I intended to keep it. "It's not the same." He was deflecting, and I couldn't allow that. "Again, what was that about?"

"It's *business*. Part of *my family business*, which you *aren't* part of. You aren't my blood." He pointed to the stairs. "Now, I have a pressing issue to deal with. If you must stay, then stay in the guest room, and keep out of the way."

The guest room. That burned. It had been my room, but as soon as I'd moved into my dorm at UNC Chapel Hill, he'd taken it over and thrown my stuff away like I was a nuisance he'd gotten rid of.

"Peter—" I started.

He lifted a hand. "Seriously. I don't have time for this. Your sister's future is in my hands."

I froze. My sister? What did Eva have to do with his meeting with Drake? "Is that what Mr. Hale was talking about?"

"For fuck's sake, Everly." His nostrils flared. "Get out of my hair. Now."

My eyes burned. I should've known he wouldn't talk with me, but I'd hoped he might see that I could help him work out the problem. "Fine. Just let me know—"

"Leave!" he shouted and slammed his hands on the desk.

Any sense of dignity I had left was gone, but I refused to leave like a coward. Instead, I lifted my chin and slowly walked back upstairs.

With every step, my heart pounded harder. I worried that whatever had happened had endangered my sister, but that made no sense. Neither twin worked for my stepdad.

When I reached the top of the stairs, I went into the kitchen. With the open floor plan, I could see Eva and Elliott still engaged in their video game as if nothing had happened.

I wished I could be so oblivious.

I rushed past the rectangular white oak dining table that sat close to the windows and snatched my car keys off the cream-colored granite countertop of the cherrywood island marking the entryway into the kitchen. The cabinets and countertops matched throughout the room, and a glossy baby blue backsplash gave the space a modern edge.

Mom and I had picked out this kitchen when she'd been diagnosed with cancer. She'd wanted to do something special with me since I was losing my last parent, and she'd wanted this house to feel like home to me even after she was gone.

The familiar twinge of hurt zapped me, but I blinked hard, regaining focus. If Peter wouldn't tell me, then I had to find Drake to determine what was going on.

Marching past the sofa to the front door, I said, "I'm heading out for a little while."

Neither of the twins responded, as if I weren't even there. Like I was invisible.

As I stepped onto the long porch, the chill of twilight caused me to shiver. I should've grabbed a sweater on my way out, but I didn't want to waste time going back for one. I scurried to my white Audi A4 and slid into the black leather driver's seat.

If Drake had stayed around town, there was one place I could likely find him. He owned Dragon Alley in downtown Asheville, a luxury bar frequented by the city's elite and a handful of residents who were splurging for a special occasion. My stepdad had mentioned it when I was in town for Christmas.

Luckily, it was only a ten-minute drive away.

When I pulled up at the bar, I found a metered spot nearby. On a Friday night downtown, most people would want more than one hour's time, but that would be plenty for me.

I paid for the meter on my phone and climbed out of the car. As I shut my door, a pleasant, almost tickly sensation ran down my back. I glanced around, my gaze drawn to a black sedan two parking spots down on my side of the street. A man sat in the vehicle, his gorgeous sky blue eyes on me. His baseball cap and the dim streetlights cast his face in shadow, but those eyes gleamed in the dark like beacons. From what I could tell, he was very attractive.

Everly! Get a grip. I couldn't believe I was standing here like a crazy person when I had to figure out what was going on with my stepdad and, more importantly, my sister. Forcing my attention off him, I walked to the thick wooden door that had the bar's name written on it in an elegant script.

Before I could reach the handle, a young man dressed in a black button-down shirt and slacks, who I hadn't even noticed standing there, opened the door. He smiled. "Welcome to Dragon Alley."

I walked into the most whimsical bar I'd ever seen. The floor was hardwood, each board alternating between dark and light. The bar and tables were made of a coffee-stained wood, and the underside of the crowded main bar was lit with warm, yellow-toned lights. The overhead lighting was perfect, neither too bright nor too dark, but rather the sort of soft illumination that felt like an invitation to curl up and read one of my favorite contemporary romances. Varying shades of brown bricks accented the walls. The low hum of intimate conversations and soft jazz music added to the ambiance.

Unsurprisingly, there were no open seats. Even though everyone was dressed up, the place was trendy and welcoming.

Drake and his two shadows were sitting in the back at a corner table away from everyone else.

Even as the weight lifted from my shoulders, something hard settled in my stomach. Panic, maybe?

"If you'd like a drink, you can wait—" the host started.

But I had no desire to listen. Instead, I marched toward the person I'd come here to see.

"Ma'am!" the host called after me. "You can't go back there."

Like hell I couldn't. Drake might be rich and influential, but he couldn't just barge into my stepdad's house and threaten him, especially if that threat involved my sister.

Drake sat at the end of the table, facing the door. His attention locked on me, and he said something, causing his two shadows, who were facing him, to look over their shoulders at me.

Arching a brow, Drake tilted his head, observing.

As I grew closer, something inside me urged me to turn around and run. But that wouldn't get me any answers.

I stopped at their table and placed one hand on my hip.

"Ma'am!" the host exclaimed. "This is the owner's private—"

"Leave her," Drake commanded as he ran a hand along his chin. "She can stay."

Footsteps hurried away as the host left us.

"Sir," the cobalt-eyed man said.

"Falkor, Ladon, get us a round from the bar." Drake motioned for them to go.

Jaws twitching, the two men growled but obeyed, leaving Drake and me alone.

"How can I help you?" Drake placed his hands on the table.

"Tell me what that was about back at the house with my step-dad." I tensed as every cell in my body told me to run.

He chuckled humorlessly. "Your *stepdad* embezzled from my company. He hasn't deposited all the cash payments from the tenants for a few years now, and he needs to pay me back the missing money or provide something of equal value."

My stomach roiled. "My *sister*? What are you going to do? Pimp her out?" I clenched my hands, ready to punch the smirk off his face.

"Of course not. It's hard to find women who aren't after my money. Your sister has the proper status and education to suit my... specific needs. We'll be legally united with no way to sever ties." Drake tapped his fingers on the table. "She'll never want for anything, and she'll bear the heirs I need to carry on my legacy."

My sister would be forced to marry this man and have his chil-dren as repayment for my stepdad's crime? That was disgusting. "How much does he owe you?"

"One million dollars. Give or take." He grabbed the half glass of brown liquid sitting in front of him and drained it, his eyes remaining locked on me.

I inhaled. My mother's dying wish replayed in my head. I couldn't abandon my sister to that fate. There had to be another way out of this situation; it wasn't Eva's penance to bear.

"Take me in her place."

CHAPTER TWO

HE CHOKED and coughed as he placed the glass on the table a little too hard, trying to play off his shock. Then he cleared his throat and blinked a few times, his angular face somehow appearing sharper. "You want to take your sister's place and be at my beck and call?"

When he put it that way, it sounded even worse. That one phrase exposed what marriage to him would be like: being controlled. But my sister had turned eighteen last month, in April. She deserved to go to college and enjoy this time of her life. Though I was supposed to start my formal premed education in two weeks, I'd had four years of college and graduated with a bachelor's degree. I'd had more time to live—granted, I'd spent most of my time, including weekends, either studying or working at a local coffee shop, but at least I'd had the choice.

I straightened my shoulders. "I'm not kidding. The offer is sincere. I'm older, and..." Spilling my heart out to anyone, let alone a peculiar, good-looking man, wasn't something I was comfortable with. I sighed. "Does it matter why? Besides, you should know that Eva and Elliott are twins and very close. If you take one, the other will be there all the time." Maybe if I focused on him having a frequent visitor, it would sway him to my side.

Pursing his lips, he rubbed his finger along the rim of his glass and stared into space as if he were deliberating. Finally, he exhaled. "I hadn't considered that. But won't they do the same for you?" He observed me.

The question was legitimate, but it felt like he'd stabbed me in the heart. My throat went dry, and I tried to school my expression. I wanted to lie, but I suspected it wouldn't do me any favors. If I wanted him to trust me, I had to be honest. "No, they won't. Though I believe my siblings care about me, we aren't close. If I didn't come home, I would never see them."

He steepled his fingers and tapped them against his lips. "And your father wouldn't—"

"*Step*father," I interjected. I didn't want him to get confused about my relationship with Peter. He was the only parental figure I had, but he was upfront about not wanting me to view him that way. "And he doesn't care about me." I cringed. Maybe I should've left that last part out. If taking my sister was a way of collecting the million Peter had embezzled, then Drake might be seeking someone Peter cared about as punishment.

"This gets more interesting." He scratched at his scruff. "How old are you?"

I wasn't sure how that was relevant. He was drinking at a bar, so we were close enough in age that it shouldn't matter, but I didn't want to risk sounding ornery. "Twenty-two."

He smirked. "An older woman by a year."

My blood turned cold. He was truly considering this, which was what I wanted, but it also terrified me. Though I didn't want Eva trapped in that situation, I didn't want to be, either.

But I'd made a promise.

Dropping his forearms onto the table, he nodded. "In a way, it's better that you're volunteering. We're closer in age, and you seem more mature, seeing as your nose isn't shoved in some video game."

He rolled his eyes. "I won't have to contend with a disgruntled teenager who pouts about being locked in with me or visiting family since you're estranged. You'll be all *mine*, which is exactly what I want."

He stood, and I took a step back. I didn't want us to be too close, which, given the circumstances and the offer I'd made him, was somewhat ironic, but I didn't know him. My gut screamed that the more I learned about him, the more I'd dislike him. Though he was attractive, he was intense in a disturbing kind of way. There was something animalistic and raw about him, like a predator circling its prey. Unfortunately, I was that prey.

Placing a finger under my chin, he tipped my face up.

His pupils slitted as he surveyed me from my face to my toes.

I swallowed hard. That was the second time they'd done that. But when I blinked and looked again, his eyes were normal.

The stress of exams, missing my graduation next weekend, and coming back here where Mom's memory haunted me even more must have been getting to me.

He nodded. "Your face is symmetrical. Your light gray eyes are alluring. And your full rosy lips will make many men jealous of me."

Then he turned my head to one side and the other, evaluating my profile.

My skin crawled. I felt like an animal in a show. I couldn't believe he was judging my attributes as if I had no feelings. My hands clenched, ready to punch the jerk in the face, but I couldn't. Then he would take my sister.

He continued without a pause, "Your fair skin is a little much, but we can fix that. Your alignment and body shape are sufficient, though I don't much like the golden shade of your hair. Still, the length and fullness are adequate."

Heart pounding, I swallowed the anger swirling inside me. I'd inherited my golden hair from Mom, and I wasn't willing to change it, not even for him. "Thanks for listing all my pros and cons." I couldn't hide my disgust.

"Watch that tone, *dear*. After all, you came here looking for me." He smirked and dipped his head closer.

This guy was a narcissistic asshole, but he had all the control, and he knew it. Stomach souring, I swallowed again as bile inched up my throat.

He dropped his hand and nodded. "Overall, I suppose you're pretty enough, and with my dominant features, my heirs will stand apart from all others." He held out a hand. "I accept your offer. You'll be picked up in three days, as I informed Peter. After all, I *am* a man of my word."

I'd heard rumors of his arrogance among some of the people in the city. How their rent would increase, and Drake would laugh when they complained, asking what they were going to do about it.

I'd assumed they were making him out to be more villainous than he was, especially since he was so young, but now I was certain they hadn't made Drake sound horrible enough.

"That's only *if* we don't come up with the money." He was acting as if there weren't an alternative, but I wouldn't just hand over my freedom without a fight.

His dark eyes lightened with mirth. "Of course, darling."

The back of my throat burned. He enjoyed making others feel inadequate.

There was no way I could marry him.

"Good." I straightened my back and shook his hand, sealing the deal. As soon as I could, I released him and pivoted toward the door. "I'd better get to work."

He grabbed my arm, jerking me back toward him. His fingers dug into my skin. The urge to get out of his grip was damn near uncontrollable, but I had to be complacent, or he might change his mind.

"I want to be clear. If you plan on keeping our agreement, make sure you don't do something disgusting and soil the goods." He waved a hand from my mouth to my crotch, his insinuation clear. "I won't accept someone who sleeps with people for money. I don't share what's *mine*. Do you understand?"

My cheeks burned. "Isn't that what you're forcing either my sister or me to do?" I wasn't good at keeping my mouth shut when I was angry. Since Mom's death, I tried to let Peter's indifference and the twins' obliviousness roll off my back. I didn't want to alienate myself from my family more than I already was. If I stood up to my stepdad and became too much of a nuisance, I wouldn't be welcomed back. So, for the most part, I took it.

But I'd just learned that I had my limits.

"No, *darling*." He lowered his mouth to my ear, his hot breath hitting the sensitive shell. "You'll be treated like a princess. It's not the same, so don't try to cheapen it."

I shivered, but it wasn't from desire. I wanted to get away from him. "That thought hadn't crossed my mind."

His grip went slack, and the blood rushed down my arm, causing it to tingle, but his mouth stayed right next to my ear. "That's a good girl."

Something was seriously wrong with him. I had to leave before I did something I regretted in the morning. "I'll get Peter to contact you when we get the money." I inhaled as I walked toward the door, refusing to look back. I was certain I *would* vomit if I did.

"Remember, three days, darling," he cooed, then broke out in loud laughter.

It was the last thing I heard before the bar door whooshed shut behind me, chilling me to the core.

I rushed to my car, shaking from the meeting. There was something sinister about Drake, and it unnerved me.

As I approached my vehicle, I looked for the man with striking blue eyes, but the spot where he'd been parked was empty.

Somehow, that chilled me even more.

THE THREE DAYS passed more quickly than I'd thought possible. I stood in the center of the *guest bedroom*, taking a deep breath as the realization of my horrible situation sank in.

I'd painted until my wrists had flared up with tendonitis and then painted some more. I hadn't completed a single painting since Mom had passed, but in the past three days, I'd done six detailed and intricate pieces and rushed to the local gallery to offer them for sale. Luckily, they'd honored my previous agreement without hesitation since I'd sold several paintings through them while I was in high school. They'd reached out to me several times after Mom's death because a customer had asked for more of my artwork, so I could only hope the customers were still interested.

Mom had loved my portraits of downtown Asheville and my landscapes of the woods and mountains that surrounded our city. I'd been painting since I was quite young, and I'd earned money for college and a reputation locally for my work. I should've been able to sell these pieces for decent money, but the inquiring customer hadn't dropped by, and no one else had purchased them yet.

Between that and driving for Uber at night, I had hoped to come up with a portion of the payment to help my stepdad with the total, but as soon as Drake had informed him that he had switched plans to me, my stepdad hadn't even tried to repay him.

No wonder Drake had laughed so hard when I'd left the bar.

I stood at the window next to the black, iron-framed queen-size bed. The window overlooked the driveway where Drake would be pulling up any second.

Each heartbeat was a stark reminder that I was closer to losing my freedom. I wasn't sure what to expect once I left here, but I was certain I would lose touch with the twins. At least it was because I was fulfilling my promise to Mom.

Tearing my gaze from the view, I walked halfway through the wide-open attic room with its slanted ceiling. It was one of the largest bedrooms in the house, but there was no connecting bathroom or closet. I suspected that was why I'd received it when we'd moved in with Peter.

I walked to one wall and touched the light blue paint. Underneath my fingertips, I could feel the slight indentations of what Peter had covered up—the painting Mom and I had done together when we'd moved in and made the room mine.

My heart fractured from the bittersweet memories. God, how I missed her.

An engine rumbled below, and my lungs seized. I didn't bother checking the window because I heard two car doors open.

Drake was here to collect his *property*.

Me.

I exhaled, forcing myself to breathe. Passing out wouldn't accomplish anything.

With more self-control than I'd believed possible, I strolled to the bed and picked up the two dark duffel bags of belongings I'd brought back from college. It was everything I owned, and it had been hard to realize that my life could be packed up so easily.

The doorbell rang, and I turned around in the room, giving it one final look. Despite the agony cutting through my chest, I pulled up the memory of what the room had looked like with the mural Mom and I had created—a sunrise over downtown Asheville in front of Mom's and my favorite coffee spot.

"Everly!" Eva yelled, her voice sounding strange. "You have a visitor."

If only it were a visitor and not my new "owner."

Part of me wished I hadn't left campus early and skipped my graduation ceremony. Then I wouldn't be in this predicament. But Eva would be. I had to remember that.

I glanced at the bracelet on my wrist, a gift from my mother. She'd given it to me the day she married Peter, a reminder of what I meant to her. I hadn't worn it since she'd passed, the memories stinging and too fresh, but today, I needed it. I needed her. It was white gold and formed with interchanging small hearts and diamonds, with two bigger hearts hanging down and inscribed with *Everly* and *The love between a mother and daughter is forever.*

My eyes burned with tears.

"Everly!" my stepdad yelled.

Blowing out a breath, I opened the door. I knew better than to delay the inevitable. It only made things harder. I walked downstairs, each step slow and steady, and when the front door came into view, I stopped, surprised.

Drake wasn't there.

Instead, it was the same two guards who had shadowed Drake the other day, plus a tall, beautiful girl I'd never seen before.

She lifted a brow as her mocha eyes examined me. Long, curly, dark brown hair flowed over her shoulders and stopped midway down her back. Where Drake had pointed out that I was pale, she was the opposite—a gorgeous bronze. She stood about two inches taller than my stepdad, bringing her in at around six feet. Her height only added to her allure.

My five-foot-eight height made me taller than most girls, but now I felt short.

The girl glanced back at the guards. "Not what I was expecting, but it makes sense."

"Does it?" Falkor grumbled.

I wasn't sure how to take that, but I didn't give a damn.

"Hi, Everly." The beautiful girl turned back toward me. "I'm Saphira. Drake couldn't come to pick you up today, so I'm here in his place."

That was more than okay with me. I nodded, not trusting myself to talk.

"Take her bags and go upstairs to get whatever else she needs," Saphira ordered the two men.

Falkor took the two duffel bags out of my hands as Ladon stepped toward the stairs.

"No need. This is all of it." I cleared my throat.

Both twins stood by the couch, watching everything. My stepdad was at the door, holding it open.

Saphira's head tilted back, but then she shook it. "No worries. You'll have more than you'll ever want or need once we get you to your new home."

"Her home?" Elliott crossed his arms. "Her home's here. What are you talking about?"

I hadn't told them anything. Partly because I was a coward and didn't know what to say, and partly because they'd been busy the past few days, and I hadn't seen them.

"Your sister's future is with Drake Hale, and she's moving in with him." My stepdad seemed jovial. "This is a very good thing for our family."

No, it was a very good thing for *him*. He was the reason I was in this mess.

"Wait. That seems fast." Eva bit her bottom lip. "I didn't realize you and Drake were dating. Of course we'll come visit."

"That will be up to Drake," Saphira interjected.

As expected, he was going to remove the last members of my family from my life. My shoulders shook, but I couldn't fall apart.

"But—" Eva started.

"You heard her." Peter waved his hand, telling me to leave. "We aren't invited, and Drake is waiting for her. We don't want to hold her up."

"We do need to go." Ladon returned to the door. "Drake will be waiting."

I was sure he would be.

Saphira, Ladon, and Falkor walked out the door, and I followed, each step harder than the last. I was heading toward a future I didn't want, and I was at the mercy of fate.

As I turned to the twins to say goodbye, I was surprised to find them right behind me. They pulled me into a group hug.

"Be careful, E," Eva whispered.

I hadn't been prepared for concern. They must have sensed

something was wrong. I returned their embrace, taking a deep breath and committing their scents and how they felt to memory. Then I pulled myself away before I couldn't.

"Hurry up," my stepdad gritted. As soon as I stepped onto the porch, Peter said, "It's about time she was useful." Then the front door slammed shut.

What was left of my heart shattered, and I couldn't even feel my legs as I made my way to the black sedan. Falkor held the door open, and I slid into the leather back seat, next to Saphira.

She frowned. "I'm sorry your stepdad is an asshole. No wonder you're here."

Out of everyone I knew, she was the one who'd understood in seconds what people who'd seen my relationship with Peter for years had never picked up on—he didn't treat me like a daughter.

Afraid to speak, I only nodded. I couldn't risk breaking into tears.

The car pulled away, and I laid my head on the headrest. I didn't need to watch the city pass by. Memories of Mom haunted me, and every mile toward the mountainous outskirts of the city only added to the pain. That had probably been the last time I'd ever see my brother and sister.

After we'd driven for twenty minutes, Falkor shouted, "Holy fuck!"

CHAPTER THREE

MY EYES FLEW OPEN, and I inhaled sharply. I glanced around, searching for the other vehicle with which we surely had to be on a collision course, but all I saw was the empty two-lane road leading us into the isolated peaks of the Blue Ridge Mountains.

"Brace yourselves!" Falkor yelled, and clutched the steering wheel hard enough that his knuckles blanched.

He was frantic, but there was *nothing* on the road. We were surrounded by freshly sprouted trees.

Following Ladon's focus to our right, I squinted into the trees. Something barreled toward us.

I gasped.

It was too big to be a bullet.

I yelped as Saphira grabbed my shoulders and pushed my upper body out of view of the side window.

Instead of a crashing noise, something thumped outside our car.

"Dammit, the tire blew," Falkor gritted.

"Keep driving!" Ladon exclaimed.

I tried to sit upright, but Saphira shoved me down again. Her strength was remarkable, even for her larger stature.

My back ached from crouching over my knees, but I supposed that was a better alternative to dying.

The car jerked, indicating the tire had deflated. We could drive for a while on the rim, but I wasn't sure for how long. Every few seconds, the vehicle would lurch, forcing Falkor to slow down.

Ladon growled, "Here comes another fucking arrow. What year is this person living in? The Middle Ages? Use a damn gun!"

A second thump told me everything I needed to know. Another tire had been blown, and it sounded like it was the one right behind me. Robin Hood was attacking us. That was the only rational explanation I could come up with.

"We have to stop," Falkor said with disgust. "Whoever is attacking us will catch up, so it's better if we get out and prepare to fight."

These guys were idiots. Yes, we were moving slowly for a car, but we were going at least twenty miles per hour. No person could catch up with us at that speed. "Just keep going!"

Saphira exhaled. "We would if that were an option."

Lovely, she was on the same page as these morons. We were going to die. Granted, if we drove far enough, we'd get out of range of the archer, and if we kept a steady pace to God knew where, we might make it out of this alive.

"I want it noted that I believe this is a horrible idea," I said as I sat up again.

Saphira glared at me, but if we were climbing out of the car, there was no reason for me to hide.

The two men opened their doors. Falkor called over his shoulder, "You two stay inside. We'll eliminate the threat and go from there." He slammed his door shut.

I detested their sexist manner, but I remained silent. Though I disliked their arrogant implication that two women couldn't fight, for myself, I couldn't disagree. I'd dedicated my life to improving my painting techniques and studying. Self-defense hadn't been part of that program, and just ten minutes on an elliptical kicked my ass.

I rolled my eyes. "We should've kept *driving*."

"Falkor and Ladon are highly skilled warriors trained to assess danger." Saphira leaned forward to look out my window. "If they say this is the best option, it is, even if we don't understand it."

Of course she would take their side. She was with them. The best thing I could do was remain silent and pray their stupidity didn't kill us.

I pulled out my cell phone and dialed 911, one of the first things people trained to react to dangerous situations would do.

"What are you doing?" Saphira asked as the phone rang.

"Calling for help, since no one else is." For six years, I'd had to shut down my attitude and behave. In the past three days, that control had been ruined, all due to my affiliation with Drake. My future wasn't looking very promising.

She snatched the phone from my hand and pressed the red button, cutting off the line. "We are *not* calling for help. Falkor and Ladon have it covered."

Great, she was an idiot, too. Maybe this was par for the course with all people tied to Drake.

A loud roar shook the car, and my heart jumped into my throat. I turned to my window.

My entire world stopped...because what I saw was impossible.

It only existed in fiction.

A huge, shimmery plum dragon flew by the car toward the warriors. Its scales were the very color I favored when painting the night sky.

I froze, unable to do anything but gape.

This had to be a dream—no, a nightmare. Maybe this situation with Drake and my time back in Asheville was an elaborate anxiety dream fueled by my exams.

That was the only plausible explanation.

Doing what I'd seen countless people do in television shows and movies, I pinched my arm.

The sharp sting forced my lungs to expel air, and I couldn't mask my grunt. *Ow. That hurt.*

"What are you *doing?*" Saphira scoffed. "I don't think bruising yourself will make the dragon go away."

Her confirmation of what I'd seen didn't make me feel better. In fact, my vision blurred as the car seemed to close in on me, suffocating me.

"Dra...gon?" I gasped, hoping that saying the word would make sense of everything.

It didn't.

The world spun, and I reached forward to steady myself.

"Everly!" Saphira shouted...or I thought she did. However, noises were gurgling as if I were under water.

Something hard smacked me on the cheek, and the world righted itself as my skin stung.

"Listen to me. I need you to stay focused. That dragon is after something, and I'm not sure what." Her face twisted in anger. "We may have to run for it."

Falkor and Ladon stood beside the car, ready to face down a *dragon.*

I reached for the handle to open my door. "They need to get back inside the car!" But my hand stilled as Falkor's clothes ripped from his body and yellow-green splotches dotted his skin, becoming what could only be described as scales.

My mind turned to mush. This *had* to be a dream. But as I kept my eyes on Falkor, his body quadrupled in size, and wings sprouted from his back. He flapped his wings and soared toward the silvery plum dragon.

As he rushed our attacker, I shook my head, ready to open the door again to get Ladon inside, but then *he* began transforming, too. Pine green scales covered his body as his black suit ripped to shreds and fell off him.

No wonder Saphira had trusted them to handle the situation. But that didn't comfort me. I'd been riding around with *dragons* without a clue. What else didn't I know about what I'd signed up for?

"Shit!" Saphira exclaimed, bringing me back to the present.

I followed her gaze in time to watch the gorgeous silver-plum dragon breathe fire at Falkor, who darted below the stream, dodging the flames. As he shot upward, the dragon swung around and used his long, thick tail to smack Falkor in the head.

Falkor dropped, but the dragon didn't let up. He darted after him, and as Falkor regained his balance and flapped his wings, the dragon bit into Falkor's shoulder. He threw his head back and roared in pain.

Now that Ladon was fully shifted, he soared toward his friend. Smoke trickled from his nose, conveying his rage. I wasn't a dragon, but even I understood what was going on there.

Attacker Dragon released his hold on Falkor and shot up high enough to kick the dragon in the head. Falkor flew backward and rammed into the thick Fraser and balsam firs and red spruces. The earth shook, and the crash confirmed I wasn't imagining things.

Saphira was counting on them to protect us, but I didn't have the same good feeling about it. I cleared my throat and winced. The skin felt raw. "Isn't Falkor in charge?"

"Yeah, but Ladon is a strong fighter, too," Saphira said, then jumped over the center console into the front seat.

She wasn't growing scales...yet. "That's not reassuring!"

"I'm not trying to reassure you. You're a grown-ass woman. I'm just telling you what I know." She pressed the start button on the car and let out a huge sigh. "Thank gods he left the keys in the car. At least he was thinking on his feet."

"Or the keys dropped to the ground close to the car when he was, you know, becoming a *dragon*, and as soon as we drive too far, the car will stall." I didn't understand how she could remain so rational. We were under attack, and the *men* who were protecting us weren't even human. Maybe that should've been comforting, given our attacker wasn't, either, but it wasn't.

Saphira snarled in a way that wasn't *human*, and I sank into my seat.

"They're right here." She reached into the cup holder and lifted the black keys. "So you can stop being a drama queen and maybe yank that stick out of your ass." She shifted into gear and took off way faster than she should have with two blown tires.

Somehow, moving forward eased some of my anxiety. I recognized what this was—a false sense of security—but I'd take it.

I glanced out the back window to see Ladon and Attacker Dragon engaged in a battle. Instead of being on the defensive, Ladon was now the one landing blows.

Though I was petrified, watching Attacker Dragon fight was like watching an artist paint. He was skilled, and every movement flowed into the next, unlike Ladon, who struck fast and hard in spurts.

Attacker Dragon jerked his head to look at us. Smoke poured from his nose as he focused back on Ladon, barely ducking his head in time to avoid a strike of his front paw.

With Attacker Dragon's body not where Ladon had expected, Ladon's dragon form overshot and flew over Attacker Dragon. Attacker Dragon tilted his head back and blew fire at Ladon's underside.

Ladon released an ear-shattering screech, and I covered my ears to block out the cry. Attacker Dragon then slammed his chest and front claws into Ladon's burned stomach.

After being lifted at least fifty feet high, Ladon came crashing down. He moved his wings, trying to fly, but wasn't fast enough. As he barreled downward, Attacker Dragon spun and nailed him in the head. Ladon tumbled to the ground, meeting the same fate as his friend.

The car shook, and Saphira glanced into the rearview mirror, her face pale. "Please tell me that was the purple dragon and not Ladon."

"I could, but then I'd be *lying*." I ground my teeth, sending a jolt of pain through my jaw. That was a sign that I was stressed out and needed to relax and get my emotions in check.

"Of course not. That would be too easy," she spat, and glanced out the window. "I can't see him from this angle."

I redirected my attention outside, and my heart dropped into my stomach. This day kept getting worse, but I'd bet we hadn't hit a low yet. "He won't be out of your sight for long." Attacker Dragon hurtled toward us. "Whatever he wants must be in this car."

She pressed the gas harder, and the car lurched even more.

Screw her. I leaned over and snatched my cell phone from where she'd placed it behind her. I dialed 911 again and placed the phone under my butt to muffle it.

"Everly, hang up the phone *now*," she commanded. "What are you going to say? A huge-ass dragon is chasing us?"

"No, I'm going to tell them we need help and we're driving on our rims like maniacs because someone is chasing us." The car shuddered from the flat tires, and my stomach jiggled nonstop. I could easily throw up. "Even if the dragon doesn't catch us, our vehicle could smash into a tree and leave no survivors. So, I'm sorry, but I want to live."

I could be snarky, too.

"Drake's going to *kill* me," she rasped. "But he'll be more upset if I don't get you to him in one piece."

That was an odd thing to say. I was certain Drake didn't care about me. He wanted me for babies and status, so it was what I could do for him that he wanted to protect.

But I'd take it.

I looked out the window again and yelped. Attacker Dragon had caught up to us, and his head was lowered so it was level with my door. Sky blue eyes focused on me with humanlike intelligence despite the elongated pupils. The eyes were bright, gleaming like those of the man I'd seen in the car outside the bar. My stomach tightened. If Falkor and Ladon were both human and dragon, it stood to reason this dragon was also human.

Something tugged inside me. My head screamed at me to move to the other side of the car, but I was helpless. All I could do was stare into the beast's mesmerizing eyes. Something about them called to the void inside me.

The dragon flew faster, and one of its large feet reached for the handle of my door.

Self-preservation kicked in *finally*. I flipped the lock and slid to the other side of the back seat. "It's trying to open my door!"

"I *told* Drake it was stupid to tell the entire château about you," she seethed. "Hold on tight. It's about to get rough." If *this* wasn't rough, I feared what was about to happen next.

Wait. Château?

The car lurched as she slammed on the brakes. The right side of the car skidded, and sparks shot upward from metal dragging on asphalt. She cut the wheel hard, and the sedan lifted to the left side as she spun the car in the opposite direction.

My body was jostled everywhere in the back seat, and I wished she'd been more explicit with her warning.

We barely missed the metal railing on the other side, and she pushed the gas hard again, racing back toward the city. This was a better strategy; we were no longer going up a freaking mountain, and we were probably closer to the city than wherever Drake lived.

The dragon roared behind us, and when the car settled, I turned around to see it had already eliminated the distance between us. It sped toward us, gaining despite our speed.

"It's—" I started, but the ceiling of the sedan made a sound like crumpling plastic. My head jerked upward. Talons had pierced the roof.

We weren't getting away.

CHAPTER FOUR

MY HEART RACED, and my ears rang like I'd just left a concert. I'd imagined myself in many different scenarios, but *this* had never crossed my mind.

Silver-plum scaly wings flanked the car, and the ceiling groaned as if the dragon had landed on it. I grabbed the headrest of Saphira's seat. "What do we do?" I tried to say, but barely any noise left my mouth.

"I don't *know*," she spat. "But I hear sirens. 911 must have traced your call."

Holy shit. She'd heard me. I wasn't sure how, but I already suspected she was one of *them*. They must have excellent hearing, or that was what the few books and movies about dragons I'd heard about portrayed. Now I sort of wished I'd enjoyed those stories like Mom had. Maybe then I'd have an idea about how to get out of this situation.

All I could do was focus. "That's good. We need help." I waved my arms around. "We're about to get smushed."

"Not *that* kind of help, Everly." She stomped on the gas. The car lurched, and more sparks flew off the rims. Every few seconds, the car clunked as if we were rolling from rim to tire.

The ceiling caved in further as the dragon put more weight on it. Was he going to squash us alive?

"He wants something from one of us, so he won't *smush* us. And unless you consider flattening humans like pancakes a good thing, you've involved humans who will get hurt in the crossfire. This dragon won't give up until he gets what he wants, and humans can't find out about our kind." She glanced in the rearview mirror at me.

I hung my head. I hadn't considered that I might have sentenced the police to their demise. I'd been so stupid.

She slammed on the brakes, and I jerked forward. The downward right tilt of the car made it impossible to stay in place. A loud screeching noise came from the roof, and I steadied myself and glanced up as claws pierced it again. This car would soon be a convertible.

The *whoosh* of the flapping wings grew louder, and the sedan groaned as we were lifted off the ground.

I gulped.

Our attacker was strong enough to lift a fucking car.

Needing comfort, I ran my thumb over the bracelet Mom had given me. I had a feeling I'd be reuniting with her soon. I'd always hoped that when the time came, the idea of seeing her again would comfort me, but I didn't want to die. I had so much I wanted to do. I snorted. "At least the car's level now."

Saphira turned around and gaped. "Have you lost your damn mind?"

"Let's see." When I was stressed out, I made bad jokes. I could admit it wasn't one of my best attributes, but it was how I coped. "Until twenty minutes ago, I didn't even know *dragons* existed, and now I'm being carried off in a car by one. I'm going with yes, and I hope I wake up from this horrible nightmare, pronto. Someone must have drugged my coffee this morning."

"*This* isn't a bad trip." She leaned over and popped open the glove box. "This is your life since you agreed to be Drake's."

That was enough to slam my sanity back into me. I wanted to ask if he was a dragon, too, but I had a pretty good guess that he was, and I wasn't sure I could handle it if she confirmed my suspicion.

She reached inside and removed a black pistol. "Thank gods those two are always prepared."

If this dragon could pick up a car, I doubted that a gun would work on him. "Why don't you shift?" That made the most sense, given the situation.

"If you want to die, I can." She lowered the gun and moved like she was putting it into her pocket. "If I shift in here, I'll destroy the inside of the vehicle, including you. And if Falkor and Ladon couldn't take him in dragon form, I don't have much hope."

That was great. "You're not a warrior?"

"No, I'm not. Drake asked me to come and welcome you since he's dealing with a situation." She exhaled.

For some reason, even though she was a dragon, she didn't scare me. Not like our attacker and the other men.

I hated that she was in this mess because of me.

I glanced out the side window. The road was far below us, and I had no way of telling how high we were. I could see the flashing red and blue lights of the approaching police, but they were like tiny little toys. By the time they made it to where we were, we'd be out of sight.

I inched to the middle of the bench seat in the back and clutched the driver's and passenger's headrests. I wasn't sure what I feared more, the talons over my head or the possibility of the dragon releasing the car and us falling. Either way, I was terrified.

Saphira's brows furrowed. "Are you okay?"

I shook my head. I hadn't been this frightened since Mom had died, leaving me all alone.

"I'll do everything I can to protect you." Saphira placed a hand over her heart. "I promise."

I believed her, which was insane. Even though we'd known each other for less than an hour, she'd already proven she would follow through on that promise.

The car groaned and tilted forward slightly. The trees grew larger and the ground closer, and my mouth went dry.

"We're landing," Saphira said and rolled her shoulders. "Just... stay inside and let me handle this."

She was being vague, and there had to be a reason—the dragon overhearing, I assumed. If she could hear sirens from miles away, then the dragon could hear anything we said inside the car.

A shiver ran down my spine. I didn't like that thought *at all*.

The trees rushed toward us, and I closed my eyes. I clutched my bracelet with my free hand and focused on the last moment I'd shared with Mom before she was hospitalized. She'd been at home in her own bed, and we'd sipped on our favorite lattes while watching *I Am Dragon*, a movie she'd claimed was one of the most epic love stories of all time. *How ironic*. The woman in the movie had been kidnapped by a dragon.

Branches screeched against the glass, and my eyes flew open. We were almost to the ground.

The car shook on impact, and my head jerked back. Though it hadn't been a fast drop, the landing hadn't been graceful.

The dragon removed its talons from the top of the car, leaving holes in the roof. It lifted into the air and flew away to the right.

My breathing calmed. I whispered, "He's leaving."

Saphira glanced over her shoulder and rolled her eyes. "He wouldn't take us, then leave. He's likely shifting back into his human form. *That* must be his ride." She gestured to a black, four-seat ATV parked twenty feet from the car under a huge Fraser fir.

There went any sense of clarity I had. "Then we need to run *now*." If he was shifting, this could be the chance we needed. I pushed open my door and climbed out. My black, strappy high heels sank into the ground, and a twig scraped my ankle.

Son of a gun. That hurt.

Not a second later, Saphira got out of the car and glared at me. She mouthed, *What are you doing? I said stay in the car!*

I hated that I could make out her words. I would *not* just sit here and wait to be taken, killed, or tortured.

Ignoring her, I yanked off my high heels and tossed them back into the car. *There. One problem solved.*

Saphira stared at me as if I'd grown a second head. After today, I wouldn't count it as implausible.

I tiptoed around the vehicle, not making a single sound. Ha! Who said I couldn't make it outdoors? Mom had said I could do anything if I put my mind to it.

I was halfway to the ATV when a deep voice on my right called out, "What do you think you're doing?"

Placing my hands over my mouth, I held in my scream and pivoted toward the voice. Then my brain short-circuited.

It had to be the man from outside the bar because those eyes matched. I'd known he was attractive that night, but in full daylight, he was the sexiest man I'd ever seen. He stood about ten feet away from me, past the car. His medium-brown hair hung in his eyes, and his tan complexion made him look like a model. He was shirtless, and everywhere my gaze landed was full of muscles—all seven and a half feet of him. However, his eyes revealed everything I needed to know —this was the plum dragon that had attacked us.

Saphira pinched the bridge of her nose. "I believe she thinks she was being quiet."

His attention swung to her. "Well, she's not your problem anymore."

Alarms rang in my head, and shock had me at a loss for words. Why would someone like *him* try to kidnap me? I was no one of value. Hell, even my own stepdad had handed me over as if I were an object to be traded.

"Like *hell* she isn't." Saphira removed the pistol from her side and aimed it at our attacker. "*You* won't be my problem anymore." Her hand shook, but she pulled the trigger.

Our attacker spun around, and the bullet hit a spot five feet away from him. She would've barely nicked him if he hadn't moved.

He ran to the tree line and ducked behind a huge red spruce.

Keeping her focus on the spot where he'd disappeared, Saphira ran toward me and said, "Check to see if the key is in the ATV."

I stood there, unable to move.

"Everly!" she snapped as she caught up to me. "Do you *want* him to catch you?"

Even if the guy was drool-worthy, I didn't want to be forced to go somewhere against my will...again. Catering to Drake was enough.

My feet finally moved, my sense of self-preservation kicking back in. Thank goodness for that instinct.

I hurried to the ATV and leaned into the vehicle. My eyes burned. "They're not in here."

She growled. "Go to the back and get the VIN number off the ATV. It'll be on the bottom left."

I listened to what she said and found the tag. I rattled off the number to her, and she didn't even jot it down. "Do I need to find something—"

"No, I'm good with numbers," she replied, her hands shaking harder. "We're leaving," she called. "You stay there, and no one has to get hurt."

For a second, silence greeted us. Then the man sighed. "I wish that were true."

Saphira's jaw twitched. "Everly, *run*." She glanced at me, her irises darkening. "*Now*."

I stumbled back a few steps, unsure what to do. Leaving her behind didn't feel right, but she was a *dragon*. If anyone was going to kick this guy's ass, it was *not* me.

The guy ran from behind the red spruce, and my mouth opened to warn her, but no words came out.

She jerked her attention back to him and fired the weapon a few more times, but each bullet missed as he charged toward us.

When he was five feet from her, she aimed the gun right at the center of his body. At this proximity, I doubted she'd miss. As she pulled the trigger, he spun to the right, away from the car, and lunged at her. He sacked her, and she fell on her back with him right on top of her. He forced the hand holding the gun over her head.

Growling, she clawed at his chest and tried to kick him between the legs.

He shifted his weight, blocking the cheap shot with his thigh, and punched her in the face. Her head jerked, and her eyes rolled into the back of her head.

My throat closed. He'd knocked her out with one blow. Now I was alone with the psycho.

Once he'd pried the gun from her hand, the man rose to his feet. I backed away, not sure what to do. If I ran, I'd be like prey he could hunt, but if I stayed, he'd definitely take me. But how could I leave Saphira after she'd tried to protect me?

"Please don't run," he said. "Then I'll have to chase you...and I will if you make me."

I shook my head, taking a few more steps back. "I don't know what you want from me. I have nothing."

He blew out a breath. "If you don't get on the ATV, I'll be forced to hurt your friend. Is that what you want?"

"No, but I don't want to go with you, either." I gestured to the woods. "Let us go."

"If I could, I would." He charged at me.

I opened my mouth to scream, but he was already there, sticking a needle into my neck. The world tilted as my body went slack, and I fell into his arms.

He whispered, "I've got you."

I wanted to laugh. *He has me.* He was the reason I was drugged, but my tongue grew thick, and my eyes closed, forcing sleep upon me.

Something pounded rhythmically, waking me. My head throbbed, and I touched it, wondering if my pulse was making the noise.

Another round of thumps echoed in random succession...not my pulse.

I opened my eyes and found myself in a room I'd never seen before. The stark off-white walls reminded me of my dorm and hurt my eyes, even though the lights weren't on. I lay on a queen bed, covered by a light blue sheet. A dresser sat in the right corner of the room, next to a window with steel bars over it.

In the opposite corner, an open door revealed a small bathroom with a toilet and a shower.

I sat up quickly and groaned. The room spun from whatever drugs were wearing off.

Drugs.

Bars.

The air sawed through my lungs.

That man had captured me.

Saphira.

She wasn't here with me. I jumped to my feet and lost my balance, falling into the wall.

A HARD *BANG* hit the wall above my head, the sound desperate and determined.

It had to be Saphira.

She was alive and here. The room swirled around me, and I placed my hands against the wall to steady myself.

"Saphira?" I croaked. I swallowed to ease the dryness in my throat, but it didn't help.

Silence.

Maybe I'd been imagining things, or she couldn't hear me—which would make sense, because I couldn't hear her. I cleared my throat and winced, but I forced myself to speak louder. She had dragon hearing, after all. "Saphira?" My throat felt as if it were bleeding.

Something thudded against the wall again, but it sounded different...as if her head or body were leaning back on it.

That had to be her. I chose to believe it, even if it was wishful thinking.

I laughed, the sound not unlike a whale's mating call. My body was functioning at half-capacity from whatever tranquilizer our attacker had used on me.

The pummeling started back up, confirming it was her. If it was our attacker, and if he was that desperate to see me, he'd be waltzing in right about now.

My stomach soured. He couldn't be far away.

Needing all my focus, I used the wall to support myself and took two steps back to sit on the bed. The springs creaked under my weight, and my head pounded harder. This felt worse than what I imagined a hangover would be like, and that was saying something.

I gripped my head with one hand and placed the other on the mattress to steady myself. Something cool pressed into my palm.

I lifted my hand to find my bracelet lying there...broken.

A sharp pain struck my heart, and my breathing turned ragged. This had been my worst fear and one reason I never wore the bracelet. The clasp was broken, and I couldn't fix it, especially here.

I ran a finger over the quote, the engraving scraping my skin.

My chest shook, and I tried to hold in my crying, but a sob broke through, and tears dripped down my cheeks.

The banging on the wall started all over again.

She must be able to hear me. I should have tried to reassure her, but between the heartbreak and my head swirling, I could barely stay upright.

Footsteps sounded, and I jerked my head up and focused on the thick oak door. A square cutout had a metal flap over it like a small access panel in a prison cell. The doorknob jiggled, and I brushed my tears away.

It was him.

Attacker Dragon.

Something slid into the handle, and I held my breath. *Please don't let him come in here.* He'd drugged and kidnapped me. There was no telling what he might do next.

The door opened...and the first thing I noticed was his eyes.

Even after all the horrible stuff he'd done, they intrigued me.

Oh, hell no, Everly, I chastised myself. *You will not develop even the slightest version of Stockholm syndrome. You're not that desperate for an emotional bond. You've been fine on your own for the past six years.*

He scanned me as he entered the room and shut the door behind him with a bare foot. His nose wrinkled. He carried a plate with a sandwich on it and a glass of water, both of which he held out to me, muscles bulging under his black cotton shirt. "Here. Eat this so you stop crying."

My bottom lip quivered, but I straightened my shoulders. I refused to look weak, even though we both knew he had all the control. I'd pretend to have my dignity—like I'd done for a long while now. "Eating won't make me feel better," I rasped. "You were outside Dragon Alley the other night. I *saw* you."

"Yes. I have to keep an eye on my enemies, and fortunately, I was there—because it led me to you." He walked to a small table underneath the window and set down the plate, then turned his back to me for a moment, not worried about me running away.

"Did you hear me? I don't want it." I clutched the bracelet and wished the sluggishness would go away. I was acting childish, but I couldn't help it.

"Oh, believe me, I can *hear* you." He spun around and sneered. "I hear you and *your friend* everywhere in this damn cabin. If you two would just be quiet, we could all get some rest."

Thank good. It *was* her. I sniffled, trying to pull myself together. A snotty nose wouldn't help matters. "I *just* woke up, so clearly, I'm not the issue."

"You weren't until you started bawling like a toddler." He gestured to the food. "So eat up, and stop acting so emotional."

"Excuse *me*." I attempted to stand, but the wood floor seemed to move, and I landed back on my butt. The disorientation from whatever barbiturate he'd given me was awful. If he was uncomfortable with noise, I'd make his life hell, offering him the same courtesy he'd afforded me. "Let's see. You're a fucking dragon. You kidnapped me by flying me away in a car. Then you *drugged* me. Let me tell you: death feels pretty damn imminent. And you broke the last meaningful thing my mother gave me before she died, so yeah, *I'm* being *emotional?*" The words raked against my raw throat, but that pain was nothing compared to the trauma he was putting me through. "I'd say that makes you criminally insensitive."

A loud flurry of thumps sounded again.

The attacker winced but kept his focus on me. His jaw twitched. "I don't care if you think you're being overly emotional. You've made me out to be a bad guy. I haven't hurt you—"

"Yeah, right. You merely *drugged* me and knocked Saphira out." I should keep my mouth shut. I knew the side effects of tranquilizers, and I was experiencing at least three: impaired judgment, mood swings, and anger. "Yet you come in here and bring me a sandwich and water like you care."

He snorted, his damn face sexy even with a scowl. "Because I'm clearly an insensitive bastard."

I frowned. How could I argue with that? And agreeing with him didn't make it satisfying. This was *not* how this conversation was supposed to go. "Uh...*yeah*." I threw out a hand...and toppled over.

Saphira slammed into the wall, and it vibrated from her assault. I didn't understand how she hadn't broken through.

In fact, I needed to get off this bed before she did break through so I wouldn't be in her way.

When I stood, the floor didn't shift under my feet. I glanced at our attacker, who didn't seem concerned about her at all.

He rolled his eyes. "I haven't touched her."

Of course *he* could hear her. I was the lone wolf—no, *human* here and didn't have the equivalent of Spidey-senses for dragons.

"If you haven't touched me, then how did I get into this bed?" I lifted a brow and sidestepped, trying to regain my balance. Maybe I should eat. I didn't like feeling this way.

His breathing turned ragged. "Would you rather I'd left you unconscious outside for a hungry animal to find?"

No, he didn't get to act like a hero. "If you hadn't drugged me, that wouldn't *have been* a problem!"

Saphira redoubled her attack on the wall.

"It doesn't matter why you're here. It only matters that you *are*." He rolled his shoulders, looking rugged and strong. "Eat the sandwich or don't. I don't give a fuck." He shrugged as if he couldn't care less. "I'm providing you with what you need to survive. It's up to you to care enough to do it."

My lungs wheezed at the truth he'd laid out. He could let us slowly starve and fade away, but instead, he'd brought food. Squeezing the bracelet tightly in my hands, I used it to anchor myself. I was making the situation more volatile. I needed something, *anything* on which to focus this anger and frustration.

Instead of answering, I breathed through my nose to calm the raging storm inside me. My body was shaking, and I hated it. When I got super upset, I always looked scared or worse. I didn't want to give our attacker more of an ego boost because he didn't need any help in that department.

He held out his hand. "Give me your bracelet."

I shook my head and clutched the hand holding the bracelet to my chest. He'd already broken it; there was no way I was handing it over.

His pupils slitted, hinting at the dragon within.

My knees locked, and I swayed again. The hair on the nape of my neck lifted. The last thing I wanted was to be stuck in a room alone with a freaking dragon. For some reason, though, he didn't seem as scary in human form, but the beast was in there somewhere.

He moved closer and loomed over me. He was almost two feet taller than me, and I had to tilt my head back to stare at his face and not his chest. His mouth tightened, and his minty-amber scent, mixed with a hint of sulfur, swirled around me. "I didn't ask, *human*."

He was trying to intimidate me, and I hated that it was working. My heart raced so quickly that my chest ached, and I swallowed back a scream. A tiny squeak escaped.

Saphira quit banging, and a loud *thud* echoed in this room as if she'd run full speed into the wall.

I winced. The sound was bad enough on this side. I could only imagine how hard she'd hit her side of the wall.

"I can't part with it," I whispered, emotion thick in my voice. The thought of him taking it from me had me damn near falling to pieces.

He pulled the hand holding the bracelet away from my chest. His touch was uncomfortably hot, as if he'd just stepped out of a steaming shower. With his other hand, he dug his fingers into the flesh between my fingertips and my palm, loosening my grip on the bracelet.

"No!" I shouted, and yanked backward, slamming into the wall across from the window and close to the door. "Please. Don't take it." I hated begging, but that was all I had to work with. He couldn't take the last meaningful thing I possessed.

A very muffled scream came from the other side of the wall, and our attacker rolled his eyes. He yelled, "You know you can't get through that. The entire room is sealed with Wolfram Dwiin." And he pried the bracelet from my hands.

Heat ran through my blood as my anger took root. I didn't care if he was a dragon—that wasn't his to take. I threw myself against his chest and pounded my hands against him. I channeled strength from the rage inside me. It felt as if I were hitting steel, but I didn't let that deter me.

"Stop!" he bellowed.

That only encouraged me. Maybe I was stronger than I realized? For a moment, I allowed myself to believe the illusion. I thrashed against him and groaned in complete frustration. My hands ached, but I had to believe it was because I was making the impact I desperately needed.

"Dear gods," he snarled. He grabbed me by my shoulders and lifted me off the floor. My feet dangled, giving me another opportunity to attack him. I kicked and grabbed his muscular chest, digging my fingernails into his skin.

I might as well have been kicking a damn rock. My toes ached from the impact, and my fingernails hadn't made as much as a dent in his skin. He tossed me onto the bed, and my head jerked back, causing the walls to spin once again.

"I said *stop*." His voice rang with power. "Don't make me hurt you."

I laughed manically, the last of my sanity leaving me. "You already have. You're taking away *everything*."

"You're about to see what pain feels like," he snarled.

Saphira's barrage on the wall kept time with my pulse pounding in my ears. As I stared at my attacker, I realized he meant every word. He would hurt me if I didn't stop, so I wrapped my arms around my legs and pulled them against my chest. I rocked myself, trying to focus on any good memories, but they all slid away like my freedom.

He was silent for a moment, and then he huffed. "Look, if I put you in the same room as your *friend*, will that calm the two of you down?"

I went still. I hadn't expected that after he'd threatened to hurt me. Being with her would be more comforting. I nodded, afraid if I said the words, my voice would break.

Lines creased his forehead, and he ran a hand down his face. "I'm not doing it for you. It's for me. I need sleep. *Good* sleep. And that can't be achieved with *you* crying and *her* trying to get out of that room, even though it's impossible." He moved his hair, flipping it out of his eyes. "I'll put you together if you promise to calm down."

I'd rather have my bracelet, but that wouldn't happen. "Fine."

He pointed at the door. "Come on. You're moving in there with her, not the other way around."

I jumped to my feet, not wanting to give him time to change his mind. I hurried to the door and threw it open.

For some reason, I hadn't expected to step into a hallway. I glanced left and noted another bedroom that looked similar to the room I'd been in. The hallway stretched from that room to the other end of the house, but I couldn't make out anything more.

Dammit, I'd been hoping to get a sense of the layout.

"You know which direction her room is in," the man growled behind me. "*Move.*"

He must have realized what I was trying to do. He did seem intelligent.

I turned right and hurried to the last door on that side. I grabbed the doorknob and turned, but it was locked.

"Did you really think it'd be open?" he asked sarcastically. He moved beside me, pulled a key out of his pocket, then slipped it into the lock.

"One wrong move, and this is over," he said and lifted a brow at me. Then he addressed the door, "When I open this, nothing had better happen."

After a second, I heard someone move away on the other side.

She must have been waiting for an opportunity to escape. Why hadn't I thought of that? I was so desperate to get to her that I hadn't considered running.

He opened the door and pushed me inside so fast that I tripped over my own feet.

CHAPTER SIX

BEFORE I COULD HIT the floor, Saphira caught me under my arms. The room swirled again, though not as quickly. The drugs were wearing off.

The door slammed as she growled, "What the hell was that? I wasn't trying anything."

"I wasn't going to wait to see." He exhaled on the other side of the door. "She was already snooping while just moving rooms, and I don't trust either of you."

She steadied me on my feet, and I surveyed the room. Dark metal covered the entire space from the floor to the ceiling. The bars over the window were the same as mine, but the door was covered with the same metal as well. "What *is* that?"

Her room was similar to mine with the bed against the outside wall, a window to the left, and a small dresser in the right corner. A tiny bathroom backed to the one in my room, hers in the far left corner. Like the bedroom, the bathroom was covered with metal, and I wondered how the hell he expected her to take a shower on a wet metal surface.

Shit. I was already thinking that we would be here long enough to need to bathe. My feet were caked in dirt from running barefoot in the woods.

"Your room isn't covered in Wolfram Dwiin?" She reached out and touched the wall.

"If that's what you're calling this metal, no." I'd never heard of it before, which was peculiar. I'd taken a ton of chemistry classes for premed. "It looks like aluminum foil." I slid a foot against the floor and realized the metal wasn't as smooth as it appeared. It was a little grainy to the touch. "Except it's not smooth."

Interesting.

I studied the wall to see what made it feel like sandpaper.

She snorted but somehow still seemed elegant. When I snorted, I was fairly certain I resembled a pig.

"This is most definitely *not* aluminum foil." She flicked her wrist. "This is dragon tungsten. It's the strongest metal in the world, forged by dragon fire."

Tungsten I'd heard of, especially with all the commercials about wedding bands.

"Any dragon can make it?" I laid my hand on top of it and pressed. It felt like one of those pin art boards I'd played with as a kid. It didn't hurt, but it wasn't comfortable.

"Only the strongest of our kind can." Saphira's tone hardened. "Which means our captor has a powerful friend."

"Why couldn't it be him?" I asked as I turned my head toward her.

She sighed and moved to her queen-sized bed, also with blue sheets. She plopped down on the mattress and touched the left side of her head, where our attacker had hit her. "The strongest of our kind are the royal line, and neither Drake nor his father would *do* this."

I swallowed hard. My curiosity and the drugs had dulled my anxiety, but now my shoulders tensed. "What do you mean, *royal* line?"

She dropped her hand. "What *did* Drake tell you?"

"That he wanted someone who wasn't after his money to be his wife and have his heirs." My skin crawled, but I held my body still. Drake had trusted her to come get me, suggesting they were friends. That relationship didn't add up. She seemed like a nice, caring person. I doubted Drake would've protected me the way she had.

She stared at me and opened her mouth, exhaling. Placing her hands on her lap, she shook her head. "That's surprising. Prince Drake is never one to hold back about his status or his wealth."

"Then maybe he planned this." Narcissists did anything for attention and empathy. They strove for control and power, and during the handful of times I'd seen Drake, I could tell those were his priorities. "This is a good way to make him out to be a martyr."

"Please." She waved a hand. "He's all about power. Your kidnapping will make him appear weak in the eyes of our people. Believe me, this is *not* his doing, and the king wouldn't do anything to upset his son. Maybe this guy found some Wolfram Dwiin that was made a long time ago. I thought it was all locked up somewhere central, but there could be more."

When she put it that way, I understood. I could see that about Drake. "I'm assuming Drake's award-winning personality is why we're in this mess. Has he pissed off enough of his subjects, or is the *prince* title a formality with no real meaning?"

"Wow, you sure jumped in without knowing the facts." She pursed her lips. "You seem like a 'think things through' type of girl, not one who leaps without knowing what she's getting into."

"Oh, believe me, I am." I sat beside her on the bed and clutched one of the pillows in my lap. "I didn't realize 'What species are you?' was a legitimate question. You all *look* human. How was I supposed to know there was a dragon hidden inside him?" I still didn't understand how that was possible. I squinted as I stared into her eyes, trying to see a hint of the creature within her.

She laughed, her worry fading as her face smoothed into a genuine smile. "That's fair. We hide our existence from humans. And there isn't a dragon inside us. It's more like the soul of a dragon courses through us."

My heart fluttered as my body overheated. Somehow, that explanation freaked me out more. The thought of an animal soul being inside them made them sound unstable.

"Do you need to use the bathroom?" Saphira bit her bottom lip and scooted to the edge of the bed.

Here I was, feeling unsettled, and she was the one inching away from me. "No. Why?"

"You're flushed, and you look sick. Are you going to puke, or is it about to come out the *other* end?" Her face wrinkled as if she smelled something bad. "Even though I'm a dragon, I have a weak stomach when it comes to *that*."

I covered my face with my hands. There was no telling what my expression had looked like for her mind to go there. "No, I'm not going to puke or...poop." Wow. That last part had been way too hard to say when I wanted to become a doctor. "But if an animal's soul is loose in you...doesn't that make you, like, constantly at odds?"

Her eyes widened. "Oh, that's what's wrong with you? You think I could go all dragony at any second?"

Well, yeah. "That's not an unreasonable assumption."

"And this is why we don't tell humans." Saphira rubbed her temples. "Which is probably why Drake didn't tell you. Though I bet he wanted to tell you he's a prince. He brings it up in every conversation, despite each of us being well aware."

"At least it makes more sense that he was so focused on my appearance. He said that with his dominant features and my symmetry and figure, his heirs would be appealing." Though I wasn't sure it made his comments *that* much better. He'd still treated me as less than a person, but perhaps, since I wasn't a dragon, he naturally viewed me that way.

She rolled her eyes but readjusted herself on the mattress, comforted that I wouldn't hurl on her. "That does sound like Drake. He's a little intense."

That was an understatement. "Can you explain the dragon thing?"

"Oh, yeah." She stood and paced the small area between the bed and the wall. "It's not like our animal is constantly trying to take over or battle for control. Our dragon is deep inside us, and for the most part, it's content. Magic pumps through our blood, and when we call forth the dragon to either fly or fight, our shift is a natural transformation."

I leaned forward, hanging on to her every word. Though I was listening, I still had to be missing things. However, I took away the key idea that was relevant to me—they called forth the dragon, not the other way around. "Does it ever take over?"

When she stopped in her tracks and frowned, my entire body froze.

"If we don't shift often enough, yes. Our dragon can get anxious and try to take control." She pushed her long curly hair behind her shoulders. "Our dragon side is as much a part of us as our human side. We're neither human nor dragon but shifter. All shifters have similar struggles."

The information crashed over me like a wave pulling me under. "How often do you need to shift? And there are other types of shifters out there?" All my life, I'd studied as much about the world as possible, but now I wondered if I actually knew anything.

"There are also wolf shifters and bear shifters." She placed her hands behind her back. "But not any other kind that I know of."

At least there was that...I guessed. Right now, I needed to learn most about my immediate threat—dragons. "You didn't answer my question about how often you need to shift." Was she avoiding telling me? My palms were sweaty, and I wiped them on my black shorts.

"Once a week at minimum," she whispered. "But I shifted three days ago, and we'll find a way out before then."

A lump formed in my throat. We had four days until her dragon took control, and since this room wasn't big enough to hold her in that form, I wasn't sure what that would look like. One thing I was fairly confident about was that if I didn't find a way out of this room before she had to shift, I would likely get crushed and die. "What if we *don't* and I'm in here with you? I'll be squashed."

"I can't shift in this metal prison. If we stay here that long, I'll lose my mind as my dragon tries to take over but can't." She smiled sadly as if she was trying to reassure me.

That didn't help *at all*. "Uh…so I'd be stuck in here with a woman whose dragon soul is trying to take control and failing. That doesn't sound much safer."

She placed her hands on my shoulders and stared into my eyes as she vowed, "We'll find a way out of here before then."

I smiled. She was reassuring me the same way Mom would have. It was the most kindness anyone had shown me in a long time, and I didn't want to dismiss it. "Let's take it day by day."

"That's all we can do." She stood up and winced as she clutched her head.

She might have a concussion from getting knocked out. The best thing she could do was lie down and rest.

"First, let's get some sleep." I slid off the bed and landed on my knees. "We both need it if we're going to find a way out of here."

Exhaling, she nodded. "That's a good idea." She stared at me. "Why are you on the ground? That metal will *not* be comfortable to sleep on."

Though it was grainy, I was tired enough that I was certain I could fall asleep. "It'll be fine."

"We just got kidnapped together." She pointed to the side of the bed by the window. "You take that side, and I'll sleep here."

My heart expanded, tightening my chest. She was taking the side of the bed closest to the door. "Uh…thanks. Let me wash my feet before I crawl into bed." I'd rather take a shower, but I had no clean clothes to change into. Another issue for tomorrow.

She nodded, and I rushed into the bathroom. The metal-coated shower was just big enough for one person to stand in, and I almost cried when I turned on the water and it ran. The toilet wasn't metal, but the sink was covered with it.

Our kidnapper must have thought that we wouldn't risk trying to escape via the toilet. He wasn't wrong.

There was a bar of soap on the sink and in the shower, along with bottles of shampoo and conditioner, which I found odd. He'd kidnapped us but made sure we had toiletries. Not wanting to over-think it, I washed my feet quickly and searched for a towel. The only one I could find was the hand towel by the sink, but that would have to work.

Once I got clean and used the toilet, I headed back into the room. Saphira was already lying on the bed with her eyes closed. The sun was just setting, but it wasn't like we had much to do, so I slid in beside her and was out within seconds.

***

SOMETHING CLICKED, stirring me from sleep. Was my roommate waking up to go to class?

When the mattress moved, reality crashed over me. I wasn't at the university. I'd been kidnapped, and there was no telling where we were.

A low snarl came from Saphira, and I opened my eyes, finding myself staring at the window. I sat up just as the door opened.

Our attacker strolled in and shut the door, blocking it so Saphira and I couldn't go around him. He held two cups of coffee. Steam drifted from the tops, and I leaned toward him.

After a night of not drinking anything, I needed something for my throat.

His hair was wet from a shower, and his white shirt clung to his skin, emphasizing each muscle. His dark jeans molded to his legs, and the sad truth was, if I'd met him outside of this horrible situation, he would have interested me.

He held out one cup to Saphira and the other to me. "I thought you two might want some coffee while I make breakfast," he rasped.

The last thing I wanted to do was accept a cup of coffee from him, but my pride wasn't stronger than my need for caffeine and something to drink. I rolled across the bed, and when I tried to stand, I fell hard onto the floor and onto Saphira's foot.

Okay, maybe all the drugs weren't out of my system.

Saphira grunted and yanked her foot out from under me, and my face burned as I got up.

Now that my pride had completely vanished, I was certain there was no salvaging it.

He stretched the cup of coffee toward me and chuckled. "You clearly need this."

A few choice responses popped into my head, but I swallowed them down. I might not trust him, but if I didn't drink or eat something, I wouldn't last very long.

Saphira must have had the same thought because she grabbed her cup at the same time I did, our attacker watching our every move.

There it was. He was still in attack mode, ready to spring into action.

As I put the cup to my lips, our attacker said, "Oh, and I've got something for you."

He reached into his pocket, and I tensed.

CHAPTER SEVEN

I HAD no clue what to do. He'd brought coffee, which seemed too good to be true. He must be using the caffeine to distract us from whatever was in his pocket.

Even if I had taken a self-defense class, it wouldn't have helped me. This guy was a *fucking dragon*. I was confident that even if I could remember the moves I'd learned, they wouldn't work against him.

Saphira paused with the coffee cup half an inch from her lips.

I wasn't the only wary one.

He struggled to remove whatever was in his pocket, putting me more on edge. My heart raced, and my body tensed. I hated feeling helpless.

"Finally," he grumbled as he withdrew his hand.

A scream lodged in the back of my throat as Saphira thrust her coffee at me, and I took it. A little bit of the hot liquid splashed over the rim onto my hand, but getting burned was the least of my worries.

She stepped in front of me...just as he removed my bracelet from his pocket.

His brows furrowed as he glanced at Saphira and me. He lifted the bracelet by the newly fixed clasp and said, "What the *hell* is your problem?"

"What in the world?" Saphira gestured at the jewelry. "You brought us a *gift?*"

I pivoted around Saphira and shoved both mugs of coffee into her hands. I blinked as my shaky hand reached out to snatch the jewelry from him, but I stopped short. This could be a trick. "That's *my* bracelet. He broke it yesterday and took it from me." He had to be playing some kind of demented game.

"I...fixed it." He held out the bracelet to me. "I thought you'd be happy."

Kidnappers didn't do things out of kindness, and I wasn't stupid. We'd seen his face.

Unbridled rage soared through me. Now that it'd been released, the flames were hotter and brighter. "I'd be happier if you hadn't *kidnapped* us. Then you wouldn't have needed to fix it in the first place!"

His jaw twitched, and his pupils slitted. The flames cooled as fear rooted inside me. If we were going to die, I didn't want to make it happen earlier than he planned.

"No wonder Drake picked you." Our kidnapper scowled. "You're as entitled as *he* is."

The words cut worse than anything physical he could've done. I despised Drake, especially since he'd locked me into marriage without telling me what I'd become a part of. "I'm not entitled. Did you really expect a *thank you?*" I swallowed, trying to keep my voice even.

"What are you trying to accomplish?" Saphira squinted at him. "I'm not buying this whole 'nice guy' act."

He laughed bitterly. "Oh, and you're such a *nice* girl. *She* didn't even know dragons existed until the attack."

I placed my hands on my hips. "How did you know that?"

"The fear you displayed yesterday and now," he answered

smugly. "You don't even want to reach out to take back the bracelet that means so much to you."

I hated that he'd guessed that. I'd worked hard since Mom had died to hide my emotions behind a perfect fake smile. Current circumstances had ruined that completely, and I was afraid I'd never be able to pretend again. A chill ran down my spine.

Was this my life now—a lifetime as his or Drake's servant, doing whatever they desired?

"Fine. You want her to have her *fixed* bracelet," Saphira snapped, and handed me back my coffee. She reached out and took the bracelet from him. "There. Consider it done. You're obviously such a *nice guy* and wanted to take care of us." She lifted the bracelet and the coffee cup, emphasizing her point.

His neck corded, and his hand blurred as he clasped Saphira's cup. "Treating you like prisoners will make this easier for *me*." He pulled on the cup, and the liquid spilled.

I stumbled back a few steps, not wanting to be caught near these two as they fought each other. They could land on me and squash me like a bug. I gulped in a breath, trying to remain quiet.

"Wait!" Saphira exclaimed and lowered her lips to the rim of the cup.

What in the world was she doing?

"Prisoners don't get to make demands," he snarled and jerked the cup again.

Saphira had already placed her lips on the cup, and her whole body moved with it. She raised the hand with the bracelet and pressed it against his chest for balance.

She tipped the mug, taking a large sip before he pushed her off him. He frowned as his attention flicked between the mug and her. He tipped the mug up and drained the rest of the liquid. His attention then homed in on me, and he swiped my mug and drank it all, too.

The coffee had been super hot, more so than I was used to. The liquid had scalded my hand, so I had no idea how he'd drained two full mugs that quickly. Then I realized he was a fire-breathing dragon. That liquid was probably like a cool drink of water to him.

That all-too-familiar trickle of fear clawed in my chest, weakening my knees. I didn't regret my decision to take Eva's place, but damn, I wished I weren't here.

"You *bastard*," Saphira growled.

Our attacker's face hardened as he glared down his nose at her. He sneered, "I tried to be nice, but you complained, so we're back to square one. Watch your tone, or you won't get any breakfast. I know the human can last longer than *you* can without food. Behave, or I won't even provide the essentials."

Her irises flashed with anger, and smoke trickled from her nostrils.

I froze. This further proved how little I knew about dragons.

"What do you want from us?" I whispered. "I don't know you."

The angry lines on his face smoothed. "It isn't you that I'm after. You're just a means to an end."

Once again, I was missing something. "What could capturing me accomplish?"

Saphira pressed a hand to her stomach. "He wants something from the *prince*."

It took a second for me to understand. Even though Drake had entitlement issues, I didn't yet correlate that with "prince." In my mind kings, queens, and princes should do everything they could for their people and be selfless, hardworking, and caring. Three qualities I was confident Drake lacked. "I hate to break it to you, but I don't mean a damn thing to him. I'm replaceable."

Our kidnapper snorted. "Did you think it was smart to agree to belong to a man you don't know? Were you that hard up for money or attention? Because you're in over your head with no fucking clue what's going on."

His sinister tone caused me to step closer to Saphira. Though she was a dragon, I felt safe with her.

"And now you're looking for safety with someone who also

doesn't have your best interest at heart." He gave an exaggerated eye roll. "Maybe you should work on your instincts before they get you killed."

Despite his cruelty, there was truth behind each word. Either that, or he was an amazing manipulator, but something about him made me *want* to trust him.

Oh, hell. He was right. My instincts were messed up.

Saphira edged in front of me and pointed a finger at him. "I don't know who you think you are or what you know about me, but you're wrong. Drake may be my prince, but I think for myself. I don't need a *man* telling me what to do."

"So you have nothing to hide?" The corners of his eyes tightened as he watched her. "Nothing you would rather she not know?"

"Of course not." Saphira glanced at me and back at him. "Drake asked me to pick her up because the king needed to meet with him. I obliged. That's all."

He gestured at me. "You think she knows what she signed up for? She didn't even know he was a dragon."

She flinched.

My skin prickled, and I stepped away from Saphira. He was trying to turn us against each other, but I sensed there *was* something more I didn't know.

My vision dotted as I grew short of breath. "What else is there?" My voice squeaked.

"Tell her," our kidnapper taunted.

She turned to me, her cheeks turning a faint pink. "I truly thought you were aware of everything."

"All I knew was that I agreed to marry a *man*." I took a few steps back, wanting to get away from both of them. "Now there are dragons, and there's something else I don't know."

Saphira cringed, and our kidnapper laughed humorlessly.

I gasped, trying to catch my breath. The room suddenly seemed devoid of oxygen.

"Is *that* what you think he wants you for?" the kidnapper asked. "As a wife?"

My mind replayed our conversation at the bar. "He said he needed someone to be his, someone he could trust not to be after his money and to provide heirs. What else—"

"Your future is as his *breeder*," the kidnapper spat. "He'll marry another dragon while you're kept somewhere in the house, at his beck and call."

The world tilted, and I clutched the footboard of the bed for balance. "No." I locked eyes with Saphira and croaked, "Tell me that's not true."

She averted her gaze to the floor. "I..." She trailed off, unsure what to say.

My chin trembled. After she'd gone all out to protect me, I'd trusted her, thinking she was a good person. Now I knew the *real* reason. "Why? Why does he need *me* if he'll have a dragon as his queen?"

"Because dragons have a hard time reproducing, and our numbers are dwindling," Saphira answered in a rush. She hung her head. "We're trying to find a quicker way to reproduce."

"Trying?" This kept getting worse. "Like...this hasn't been done before?" My heart jumped into my throat. I hadn't considered carrying a *dragon baby* inside me. How would that even work?

She picked at her fingers, not answering.

My kidnapper had no problem filling me in. "You'll be one of the first humans they try this with. There's no telling if it'll work or if you'll survive."

No wonder Drake had wanted someone without strong familial ties. I could die, and it would be years before anyone asked about me...if they ever did.

Tears burned my eyes. I'd thought I'd felt worthless before, but boy, had I been wrong. *This* was the epitome of worthlessness. "And you knew?" I glanced at Saphira. I needed to hear her say it.

"Everly, until we spoke today, I thought *you* knew." Saphira twirled a piece of her hair around her finger. "I swear. I know Drake is self-absorbed and has borderline ethics, but I didn't realize he was this far gone. I didn't know how to tell you or if I should."

She could justify it all she wanted. At the end of the day, I was a human, so I didn't count. I was a means to an end, even if it resulted in my death.

I laughed. I hated to admit it, but the kidnapper had a point. "I didn't know about the supernatural world, so even if I had known about the breeding part, I wouldn't have known I might *die*."

She opened her mouth and closed it.

Good. At least she wouldn't talk out of her ass anymore.

I straightened my shoulders. "Take me back to my cell."

"What?" Her mouth dropped open. "No! We need to stay together."

I laughed again, the sound making my stomach roil. "Why? To protect me so I can die a brutal death when a dragon baby rips its way out of my body? I'd rather take my chances with *him*." I pointed at our kidnapper.

Something like sadness reflected in our kidnapper's eyes, but it had to be a figment of my imagination. I was done trusting anyone... especially *dragons*.

"I'll take you back to your room." He turned and grasped the door handle.

Saphira grabbed my arm. "Everly, don't go. I get it, I messed up. But when I came to collect you, I seriously thought you knew everything. *I'm sorry*. Please stay here with me."

Something tugged at my heart, but I pushed it away. I wouldn't keep making foolish decisions. "I need space."

I jerked my arm, expecting her to hold tight. She could make me stay if she wanted to, but she released me.

"Please. Stay," she begged again.

"You heard her." The kidnapper opened the door and plucked the bracelet from her hand. "She wants to go back to her room, and I don't blame her. All you people are out for yourselves."

He spoke as if he had experience.

Once I walked out the door, he shut it and locked it behind me, and panic set in. He had me alone again without Saphira for protection.

I'd let him play me, and now I wondered what he'd do.

CHAPTER EIGHT

I REGRETTED LEAVING SAPHIRA, but I couldn't stay with her, either. I no longer trusted her. The kidnapper had made her allegiance to Drake clear.

Hurt ripped through me, and I hated that I'd let my guard down. I guessed that was what happened when you were thrown into a chaotic situation with people you didn't know. Saphira and I had forged a bond of captives, but I would be a captive at Drake's place as well. She'd be free.

This was why I didn't let anyone close. I always got hurt.

Our kidnapper slid around me and slipped the key into the lock of my room. He opened it and pointed inside. "No funny business."

I didn't have it in me. The sting of betrayal was fresh, and I blinked several times to hold back tears.

I stepped back into the room and inhaled deeply. I scanned the space and realized the sandwich he'd left me yesterday was gone.

He must have cleaned up behind me.

Holding both mugs in one hand, he came in and shut the door.

I'd expected him to lock me in and leave, but nope. There he stood.

His features softened, taking away the dangerous edge. I needed it back because my stomach started fluttering without it. There was no denying that he was sexy.

I sat on the mattress and ran my hands over the sheets, the void of loneliness growing colder inside me.

He strolled over and held out his hand, letting the bracelet dangle. "Here. Take this."

Unable to fight the urge, I obliged. Part of me expected him to yank it away and make fun of me, but when warm metal touched my fingers, he released it. His hand had heated it up.

I swallowed hard, the years of manners Mom had ingrained in me coming forward. "Thank you."

His brows furrowed. "That's the last thing you should say."

"Huh?" My brain was struggling to keep up. My thoughts kept flitting back to Drake and Saphira instead of focusing on our conversation.

"You just thanked me." He shook his head, his long bangs blocking part of his eyes. "You shouldn't. Fixing your bracelet is the least I could do."

If I hadn't known any better, I could've sworn I was talking to a different man. Yet I was still a prisoner locked in a bedroom, so this had to be a game. "I don't know what you're trying to accomplish, but you can quit being nice. Yes, you called Saphira out for what she's part of, but that doesn't make us *friends*. I'm still your *captive*...unless I'm not? In which case, I'd like to get the *hell* out of here."

"I can't let you go. I'm sorry." He bit his bottom lip and frowned. "I wish I could, but there's a reason for all of this."

I'd heard the same refrain over and over again since Mom's death. Reasons always abounded, and they always benefited someone else. I was expendable...a means to someone else's ends. "Don't. I get it. There's something you want that's more important than me."

"Look, I don't know you, but you have a jaded view of yourself. You're beautiful and strong and—"

"Stop." Was this guy for real? He must have thought I was so hard up that throwing a few flattering words at me would make me stay here willingly. "Don't pretend to be a nice guy. Just stay the asshole we both know you are."

I was usually good at biting my tongue and playing whatever role my audience wanted, but I was so damn tired. This whole "taking my sister's place to become a dragon prince's mistress and bear his heir that could possibly kill me at any time" development had broken me. That didn't take into account getting kidnapped. Every time I thought things couldn't get worse, something out there proved me wrong, not that I believed in a higher power or anything.

He nodded. "I can do that." He opened the door and glanced back at me. "But I am sorry. You don't deserve this."

Gritting my teeth, I readied myself to yell at him to get out, but he was already closing the door. I flopped onto my bed and stared at the ceiling, rubbing my thumb around the inscription on my bracelet and trying not to think about what would happen to me.

THE DAY CRAWLED BY, and my boredom reached the point where I'd stand at the window and try to count all the raindrops that fell from the sky. The light dimmed as the sun set behind the leaden clouds. Dragon Guy had brought me some basil chicken and pasta for dinner, and I was now eating at the table, still staring at the raindrops.

I cut off a piece of chicken with the butter knife and the fork he'd provided and continued my impossible task. I was up to one hundred thousand, and I knew, without a doubt, that wasn't even one-millionth of what had fallen.

At least the room was dry and warm. He could have stuck us in a basement or something not even half this nice.

A door somewhere in the house slammed, and I held my breath, listening. Could he have possibly gone? I hadn't heard that noise before. But he hadn't left the house since Saphira and I had arrived, so that would be a first and most likely wishful thinking.

Placing my fork and knife on the edge of the plate, I leaned forward. My forehead hit the cool metal bars, blocking me from seeing out of the corner of the window, where I assumed a road was, since I could see trees to the left.

An engine rumbled, and I took a step back just as a large, white, beat-up pickup truck rushed by. The silhouette of the person inside was huge, confirming it was our kidnapper.

Blood buzzing, I pressed my face to the window again, watching the taillights shrink and disappear from sight.

He'd actually left and taken a truck and not the ATV, and I hoped that meant he was driving somewhere far away.

This might be my only chance to get out of here and call for help. I spun on my heels and ran for the door. I clutched the doorknob in my hands and turned, praying it opened.

The knob didn't budge.

Dammit. That would've made this whole thing go a lot more smoothly, but that also would have meant that my kidnapper was not intelligent. Unfortunately, that wasn't the case.

I'd just have to be smarter.

I faced the room, pressing my back against the wooden door. I scanned the area for another way out, and my gaze stopped on the end table.

That was it. I would smash my way out.

I placed my plate of food on the floor and grabbed the thin wooden legs of the lightweight table before hurrying back to the door. I grunted as I swung the table against the door with all the force I had. The *bang* was loud, but nothing much happened. The only damage was a small dent on the door and a much larger ding on the edge of the table.

"You've got to be *kidding* me," I muttered. Frustration fueled me, and I lifted the table over my head and slammed it into the same spot.

Something *cracked*, and my heart picked up its pace. It was about damn time something good happened to me, but when I lowered the end table, the thick wooden section on top dropped to the floor with a heavy *thud.*

And the door didn't look much worse than it had moments ago.

Of course he'd pick a sturdy door for this room. That wasn't surprising, considering Saphira's room had all that aluminum foil inside to keep her locked in. This guy had thought everything through.

Something banged against the wall separating Saphira and me. She must have been worried.

I pulled at the ends of my hair, feeling crazy. I wished I could communicate with Saphira somehow. If I'd had her hearing, I was certain we could have, but with my human ears, I might as well be alone.

Unsure what to try next, I dropped the wooden legs and hurried to the bathroom. Maybe there was a way out through there.

I turned on the lights and studied the tiny room. There was a small tub, a toilet, and a sink all crammed together. The room was windowless.

My heart pounded so hard that my ears rang. The sink was a pedestal style, so the wall was exposed on the sides underneath, between the wall and the toilet. Maybe I could knock that out.

I kicked at the drywall, determined to break a hole through it.

It was like hitting a pole.

Right. Dammit, Saphira's bathroom was on the other side and covered in that special metal. If a dragon couldn't get through it, there was no way *I* could. I was only wasting time and energy.

There had to be another way.

I rushed back into the bedroom, my attention locked on the bars over the window. I could try breaking those.

I picked up the two broken-off table legs and circled back to the window. Swinging them as hard as I could, I pounded the middle of the five bars over and over, using all the force I could to crack the metal. With every strike, wood splintered from the legs.

I continued to push, hoping like hell *something* would give.

One leg broke in half, the loose part flying backward and hitting me in the forehead.

Pain exploded from the impact, and I damn near fell over. I side-stepped and caught my balance as something warm ran down my face. Tears welled in my eyes as I tossed the wooden legs on the bed and rushed back into the bathroom to take care of my injury. If I didn't get the wound to clot, I would be in worse shape.

Another round of banging came from the wall, but I ignored it as I snatched some toilet paper and pressed the material to my head. That should keep the gash from getting worse, even if it wasn't the most sanitary treatment. That was an issue for later.

My head throbbed, and I couldn't believe I'd been so foolish. I was so intent on getting *out* that I wasn't using my brain. There was no telling how long he'd be gone, so I had to think critically instead of repeatedly injuring myself.

Stepping back into the room, I took deep breaths to calm my flight instincts and allow the adrenaline to clear my head. I rolled my shoulders, and my gaze landed back on the door.

Breath catching, I developed a different plan.

The hinges. That was my best bet.

But I didn't have a screwdriver or hammer, so how could I get this to work?

I growled and clenched my free hand. Every damn time I got close to thinking of a solution, the plan fell through. It'd be nice for *something* to work while I had the chance.

My attention went back to my dinner plate. The only good thing about being here so far had been the delicious food. I was wondering how my kidnapper had learned to cook so well when light reflected off the knife.

Body tensing, I feared I might cry tears of relief.

Still clutching the paper to my cut, I stumbled to the butter knife and fell on my knees. That stupid table leg had hit me hard enough that it was messing with my balance. I had to get out of here.

I grasped the knife and slowly marched to the door. Head spinning, I decided to start with the top hinge.

The hinge was new and unpainted, which was what I'd expected. Our kidnapper had gone to great lengths to set this place up to contain us, which meant he'd bought new stuff. The top of the hinge was capped and styled like the more modern version, so I couldn't twist the top off with my fingers.

This butter knife would have to do the trick.

I placed the edge of the knife between the top hinge and the tip of the pin, but I couldn't get the blade to slip through. I hissed, tired of everything working against me.

Removing my hand from the toilet paper on my head, I waited to see if it would fall. It stayed, as I'd been hoping from the few times I'd seen my stepdad treat a razor cut.

I hit the butt of the knife with my fist and wedged the blade between the hinge and pin, but not enough, and it hurt like the dickens. I couldn't hit it any harder. I needed something to use like a hammer...like the table legs.

Moving as quickly as possible, I snatched one wooden leg from where I'd tossed it on the bed and moved back to the hinge. This time, I held the butter knife at the base of the handle and smacked it repeatedly with the leg. The pin started to lift away from the hinge.

My stomach fluttered, and my senses sharpened. I might make it out of here. I worked diligently while listening for the rumble of the engine, and soon, I was yanking the hinge out.

I got to work on the middle one.

The process felt as if it took forever, but when I finally got the bottom one loose, I could hardly believe it.

With all three pins removed, I stood back and examined the door. I had to separate the hinge so I could get through the opening. I placed my thumb on the top part of the hinge with my fingers underneath it, pulling it toward me. It wasn't easy, but I gritted my teeth and yanked harder, and finally, the hinge separated.

I followed the same process for the middle and bottom ones, and I had the door open enough to slide through. I glanced out the bedroom window to see it was pitch black outside. It'd taken longer than I'd realized, but our kidnapper wasn't back yet. I had time to try to get Saphira out.

Head pounding, I stepped into the hallway.

A faint rumbling hit my ears.

Our kidnapper had returned.

CHAPTER NINE

I FROZE. Everything inside me screamed to get Saphira out, but there was no time. It had taken me all evening to get myself out, and she was in a dragon-proof, metal-encased room.

The rumbling grew louder. It was definitely the truck from earlier and not someone driving by. Our kidnapper was almost back. I had to escape *now*, or all of this would have been for nothing. Once he saw how I'd broken out, I wouldn't have another opportunity.

Counting on Saphira's superb hearing, I said, "I'm sorry. He's almost back, and I've got to leave, but I *promise* I'll bring help."

A small bang on the door was the only response I could hear. The lack of frantic loudness led me to believe she was giving me permission.

With every passing second, he grew closer. The dragon was already so much stronger and faster than me. I needed a head start.

I ran to the end of the hallway. To my left was the front door with a small rectangular window that revealed headlights flickering between tree branches. Adrenaline coursed harder through my blood, making the engine sound louder, as if I were in tune with my surroundings.

Pivoting right, I rushed into a den. The dark charcoal walls gave the place a more modern feel, and two black futons were the only furniture. This couldn't be where he lived.

My eyes found a white-painted back door with a window at the top revealing more of the looming forest.

There was my exit!

I held my breath as I turned the lock. *Please don't let this set off an alarm.* When it clicked, I exhaled and threw open the door. I stepped out onto a small cement porch, and my shoulders relaxed when no alarm blared to notify him of my escape. I forced myself to pause and shut the door, not wanting to alert him right away that I'd left. I needed as much time as possible before he began to hunt for me.

A shiver ran down my spine as the door shut. Then I was sprinting over the grass, the soggy earth underneath already clumping between my toes.

Gross. I hated being barefoot, but high heels would have impeded me more.

Rain still poured from the sky, and my shorts and shirt were drenched before I reached the tree line. Maybe this weather would help me. The rain should hide my noises and scent.

As I reached a Fraser fir, I pushed myself harder, racing into the woods. The engine was now loud. He'd be at the house momentarily and heading inside.

With every step, my feet sank into the ground, making it hard to gain traction. This must be what quicksand felt like, but at least I could move forward.

My breathing was rapid, and I tried to get it under control. I didn't know which way was north, south, east, or west. I'd never gone camping and had always brushed off learning survival skills—and boy, did it show. I needed to find a road or someone's home.

Scurrying noises had my heart stopping. I'd been so focused on escaping that I'd forgotten about wildlife. I reminded myself what I'd learned during my time volunteering at a veterinary office: most animals took cover from the rain, just like humans, so this weather made the woods safer for me.

I paused to get my bearings. The heavy rain and darkness made it hard to see much farther than a few feet in front of me. I'd have to run until I found something to follow. Staying put wasn't an option.

Something charged at me, and I clamped my hands over my mouth to hold in a scream. *This is it. I'm going to die.*

A squirrel rushed by me to a tree for shelter.

I let out a maniacal laugh. I was letting my anxiety get the best of me. People went hiking all the time, and most of them made it out alive. I was being a drama queen.

A thick branch lay at the foot of a red spruce, and I snatched it up to carry as a weapon.

No more being scared of squirrels unless they shift into humans, I chastised myself. I was letting fear control me. I had to get away, send help for Saphira, and find my way back to Eva and Elliott. If I could convince them to leave with me, maybe the three of us could start fresh somewhere Drake could never find us. And if they refused to leave my stepdad, I guessed I'd deal with Peter as long as it kept us all safe.

That was worth risking everything. If I was going down, it would be swinging and not as some pathetic martyr.

From not too far away, I heard the door of the truck close. Shit, I hadn't made it very far, and he was already out of the vehicle.

I picked up my pace, trying my best to navigate the weeds and ground cover. Every few steps, a twig or rock stabbed me, but I gritted my teeth and refused to give up. I kept hoping my eyes would adjust to the darkness, but they hadn't. I began to move more quickly and focused on the ground right in front of me, dodging trees. I wanted to run, but I couldn't risk being careless.

"Everly!" a deep, sensuous voice called from behind me.

I startled and clamped my hands over my mouth to hold in my scream, forgetting I held that branch. It cut my lips, but I didn't feel the pain. *He* knew I was gone.

I had to go.

I pumped my arms and hurried, trying to prevent the branch from hitting me as I ran. I stumbled over a hidden root as the rain slanted, hammering my face. Lovely. Yet another hindrance that would make things more challenging. But that was the one thing that drove me—a challenge. And I'd be damned if I gave up now.

I got into a rhythm and only tripped over my feet every few steps. The rushing of a stream caught my attention, and I turned toward it. I'd read something about following a stream when you were lost in the woods. Water ran downhill, and I needed to remain at least a hundred feet away to reduce the chances of meeting wildlife, slipping, or running off a cliff.

As I made my way toward the water, an uncomfortably tight sensation shifted inside me. Something was definitely wrong, and I didn't need to be a genius to know what. I was being hunted.

The feeling of being prey once more twisted through my stomach. My hands shook, but I didn't slow. He would only catch me faster.

The sound of rocks jostling came from the direction of the water. With the loud noises, I imagined it was a large animal—like a bear.

I stayed on my path and didn't move any closer to the water. A stitch flared in my side, the pain worsening with every step. I was extremely out of shape, but I couldn't afford to stop and rest. Though he hadn't called out again, I could sense he was near.

I inhaled through my nose and breathed out of my mouth to see if that would calm my nerves and ease the discomfort. One time, a gym instructor had recommended that I hold my hands over my head to catch my breath faster, so that's exactly what I did. There was no point in worrying about looking stupid now.

Surprisingly, the tactic worked, and it also blocked a bit of the rain from hitting my face.

Despite my attempt to keep the same distance from the stream, I broke through the trees, and the bank came into view. It had cut to the right and intersected my path. That was what I got for having human ears in a torrential rainfall.

The stream was sizable, likely due to all the rain, and rocks led down to the water. Every ten to fifteen feet, the stream dropped down a short hill.

Under normal circumstances, I would have marveled at the sight. It was worthy of a painting. But now was *not* the time for inspiration.

I turned right to keep a hundred feet between me and the stream, but a tree branch just above my head shook. I screamed and dodged left, desperate to get away from whatever was about to attack me.

"Everly!" my kidnapper yelled. "I'm coming."

His words added to my fear, and tears ran down my face, mixing with the rain. An owl flew from the branch above me, not some evil raccoon desperate to eat me.

Now he had a better sense of where I was.

My foot hit smooth stone and slipped. I tumbled to the ground, and my knees hit rock, scraping off skin. I groaned as the sharp pain took hold, and I tried to get up but only slipped again.

This couldn't be happening. I had to get out of here. Gritting my teeth, I released the branch and forced myself to get slowly to my feet, ignoring the agony in my knees. I inched toward the muddy, twiggy ground and away from the slick, smooth rocks.

Once on solid footing, I hurried ahead, knees aching.

I touched the tree trunks to steady myself. I had to keep a level head, or I'd wind up hurt worse than I already was, no kidnapper needed.

The stream rushed beside me, and I made sure to keep it in view. After a few minutes, the sound of loud, crashing water made a lump form in my throat.

I knew that sound all too well. A waterfall.

As if confirming my thoughts, the trees broke away, revealing the drop-off. I couldn't see how far down it went. I'd have to find a way down from here.

Reaching the edge of the cliff, I clung to the trunk of a fir and glanced over. Jagged boulders framed the waterfall. I'd have to go down using the trees. It would take a while, and the drop was steep, but it was nothing like the rocky waterfall on my left.

But as I moved deeper into the trees and away from the water, the earth under my feet crumbled away. I tried to jump back onto solid ground, and I gripped a tree trunk, the wood rough beneath my fingers. As my hands slipped, splinters cut into my palms. I wasn't strong enough to hold on, and I couldn't get any purchase with my feet. I yelled, "Help!" At least, if the kidnapper found me, I wouldn't fall. All my life, I'd tried to do things the smart way, and here I was, about to die in a mudslide.

"I'm almost there!" he exclaimed, sounding concerned.

Or maybe I was delusional.

"I can't hold on!" I exclaimed as my grip slipped.

Sky blue eyes appeared through the darkness just as my fingers slid from the trunk.

"Everly!" he yelled as I fell.

I tumbled backward down the incline. Rocks dug into my skin, and dirt crumbled around me. I threw my body out of its backward roll, but I lurched sideways and kept sliding, hitting what felt like every rock and branch in my path.

My body slammed into something, and the back of my head took the brunt of the impact. Bright sparks and then black spots flashed across my vision.

Through my blurry gaze, I saw the shape of my kidnapper running down the incline. Where I'd slipped and fallen, he expertly navigated the terrain. He hunkered down next to me, and my vision narrowed to a pinpoint.

His gorgeous blue eyes were the last image I'd ever see.

He brushed my hair away from my face and whispered, "I've got you, Everly. I'll save you."

For some reason, I believed he would.

CHAPTER TEN

DARKNESS SURROUNDED ME. I was dying. I kept waiting for the blinding light that people saw during near-death experiences, but it never came. I'd thought running through the dark, rainy woods had been the bleakest moment of my life, but that was nothing compared to being submerged in unending darkness.

I couldn't see my hands or body, and it felt like there was nothing around me.

Maybe I wasn't in a physical form.

Something brushed against my face, but as I reached up to touch the sensation, all I felt was air.

I tried to move my legs, but nothing happened. Fear settled heavily inside me.

A tickle started somewhere within. The sensation spread throughout my...existence? Because I no longer had a body.

No matter what I did, I couldn't get away, and the tickle strengthened into a tingling sensation. The odd sensation was hot, uncomfortably so, but maybe that was from my body temperature dropping after getting soaked by the rain in the dark.

I had to be dying, and my subconscious was the only thing

processing the stimuli. What should have been my chest tightened at the realization, and I'd have done anything to caress the bracelet my mom had given me.

Scorching heat swirled through me. I wondered if the kidnapper had changed into his dragon form and was breathing fire on me. That would be one hell of a convenient way for him to hide dead bodies.

Flames licked through me, racing toward something deep inside.

My heart.

Maybe this was what being burned alive felt like when you were unconscious. No one could endure something like this and live to tell the story. I'd never believed in a higher power, but with the agony searing through me, I was ready to plead and beg someone, *anyone*, to take this misery away.

Then something *snapped* inside me, and my consciousness slipped away.

A BANGING REPEATED in sync with the throbbing in my head. Something else pressed into my back, and I fidgeted, too tired to even attempt to open my eyes.

Faint footsteps sounded, and a deep, sexy voice said, "Cut it out. She's *fine* but needs rest."

"What did you do to her?" a strong female voice replied, sounding very similar to Saphira. "If you put so much as a *bruise* on her, I'll kill you when I get out of this prison cell."

The past several days replayed in my mind, and any hope of getting more rest vanished. The memory of tumbling down the steep incline and banging my head had my eyes popping open.

I shouldn't be alive.

The world swirled in front of me, and I sat up so quickly that I nearly tumbled to the floor. My clothes clung to me, still drenched from the rain, and the scent of copper almost had me dry-heaving. I scanned the room I'd escaped not long ago, searching for the horrible smell, but nothing stood out. The room looked the same but also different.

Shaking my head, I closed my eyes and opened them again, but the view didn't change. The room was more detailed with elements I hadn't noticed before. The dark charcoal walls were actually several individual colors swirled together—black and white with faint touches of orange and yellow to provide warmth. Everything that a true painter knows, but never had I seen colors quite like this.

There was only one explanation—a brain injury. I needed to get to a hospital quickly. I wasn't sure how I'd survived this long.

When I touched the back of my head where it had hit the trunk, there was only mild discomfort.

"I didn't hurt her, for gods' sake," our kidnapper replied. His voice was sexier than I remembered, the sound alone calling to something deep inside me.

Something brushed against my mind, and I jumped to my feet and turned around, searching for the danger, but nothing was there. The room spun faster than it should have, and I noticed a tiny spider hiding in the far corner twenty feet away. It wasn't much larger than a pen tip, but I could make out all eight legs.

A strangled groan left me as my heart pounded.

Footsteps hurried toward me, and my attention swung to the doorway. My kidnapper stepped in...and my heart stopped as the world tilted on its axis.

There was a hint of a scar on his chin, something I hadn't noticed before, and it added to his rugged good looks. His sky blue eyes were even more breathtaking with the white and blue shades so beautiful. I could stare into his eyes for the rest of my life and never grow tired of them.

He lifted his hands as if he were approaching a rabid animal. "Everly, you're safe."

I laughed, not sure why. The sound wasn't normal, and it echoed as if I were in *someone else's* body. Something was very wrong.

I took several steps back until I hit the wall behind me. "I need a hospital." The person who'd spoken sounded elegant and scared. The scared part fit me perfectly, but not the elegant part.

"No, you don't." He shook his head and took one step closer. "That's the last thing you want. Trust me."

Rage blazed through my blood as I clenched my jaw. "*I* just finished a premed degree. Did you?"

He opened his mouth to respond, but I wasn't done.

"I *know* I shouldn't be standing right now, but I am. I'm seeing colors I never knew existed, and I can see a fucking millimeter-big spider in great detail across the room! So please forgive me if I don't *trust you.* I'm *here* because of you."

Hanging his head, he kept his attention locked on me. "That's fair. You're right."

Something inside tugged at me to close the distance between us and tell him it was okay, almost like I had a split personality. I reached for my bracelet, but all I felt was my skin. The bracelet was gone. A sob built in my chest.

"Hey. Wait." He reached into his jeans pocket and pulled out the bracelet. "It's right here."

The asshole had taken it from me again. Even though I was angry at him, I also wanted to kiss him. Something was truly off with me. "Give it back," I demanded, sounding like a petulant child.

"I will, but don't put it on." He tossed the bracelet to me.

It came at me in slower motion than normal, and I easily caught it as something brushed against my mind again.

Clasping my fingers around the bracelet, I breathed rapidly, not even upset that he'd told me not to wear it. "Something is seriously wrong with me. Things are moving slower, and I can feel something weird inside. I've injured my brain and need medical help."

He pinched the bridge of his nose, and his brows furrowed.

The overwhelming urge to rub my fingers over the indentation and smooth out his worry had me taking an involuntary step forward. Oh, *hell*, no. I had to get my act together.

"Everly," he breathed. The sound was like a paintbrush running over a blank canvas—magical and full of promise.

My body warmed in a way that was inappropriate and foreign to me. Ever since Mom's death, I'd vowed to stay away from men and focus on my studies. And though my captor was delectable, he would *not* tempt me. I clenched my free hand and chanted internally, *Go away, Stockholm syndrome.*

"You fell and got hurt," he said, moving another foot closer to me.

Some of the warmth froze, and I sneered. "Yeah, I was there and *experienced* it. The tree won, which is why—"

"I *couldn't* take you to a hospital." His irises darkened, and he rasped, "You wouldn't have made it. Your skull was cracked. When I examined it to see how bad it was, I changed you."

My heart pounded like the drums of war. I had no idea what he meant, and I didn't want to. Whatever he'd done was why I was feeling so strange. However, I refused to ignore my problems. Denial often made a situation unsalvageable. "What does that mean?"

Licking his lips, he lifted his chin as if he was ready to face me head-on. Sweat pooled under my arms.

"I..." He blinked for a long moment.

If he didn't spit it out, I'd be forced to rush over there and rip his clothes off to show him who was boss. I froze, my sexually infused trigger startling some sanity back into me so I didn't follow through on that threat. I'd been attracted to men before, and I'd never had trouble keeping my mind focused. Why was I struggling with *him?* Maybe it was the near-death experience.

He cleared his throat. "I turned you into a dragon shifter."

I stood there, dumbfounded. Pressure built inside until I might explode. I examined my exposed skin for a bite. All I could see were cuts and bruises where twigs and rocks had hit me, but nothing that looked like teeth marks. I ran my fingers along my neck, searching for puncture wounds, but all I felt was smooth skin.

He inched closer to me. "What are you doing?"

"Stay back." I threw my hands forward, making sure the one still held the bracelet. That was when I noticed blood on my hands from where I'd touched the base of my neck. They shook as I turned my palms toward me. Blood stained them, too. "Did you bite me on my scalp?"

"What?" he asked loudly.

I jumped back, hitting my head on the wall supporting me. A twinge of discomfort wafted through me but disappeared.

That wasn't possible...for a human. But I wasn't human anymore.

"Shit. Sorry." He groaned. "I'm not trying to upset you, but you caught me off guard. You can't change someone by biting them. The blood is from your head injury."

The last part was the only thing that made actual sense. Though learning he hadn't bitten me eased some of my tension, lightheadedness swept in. "Then *how* am I a *dragon*?" The last word came out in a squeak.

"It's a special ability I have. I couldn't let you die." He blew out a breath. "So I changed you."

"You didn't ask for my permission!" I wiped the blood on my shorts and clutched my bracelet tightly, needing something to ground me. Mom always did that, and I needed any part of her I could find at that moment.

My captor flinched. "True, but I couldn't. You were unconscious and dying."

"That doesn't make this *okay*." All my life, the only thing I'd had of my own were my choices: what degree I wanted, where to go to school, and whether to keep in touch with my brother and sister. I didn't have close friends, a loving family, or someone to confide in. And the one thing I could count on—making decisions for myself— had been stripped away by someone who'd made the largest decision possible for me.

He laughed, and the cruelness on his face yanked at something deep inside. I'd hurt him, and I wanted to ease his pain, which wasn't rational. I dug my feet into the hardwood, refusing to budge from my spot.

"You want to be a doctor." He waved a hand toward me and stalked forward, a dangerous edge to his glare. "You're telling me that if a patient was dying, and you could save them, you *wouldn't* unless they gave you permission?"

I straightened my back. "They'd be in a hospital, so that would be my permission."

"Not if they were in a wreck and were found unconscious. Or what if you stumbled upon someone struggling in a park?" His jaw twitched as his pupils slitted.

He said something else, but I couldn't hear it. All I could do was stare at his dragon peeping through. When his pupils had slitted before, it had terrified me, but now I was intrigued...uncomfortably so.

He growled, "Would you? Answer me."

I shook my head, trying to focus on the conversation and not him. He was so close I could feel the warmth wafting from his body and breathe in his delicious minty-amber scent. "Yes, I would, but I wouldn't be changing them fundamentally."

"I'd rather you *hate* me than be *dead*," he said with conviction.

"Oh, don't worry. I've hated you since you attacked our car." I was done letting him bully me. "You're going to kill us, anyway. Don't pretend. We've seen your face. You can't let us go. You might as well tell me your name. There's no reason to hold back now."

"Thorn," he murmured. "My name is Thorn, and I won't kill you. Either of you. Why would you think that?"

"Don't you dare play the good-guy angle again." I stuck my finger in his chest, and something *zapped* between us.

He gasped, feeling the sensation, too, but I schooled my features into a mask of indifference. My expression was one thing I was good at controlling. I'd learned to do it after losing Mom so I wouldn't anger my stepdad with looks of hurt or disgust.

"You, *Thorn*, kidnapped Saphira and me, locked us up, chased after me when I tried to escape, then changed me into a *dragon*." I let my anger flow through every word, wanting him to feel how much I despised what he'd done. "You are *not* a nice guy. You're a *monster*."

His lip curled, and pain flashed across his face. His eyes turned cold. "Let me show you a monster." He yanked my arm, dragging me into the hallway.

I planted my feet on the hardwood, trying to fight his hold, but he was too strong.

Terrified, I wondered what I'd unleashed.

CHAPTER ELEVEN

NO MATTER WHAT I DID, Thorn was too strong to stop. I could have still been human with how easily he was dragging me through the living room and back down the hall. His fingers dug into my skin, adding more discomfort to the electricity sizzling between us. The pain was as agonizing as it was pleasurable.

"What are you doing?" I rasped, trying to yank out of his hold.

I might as well have been a baby doll because he didn't even miss a step and continued moving at the same quick stride.

"If you want to be a prisoner, you'll be one," he growled.

My throat hurt as my legs gave out. I fell to my knees, and with one swoop, he picked me up and carried me around the turn in the hall.

The door to the room I'd been staying in was exactly how I'd left it. It hung crookedly in the doorway, each hinge still undone. I wasn't sure what he thought putting me back in there would accomplish, but then he walked past it to the last door in the hall.

Saphira.

"What are you doing to her?" Saphira shouted and banged on the wall.

Instead of responding, he dropped me and pulled out the key to unlock her door.

This was my last chance to get out of here, and I had to try.

I leaped away just as his hand grabbed for me and caught my hair. The door clicked open, and he yanked on me, setting my scalp on fire.

"Shit!" he hissed, and let go, then promptly caressed the base of my skull where it had hit the tree trunk.

My eyes burned with tears. As the door opened, he wrapped his free hand around my waist and threw me inside. Saphira yelped and jumped away, and I sailed onto her mattress.

Before I could even glower at him, the door had slammed shut, the sound echoing over the metal. I yelled, "Asshole!" feeling a lot braver with him on the other side of the door.

"Everly!" Saphira hurried to me. "You're hurt!" She reached out to inspect my skull, her eyes wide with concern.

Her worry caused my tears to break free and stream down my face. No one had even pretended to care about me in so long that even though she'd been willingly taking me to Drake to become his breeder, I couldn't stay mad at her.

That was how pathetic I'd become.

I caught her hand and shook my head. "I'm fine. Thorn saved me."

Her eyes bulged, and she stumbled away from me and into the wall next to the door.

With everything Thorn had done, including tossing me in here so cruelly, I couldn't blame her disbelief. "I know. I was surprised that he saved me, too, but he needs me for *something*."

Her smooth, dark skin blanched, and she lifted a shaky finger. "Who the *hell* are you?"

I stood, not wanting my clothes to soak the sheets and because her reaction had unsettled me. "What do you mean, who am I? You picked me up from my stepdad's house yesterday."

"No." Saphira jerked her head from side to side. "You look and sound just like Everly, but you aren't human."

Was that what was tripping her up? I rubbed my hands together, needing to expel my nervous energy. "I *know*," I croaked. "I escaped from the room and ran into the woods. I tried to get away, but I slid down a huge incline and cracked my skull. I should be dead, but Thorn found me, and I woke up like *this*." I waved a hand in front of my body. "My vision is funny, I'm hearing things, and there's something messing with my mind. He said he had to change me to save me." Maybe I was supposed to die, and this was me cheating death.

"That's *insane*." Saphira raised a hand and held it in front of her. "We're born as dragon shifters, not *turned*. Stop with whatever *game* this is, and tell me how you were able to hide your dragon before!"

None of this made sense. Thorn had told me he'd changed me, and now she was saying that wasn't possible. I wasn't sure who to believe. Each of them had a reason to lie to me.

Just when I thought someone cared about me, I was proven wrong. If that wasn't proof that I was destined to be alone, I wasn't sure what was. "I wasn't hiding anything." I was so tired of trying to be enough for everyone. Maybe that was the point—I needed to be content with myself from here on out. "But believe what you want. I don't care."

I glanced down at my soaked shirt and shorts. Blood stained the shoulders of my white lace top, and the bottom half was covered in mud. My black shorts had mud caked on them as well, and I looked like a drowned rat.

The panel in the door opened, and clothes were dropped onto the floor, followed by two towels.

Thorn cleared his throat. "I know I said I'd be a monster, but Everly needs to take a shower after her *outing*, and there's extra there for Saphira. The clothes will be too large for Everly since she's short, but she can roll them up to an acceptable length."

I wanted to wave my middle finger high in the hopes he'd see it, but getting out of these soaked, muddy clothes sounded too good to pass up.

I approached the clothes as if they were a weapon, making sure there weren't any surprises. All I found were two thin, white cotton towels, two pairs of women's sweatpants—one gray and one black—and two medium black cotton shirts.

Something twisted hard in my stomach. Where the hell had he gotten these women's clothes? Worse, why did it bother me that he might have a girlfriend or a *wife?* My breathing quickened as anger slammed through me, and something sulfuric lodged in my throat.

"Whoa!" Saphira exclaimed and lifted her hands. "You need to calm down."

Oh? *Now,* when I was barely hanging on to my sanity, she decided to talk to me. That same odd feeling brushed against my mind and roared.

Something growled nearby, and I staggered back a few steps, trying to locate the threat and get away. I couldn't find it, despite the growling growing louder.

"Holy gods. You weren't lying." Saphira gasped and hunkered down. "Everly, you need to calm down, or you will attempt to shift, which is impossible in this room and will only drive your new dragon crazy."

Shift.

The new, foreign part of me—the part that roared—*really* enjoyed the sound of it.

"You're angry, hurt, or scared. Hell, from what you told me, you're most likely all three, and it's causing your dragon to want to take control." She spoke slowly and calmly, reminding me of when Mom would sing the twins a lullaby to calm them and get them to sleep. "I need you to breathe slowly and deeply. Clear your mind, and take yourself to a happy place."

For a second, I felt like I was listening to a clip from *Peter Pan.* But instead of flying, I was trying to stay...human.

I kind of wished it were the pixie dust issue instead.

The heat in my throat strengthened, and I opened my mouth, only for smoke to trickle out. *I'm breathing out black smoke.* She hadn't been exaggerating. I would shift if I didn't get it together.

The panel opened again, and those breathtaking eyes locked on me through the hole. "Everly!" His voice was filled with fear.

"Don't come in here," Saphira said. "You'll make it worse. I need her to focus on something *happy, not* our *kidnapper* who got us into this mess. If she attempts to shift in here, it's going to be very problematic."

His eyes had a calming effect on me. I stared into them and focused on how it had felt to paint during the past several days. Though I'd been under pressure to make money, there'd been something freeing about it. To see something blank come to life with whatever image I envisioned had brought *me* to life for that short time.

The dark purples I loved to use for the sky flitted through my mind, reminding me of Thorn's scales. The various blues and whites I'd used to capture the essence of the city skyline were similar to my kidnapper's eyes.

"You're doing it," Saphira encouraged. "Keep it up."

Her voice brought me back to the present. The roaring wasn't in my head anymore, and the smoke had gone. Instead of anger, I felt exhausted. "Thank you."

"You're welcome." Saphira forced a smile, though it didn't reach her eyes. "Why don't you take a shower and clean up? It might make you feel..." She trailed off, searching for the right word, then settled on, "Better."

I wondered what word she'd been about to use, but it didn't matter. A shower would give me some alone time to begin to deal with my new fate.

I bent down and snatched a towel, the black sweatpants, and a shirt. The idea of blending into the darkness was alluring.

Although...now that I had dragon vision, that would be impossible, much to my chagrin.

I headed to the tiny bathroom, seeking isolation. As I turned to shut the door, my traitorous gaze landed on him.

He was still watching me.

Something inside me vibrated like a cat purring, and a lightness filled my chest. Two very strong reactions that *he* shouldn't inspire.

Once I shut the door, I leaned my head against the wood and breathed. I put the bracelet on my wrist, not wanting to lose it again.

There was movement in the outer room, followed by Saphira murmuring, "How did you make her a dragon?"

That was an answer I would also like to know, and I held my breath.

Instead of words, I heard the door panel slide shut. That was answer enough—he wasn't going to tell her.

I slumped and forced myself to turn on the plastic-walled shower. As soon as I could, I stepped into the hot water and washed my concerns and fear away.

I WASN'T sure how long I remained in the shower. The water never rose to a warmth I enjoyed, and even though I tried like hell to focus on getting clean, I couldn't get the demons that plagued me out of my mind.

My only reprieve was the long stretch of solitude.

I towel-dried my hair, the back of my skull still tender. I couldn't fathom how I'd survived. The injury I'd sustained should've left me incoherent for days. But here I stood, brushing my wet hair with my fingers, unsure how I looked because there was no mirror.

I quickly pulled on the clothes Thorn had set out for me. Disgust with myself settled hard in my stomach as I pathetically smelled them, wondering if I could pick up the scent of the person they belonged to.

They didn't smell like anything except Thorn, from when he had handled them.

The clothing was a size too large for me and definitely too long, as he'd suspected. My heart fluttered at the fact that he'd paid enough attention to me to notice, forcing me to get angry at myself. I would *not* allow myself to feel soft, warm feelings toward a man who'd done nothing but hurt me.

Footsteps padded to the bathroom door, and I opened it before Saphira could knock. I didn't want her accusing me of anything else or asking more questions I couldn't answer. It would only frustrate the both of us.

I forced a smile, but when she flinched, I figured it hadn't hit the mark. Mom had told me to fake it until I made it, and I'd been taking that piece of advice ever since I'd left her grave.

"Your turn," I said, trying to sound happy.

She narrowed her eyes and brushed past me. She glanced around the bathroom, and I followed her gaze.

Steam rolled out of the tiny room, and the lights were off. I realized I'd showered in the dark. The steam wasn't an anomaly, except the shower had felt cool the entire time, so that much steam seemed weird. The darkness was most definitely not normal...not for me.

"I'm assuming you're okay with sharing the bed again?" She arched her brow. "Otherwise, one of us is sleeping on the floor."

I shrugged. "We might as well get comfortable with each other. We might be here for a while." He couldn't put me back in the other room because I was a dragon shifter now. I was stuck in this aluminum can with her.

"That's what I was thinking," she agreed before shutting the door.

I went to the bed and stared at the mud-stained sheet. At least it was the sheet and not the mattress cover. I removed it from the bed just as the lock on the bedroom door clicked.

Thorn was back. The door swung open, revealing him with a new blue sheet, pillow, and a lavender blanket. My throat tightened.

He had changed into gray sweatpants that left very little to the imagination, and his white cotton shirt hugged his body, each curve of muscle on full display. If I wasn't careful, drool might run from the corner of my mouth.

He stayed in the doorway and held out the items. "Here, I thought you might want some clean stuff since I kinda threw you on the bed." Regret lined his face.

"That isn't very monstrous of you," I said as I took the items from him. "Or are they lined with itching powder or something to hurt us?"

"I am *not* going to hurt you." He placed a hand on his chest and stepped closer to me.

Electricity surged between us, leaving me breathless.

"I promise." His eyes locked on my lips. "That was never my intention, especially not now."

The last three words replayed in my head, but my mind couldn't focus. I edged toward him, each of us drawn to the other like magnets.

"Why did you take me?" Something inside me was desperate for him, but I couldn't want someone who could be so careless.

"Because—" he started, but the bathroom door opened.

CHAPTER TWELVE

THE ROAR RANG in my head again as both parts of me were angry over the interruption. I was desperate to know *why* Thorn had taken me, and I was damn close to getting the answer.

Thorn took a hurried step away as if we hadn't shared some sort of inappropriate moment.

"Did I interrupt something?" Saphira asked, and I looked at her to find her gorgeous skin back to its normal brown color and her face scrunched in puzzlement.

The clothes hugged her body. One size too small, they fit her like a glove, as if she purposely wanted to show off her figure. I wanted to shove her back into the bathroom and slam the door. She was captivating—worthy of painting. I didn't doubt where Thorn's attention would be now. I couldn't compete with her.

Not that I was *trying* to compete. I had to get my head on straight.

"I was just dropping off clean sheets," Thorn rasped.

Oh, I bet I knew why his voice was gravelly. My jaw ached from clenching my teeth. My stomach burned, and my attention darted to Thorn.

The burning was extinguished as quickly as it had come.

His eyes were locked on me, his pupils slitted, and my heart jump-started, calming the crazy whirlwind of emotions.

"And you were about to tell me why you kidnapped me." I wouldn't let him off the hook. If I didn't push, I would never gain clarity. I moved so I could shift my attention between him and Saphira. The last thing I needed was for them to realize I was attracted to *him*. One, he could use that to his advantage if he wasn't already, and two, I didn't want Saphira to judge me more than she already had.

Saphira crossed her arms, enhancing her chest, and a snarl rang inside my head. She shook her head. "There's a far more pressing question. How the *hell* did you turn her into a dragon shifter? Do you realize what you've done?"

Thorn's gaze ripped from me to her. Instead of desire, though, his face turned pink, and his nostrils flared. "Yes, I do. I *saved* her. Would you rather I had let her die?"

I swallowed. He had saved me, but I didn't need to believe he was a hero. If he hadn't kidnapped us, I wouldn't have almost died.

My heart dropped at the thought of him not taking us. What the *hell* was *wrong* with me?

"I'm not buying it." She lifted her chin and sneered. "You took us against our will. I don't believe you give a shit what happens to us. You need to keep her alive for whatever your plan is."

"Says the woman who was willing to take Everly to a dragon shifter so she could be his human breeder." Thorn wrinkled his nose as he spat, "At least I've put off that horrible future."

Put off. Not *ended.* The wording was particular.

My insides ached at the thought of him leaving me.

No, it had to be heartburn. I *didn't* like this sexy man—er—man. *Just man. Not sexy. Ugh, Everly, keep your head on straight. Don't let your hormones get the best of you.* I'd never had this problem before, and of all the times and places, I'd rather it not be *here* with *him*.

Needing to prove to myself I hadn't completely lost it, I straightened my shoulders. "You're deflecting instead of answering her question. How did you change me? You said it wasn't a bite. Was it a scratch?" It had to involve the mixing of bodily fluids or a virus or whatever it was that made someone a dragon shifter.

The corners of his mouth tipped upward as his attention settled back on me. His face softened as he said, "No, it wasn't a scratch, either. DNA doesn't make up a dragon shifter."

"Exactly!" Saphira exclaimed as she pointed a finger and marched to the bed. "That's why *this* shouldn't be possible. If I hadn't seen her nearly shift, I wouldn't have believed it. I would think you and she were in cahoots and had a witch involved, but she was terrified. That's something you can't fake. Drake and King Arman will be very intrigued when they learn what you did."

Thorn's face hardened, and an alarming glint appeared in his eye.

My body warmed from the danger he emanated.

"King *Arman* will know *exactly* what it means." His voice was deep and low, reminding me of the various red and orange shades I used in a painting to convey that type of emotion.

His hurt and anger called to something inside me. I hadn't noticed that I'd moved toward him until my hand touched his arm.

The electricity between us sprang to life, and I gasped at the pure intensity, as if his emotions had amplified our connection.

His irises glowed faintly, reminiscent of light breaking through the clouds on an overcast morning, as if my touch had given him peace or hope.

Then he flinched and jerked his arm away from me. His usual indifferent façade slipped back in place.

The rejection stung, and I dropped my hand as my face burned. I couldn't believe I'd tried to be there for him after everything he'd done, and worse, that he'd disregarded me.

Saphira's brows furrowed as she glanced between us, but before she could say something, he stepped toward the door.

"That's the beauty about this situation." He yanked open the door. "I don't have to give you anything. You eat when I allow it. You shower when I decide you can. Anything you want or desire has to come from me, and tonight, my generosity has ended." He stepped outside and shut the door, the sound echoing against the metal in the walls.

His absence caused my head to swim, as if he were the oxygen I needed. Unshed tears burned my eyes. He shouldn't have this effect on me.

"Asswipe," Saphira growled and banged a fist against the wall.

I could hear his footsteps in the hallway, but then he was gone. All I could do was stand there and breathe in the last of his scent before it vanished. Needing comfort, I wrapped my arms around myself.

"Help me make noise so we..." Saphira trailed off and looked at me. Her hand went still and dropped to her side.

Great. She must have realized that something even weirder was going on with me. I didn't have the energy to answer questions about why I found Thorn attractive, especially since I didn't understand it myself.

"Gods." She sighed and dropped her head. "You're a huge mess."

At her assessment, a tear streamed down my face. The truth hurt.

"I'm sorry," I whispered. I tried not to show emotion around others, but I couldn't get myself together. "I—"

"You do *not* need to apologize." Saphira smiled sadly as she removed the dirty sheet from the bed and unfolded the new one. "You haven't connected with your dragon, which is difficult to do at ten, let alone your age. You'll feel all sorts of crazy until we can get you outside so you can shift."

The hold on my heart loosened, and I wiped away the tear. "Wait. This is normal? I feel like I'm losing my mind."

Saphira plopped onto the side of the bed closest to the bathroom, grabbed the extra pillow, and placed it on my side. She patted the spot next to her. "It is normal. When you shift, you get to know your dragon. Right now, it's like there's this foreign entity in your body with its own emotions and thoughts because you haven't truly merged."

Thank goodness. I must have confused that struggle with my attraction to Thorn. I had a valid reason: I was misunderstanding my dragon. "Ugh. I don't know if I can go on like this much longer." I plopped onto the bed, reminding myself not to get too comfortable with Saphira even if I needed a friend. She had Drake's interests at heart, not mine. But she could provide me with insight to help me get a handle on my new dragon.

"It will be hard, but you'll manage." She pulled her hair to the side and lay back on her pillow. "I could tell you were strong the moment I met you and saw how your stepdad treated you."

Now that I knew how good her hearing was, I'd bet she'd heard Peter's words: *It's about time she was useful.* He'd never hidden that he didn't like my presence. "I wouldn't call it strong. I would call it learning to survive."

"They're one and the same to me." She shrugged as her wet hair turned the light blue pillowcase a shade darker.

"That's why you didn't have a problem handing me off to Drake?" The words were out before I could think them through. I usually didn't hold people accountable for their actions. It didn't actually change anything, besides making everyone uncomfortable. I liked standing out academically, not through confrontation.

She pursed her lips. "I honestly thought you knew what you were signing up for. I didn't realize he'd let you believe you were agreeing to marry him—a *human* him."

Now that I reflected on our past conversation, he hadn't. "He used words like *mine, belong,* and *heirs.* I just assumed that was what he meant."

"Please. If he left out the words *dragon shifter, breeder,* and *mistress,* knowing you were human and unaware of our world, then what else could you have thought?" Saphira rubbed her temples. "That's not okay. In our world, agreements are binding, but he can't hold you to the agreement because he didn't disclose everything."

"It wasn't in writing." I shrugged. "So I'm not hopeful on getting out of it." That would've been smart of me to demand, but I wasn't one to confront people and protect myself when it came to my siblings—hence why I'd been taken advantage of by my stepdad and Drake.

Saphira cringed. "It doesn't matter if it's not in writing. An agreement can't be misleading, and *this* was. If we get out of here, I'll take you home."

My breath caught, and I tipped my head toward her. "Are you serious?" I hadn't expected her to go against Drake's wishes. He was also her prince.

"Of course." Saphira touched her chest. "He may be my future king, but that doesn't mean I have to go along with him when he's wrong. I thought he was doing questionable things before, but *this* confirms it, and he's gone too far. I'll get my dad to talk to King Arman and inform him of what Drake was trying to pull."

I didn't want to cause Saphira problems, but I didn't have a choice. "I appreciate what you're doing, but I can't go back. *If* we get out of here, I'll follow through on my promise, especially if an agreement is binding in your world."

"I told you we have a case for why it can't be upheld." Saphira rolled onto her side toward me and propped her head on her hand. "It'll be fine. We'll make sure to get the king involved."

"No, *you* don't understand." There was no doubt in my mind about what would happen if I didn't show up to take the role. "If I don't go, he'll take my sister instead."

"Why would you say that?" She shook her head. "I'm telling you—"

I already knew she was going to regurgitate that I'd be allowed out of the agreement. "Because my stepdad stole money from them. I heard the entire conversation Drake had with Peter. If my stepdad couldn't repay the money, Drake said he'd take my sister as payment."

Saphira's jaw dropped. "What? That's crazy. He was blackmailing a *human* for his daughter?"

"Yes, he was. When Drake left, I tried to talk to Peter. He wouldn't tell me anything, but the more I thought about Eva being forced into a loveless relationship..." I trailed off, the emotions clogging my throat. I jumped to my feet and paced in front of the door. "I couldn't allow that to happen."

I paused, chest heaving, trying not to melt down more than I already had.

Something pulsed through my veins like a jolt, and I had no doubt it was my dragon.

"Wait. If he wanted your sister, how did you get involved?" Saphira bit her bottom lip, looking like she was trying to solve a complicated math problem.

That part should've been obvious. "I remembered Peter talking about a bar that Drake owns downtown, so I went straight there and found Drake. I demanded he take me instead of Eva if we couldn't come up with the money. I thought I'd figure a way out of it. I even took paintings to my local art gallery, but not one of them sold. Then my time was up, and you showed up to take me to him."

"I asked him why a human would agree to his terms, and he just smiled, saying it was part of his charm." She closed her eyes. "I figured he'd promised you nice things in return. I had no clue he'd gotten *that* bad."

Footsteps pounded down the hallway toward us, but I couldn't seem to care. I was too focused on needing to convince her that none of that mattered. "Either way, I have to go to Drake. Otherwise, he'll take my sister." Then *all* of this would've been for nothing.

A loud growl came from behind the door, followed by a click. Thorn stepped inside, smoke trickling from his nose and his hands fisted at his sides.

My dragon roared in approval while I froze in terror.

CHAPTER THIRTEEN

EVEN THE PART of me that was terrified didn't want to tear my eyes away from Thorn. The image of him before me needed to be immortalized, and I tried desperately to capture the memory in detail so I could recall it later and do it justice.

"He *forced* you to be his?" he rasped, each word followed by a trickle of smoke from his mouth. "You weren't willing on your own?"

Saphira scoffed and sat upright, placing her body slightly in front of me on the bed. "Why does that matter to you?"

That was a valid question, but that foreign entity within me brushed against my mind, and the urge to grab a fistful of her hair and yank her out of my way surged through me.

Great, he'd blessed me with a violent dragon. What else could go wrong? I winced. Though I didn't believe in fate or anything else, for that matter, especially since there was no proof it existed in medicine or science, I didn't want to jinx myself. *I take it back,* I thought, sending that out to the universe just in case.

"That's none of *your* concern," he growled, and marched to my side of the bed. He hovered over me. "You were *forced* into this?" He searched my face for answers.

The heat from his body rolled over me, despite several feet separating us. My dragon calmed at his nearness and the fact that we had his attention.

His body quivered as his face twisted in a combination of anger and agony.

"Shit!" Saphira hissed and jumped to her feet. "Get yourself under control. You can't shift in here, and you'll wind up hurting us if your dragon goes crazy."

Somehow, I knew I was the reason he was out of control. "Yes and no. Technically, it was my sister, but she just turned eighteen, and I promised my mom on her deathbed that I would protect her and my brother. I had to take her place."

His breathing slowed, and his face smoothed. I sort of wished he could shift in here. I wanted to witness him shifting into his dragon form because it would be mind-blowing.

"So...you don't have feelings for him?" he murmured.

If I'd been just human, I wouldn't have heard the question. Even now, his words sounded like a rush of wind. "No," I answered loudly and scrunched my nose. "His personality ruins everything about him."

"Why is that relevant?" Saphira placed her hands on her hips. "It doesn't matter if she finds him attractive. She agreed to take her sister's place."

A snarl vibrated deep in his chest as he glared at her. His jaw twitched as he spoke through gritted teeth, "It matters because he's forced a *human* into our world against her will. I see that his ethics don't fall far from the *king's*." He said the last word as if it were vile.

"Well, it's not a problem anymore." Saphira gestured to me. "Because she's not human. And the king is *nothing* like his son."

Thorn laughed bitterly. "That's what he wants you to believe."

Despite the anger and malice lacing his words, there was a hint of heartbreak, too. If I hadn't heard that tone enough in my own voice over the years, I wouldn't have picked up on it, but the sound tugged at something deep inside me. I threw my legs over the bed and leaned toward him, catching myself before I reached for him.

My reaction to him perplexed me. When I met him, I'd found him handsome, and he had intrigued me, but ever since I'd changed, it was like I *needed* him. It had to be a type of sire bond. All the vampire and a few werewolf shows and books talked about that, so it made sense that it would happen with dragons.

"I *know* the royal family." Saphira lifted her chin, staring down her nose at Thorn. "I grew up around them. My father is the king's trusted advisor, so don't act like I'm misinformed. Your opinion of them stems from your own ill-perceived views."

"Ill-perceived?" Thorn grimaced. Anger and hurt were etched into his face. "I can promise you that is *not* the case."

Whatever had happened to him was personal. I wasn't sure how I knew that, but something inside me screamed it was true.

Saphira fisted her hands. "I don't have anything to prove to you. Obviously, you aren't willing to see reason." She raced toward the unlocked door, trying to escape.

I'd been expecting it to happen. If she got out of here, she could lock Thorn and me in the room while she went to get Drake.

I should have joined her, but I didn't budge. It was as if my survival skills had vanished into thin air.

Thorn didn't waste a second. He rushed after her.

As Saphira reached for the doorknob, Thorn slammed into her side, knocking her into the wall.

He planted himself in front of the door, blocking her escape. His pupils slitted as he shook his head, frowning. "And here I was, hoping you actually *wanted* to listen to my story to see if there was any truth to it."

She groaned and rubbed the right side of her arm. Wet hair stuck to her face, making her seem less elegant than usual.

"Yeah, I'm the misguided one." He snorted and tromped to the door. "I'm done talking." As he opened the door, his gaze settled on me, and he said gently, "Get some rest. The tenderness in your head should be gone by morning if you get a solid night's sleep."

Before I could respond, he shut the door, and the lock clicked into place. His footsteps were muffled as he walked slowly away. With each step, the weight in my chest grew heavier. I put a hand over my heart to ease the discomfort.

"Something weird is going on," Saphira murmured, her head tilting.

I didn't understand why she was whispering. Thorn was far enough away that we couldn't hear him anymore. "I don't know what you're—"

She placed her finger in front of her lips.

I had no clue what the gesture meant in dragon. "What are you doing? Flipping me off?"

Dropping her hand, she bit her lip. "Telling you to be quiet. Is that how *you* flip people off? Because most people know what that means. It's even in the opening to *Pretty Little Liars*."

I was so confused about what shushing me had to do with a television show. "I know it means 'be quiet,' but you're a *dragon shifter*. I thought it might mean something different to you."

She shook out her arms. "We live in the same world as you. We may have dragon magic, but overall, our gestures are the same as yours."

"Good to know." At least I could rely on nonverbal communication. "I can't hear him anymore."

Motioning to the metal, she answered, "That doesn't mean he can't hear *us*. The Wolfram Dwinn is not only stronger than a dragon, but it also limits the noises we can hear while we're surrounded by it."

His reappearance after I'd told her everything about why I'd agreed to Drake's terms now made sense. He'd listened to our conversation from wherever he'd been in the cabin.

My stomach soured. There was no telling what else he might have overheard that I'd rather he not know.

I wrapped my arms around my waist. Not knowing how dragon stuff worked was getting on my last nerve. "Anything else you might want to share with me?"

"Not that I can think of." Saphira plopped down on her side of the bed and pulled the covers over her legs. "It's not like there's an instruction manual. You're the first turned dragon I've ever known."

Her words hit the mark, and I sucked in a breath. "That's fair. It's just frustrating not knowing things that every other dragon knows. I'm trying to paint a realistic picture when I haven't mastered the fundamentals yet."

Brows creasing, she popped her lips. "I'll pretend I understood your point and tell you that you'll have to think of this as a work in progress. I'll be right by your side, guiding you."

There was one thing I knew for certain: of every dragon shifter I knew, though that group was limited, I trusted her. "Okay." I had no other option, anyway.

I crawled into bed and turned my back to her, facing the window and not the door. That was for the best. If I stared at the door, I'd be willing Thorn to reappear just so I could see him again. At least, with the window, I could only see outside. "Like Thorn suggested, I should get some rest." I forced a yawn, hoping to prevent her from asking the question from earlier again.

"Fine. I'm tired, too," she grumbled and dropped her head onto the pillow.

Silence descended, and I stared at the metal wall. My reflection stared back at me. My blonde hair was drying and looked fuller than ever before, and my gray eyes were more vibrant. My normally ivory skin had a hint of olive to it, giving me a natural glow. I barely recognized myself.

Time moved slowly as I waited for fatigue to overtake me. My mind raced with everything I'd learned. Over the past few days, my life had taken a tremendous curve, and these progeny-like feelings I had for Thorn disturbed me. I shouldn't care this much about someone who'd kidnapped me.

Just when I figured sleep would never come, my eyes closed.

Loud footsteps hurried down the hallway toward the door, waking me from my slumber. My eyes popped open, and I tried to get my bearings.

This was definitely not my dorm.

The world was brighter than ever before with colors I'd never known existed reflecting off the metal wall in front of me.

The bed jostled as someone clambered to their feet.

With that, I remembered where I was and who I was with. Now the colors made sense.

I sat up to find Saphira glaring at the door.

A key slid into the lock, followed by a *click* and the door opening. The scent of bacon wafted into the room, but that wasn't what made my heart stop.

Thorn's tall, rugged body came into view, stealing my breath. His full lips were pressed in a line, and his hair hung in his face, making him look like the *perfect* supermodel. He deserved to be painted so the memory of him would last forever and not just in my mind.

"We have a problem," he said gruffly. "A police car is on its way here."

I blinked. "Did Drake find us?"

He shook his head. "I left last night because my perimeter alert system went off. I drove away so I wouldn't alarm whoever was near the cabin, then scouted the area. I found squirrel hunters out there. When I returned, I saw that you'd escaped. I can only assume that one of them saw me carrying you and called the authorities. The monitor I have on the driveway just went off, and I was able to catch the vehicle on camera."

My heart pounded. This might be the way out of this horrible situation.

Saphira snorted. "They'll want to check the house, and you don't want them to find Everly and me locked in a room."

He frowned. "Yes."

An engine grew louder. I turned to the window and saw the police car about five hundred feet away. The officer would be here momentarily.

She beamed. "So you're letting us out?"

"Yes, I have to." He exhaled, and his jaw twitched. "I'm going to tell you something, and all I can do is ask you not to say anything to give us away. I took you to save my parents. I have no intention of harming either of you, or I would've done so by now. I promise when the police leave, I will tell you *everything*, including how I changed Everly into a dragon." Face lined with worry, he moved to the side and gestured for us to leave our prison cell.

I blinked several times as I stared at him, my breath catching. *His parents.* That's what this was all about?

I *needed* answers.

And I needed to understand why his parents were in danger and how he'd turned me into *this*.

Saphira nodded toward the door, telling me to go first. I stood and marched past Thorn and out the door. I had to use every ounce of self-control not to brush my arm against his body. I was jonesing for the electricity that pulsed between us, desperate for my next fix.

But Saphira was watching me, and I didn't want her to ask questions I couldn't answer.

I scurried down the hall with Saphira on my heels.

Boots scuffed the ground outside, and I realized there were two officers. They wouldn't come without backup to check a threat.

As we entered the living room, my gaze followed my nose to the kitchen, which was wide open to the living room. I hadn't noticed much about it before because I'd been focused on escaping.

A rectangular table sat in the middle of the kitchen, which had black counters on top of white cabinets against one wall with a sink and a dishwasher, and the stove against the wall that faced the front of the house. Bacon and eggs were piled onto two pans on top of the stove.

My stomach growled as intense hunger swamped me.

A loud knock sounded on the door, and Saphira and I glanced at each other as Thorn tensed.

He sighed as he walked to the front door then turned around and glanced at us again. He murmured, "Please."

When neither she nor I responded, he turned around and opened the door.

CHAPTER FOURTEEN

I WASN'T sure what to do. Part of me wanted to proclaim I needed help while an equally large part wanted to remain quiet. I had no doubt that Thorn had answers. Was getting them worth the risk of remaining his prisoner? I wasn't sure.

In the doorway, two men in black police uniforms towered with their hands near their holsters.

The taller officer stood on the right, his dark eyes searching the inside of the cabin. His raven hair was cut short, and his sideburns bled into an obsidian, short-trimmed beard. His dark skin wrinkled around his eyes from constant tensing. "Good morning. Sorry to bother you, but we're checking out the area."

The chestnut eyes of the shorter officer homed in on the two of us where we stood behind the couch. His brown skin was lighter than his friend's, and his face was a little rounder, lending him a more friendly countenance. However, his jaw was set as his gaze swung between us and Thorn.

"Of course, Officer." Thorn gestured for them to step inside. "We were about to sit down and have breakfast."

Saphira took an eager step toward them, and my dragon roared and brushed my mind. I moved so our shoulders bumped, and her gaze landed on me. Her brows furrowed, and I shook my head.

The shorter officer strolled over to us, and I swallowed hard. He might have noticed our interaction.

"We had a call late last night from some hunters who saw a girl running through the woods. They then said that a man carried her back toward where she'd run from," the taller officer said as he stepped farther inside. "Your cabin is the closest to the incident, so we thought we'd check in and make sure nothing was amiss."

Thorn had been right in his assumption about the hunters. At least there were still good people in the world who called in something concerning. Not everyone would've done that.

"One mentioned it looked like the girl had blonde hair." The shorter officer studied me.

With the six years of practice at keeping my face neutral around Peter, my expression remained indifferent.

"I, for one, am glad you're here," Saphira started and lifted her chin.

Without thought, I interjected, "It was me. I was the girl out there."

Thorn closed his eyes and hung his head, which pulled at my heart.

"Thank gods. For a minute, I thought you'd lost your mind." Saphira sighed and leaned back against the back of the couch.

The taller officer reached for his handcuffs, and my stomach dropped.

I couldn't rat Thorn out. I *needed* answers. "I got restless being cooped up all day, and I went for a run."

"Everly." Saphira's jaw dropped. "What are you *doing?*"

I couldn't fault her. I probably wasn't being smart, but I was going with my gut. And my gut said I needed to hear what Thorn had to say. I believed that he wouldn't hurt either Saphira or me. "I *know*." I rolled my eyes and cringed. "I can't believe I'm telling them this, either. It wasn't my finest moment."

"You're telling us you went running into the middle of the forest in the dark while it was pouring rain?" the shorter officer asked slowly and squinted.

Thorn lifted his head, a strange expression on his face.

"Like I said, it wasn't my finest moment." I forced a laugh and twirled a piece of hair around my finger. "I worked at a vet's office a few years ago, and I learned that rain makes it safe to explore the woods if you're going to do it. Critters don't like being out in it any more than humans do, so I figured, why not?" I shrugged, hating how dumb I sounded.

Clearing his throat, the taller officer moved his hands back to his sides. "You do realize that...um...dangerous *critters* can still be out there. Bears roam these parts."

He had me there, but in fairness, I had been running for my life. I hadn't been sure at that point that Thorn wouldn't hurt us. I bobbed my head. "I had bear spray, and those critters are so big that I *totally* would've heard one." If there was an afterlife, I hoped Mom was *not* watching me now. I was certain she would not be proud of me.

All four of them blinked at me like they couldn't believe what they were hearing. Yeah, me, neither. But I was already in deep, so I continued to tread water.

"Okay, but that doesn't account for you being hauled back here by a man." The shorter officer scratched his head.

I could imagine what he was thinking, and it was probably best I didn't know for sure. "I got myself into a wee little pickle." I lifted my fingers and held my thumb and pointer finger close together. "I got lost, and fortunately, I found a spot where there was a bar of service and sent Thorn a text, informing him I was near a waterfall."

"I know the area well and had a good guess where I could find her," Thorn added, placing his hands into his jeans pockets.

"Did you, now?" Saphira pursed her lips, not helping the situation.

I sauntered over to Thorn, looping my arm through his. I almost gasped at the spark from his skin. "Ignore her. She doesn't approve of our relationship, but she's my best friend, so I brought her along."

Thorn forced a smile and wrapped an arm around me. Wanting to sell the story, I stood on my tiptoes and pecked his lips. The jolt made me gasp and grow lightheaded. I sagged into his side, the electricity strengthening between us.

"What the *hell!*" Saphira snarled.

"See." I gestured at her. "Anyway," I said flippantly and nuzzled into his side. I wanted to sneak another kiss and rub against him like a cat. Yeah, maybe I shouldn't have tried to pull off the act so convincingly. "When he found me, I thought he was a big bear and ran. I slipped and tumbled down an incline. I hurt myself, and he had to carry me home."

"That's an interesting story." The shorter officer swung his attention to Saphira. "Do you have anything you'd like to add?"

Mouth drying, I held my breath. I'd tried, but I couldn't force Saphira to remain quiet. If she wanted to tell them the truth, I couldn't do a damn thing about it.

Saphira exhaled and glanced at me, then Thorn. "I wish there were, but how could I top that?" she asked through a frown.

I released the breath I'd been holding, and Thorn's arm relaxed around me.

The two officers glanced at each other, then back to Saphira and me. The taller one asked, "You two aren't in trouble?"

"No more than usual." I beamed. That was true. Being held captive here was the same as being forced to be around my stepdad regularly.

"Well, all right." The shorter one removed a wallet and pulled out two cards. He handed one to Saphira and one to me. "If anything changes, this is how you can get ahold of us."

I examined the card, making sure they saw me take note of it. "Thank you so much. We sure will."

The two officers turned and headed to the door.

Saphira glared at me and mouthed, *We should tell them.*

I shook my head and replied, *I need answers.*

She looked at the ceiling but didn't say another word.

When the officers got to the door, they turned around and looked at Saphira and me again. I smiled widely and waved, hoping to come off as carefree.

The taller one nodded. "Thanks for your time."

"No problem," Thorn replied as he headed to the door. "Let us know if you need anything else."

"Will do," the shorter officer said, and the two of them walked to the police car.

When the door shut, I heard the taller one grumble, "That girl's not smart."

"But she's pretty, so at least the guy's got that going for him," the other officer replied.

The three of us remained silent until the car engine started.

Then Saphira growled, "I hope we don't regret that."

I couldn't blame her. I hoped we didn't, either, especially since I was the one who had ultimately made the call.

Thorn's attention was locked on me, his jaw slack. He murmured, "Thank you. I didn't expect you to do that."

His surprise settled hard in my stomach, and I slumped. He must not be used to people protecting him.

I couldn't allow him to see how his reaction affected me. "I didn't do it for you." That was a lie. I partly had, but I controlled my breathing, hoping he didn't pick up on it. "I just want answers."

"That's fair." He chewed on his bottom lip. "And I promised them. Where should I begin?"

"At the beginning." Saphira straightened her shoulders. "After what we just did, I want to know *everything,* including how you changed Everly into a dragon. I only played along to get answers."

"Then I'll start with the king betraying me many years ago."

Thorn's face hardened, and his lips curled as if he'd tasted something awful. "That's what set everything into motion."

"Impossible. I've *never* seen you before." Saphira glowered. "You haven't been in this area before, or everyone would know. You must be part of a local thunder indirectly tied to the king. That means there's no way you've been around him enough to judge whether he's a just man. One of your own leaders likely did something wrong and blamed the king."

"You're right. I am part of a small thunder." Thorn rolled his shoulders and moved into the kitchen. "One that's made up of just Mom, Dad, and me."

It was as if they were speaking a different language. "What's a thunder?" I asked.

Thorn looked at me, the angry lines smoothing into his normal, kind face. "It's what a group of dragons who live close to one another and regularly interact is called."

"So...I don't have a thunder." That figured. I'd been a loner for a long time, so why should it change now? My heart panged with loneliness, but I pushed the annoying twinge away. It was better not to count on anyone but myself. I had to remember that.

"No." Saphira smiled sadly and touched my shoulder. "But if you follow through and give yourself to Drake, you'll automatically become part of one of the largest thunders in the world."

Thorn's neck corded, and he clenched his hands. "If you want to be part of a thunder that forces people into servitude and tortures, kills, and kidnaps people, it's a great group to join."

I snorted, then clasped my hands over my mouth. I couldn't get over the irony of what he'd said. "Really? You're bringing kidnapping into this? Isn't that the pot calling the kettle black?"

Saphira smirked. "She has a point. You're criticizing Drake for the very thing you're guilty of. And don't play dumb. We've been living in a room lined with Wolfram Dwiin so we can't escape."

"Don't compare me to *him*." Thorn pounded his chest. "I'm not forcing either of you to have sex with me so you'll give me an heir. I'm not getting *any* pleasure out of this."

There was the opening again, and I had to take it. "Then why did you kidnap us? What in the world could Saphira and I possibly get for you?"

"The answer to that proves how little either of you knows about your *king* and *prince*." Thorn pointed at the window in front of the table, but I saw nothing out of the ordinary. "It's more about you, Everly, than Saphira." He looked at her. "I'm sorry you were collateral damage, though having you both will be more effective. In Drake's mind, someone has made him look weak by taking what he considers his property. It will drive him slowly insane, and I will use his insecurity to save the two people who mean the world to me."

My mouth went dry. I hated to admit it, but his plan might work. Drake had treated me like an object, and although I wasn't irreplaceable, someone had stolen me from his guards.

Saphira lifted her hands. "That may be true about Drake, but the king is a *good* man. He wouldn't harm anyone who didn't deserve it."

"And you have no doubt about that?" He bared his teeth and clenched his hands. "That he wouldn't have marked a young boy and his nanny for death?"

She went still and swallowed, remaining silent.

That was a very specific comment. A shiver ran through me as the silence stretched.

"I don't doubt that something horrible happened to the people you love," Saphira said slowly, weighing each word. "Otherwise, I believe you wouldn't have done this. You haven't deliberately hurt us, and you have provided us with certain comforts. *Something* drove you to kidnap us."

Some weight lifted off my shoulders. I wasn't alone in those types of thoughts. His attitude went back and forth like a yo-yo, but I was beginning to realize there was far more to his story than we knew.

"I think someone is using the king's name to justify their own actions," she continued.

"I know every person involved." Thorn stared off into space. "The blame isn't misplaced."

I wondered where his mind was at that moment. With his narrowed eyes, it was as if he were seeing a different world. I took a step toward him, the electricity increasing between us, but he didn't move.

I whispered, "What happened?"

CHAPTER FIFTEEN

HIS SHOULDERS BOWED AS if carrying a heavy burden.

I had to stop myself from rushing over to help him carry it. He probably wouldn't appreciate the support, and Saphira would lose her mind. Most importantly, it wasn't my place...even if I wanted it to be.

"Any *day* now," Saphira sniped as she strolled toward the kitchen and grabbed a handful of bacon. "Unless this is your way of trying to get out of *telling* us something."

If she would just stop and watch with an open mind, she would see that whatever he had to say was difficult for him. I wanted to chastise her, but that would only delay us in getting answers.

She popped a piece of bacon into her mouth, and for the life of me, I didn't understand how she could eat at a time like this.

"Just...give me a minute to gather my thoughts," he rasped and crossed his arms.

I smiled sadly at him. "Take your time. We're not going anywhere."

"We could've," Saphira grumbled. "But you made it clear that you want to stay here, and I stupidly went along." She took another bite of bacon. "At least I'm getting to eat. That's a silver lining."

My stomach grumbled, and my mouth watered. I'd questioned her for eating at a time like this, and now I wanted to do the same thing. Eating *would* be better than scolding her...or that was my justification.

I hurried over and grabbed a piece of bacon. When I took a bite, the taste exploded on my tongue. It was better than it had been when I was human, the salt and grease like an orgasm in my mouth.

Saphira and I chowed down, waiting for Thorn to start.

After what felt like hours, he finally spoke. "A young, beautiful nanny took the six-year-old boy in her charge for an early morning walk." His tone softened, and a faint smile spread across his face. "She told him he didn't have time for breakfast, or they might miss the elk in the area."

Warmth exploded in my heart. I loved watching the elk in the mornings or late evenings. Mom would take me with her on hikes in the woods, and I would go begrudgingly. Even though I loved painting nature, I wasn't fond of actually being out in it. But for the longest time, I was the only person she had to go hiking with. To make her happy, I'd swallow my complaints because she'd sacrificed so much for me. The few times we'd stumbled upon the elk in the woods had been magical, making the miserable experience more than worth it.

"You see, the boy *loved* seeing the elk and the deer in nature. Whenever it happened, it was the highlight of his day, so he followed his nanny dutifully." He leaned his back against the wall without missing a beat in the story. "They took in the cool morning, enjoying the breeze on their warm skin. That was when they heard a rustling in the woods nearby."

He licked his lips as the corners of his mouth dipped. "At first, the boy thought the sounds were an elk or a deer, but the nanny had tensed. She encouraged him to turn around, saying they should hurry back to eat breakfast."

I turned to Saphira to see her reaction. This story had to be part of what was driving Thorn to do everything that he was doing.

Saphira's brows were furrowed, but she didn't slow down on eating. I was fairly certain she could eat during a natural disaster.

My appetite had been ruined. His story had already captivated me.

"Another rustling noise sounded as they headed back, and an arrow came a few inches from hitting the boy in his calf. The nanny screamed for the boy to run as she stayed behind to protect him." His breathing picked up, and his eyes glistened. "The boy didn't want to run, but he wanted to make his nanny happy. So he took off...until he heard the sound of her body hitting the ground. She'd been hit by an arrow, one lodged deep in her back."

Heart hurting, I rubbed my chest. I couldn't imagine an innocent little boy going through this, and to hear how the nanny had loved that child...they must have had a special bond.

"When the man stepped from the woods, the boy knew it was over. That both he and his nanny would die. But the man stopped in his tracks and hurried to the woman and the boy." A cruel smile stretched across Thorn's face. "He said he hadn't signed up to kill a child."

Saphira laughed and wiped her greasy hands on her sweatpants. "Let me guess: the king sent the assassin."

"Yes." Thorn's irises darkened to cobalt. "He did."

"Why would you believe that?" Saphira rolled her eyes and leaned against the countertop next to the stove. "The assassin could've blamed anyone for that."

"He could have." Thorn shrugged and narrowed his eyes, taking a step closer to us. "But when the assassin instead hid the boy and nanny away, why did the king's guards hunt them down and try to kill all three of them?"

"That could've been for *anything*." Saphira sneered. "Why would *that* boy be so special that the king would want him dead? And you weren't there. How would you *know*?"

He lowered his head and locked on her eyes. "Because that boy was *me*, and the king fears *me*."

Her jaw dropped, and she blinked. "Wait." She jerked her head toward me and asked, "Did you say his name was Thorn?"

I nodded, and she blanched.

My pulse skyrocketed. Who *was* this man? And what had he done? By her reaction, I thought maybe we should've left with the police, but my dragon huffed as if she could hear my thoughts.

The tension and silence in the room smothered me. Saphira's eyes bulged as she stared Thorn down and whispered, "That's not possible."

Though I usually kept my head down and stayed away from others, patience was not one of my virtues. I'd had enough of waiting. Earlier, I'd swallowed my frustration because Thorn had been struggling, but with the cruel smirk on his face, my sympathy was gone. "What's not possible?" Whatever Saphira's revelation was, I needed to be in on it.

He lifted a brow and smiled smugly. "Oh, the king does fear me."

She let out a shaky breath. "What's your last name?"

"Wight." He crossed his arms and winked, watching her reaction. He stalked across the room, mirth in his eyes as he stood only a few feet from us.

As expected, that name meant nothing to me, and I wanted to slap the smug look off his face.

Saphira stepped closer to him, and I stumbled forward, ready to shove her back. I didn't like her getting too close to Thorn.

She pressed her lips together. "Is that the last name you were born with?"

What an odd question. All my aggression at her proximity left me. I stared at Thorn, trying to put the missing puzzle piece into place.

The smirk vanished from his face. "No, but I suspect you already know the answer."

"But..." She touched the base of her neck and grimaced. "He said you were attacked and there was nothing left of you to recover."

"Yet here I am." Thorn dropped his hands and stood to his full height. Pain darkened his irises. "The king isn't the man you think you know."

Every cell in my body screamed at me to wrap my arms around him. However, I wasn't foolish enough to believe *I* could comfort him. He was hands-down the sexiest man I'd ever seen, and I was certain he could have any woman he desired. Not that it mattered. He'd kidnapped me, so I didn't want to be with him, anyway. I'd *only* stayed for answers.

I cleared my throat, needing to exert some independence. I wanted to tap my foot, but I forced my legs to stay still. "Fill me in."

Saphira jerked her head my way, her bottom lip quivering. "Do you remember how I told you it's impossible for a human to be *turned* into a dragon shifter?"

"Of course I do." I threw my hands out to my sides. "It *just* happened last night."

"What I told you is true with one exception." She waved her hand at Thorn. "It can be done by a dragon shifter I was told died when he was a child."

My head hurt, and I was rather confident it wasn't because of my fall. I bit the inside of my cheek and regarded him. "You can make dragon shifters? How? And why would the king *fear* that?" Instead of using humans for breeders, they could find willing humans who wanted to become dragons. That seemed like an easy sale.

"I was born with a certain mark, and such is the burden of the curse," Thorn answered in a deep, raspy voice.

I rubbed my forehead where the pain was centered. "I know I called you a monster, but you turned me without my consent. I didn't mean to make you feel as if it was a curse."

A tender expression softened his face. "That's not why I called it that. It's truly a curse."

"Why would the king wait so long to have you killed?" Saphira shook her head. "You were six when someone tried, but you were born with the dragon mark on your back. Why not kill you right then and there?"

When he'd said *marked*, I'd thought he meant under a full moon or something that would reveal him as the cursed one. I hadn't pictured a physical mark on his body, but now I desired to see it...for educational purposes. Not because I wanted to see him shirtless.

"I believe he hoped the power would remain dormant." He spread his fingers and glared at his palms. "But when I was six, the magic appeared. The king and I were playing chase in the backyard, and when I raced after him to tag him, the magic surged inside me. I thought it was just a tickle in my belly, but when I touched him, I took his dragon from him."

I'd always been able to follow stories and lectures with ease and never struggled with comprehension. That was one reason my grades had been stellar during my four years in premed, but I couldn't wrap my mind around this information. Every time I thought I was on track with him and Saphira, I was proven wrong. "Why would the king be playing chase with you? I don't understand. Or...a human king probably wouldn't have a random boy in the backyard playing chase with him. And I thought you could *create* dragon shifters, not make a dragon shifter *human*. Did you give me the king's dragon?"

"No, you don't have the king's dragon. I gave it back to him as soon as I realized that I'd taken it from him by mistake. But the real answer to your questions is that I can do both—make humans into dragon shifters and take away a dragon shifter's magic." Thorn tugged at the hem of his shirt. "I don't know how to describe it, but when a dragon passes, their magic is released back into the world. I can pull the magic from the air and push it into a human, making them into a dragon shifter. It's a mixture of magic, so the dragon is unique to the person. The opposite happens with a dragon shifter. I pull their magic into my body, and I can hold on to it for a short moment or release it into the world, just as if the person died. I can't, however, pass someone's dragon to another. Their body isn't the same, and the magic would be altered."

Though the concept was foreign, I relished the fact I didn't have the king's magic inside me. I was fairly certain the king would kill me if that were the case. "But how is there enough magic to do that? I mean, there's what, a handful of you all?"

He huffed. "There are hundreds of thousands of us across the world, and we've existed as long as man."

I shouldn't have been surprised. I would be foolish to think these were the first dragons ever.

Saphira poked her tongue into her cheek. "But you gave the king his dragon back. Was it not fully his dragon? Because that could be why he tried to kill you."

"That's a good question and one I've always wondered about but never had a chance to ask because of, you know, the fear of *being murdered*." Thorn exhaled and raised his hands. "I immediately gave him his dragon back without any of his magic escaping my body. It was completely *his* magic. But I was able to get one answer over the past twenty-one years. He was afraid that I would take it away from him again and not give it back. And how can a king rule dragons if he's lost his own?"

My head reeled. The king's fear made sense, but it wasn't right to punish a six-year-old boy for something he hadn't meant to do. Furthermore, the boy had given him the dragon back. "Why didn't he just banish you from his house?" That would've resolved the problem without needing to kill a sweet, innocent boy.

His face scrunched as he swallowed hard. He took a deep breath, steadying himself to speak.

CHAPTER SIXTEEN

THE BACON I'd eaten churned, and the anticipation was worse than actually hearing the answers.

He exhaled and said, "That would have been impossible because I was his son. He couldn't banish me and have our people find out."

I blinked as I processed what I'd heard. I swore he'd said he was the king's son, which would make him a prince *and* Drake's brother. Drake, the very person who intended to breed me for heirs. I tried to keep the food from coming up again. "You're a prince?" I croaked.

"*Was* his son." Thorn karate-chopped the air. "I'm not anymore. I'm Vlad and Cassidy's son. *They're* my parents in every way that counts."

Two names, male and female...like the nanny and the assassin who'd saved them. "Is that who was with you in the woods that day?"

He nodded. "And I'm alive because of them. If it hadn't been for *both* of them, the king would have succeeded."

Saphira laughed. "Wait. You're saying that the man who nearly shot you in the leg and shot your nanny is the same one you consider your *father*?"

His lips pulled back, and he spat. "Yes. Arman didn't tell him who his target was, and when he realized that he'd been sent to kill the prince—who was a child—and his nanny, he saved us. He and Cassidy also risked their lives to keep me safe and raise me. My loyalty is with *them* and no one else."

All my life, I'd reminded myself there were people out there with harder lives than mine. Even when my stepdad would suggest I shouldn't spend the holidays with my siblings, or when no one showed up for my high school graduation or awards ceremony, I'd pushed my tears away and tried to keep things in perspective. Thorn's story was exactly that: heartbreaking. His father had turned him away, but it was far worse than that. Thorn had lived every day with this curse, a reminder that the very people who should've protected him had set him up to perish. At least, for the first sixteen years of my life, I'd had my mom solidly by my side. "I'm sor—"

"No." Thorn's hands shook at his sides. "Don't. Cassidy and Vlad were the best parents I could have asked for. We don't have the same blood, but that doesn't matter."

I nodded, unable to say more. I hadn't meant to upset him, but he needed to realize that not everyone would've done that to him.

"Why show up now?" Saphira rubbed the arm that had hit the wall. "Why make your presence known if you've been in hiding for the past twenty-one years? That seems pretty stupid, if you ask me."

He planted his feet wide apart and breathed noisily. "I didn't have a choice. Believe me, I'd rather be far away from here, living a simple life. But the *king* wouldn't have it."

I rubbed my hands together, trying not to fidget. I didn't want to do anything to make him think I pitied him after I'd tried apologizing for something I'd had no influence over. However, seeing him so torn up broke what was left of my heart in two.

"A little over a month ago, Vlad and Cassidy left the city to shift." He pressed a fist to his mouth. "I couldn't go with them because I was called in to work at the last minute. They should've gotten home before me because I worked a twelve-hour shift, but when I got back, the place was empty."

Saphira put her hands on her hips. "That doesn't mean the king has them."

He continued as if she hadn't said a word. "I thought maybe they'd gone on a date or made a detour, so I called Cass's phone. Falkor answered, informing me they had her and Vlad."

For once, I knew who they were talking about. That was one of the guards who'd come with Saphira to pick me up. He was definitely not the warmest person, so Thorn's story was plausible.

When Thorn didn't continue, I asked, "What did he say?"

"If I wanted them to be freed, I had to turn myself in." Thorn's shoulders sagged.

"And you figured you'd kidnap Everly instead?" Saphira snorted, and her nose wrinkled with disgust. "What if they aren't willing to make that trade?"

Actually, that wasn't a bad idea. I couldn't fault him for trying to find a solution to save all three of them, and ultimately, I would wind up back with my intended fate—Drake.

My dragon roared inside my head and brushed my mind, causing my blood to thrum. I had no clue why she was acting this way, but I felt like I might lose control.

"I told you before—Drake will be desperate to retrieve Everly so he doesn't look weak," Thorn growled, his words barely forming.

"What in the scales is wrong with the two of you?" Saphira glanced from him to me. "It's like you're going to shift." She scoffed. "Both of you, take some calming breaths and get your act together."

She was right. If I were ever going to shift, I wanted the experience to be *my* choice. I suspected if the dragon thought she could control me, my human side would always be at her mercy, and I refused to be controlled by anyone or anything. I slowly filled my lungs, remembering all my yoga classes. Meditation had helped me get through things with my stepdad and siblings. Little had I known I was preparing myself to be a dragon shifter.

I closed my eyes and took a full, deep inhalation through my nose. As I exhaled, I opened my mouth wide and stuck out my tongue, making the encouraged *ha* sound. Even after just one round, the thrumming eased, and the dragon's roar quieted. I repeated the breathing technique a few more times. When I opened my eyes, I found Thorn and Saphira staring at me strangely.

"Were you coughing up a hairball?" Saphira waved her hand up and down at me. She looked at Thorn. "Maybe your magic got confused and turned her into a cat instead of a dragon."

"No, I didn't have a *hairball*." I scratched my head. "It's the lion's breath breathing technique used in yoga."

"Oh, dear gods." Saphira pinched the bridge of her nose. "This girl is definitely human."

Was she seriously judging me? I swirled a finger at her. "It got my dragon under control, which is what you wanted, so *you're welcome*."

"Can we get back to the matter at hand?" Thorn grumbled. "Or should I put you two back in your room?"

After all this, he still planned on locking us up? Lovely. "We're fine," I said quickly. "But how did you expect to get word to the king that you have me?"

He nodded. "I've been watching the dragon net. That's how I found out about you heading to Drake's. When the guards realize the trail has gone cold, they'll post something there, which will include a way to contact them."

"What's a dragon net?" That sounded straight out of a sci-fi movie.

Saphira rolled her eyes. "It's an intranet site for all dragon-related things. It's one of the main ways the king communicates with every-one. I told Drake he shouldn't have told the entire house about Everly because it was bound to get out."

Cold realization washed through me, making my palms sweaty. "Drake wanted a human to breed with, and I'm definitely not that anymore. He may go after my sister again, and I have to protect her. No matter what." My chest seized as I hurried to Thorn. "I need you to take the dragon away from me."

Thorn's head dropped, and he winced.

There was something he wasn't telling me.

I waited for a second, but he remained quiet. The urge to scream nearly took over, but it didn't compare to my dragon inside. She roared, but this time, she didn't try to overtake my senses. I knew that her reaction was more personal—she was pissed at me. She must not have been overjoyed with me asking Thorn to remove her.

"*Now* you decide to be quiet." Saphira blew a raspberry. "Unbelievable. You wouldn't shut up a second ago, but Everly asks you a question, and suddenly, that cat has your tongue."

Shaking my head, I cut my attention toward her. "Another cat cliche? Really? I'm beginning to think you have a thing against cats."

"Gross." She scrunched her face. "I love kittens and actual cats. There are cat shifters in the world, but not in the U.S. Thank gods. Those I don't like. A lion, jaguar, or cheetah is definitely not cute and way too predatory for my liking—not that I would have an issue taking them on. I'm a dragon, after all. But a true kitty cat—I'm a huge fan and have two waiting for me back home."

A dragon with pets. That surprised me, but maybe her human side liked the companionship. Because I was certain her dragon would prefer to eat them. "I didn't see you as a cat lady."

"Well, you clearly aren't good at reading people." She shrugged. "You did agree to be a dragon shifter's human breeder."

I flinched. She had a point there. "Yeah, but it's not like I thought he was a good person or..." I trailed off. This wasn't helping my case.

Thorn emanated a deep, threatening growl. It diverted my attention back to the man I needed an answer from.

My heart leapt into my throat, but I forced myself not to cower in fear like before. After all, he *needed* me. He wouldn't risk killing me, or he would've let me die at the base of the cliff. "Seriously, I need you to remove the dragon you put in me. I can't risk him going after my sister. I promised my mom I would protect her."

His growl disappeared, and he rubbed his hands together. "I...I don't know how."

Head tilting back, I lifted my chin. "That's not funny." He'd told

Saphira and me that he'd taken the king's dragon from him and given it back. He'd also *changed* me.

He rubbed a hand down his face. "I seriously don't know how to do it."

"Not to state the obvious, but neither Everly nor I is buying that." Saphira tapped her foot.

"I don't blame you, but every time I've used the curse, I haven't *meant* to." Thorn stared at his palms as if they held all the answers. "With Arman, it was a tickle when I tagged him. My heart was pounding, and as soon as I saw his expression and felt something strange inside me, I panicked and gave it back to him. With Everly, I was checking her injuries and trying to calm her, even though I was scared she was going to die. The process was so fast that I didn't notice what I had done until her red-berries-and-pear scent changed to include a faint trace of brimstone."

Shit. If he didn't know how to remove the dragon inside me, I wasn't sure what to do. I guessed I would hand myself over to Drake and hope and pray he wouldn't go after my sister. That was the only option I had. "Can't you figure it out?" I wasn't above begging.

He blew out a breath. "I can try, but I'll need time."

That was fair. However, I wasn't sure how someone went about figuring out how to make magic work. "I'm not going anywhere anytime soon, and I kinda need you to remove it. Seems like you have the perfect person to work with."

Dark circles were beginning to appear under his eyes, and I'd bet it wasn't from a restless night. It had to be from the emotional trauma of the story he'd shared with us. I could see the toll his past had taken on him, and I wished I could soothe the pain.

I believed that a person's situation informed their decisions, and not necessarily how they were raised. That view always garnered harsh criticism, but it was clear that the critics lived in a more cookie-cutter world than I did. I blended in to avoid my stepdad's cruelty, not because Mom hadn't raised me to be strong and independent. I'd done what I'd had to do to survive two years under his roof until I turned eighteen. After that, I'd conformed so I could visit my brother and sister. I'd molded myself into what I needed to be to fulfill my promise to Mom.

Thorn was another perfect example. He'd been traumatized, forced into hiding, and raised by two people who had chosen to take care of him. They'd blended in with humans for over two decades, only for the king to capture his mom and dad. He was doing the only thing he could to protect them, including capturing me.

Though I didn't agree with his choices, I couldn't fault him. He was fighting for his family.

My heart ached, and I desperately wanted to throw myself into his arms. Even after everything he'd done to me, my attraction to him kept intensifying. I hated that I'd give anything to know the taste of his lips or how his breath felt against my neck. As my body warmed, I knew I had to get it under control. "Maybe you should take a nap. We can try after you wake up."

"A nap?" He gestured at the eggs and bacon. "It's morning."

Saphira spun back around and grabbed a plate next to the stove. "It's fine. You can sleep. I'm sure I can take care of this."

A cell phone rang, and my eyes zeroed in on the one sitting on the kitchen table. I hadn't noticed it until now.

Snatching it from the table, Thorn scowled. "It's Falkor."

I swallowed hard. "I...I thought you killed him." I'd seen the guards' bodies fall from the sky and land hard in the woods that day Thorn had captured us. It was crazy to think that was only two days ago.

He flinched. "I knocked them out. I couldn't bring myself to kill them."

I was fairly certain I'd hurt his feelings, but what was I supposed to think?

The last remaining restraints around my heart shattered. My gut said he was a good man, and he was finally showing me that he was. Most people would've killed the guards who'd captured their parents. If it had been Mom, I might not have been so kind.

"Maybe he's calling to see how you're doing?" Saphira suggested, though the joke fell flat.

Not bothering to address her, I shook my head. "Don't answer it."

"I have to. It could be about my parents." He swiped the phone and held it to his ear. "Hello?"

CHAPTER SEVENTEEN

JUST AS WE were making headway with Thorn, the dragon guard had to call. I wanted to growl in frustration, but I understood that Thorn had to take it. If they'd had my family, I'd have done the same thing.

Thorn paced in front of the couch, though his attention stayed firmly locked on us.

"So…it took me a few days to recover and connect the dots," Falkor said hatefully on the other end of the line. "Just as the king predicted, you grew into the exact thing he *knew* you'd become. Someone who would attack your own kind instead of handing yourself over."

I gripped the edge of the countertop, surprised I could hear the guard so clearly.

"I'll bring you Ev—er—*the girl* in exchange for Cassidy and Vlad." He grimaced and cleared his throat. "It'll need to be a place I name, and our meet-up will need to be within an hour of receiving the location."

My dragon roared inside my head so loudly that I wanted to cover my ears. Between the noise and the sharp sting ripping through my chest, my knees buckled. I had no idea what had caused this reaction. I knew I had to go to Drake. Maybe it was because I wasn't human anymore and I feared what Drake would do if I showed up as a dragon. But there was something else—I didn't want to leave Thorn.

I pushed those feelings aside. That part *didn't* matter.

"That's not how this works." Falkor chuckled darkly. "You forget you are no longer viewed as a prince, and your demands mean *nothing*. You're the *enemy*. Now let me explain how this will happen."

Thorn's pupils elongated, and he bared his teeth. "I have *your prince's* breeder. You don't get to make the demands here."

"And we have your *parents*," Falkor spat.

"So we're on even ground." Thorn's free hand fisted at his side.

Falkor snorted. "Sure. But here's the thing: Drake can find another human. She was convenient, but not the be-all and end-all. Can you say the same about your parents?"

My head sagged as terror squeezed my chest. His words validated my worst fear. I had no doubt the next human Drake "found" would be Eva. I *couldn't* allow that.

Thorn's nostrils flared. "That's not true. The king doesn't realize that Drake wouldn't—"

"If you don't turn yourself in and bring the girl with you, we'll kill your parents," Falkor interjected. "It's that simple. We'll start with Vlad since he's the traitor who didn't finish the job."

Thorn growled, his irises glowing. My dragon purred, and I understood his dragon was peeking through.

"What the crap?" Saphira stomped and pouted. "What am I? Chopped liver?"

"If you harm either of them, you will *all* regret it." Thorn's chest heaved.

I patted Saphira's arm while remaining focused on the conversation.

Falkor laughed abruptly. "Please. You can't do anything. We'll shoot you before you can get close enough. You have until noon

Saturday, and if you and the girl aren't at the place in the woods where Vlad attacked you, Vlad will die." There was a quiet click, and the line disconnected.

The house fell silent.

After a long pause, Saphira sniffed. "Seriously, they didn't even ask if I was with you. They know I haven't come home. How can they be that heartless? I grew up with them."

Thorn tossed the phone onto the couch. "I told you they aren't who you think they are. And you thought I was the liar."

I hated that we were all struggling. I understood feeling unimportant and abandoned. I'd felt like that every day for the past six years. It was one reason I hadn't stayed behind to attend my college graduation. No one had been there for my high school graduation, and I hadn't wanted to live through that again. If someone had threatened Mom's life like that when she'd been alive, I would have been falling apart. It proved how strong Thorn was.

Also, the phone call had backed up his story. Even Saphira couldn't question it. The king had tried to kill him, and the very guard who'd escorted Saphira and me had just confirmed it.

She stumbled to the wooden table and sat in one of the matching wooden spindle chairs, placing her elbows on the table, and sank her head into her hands.

"You can't turn yourself in." I lifted my hands and stared at him. "You'll die if you do."

"If I don't, my parents will die." He ran his hands through his hair, pushing his shaggy bangs back. "I couldn't live with that."

I swallowed. I didn't know why it was so damn important to me, but the thought of him handing himself over made me want to kill someone. If he didn't see reason, I'd find a way to lock him up in the dragon-proof room.

"There has to be another way," I said as I walked past Saphira into the living room and stopped a few feet in front of him. "If you hand yourself over to Falkor and they release your parents, your parents will come back for you, especially if they think the king will kill you. Either way, I have to be handed over, and I need to be human when that happens."

He huffed and tipped his head back. "You're right. I have a little over two days to figure out how to make this work." He gestured to the hallway. "You two need to go back to your room."

"What?" Saphira slapped her hands on the table. "You're going to lock us up?"

"I need to leave." He winced but stood tall. "And I don't trust you two enough to leave you loose in here while I'm gone. As you can see, trust doesn't come easily to me."

"I can help." Saphira stood and leaned over the table. "My uncle is close with my dad, but he lives about fifty miles away from the mansion at the edge of dragon territory. He isn't a fan of Drake and is lukewarm toward the king. I bet I can explain the situation and get him to help. I'll ask him to find out where they're keeping your parents."

This was new information. With Saphira so convinced the king was a good man, I found the fact that her uncle wasn't a fan shocking. "Why isn't he a fan, especially if your dad is the king's advisor?"

"It's my cousin." Saphira bit her bottom lip. "He got into a fight with Drake about five years ago. He was thirteen, and it was about me. Drake had said that my opinion didn't matter and the only thing I was good for was breeding. We were in the garden behind the château while my uncle, Dad, and the king were meeting inside to discuss a situation outside of Atlanta.

"Drake told Tyson to mind his business, but Tyson told him I was smart and deserved respect. Drake shifted and attacked him. Tyson shifted, too, to defend himself. Striking hard and fast, Drake clawed deep into Tyson's back at the base of one wing. Tyson never fully recovered, and Drake told the king that Tyson had been disrespectful, but Drake hadn't meant to hurt him. I'd seen what really happened, but when I tried to speak up, Tyson cut me off, and the king fired my uncle as his financial advisor and evicted them from the home provided for the king's advisors. That's why they live on the outskirts of dragon territory. My uncle knows the truth and resents the king for believing his bratty son, and Drake for harming Tyson on purpose."

Her cousin had protected her the only way he could. He'd protected her dignity, and then he'd kept her from being another target.

"That's a horrible story, and I believe every word, but I don't want to make your relatives a target again." Thorn's face softened. "They've gone through enough."

He wasn't accepting her help, and that was frustrating. I understood that he felt like he was alone, but we should rely on one another. "What are you going to do? Besides trying to change me back into a human?"

"I...don't know. But sitting here isn't an option." He placed his hands behind his head, his shirt inching up and showing off a small section of his stomach.

Drool puddled in my mouth, and something flamed inside me.

"The king and Drake don't have to know my uncle helped you." Saphira marched around the table and placed her hands on the back of the sofa. "Once we know where your parents are, we can plan a way to free them. I can think of a few places where they might be so the servants don't know. If it's one of those locations, I can say you beat it out of me."

His pulse thudded in his neck. "Why don't you just call him? I can't risk you leaving and not coming back, or bringing warriors with you."

"Please." She rolled her eyes. "First off, he needs to see me so he can tell I'm not under duress and legitimize your claims. And Everly would stay here with you. Do you know what Drake would do to me if I came back without her? He'd know that I left her, and that wouldn't sit well with him; he's not even negotiating for my return. Besides, I like Everly, and you need to turn her back into a human before he finds her. If I don't come back, I'll have no way of knowing if she's human again."

"Okay, then you'll tell him our location." Thorn shook his head. "I can't risk it."

I understood his hesitation—he had kidnapped us and held us prisoner—but I figured it wouldn't hurt to put in my two cents. "What choice do you have? If she betrays you, they'll find us, and your parents could die. You're the one they want. If you let her go and she follows through, you might be able to save your family without turning yourself in."

Thorn's face flushed. "Why the hell couldn't they just leave us alone? We were hiding away from all the dragons. We were completely immersed in human life. The only exception was needing to shift once a week, but we kept the time short and sweet. We were trying to stay invisible."

"I promise I won't tell anyone this location." Saphira placed a hand on her heart. "I will come back here alone and give you whatever information I can."

I'd always heard that when someone lied, there were physical signs: increased heart rate, sweating, and an inability to maintain eye contact. Her heartbeat was steady, her skin maintained its same gorgeous complexion, and her attention was locked on him.

I had to say something. "I believe her."

He exhaled and pinched the bridge of his nose. "Fine. Go. I just hope this doesn't bite me in the tail."

"It won't." Saphira rubbed her hands together. "I'll go now so we'll have time to plan tonight. But first, I need to know where we are."

"The dragon lands are fifty miles north of here." Thorn rocked on his feet. "You can't miss it."

"All right. I'll go into the woods and shift." She headed to the front door, eager to leave.

I was certain that made Thorn more anxious, but we'd been locked in here against our will, and she was antsy to get out of the cabin.

Thorn nodded. "Remember, there are hunters in the woods, so be careful. The cops already came here to ensure Everly was okay. We don't need someone else calling about dragons."

She winked. "On it. This isn't my first rodeo." She opened the door.

"Wait," I called out. I hurried to her and pulled her into a hug. "You're also risking yourself by doing this. I don't want you to get hurt, either."

At first, she tensed, but then she returned the embrace with vigor. "Thank you. You've only known me a few days, and you already care about me more than the royals do. I'll be careful, and we'll find a way to get you out of this commitment with Drake."

"As long as we don't put my sister at risk." We had to figure out a way to free both of us from the narcissistic asshole.

She pulled back and smiled sadly. "Got it. I'd better go."

This time, I didn't stop her and watched her walk off the front porch and hurry across the driveway into the woods on the other side. The door shut before she broke through the tree line.

A low rattle sounded from behind me, and the back of my neck tingled. I spun around to find Thorn with his eyes closed, his chest shaking.

Something was wrong.

I hurried toward him as a lump formed in my throat. If something happened to him, I wouldn't know how to help him. Then his eyes opened and locked on me, stopping me in my tracks.

The air between us sizzled with electricity. Maybe Saphira shouldn't have left because now we were alone. Though I believed he was a good guy, he hadn't been honest with me. That wasn't something I could just forgive and pretend never happened.

"What's wrong?" I asked, focusing on the agony that had been there just moments ago.

He snarled, "You can't go to him. You won't have a life. He'll never let you go, even if he decides he doesn't want you anymore."

I chuckled humorlessly. "You think I don't know that? But my sister just turned eighteen, and she has our brother. They're twins and have a close relationship, so he would get hurt in the crossfire as well. It's better if it's just me."

Closing the distance between us, he lowered his head and stared into my eyes. Between the energy surrounding us and his delicious scent swirling around me, the world tilted. If I hadn't known better, I would have thought he was staring into my soul. I felt raw and bare before him.

"You don't deserve this," he whispered and lowered his head toward me. "You should've never been thrust into this dangerous world."

I swallowed and licked my lips. The peck we'd shared had been mind-blowing; I wondered what a full kiss would be like.

When his lips were just millimeters from touching mine, I realized I might get the answer to the most important question in the entire world—how he tasted.

CHAPTER EIGHTEEN

BUTTERFLIES FLUTTERED in my stomach as his lips came closer to mine. This kiss would be my undoing. If a peck had felt amazing, this would rock my entire world, and I might never want to stop.

That wasn't an option.

Right when his breath hit my face, I took a step backward.

Everything inside me protested, and I almost stumbled toward him, wanting to finish what we hadn't even started. However, the risk of what he might take from me—my heart—might not be something I could survive, and I had to protect my sister.

His face scrunched, and he jerked upright. He cleared his throat and muttered, "I'm sorry."

Now I was the asshole, making him feel awkward and embarrassed. "You have nothing to apologize for. I'm giving mixed signals. It's just...I don't want to complicate things more between us when we have people we love at risk."

He shook his head, and his long bangs fell into his eyes. "Let's not forget I kidnapped you. I'm sure that's part of the equation as well."

My face burned, but I lifted my chin, refusing to appear guilty. It was an excellent reason not to want to kiss him, but I'd forgotten that fact momentarily. I'd seen my dormmates act foolish over guys, so I knew firsthand how lust could make anyone stupid. But I'd thought I was above that, and oh, how the mighty was eating her own words. "Well, we're allies, right? That didn't seem like a good point to bring up when we're trying to trust each other and work together."

"Then I won't bring it up again." He rubbed his hands and backed up more.

Something tugged inside me, and I almost followed him. I had to stop acting hot and cold toward him and settle for one—er, I meant choose cold.

"Maybe you should warm up some breakfast and eat before you try to change me back into a human." The few pieces of bacon I'd scarfed down had formed a lump in my stomach. Even as a human, I could eat more than that, so stress must have been getting in the way of my appetite.

He exhaled and headed toward the kitchen. "Yeah, let me grab something. Don't you want anything else? You only ate half as much as Saphira."

"I'm good." The thought of eating anything more made me certain I would hurl. I hated vomiting in general, but I'd die if I did it in front of him. "The whole situation is making me tense."

"I understand that all too well, but to figure out how to use my magic, I'll need my strength." He strolled to the eggs and what was left of the bacon—a mere five strips. He took a plate from the cabinet to the right of the stove and filled it with food, popped it in the black microwave over the stove, and started it.

Not sure what to do, I rubbed my hands down my sweatpants. Though they were comfortable, they were too long and not my normal style. I would've liked a pair of high-rise skinny jeans and a flowy top instead of these.

"I would *love* a cup of coffee." I went into the kitchen and searched for the Keurig. When my gaze landed on a traditional coffee maker, I stopped. "An old-school drip machine?" Though I'd worked in a coffee shop, I'd handled the lattes and frozen drinks, never the coffee makers, and at home and the dorms, I'd had Keurigs.

The microwave beeped, and he removed his food. He turned to me and lifted a brow. "Yeah. I'd been about to start coffee when the cops pulled up."

I wished he had. "That's cool. I can do it." I scanned the countertop and saw white filters in a bag and a container that had the label *coffee* on it. I grabbed the container and lifted the plastic lid to find ground coffee inside. Luckily, I'd watched my coworkers work the commercial version of this, so I knew what to do. I pulled open the place that held the filter in the machine and put a filter inside, but then I realized I had no clue how much coffee to put in it. "How many scoops?" I tried to sound strong and steady.

"Four, unless you don't like it as strong." He sat at the table and took a bite of his eggs. His nose wrinkled as if the food didn't taste good, but he continued to eat like he was on a mission.

Following his directions, I added the coffee to the filter and poured water into the side. I pressed start and almost cheered when the liquid came out looking normal. There were already three sizable brown coffee mugs set to one side.

I turned to him and pressed my back against the counter as the brewing coffee filled my senses. Since it was just him and me, maybe this was my chance to ask questions I might not get answers to later on. "Your magic doesn't sound like it's necessarily a *bad* thing. By using your magic on me, you saved my life. So...why do you call it a curse?"

He finished chewing on a piece of bacon. "Well, my biological father tried to kill me over it, so we can start there."

I winced. "Fair point." I hadn't meant to pick at the scab. "But for him to react so violently, something must have influenced him to view it that way. I'm just—"

"Are you defending him?" Thorn tilted his head back, and his nostrils flared.

Asking this question hadn't been wise. He was taking it personally, and I couldn't blame him. "Of course not. You mentioned you were born with the mark of the curse. It didn't start when you accidentally stole the king's dragon. It was like your...*the king* had expected you to do something."

"You're right. I'm sorry." He licked his lip. "Being here while my parents are in danger has me reliving the very occurrence I've tried to forget."

The coffee machine sputtered, and I welcomed the distraction. I spun around, grabbed two mugs, and filled them. "I didn't mean to make this situation worse. Forget I asked."

I sat across from him and handed him a mug.

"Thank you," he said gently. "No, it's a fair question and one you have a right to ask, especially since I changed you."

Some tension left my body. I liked getting answers. My life had enough mysteries, such as why my stepdad resented me.

He took a sip of his coffee and set it back on the table. "In the last millennium, only a handful of dragons have had this gift. No one knows why, and little is known about the first few who had the magic. The last king who did had stories written about him. His legacy lives through some of the older dragons who are still alive after his reign. He was my grandfather."

My stomach clenched. I sensed the stories weren't good.

"He died before I was born, but I learned he used the magic unabashedly." Thorn leaned back in his chair. "He created a handful of dragons for people he deemed worthy, usually because a dragon shifter had fallen in love with a human."

I didn't understand the issue. "He was allowing people in love to be together? That sounds like a good thing."

Thorn grimaced. "It was usually a human that a dragon had become obsessed with, and my grandfather turned them against their will. That's why I'm surprised the current king is okay with Drake's plan for you, but maybe he can't afford to lose his last heir." He shrugged.

If the king was letting Drake get away with something he'd been vehemently against when Thorn was young, that had to be a bitter pill for Thorn to swallow. I laid a hand on the table and forced myself not to reach for him. I wanted to comfort him.

He ran a finger along the rim of the mug. "But what my grandfather was known for was taking people's dragons."

"Permanently?" My eyebrows rose. "Because they did something bad?"

"If disagreeing with him is a valid reason, then yes, because they did something bad." Thorn pushed his half-full plate away.

I had to be missing something. "During riots or a rebellion?" There were times in history when leaders took a firm stand to prevent a bigger problem from occurring.

"Nothing like that. People were too scared to rebel." His lips pressed into a line. "If they disagreed with him about *anything*, right down to the color of his tie, he'd remove their dragon. Most people believe his magic corrupted him because he got worse the older he became."

"He was a tyrant."

He nodded. "And since I was born with the same magic, that's what people believe I'll become."

My belly roiled. "I'm sorry." I wasn't sure what else I could say.

"It isn't your fault. I am sorry you got wrapped up in our world." He stood and gestured to the living room. "Why don't we move to the couch, and let me see if I can figure out how to undo what I did to you without permission."

I had more questions, but this was his way of moving on from the conversation, and I didn't want to push him.

I took a large sip of coffee, surprised it didn't burn my throat. One perk of being a dragon was that I could breathe fire, I guessed.

I headed to the living room, ready to entertain myself while he got his bearings.

An hour later, Thorn hadn't achieved anything. He'd been sitting right beside me, trying to connect with his magic, while I'd clasped my hands, desperate for a way not to touch him. The jolt between us stole my breath and made me dizzy, and I yearned to feel him, kiss him, and be with him.

He huffed and placed his head in his hands. "I don't know how to do this. I don't feel anything different inside me. All I can sense is my dragon."

He'd been growing more frustrated with each passing minute, and I feared he might be at his breaking point.

"Okay." I turned toward him. "When I fell and hit my head last night, did you feel anything before you touched me?"

Sitting back upright, he squinted and stared at the wall underneath the TV. "Actually, I didn't. It was when I touched you."

At least we had one piece of the puzzle solved. "So try that now." I inched toward him, eager for the distance between us to disappear.

He swallowed, and his Adam's apple bobbed. "You want me to touch you?"

The way he said it made my chest feel funny, and I tried not to take the words like a sexual innuendo. "If that worked before."

"Right." He cleared his throat.

The way he was acting awkward despite being devastatingly gorgeous made him more endearing. He could have any woman on the planet, but he wasn't arrogant in the least. That made me more attracted to him, and there was nothing I could do to stop it.

He held out his hands and paused before touching my shoulders. Electricity sprang to life between us, sizzling from my shoulders down my spine, and to my core. I gasped from the pleasure.

He dropped his hands. "Did I hurt you?"

Great. He must not have felt the same thing I had. This was all one-sided. "No, sorry. Still getting used to being part dragon."

"You may not have to be uncomfortable much longer." He smiled sadly and touched my shoulders again.

The pleasure washed through me once more, but I'd expected the sensation and stayed relaxed.

He closed his eyes, and I stared at his long lashes. Now that he wasn't looking at me, I could take in every gorgeous feature. His cheekbones were angular and his lips so full that I'd bet they were soft as a feather. Between his looks and his love for his parents, there was no doubt he would make a woman very happy someday.

I wished that woman could be me.

Something trickled into my body, a warm energy I'd never felt before. My dragon roared in my brain, and I jerked. She'd been so quiet. The magic swirled around inside me, floating within my body.

"I feel something," I whispered.

His fingers dug into my skin as he gritted out, "I know, but I can't get my magic to attach to your dragon." His brows furrowed, and more warmth flowed into me.

My dragon mixed with the magic, and my heart dropped. He was taking her from me, but I wasn't relieved like I thought I'd be. Inexplicably, I wanted her to stay. I couldn't be attached to her. She'd been part of me for less than twenty-four hours.

His hands began to shake on my shoulders, and I focused back on him. Sweat beaded his face as he grimaced. He was trying like hell to change me back into a human, and it was taking a huge toll on him.

"Hey," I said, but he continued to funnel his magic into me.

I cupped his cheek, and his eyes flew open. His irises glowed, his pupils slitted, and my dragon stirred. Our faces were so close, and everything inside me ached for him. There was no way I could go another second without him knowing how I felt.

"I'm sorry," he murmured, but before he could say anything else, I kissed him.

He wrapped his arms around me, pulling me against him as we opened our mouths to each other. Electricity jolted between us, and his faint vanilla flavor filled my mouth, overloading my senses.

All logic escaped me, and all I could focus on was his mouth, taste, and the way his body felt against mine. Our tongues danced together, and I threaded my fingers into his shaggy hair, loving how easy it was to grab on to.

My breathing quickened, and I moved to straddle him.

Something jingled, breaking through the bubble of desire. The doorknob turned. We weren't alone.

I jerked away, trying to break us apart, but Thorn clung to me.

Saphira couldn't find us like this.

HIS TONGUE BRUSHED MY LIPS, and my brain fried. I'd been crazy to pull away. The connection between us buzzed like a high, making the deliciousness of his touch and kiss more intoxicating.

"What the *hell*?" Saphira yelled as she slammed the cabin door behind her.

I flinched as reality crashed over me. *That* was why I'd tried to pull away.

Thorn jerked back, making my dragon whimper and my heart ache.

Feeling that way was ridiculous, especially since I'd retreated first. We'd admitted, not even a couple of hours ago, that kissing wouldn't be wise, especially since there was no future for us together.

His magic had spurred something inside me and made me lose my mind.

Saphira stomped toward us until I felt her hovering at my side.

I wanted to hang my head and avoid eye contact, but that would make this situation more uncomfortable. I'd learned the hard way that facing issues head-on helped the confrontation. Well, that and taking full responsibility, even if it wasn't your fault.

In this instance, I *was* to blame. After all, I'd kissed him this time around.

With every ounce of self-control I possessed, I turned my head toward her.

Her long, curly hair was windblown, and her brown skin glistened in a way it hadn't during the past few days while we'd been locked in the cabin. She was a vision, and again, I wondered why Drake hadn't chosen her to be his...breeder.

Then I remembered. He needed a human, which I wasn't anymore.

"It was my fault," Thorn said and lifted his chin as if ready to fight. "Our magic melded together, and I kissed her."

My chest expanded, and my attraction to him deepened, which I hadn't thought possible. He was willing to take the blame.

"So you *take* anything you want?" Saphira pointed a finger at him. "Kidnapping Everly and me, locking us up here, and now pushing yourself on her?"

There was no way I would let him do this, especially since he and Saphira had gotten on the same page before she left. "It wasn't him. It was me. He's trying to protect me from your wrath. I kissed him for the reason he said. His magic was all inside me and mixing with my dragon. I got wrapped up in the moment and lost my head."

"Seems like more than losing your damn head," Saphira snarled as her eyes widened. "I get that maybe he isn't the villain, but he *kidnapped* us and changed you into a dragon."

Normally, I would back off, but I couldn't let this go. She was attacking Thorn, and it wasn't fair. "Oh, so he should've flown up to the car door while you were driving away and asked you to roll down the window so he could plead with us to come with him? Oh, wait, he was in *dragon* form."

Thorn gave me that same strange gaze he had when the cops had been present. His brows were furrowed, but his eyes were filled with...not confusion, but adoration.

Saphira's jaw dropped. "Are you *defending* him?"

"Yes, I am. He's in a horrible situation with no good answers. A situation we're involved in. Do you think it was a good decision to get your uncle involved?" I stood and crossed my arms.

She rolled her eyes. "No, because now he's at risk. But it was the best option we had because Thorn and his parents don't deserve *this*. Besides, I want to help so I can see what the king has done. If what Thorn says is true, then the king and the prince have been abusing their powers."

"And that's the conclusion Thorn came to when he captured us." I aimed to be pragmatic. If I didn't think rationally, emotions would take over, and that would be bad. That was one reason I enjoyed medicine. It was filled with facts and diagnostics. If you kept searching, finding an answer was inevitable. Reacting emotionally often made things worse. "If he turned himself in to free his parents, they would come back for him, risking them all, so he had to find another solution...which happened to be us."

"I'm really sorry for dragging you two into this." Thorn licked his lips. "I wish I'd figured out something else instead."

Saphira's expression softened. "*Fine.* I get why you did what you did. I'd do anything for my family, too," she said begrudgingly.

Wanting her to realize something else, I added, "And he took the blame for something I started to save me from *this*." I gestured at Saphira.

"That was my fault as well." Thorn smiled sadly. "I didn't stop you."

I glared at him. He was *not* helping.

"Oh, gods," Saphira growled. "No more kissing." She tilted her head at me and said, "You do plan on handing yourself over to Drake, don't you?"

Thorn's jaw clenched.

He wasn't taking this well. That might be due to his brother having so much control over everything. "Of course I am. I can't risk Eva. When I turn myself over, I'll need both of you to keep an eye on her to make sure she and my brother stay safe. I won't be able to watch over them like my mom asked me to. So far, Thorn hasn't been able to take back my dragon."

"I will." Saphira placed a hand over her heart, but then she wrinkled her nose. "Maybe it didn't work because you *attacked* him."

I scoffed and puffed out my chest. "I did not *attack* him. I ki—"

She lifted a hand. "Stop right there. We're going with attacked because I need to unsee what I walked in on. I'll have nightmares for months. I seriously thought you were eating each other."

That image was *so* not sexy. He was the first man I'd ever really kissed, so maybe I'd been horrible at it. My stomach dropped as my neck and ears grew uncomfortably hot. I was certain I'd never be able to look at Thorn again without wanting to hide.

Thorn cleared his throat. "That's not why I couldn't turn her back. I don't know how long I funneled magic into her, but I *couldn't* latch on to the dragon. Then my magic actually rejected taking her dragon from her. I pushed more into her to override it."

I'd wondered why he'd increased the amount flowing into me. I faced him again. "I thought you took the king's dragon."

"I *did*. My magic latched on to it easily, just like I gave you yours without a struggle." Thorn lifted clenched hands. "I don't know what the hell the problem is."

"Maybe you didn't try?" Saphira rocked back on her feet and leveled her gaze at him. "Keeping her a dragon is one way to stick it to Drake and thwart his plan."

She was right, but I'd *felt* everything he'd done. I insisted, "His magic swirled around my dragon. I felt him trying to connect with her, but it wasn't happening. My dragon wasn't even worried."

"Forgive me for thinking you might be biased." She cocked a brow.

"Turning her over to Drake like *this* while the king has my parents doesn't bode well for me, either." Thorn inhaled slowly and lowered his arms. "Believe me when I say I tried."

Saphira shook her head and grimaced. "You're right. I'm sorry. This whole situation would be easier if you were the bad guy."

I understood that sentiment far too well. "Did you learn anything from your uncle?"

Thorn stood and crossed his arms. He swallowed hard and remained quiet.

"No, but I didn't expect to. I told you both that." She raised her hands. "But he'll talk to Dad and get us some answers. There's a catch, though."

Thorn glanced at the door and rasped, "Did you tell them where we are?"

"What? No!" she exclaimed. "You really do have trust issues."

He bared his teeth. "When your father tries to kill you and hunts you for the rest of your life, lack of trust gets ingrained in you."

We were losing focus, and I wanted answers. "What's the catch?"

"He was hesitant to get involved and told me to stay out of it. He says going against the royals will cause me grief." Saphira wrung her hands, not looking like the confident dragon she was. "So...I told him who our kidnapper is."

"*What?*" Thorn snarled. "Why would you do that?"

"To get him to *help* us." She stomped a foot as she glared at him. "He didn't believe it. He told me to come back tonight with *you*, and he'll give us the information. He has to see that you're alive with his own eyes. Everyone believes you're dead."

Well, she was certainly blunt. I sighed. "We're aware everyone believes that, Saphira."

Thorn chuckled, and my stomach flipped. "He wants me to come to dragon lands to visit him. Really? I might as well hand myself over to the king."

I didn't know how the dragon lands were set up, but I could see why he was hesitant. If there were guards on its perimeter, they would be watching the area closely now that Thorn had Saphira and me.

"He wants to meet with you twenty miles south at a stream where Tyson and I used to go when he wanted to get away from the thunder after his injury." She rocked on her feet. "We never saw humans there, and it's a safe location. It's deep enough in the woods that humans rarely travel there and close enough to the thunder that a rogue dragon wouldn't hang out that close to our homeland."

It did sound like a happy medium. "I understand his hesitation. He probably wants to see who Saphira has been with since she went missing."

"Are you sure he can be trusted?" Thorn scratched his neck. "Can't I call him instead?"

"I trust him, and he wants to see you. He hopes you *are* alive." Saphira closed her eyes, and her face twisted in agony. "He hates the king and Drake. I think he wants to meet you to see if you became what everyone said the curse would make you. If I know him, he's hoping you're a decent man and might want to take your place in line to the throne. Tyson gets ridiculed and barely ventures outside the house unless it's with me to go to the stream I mentioned."

Thorn leaned his head back and stared at the ceiling.

"It's up to you," I said. I understood the risks of going and the risks of remaining here. "One way, we might get answers, and the other way, we have to hope we can find where your parents are being kept. As soon as the warriors are alerted to your presence, they'll call for backup. We need to know exactly where we're heading."

"Either way could go badly." He chewed on his bottom lip and turned to me. "What do you think?"

My heart pounded. Outside of the classroom, no one ever asked for my opinion. I fidgeted and pulled my thoughts together. "I trust Saphira, and if she believes her uncle just wants to see you to confirm who you are and that he might have hope, it's worth the risk. It's not like the king isn't aware you're alive."

"Okay." He nodded. "That's what we'll do. What time are we supposed to meet him?"

Saphira smiled. "Midnight. That way, he has time to talk to Dad. Luckily, my uncle lives on the edge of dragon territory and is out of favor, so guards don't patrol there. He can sneak away." She leaned toward us over the back of the sofa. "I promise you he wouldn't betray me. We can fly in and out with no problem."

Fly.

My stomach soured. "Wait. I haven't done that before."

"You'll be fine. You'll have to learn, anyway, for your dragon to fully sync with you." She waved my concern off as if it were silly.

I tensed. "Okay, but that isn't comforting."

Thorn placed a hand on my arm. "We'll be with you the entire way. Saphira can shift with you, and I'll stay nearby in dragon form in case we run into any issues. You'll have the two of us to help you."

His words released some tension in my stomach, but my lungs struggled to work as I tried to fight my nerves. Saphira was right: I'd have to try eventually, and it would be better with them there to support me.

There was one thing that would take my mind off having to shift... "Why don't we have lunch? Is there a pizza place we can order from that delivers here?"

"You do realize we're in the mountains?" Thorn grinned at me.

"Yeah, but people still like pizza out here, right?" I didn't know how to cook, so pizza was the default when I decided to stay in. "Or we can order something else and DoorDash it."

"With how far they'd have to travel, that would be expensive." Thorn shook his head.

Apparently, I was that easy to read. "Does someone know how to make something? We always ate out or brought food in."

"And if your father is the king's advisor, you're probably as spoiled as she is," Thorn said, nodding at Saphira as he strolled into the kitchen.

Saphira stuck out her tongue. "Maybe. But I'm sure Everly and I could manage *something*."

"Leave the cooking to the experts." He pulled out a skillet. "I make a mean grilled cheese."

I smiled. At that moment, it felt like we were three friends hanging out and at ease. I just hoped that didn't change between now and when we left.

THE REST of the day passed in a blur. Saphira and I played checkers and talked fashion while Thorn watched a baseball game on TV. My competitive side leaked through every time I won a match, a vice I was well aware of. However, wanting to be the best was the main reason I was at the top of my premed class, and it had helped me get into the medical program at the school.

But my impending shift hadn't strayed far from my mind.

Thorn entered the house, his pupils elongated. "The coast is clear of humans. We can go outside and shift."

Soon enough, the three of us were walking out the front door to meet Saphira's uncle, Thorn with a large duffel bag slung over his shoulder. The importance of what we were about to do struck me, and my lungs seized. How was this my life? I hadn't even processed that I wouldn't be attending classes this summer or, more than likely, ever again. Protecting my sister was costing me not only my freedom but also my dream of helping others. In all the turmoil, I hadn't thought through everything I was giving up.

"Hey, I don't need you freaking out, too," Saphira grumbled and bumped shoulders with me.

If I'd been human, I would've fallen and skidded across the gravel driveway. Now, her mild razzing was a mere annoyance.

"Sorry, I was lost in thought." Thinking about how my entire life had changed in the blink of an eye, all because my stepdad had embezzled a million dollars from a dragon prince.

I wondered if that was why he'd been acting so strange the last few months while Mom had been alive. He'd grown cold and distant, mainly toward me, but he'd put up a barrier between himself and Mom and my half siblings as well. He'd just tolerated them better.

The moon shone down in a cloudless sky, and when I looked up,

I went still with amazement. My entire human life, I'd believed the night sky was dark blue, but my dragon eyes told a different story.

The sky still appeared mainly dark blue, but there were green and yellow splotches throughout the atmosphere. Yet what made it so breathtaking was how brightly the stars shone, like beacons and spots of cobalt and pink swirls from the center of the Milky Way.

When things calmed down, I would have to paint this image for humans to see.

"Are you okay?" Thorn paused beside me and followed my gaze skyward. "Do you see something concerning?"

"I've never seen the sky like this before." I winced at my breathy tone. I probably sounded very cliché to him. "Human eyes don't see all the colors, and they're breathtaking."

"Well, you'll have the rest of your life to see the sky since Thorn can't turn you back." Saphira looped her arm with mine and dragged me toward the tree line. "Let's hurry up so we aren't late to meet my uncle."

She was right. I was dragging my feet. I glanced over my shoulder and saw Thorn's scowl before he hurried after us.

The closer it got to eleven-thirty, the more stoic he became.

Soon, we were walking into the tree line, and I stared at the surrounding red spruces and balsams, seeing patterns and colors in their branches and remaining leaves I'd never known existed.

Thorn tossed his duffel bag to the ground. "I brought clothes for us to change into once we arrive."

I nodded and swallowed hard. I'd been dreading this aspect for a while, but Saphira had sworn that my dragon would take control and the transformation would come naturally. Thorn headed deeper into the woods, and I heard noises of something large nearby—he'd already shifted into dragon form.

Saphira stripped down next to me and waved her hands, encouraging me to go on.

I inhaled shakily. "Let's see how this goes."

"Remember to allow your dragon to take over. That will be the hardest part, but if you do that, everything else will fall into place," Saphira reminded me.

She stared at me, making my skin crawl. "Got it." I closed my eyes, not wanting to see her watching me, and searched for my dragon.

Finding her wasn't hard. She immediately brushed my mind. Forcing my body to relax, I waited.

Nothing happened.

What the hell? By being calm, I was letting her know she could take control, yet she sat there as if waiting for an invitation.

Of course I struggled with the one thing that was fundamental to being a dragon—shifting. I wasn't sure what she wanted, and we needed to go.

"Don't get upset. Just talk to her like you would a friend," Saphira murmured beside me.

Lovely. This wouldn't be awkward at all. *Please, dragon, work with me, here.*

At that, she wrapped gently around my mind, and her magic streamed through my blood. My body expanded, growing larger, and I couldn't believe it. The dragon *had* needed a freaking invitation.

I opened my eyes. Silvery scales shimmered all over me. I lifted my head, and the ground underneath me appeared farther away than usual. I regained my equilibrium, and my dragon urged me forward, tugging me around the bush to see the object of my desire.

Thorn.

Then something jolted through my heart and changed my whole world.

CHAPTER TWENTY

THORN'S SILVERY plum scales were more gorgeous through dragon eyes. I grew dizzy as I noted the moonlight reflecting off them. The silver glistened, further enhancing the purple. He was the most gorgeous creature I'd ever seen, human or dragon.

Something settled deep inside my heart, and it felt lighter as I edged toward him. Even if I'd wanted to stop, there was no way I could. I was *meant* to be beside him.

His sky blue eyes took in every inch of me, too.

The thought that my first time flying would be with him made the situation more extraordinary. I finally understood what it meant to be alive. The electricity that had shot through me in human form had been a mere taste of what it was in dragon form.

With every step closer to him, the electricity changed to something like a lightning bolt that constantly sizzled between us.

A loud huff sounded next to me, and something rammed into my side.

Saphira.

She'd shifted.

I'd expected to stumble from the pressure, but my dragon countered the momentum, and I didn't budge.

Thorn emanated a low, threatening growl.

I was certain he didn't like how she'd rammed into me, but we couldn't converse in dragon form. It was the only way she could get my attention, seeing as I'd been transfixed by Thorn.

Saphira moved in front of us, her footsteps shaking the ground. Her butterscotch scales shimmered and contrasted nicely with her mocha eyes.

I jerked my gaze back to Thorn, wondering if I'd lost his attention to her. The mere thought made my dragon angry, but my chest relaxed as he took a protective stance beside me and glared at her.

She rolled her eyes, a hint of her human side peeking through, and tilted her head skyward.

I understood what she was saying: we needed to go.

Though my hands and feet were touching the ground, my left talons rubbed what would've been my right wrist, searching for Mom's bracelet out of habit. My stomach dropped before I remembered Saphira had told me to leave it behind. I'd left it on the kitchen table where I could pick it up first thing upon our return.

I brushed my head against Thorn's long neck. I wanted to calm him, and my dragon had taken control, knowing our touch would do just that.

He huffed at her and nuzzled me back.

Butterflies took flight inside me. I was way too giddy in this form.

Saphira shifted her weight back and used her front right talons to kick at the ground.

Her show of impatience was similar to that of a horse. My dragon snarled in my head.

Great. She and I were getting along *so* well in this form.

Moving a few steps away from me, Thorn spread his wings. He flapped them slowly but didn't lift into the air.

After a second, I realized he was showing me what to do.

Though I understood the theory, I wasn't sure how fast to move them or how far to lift and lower them. What if I got high into the sky and lost momentum? I'd been so concerned with shifting that I hadn't realized I'd also have to fly.

Following his lead, I spread my wings, the sensation foreign as my back moved in a way it never had before. I raised and lowered my wings like he was showing me, but they shook from a lack of control.

Saphira stood back on all four legs and moved her wings in the same way as Thorn but faster, and she rose slowly, hovering several feet off the ground, showing me how it was done.

There was no way I'd be that graceful, but we had somewhere to be. I couldn't just stand here like an insolent child.

Taking a deep breath, I moved my wings faster, and my large body shot skyward. Tree branches smacked my face and chest, but I couldn't dodge them as I zigzagged up.

When I broke through the trees, I took a deep breath and tried to get my bearings...which was a horrible idea. My wings stopped moving as quickly, and I tumbled down.

Thorn and Saphira raced toward me, but I was already dropping back into the tree cover. Limbs cracked, and one branch stabbed me in the side. I flipped over so I was staring into the night sky, and then I slammed into the ground, my rump taking the brunt of the impact.

Pain shot through the back of my head, and I roared as I attempted to get up. Unfortunately, I'd wedged myself between two tree trunks, my body stuck tight. I wasn't sure how the trees hadn't toppled over. I couldn't roll, and with my back aching, I wasn't strong enough to sit up.

I was trapped.

Thorn crashed through the treetops, rushing toward me. Though it was hard to tell his expression in dragon form, I could sense his emotions through his eyes—he was worried.

My dragon grumbled inside my head, angry over how silly we looked now that Thorn was here. I didn't need to hear her displeasure. I already wanted the ground to open up and swallow me whole. I'd never been athletic, and that had carried through to my shifter form.

He landed near my head and checked on me. Once he realized I wasn't seriously injured, he slid his front legs—arms?—under my shoulders.

The familiar bolt of lightning coursed between us, and I was tempted to lie there and enjoy his touch. Then Saphira appeared.

I didn't want another lecture once we got back. This time, when Thorn pushed, I tried to sit upright and got unwedged.

Soon, I was able to stand, easing the pain from my entire weight pressing onto my back.

Saphira shook her head, communicating enough for me to know that she was either appalled or found my attempt to fly hilarious. Either way, I'd never hear the end of this.

I wanted to shift to human form and tell them to go on without me, but that wasn't an option. I didn't need to give Thorn a reason to abandon the plan, and he wouldn't leave me behind.

I would have to learn to fly.

Thorn blew out a breath, his irises darkening with concern.

If I didn't do something soon, he'd shift back. Asking my dragon for help to shift earlier had worked, so I might as well try that again. I closed my eyes and thought, *Can you help me fly?*

Though I couldn't see my dragon, I could sense her inside me. She growled and brushed against my mind. My natural instinct was to not let her in, but maybe she needed that to fly.

I took a deep breath and relaxed, and her magic flooded through me. When I opened my eyes, my sight was the same, but I could sense life all around me. Before, I'd only seen and heard the woodland animals. Now I could tell that raccoons and opossums were scurrying through the underbrush as far as a few miles away, close to the stream.

My wings flapped, the motion fluid and natural. They didn't feel like a foreign part of my body but rather like they had always been there. The weight on my limbs lifted, and soon, I felt nothing underneath them. The best part was that I was no longer petrified of falling. Granted, I was only a foot off the ground, but I'd take the win.

Saphira nodded and flapped her wings, following my lead. Thorn stayed on the ground, afraid that I might fall again, which annoyed me.

Instead of waiting for him, I flew higher. We'd planned not to stay on the ground too long in dragon form to avoid detection. Even though I couldn't sense any humans nearby, I didn't want to take chances.

Saphira and I pushed our wings harder and broke through the treetops. As the cool night air brushed my scales, an exhilaration I'd never experienced before surged through me. This high in the sky, no one could touch me. Not my stepdad, not my debilitating tendency to please when it came to my family, and not even my perfectionist side where I had to be the best to prove I was worthy. I was so high up that if there was a Heaven, I had to be close to it, and I had no doubt that was exactly where my mom was.

The beat of strong wings echoed behind us, and I didn't have to look to know it was Thorn. Not just because he was the only other dragon around, but the *zing* that surged between us was growing stronger, indicating he was catching up.

Saphira pulled in front, leading us to the place where we were to meet her uncle. It was almost comical seeing her fly with the black duffel bag clutched in her talons.

I didn't rush to catch up, enjoying my current pace. I surveyed the ground, reveling in the clear night that allowed me to see everything below. Even this high—an altitude I'd been close to only on an airplane—I could make out a handful of cars spiraling down a windy two-lane road.

As Thorn caught up to me, his tantalizing scent of minty amber and brimstone filled my nose. It was the best scent in the entire world. The only thing as delicious had been his faint vanilla taste when we'd kissed.

My attention was locked on him. As a dragon, I could tell that Thorn was as strong in this form as in his human one. I doubted there was any dragon who could rival him in strength and size. He was thirty feet tall, at least ten feet taller than my dragon. The diamond flecks in his sky blue eyes captivated me, and I tried not to focus on my fear of never seeing him again once I surrendered myself to Drake. The thought was too painful.

Saphira glanced back at us, then nodded down and to the right.

My gaze followed where she'd indicated, and I saw a stream. That had to be where we were meeting her uncle.

My body suddenly felt heavy. I didn't want this moment to end. I couldn't believe we were already at the meeting place, but at least I had the return flight to look forward to.

There were no hints of humans. The closest car was at least thirty miles away.

We began our descent, and Thorn's wings tensed and flapped more briskly. I hated the turmoil plaguing him. Not only did the king have his parents, but now he had to face someone he'd once considered one of his people.

By the stream stood a man who had to be Saphira's uncle. He watched us descend, his emerald eyes and bald head reflecting the light of the sky. He rubbed a hand over his raven goatee as the dark skin around his eyes tightened.

He didn't seem comfortable about the meeting, either, and I wondered why he'd demanded to have it.

The three of us landed half a mile away, where red spruces and balsams grew thick. We'd have cover when we shifted back into human form. As my feet touched the ground, I wanted to shoot back into the sky. But my sister's freedom was at risk, and who knew what kind of prison Thorn's parents were being held in?

Thorn glanced from side to side, getting a feel for the place. I didn't sense anything odd, but he had been a dragon much longer than I had. After a pause, he snorted and walked into the trees.

As soon as his handsome, strong tail was out of view, Saphira tossed the duffel bag in front of us.

Now *I* had to shift. That would be fun.

Beside me, Saphira's form began to shrink. She didn't struggle at all, but then she had been at this her entire life.

Last time, talking to my dragon had helped. *Can you help me shift back into human form? We need to protect our sister.*

Unhappiness coursed through me. My dragon wasn't ready to relinquish control, but I felt her separate from my mind, and when she did, my body shrank.

Back in human form, Saphira unzipped the duffel bag. "Look at you! You shifted right back without issue. Call me impressed."

When the wind blowing against my body became chillier, I glanced down to see I was back in my naked human body. "My dragon and I are starting to have an understanding."

"Good," she said as she tossed me the smaller pair of sweatpants and a shirt.

I quickly dressed, not wanting to risk her uncle searching for us and finding me like this. I slipped on some tennis shoes that were a size too big and exhaled, feeling more like myself and able to meet someone.

"Thorn! It's your turn. Everly and I will go meet my uncle," she said as she looped her arm through mine.

The ground shook as he approached us. I wanted to hide and watch him shift, but Saphira wouldn't release her hold on me and dragged me away.

That was for the best. The last thing I needed to be was a creeper.

We walked through the tree line and found her uncle standing where he'd been when we'd flown in.

"Saphy." He smiled and placed his cell phone into his pocket. "I was beginning to wonder if you'd be here."

"Sorry. We had some strange delays." Saphira glanced at me but didn't tell him it was my fault.

Interesting.

"Where's the *supposed* prince?" Her uncle looked past us into the woods.

"He's shifting and getting dressed," she answered, and placed a hand on my shoulder. "This is Everly. Everly, this is my uncle, Brenton Asher."

Normally, I was good at meeting people, but this was the first dragon I'd met as a dragon myself, and I wasn't sure what the right greeting was. "Hi, Mr. Asher. It's nice to meet you."

"I wouldn't be so certain." He bit his bottom lip and wiped the sweat from his brow.

"What's wrong?" Saphira stood straight. "Is Tyson okay?"

"Nothing. He's fine." He cleared his throat.

A branch snapped, and that bolt of lightning shot down my back. I hadn't expected that intensity in human form, and I gasped.

Thorn's footsteps hurried, and soon, he reached my side. "Everly, what's wrong?"

I was certain I shouldn't answer that question. "Sorry, just a little overstimulated."

My feet were traitors that inched closer to him.

"Oh, dear gods," Brenton gasped and stumbled back. "It *is* you. I thought Saphira had gotten it wrong."

"Clearly, I didn't. But why are you so sure?" Saphira tilted her head.

"Even though Thorn didn't know me, I was around the castle when he was small. I saw him with his nanny often." Brenton placed a hand on his chest, looking as if he'd seen a ghost. "He's an exact mixture of the king and queen."

That was funny. Even though Thorn and Drake had similar features, I wouldn't have thought they were siblings right away. Drake's features must favor one parent.

"I've seen many people as a child, but I don't remember them."

Thorn moved so our arms brushed. "Did you find out where they're keeping my parents? I need to rescue them."

"Oh." Brenton pulled at the collar of his thin white cotton shirt. "Yes. Well, I didn't quite get an answer. I tried talking to your father, Saphy, but—"

Thorn tensed beside me and looked at the sky. "We've got incoming."

CHAPTER TWENTY-ONE

JUDGING by the way Thorn's body thrummed and our proximity to dragon territory, the "incoming" wasn't a good thing.

A lump formed in my throat, and I glanced at the sky for the threat.

"I thought you said we could trust him," Thorn rasped and glared at Saphira. "Are you in on this?"

"No! Of course not." Saphira shook her head, and her brows furrowed as she gaped at her uncle. "What did you do?"

"I—" he started.

Thorn cut him off. "We don't have time for this. Everly, get out of here. I'll be right behind you."

I laughed, surprising myself, the sound maniacal even to my own ears. "You think I'm going to leave you?"

Then I sensed the presence Thorn had. The threat wasn't coming from the sky, but rather from the ground. My attention focused over Brenton's shoulders as two figures dressed in black raced toward us. One of them was Ladon, and the second was a woman.

Even with the black helmets, I could make out the edges of the woman's bleach-blonde bangs falling a little over her cinnamon-brown eyes.

The strength of my vision as a dragon shifter still unsettled me.

Ladon and the woman carried huge rifles on their shoulders, the barrels larger than normal, which looked odd.

"Yes, you'd better leave," Thorn snarled, as he lifted me by the waist and placed me behind him.

The lightning that bolted between us wasn't enough to quash my anger. These warriors were after *him*, not me. If anything, he needed to leave.

A *click* sounded behind me, and I spun around to find Falkor looking out from behind a red spruce about a hundred yards away, rifle pointed at us. He pulled the trigger.

I pivoted and tackled Thorn from behind, and he fell forward. He had about a hundred and fifty pounds on me, but he hadn't been expecting my assault and toppled like a tree.

His knees and hands hit the ground as I plastered myself over his back. Something *whoosh*ed over our heads. The bullet punched into the earth, and dirt was launched into the air.

Jerking my head up, I spotted the bullet a foot shy of hitting Brenton. Wait, that wasn't a bullet. It was a dart.

Saphira hissed, "They've got tranq guns."

I must have misunderstood her. That was something people used on *animals*.

My heart sank. That was *exactly* what we were.

My human part wanted to freeze, but my dragon appeared, forcing me to my feet. Thorn stood as well, and his jaw twitched. Just as I glanced back at Falkor, Thorn sacked me.

Unlike him, my whole front hit the ground, the overgrown grass getting stuck in my teeth. To make matters worse, he settled his entire weight on top of me. He was so heavy, I couldn't breathe. Something hit the ground close to us, and I realized he'd protected me from a dart.

That wasn't how this was going down.

I bucked underneath him, but it was like slamming into a brick house. I got that he was a dragon, but his strength should have been impossible.

My lungs screamed, and I muttered, "Can't breathe."

His full weight lifted off my body.

"If we stay much longer, they'll capture you," Saphira said from her spot beside us. "They have Jessie and Cedric with them."

I had no clue who they were, but by the way Thorn sucked in his breath, I thought he did.

"Of course they'd bring their four strongest warriors." Thorn rolled off me and glanced in both directions. "We have to run. We're sitting ducks here."

I wasn't a strategist, but his analogy fit our circumstances. "Then let's *do* that." I was an action-type person...unless I was frozen in fear. Go figure.

Not wanting to stick around to see who went first, *I* moved. But instead of running away, I figured why not run directly at the warriors? They wouldn't expect that, and they weren't targeting me.

Since Falkor was the only one shooting, I'd start with him. I pivoted toward the warrior and ran at him, hoping my path would block his easy shot at Thorn.

"Everly!" Thorn roared. "What the *fuck* are you doing?"

"I'm not a rocket scientist, but I'm pretty sure she's running toward Falkor instead of *away*," Saphira answered. "She's not thinking clearly."

Arms grabbed my waist, but the jolt was missing. Saphira's freesia smell filled my nose as she yelled, "Thorn, *go*." She tossed me toward the stream.

My body soared, the air whipping around me, but I landed on my feet. Now I was out of range of the warriors' current target.

Thorn and Saphira raced toward me. Two darts landed where they'd been a second before.

Heart pounding, I fought the urge to race toward them. That would only slow them down.

A dart whistled through the air and hit the back of Thorn's foot.

No. This couldn't be happening.

Instead of collapsing, Thorn continued to run, his speed not impacted. His nostrils flared as he pointed behind me. "Move!"

"Your foot," I spat as he and Saphira reached me.

He glanced down and paled. He reached below and yanked the dart out, and my heart began to beat again. The dart had hit the sole of his shoe. *That* we could survive.

"Thank gods," Saphira sighed.

With the immediate threat handled, I took off to the left, unsure where to head.

As I took a few steps, someone ran up behind us. I looked back to see Brenton right behind Saphira.

She clenched her hands at her sides. "What do you think—"

Thorn rushed past her and punched Brenton in the nose. Brenton's head jerked back, and blood gushed down his mouth and chin.

Former Everly would've been appalled, but Dragon Everly knew the bastard deserved it.

The hairs on the back of my neck rose. We'd stopped for too long. Falkor, Ladon, Cedric, and Jessie were almost upon us. Knowing that Brenton was injured and would likely slow because of that, the three of us moved in sync and took off running.

"There!" Ladon yelled from our right.

They were rushing to intercept us instead of shooting.

"Saphira, you know the area. Run!" Thorn murmured urgently.

"Don't shoot unless you know you can hit Thorn," Falkor yelled. "We're low on tranqs. He's the actual threat."

At least they didn't have unlimited ammo. That was one silver lining.

Saphira took off, damn near blurring past me. Thorn gestured for me to go, and he would take up the rear.

That wasn't smart—there was no way I was even half as fast as Saphira—but I'd learned he was stubborn, so the best thing I could do was move and find a way to get behind him.

I ran as fast as I could, which was nothing to marvel at, though I moved quicker than if I'd been merely human. Maybe it would be best if I shifted into dragon form?

Saphira was almost out of sight ahead of us, but there wasn't a damn thing I could do.

"Tap into your dragon," Thorn commanded from behind me.

He made it sound simple, which it was for them, but not for this newly turned dragon. That would be like me scoffing at him after he bought his first paint set and tried to recreate *Girl with a Pearl Earring*.

Impossible.

"This is going to be a piece of cake," Jessie said from way too close for comfort.

A shiver ran down my spine. They were going to catch us.

As if fate was real and a legit bitch, a man I'd never seen before appeared on my left, just past a balsam fir I was running by, and steamrolled me. My body lurched to the side from the impact, and the man spun me around so he was at my back and we were both facing Thorn. His hot breath hit the top of my head.

"Let her go, Cedric," Thorn commanded.

"You're not a prince anymore," Cedric seethed. "Just a criminal to bring to justice."

I snorted, wanting to draw the warrior's attention away from Thorn. "Why is he a criminal? Because he has magic you idiots don't understand?"

Cedric breathed rapidly just as Falkor walked out of the trees to Thorn. On the other side, Ladon and Jessie stood across from Falkor, their dart guns trained on Thorn.

My dragon surged and brushed against my mind. Amazingly, I understood what she was telling me. Falkor didn't have his gun raised, so he was likely out of tranqs.

In the commotion, all four of them had been focused on who they viewed as the threat.

But they weren't expecting *me*.

All right, friend, I thought to my dragon, keeping my mind open to her. *Let's have a little fun. Let's shift and protect Thorn.*

My dragon roared with excitement and melded with my mind.

Unlike the first time I'd shifted, there was no resistance. I could sense my dragon's magic flooding throughout me, indicating the shift was underway.

"What the—" Cedric gasped as his grip on me loosened.

I wasn't sure if it was because he was surprised or because my neck was expanding. It didn't matter either way.

The larger I grew, the more uncomfortable I got, as if there was something lumpy underneath me.

Ladon and Falkor stared at me, jaws slack.

My attention landed on Thorn, ready to protect him, but he'd used the distraction to rush Falkor.

The cobalt-eyed warrior heard Thorn, and his hand went for the knife sheathed at his waist.

My stomach churned with acid. I couldn't allow Thorn to get injured.

I went to rescue him, but Thorn reached Falkor and punched him in the face. Falkor swung the knife at his neck, but Thorn jerked back, and the knife missed the mark.

"I thought you said she was *human,*" Jessie gasped from below. "If we'd known, maybe Cedric wouldn't have been *sat on.*"

Oh, so that was the lump under my ass. I'd rather have not known that fact. Now I was very uncomfortable with both the lump and *the reason* it was there.

"She *was,*" Ladon said with shock. "He must have changed her."

Since Thorn had Falkor handled, I'd focus on these two.

Something hot inched up my throat. Great, I was going to throw up in dragon form. At least I had two places to target.

Smoke trickled from my nose.

"Shit, she's gonna blow!" Ladon exclaimed. "Run! We need to stay human to use our tranqs."

The two of them turned and ran back the way they'd come as I opened my mouth and flames shot out.

I couldn't believe my eyes. The human part of me was both panicked and mesmerized, but my dragon was in full control.

Both warriors were out of harm's way, which had been my dragon's plan. Neither she nor I was a murderer. We were two parts of the same person.

Thorn had Falkor's knife and used the butt of the weapon to knock the guard in the head. Falkor dropped like a sack of potatoes, knocked out again.

Good.

I flapped my wings and glanced downward to find Cedric knocked out, too. His chest was still moving, but he wasn't a threat.

I soared upward and flew after Ladon and Jessie. They'd split and were running in opposite directions. I roared in frustration. All four warriors were trained and would be strategic.

I sensed Thorn racing after me. Instead of rushing to safety, of course his ass was coming to help me. He had to be staying in human form so he could communicate with Saphira and me.

"I'll take Ladon," Thorn called from below. "You take Jessie. Be careful." He took off after Ladon.

As I flew over the trees, I quickly gained on Jessie. She was running hard and fast, better than I had before I'd shifted, but I easily kept up with her.

She jumped over the large trunk of a fallen tree and crouched in a thick section of brush.

She was up to something, and she wanted me to fly right to her.

I might not have military training, but that didn't mean I lacked critical thinking. I slowed my flight and darted a few trees over behind her.

As I moved, the sound of approaching dragon wings filled my ears, and Saphira's butterscotch dragon soared into view. She was gliding toward Thorn, and my shoulders lightened. Thorn would have backup as he chased Ladon in human form.

A *click* refocused me on Jessie. Even though Thorn was getting help, we weren't home free. I flapped my wings harder, wanting her to think I was planning to fly higher or away.

Hearing the *snick* of the trigger, I stopped moving my wings and crashed.

My body slammed into the ground, and pain exploded in my legs. I could only pray my plan had worked and she hadn't expected me to plummet. Pushing the discomfort aside, I flapped my wings hard and raced toward her. I didn't want to give her a chance to reload the gun.

That uncomfortable rumbling started in my stomach, and I knew it was fire. Boy, did it feel like indigestion. I blew flames into the brush where she was hiding. The green leaves shriveled and died from the heat.

Jessie raced out of her hiding spot, and I snaked after her, staying low to the ground while extending my talons. When I hovered over her, she lifted her rifle and aimed at my belly.

She'd been waiting for this moment. That was why none of the warriors had shifted. They were planning to take us down with their tranqs, and I'd fallen into her trap.

As she pulled the trigger, I darted to the right behind a large red spruce. The dart barely missed my tail, but as the old saying went, *almost* didn't count. I hadn't been hit.

I twisted around, knowing she would either be out of darts or needing to reload. I had to get her to run so I could knock her out.

Then I heard Thorn scream, "Saphira, no!"

My throat went dry, and not from breathing flames.

CHAPTER TWENTY-TWO

EVERYTHING inside me screamed to rush toward them, but my dragon didn't budge. We hovered in the air, doing nothing. Clarity descended upon me as if the dragon and I were finally merging from battle. If we flew off, Jessie could call in reinforcements and have time to strategize. Right now, both sides were on even ground, making decisions in the moment. If I reacted, the odds could switch in their favor. I had to trust Thorn and Saphira to handle themselves.

Though it went against my nature, I focused on my target, channeling my frustration into catching her.

She'd gone back into her hiding spot in the thick bushes. I had to destroy it.

I pumped my wings faster, letting my dragon take control. She was better at this than I was, and I needed to stop fighting her.

The breeze cascaded over me, invigorating me as I flew toward the bush and extended my talons. A good way to fight an enemy was to prevent them from hiding.

As I drew closer, I listened for a *click* to indicate she was readying to shoot and made my move. My talons slashed through the bushes like a knife through butter, with barely any resistance, revealing Jessie.

She was crouched with her rifle strapped to her shoulder. Instead of aiming the rifle, she held a dark metal dagger. She swung the blade at me, and my dragon form veered back, but not quickly enough: the tip of the dagger sliced the edge of my leg.

Something cold crashed through my body, numbing my magic. I dropped and landed on my butt. The ground shook...or maybe that was just my mind. My body shrank as my dragon removed herself from the center of my mind, as if she'd lost control.

Snickering, Jessie stood and tossed the rifle back into the brush to keep it hidden should someone stumble upon us. With the dagger in one hand, she removed an oversized metal bracelet from the back of her belt. "You have no idea what you're up against."

As my scales turned into skin, I felt something large heading our way, but as soon as I was human, I could no longer sense it. My magic was on the fritz.

The breeze, which had been comforting a few minutes ago, blew my hair around my shoulders, reminding me that I was sitting here buck naked. I folded my arms over my breasts and crossed my ankles, completely exposed. "How did you do that?"

She frowned. "He should've never changed you. You're clueless about this world, but that's what you get for being a greedy human." She lifted her dagger. "It's made of Wolfram Dwiin, tungsten metal forged—"

"By dragon's fire." My blood boiled at her condescending tone. "Not just *any* dragon but a royal."

Head tilting back, she scanned me again. I wished she'd look away because I severely underdressed.

"Color me surprised, but that doesn't change what has to happen." She lifted the gigantic handcuff. "We can do this the easy way, or I'll be forced to hurt you again." She came toward me.

My skin jolted like it did any time I was close to Thorn. My dragon roared and pressed against my mind, wanting to take back control, but it was like she couldn't enter.

The sound of wings flapping made me dizzy. Considering the way my body was reacting, I was pretty sure it was Thorn. I was *attuned* to him.

Jessie snarled and turned her head toward our new arrival. Now that she was distracted, I took the opportunity to do the same.

Thorn's gorgeous dragon form soared toward us between a red spruce and Fraser fir. His plum scales glittered more silvery in the moonlight. Smoke trickled from his nose, and his sky blue eyes focused on me. He roared so loudly that my body vibrated. Then his attention locked on Jessie. He zoomed across the clearing, and I yelled, "She's got a Wolfram Dwinn dagger and a handcuff!" With his background, he probably already knew that, but I didn't want to assume and have him stuck in the same situation I was in.

Unthreatened by me, Jessie turned to Thorn. She clutched the dagger in her hand, and when Thorn got close, she swiped at him as she had with me. Unlike *me*, however, he was prepared for it. He drew his dragon legs close to his stomach...and breathed fire.

She rolled to the side, avoiding the flames, and climbed back onto her feet. She stood with her legs shoulder-width apart, waiting for Thorn to attack again.

This was why I needed to get in shape. Even at twenty-two, I was convinced that if I tried that, I'd break a hip.

My dragon grumbled, unhappy with me sitting here, covering my privates, while Thorn was under attack. She was right. I needed to do *something*.

But what?

I scanned the area and noticed that Jessie was inching back toward her hiding space. A lightbulb went off: she was moving toward her rifle so she could tranq Thorn.

Not if I got the rifle first.

Whimpering, I climbed to my feet, keeping my hands over my

breasts. There wasn't much I could do about my lower half. Though I had a plan, that didn't mean I was willing to run through the woods naked. I needed to find some clothes, *pronto*, but after I took the rifle from her.

Thorn glanced at me, his eyes reflecting worry. He obviously thought something was wrong with me, which I could use to hide my intention. A strange growl emanated from his chest, sounding more threatening than his roar. I'd never heard the sound before. I still knew very little, as Jessie had reminded me.

I stumbled a few steps, trying to appear disoriented, which unfortunately wasn't hard. I suspected that it was less acting than I'd have liked to imagine.

As Thorn swooped down to attack Jessie, I walked in a zigzag, hoping like hell she didn't realize what I was doing. I was praying her entire focus was on her battle with Thorn.

The closer I got to her hiding place, the more difficult it was to hide my destination. Out of the corner of my eye, I watched as she swiped the dagger at the tip of Thorn's wing as it descended, changing her strategy. He jumped back into a tree. Her gaze landed on me.

"Oh, *hell*, no," she spat and ran toward me.

Losing all sense of modesty, I pumped my arms at my sides, rushing the last ten feet to the rifle.

The sound of wings flapping told me that Thorn was already getting into position to hold her off. With her speed, I needed every ounce of help I could get. I was *not* a fast runner, especially not in bare feet.

As I lunged for the rifle, Jessie screamed, but it could have been a distraction. I reached the thicket, unsure where she'd put the gun.

Her footsteps started toward me.

Moonlight glinted off a dark piece of metal, and I snatched up the rifle. As I straightened, a body slammed into me, knocking me into a tree trunk behind the bushes. I kept my grip firm on the rifle, not willing to lose it, and as I steadied myself, Jessie punched me in the cheek. My head snapped sideways, the pain blinding. I'd never been in a fight before, except for the one with the cliff before Thorn changed me.

My dragon surged, brushing my mind, and instinctively, I jabbed the butt of the rifle into Jessie's side. She stumbled back a few steps. Thorn appeared above her, and his talons dug into her shoulders and lifted her off the ground.

She smirked sickeningly as she raised her dagger.

I lifted the rifle, aimed at her chest, and pulled the trigger, hoping the gun was loaded.

I chanted internally, *Please don't hit Thorn.*

A tranq shot out of the barrel, and I held my breath. Jessie stabbed him in the leg a moment before the dart hit her calf.

Not exactly the spot I'd been going for, but at least it had hit *somewhere.*

Thorn's huge form shrank as the metal took effect, and he tumbled from the sky. He released Jessie, and she crashed like dead weight. Thorn still had wings and lowered himself to the ground before dropping the remaining ten feet.

Saliva filled my mouth as I hurried over to him. There was no telling how deep she'd cut him. I dropped to my knees at his side and pushed the hair from his eyes. I murmured, "Thorn?" I didn't want to be too loud in case someone else was close by.

Our skin sizzled, and his eyelids cracked open, revealing his beautiful, glowing eyes. My own burned with unshed tears. Thank goodness he was at least coherent.

"Jessie!" he exclaimed, sitting upright quickly.

I became very aware that he was *naked.* And so was I. My eyes acted on their own will and scanned his large body. And boy, did I mean *large.* Most might even say gigantic, and not in just one thing. *Everything* about him was large. His chiseled abs, the curves of his muscles, and his pleasure seeker.

I cringed. What was I, an old lady or a young teenager? I was studying to be a *doctor,* for goodness' sake. I should be able to call it by its *technical* name—penis.

He stood, putting his pleasure seek—er, penis right in front of my face. If anyone saw us, they'd find me on my knees in front of him and get a *very* wrong idea about what was going on. Unless they saw the unconscious body several feet from us...and that would either make them realize something weird was going on or make them think we were super kinky.

Why couldn't I get my mind out of the gutter?

"I...uh..." I couldn't concentrate, so I jumped to my feet. Clearly, that had been a bad idea. Now his gaze was on my breasts.

Something spicy filled the air, making me salivate.

Jessie groaned, slamming me back into the present. I needed clothes for him and me as soon as possible.

"I tranqed her." I lifted the rifle, refocusing his attention before we got too distracted, or worse, I mumbled something about his pleasure seeker. Then I remembered him hollering Saphira's name. "Where's Saphira? Is she okay?"

"She'll be here soon." He cleared his throat and jerked his head away. "I'm sorry if we worried you, but I had to distract Ladon, so I yelled. She stayed to fight him while I shifted and came to check on you."

I licked my lips. "How are we supposed to get out of this situation?" I waved my hand at him and me. "How long until we can shift back into dragons?"

"Just a few minutes." He ran a hand through his hair, his bicep bulging. "You might be able to shift now. The fumes prick the skin and vanish rather quickly. They do that to force a shift and then put on a Wolfram Dwinn collar."

My world dizzied. If a room covered in Wolfram Dwinn could stop someone from shifting, I'd bet a collar would do the same.

Wings whirred toward us, and Thorn and I turned in the direction he had come from. I spotted a hint of butterscotch scales.

Saphira.

Some of the weight on my shoulders disappeared. She was all right and heading toward us. "I'm so glad to see her." I ignored my dragon and the part of me that was not thrilled about her seeing Thorn naked. This was a high-stakes situation, so our safety was more important than me worrying about her seeing him.

"Ladon was injured. I know you care about her, and I wouldn't have left her unless I was sure she could handle things," Thorn assured me with a sad smile, and my heart skipped a beat.

He was so damn handsome that even a painting couldn't capture his perfection. But I feared that if I didn't try once things were settled, I'd never be able to remember him well enough. It was inevitable that we'd part, even if I didn't want that. I'd learned the hard way that wishes and desires didn't change a damn thing. In certain cases, like with Thorn, they only broke your heart, time and time again.

"I know," I said softly, not questioning if he could hear me.

Adoration filled his eyes, but then it vanished. "Why don't you try to shift again? We need to get out of here." He turned his back to me, and my heart panged.

Now wasn't the time to push him. We could be attacked again at any moment. Anything I wanted to say to him could wait. But what was the point? We wouldn't be with each other much longer.

Pushing away my trivial concerns and focusing on our safety, I inhaled deeply and let my dragon brush my mind once more. This time, she was able to enter it, and her magic thrummed through me. My body grew larger as I stumbled away from Thorn and shifted.

If Thorn couldn't shift soon, I would carry him back to the cabin.

As Saphira approached, she snarled and darted the last ten yards toward us.

I noticed something to my left, behind the trunk of a red spruce: a rifle lifting in our direction.

Falkor.

My human side froze, but thank goodness for my dragon. She sprang to life.

I roared and took flight, using one of my legs to shove Thorn out of the way. He hit the ground hard.

As I leaped toward Falkor, he turned the gun on me. He pulled the trigger, but Saphira appeared, blocking me from the tranq. The thud of the dart lodging into her scales rang in my ears. Instead of crashing, she flew toward Falkor. She roared, and my dragon understood what she was telling me.

She wanted us to go.

Her wings slowed, and her body shrank. There was no way I could reach her to carry her out of here. Not with Falkor right there.

"Everly, go. I still can't shift," Thorn said behind me. "You need to get out of here."

If he thought I was leaving without him, he would soon learn otherwise. Turning, I swooped down and picked up Thorn in my front claws. I flapped my wings hard, pushing myself to get us out of this hellhole.

When Saphira's body fell to the ground, my heart stopped. She'd sacrificed herself to give us a chance to get away.

We broke through the treetops, my heart squeezing as if it were trapped in a vise. I hated that I'd left Saphira behind.

"Don't slow down," Thorn commanded. "We aren't alone."

CHAPTER TWENTY-THREE

HIS WORDS ECHOED in my head, but I couldn't sense anyone chasing after us. Falkor had Saphira down below.

Then my dragon senses alerted me that Falkor's form was getting bigger.

A lump formed in my throat. Falkor was the person in command. I wasn't sure how *I* was supposed to go up against him.

Pumping my wings as fast as they'd go, I soared back toward the cabin, Thorn fidgeting in my grip. Even though I couldn't see him and I was four times his size, I could feel the hard cut of his muscles where my toes wrapped around him, and the lightning jolt between us was sparking throughout my body.

I was unsure what to do, and I wished I could talk to him. However, remembering how slowly I'd run, I didn't want to land and shift back into human form. In this state, I could move faster than on my human legs.

"Listen to me," Thorn said as he placed his hands on my top claw. "You have a head start and can fly fast. Push yourself, and don't head straight back to the cabin, or we'll lead them right to us. They can follow our scent."

Oh, great. So I was going to be flying around forever while holding his naked body. I cringed. That didn't sound horrible, except for the warrior chasing us.

My goodness. My hormones were getting the best of me, and we were in a life-or-death situation. I'd heard lust made you stupid, and I could attest to that fact, unfortunately.

I made a strange noise, a cross between a groan and a growl. Instinct told me to go in the opposite direction, but that would lead us closer to the dragons that supported the king and Drake, which wasn't smart.

What was a girl to do?

My dragon took control just as Falkor crested the trees. She turned my body toward Asheville. I almost fought her, but then awareness seeped into me.

If we were around humans, Falkor would behave better. And, dare I say, he might have to give up the chase. The only problem was that Thorn and I would be *naked* in the middle of the city.

That was better than death.

Unless a woman saw Thorn naked. Saphira and Jessie were bad enough. My tolerance of more women seeing him this way had vanished.

That split personality I felt whenever I thought of Thorn fought against itself. I'd hoped that things would get better, but this sire bond situation was strengthening instead of subsiding. I wasn't sure what to do about it since staying away from him wasn't an option right now.

I flew higher, ensuring no one could see us. There was a reason dragons hadn't exposed themselves to humans yet, though I wasn't certain what it was. Another question I'd eventually want answered.

Falkor roared as his wings flapped urgently, showing his desperation to catch us. Every part of him was green except for the undersides of his wings, which were burnt orange. He looked like a warrior dragon, moving gracefully and precisely, his entire focus on me.

"Stop watching him," Thorn commanded, his body tense. "It'll slow you down. Trust your dragon—she's part of you now—and move."

Looking forward again as we headed toward Asheville, I obeyed Thorn and repeated to myself what he'd said. At first, my dragon and I had felt like separate beings, but the gap was narrowing. We were at odds about little things, especially when it came to *him*. He was the driving force that made my two sides fight each other, which had to be from the sire bond or whatever the dragon version of that was called.

I shoved that portion of my dragon and my bond from my mind, wanting us to work in tandem.

Falkor's bulky frame was slowly catching up to us. My lungs struggled to fill as my dragon pushed us harder. We picked up a little speed, but all that accomplished was keeping Falkor the same distance away. I wasn't putting more distance between us.

The starry night was still gorgeous. The colors I'd marveled at before swirled around us, and the air smelled clean, like before a good snow. The temperature was colder up here, high in the sky where no human could see us shrouded in darkness.

One day, I wanted to fly when we weren't in danger. It was freeing, especially with the surrounding sky lights so beautiful to be part of.

"Where are we heading?" Thorn asked below me.

I wanted to roll my eyes but didn't waste the energy, especially since he couldn't see the gesture. Instead, I nodded toward the lights of the place where I'd spent my whole life. Though we were still twenty miles away, we could see the gorgeous mountain city. Although it was one in the morning, the lights were bright, illuminating its beauty.

He cleared his throat. "Everly, I don't know what you're planning, but we can't let humans know about us. Even though we're stronger, there are more humans than dragons, and they have military weapons at their disposal. They'd likely try to eliminate or control us."

His assumption that I was planning to expose us boded well. It was exactly what I wanted Falkor to suspect.

I began my descent. This late, there weren't any cars driving below, but I wanted to get close enough so that if Falkor did damn near catch us, we could use the small population of people who were out this late to distract him. The threat of me outing us to the human world had to count for something with him. I suspected the king wouldn't be happy about it, or the world would already know about dragons.

Behind us, Falkor growled, maybe to communicate his concern.

A memory floated through my mind, giving me an idea. I darted downward, not wanting to risk getting any closer. We were ten miles shy of the outskirts of the city. I barreled toward an area where Mom had often forced me to hike with her. It had yielded the prettiest pictures, which we'd used as inspiration for our paintings. A sizable spring surfaced nearby. Its stream went on for miles and ran into a large waterfall that was popular with tourists during the day, but at night, that shouldn't be an issue. Not that I planned to go *that* far.

With the lead we had on Falkor, I should be able to drop into the spring and shift into human form. Hopefully, we could use the water to hide us and mask our scent.

My dragon pushed harder, and the trickle of water over the rocks caught my ear. Luckily, it was May, which meant there was more rain than normal and the water level was higher. Exactly what we needed.

As I breezed through two stands of red spruce, my dragon withdrew from my mind, and something pinged my dragon senses, but the shift back into human was already underway. All I could tell before I lost my awareness was that it was a couple of large animals, likely bears. At least Falkor couldn't see us now that we were just above the water.

"Let me go," Thorn rasped. He knew I was struggling to keep him in my grip.

Even though I didn't want to drop him, I didn't have a choice. As my body shrank to half my dragon size, he slipped from my reforming hands. My wings kept me from completely descending so I wouldn't land on top of him.

As he crashed into the water, my body completed the transformation, and I dropped the remaining five feet after him. I gulped a breath moments before I splashed into the frigid waters. Thank goodness I was a dragon, or I'd be freezing.

At first, I was disoriented. I'd never been a strong swimmer, but I was good enough not to drown. I hoped there might be campers around, or hunters, to prevent Falkor from combing the area too long.

My vision was clear, but the water was murky with mud from the recent rains. I could feel ripples coming from Thorn swimming a few feet in front of me. I waited for my lungs to burn from holding my breath too long, but instead, a strong arm grabbed my waist, and before I realized what was going on, Thorn had pressed me against his body. The world spun from the lightning jolt between us, but he guided me to a spot and brought us up for air. Then I realized that this part of the spring was lined by thick brush instead of the rocks I was used to. Clearly, Mom and I had never seen this section of the spring.

We hunkered shoulder-deep in the water, our heads just above the surface and shielded by branches and our bodies hidden by the murky water. Even dragons couldn't see through dirt, but Falkor would sense us if we weren't careful.

I tried to stay still and held my breath as Falkor swooped into view. My mouth went dry as a scream bottled in my throat. I needed to swallow, but I remained frozen, afraid to move a muscle.

"You all, stay in the tent," a man said, sounding concerned. I estimated he was about a quarter mile away. "I'll check things out to make sure we're safe here. If I scream to run, you take the kids to the car, Joy."

My heart hammered. Those "bears" were actually human campers. My dragon had tried to alert me before she'd retreated, and I hadn't picked up on what they were. However, Falkor could.

Falkor relented with a low growl of disgust, but he soon ascended into the sky to get away before the human reached us. I wanted to run away, too, but we needed to stay here a little longer to make sure Falkor was too far away to spot us.

"We're not out of the woods yet," Thorn murmured.

I flicked my attention to his face, the worst thing I could have done. I was pressed against his chest, naked, and now my eyes were focused on his mouth. I licked my lips, desperate to taste his, and need slammed into my body. Even the frigid waters of the spring couldn't smother the fire raging inside me.

He hissed, his irises glowing. Then I wrapped my legs around his waist.

Yeah, I'd lost my mind. I was climbing my kidnapper, who'd changed me into a dragon, while we were hiding from another dragon, naked, in the water with a human checking out the area. Those were things I'd *never* imagined would apply to me.

"Dammit, Ev," Thorn growled as his lips captured mine.

The world faded away, and I could only vaguely hear the human coming closer through the darkness as Thorn and I devoured each other. His tongue swept over mine, and I clung to him. He tasted minty, even after breathing fire, and each stroke and touch made the world fade further from my mind.

He gripped my hips and pressed his pleasure seeker against me.

"Who's there?" the man asked from the embankment, and reality filtered back into my mind.

My face burned. We should've been quiet, but we'd gotten caught up in kissing and crushing our bodies together.

Thorn laid his forehead against mine and closed his eyes.

The man swept a flashlight right where we were hiding and said, "Come out, or I'm calling the cops."

For him to know exactly where we were indicated we'd been making more noise than I'd realized.

"Stay here," Thorn murmured as he untangled me from his body.

I came close to whimpering. I didn't want to release him, but we definitely didn't need to get the cops involved. I behaved and placed both feet on the rocky spring bed, sinking into the water.

"Hey, sorry." Thorn stepped out of our hiding spot into view of the flashlight. "I...decided to go for a late-night skinny dip and don't want you to see my dangly bits."

My shoulders shook with quiet laughter. He hadn't lied, making his delivery sincere.

The man's stern face relaxed, and his brows furrowed. "The water is still cold this time of year. You need to get out before you get sick."

"I will." Thorn pushed his wet bangs out of his eyes. "I heard something else out here, but I think whatever it was is gone."

The man rolled his shoulders. "Yeah, it must have been an animal." He turned to head back to his family but paused. "Do you need help? I have a cell phone if you need to call someone."

Times like these restored some of my faith in people. Most people I'd come into contact with had wanted me for *something*. To help them make a good grade, cover a shift at the coffee shop, or go away. This man...this *human*...was concerned about Thorn, even though he didn't know him.

"Nah, my girl is around here somewhere. I need to get back to her, but thank you," Thorn said kindly.

"Yeah, okay. But seriously, get out of the water." The man turned away and hurried back to his family.

When he was out of sight, Thorn rushed to me. "We need to shift and fly around before heading back to the cabin. He may still call the cops."

"Okay." If I were that man, I'd call the cops and have them come by to make sure Thorn was okay and not doing anything shady. The man was far enough away that if we shifted and flew off quickly, he probably wouldn't notice us.

Without another word, we let our dragons take control. After the man got back into his tent, we took flight, careful to watch for Falkor.

Luckily, there was no sign of him, but the tightness in my

stomach wouldn't release. Even though Thorn and I had gotten away unscathed, Saphira had likely been captured, and Thorn's parents were still locked up. We'd already burned a day, and we had less than twenty-four hours to determine another plan before Thorn had to choose to turn himself in or risk his parents' lives.

I already knew which one he would choose: he'd give himself up.

My heart fractured. The world *needed* him. He was the light that a corrupt king wanted to extinguish.

Even flying didn't feel as nice with the weight of the situation on my mind. We'd hoped to get answers, to determine a solution, but all we'd done was tip them off that we were trying to save his parents without Thorn turning himself in.

After a few hours of flying around in every direction to confuse any dragon that might be tracking us, we arrived back in the woods in front of the cabin.

The two of us shifted into human form, not bothering to hide from each other.

As we entered the warm cabin, I hugged myself. The urge to ogle Thorn surged through me, but I kept my eyes averted to the floor. I was about to ask him where the clothes were when Thorn cleared his throat.

I glanced up into his eyes...and the world went still. A sweet, spicy scent swirled between us, and the lightning bolt shot down my center, even though we weren't touching.

At the same time, we closed the distance between us. I stood on my tiptoes to reach his lips, but he whispered, "Wait. We need to talk."

CHAPTER TWENTY-FOUR

I STOPPED BREATHING. A shiver ran down my spine like a cold shower. His words were more frigid than the spring waters we'd been in hours ago and didn't bode well for a happy conversation, especially not when the two people involved were naked.

Though everything inside me wanted to rub my body all over Thorn, I forced myself to step back. I crossed my arms over my breasts and turned half away so I could conceal most of my full-frontal view. However, my traitorous eyes kept trying to scan his body, and I became disgusted with myself. I understood how a guy might struggle when a woman said, "My eyes are up here."

But if I went to get dressed, Thorn might change his mind about saying whatever he wanted to say. If he was going to reject the idea of us, I needed to hear him say it. Otherwise, I would continue to pine for a man who wasn't interested in me. It was better to have my heart shattered than continue to hope.

Hope made you do foolish things.

"Sure." I straightened my shoulders, trying not to look awkward and self-conscious.

He grimaced and scratched the back of his head.

My heartbeat quickened, but not from desire like before. Sweat pooled around my hairline, and I wanted him to spit it out so we could get dressed. Well, okay, I didn't really want *him* to get dressed, but that was the problem. "Here. I'll help you out. You aren't interested in me." As soon as I'd said the words, I wanted to take them back. "Not that we have a future, anyway." My dragon roared in anger so loudly that I nearly clutched my head.

His face twisted in agony, and he exhaled.

I was making things worse. But this was the first time I'd felt like this toward anyone, and the feelings were strong and all-encompassing and making me stupid. So what did I do? I continued to talk. "Because I have to go back to Drake and be—"

A low growl rumbled from his chest as he stalked toward me and wrapped his arms around my waist, pulling me flush against him again. He rasped, "Do *not* finish that sentence."

My body warmed again from the lightning shooting between us. My brain fuzzed as I tried to remember that he'd put the brakes on things. I shook my head, needing to do something other than *kiss* him. He'd essentially said no, and I would never force myself on anyone.

"I'm just saying you don't have to explain. I understand that you don't want to complicate matters." I licked my lips, tasting him. I tried to sear it into my mind, along with his features. I suspected I'd be reliving these stolen moments for the rest of my life, and I needed to remember as many as possible. The mind had a way of darkening memories.

He smirked, but the humor didn't reach his eyes. "You think things can get any more complicated? My thoughts revolve around you. You've already become the center of my world."

I gulped as tingles and the thrumming of our connection erupted all over my body. I grew lightheaded from the high, and I never wanted to come down. But I had to remain logical. He'd pulled away for a reason. "Then why did you stop me from kissing you?"

"I need to make sure you understand the consequences," he

murmured as he cupped my face. "That we have a special connection, and it will only strengthen, especially if we make love."

A shudder ran through me. The fact that he'd called it *making love* instead of *having sex* made my stomach flip-flop. He was also trying to tell me about our sire bond. "I already know."

His brows rose. "What? How?"

I stared into his gorgeous irises and replied, "I feel our connection through my entire body. It's like you're anchored to my soul."

His breath caught. "I'm sorry. I didn't know it would happen."

"Stop apologizing." I wrapped my arms around his neck and twisted my fingers in his hair. My breasts pressed into his chest, and my body thrummed with hot desire. "You *saved* me, and you tried to change me back into a human. If it weren't for you, I'd be dead, and I'm sorry I reacted so strongly. Even if our feelings are making this situation messy, I wouldn't change a moment of our time together, including the rough start."

Adoration filled his face as he stared into my soul. He whispered, "Same. I wish our meeting had been different."

My heart ached. "Me, too, but right now, I need you to shut up and kiss me."

His hands cupped my ass as his breathing turned ragged. "Ev, are you sure—"

The nickname expelled the last of my sanity, and I pressed my lips to his. "Yes. Now take care of me."

"Always," he promised and returned my kiss with vigor.

That wasn't a promise he could make, but I pushed the negative thought away. He and I deserved a night together. Even if, tomorrow, it would change everything.

I parted my lips, and his tongue entered my mouth. His faint vanilla taste filled my senses. He lifted me by my ass and, with one hand, made sure the front door was locked before hurrying down the hallway into the first bedroom. The one I hadn't been in before—his.

He laid me down on the mattress gently and quickly climbed up beside me without breaking our kiss once. A hand inched down my stomach, and he pulled away from my mouth to suck on one of my nipples.

My body quivered, and I trailed my fingers along his abs, enjoying his attention and the hard curves of his body. He was more perfect than any sculpture, and I was thrilled that I was one of the few who would be able to enjoy it. My dragon growled at the thought of him with anyone else, and some of the pleasure dimmed.

He went still and straightened. "Did I do something wrong?"

"What?" I couldn't process the question because it was so absurd. "God, no. What you're doing is perfect. It's just...I couldn't help but think about why you know exactly what to do."

Jaw going slack, he blinked twice. "You think I've done this before?"

My body tensed. "Well, look at you. I mean—"

"Ev, I've been hiding my entire life and keeping everyone but my parents at arm's length." He smiled tenderly. "If I'm doing anything right, it's solely because of our connection."

His confession had my body melting, and I refused to think about our future. At least this was something we could share with each other. "I'm a virgin, too."

He beamed, and I forgot how to breathe. He was that damn perfect. My body ached for him in a way that was almost too painful.

"No more talking," I whispered as I kissed him.

He chuckled deeply, and my body blazed. In this moment, he seemed truly happy, and I was going to allow myself to believe it was because of me.

His fingers slipped between my legs, and he circled a sensitive spot that forced me to stop kissing him and lean my head back. Wanting to give him the same type of pleasure, I touched his shaft, thrilled with what I found. He was just as ready for me.

Mouth on my breasts, he worked my body like an artist creating a masterpiece. The friction slowly built as his scent and taste filled my entire world.

He moaned as he circled my spot faster, and my body exploded with pleasure...but it wasn't enough. I pulled away from him, and he hissed in disappointment.

"I'm not done with you—" he protested until I straddled him and lowered myself so he entered me. He grabbed my waist and murmured, "Slow down. Don't hurt yourself."

My chest expanded. Instead of worrying about his own pleasure, he wanted to take care of me. "Don't worry, I won't. But it's my turn to pleasure you."

His pupils slitted, and my stomach clenched with unfathomable need.

Even if I hadn't wanted to take my time, I didn't have much choice. He was gigantic, and I had to continually let myself adjust to him for a few seconds before lowering myself another inch. He scooted to the headboard and sat up as the dark purple sheets bunched around us.

"You're so damn beautiful," he said as he lowered his head to my breasts.

As his tongue stroked my nipples, warmth curled in my stomach, and I finally got him all the way inside me. I moved my hips, the burn of my first time a little uncomfortable, but after a few thrusts, that discomfort was replaced with something mind-blowing. I increased our pace.

Thorn leaned back against the headboard and clutched my waist. "Oh, gods. You feel so damn amazing," he groaned as he bucked underneath me.

Our bodies slick with sweat, we moved in rhythm. If I hadn't known better, I'd have believed we'd had sex many times. He knew exactly what I wanted, and each one of his sighs and moans encouraged me.

Friction built inside me, and my body clenched as if preparing for an explosion. I locked eyes with him, his irises glowing as his pupils elongated and his dragon peeked through.

My dragon stirred in response.

"I love you," he confessed, his sincerity in every line of his face.

Despite the short amount of time we'd spent together, there was no question about how I felt in return. "I love you, too."

Another orgasm ripped through my body, and he pumped harder, his body shaking from his release.

Something inside me *snapped*. Suddenly, his emotions and mine intermingled. The ecstasy intensified, his pleasure mixing with mine, and the world shook. Our dragons roared in unison, the way our two halves were meant to be.

I wasn't sure if it was minutes or hours, but it didn't matter—the amount of time wasn't long enough as our bodies quieted and stopped thrumming with bliss. I sank onto his chest, and he wrapped his arms around me.

At least we had this moment, I thought.

His arms tensed. *We'll have these moments repeatedly for the rest of our lives.*

I stiffened and tried to roll off him, but he held me tightly. I'd heard his dragon in my head just moments ago, but I'd been so drunk on our sex high that I hadn't paid attention. Now I was hearing his voice in my head, too. "Why can I hear you?"

He turned us to one side so we were facing each other and smiled tenderly. "Because of our connection. We've completed the bond."

None of that made sense. My heart dropped. "You're going to have sex with every human you turn into a dragon?"

He blinked, and his brows furrowed. "What? No! You're my *first, last,* and *only.* Why would you think that? Not that I'm planning to turn any more humans into dragons, anyway."

"Because of the sire bond." Some of my hurt ebbed, but not my confusion. "I thought it was formed from you changing someone, but I guess you have to have sex with them, too."

"Sire bond?" His nose wrinkled. "What in the *hell* are you talking about? We don't have a *sire* bond."

I felt incredibly stupid. "But...after you changed me, my attraction to you increased a hundredfold. Since then, it's been getting stronger."

"You thought it was because I changed you?" His arms loosened. "Gods, no. At first, I was surprised by how I responded to you when you were human, but once you became a dragon, everything clicked into place." His hand rested on my cheek, the lightning bolt surging between us.

I would never get tired of this. "Mind filling me in?"

"When you were human, we were soulmates," he whispered.

Soulmates. The very thing so many stories and movies were made about. A person designed specifically for you. "Were? What are we now?"

"Fated mates," he said softly, his irises lightening to the shade of blue that was quickly becoming my favorite. "Two halves of the same soul. Now that you're a dragon, too, we've completed the bond, and our souls are merged. We are linked for the rest of our lives."

I loved the sound of that...except we wouldn't have that opportunity. "What happens when I have to hand myself over to Drake? Will he know?"

Thorn's nostrils flared as he held me tight. He damn near bellowed, "You will *not* be handing yourself over to Drake. You are *mine*, and I won't share you with anyone."

All my life, I'd known that I would never put up with someone being possessive. Oh, yet again, how wrong I was. My throat actually emitted a purring sound.

That noise must have calmed Thorn because he smiled at me and chuckled. "Did you like that, babe?"

Babe.

Between all the sensations coursing through my chest and my stomach, I was beginning to worry I had indigestion. That would be very unfortunate. "Kinda, but I never thought I would."

"Humans think it's unhealthy because the jackasses who are like that are usually controlling. But not with shifters. We're possessive because we love the other person so much, it makes us crazy thinking about someone else touching them, harming them, upsetting them." He kissed my nose. "I want you to be happy, and if that takes cutting off Drake's testicles to ensure he has no use for you, I'm more than happy to do it."

I giggled, the sound foreign and unfamiliar. For this brief moment, I was high on all things Thorn.

"And that right there is what I plan to do every day for the rest of our lives." He tucked a piece of my blonde hair behind my ear. "Make you smile and laugh."

Tears threatened to spill as my throat thickened. I was blissfully happy, but doom was around the corner, choking me. "We both know that can't happen."

Jaw clenching, Thorn rolled on top of me, pinning me underneath him. He rasped, "You will *not* be getting close to Drake. We will figure out another solution. Giving you up is *not* an option."

There was so much power in his voice that I believed him. Thorn was a kind and loyal man but viciously protective of those he loved. And now I was one of them. Maybe we *could* find a way to keep my sister safe and save his parents and Saphira. I nodded, staring at his full lips.

"Good," he murmured and kissed me.

My body was already warming for round two. I wrapped my legs around him, eager for him to slide in.

He groaned and pulled back. *No, you need a chance to heal first. This was your first time, and even though I want to claim you again, I need to take care of you better.* I pouted as he reached behind his back and untangled my legs from his body. *Go take a shower. I'll change the sheets and make us something to eat before we sleep. We need to rest so we can figure out what to do next.*

All the lightheartedness vanished. The threat hung over us again, and even though I wanted to sex him up, I *was* sore. A warm shower would do me good. "Fine, but we will do this again soon."

"Definitely." He winked.

He stood and took my hands, helping me to my feet. His voice said in my head, *Now go take a shower before you make me* not *treat you like the special treasure you are.*

My heart skipped a beat. The way I felt about him shouldn't have been possible, but I loved him more than anything else in this world. *Fine.* I glanced at the bed, wanting to see visual evidence of our time together, and noted blood on his sheets.

I cringed. No wonder he wanted to get out of bed and change the linens. *I'm sorry.*

He placed his finger under my chin, forcing me to look him in the eyes. "That is the most wonderful thing that could've happened." He motioned to the bloodstain. "Don't you *dare* apologize for it."

Warmth poured through my chest, near my heart, as his love and sincerity filled me. My cheeks hurt from grinning ear to ear. He'd said I was his special treasure, and I felt like just that.

He grabbed my shoulders and turned me toward his bathroom, then smacked my ass. "Get into the shower, and when you come out, head to the kitchen. I'll make us some grilled cheese sandwiches and vegetable soup."

As he left the room, my stomach gurgled in anticipation.

Now that I wasn't staring at him, I took in the space. It didn't tell me more about him. The room had the exact same layout as mine, with the same wall color and furniture style, though his bed had purple sheets.

I quickly entered the bathroom, not wanting to be apart from him for long. His was double the size of mine and Saphira's. There was a much bigger sink with a cabinet underneath it, and a tub about three times larger.

In other words, we could have shower sex.

Wow. I had a one-track mind.

I opened the cabinet and found several clean towels. I snatched one and threw it over the shower rod. The shower curtain's shimmery light blue color reminded me of Thorn's eyes.

Eager to get back to him, I hurried through my shower, taking enough time to clean myself without dawdling.

When I entered the bedroom, I paused. I found the duffel bag I'd packed to take at Drake's at the foot of the bed. I connected, *My stuff.*

I figured I was long overdue giving it back to you, he replied, a twinge of regret floating through. *And I thought you might like to check in with your siblings.*

I love you, I connected and hurried to my bag. *You were doing what you had to do for those you love.* I snatched my favorite pair of pajamas from the bag—a shirt and shorts that resembled a colorful abstract oil painting with various shades of blue, yellow, and orange. Once I was dressed, I dug out my phone and charger. As expected, the battery was dead.

The warmth in my chest chilled, and I understood what that meant. Something had upset Thorn.

I hurried toward him. When I stepped into the living room, my eyes locked on him. He was sitting in front of a laptop but frowning at his phone, his back rigid.

When the screen from his cell phone came into view, my knees nearly gave out. I muttered, "Oh, no."

CHAPTER TWENTY-FIVE

AS I DROPPED, Thorn spun around and wrapped an arm around my waist, pulling me against him. The jolt of our connection thrummed between us, but all I could do was gape at the phone's screen.

Saphira.

She wore the collar I'd mistaken for a handcuff around her neck. The dark Wolfram Dwiin metal shone against her skin. She had cuts on her face and a black eye. They'd beaten her after forcing her to shift back into her human form.

She stood in the middle of a grove of red spruces and Fraser firs, which didn't help pinpoint where she was. The trees were common throughout the Blue Ridge Mountains, and the woods were everywhere.

"Thorn, who sent that?" I rasped, my lungs barely moving. I wanted to shut down, but that wouldn't get either one of them out of this situation.

His hand tightened around my waist, and he answered, "It was texted to me a minute ago. I thought it was from King Arman about my parents, but I was wrong."

My throat hurt, but I forced myself to swallow. "What do you mean? Who is it?"

He turned my body toward him and rasped, "It's Drake. Somehow, he got my number."

I furrowed my brows. "But why would he think you care about Saphira? Unless—"

"The message was for both of us," he finished as his face scrunched in agony. "He's trying to get a rise out of you since his efforts haven't worked on me so far."

That might be true, but I still needed to watch it. "Replay it."

He shook his head. "That's not a good idea."

My jaw twitched as boiling anger swirled around me and leaked into the connection we'd formed. I growled, "Correct me if I'm wrong, but I didn't ask for your opinion."

He flinched, and his hurt wafted through me. He inhaled slowly and straightened his shoulders. "I know that. I want to protect you."

I tensed as my heart sank. "I'm sorry, I didn't mean to snap at you." I'd reminded myself of my stepdad, and that was definitely not how Thorn should be treated. He was a good man, and I should've known his reluctance was coming from a place of concern. "It's just...*seeing* her like that..." My gaze went back to his phone, the screen dark due to inactivity.

Warmth seeped into me, and he stepped to the side so his face blocked where I'd been looking. He said, "Believe me, I get it. That's why I'm *encouraging* you not to watch it." He took my hand and placed it against his chest where I could feel his heart beating.

The *thump-thump* was better at calming me than even painting, but it didn't change anything.

I pressed my lips together as I stared at him with such adoration. He was trying to protect me, but I was a grown woman, and I couldn't be protected from everything. "If you saw a video of someone you cared about who'd been beaten up, would you listen to me if I told you not to watch it? That it was for your own good?"

His eyes narrowed. "That's playing dirty, Ev. And not the kind of dirty I approve of."

Snorting, I couldn't help but smile. "Because you know the answer."

"I would be adamant that I needed to watch it. For clues, if nothing else." He dropped his forehead to mine and whispered, "But I would still encourage you to try a different strategy."

"Noted, but *this* certain piece of advice will be ignored." I placed a hand on his cheek and pressed a quick kiss to his lips. I connected, *But I did listen, if that counts for anything.*

It does. He pulled away, frowning deeply. *That won't make this any easier.*

My mouth dried. The video had to be bad if he was that eager for me not to watch it. But if I didn't and something happened to either one of them, I would never forgive myself.

He interlocked our fingers and led me to the table, then swiped the phone and pressed play.

On the screen, Drake strolled next to Saphira, all decked out in a black suit with a sinister smile on his cruel, hardened face. I wasn't sure how I'd ever found him attractive. This was the face of a *monster*.

He wrapped an arm around Saphira's neck, placing his face close to hers. Saphira flinched, and he chuckled as his onyx irises glowed.

The jackass was getting off on her fear.

He stared straight into the camera, and I could've sworn his gaze locked on me.

"I learned some unfortunate news tonight." He forced a frown, but his irises couldn't hide his mirth. "Something that belongs to me may have willingly aided my mortal enemy."

Acid roiled in my stomach. He had no problem making the fact that he viewed me as his property clear to anyone who watched this.

"Because I feel that aid was coerced, I'll give you one last chance." He refocused on whoever was recording. "Despite you becoming a *dragon* shifter, I'm still willing to keep our bargain. You come here and be *mine*, and I'll let Saphira go back to her father. I hear you two have become close, so it's that simple."

He steepled his fingers. "Your deadline is the same as my enemy's. You have a little over twenty-four hours. If you and the *abomination* don't show, then Cassidy, Vlad, and Saphira will lose their lives." He smirked.

Something *cracked*, and I glanced down to find that I'd broken the top piece of wood on the chair in half. I couldn't muster up the energy to care, but I released my hold.

"*Thorn*. Everly. The meeting spot is still where this story began." Drake tugged on his suit jacket. "I'll have guards there, waiting for you whenever you decide to return." He turned to walk off camera, then paused. "As long as it's before your deadline." He winked, and the video ended.

Black smoke trickled in front of me.

Thorn's strong arm wrapped around me, pulling me to his chest. Our bond thrummed between us and eased some of the turmoil in my soul, helping me see the situation more clearly.

I'm sorry, Thorn connected as he ran a hand over the back of my head. *This is all my fault.*

He didn't get to take the blame for this. I pulled back and homed in on his eyes. "Did you force Drake to find a breeder?"

His head jerked back. "Of course not."

"Did you call the king and tell him where to find your parents?" I arched a brow.

"Again, no." He searched the room as if to understand why I was asking these questions.

For someone so smart, he was missing the point. "Oh. Wait. Did you beg to be born with your extra magical powers?"

"Gods, no." He cringed. "Until this past week, I would've given anything to be a normal dragon."

I blinked. "Until this past week?"

"Yeah." He smiled tenderly. "Until you. *All* of this was worthwhile because by changing you, I revealed my fated mate. Our bond would've worked with you in human form. We would've still maintained a connection, but not one as strong as this." He brushed his thumb over my bottom lip. "Not one where we can mind link and be as close as two souls can possibly get."

My heart expanded to the point of physically hurting. That was the most romantic thing I'd *ever* heard anyone say.

He grinned, obviously feeling how his words had affected me.

But he was derailing me from my point.

"You didn't force Drake to take a breeder, you didn't rat out your parents, and you didn't ask for your magic." I held up three fingers. "Please explain why you're apologizing and saying this is all your fault?"

His face fell, but his arms tightened around me. He linked, *You're playing dirty again. If you keep doing that, we'll need to adjust things so you're only like that in bed.*

Desire flared inside me, but I had to tamp it down. We had to save Saphira and Thorn's parents. Sex would have to wait. "I'm being rational, and if we're going to save them, you've got to start thinking that way, too."

"You're right," he said and released me. "We need to eat and sleep so we can *both* think clearly. The good thing is that all three of them are dragons, and Vlad is a warrior." He removed two plates from the counter that held grilled cheeses wrapped in aluminum foil to keep them warm. Then he ladled soup into two bowls. He placed them on the kitchen table, where two glasses of water were already positioned, and moved the broken chair out of the way. "And what did that chair ever do to you?"

I chuckled and went to the outlet under the window to plug in my phone before taking a spot in front of one of the servings of food. "Wrong time and place is all. I'll figure out how to fix it."

"I'll handle it." He sat in the spot next to me.

The two of us ate in silence.

I hated to bring up the video again, but I still didn't know so much. "Where does he mean by meeting where it all began?"

"That's easy." He took a bite, which equated to half of the grilled cheese. "The place where Vlad attacked us."

"Not where you took your da—er, King Arman's dragon?" To me, *that* was where it had all begun, so to speak, even if that wasn't the case. "Or the place where you were born?"

"I was born in the château, and I temporarily took the king's dragon in the backyard of the same château." Thorn took a sip of soup. "He wouldn't risk doing this too close to home. He doesn't want anyone to realize you were taken. So...the next logical place is where I was *supposed* to die. It's where Falkor also told me to go."

I wasn't sure if that could be considered the beginning, but it was the place that marked the start of Thorn's new life. Maybe that was why Drake had thought of it.

"Château, eh?" I lightened my tone. "Sounds fancy." I lifted my glass, extending my pinky.

He laughed, the sound soothing like a brush stroke. "It is. *Mansion* doesn't convey royalty, but we can't use the term *palace* for fear of humans overhearing. So *château* is the compromise."

"Is it in the heart of the dragon lands?" I set my glass down and grabbed the napkin by my plate. I wanted to learn everything about him, including his horrible past, if he was willing to tell me. Besides, I was a dragon shifter, which meant Drake and King Arman were my leaders.

He nodded. "It is, and it has the most acreage of any dragon property. The servants' homes are on part of the thousand acres, and the woods take up over half the space."

Licking my lips, I tried to fight off fatigue. "Are the homes all lumped together in one section, or do they have woods between them?"

Putting down his spoon, he leaned back in his chair and observed me. "They're clustered together so that the woods are wide open. Why?"

"I want to get an idea of what we're up against. If we're going to rescue them, I need to know how the area is laid out." I took a deep, calming breath to steady my heartbeat.

"Let's talk about it after we sleep." He placed a hand on mine. "We'll figure out a way to save all three of them tomorrow. I *promise*."

That was the thing: I wasn't sure he could make that promise. "What if we can't?"

"Vlad and Cass spent half their lives evading the royal guard and staying off the radar. If ever three dragons had a chance to escape, it's them. Besides, there's no way in *hell* we're handing you over." Thorn shook his head. "I don't care about the consequences. You have a lifetime of happiness ahead of you."

What he wasn't saying was telling. "What about you? You're only talking about me. If you're turning yourself in, there's no way in hell I'm staying behind."

He pinched the bridge of his nose and hung his head. "My parents made me swear that if they got captured, I wouldn't risk myself to save them. I had no intention of keeping that promise, but if it's the only way to keep you safe—" His turmoil swirled between us like a raging tornado.

My heart fractured from his pain as his love flowed into me, taking me by surprise. He was contemplating *sacrificing his parents* for me. "Thorn—"

"Look, let's take a moment to enjoy each other's company." He squeezed my hand gently. "We'll strategize a way to save them all. But Ev, you're the most important thing to me. A precious gem that sparkles through the night, giving me my first sense of peace since I was a young boy. I can't lose you. I *won't*."

The way his irises glowed as he locked gazes with me informed me of his resolve. I couldn't talk him out of this. However, I also knew what it was like to lose a parent. It shredded your soul in ways you couldn't imagine. And every day, as their voice and laughter faded from memory, part of you went along with it.

If I gave myself up to Drake, even if Thorn and I couldn't be together, at least his parents and I would all be alive, and he would survive. But there was no way I could convince him of that, and I feared that if he chose me over his parents, he'd grow to resent me as we got older. "I want you to be happy, too. I can't lose you, either."

"I am happy and will be forever, as long as we're together." He smiled adoringly.

I leaned over and kissed his lips. "I can agree to that." He was right about one thing: the three of them were dragons. If he believed that much in Vlad and Cassidy, I would, too.

His body relaxed. "I'll go shower. Why don't you get ready for bed? Then we can get some rest."

"Okay." I smiled, scanning his chiseled face. The existence of someone so gorgeous shouldn't have been possible, yet here he was... my *mate*. My dragon purred.

He stood from the table and picked up his plate.

"Hey, you cooked. I'll clean." I clasped his wrist. "It's only fair." I'd never had someone take care of me the way he did, and the last thing I wanted to do was take advantage.

"But—" he started.

"Seriously. I'd like to take care of you, too, so let me do it from time to time." My cheeks hurt from smiling again. The sensation used to be foreign to me. "Forever is a long time for me to sit around. I need to stay limber."

He winked. "You just took care of me in the bedroom. *That* you can do any time you want."

My body heated with desire, and he grinned like a dragon that ate a cat that ate the canary.

Nope. He was getting too big of a head already. "Just go. I'll clean up."

"Fine, but tomorrow, you'll be punished for back talking," he said, brushing past me so my arm touched his groin.

Unable to resist, I watched his ass as he strolled from the kitchen and out of view.

He might be the death of me.

Once he disappeared, my gaze landed on my phone. It should

have enough juice for me to turn it on and see if the twins had tried to reach me. Eva had actually looked distraught when I'd left. I took my last bite of grilled cheese, then walked over and powered it up.

As soon as the phone cycled through the welcome, my phone dinged with text messages. Several were from Eva.

The shower turned on in the bathroom as I read through them all. She was concerned, asking me why I wasn't answering. The last text read, **Please call me ASAP.**

She'd never asked me to call before.

The shower curtain closed as Thorn got into the shower. I hit the call button.

She picked up on the first ring. "Everly?" Her voice was thick with tears. "Is it really you?"

My lungs seized. "Yes. What's wrong?"

"I've been kidnapped," she breathed as a sob racked her body. "Drake took me."

The walls closed in on me, and my vision darkened around the edges. "Is he there with you?"

"Yes, him and a girl named Saphira," she answered.

A dark chuckle echoed from the other side of the line, followed by Drake saying, "Tell your sister that if she doesn't want you to take her place, she has to turn herself over."

Eva whimpered. "He said—"

I wouldn't force her to repeat that. "I can hear him."

"Oh, that's right. She's a *dragon* now," he growled.

It sounded as if Eva was hyperventilating, and my heart squeezed.

"If you hurt her—" I started.

"If you don't want your sister to become my personal breeder, I expect you to return to me within two hours. I'll even sweeten the deal. If you hand yourself over in that time, I'll release your sister, Saphira, *and* Thorn's parents. You have my word."

Razor-sharp pain slid through my entire chest, as if my saliva had turned into a weapon.

Babe, what's wrong? Thorn connected.

He had to be feeling my turmoil like I'd felt his. *Just stressed.*

"Everly, you can trust his word this time," Saphira said. "He has witnesses, so he can't go back on it."

She knew how desperate I was to protect my sister, but she didn't realize I would have to give up my fated mate to save her.

CHAPTER TWENTY-SIX

MY BREATH CAUGHT, and the water from the shower turned off. I'd run out of time.

Eva started sobbing, and my entire world crumbled. "Fine." The word felt like sandpaper rubbing my throat raw.

"Aw, the love you have for family. It's endearing. Continue straight past where you met Brenton, and you'll find the château. It's two connected houses. Then fly south. You'll find us." His voice grew louder as he took the phone. "Two hours." The line went dead.

I stared at my phone, wondering what the hell had happened. But this solution would not only save my sister but Saphira and Thorn's parents as well. This was the best option, and it had to happen tonight.

My mind raced. Thorn and I were exhausted from the long night, the flight, and completing our bond. I'd barely been able to keep my eyes open...until now. I couldn't sleep, knowing I had to find a way out of here without alerting Thorn.

I promise it'll be okay, Thorn connected as his footsteps drew closer. *Where are you? I thought you'd already be in bed.*

I placed the phone back onto the table, making sure the screen was off. I didn't need him to notice anything out of the ordinary. I quietly climbed to my feet and cleared the table. *Sorry, I finished eating and was tidying up.*

He entered the living room and kitchen as I placed the plates, bowls, and cups into the sink.

I turned and stared at him. He was more gorgeous than any painting or sculpture I'd ever seen. His hair was wet and hung across his forehead, his sky blue irises sparkling. He wore dark gray pajama pants, but even through them I could see his *outline*, and even better, he was shirtless. His wide, muscular chest was on full display, his six-pack begging me to touch it.

"I know you want to clean up, but this can wait a couple of hours so we can get some rest," he said through a yawn. He took my hands and led me toward the bedroom.

The bolts of electricity sizzling between us stole my breath, but I managed to quirk a brow. "Are you putting me back into the room I shared with Saphira?"

"Nope." He grinned wickedly. "I want your dragon to come out and play whenever she wants."

My heart fluttered as he picked me up like a princess and carried me the rest of the way before laying me down on the bed, which now had lavender sheets. He kissed me and connected, *Besides, this is our room now. We share everything.*

That was like a punch to the gut. He might be sharing everything, but as of five minutes ago, I was not. My dragon grunted, but she didn't roar in anger. I realized she was just as desperate as I was to protect our mate emotionally. I replied in the most honest way I could. *I love you.*

He scooted me over and crawled into the spot beside me. He wrapped his arms around me, and I felt safe and cared for. Tears burned my eyes. I'd never felt anything like this before—hadn't felt protected in forever.

"Hey, I love you, too," he murmured and wiped the tears off my cheeks. "What's wrong?"

So much. I knew I'd never feel this serenity again. As soon as I'd found it, I had to lose it. But *he* was worth it. I'd rather him hate me than himself. I forced a smile. "You make me so *damn* happy."

"Well, I don't want to be the reason you cry, even if they're happy tears." He tightened his arms. "My life's goal is to make you smile as much as possible and protect you."

He couldn't have said more perfect words.

Needing to taste him again, I kissed him. When he responded, I tried to deepen the kiss, wanting to make love with him one more time.

He pulled back. "Babe, I want you so damn bad. Don't make this any harder."

A smile spread across my face. "That's kinda the point. I want to make you harder."

"Naughty girl," he chuckled, warmth spreading through our bond. "But my desire for you is only outweighed by my love. You need time to heal, which means you need rest. When we wake up in a few hours, I'll let you ravish me."

My body tensed. There wouldn't be a next time, but if I pushed, he'd know something was up. "Okay, but one more kiss?"

He kissed me, his tongue swooping into my mouth. I closed my eyes, relishing each touch, stroke, and sizzle that soared between us. When my fingers brushed the curves of his stomach, he shuddered and ended our kiss.

"I know what you're up to, and it's not happening. We aren't in a rush. We have the rest of our lives to have tons of sex." He kissed my nose. "Sleep before I have to handcuff you to the headboard."

He was teasing, but I didn't want to take the chance, especially since I needed to get out of here.

"Fine," I huffed, which caused his shoulders to shake.

Goodnight, my love, he connected as he breathed in my hair.

A sob built in my chest, but I swallowed it down. *Goodnight, Thorn.* I *wanted* to say more, but I couldn't.

I had no doubt that by the way Drake had worded his reply, if I waited too long, he'd rescind the offer. I couldn't risk Thorn's parents, Saphira, or my sister. Most importantly, I couldn't risk Thorn. I believed if it came down to it and we didn't find another solution, he'd give himself up to save them all. The difference between him and me doing it was that my way kept Thorn alive. If he turned himself in, the king would kill him.

I lay still in the arms of the man who now owned me, heart and soul, and listened to his steady heartbeat and the sound of air filling and leaving his lungs.

All too soon, his heart rate slowed, and his breathing steadied. Our connection cooled, indicating it would soon be time for me to make my move. I waited a few more minutes, then wiggled as if to get comfortable. I murmured, "So hot," as if that would make a difference.

He immediately released me, despite being sound asleep, and scooted over half an inch. Close enough that the electricity pulsed between us but far enough away that the cool air hit me.

Even in his sleep, he was taking care of me.

My heart shredded, the pain worse than anything I'd experienced before, and my body ached for his warmth. But I had to remember why I was doing this—for him.

I inched out of bed, the mattress barely shifting. Becoming a dragon had made me a lot more graceful. When I placed a foot on the cool wooden floor, my ankle nearly gave out. I balanced myself on the mattress, causing it to bounce, and steadied myself before my ass hit the floor and made a ton of commotion.

Maybe there was a higher power, fate or karma, making sure I stayed grounded, literally and figuratively.

His eyelids fluttered, and I whispered, "Hey. Sorry. I'm just getting a drink of water."

Hurry back, he connected and closed his eyes.

Not wanting to lie and wake him further, I tiptoed from the bedroom toward the living room and kitchen. I went directly to the sink and turned on the faucet. I had to at least pretend I was doing what I'd said. Our connection cooled again, and he fell deeper asleep.

Using the sound of the water, I strolled to the window in front of the kitchen table, which overlooked the side of the yard. I unlocked the latch and eased the window up so it didn't make any noise. When it was halfway up, the opening was large enough for me to fit through.

Needing to keep up the illusion, I went back to the sink and turned the water off. Our bond was still cool, but I suspected it wouldn't stay that way for long.

I had to go.

I rushed past the kitchen table and slipped out the window. Once my feet hit the ground, I ran as quickly as possible toward the tree line we'd come through earlier. The night sky was lightening, hinting that the sun would rise soon.

When I reached the trees, I quickly undressed, and my dragon surged forward. I didn't even have to ask, and I hoped that meant we were growing more in sync. I tried to pick up my clothes with my talons but couldn't grab them.

Damn big dragon hands. I tried again more slowly and snagged them.

Soon, I was flying high in the sky toward the dragon homestead. From Drake's directions, I should be able to find the château. If his arrogance was any indication, it wouldn't be hard to miss.

Each flap of wings that took me farther from Thorn broke my heart. I tamped down my emotions, not wanting to alert him to what was going on. If he found out too soon, he could stop me, so I had to keep a level head. I'd heard that people could die of a broken heart, but I'd never believed it. Science didn't support that theory, but I feared I was about to learn how wrong I'd been before I even made it to Drake. I hadn't believed anyone could feel the sort of torture now ravaging my soul.

My dragon's pain blended with mine. The separation of animal and human blurred more every time I shifted into dragon form. Maybe that was why dragon magic made dragons shift so often—to ensure they didn't become separate beings like we'd been before I shifted.

That was something I could research and focus on later once my future as Drake's property began.

All too soon, I passed the place where we'd met Brenton, the very person who'd betrayed us when we'd foolishly hoped we could save everyone without losing anything. I forced myself to look elsewhere, not wanting to feel the stab of betrayal all over again.

I took a deep breath to regulate my emotions. I had to be strong; otherwise, Thorn would know exactly where to find me, and I needed him to stay asleep for as long as possible.

Following Drake's instructions, I passed over the houses. They started out small but soon became bigger. I was getting closer to the château.

After a few more minutes, I flew over a huge mansion that looked like two connected homes. The gigantic house was sunflower yellow with gray trim and a beige roof that slanted down into a sizable terrace in front of an immaculate green backyard.

My stomach clenched. That had to be where Thorn had been playing tag with the king when the incident had happened. An accident where an innocent, sweet boy's life had changed due to fear.

My connection to Thorn warmed in my chest, surprising me. I'd lost focus on staying level-headed as I'd searched for Drake and the others. Even in dragon form, my eyes burned with unshed tears.

Ev? Thorn connected.

My breath sawed through my lungs in a gasp. I wasn't sure how to respond. I hadn't reached Drake yet.

Flying lower, I entered the woods behind the château. I'd be there soon.

Why aren't you back in bed yet? Thorn asked. *Why are you upset? What's wrong?*

I'd been gone only thirty minutes, and he was already awake and searching for me. I'd hoped his parents would be on their way to him before he realized I'd left. *Thorn, I'm sorry.*

Warmth spread through me as he replied, *Babe. Nothing to be sorry about. Just come back to bed before I make you.*

My heart stuttered just as Drake, Eva, Saphira, and two people I'd never seen before came into view.

Eva's steel blue eyes bulged with fear, and her long, dark brown hair was messy. She wore her favorite sleep outfit—a heather gray shirt that said *OMG aRe YoU a GIRL GaMeR?* in purple, with a purple controller underneath, and matching purple plaid bottoms. It had been her Christmas present from Elliott last year.

The strange man had greasy caramel hair plastered to his face, his ivory skin so pale it appeared ghostly. His cornflower eyes looked sunken, but the way they widened as he watched me approach made my blood run cold. The woman's golden brown hair hung limply past her shoulders, her tanned skin splotchy as if she hadn't been eating well, and her hazel eyes were dark with pain.

They had to be Thorn's parents. Just like Saphira, they each had a collar locked around their necks.

Drake's dark gaze was already fixed on me, and cold fear spiraled through my gut.

What's wrong? Thorn asked as alarm rang through our bond. *Ev, where the fuck are you?* Hot anger and icy fear followed the alarm.

He already knew, so I didn't need to tell him. Instead, I said, *Drake had Eva contact me. He kidnapped her and threatened to use her as his breeder if I didn't turn myself in tonight. He promised to release not only her but Saphira and your parents. My life for four. I know what it's like to lose a parent, and if there'd been a way I could've saved my mom and didn't, I wouldn't have been able to live with myself.*

Everly, get your ass back here right now. *You can't trust him,* Thorn commanded. *I'll be fine just as long as you're by my side. We'll figure this out together. I can't live without you.*

Saphira told me his word is good because there are witnesses. This is how I can save all four of them. I had to do it. You think risking me is too great of a cost, but... What was left of my heart shattered. *I'd rather you hate me than yourself.*

He lies, Everly. He'll do anything to get you there. And I could never hate you. None of this is your fault. Besides, don't you realize I'll just come after you? His love surged through our bond. *If you don't know that, you clearly didn't think this through.*

My heart ached. *I can't risk you dying. Nothing is worth that.*

And nothing is worth losing you. His determination slammed into me, stealing my breath. *Now turn around and come home to me.*

Home.

Thorn was my home. I hadn't realized that was how I felt about him.

Everything inside me wanted to head *home,* but I couldn't. *I'm already here.*

His dragon's roar echoed in my head as I landed in front of Drake, my attention locked on my sister, who was shaking so hard, her teeth chattered.

My dragon form had to be taking my emotions over the top. I lifted the talon that held my clothes and nodded toward a section of thicker trees.

"I shall allow it." Drake's attention flicked to the tree line, where I sensed ten guards scattered about. "Jessie, go with her and keep an eye on her as she shifts back. If one of the men even glances at her while she's naked, kill him on the spot."

He wasn't protecting me; he just didn't want anyone to see his property nude. I didn't bother waiting, just turned and headed for the trees. Jessie stepped out from my left and followed me as I headed to the right.

If he touches you, his death will be slow and painful, Thorn connected as his boiling rage swirled inside me.

That should have scared me, but his words thrilled me.

In the trees, my dragon receded, and I was back in human form. I dressed, trying to become logical. *Thorn, if you come here, they'll kill you. You'll be outnumbered. Don't. If you're determined, wait until your parents come back, and plan something with them.*

I'm coming for you, he replied. *Waiting is not an option.*

I turned to find Jessie with her hand on her rifle, but I ignored her. I needed to get out there and make sure all four prisoners were released. I knew Thorn's parents wouldn't let him do something this risky.

I marched past her and back into the small clearing. Thorn's parents and Saphira were still collared, and Eva had her arms wrapped around her.

"I'm here. Release the four of them like you promised." I marched until I stood a few feet in front of Drake.

"Everly?" Eva gasped. "When did you get here?"

Stupidly, I hadn't been prepared for this question. Of course she didn't know I was a dragon shifter. I'd been so focused on Thorn that I hadn't realized my sister would learn what I'd become. "Just now."

Drake laughed cruelly. "She's the dragon that appeared not five minutes ago."

"It's true?" Eva's face blanched. "*You're* one of them? No."

A sour taste filled my mouth, but there was no time for me to address her reaction, and I refused to let Drake watch this exchange. I glared at him.

He lifted his chin, staring down his nose at me. "You do realize I'm the one in control here? Not the other way around."

Games. He loved playing them, but I was tired and not in the mood. I needed him to release Thorn's parents. "You promised that if I came here, you would let the four of them go."

"I did. You're right." He tapped his finger to his mouth. "But...I changed my mind." He sneered, his dark eyes glowing.

My vision blurred. "I came here within two hours as agreed. You can't renege."

"That's the thing, Everly. I never had any intention of releasing any of them." He walked a few steps closer and sniffed me. "I said it to get you here, but *this* is a surprise. Not only did you somehow become a dragon shifter, but you also *mated* with someone."

My world tilted, and I glanced at Saphira. "You swore he'd keep his word."

Saphira nodded, her jaw clenching. "I heard him agree to it. Drake has to let us go."

"Stupid women." Drake rolled his eyes. "I'm the king's heir. Those laws don't apply to me. I can do whatever *I* want. I am the *law*."

"If King Arman—" Cassidy started.

Drake cut her off with loud laughter. "My father won't do anything to me. I'm the golden son. So shut your mouth, or your death will be imminent."

"Don't you *dare* talk to her like that," Vlad snapped, seething.

"Or what?" Drake lifted his arms. "You can't do anything."

This situation was growing worse by the second. "Fine," I said. "If you won't honor that agreement, then honor the first. Let Eva go."

"No." Drake's irises darkened. "You're a dragon, and I need a human breeder. But now I have something else that the abomination will do anything for—*you*. This is a bonus." He leaned into my face. "My plans were to capture his parents and hope that he came, but with his fated mate in my power, there's no question he'll come."

When I flinched, I heard him inhale as if he were absorbing all my disgust and fear.

Thorn, the king didn't capture your parents, I hastily linked. *It was Drake.*

What? Thorn's shock registered, then turned into disgust. *He'll regret ever being born.*

"You've been given a new role," Drake whispered, his breath hitting my ear. "My wife. And your sister will be my breeder. We'll be one happy family, especially once I kill Saphira, Cassidy, Vlad, and the abomination."

My legs wobbled, but I forced myself to remain upright. I

wouldn't crumble in front of him. *I'm sorry. I fucked up. He won't let any of them go.*

"Half of you, take my prisoners back to their hiding spot. We'll execute them in twenty-four hours, hopefully with the abomination in tow." Drake flicked his hand at the guards. "And half of you, take my *future wife* and *breeder* to the guest portion of the château. I'll make my father aware that we'll be organizing my wedding in the morning."

The guards came as ordered. Saphira, Vlad, and Cassidy stood there, waiting to be escorted away. They didn't fight, cry, or beg but remained calm and collected. I suspected they were biding their time.

Falkor strolled to my sister and pointed at the château.

Tears poured down my sister's face. "No, please. Let me go."

Black dots obstructed my vision as my heart thrashed in my ears. I had come here to prevent this, but instead, I'd made things worse.

Thorn would fly right into their hands.

My knees gave out, and I dropped to the ground.

There wasn't a damn thing I could do to protect any of them. I'd broken my promise to Mom, and I'd ripped my own heart to shreds by foolishly leaving Thorn behind.

With cold tendrils of fear weaving through me and binding my chest, I realized I had led my fated mate to his death.

JEN L. GREY

MARKED DRAGON

THE MARKED DRAGON PRINCE TRILOGY 2

CHAPTER ONE

FEAR STRANGLED me as my sister, Eva, sobbed while a gigantic six-and-a-half-foot burly guard hovered over her.

Her steel blue eyes glistened from the tears that streamed down her cheeks and dripped onto her heather-gray pajama top, which asked *OMG aRe YoU a GIRL GaMeR?* in purple lettering with a purple remote underneath it and matching purple plaid bottoms. Her long, dark brown hair was messy, and strands stuck to her wet face.

"Move your ass, *now,*" Falkor threatened. His cobalt eyes narrowed, and every muscle in his arm bulged as he pointed toward our new prison, the royal dragon chateau. He was bulkier than anyone here, and his every word dripped with malice. He and Ladon were Drake's favored guards.

Drake's onyx eyes were locked on me. More than seven feet tall, he towered over my five-foot-two-inch body. His white button-down shirt hugged his muscles, and his black trousers showed not one wrin-kle, despite the time being nearly five in the morning. His brownish black hair remained perfectly styled in short, upward spikes, making him look every inch the regal prince he was. At one point, I'd found him handsome, but now, all I saw was the face of a monster.

Five guards I'd never seen before surrounded Saphira, my loyal friend, and Thorn's parents, Vlad and Cassidy. Drake had instructed the guards to take them back to their *hiding spot*, giving no indication of where that was.

He must have known I would tell Thorn—my fated mate.

Everly, what's going on? Thorn connected, using our bond. *I'm halfway there. I won't be much longer.*

I tried to swallow around the lump in my throat, but my mouth was so dry that it was impossible. I'd messed up by coming here. Okay, *messed up* was an understatement. *Fucked up* was way more accurate but still didn't quite capture the awfulness of my decision. Drake had promised that, if I came within two hours of my phone call with Eva, he would let Eva, Saphira, and Thorn's parents go. According to dragon law, a spoken agreement was binding, but apparently, since Drake was the dragon prince, his position superseded that. *They're taking Saphira and your parents back to their hiding spot, and Eva and me to the chateau.* But that wasn't the worst of it. *Thorn...I'm so sorry. I should never have come here. I should've told you everything.*

Yes, you should have, he replied. *But I understand why you didn't. I just need you to hold on until I get there.*

You can't come. My heart clenched. *You'll walk right into the trap, and there won't be a way for any of us to escape.* I wanted him here. I wanted to be in his arms again, but it wouldn't happen if he didn't think logically.

Ev, he connected, his turmoil building through our bond.

I'd never liked nicknames. Well, not since Mom died. Mom had called me her little da Vinci because I shared her love of painting, and because I'd sold more paintings during my high school years than many artists did in their entire life. After her death, I'd wanted to be called by my full name...until *him*. *Thorn, I need you, so we need to figure out a way to save us and for you not to die.*

Saphira's mocha eyes homed in on mine. "So you want us to head back—"

A low growl sounded, and a thick hand punched her in the face.

My friend's head snapped back, and Ladon fisted her long, curly, dark brown hair at the base of her skull. Her bronze skin blanched, but otherwise, you wouldn't have known she'd been affected since her face remained a mask of indifference.

"Don't even *think* about hinting at where you're located," Ladon seethed, his ice-green irises colder. He was huge, only slightly smaller than Falkor in height. Both could easily be MMA fighters.

Vlad hissed and stepped forward. "Why don't you pick on someone your own size?" His cornflower-blue irises darkened in disgust, and his jaw twitched. Even though he was overly pale from being held captive for so long, his greasy hair plastered to his face, he wasn't cowering.

No wonder Thorn was such a strong man. His role model, the man who'd saved him from death, was fearless.

The female guard, Jessie, grabbed the chain that connected Vlad's Wolfram Dwinn collar to his handcuffs and yanked him back. She sneered as her short bleach-blonde bangs fell over her cinnamon-brown eyes and brushed the shaved section of her dark brown hair. "If you're looking for a fight, I can handle you."

"Why don't you focus on getting us back to the *hiding spot*," Cassidy said. "Then there won't be an issue." She rolled her shoulders as if trying to get comfortable. She looked worse off than the other two. Her dark golden-brown hair hung limply, her hazel-green eyes were sunken, and her splotchy tan skin made her appear sickly.

"She's right. Take the three of them away. We need to focus on the abomination's arrival." Drake flicked his wrists.

Abomination. No wonder Thorn couldn't stand the royal family. Between the king trying to have Thorn—his own son—killed, and his brother's actions, I would hate their guts, too.

The guards took Saphira and Thorn's parents away, and I took a step after them.

Clenching my hands, I tried to keep my breathing steady. "Saphira's dad is your father's advisor. Shouldn't she come with us?" I wanted Saphira by my side. She was my friend and our best chance at strategizing a way out of this.

Four guards surrounded me, cutting me off, blocking my view of Saphira and Thorn's parents as the other five guards led them away.

"Now, Everly…" Drake snickered. "She betrayed me. She was going to help my brother, the very person who desires to take my kingdom from me. That's unacceptable and punishable by death."

Death.

He planned to kill all three of them.

Eva gasped and wrapped her arms around herself, her gaze begging me to get her out of this.

Ironically, I'd tried to save her and made a worse mess of things. Acid roiled in my stomach.

The guard in front of me with yellow eyes removed a collar from his back pocket. He lifted his arms to place it around my neck.

They were going to cage my dragon. That was probably why Vlad and Cassidy didn't look well—there was no telling how long it had been since they'd shifted.

My dragon roared so loudly that my ears rang. I whimpered, "Please. No."

"Aw, see," Drake cooed, strolling toward me. His dark irises twinkled, and it wasn't from the moonlight. "She's going to behave, so that's not needed."

My skin crawled as he stroked my cheek, and I yearned for the jolt of the fated-mate connection with Thorn.

What's wrong? Thorn asked, sensing my distress.

I had to learn to lock down my emotions, or Thorn would do something irrational. I could feel his urgent desire to come get me, and I didn't need to fuel it. *Eva's upset, and Drake is disgusting.*

Eva whimpered, and my vision spotted. I had to get us moving to the chateau. Maybe there, she'd settle down.

Drake tilted his head, watching me, and sneered, "You're talking to *him*, aren't you?"

Refusing to cower in fear, I straightened my shoulders.

He chuckled, and a sinister smile spread across his face. "Perfect. Keep doing that."

I gritted my teeth. I was giving him what he wanted—fear and disgust, two emotions that would make Thorn more desperate to reach me. I'd cowered and given in to my stepdad my entire life to stay close to my twin half siblings and fulfill my promise to my mother to protect them. But this unhealthy cycle ended now...starting with Drake.

Thorn, he's toying with me to get you to come here without a solid plan. I had to keep Thorn from rushing in. *You have to fight him strategically, not with anger and fear clouding your judgment.*

Sort of like what you did, he bit back.

I flinched, a pang of regret shooting through my chest. My eyes burned, but I managed to swallow and hold my tears at bay. *I thought I was doing the right thing. Saphira told me I could trust his word. If it had worked, I would've saved four people.*

His regret wafted through. *I'm sorry, babe. That wasn't fair. Saphira still has her blinders on when it comes to the royal family. You can't listen to her. Just knowing you're there with him is driving me insane.*

No, I deserve your anger. I was foolish, but I truly thought this was the best solution. The only good thing is that I'm with Eva. I always strove to be smart. That was why I had a perfect GPA despite the challenges of completing a premed degree. But my intelligence hadn't stopped me from making a stupid decision. I'd trusted Drake's word when I knew he was a bad person.

I had to focus on the two most important things I had influence over: getting Eva and me to the chateau and getting Thorn to stop and think. "Are we going to stand out here all night?"

Drake nodded. "Good point. It'll be harder for him to reach you in the chateau with all our security measures."

That hadn't been my point, but whatever.

"Go," Drake commanded again and shoved my sister in the back.

She stumbled and fell, barely able to hold out her hands in time to catch herself. Though she was eighteen and technically an adult, she was still very young.

I started toward her, but Drake clutched my shoulder. "Where do you think you're going?"

My dragon roared, and my right hand fisted. I wanted to punch the prick in the face, but that would only make this situation more volatile and worse for Eva. "To help my sister."

Drake rolled his eyes. "She can get up on her own. She may not be a dragon, but dammit, she will learn her place." He turned to her and snarled, "Get on your feet and move."

Eva's shoulders shook with quiet sobs as she slowly climbed to her feet. Her eyes were bloodshot from tears, and I held out my hand to her. I said soothingly, as if she were a child, "Come on. We can walk together."

Nodding, she hurried toward me.

Falkor arched a brow. He glanced at Drake and asked, "Sir?"

I growled, unable to hide my disdain as my dragon surged forward.

Eva stopped and stared at me, her eyes full of fear. I wrestled myself under control. I didn't want my sister to be afraid of me.

"It's fine," Drake said and winked at me. "It's great that my future *wife* and my *mistress* get along. Hell, if I'm lucky, they'll both be pregnant at the same time at least once."

Bile inched up my throat, but it didn't burn thanks to my new dragon shifter form. He could say *wife* all he wanted, but there was no way in hell I'd ever say, "I do." There was only one person I was willing to marry, and it was most definitely not Drake.

I kept my expression neutral as I extended my hand to Eva. She hesitated before hurrying over to clutch my arm.

Ladon flanked my other side while Yellow Eyes moved to my sister's other side. Drake followed us, and the other three guards took up the rear.

Of course, he'd put himself in the middle. He wouldn't risk not being completely protected.

We headed to the chateau, and I held tight to Eva. I didn't know how to protect her, but I hoped holding her to my side would bring her some comfort. I'd meant to save her from this hellish future, but instead, I'd gotten us trapped in it.

Thorn, please tell me you won't do anything rash, I connected with him. I needed to hear his promise, but I was also desperate to just hear him.

I won't, he answered. *But I won't stay back, and hope Drake and the king develop a conscience. I'll determine a way to get you and my parents out of there today.*

I nearly sobbed. He and I had agreed to figure out the plan together. Then I'd seen Eva's text, and I'd called her and run off alone, getting us into this mess.

Falkor had promised Thorn that his parents would be freed tomorrow morning if he turned himself in.

I didn't believe him. If Thorn came, Drake would kill him along with his parents. Thorn was in a time crunch, and though I didn't want him to risk his life, how could I ask him not to? I had done the same, though my life wasn't at stake—just my freedom.

The gigantic sunflower-yellow chateau with gray trim came into view as we exited the woods. The sizable terrace was immaculate with the greenest grass I'd ever seen. The beige, slanted roof gave the chateau a regal appearance.

Ladon and Yellow Eyes herded us to the right, away from the terrace and back entrance. When I'd flown over the estate on my way here, I'd noted that the house looked like two separate homes that were connected. He'd told the guards to take us to the guest home, so my observation appeared to be accurate.

When the other portion of the chateau came into view, I noticed the houses were connected by an enclosed walkway. The back of what I assumed was the guest side had a smaller terrace that was just as nice with a wooden door leading into the home.

As we stepped onto the gray-painted wood terrace, the back door opened, and an older man in a suit stepped outside. He was bald with gray hair at the base of his skull. Shadowy hazel eyes glanced at Eva and me before locking on Drake. "Your Highness, I've had both bedrooms prepared. I'll have maids assigned to the suites as requested."

"Make sure it gets done, Sinclair," Drake snarled, not bothering to thank the older man.

My feet stilled. Going into this house would make it all official, and everything within me screamed not to enter.

"Move," Drake muttered. "*Now*."

My chest constricted as I entered with Eva and looked at the place that could very well be my home for the foreseeable future.

The interior was gorgeous with dark cherry wood floors and off-white walls. There was a white painted fireplace with a roaring fire. A breathtaking painting hung over it. Mesmerized, I walked past an obnoxious white couch that was clearly never used and a glass coffee table to stare at Mom's most favorite painting in the world.

It was a replica of one of *Water Lilies*, a series of oil paintings Claude Monet had created over one hundred years ago. Mom had said that the way he painted the faint ripples in the water, washing over the leaves, made her hear the faint rush of the breeze. My chest constricted at the flood of memories.

"I said *move*!" Drake bellowed.

I turned my head to find Eva stumbling over her feet again.

My dragon roared. Oh, *hell* no. This wasn't happening.

CHAPTER TWO

I PIVOTED past the coffee table, hot rage boiling within me. Eva wobbled and fell backward.

I managed to reach her and wrap my arms under her armpits before her ass could smack onto the wooden floor.

Drake hadn't even tried to help her.

She gripped my arms, and I helped her back onto her feet. When she was steady, I spun toward Drake and snarled, "What the *hell* was that?"

He stepped toward me, moving into my bubble. His scent of leather and brimstone hit my nose, causing my head to twinge.

Great. I hadn't gotten a migraine in forever, but his presence was making one rear its ugly head.

"Let me make this crystal clear," he breathed, a hard glint in his eyes. "You may become my *wife*, but that doesn't give you any power in our relationship. I will do what *I* want. If your sister moves too slowly, she'll get stomped on. I don't give a *shit* if you have a problem with it."

I laughed bitterly. "You're delusional if you think I'll be your *wife*."

He held my gaze, challenging me. He said cruelly, "Oh, you will be." He brushed his fingers across my cheek.

I forced myself to remain still, hiding the disgusted chill coursing through my body. I swallowed the vomit and lifted my chin. "I will *never* say, 'I do.' There's nothing in this world that could coerce me now that I know you can't be trusted."

He gripped my jaw, digging his fingers into my skin. His pupils slitted as he murmured softly, "Who said anything about *you* needing to say, 'I do?'"

My heart dropped into my stomach as Eva whimpered beside me.

Laughing, he dropped his hand and studied me. Whatever he saw made him giddy, but I couldn't stop the horror from sawing through my lungs. I'd thought I knew what being powerless felt like. Now I understood how devastating having your power stripped away was. At least, my stepdad hadn't physically hurt me. He was just indifferent and lashed out when I came around to see my siblings. Yes, I'd bitten my tongue and been submissive, but I'd made decisions for myself: my major, which college I went to, and whether I dated. I had a nagging suspicion that if I breathed too loudly, Drake would get on me. Hell, he likely would if I breathed at all.

How am I supposed to remain rational when I feel the terror swirling from you? Thorn connected, his concern slamming into me and warming my cold heart.

I didn't know how to answer that. I barely knew anything about being a dragon, and this fated-mate bond was newer than that. *I need you to. Several lives depend on it.* I wanted to tell him what Drake had said, but I feared that would tip him over the edge.

I had to get my shit together and be strong. Otherwise, Thorn would come here and save me before they had a good plan.

Inhaling slowly, I schooled my expression and shoved the cold tendrils of fear deep down inside me. I had experience with this, or I'd fake it until I made it. "Marriage vows require *both* parties to make the promise."

"Human marriage." He tapped his chin. "By dragon law, only the man is required to say it. After all, we are the *stronger* gender. Women are needed to birth children."

"Then why have a human mistress?" If dragons relegated women to their roles as child bearers, then he shouldn't need Eva. If I could get her out of here, the situation would be slightly more bearable, and I'd have kept my promise to Mom.

Falkor growled from behind Drake and said, "The *prince* doesn't answer to *you*."

If I'd been hoping to find an ally, Falkor was a sure pass on that front. He was shoved so far up Drake's ass that I wondered if he could breathe up there.

Snarling, Drake glanced over his shoulder at the guard. "Even though what you say is *true*, she will be your *queen*, and you will not talk to her like that. Do you understand?"

"Uh...yes, sire." Falkor averted his gaze, but his neck corded as he glanced at me.

Lovely. Now the guard resented me. Who would've thought that Drake would care if the warrior talked to me that way? *He* sure didn't mind doing it.

Drake turned back to me and grabbed the ends of my hair. "I will have children with *both* of you. The son, if not sons, I have with you will be the future heir, and the sons I have with your *sister* will help keep our race alive."

Sons. He seemed pretty certain. "How do you know you'll have boys?" I couldn't bring myself to say *we*. That was inconceivable.

He frowned and yanked on the ends of my hair. "Because I'm *strong*. You should know better than to ask such an idiotic question."

My dragon roared at the way he talked to me and the sharp pain in my skull, but I didn't flinch. I'd already let him feel too much in control as it was. "You know that has nothing

to do—"

He bared his teeth. "When I want your opinion, I'll ask for it. Until then, keep your mouth *shut*."

I wanted to tell him that science wasn't an opinion, it was facts, but I lodged the words in my throat. He wouldn't listen to me, even if I pulled out a science book and showed him that strength didn't influence which sex was born. Many kings in history had had this mentality, but in their defense, they hadn't had the knowledge at their fingertips that we did now. Drake was either too stubborn or too stupid to believe it.

Silence descended, and after a long moment, he smiled. "Good girl."

My hands clenched. He was a condescending, arrogant jerk, and someone needed to teach him a lesson.

Footsteps outside the terrace headed our way, causing my vision to blur. *Thorn, please tell me you aren't here.*

No, he answered, but his displeasure weighed on me. *But I wish I were. I'm several miles south of the dragon territory. Fifty warriors are patrolling the area. If you hadn't asked me to be careful, I wouldn't have noticed them. It's hard knowing he has you.*

The world righted itself. Thorn wasn't being reckless. I pushed the warmth of my love and approval toward him. *That's why I told you I needed you to stay focused. Drake is hoping you will do something reckless so he can capture you. Then there'd be no way you could help us.*

His dragon hissed, and he replied, *I know. I have to get you out of there. I'm flying around to see what sections are less guarded and how often the warriors change shifts.*

Static filled the air, startling me. Footsteps hurried past our door as if they were heading toward the other wing of the chateau.

My gaze landed on a walkie-talkie on Falkor's hip. Something was going on.

The walkie-talkie came to life, and Ladon slurred, "Falk...or. We've...got...a lil...

prob—"

Slipping the walkie-talkie from its holder, Falkor pressed the button. "Spit it out already."

"Don't waste time." Drake gestured to the door. "Everyone but Falkor, go! Ladon's with our prisoners. The abomination could be *here*."

My heart raced. Maybe they'd found a way out? Then my blood turned to ice. I linked, *Thorn, you'd tell me if you were here, right?* I hated to ask him, especially since I'd snuck out on him while he'd slept, but I hadn't *lied* to him, and I was certain he wouldn't do that to me. Still, I had to ask. Maybe he would if he thought it would keep me calm.

Of course, I'm not. I wouldn't tell you that and then show up a moment later. Hurt wafted from him.

In less than three hours, I'd hidden something from him and snuck out on him, and now I'd accused him of lying to me. I had *a lot* to learn about being in a relationship. *I honestly believed that, but something is going on here. Ladon was with your parents and Saphira, and he just reached out to Falkor, sounding odd.*

"We need to get them into the master bedroom." Falkor pointed toward the hallway past the living room. "We'll be more secure there."

My attention flicked to the door as my body tingled. Falkor was now the only guard here and had the collar. If we were going to attempt to escape, this was our chance. I'd have to signal Eva, somehow, when the time came.

Drake rushed past me toward the hallway. He wasn't concerned about making sure Eva and I were safe; he was just desperate to save his own ass.

Figured.

"Don't try anything stupid," Falkor breathed. "Drake might have scolded me for the way I talked to you, but I swear to you, he would rather I be forceful than let you escape."

I wiggled my fingers at my side. I wasn't surprised he knew what I was contemplating. He was one of the top warriors for a reason.

Needing a plan that might catch him off guard, I dutifully turned around. I steadied my breathing, remembering the tips from all the yoga classes I'd taken. That was the only type of exercise I could tolerate, preferring to work on limbering my muscles instead of running outside or touching other people's sweat smears in a gym.

Eva scurried over to me and looped one arm through mine. She was shaking, and sweat had beaded on her upper lip.

My jaw popped from how hard I was gritting my teeth, but I had to do something to control my anger. The measured breathing wasn't cutting it. Eva shouldn't even be here. She was supposed to be safe. This was meant to be *my* future, not hers.

"It's going to be okay," I whispered loud enough for her to hear, which meant Drake could probably hear me from wherever he was.

Falkor snorted as if I'd told her a joke.

I clenched my hands, my nails digging into my palms and stinging the tender flesh. The pain centered me.

Eva glanced over her shoulder at the guard and murmured, "I wouldn't be so sure."

Not wanting to say more, I nodded. "Watch where you're going." Giving her something to focus on would make her feel better...or it had worked when she was younger.

Her head bobbed, and she jerked forward, the area around her eyes tightening. We were approaching the hallway, and a doorway to our left led into a ginormous kitchen. The same hardwood theme continued throughout the kitchen with a dark cherry island in the center of the room. A huge door in the middle of the cabinets matched, and I suspected it was an oversized refrigerator. The rest of the cabinets were light gray, and gray marble countertops completed the space. The island contained a sink and a dishwasher, and several ovens and stoves were set around the perimeter.

At the end of the room was a dark cherry wood kitchen table that could seat twelve with a gigantic chandelier hung overhead.

The space was beautiful and regal, everything a chateau should be. Even though I'd grown up without hurting for money, I didn't feel like I belonged here.

"You'll have the rest of your life to get familiar with the house," Falkor said. "Hurry up."

A loud roar echoed overhead, and Eva yelped, burrowing deeper against my side.

I glanced down the long off-white hallway. Gorgeous paintings I wanted to study hung on the walls, but I forced myself not to focus on them. I needed an exit strategy.

As we approached an intersecting hallway, I turned my head and saw the front door.

My chest fluttered. It was now or never.

Drake's head popped out of the door to the right, and he snapped, "What the *hell* is taking so long? I could be attacked any minute."

"We're on our—" Falkor started, moving closer behind us.

I tapped into my dragon, and she roared. She was on board with getting out of here and back to our fated mate. I released Eva's hold on me and spun around, facing Falkor.

Falkor lifted his hands, holding the collar open. I countered by squatting and snatching the gun from the sheath on his waist.

"Everly!" Eva whimpered, but I ignored her.

I couldn't risk getting distracted.

Falkor dropped his elbows, one hitting the top of my head. The sharp throb caused my eyes to burn, and nausea rolled through me. I spun, kicking out my leg, and nearly toppled over.

Ev, Thorn connected. *What's wrong?*

Grunting, Falkor wrapped an arm around my waist. He lifted me over his shoulder upside down, my face to his stomach. The blood rushed to my head. My vision hazed, and I dropped the gun.

"Get this contained," Drake snarled, and I heard him run down the hall toward us.

A roar thundered in my mind, and Thorn connected again, *I can feel your pain.*

Unsure of what to do, I went with my gut. I grabbed Falkor's belt buckle and unfastened it. *I'm trying to escape.*

Falkor recoiled, which meant my asinine plan was working. He readjusted his weight, getting ready to flip me over, but I wasn't done yet. I yanked at the button and then the zipper of his pants, unfastening them, then shoved the pants down as far as I could reach.

"What is *wrong* with you?" Falkor growled as I got a full view of his dangly bits.

One thing became clear, unfortunately. All dragons weren't large, and my fated mate was exceptional...or maybe Falkor was one sad, lonely dragon. I wasn't sure if I meant the dragon alone because, with a penis this size, it had to be lonely, too.

Drake growled loudly. "Why did you pull your pants down in front of my future bride's face?"

I wasn't sure what made me sicker: my face full of Falkor's privates or Drake calling me his bride.

"*She* did it," Falkor rasped as he dropped me.

I caught my weight on my arms and rolled forward onto my feet. Out of the corner of my eye, I saw Falkor hurry to me, but his slacks prevented him from moving well. He squatted down. Time was running out.

I stood and reached for my sister. Then the world tilted, and it wasn't from the elbow drop.

Drake had one hand wrapped around Eva's throat; the other hand held a gun to my sister's temple.

MY BREATHING QUICKENED, and I grew dizzier.

Thorn's voice popped into my head. *Everly, you're in pain and terrified. If you don't tell me what's going on, I'm coming. Damn the consequences.*

I sank to my knees, pain and fear making the walls close in. I understood that my mind was playing tricks on me, but that didn't make it any better. If I lost Eva and Thorn, it would destroy me. *Drake has a gun to Eva's head.*

Behind me, Falkor hurried to his feet, and I heard him frantically pull up his pants and zip up his fly.

There was no getting out of this.

I'm on my way, he replied.

"You better think carefully about your next steps," Drake spat as he pressed his chest against Eva's back and placed his head next to hers. "One wrong move and I *will* blow her brains out."

My stomach convulsed. It wouldn't be long before I vomited up whatever was left in there. "*Please* don't. You said you need her, so I'm begging you not to hurt her." I connected with Thorn, *Please don't come. If you do, things will only get worse. I need you to find a way to get us all out of here. It has to be planned.*

His response was just turbulent emotions. I couldn't lock onto one in particular, but an icy and hot blend of terror, anger, and distress filtered through the bond.

The jangling of Falkor fastening his belt had despair pressing in on me. He was back in position, and soon, I'd be *collared*. My dragon hissed, but she didn't force herself forward, as if she loved my sister as well and wouldn't risk her life.

Drake chuckled sinisterly. "Do you think I can't find another human to use? I brought her here to make my future wife happy and keep her family close."

That was bullshit, and we both knew it. I was tired of taking it without calling the other person out. "You *knew* I didn't want this life for her. That's why I volunteered to take her place. Besides, it's not like anyone else embezzled money from your company, so don't pretend you'll do something we both know won't happen."

His hand shook, and his eyes flashed with anger. "Are you that foolish? I can take whoever and whatever I want. There are other ways to blackmail humans into giving up something precious. And... wouldn't it be something if, after you begged to take your sister's place, she died because you wouldn't submit to me?"

Every breath I took roared in my ears. I'd thought that I severely disliked my stepdad, but boy, he was a saint compared to Drake. Anger settled heavily in my chest, my dragon fidgeting inside my brain. "Fine, you win." I forced out the words, knowing they were the ones he wanted.

Warmth approached my back. Falkor. I closed my eyes, waiting to feel cool, rough metal sliding around my neck.

"Don't," Drake commanded. "That won't be necessary."

"But, sire." Falkor cleared his throat. "She can't be trusted. Not after *this*."

I didn't have to see the warrior's face to know what I would find. He was embarrassed.

The click of the gun had my eyes popping open.

Drake had loaded a bullet, and the end of the barrel was still in place. "Everly, tell us you'll behave."

Eva's eyes were red from crying, and her bottom lip quivered.

This asshole would pay. I wasn't sure when or how, but I wanted to be the one who knocked the cocky grin off his face. I choked, "I'll behave."

"Good," he cooed and dropped the gun to his side, releasing my sister.

My entire body wanted to give out, and unshed tears blurred my vision and burned my eyes, but I blinked them back. I connected with Thorn, *He released Eva. She's not in immediate danger.*

The lightness of his relief through our bond eased some pressure off me.

"Your Highness, this isn't a good idea," Falkor insisted as he moved to stand beside me. He had the collar in his hands and a scowl on his face. "She needs to be contained."

Though I knew better, I couldn't stop the words. "Since you obviously don't know how to prevent yourself from getting pantsed."

His nostrils flared, and his head jerked in my direction. "That was a cheap move. A true fighter wouldn't do that."

"It doesn't *matter*," Drake snapped. "You are supposed to be *trained* for *every* situation. If someone wants to get free, they'll do whatever is necessary." His gaze landed on me, and there was something odd in his eyes.

I didn't want to know what it was, but the emotion would no doubt further disgust me.

The vein between Falkor's eyebrows bulged. He'd never be my ally, but I hadn't counted on that, anyway. He was drinking whatever Kool-Aid Drake was serving.

I wondered why these guards were so loyal.

Wings flapped over the house, and footsteps pounded our way. Whatever was going on outside was still underway.

"You three need to go into the bedroom," Falkor commanded as he pivoted toward the end of the hallway and the front door, positioning himself so he could still watch me. At least, he thought I was worthy enough not to disregard me.

I clutched my head and stood, the pain intensifying. I needed a dark room, Advil, and caffeine, pronto. I couldn't run right now, even if I had the opportunity, especially since the adrenaline was wearing off and the pain continued to intensify.

Drake waved the gun at me and Eva, then at the room. My pulse raced, and my head pounded in sync with my heartbeat. I moved away from the front door and farther down the hall just as the back door opened.

"Get in there, *now*," Falkor hissed as he ran down the hall.

Eva was frozen, a few tears trickling down her cheeks. She wasn't crying as hard as before, but I was certain it was because shock had taken over, something with which I was all too familiar.

When I'd asked Drake to take me instead of Eva, I'd had no clue what I'd signed up for. I'd thought it would be a loveless marriage. Little had I known I'd be thrust into a supernatural world with a sadistic asshole *dragon prince*. Not that it would've changed anything —I still would've taken her place—but I would've been more prepared for *this* future.

I looped my arm through Eva's, forcing her to move with me. Drake was already at the door, scowling.

We passed a door on the left, and I noted that it was a bathroom. I'd have to get the lay of the house later when Drake didn't have a gun.

We were a few steps shy of entering the bedroom when the person who'd come in through the back door said, "Falkor, they got away."

My heart leaped into my throat as hope surged through me. I wanted to ask who, but I swallowed the words whole. *That* question would not go over well, especially with Drake still holding that blasted gun.

Someone needed to do something about that.

Drake marched back out of the bedroom, his face damn near the same shade as a tomato. He grabbed Eva and me by the shoulders, spun us around, then shoved us back toward the living room.

"You could've just *asked*," I growled, not liking being manhandled. This could easily go in the direction of physical abuse.

He snarled, "Move or I'll make you."

Eva whimpered, and I pulled her tighter against me. The shaking of her body didn't lessen as we picked up the pace.

Back in the living room again, Falkor was staring out one of the windows, his eyes narrowed. "We need to alert the warriors at the perimeter."

The new warrior was dressed in black like the others. He was tall, coming in at around seven feet, and very muscular, with a bald head and honey-brown eyes that weren't as cold as Falkor's.

"We already did via cell phone in case the escapees got a walkie-talkie and are monitoring our actions." The new man rolled his shoulders and glanced at us.

Drake's chest heaved as he stood next to me. He snapped, "How the *fuck* did this happen, Uther?"

Using every ounce of self-restraint I had, I managed not to roll my eyes. He had some nerve talking like that to men who risked their lives daily for a pompous jerk like him.

Uther tugged at the collar of his black shirt. "We're not sure, Your Highness." He averted his gaze and placed his hands behind his back. "They were locked in the cellar of Falkor's house, the same as they've been for the past month. Multiple people must have been waiting nearby because, as the guards were leaving, all five of them were shot with tranqs."

My breath caught. *Thorn, your parents and Saphira escaped. Finally, some good news.*

Warmth wafted toward me as he replied, *What? How?*

One second. Let me hear the whole story. But keep an eye out for them, I replied. I'd take this small win. And if I could get Eva out, I could deal with the hell of being left behind.

Drake growled. "How long were Ladon and the others out?"

"Not long." Uther lifted a hand. "Four nearby warriors noted three dragons flying away, frantically. Three of them shifted and flew after them, while one rushed to see what had happened. She found all five guards passed out on the ground and gave them the tranq neutralizer, which stirred them awake, and allowed Ladon to contact you."

That was why Ladon had sounded so groggy over the walkie-talkie.

Drake's body shook. "You're telling me *three* warriors went after them, and they still haven't been caught?"

Uther's Adam's apple bobbed. "The three prisoners are fast and had a decent head start. The warriors are chasing their scent, but they've split up, making it hard to track them."

I relayed the information to Thorn, ecstatic that he might very well get his parents back.

Vlad knows what to do. He also knows where the cabin is, Thorn linked, but I could feel his trepidation. *I don't know if I can go back and be that far away from you.*

My vision blurred, and I blinked back tears. I didn't need to break down, especially not in front of Drake. *You have to. Go see your parents and learn everything you can from them. Then find a way to bring me back home where I belong—in your arms.*

Damn straight you do, he replied. *I'll head back to meet up with them, but I won't wait long to come back for you. I need you here with me.*

Drake rushed to Uther and pointed at the door. He bit out, "Then why are you still here? Take every available resource and hunt those three down, *now.*"

Sticking out his chest as if he were unfazed by Drake's words, Uther lifted his chin. "Yes, sir. I just wanted to apprise Falkor of the situation."

"Actually, it'd be best if Uther stayed here." Falkor held out his hand for his gun. "I'll help hunt down the others. Ladon, Jessie, and I have worked closely together for years, so it'll be quicker."

"Good idea." Drake nodded and gave the gun back. "If you need anything, say the word. If anyone can fix these mistakes, it's you."

The corners of Falkor's mouth tipped upward, the first sign of a smile I'd ever seen on his face. Of course, it would be due to a psychopath's compliment.

"Watch her," Falkor commanded Uther and pointed at me. "She tried to escape earlier, so keep her close."

At the smug expression on Falkor's face, I wanted to take him down a notch. "If it hadn't been for Drake getting your gun, I would've gotten away. Let's not pretend otherwise."

The warrior glared at me, his pupils elongating.

Mission accomplished.

"That's enough." Drake tisked and crossed his arms. "Falkor, head out and manage the search. Everly and I need to get some rest before a long day of wedding planning. It's almost sunrise."

My mouth filled with saliva, and I wanted to spit. The last thing I wanted to do was plan anything with *him*, even though I longed for a dark room to get some relief from my pounding head. I worried about where, exactly, I'd be sleeping. Sharing a bed with *him* would send me over the edge.

Falkor exited through the back door, and I prayed that Thorn's belief in his dad held true, and that the three family members would find one another.

"If these two disappear while I'm gone, there will be hell to pay, Uther," Drake warned, leveling his gaze on the warrior. "She's smart and will be my bride. If anyone threatens her, they will answer to me. Do you understand?"

The warrior shifted his weight from one foot to the other. "Yes, sire. They won't get away."

"Make sure of it." Drake turned to me, and his cruel smirk reappeared. "In three hours, I'll be back here to take you to meet my father and begin planning. You better be ready. There are clothes your size in our closet."

My skin crawled. Between him having clothes for me and referring to the closet as ours, I wanted to claw my eyes out.

He chuckled, watching my every expression. He strolled over to me and hovered his lips inches from mine. The closer he got, the more I wanted to vomit.

The thing was, I'd never be desperate enough to ever let him kiss me.

HE WAS SO close that his onion breath hit my face, making me want to gag. Any reaction would only encourage him, and I'd already done enough stupid stuff for the night.

I pressed my lips together so his breath couldn't seep into my mouth. I did *not* want to taste it. The stench in my nose was bad enough. If I made it clear I didn't want to kiss him, he'd probably force the issue.

Scanning my face, he smirked. "Don't worry. Our first kiss won't be tonight." He placed a hand under my chin, tilting my face upward so we were looking into each other's eyes. "It will happen when you're clean and don't smell like *him*."

Batting my eyes, I smiled sweetly. "Then you might have to wait a while." If not bathing would get him to leave me alone, I'd happily become the stinkiest woman alive.

"Remember, I'm the one who has the power. If you want your sister to be well taken care of, you'd better behave," he warned as he pressed the tip of his thumb into my chin, causing my entire jawline to ache and increasing the pressure in my head.

Dropping his hand, he sneered. "Goodnight, my *pet*. Sleep tight.

Our first day together as an engaged couple is on the horizon, and I expect you to be polished when you meet the king."

My heart raced, and I desperately wanted to hammer a hole into my head to release the pressure.

He turned and headed toward the back door. He paused beside Uther and steepled his fingers. "Make sure you watch them. When more warriors return, I'll ensure there are several positioned around the house in case my bride tries to escape. But let me be clear—if she gets away, you know what will happen."

Eva whimpered and shuffled back, putting more distance between her and the rest of us.

Glancing over his shoulder, Drake beamed.

I would have to talk to her. If she kept showing her fear, Drake's attitude toward her would get worse. He got a high from people fearing him. She was giving him that in spades.

I moved in front of her, blocking his view. I hated what he was doing to her. Drake already knew how much I cared about my sister, so there was no point in pretending I didn't.

Realizing I had no intention of moving, he left. As soon as the door shut, my lungs worked easier, and the three of us stood in silence.

Uther placed his hands in his slacks pockets. "You two look like you've had a rough night. Why don't you head to your rooms and get some rest?"

Time alone sounded perfect. I wanted to get Eva settled and try to get rid of this headache so I could stay focused. "Which room are we staying in? I'm assuming the one to the left."

Uther winced. "Actually, your and Drake's room is on the right. Eva's is the one across the hall on the left."

Tensing, I shook my head. "I'll stay in Eva's room with her." I refused to share a room with *Drake*.

He bobbed his head and sighed. "Okay. It'll be easier to watch you two if you're in the same room."

I forced myself to exhale. His reasoning didn't matter as long as Eva and I stayed together.

I turned around and found Eva rocking, her arms wrapped around herself. Her face was sickly pale...worse than when she'd had the flu after Mom had passed.

Making my way to her, I placed a hand on her arm to comfort her, but she jerked back.

Her voice shook as she said, "Don't touch me."

My chest constricted as if she'd stabbed my heart. My eyes burned, and I dropped my hand, putting space between us. I had to remember she was going through a lot, and Elliott was the one she always turned to. Not me.

"Come on, let's go to the bedroom," I said, keeping my voice steady. I braced myself, ready for her to tell me she didn't want to share a room with me, but she turned and headed down the hallway. Some of the tension left my shoulders.

We marched past the bedroom on the right, and I purposely didn't glance inside. I didn't want to see Drake's room. I needed to get some decent sleep and not have a visual of my personal hell.

Eva and I entered the bedroom on the left, and Uther stopped at the door.

He scratched the back of his neck. "I really don't want to be in there while you get ready for bed and sleep, but I can't risk you running away, either."

In other words, he was a nice guy who was stuck working for a shitty person. I could only imagine what sort of punishment Drake would inflict upon him if we escaped. I suspected it would involve hurting someone he loved. That seemed to be Drake's style, but Uther didn't have anything to worry about because Eva and I were trapped. "All the warriors are out at the territory line, so it would be stupid to run away now."

He bit his lip. "True, but that doesn't mean you won't. I have a little girl I can't risk."

There it was—Drake's leverage against him. What sort of sick person was willing to hurt a child, especially when the dragon shifter population was dangerously low? "I promise, if I try to escape, it won't be tonight." And it wouldn't be, not with a little girl at risk, but I decided not to say that.

"Fine." He exhaled, but his face was lined with tension. "I'll stay outside the door, but if anything sounds strange, I will bust in. Do you understand?"

I nodded. "That's fair."

"You better get some rest." He arched a brow and frowned. "Trust me. You don't want to disappoint Drake."

As he shut the door, a chill ran down my spine. Ignoring the sensation, I scanned the room, taking in the dark cherry wood accents and the light gray walls. A modern bronze chandelier lit up the entire room. A king-size bed was centered against the right wall, with white silk bedding and four huge pillows. A charcoal rug ran from underneath the bed, and a dark cherry wood bench was positioned at the foot. The headboard was the same gray as the rug. Two oversized dark cherry wood nightstands sat on either side of the bed with a large bronze lamp on each one. Across from the bed, against the left wall, rested a dresser with a gigantic mirror. To the right, I glimpsed a sizable walk-in closet full of clothes and, to the left, a bathroom.

Eva stood near the edge of the bench. She appeared tiny in the enormous room. Tears streamed down her face, and the image reminded me of the preteen who'd lost her mother.

Devastated.

I eased toward her, needing to comfort her. "Eva, I promise everything will be okay."

"You can't promise that," she said brokenly as she countered each one of my steps, easing toward the room's double windows. "And don't come any closer."

The words were a punch in the gut, but I obliged. "I *will* figure something out. I came here to protect you."

She huffed. "Well, you did a piss-poor job."

"I got kidnapped on the way here, and things took on a life of their own." I didn't want to tell her too much and risk her becoming more of a target. "As soon as I learned Drake had you, I came here. You know that."

She rubbed her arms. "Maybe it was a ploy. I mean, how can I trust you? You're one of *them*."

I pressed my fingers to my temples to ease some of the agony from my head, especially since my heart was taking a beating. "How can you ask that? I'm your sister and will always look out for your best interests."

Eva rocked back on her feet. "I...I know that. I just need time to think. My life has completely changed in the past several hours, and I'm..."

"It's okay," I murmured. She was processing the situation, and I needed to be understanding. Eva had seen me in dragon form. That was a lot to take in. "Look, I'm going to take a shower." I didn't want to wash Thorn's scent off me, but my headache was getting worse. If I didn't do something to get my migraine to recede, I wouldn't be able to sleep or think clearly.

"You're going to leave me?" She hurried a few steps toward me.

"Of course not." I gestured to the door on my left. "The bathroom is right there. I'll leave the door unlocked. If you get too uncomfortable, you can join me in there."

She sat on the bench and nodded. "Just hurry. Please."

"Promise." I forced a smile and rushed into the bathroom.

I shut the door, wanting privacy as the acid swirled harder within. I kicked off my sneakers and set my feet on the cool, dark gray tiles. There were his-and-hers sinks to the right, with dark cherry wood cabinets and a white marble top. Next to the sinks was a huge white tub, and between the tub and the toilet was a stall lined with white subway tiles and a huge shower head.

I scurried to the shower and turned on the water. A cutout cradled a bar of soap and bottles of shampoo and conditioner. A small linen closet contained towels and two white robes. I snatched a towel and threw it over the glass of the shower stall as the water warmed.

I laid my head against the glass to get the throbbing under control. I closed my eyes, and Eva's traumatized face popped into my mind. I had to do something before Drake decided it was time she took on the role of his breeder.

The acid in my stomach lurched up my throat, and I rushed to the toilet and vomited.

The world crashed down on me, and I dry heaved, letting the agony take over. I had to be strong around Eva, so this was my chance to have a moment of weakness.

Ev, Thorn connected. *What's going on? You're in so much damn pain.*

I was, and there was no reason to lie to him. He could feel my turmoil through our bond. *Eva is petrified. She didn't want me to touch her. I'm sleeping in the room Drake assigned to her and not in the room he's classifying as ours.* The last word had me heaving again.

Thorn didn't immediately respond, and I realized what I'd said. I hadn't wanted to tell him about the wedding until tomorrow.

White-hot anger thrummed into the bond. He asked slowly, *What do you mean 'the room he's classifying as ours'? If you're his breeder...* His dragon bellowed. *Is he planning to* marry *you?*

Thorn, I need you to stay calm, I replied and rested my head on the toilet seat. I was beyond caring whose butt might have been on it. *This is why I need you to work with your parents and Saphira. Since I'm not human anymore, he took Eva as his breeder, and he plans to make me his wife. I need you to save Eva and me.*

Were you going to tell me? he asked as our bond constricted from his pain.

I just kept hurting him. *Of course. First thing in the morning. I wanted to make sure you had calmed down.*

Calmed down? he parroted. *I will not calm down until you're here beside me where you belong, and knowing you're keeping things from me is making this a lot more difficult.*

My dragon whimpered. He was right. I needed to be honest with him. How else could I expect him to trust me? *I'm sorry. I wasn't trying to be deceitful. I just had a lot going on, and I was petrified that you would come here, now that it's clear that Drake has no intention of letting you live.* I didn't know how to do it, but I tried to push my regret and love toward him. *I swear, from here on out, I'll tell you everything. Even if I fear you'll do something I won't like.*

His hurt ebbed and was replaced with the warmth of his love, easing some of the sickness in my stomach. He replied, *Thank you. I love you, and I promise I'll get you and Eva out of there. When is the—* He broke off, unable to say the word.

He didn't have to. I understood the question. *I don't know. I meet with him and the king in a few hours.*

Okay, let me know, immediately.

Are you safe? I held my breath.

We're all at the cabin. Vlad is on the couch, and Cassidy is asleep in our bed. Saphira opted for the room you were in originally.

They'd made it. My stomach settled, and I lifted my head. *Why didn't your parents sleep together?*

They stuck me in the Wolfram Dwiin room to make sure I can't sneak past them. His annoyance flickered through our connection.

I snorted as half of the worry weighing on me disappeared. His parents and Saphira were there, and they were making sure he didn't do something reckless.

Did they tell you how they got away? I was still stunned that they'd had someone in position to rescue them.

Thorn replied, *They have no clue. It just happened.*

Now that I'd gotten some sanity back, I stood, flushed the toilet, and made my way into the shower. Steam rolled from the top, fogging up the entire room. I stood under the stream and nearly moaned when the water was hot, even to my touch. Ever since I'd become a dragon, the showers had felt lukewarm, but this shower had obviously been made for dragon shifters.

Maybe whoever helped them will help get me out. My chest expanded with hope.

Thorn didn't feel as relieved. *I wouldn't count on it, and Drake will have you heavily guarded. We'll have to operate under the assumption that we're on our own.*

I hated the sound of it, but that was the best strategy. I turned off the water and dried my body. My head was still killing me, but it was bearable enough to sleep. As I slipped on my clothes, I replied, *You're right. I hate to do this, but I have to get some rest. I don't want to miss any detail that might help with our escape.*

Link with me as soon as you wake up. I don't care what time it is or if you think I'm asleep. I need to know what's going on.

That was the least I could do after the hell I'd put us through. *Promise. And Thorn, I love you. I'm sorry for upsetting you. I swear I wasn't trying to. I was just doing what I thought would keep you safe.*

I don't need you to save me, he replied as his dragon whimpered. *I need you back in my arms, and that means I need to know everything that's going on. I know I can't act recklessly, so I need you to trust me like I trust you.*

I do, and I'll prove it, I vowed. Actions spoke louder than words, so I needed to back mine up.

His dragon purred. *I can feel your pain, so get some sleep. I'll be here if you need anything.*

I entered the bedroom and found Eva already in bed with the lights off. She'd taken the side facing the window and away from the door, which suited me just fine. I tiptoed to the bed and crawled under the sheet, facing the door.

The sheets were cool and soft, and my body melted into the mattress. I hated that the bed was comfortable, but I felt as if I were lying on a cloud.

As I closed my eyes, Eva turned to me and scooched so close that our bodies touched. She whispered, "I'm sorry, Everly. I didn't mean the things I said earlier."

I glanced over my shoulder, not wanting to turn away from the door. If someone walked in, I wanted to see them immediately. I smiled reassuringly. "I understand, and we can talk more in the morning. I'm not upset or hurt, okay?"

She nodded. "Sleep good. Goodnight."

"Night," I murmured, and my eyes closed.

A CREAK WOKE ME. The door clicked shut quietly as someone tried to enter undetected.

Chest tightening, I opened my eyes.

CHAPTER FIVE

A LUMP FORMED in my throat as my gaze settled on Uther. He removed his black hat, confirming that his entire head was bald. Dark circles lined his eyes.

I tensed and sat up, ready to defend my sister and myself. I whispered, "What are you doing?"

His brows furrowed, and his eyes bulged as he glanced back at the door, then at me. He raised his hands and sputtered, "Nothing."

Did all dragon men think women were stupid, or was that the influence of the king and Drake? I lifted my chin, ignoring my squirming stomach. "*Nothing?* You're sneaking into the bedroom while Eva and I are asleep. That seems like more than *nothing*." I clutched the covers over my breasts, though I wasn't wearing anything revealing.

He flinched. "It's not what it looks like." He sighed and rubbed a hand down his face. "I swear. I was notified that Drake would be here soon." He gestured at his walkie-talkie. "And you weren't awake. I...I heard what he said last night and didn't want..." He winced.

He didn't have to finish. Drake wanted me ready and presentable, yet he hadn't told me what time he planned to arrive. I inhaled deeply to calm my rattled nerves. "No, it's fine. Thank you." I threw the covers off my legs and stood but paused as I stared between him and Eva. He seemed sincere, but I didn't want to let my guard down. She was human and asleep in a bed. That was as vulnerable as one could get.

"I promise on my scales I wasn't being pervy." His nose wrinkled. "I just figured the human girl could use more rest, so I was coming to wake *you*. So, you're awake, and this is awkward, and I'll be leaving now." He spun around and blurred out of the door.

If that had been Falkor or Ladon, they wouldn't have considered Eva's needs or cared if Drake got pissed at me. I'd bet they'd enjoy it. Even though I got a nicer vibe from Uther, that didn't mean I would trust him.

Knowing I needed an outfit from the other room since "my" clothes were there, I closed my eyes to calm my pounding pulse. I didn't want to go into Drake's room, but I didn't have much choice. If I wore something he knew wasn't from in there, I suspected he wouldn't let it go.

I rushed into the hall and stopped in front of Uther, pointing at him. "Do not go in there while my sister's sleeping alone. If something seems wrong, just holler. I'll be listening."

He pinched the bridge of his nose but nodded. "Understood, but you need to hurry. Drake will be here soon. He's getting ready in the main chateau."

His heartbeat remained steady, so I forced myself to enter the bedroom.

If I'd thought Eva's room was huge, I'd been mistaken. This bedroom was twice the size.

The same wooden floor ran into the room, and every piece of furniture was white. A king-size bed backed against the wall on the left, flanked by nightstands with dark gray lamps. The bedding looked the same as in the other room. The headboard was white, offsetting the silver walls, and the footboard had two drawers built into it. A dresser and a chest of drawers completed the set.

Across from the bed, in front of two oversize windows, sat a brown leather couch and a matching recliner. The sitting area overlooked the back terrace. Two doors were set in the wall on the far right side of the room. The one closest to where I stood was cracked open to reveal a large walk-in closet, meaning the other one was the bathroom.

This was where he expected us to stay. I was thankful I'd already emptied my stomach.

The walls crept toward me as my body tingled. If I didn't get out of here soon, I'd have a full-blown panic attack. I'd been weak enough in front of Drake last night. Today, I'd do everything I could not to let him get to me. Straightening my shoulders, I marched into the closet.

I snorted. It was as large as my attic room back at my stepdad's house. Each side of the room had two rows of clothing racks that were full. In the center, a gigantic island as long as the walls held more than a hundred pairs of shoes. It was topped by a long mirror that split the area into his and hers sections. The right side of the space held the women's clothing, and hundreds of pieces of jewelry sat on one half of the island counter.

A sour taste filled my mouth. This was obnoxious. One person didn't need this much. Peter had referenced how loaded the Hale family was, but I hadn't understood that until now.

If Thorn had been the prince living here, I doubted he would've been as obnoxious about flaunting his wealth.

Struggling to breathe, I strolled to the woman's side. I had no time to waste.

I sighed when I noticed there were no jeans or cotton tops, just various dresses, skirts, and jumpsuits. Whoever had ordered the clothes—most likely Drake—was sending a clear message: no casual wear for me.

My jaw twinged, and I realized I'd been gritting my teeth for who knew how long. I forced my jaw to relax and rubbed my chest where our bond was located. It was lukewarm, so Thorn must be sleeping, but I'd promised to let him know when I was awake. I connected, *Hey, babe.*

The bond warmed as I homed in on a long-sleeved, wide-legged jumpsuit. It looked like the sort of outfit I usually wore, so I removed it from the rod to get a better look. The material was threaded with shiny teal blue, silver, and gold lurex, and it had a surplice neckline and a sash.

Hey, you, he replied, but a chill ran through our bond. *Is he there?*

I undressed. *Not yet. But had the guard not snuck in to wake me—*

Thorn's dragon snarled. *He snuck in while you were sleeping?*

I had the same reaction, but he explained why. I filled him in on the incident. I couldn't blame Thorn for getting upset. I didn't like it either. *He seems like a good guy. He heard Drake threaten me about being ready, without including a time.* I put on the jumpsuit and tied the sash around my waist. The garment fit like a glove, which had my skin crawling.

Thorn's annoyance flashed. *Because he wanted to catch you off guard and use the fact that you're not ready as an excuse to punish you. You said you're meeting the king?*

Yes. I broke out in a sweat, so I turned to the island and searched for shoes. *I don't know what I'm supposed to do or say.* Halfway down, I found a pair of simple black heels that complemented the outfit and slipped them on my feet.

He'll tell the king that he wants to...ma— He cut himself off as his anger intensified and heated.

That was inconvenient for me, seeing as I was already having a hard time controlling my body heat on my own. I inhaled to steady my racing heart and bent down. I snatched up the shorts and T-shirt I'd been wearing. *Have you talked with Vlad, Cassidy, and Saphira?*

I'm waking them up now, he answered. *One second.*

Needing a task to focus on, I marched back out into the hallway. Uther stood a few feet away from the bedroom door, as if to ensure I wouldn't wonder if he'd gone inside. I walked past him into the room where Eva still slept and straight into the bathroom.

I searched the cabinets and found the items I needed still in packages: a hairbrush, makeup, a toothbrush, and toothpaste. Someone truly had prepared for Eva's and my arrival. My back stiffened.

As I stood in front of the mirror, my legs gave out. I clutched the counter to keep myself upright, my gaze boring into my reflection.

I didn't recognize the girl staring back at me.

I looked pretty much the same, but somehow...more. I still had long, golden hair but with more volume, and the same fair skin but with a faint golden glow. My light gray eyes glistened with unshed tears, but the hurt reflecting in my irises, as if they were a mirror image of my soul, had me doing a double take.

Even when Mom had passed, I hadn't looked dead inside.

So, I did the one thing that would make me feel better. I closed my eyes and pulled the image of Thorn's face into my mind.

His eyes were the first thing I recalled. That sky blue shade, with flecks of what could only be described as diamonds, had captivated me. When I'd first gone to find Drake at his fancy bar to bargain for Eva's freedom, those breathtaking eyes had stopped me in my tracks, and I'd almost forgotten why I'd gone there.

Then, the day Thorn had kidnapped me, he'd shifted back into human form and reappeared shirtless. I imagined his gorgeous, smooth, tan skin and his medium-brown hair hanging in his eyes. He was perfection, and with his chiseled features and muscular body, he could easily be a model.

And he was *mine*.

A soft knock sounded on the bedroom door, followed by Uther mumbling, "Drake is heading this way."

My arms gave out, and I fell onto my knees, the broken person I'd seen in the mirror taking control. Now that the vision of Thorn was gone, it hurt to breathe. I missed Thorn so damn much, and I'd give anything for him to be here with me.

Ev, what's wrong?

I didn't want to put pressure on him, but I couldn't lie. Not to him. Not anymore. *I miss you so much that my heart feels like it's been stabbed repeatedly. And Thorn, I'm scared.* My eyes burned, and I blinked to hold the tears at bay. *Eva's here, and I don't know how to protect her, and I don't know what to do.*

Trust me, I understand, and I will get you both out of there, he replied. *We're drawing a map of the chateau and dragon lands while trying to get a solid estimate of warrior numbers based on what Cassidy, Saphira, and Vlad know. But if you need me to stay connected with you—*

I took a deep breath. *No, keep planning. That's what I need you all to do. I'll let you know what I glean here. I've seen only one side of the chateau, so far.*

That side is intended for the prince, once he marries, Thorn explained, his emotions icy. *But he shouldn't stay there until he's wed, according to a long-standing tradition that every single dragon shifter knows.*

I clung to the hope that Drake wouldn't live here with Eva and me. *Pay attention to the conversation with them. Hopefully, you can find a way to get Eva and me out.*

Panic slammed into me, then eased. He answered, *I do need to focus. So far, our options aren't promising, but I'm here, whenever you need me.*

With shaky hands, I quickly put on makeup, going for a natural look since I was low on time. As I finished with my mascara and painted my lips a rosy pink, the back door to the house opened.

Throat dry, I took one last look in the mirror. This would have to do.

I spun on my heel and rushed into the bedroom. I shook Eva and said, "You need to get up. I'm leaving." I didn't feel safe leaving her asleep with a stranger nearby.

Her eyes fluttered open, and she touched her forehead. "Everly, I had the worst nightmare." Then her face drained of color.

"I'm sorry." I brushed my fingers through her hair. "It wasn't a nightmare."

Footsteps pounded down the hallway, and Uther said, "Sire, she's not in there."

Drake snarled, "What do you mean she's not *in there?*"

"She's in this room with her sister," Uther answered uncomfortably.

I heard a huff, then Drake's heavy footfalls heading our way.

Eva's mouth opened and closed.

"Stay in here while I'm gone." I kissed her forehead. "Be safe." I stood straight and marched to the door.

As I reached it, it opened, and Drake stepped in, coming face-to-face with me.

The hard glint in his eyes vanished, and his head jerked back. "You're ready."

That broken girl in the mirror flashed through my mind. That was what he wanted, which meant that was exactly what I couldn't become. He'd hoped I wouldn't be ready, so I batted my eyelashes, oozing innocence. "You asked me to be, so I set an alarm to ensure I wouldn't disappoint you."

Uther exhaled.

He'd expected me to tell Drake that he'd alerted me. Uther didn't trust me, either, and that, somehow, made me like him more.

Jaw twitching, Drake gazed at the bed.

My dragon stirred. I didn't like him looking at my sister, especially when she was in bed. I placed a hand on his chest and managed to only push him back gently.

His nostrils flared, and he glared at me.

That had been my intent. Blood rushed in my ears, but I held back the anger. "I thought we needed to meet the king." I'd do almost anything to get him away from her. She'd already experienced too much terror.

"Don't push me again," he warned, his expression turning to stone. He gripped my arm, his fingers digging into my skin, and yanked me toward the hallway.

Eva gasped as I moved my feet, regaining my balance.

He picked up speed, and I had to run to keep up with him. No doubt he wanted to make sure I understood who was in control.

As we passed Uther, his lips mashed into a disapproving line. However, when we entered the living room where Falkor and Ladon stood, they had the opposite sort of expression—both of them smirked. After what I'd done to Falkor last night, I'd made an enemy, but I couldn't find it in me to care.

Drake made a beeline out the back door and onto the terrace lawn. With each step, my heels sank into the soft earth, making it hard to keep up. A stitch formed in my side, but I pushed through, eager to get to wherever the hell he was taking me. The two guards followed closely behind, Falkor snickering from time to time at my discomfort.

As we rounded the yard toward the main house's terrace, the scent of sausage and eggs filled the air, followed by the clanging of plates. My stomach growled.

I counted four guards stationed near the tree line. Two ladies dressed in maid outfits stood off to one side of a round glass table with four chairs around it. A muscular man, who resembled both Drake and Thorn, was seated in the spot that overlooked the backyard. I knew this was the king, and the gorgeous woman next to him had to be Drake's mother.

The king had salt-and-pepper hair and a mostly gray, short beard. He appeared to be in his fifties, and he was just as large as Thorn. His midnight black eyes focused on me, and he reached over to take the woman's hand.

Drake continued to head straight to them, his face and demeanor transforming as he changed into a person I didn't recognize. He smiled, though it didn't reach his eyes, and slowed down, wrapping an arm around my waist as if to help me over the grass.

The woman smiled back sadly. Her striking baby blue eyes were breathtaking and held a kindness I hadn't expected. A breeze lifted strands of her dark chocolate-brown hair and settled them on the shoulders of her white, sweetheart-cut dress.

Releasing me, Drake hurried a few steps ahead and pulled out the open chair next to the queen. My throat hurt as I slid onto the seat, unsure of what was to come.

As soon as I sat, the breeze picked up again, and the queen's eyes widened. She jumped to her feet and stumbled away from me.

CHAPTER SIX

THE QUEEN'S abrupt movement jarred the table, and the coffee in her full mug splashed over the rim. She clutched her chest, breathing raggedly.

The king climbed to his feet. "What's wrong?"

Falkor and Ladon fanned out on the terrace, searching for signs of danger.

I didn't hear anything other than birds chirping. Her reaction must have something to do with me. My vision blurred.

"I thought you said she was human," the queen gasped.

Blood running cold, I took a hollow breath. Out of every scenario I'd anticipated, I hadn't contemplated this.

The two guards relaxed as they moved into positions at opposite ends of the terrace.

Brow furrowing, the king settled his attention back on me, and he sniffed the air. His eyes narrowed as he looked at Drake. "She is supposed to be human. What the *hell* is this? There's only one way this is possible."

The king didn't seem to know that Thorn had captured me. Even though Drake had admitted that he was behind the kidnapping of Thorn's parents, I had assumed the king had been made aware of it.

Drake's eyes darkened until I couldn't distinguish his irises from his pupils, but his expression remained indifferent instead of his usual cruel, stony appearance. He rolled his shoulders back and took the seat next to mine. "She is Peter's stepdaughter, not his actual blood."

Crossing his arms, the king lifted his chin. "Yes, I *know* that. I saw her, her siblings and her mother, in Peter's building several times when I met with him, and all four were human."

A long-forgotten memory flashed through my mind. I was thirteen and waiting with my mother and the twins in the lobby. A man I'd heard called Mr. Hale had come out with my stepfather, looking identical to the way he did today, as if he hadn't aged a day, but that wasn't what struck a chord with me now. It was the way I remembered him staring at me and the twins with longing.

If Drake wouldn't tell them the truth, I would. "I was human until a little over a week ago."

Drake glared at me sideways.

What were we supposed to say, other than the truth? They knew I shouldn't be a dragon shifter.

The queen's jaw dropped, and she took a few steps toward me, her gorgeous eyes brightening. "That's impossible. Unless..." She took a staggered breath. "He's alive."

Out of every reaction I might have predicted, it wasn't one I would have described as hopeful.

She took her seat again and leaned toward me. She bit her bottom lip and asked, "Where did you see this man? Was it in Asheville or another town close by?"

Drake snarled, his malice slipping through. "Mother, stop. Remember how you were supposed to meet her over a week ago? You didn't because the *abomination* kidnapped her on the way to the chateau. Falkor and Ladon nearly lost their lives."

The queen's face fell, and her eyes darkened.

I wished I could say something to contradict what Drake had said, but he hadn't lied. Thorn had done that, though not for the fun of it. I had to bite my tongue, or Eva would pay the price for my outing him. But I couldn't remain silent. "He changed me to save my life."

Hope sparked back into her gaze.

"He's a master manipulator," Drake said forcibly as he reached over and grabbed my knee. He squeezed so tightly that a whimper built inside me. He wrinkled his nose. "The real reason he changed you was that he knew you were meant to be my breeder. But that's fine. I got you back and solved that problem as well."

The king lifted a brow. "What do you mean?"

Drake's expression smoothed, and the corners of his mouth tipped upward. "Well, that's one reason I asked to meet for breakfast today. I've made a decision. Now that Everly is a dragon shifter, I want to make her my queen."

The king laughed but stopped abruptly when Drake didn't join in.

"I'm serious, Father." Drake lifted his coffee mug from the table. "I've thought about it, and there is no other person I want by my side."

Though there was a plate full of eggs and bacon in front of me, I couldn't eat without puking.

"Son, you have to be kidding." The king shook his head. "She's not dragon born."

"True." Drake shrugged. "But we ensure that information doesn't become public. We can say she didn't live in the area. She's from Asheville, and I won't have anyone else as my wife."

The king rubbed his temples. "You mentioned solving your problem. How will marrying Everly, a dragon shifter, help with our reproduction issue?"

"I'm glad you asked." He released his hold on me and took a sip of his coffee. "Since Everly will live here with me, I figured, why not make her more comfortable? So I brought her sister here to be my breeder."

"*What?*" the queen choked out. "You're telling me you chose sisters for your wife and breeder?"

He was trying to come off as considerate, but even his mom could see the error in that plan.

The king slammed his hand on the table, and the glass cracked down the center. "Have you lost your mind? You took not just one child away from Peter but *two?* All you've done is brought unwanted attention to us!"

Without flinching, Drake took a bite of his eggs. "Peter embezzled money. He knows the consequences. Besides, he was thrilled to get this one off his hands." He pointed at me.

That was like a gut punch, despite every word being true.

"Wait." The queen gripped the arms of her chair. "If Thorn took Everly, how is she here?"

"I handled the situation." Drake placed his fork on his plate and leaned back in his seat. "I located Vlad and Cassidy, used them as leverage, and voila, here she is, back with me."

She smoothed out a wrinkle in her dress across her stomach. "Is that the one—" She glanced at the king.

He nodded subtly.

I assumed she was asking if Vlad was the assassin, but I wasn't sure.

The king took a bite of bacon, chewed methodically, and swallowed. "Where are Vlad and Cassidy now?"

"Free. Getting Everly back was all that mattered," Drake said stonily as he turned and brushed a fingertip down my arm. "I want all of her, and when she returned to me as a dragon, I realized I could have her as my bride."

Needing to eat something to keep up my strength, I snatched a piece of bacon from my plate. I took a bite, and my stomach gurgled in protest. This wasn't happening.

The king swallowed and placed his hands on the table. "You did all of this without talking to me?"

"You thought he was dead. I was protecting you from making another hard decision." Drake's nostrils flared, but he kept his expression neutral beyond that. "I hoped not to bother you with anything since you both struggled with the decision you made twenty-one years ago, but with Everly now a dragon, it had to come out. If anything, this situation should reaffirm the wisdom of what you tried to do—kill him. He kidnapped her, locked her up, and changed her without her permission."

The queen flinched and hung her head. She reached over and patted my arm. "I'm so sorry you had to experience that, Everly. I... I don't know what else to say."

A scream strangled me, but I prevented the noise from escaping. This guy was more than an asshole—he was sick. I cleared my throat to ease the discomfort. "He really did change me to save me." I had to keep her hope alive. "I escaped and ran when it was dark and rainy. I fell and cracked my skull... I would've died."

Her lips quivered, but she exhaled. "He wouldn't have had to change you if he hadn't kidnapped you. There's more to this story, but it's best if the world doesn't know he's alive. He's a danger." Her eyes glistened.

Despite her remorse, I couldn't help getting angry. Blood running hot, I wanted to scream at them. *Thorn is your child too, and he's a great man.* But I'd learned from my stepdad that people wouldn't listen if they didn't want to.

Drake cut his eyes to me, giving me a clear message: *Keep your mouth shut.*

I snatched the white linen napkin from beside my plate and wiped my hands. They weren't greasy, but I needed to do something with my excess energy.

What's going on? Thorn linked, and our bond warmed.

I hated to tell him, but we'd promised we wouldn't hold back anymore, so I gave him the rundown.

Disgust charged through our bond. Thorn connected, *So, the king is acting like he didn't know about Drake's plans?*

He is. Though I'd just become a dragon and wasn't used to searching for clues that could reveal a lie, I hadn't heard any changes in the king's heartbeat or breathing. *I think he's telling the truth.*

Do not believe him, Thorn replied urgently. *The royals are skilled in covering things up, and that's what Drake is doing.*

I had no reason not to trust Thorn, but something didn't feel right about the situation.

"Enough of this conversation." The king waved a hand. "This is the first time I've formally met Everly, and Mira has never met her before. This isn't what we should be discussing when we have just learned that my son—the heir—has chosen his bride."

I'd rather talk about Thorn than *this.*

"Let's not forget his *breeder*," Queen Mira murmured. "How do you feel about that choice, Arman?"

D**RAKE TENSED**, and his jaw twitched. "Well, *Mother*, I get to choose my breeder like I get to choose my wife."

The tension was so thick it nearly smothered me. I refused to play along and act okay about my sister being thrown into this mess.

"I don't understand why you think trying to impregnate a human will work." Her nose wrinkled, and her mouth twisted like she'd tasted something bad. "Shouldn't you try having a child with your new wife first, before bringing a third person into your relationship?"

The couple of bites of bacon I'd swallowed made me gag. Here they were talking about Drake having sex with both his wife and a breeder. I'd puked enough in the last twenty-four hours that I didn't want another round, but the sensation persisted because... Drake.

"Get her in line, *Father*," Drake snapped and sneered. "If I wanted her opinion, I would've asked for it. I'm the future leader of the dragons, and I will do what I think is best."

Queen Mira grimaced and licked her lips. "I'm sorry, honey. I'm not trying to upset you. It's just...if Arman—"

"I am *not* my father." Drake lifted his chin and stuck out his chest. "I am my own man, so don't compare me to him."

She nodded and averted her gaze, and my blood boiled.

Not only was Drake an arrogant douche, but he also treated his mother like garbage. I'd do *anything* for my mom to be alive, and to see him acting so entitled and ungrateful made me want to hurt him. He had no regard for anyone but himself.

"Let's talk about this wedding." King Arman rubbed his hands together and smiled, but a vein bulged between his eyes. "It's May, so are we thinking of a fall wedding? That would give us ample time to organize everything and give our guests time to book travel and hotels."

Some of the weight rolled off my shoulders, and my lungs worked a bit easier. A fall wedding would give us plenty of time to determine a way out of this.

"Absolutely *not*," Drake rasped. "Everly and I will be wed in two days."

"Two *days*?" Queen Mira's mouth dropped. "But darling, why? We need to have her dress made, and—"

I nodded, ignoring the black spots that crowded my vision. Here I was, thinking we might have four months to plan, and of course, he'd taken that away.

I shouldn't have been surprised. He was all about claiming me and driving Thorn crazy, so he'd show up recklessly. "Drake, I'm here. Eva's here. What's the rush?"

As soon as his head snapped in my direction, I knew I'd said the wrong thing. He leaned toward me, the evil glint in his eyes bright.

I tried to lean back, but he reached over and squeezed my leg again, so hard a whimper damn near left me.

His intent was clear. If I kept doing things he didn't like, he'd hurt me. I had no doubt he'd target my sister next.

Clenching my jaw, I held still as his mouth hovered over mine.

Thank goodness, I hadn't eaten more than a bite. When his lips touched mine, my throat burned. His lips were warm but stiff and rough. They were nothing like Thorn's, and internally, I recoiled. Though the kiss lasted only a few seconds, it felt like a lifetime. When Drake pulled away, I wanted to gargle with alcohol to disinfect myself.

Ev, what's going on? Thorn connected, his worry exacerbating my upset stomach.

My eyes burned. *He just kissed me.*

Thorn's rage exploded through our connection, and my ears pounded as his dragon bellowed.

He touched what belongs to me, he connected. *I will kill him slowly and enjoy wringing out every ounce of his pain and making him squirm. No one takes my gem from me and tries to tarnish it.*

His words should have upset me, but my dragon roared in approval. Unlike Drake, Thorn didn't think of me as property but as someone who meant the most to him, like a treasure. *I couldn't stop him. I'm sorry. We're with your parents, and he threatened—*

You don't have anything to apologize for, Thorn replied and pushed the warmth of his love toward me. *He's forced you into this, and I will avenge you.*

Oh, I plan on being right there beside you. I didn't want to kill Drake, but I'd be down for making him utterly powerless.

Always and forever, he vowed, and my heart beat once again.

Drake smirked, the power-hungry glare back in place.

He could tell that Thorn and I were connecting, and he was getting the reaction he so desperately craved.

We were playing right into his hand.

Interlocking our fingers, he placed our joined hands on the table.

Drake smirked, but he didn't radiate happiness. He was as cold as an icicle. "I can't be without her for another moment. I want to do this right and not take her before the wedding, so I'm sure we can make that happen in two days. I don't care if all the guests can't make it. We'll figure out who is truly loyal to us this way."

The queen nodded. "Of course, son. We can make that happen, but Everly and I should start planning immediately."

My legs shook. I didn't want to plan a wedding to *him*, even though I prayed we wouldn't actually go through with it. There wasn't much I could do...except one thing. I smiled brightly. "Yes, we'd better. And I would love for Eva to join in on the planning. After all, she's my sister."

"That's a good point. She is important to you and in your relationship," Queen Mira said, her brows pulling together. "Drake, please have her brought into the living room to join us."

Drake stood and helped me to my feet. "Of course, Mother." Then he leaned toward me again, and I froze, fearing he was going to kiss me again.

Instead, he whispered in my ear, "One wrong move, and you will wish that Eva was only my breeder with what I'll do to her. Now, smile and laugh."

I obliged, but the sound got lodged in my throat.

He kissed my cheek and tucked a piece of hair behind my ear. "Don't worry, love. I'll be back soon."

He spun on his heels and marched away, his dedicated golden retrievers following. With each stride that took him farther away, my stomach unclenched a little. I turned back to the king and the queen and realized that King Arman had been studying me for who knew how long.

Queen Mira stood and gestured at the door to the main house of the chateau. "Come on, dear."

"Honey, why don't you and the servants go in and get things ready while I have a moment to talk with Everly alone?" King Arman said as he patted his wife's arm.

"Oh, of course." The queen laughed, but the smile didn't reach her eyes. "Drake won't let her out of his sight often." She waved the servants in and left, leaving me alone with the king.

I tried to breathe despite my lungs screaming while I waited for him to say something.

He surveyed the area, and his gaze settled on my face. "Are you mated to Thorn?"

The world shifted, and I placed my hands on the table to keep myself from falling over. Somehow, this man...the *king*...knew, and I was certain he wouldn't approve of me being mated to his eldest son.

What would he do to me?

CHAPTER SEVEN

SWEAT POOLED UNDER MY ARMPITS, and I tried to control my breathing, but the way I had to brace myself on the table had already answered his question. *The king knows*, I connected with Thorn.

"That's what I thought." King Arman ran a hand down his face, and his eyes narrowed, deepening his faint crow's feet. "That's why Drake is so set on marrying you."

What do you mean he knows? Thorn asked, trepidation leaking into the bond.

I straightened my spine. *That I'm your mate.*

Fuck, Thorn replied as his dragon snarled.

King Arman already knew the truth, so I said, "I know it's hard to believe coming from me, but Thorn isn't a monster or someone to be feared."

"Even though he kidnapped you?" The king crossed his arms.

That was a fair question, and I needed to use this opportunity to change the king's mind, if not for me and my situation, then for Thorn. "He needed leverage to free Cassidy and Vlad."

"Drake said—" he started.

"He lied," I interjected, not wanting to waste time. Drake could come back at any minute, and I suspected he'd be in a hurry. I hated what that meant for Eva. She probably wasn't ready. At least, that would buy me more time to talk to the king alone. "Thorn took me because he'd learned of Drake's plans for me. He wanted to use me as a bargaining chip."

"And what did Drake want?" King Arman tugged at the sleeves of his white and blue striped button-down shirt.

"Thorn." I ran a hand down my stomach to ease the nausea rolling inside. "He doesn't like that Thorn exists. I don't know how he found him—"

The king groaned. "I do, and no wonder the guards have been acting strangely. Falkor was my personal guard until recently, when he said he was worried that someone was stalking Drake. Falkor has to be in on it."

What's going on, Everly? Thorn piped in. *Are you in danger?*

No. Actually, the king seems bothered by all of this, I replied, trying to stay focused on my in-person conversation. "Wait, you know how Drake located Thorn?"

He placed his hands on the back of his chair and nodded. "It was because of me."

"And you're surprised he acted on it?" I scoffed and crossed my arms. Maybe it wasn't the smartest tactic for dealing with dragon royalty, but damn, he didn't get to ignore his role in this.

Growling, he focused his gaze on me and said, "I understand your predicament, but I am your *king*. Lucky for you, you're also now my daughter, but you need to understand your place."

The hair on the nape of my neck lifted, and pressure built inside me. Despite the flood of warmth in my chest from him calling me family, the strength of his stare forced my attention to the ground...as if I were submitting. My dragon grumbled, not liking it, but I couldn't fight it.

Then the sensation was gone, and I could glance up again.

"I've known where Thorn was hiding for twenty years." The king's face twisted in agony and something like regret.

Twenty years. That was shortly after Thorn had settled in Atlanta. "Why act now? Why not twenty years ago?"

"Because he was hiding." King Arman scratched the back of his neck. "And staying away from other dragons. I *couldn't* kill my son, not when he wasn't causing any harm." His shoulders slumped.

If I hadn't known better, I would've said he cared about Thorn. "Why try to kill him at all? And why would you tell Drake where Thorn was, knowing he'd be threatened by him?" My body heated, and I wanted him to spit out all the answers instead of making me ask him.

"I didn't know what to do after he stole my dragon. That was what my father had done to people who opposed him, and if Thorn decided to take my dragon and keep it, the entire dragon shifter race would be tossed into chaos." He clasped his hands. "As soon as I knew that Vlad was in the woods and in position to kill my *boy*, I knew I'd made a mistake, but I didn't know how to stop it. When I learned the attempt had failed, I was relieved."

My breath caught. I remembered Thorn telling me about his grandfather's abuse of the mark. "If you were relieved, why did you have your guards track him, Vlad, and Cassidy down a few days after that?"

"Falkor said if the truth got out about what I'd tried to do, my people would turn on me." He turned and stared into the tree line. "They were supposed to bring the three of them back as prisoners. I didn't expect a fight to break out in the middle of human streets."

I wheezed. "You thought making Thorn a prisoner would be better than killing him? Maybe he'd be breathing, but you would've stripped away everything worth living for from him and his parents."

He flinched. "Is that what he calls Vlad and Cassidy?"

I swallowed my snort and forced myself to soften my response. "Do you blame him? They protected him and cared for him when his own blood didn't." Family wasn't always forged by blood. In fact, those bonds formed outside of blood were stronger because people *chose* to forge them. I was learning that now, with Thorn and Saphira.

"No, but that doesn't mean it's easy to hear." His eyes glistened. "Shortly after that, I learned they were living in Atlanta. I told Falkor to keep an eye on Thorn. As long as he didn't leave the area or start working with other dragons, we'd let him be. I didn't have it in me to kill him, and I wanted him to be happy."

His sincerity crumbled some of my defenses. Even though his logic was flawed, he'd thought he was doing what was best for the dragons he ruled and Thorn. Something tugged at me, and I almost closed the distance between us and placed a comforting hand on his shoulder. Even though he'd called me his daughter, I was certain we weren't at that point yet. I forced myself to stay in place. "I wouldn't call that happy."

"Better than dead or locked in prison." He exhaled.

We were losing focus, and Drake would be back soon. "Why did you tell Drake?"

"I didn't. He and Falkor have grown close these past couple of years, ever since Drake took over the family business so I could focus on royal affairs." He scowled. "It had to be Falkor. He knew where they lived and where they went on weekends to shift into their dragons."

Tilting my head back, I narrowed my eyes. I didn't want to be gullible and easily trust this man, especially when he'd ordered a hitman to take out his own six-year-old son. "And you didn't notice that Vlad and Cassidy were prisoners here?"

He shook his head and frowned. "When I heard that someone could be stalking Drake, I shifted Falkor and Ladon to be Drake's personal guards instead of mine. I wanted my son protected, but shortly after the transition, the two guards started avoiding me and spending time away from the chateau unless they were with Drake. I figured something was amiss, but I never imagined *this*. Drake tends to get himself into trouble, but Ladon and Falkor are more than capable of handling it."

I clenched my hands as my pulse quickened. "Kidnapping and threatening to *kill* people isn't *getting himself into trouble*. That's way over the line of acceptable."

"You're right." He pursed his lips. "I'll fix this, but I need to handle it delicately. I can't hurt Drake. Not like I did Thorn."

Something snapped in my chest, and for the first time, I believed I might be able to kill someone. "Drake and Thorn are polar opposites. Thorn is an amazing man who is willing to do whatever it takes to protect the people he loves. Drake is nowhere close to that."

King Arman focused his intense stare on me. "Do you mean that, or are you saying it because he forced the mate bond on you?"

My body tensed as my dragon exploded in a guttural growl. I didn't care if he was my king. He didn't get to talk about Thorn that way. "He didn't *force* the mate bond on me. When I was human, even while knowing he'd kidnapped me, there was something alluring about him that I couldn't shake. After he changed me, I was even more confused because that attraction became a literal tug, and electricity sparked between us, intensifying the draw I'd experienced as a human." I chuckled, remembering my confusion. "I thought it was a sire bond and tried to fight it, but every day, Thorn showed me that everything he'd done was to save the two people who had sacrificed everything for him. Even when we were his prisoners, he took care of Saphira's and my every need and made us more than comfortable."

The king's brows furrowed. "You're his *fated* mate?"

I smiled, the words causing a lightness in my body. I wanted the whole world to know that Thorn and I belonged to each other. "Yes, and Drake is now trying to use that bond to force Thorn to do something reckless to save me before the ceremony." There was no point in lying about Thorn's desperation to rescue me. Drake already knew. It wouldn't make the situation more dire.

The king chuckled grimly and rubbed his forehead. "He learned that his brother was alive and would be considered the rightful heir to the throne despite his exile. Mira and I have given that boy everything he ever desired, which has exacerbated the problem. This is on me to fix."

A tightness squeezed my chest. I could read between the lines. They had spoiled Drake, overcompensating for what they'd done to Thorn. "Isn't it strange that the son you feared is the one trying to save the people he loves, while the one you spoiled is turning into the very thing you feared Thorn would become?"

"No." King Arman's jaw set. "That's not it. Drake is just misguided. He'll have to learn, and I'm here to teach him." He nodded toward the house. "You need to join Mira before Drake gets back with your sister."

Even though I still had so many questions, I inhaled, trying to calm my shaking hands. The king was right. Drake would be here soon, and if he found me speaking with the king alone, he wouldn't approve. "Please don't tell him about this conversation."

"I won't." He turned to me. "I will have to figure out a solution without him knowing, or he'll move the wedding up. I'll find you when I have worked something out."

I'd taken a few steps toward the door when the king said, "And, Everly."

Turning back, I looked at him, and what I saw caught me by surprise.

His hand was pressed to his chest, and a tear trickled down his cheek. "Can you tell Thorn I'm so damn sorry that I had to do what I did? That I think of him every day, and his mother and I would give anything to remove the mark and reunite our family. Isolating him was the only way to keep us and my people safe, and I want to make up for my mistake. If freeing you is the way, I'll do it without hesitation...like I did Saphira, Cassidy, and Vlad."

My throat burned and constricted as if I might choke. Even though he seemed haunted, King Arman still believed he'd made the right choice. "I'll tell him, but I want to make something clear, even if you *are* my king. You did *not* make the right choice. Thorn is loyal and knows right from wrong. He's everything Drake isn't, and the fact you still think you had to do what you did proves you don't deserve to know the man he's become in spite of you." I turned on my heels and marched into the house, desperate to get away from a man who didn't value my mate.

***

THIRTY-SIX HOURS LATER, it was the night before my "wedding." Thorn was beside himself, and I wasn't much better. I stood at the end of the bed that Eva and I had been sharing, with Uther standing guard outside the bedroom door. Falkor and Ladon were missing in action, likely from leading the charge to watch for Thorn's arrival.

"I thought you said you were going to get us out of here," Eva whispered as she crawled to the foot of the bed. She didn't realize that she no longer needed to get close to me for me to hear her whisper.

Placing a finger to my lips, I paused my pacing. I mouthed, *He can hear you,* and nodded toward the bedroom door.

Her brows furrowed, and she murmured, "What?" no doubt thinking she was being quiet.

Oh, dear goodness. I touched her arm and gestured toward the bathroom. She and I couldn't have an open conversation unless we made it difficult for Uther to hear.

She swung her legs off the bed, got tangled up in her long cashmere gown, and tumbled face-first toward the floor. I grabbed her by the waist and yanked her against my body. She landed hard against my chest, but I didn't stumble back. I still wasn't used to my dragon strength.

"I told you that gown was a horrible idea." I snickered as I helped her to her feet.

"Hey, it feels like a feather brushing all over my body." She untangled her feet and stood. "The clothes are the one nice thing about being here."

There was no way anyone would catch me in a nightgown. My skin crawled, even in the one pair of flannel pajamas I'd found in the far corner of the closet. Every inch of me, from my neck down, was covered, and I was certain someone had left them there by accident. Every other set of pajamas was some sort of cashmere gown or fancy silk set. I'd even found a piece of unnecessary lingerie. It was sheer, and *everything* showed.

A shiver racked my body over why it might be in there. If Drake ever tried something physical with me, I'd vomit all over him, and if he touched my sister, I would kill him...or die trying.

Now that Eva was steady, I hurried into the bathroom and turned on the shower. When she followed me in, I shut the door.

"They're still coming up with a plan," I whispered louder so she could hear me. "It might be best if you don't know what it is." I wanted to protect her as best I could and keeping her in the dark seemed ideal.

She shook her head. "Don't do that. We're sisters. Equals. You've taken care of me for so long—I want to be part of the plan so I can protect you as well."

My chest expanded. "Let me connect with Thorn to see if there's an update."

Leaning against the glass shower, she crossed her arms and raised a brow.

She wasn't leaving. There was no point in fighting her. I didn't want to risk her acting out and alerting the guards that we were up to something.

I connected with Thorn, *Any update?*

We're going through our options. We think one of the hidden tunnels leading into the chateau could be our best move, or possibly blending in with the help. They'll have all entrances and the backyard guarded. The problem with the help is that the warriors will be paying attention to their faces.

The wedding was to take place at noon on the terrace, with the guests sitting in the backyard. That way, the chateau would block me from view on one side, and the guards would be on the other. Broad daylight would make it easy to see everywhere for miles.

My limbs quivered. There was no good option. Drake had everything planned with no wiggle room. The king had said he'd help us, but I hadn't heard a word from him...not that Thorn trusted him anyway.

A loud knock pounded on the bedroom door, and I stiffened. We couldn't turn the water off, or it'd look suspicious. I said, "Eva, stay in here. I'll pretend you're in the shower."

She opened her mouth, but I went to the door. As I opened it, I turned back and murmured, "Please. I need you to do this."

Rolling her eyes, she nodded. I closed the door quietly and hurried to the bedroom door. I inhaled, fearing I'd find Drake's leather scent, but it was missing.

All I smelled was Uther.

When I opened the door, the guard stood there, wearing an urgent expression. He whispered, "I need you to tell me everything. It's time."

CHAPTER EIGHT

GUT TIGHTENING, I stepped away from him. "I have no clue what you're talking about. The wedding isn't for another twelve hours." *Please, if there is a higher being, don't let Drake want to have sex tonight,* I chanted internally. He'd made it clear that he wanted to wait until after the wedding, so, I assumed, Thorn would be even more desperate to reach me before the deadline.

Uther growled and glanced down the hallway toward the living room. "Now isn't the time for games. The king needs information so he can communicate with *them.*"

"This isn't a *game.*" I suspected he was trying to pull one over on me, not the other way around. "I have no idea who the king wants to communicate with." King Arman had told me he'd find me when he had a plan. This was *not* him finding me. If anything, this could be a test from Drake. After all, he seemed to trust Uther, especially when he could hold the safety of his daughter over his head.

He sighed and licked his lips. "Look, this is *risky* for me, but Drake isn't the king yet, and my loyalty lies with King Arman."

I studied him, gauging whether I should trust him. "This wasn't what the king and I agreed to." I watched his reaction to see if it would hint at his dishonesty.

"I know, but we tried to get him here." Uther shuffled his feet.

Heavy footsteps walked from the back door toward the hallway. Ladon stepped into view and arched an eyebrow. "Is there a problem?"

Uther tensed. "I was—"

"Heading into the bathroom with me," I interjected then flinched. That could get him in hot water with Drake if I didn't tread carefully, so I had to improvise. I clutched my stomach and hunched over. "My stomach has been upset this evening, and I kinda stopped up the toilet."

Ladon's nose wrinkled. "Whoa. Stop." He lifted a hand.

I groaned. "If you don't want Uther to help me, you could. I just need someone to plunge because I sorta made a mess trying to do it myself."

The corners of Uther's mouth tipped upward, but he mashed his lips into a hard line, hiding it.

"No!" Ladon slashed the air with his arm. "Uther is fine. I just heard you whispering and—"

Stomping my foot, I tried to play the part of the future, spoiled queen. "Well, I'm *sorry*. Next time I have stomach issues, I'll announce it to everyone in the house. I apologize for my discretion." My body burned, but I took a deep breath to prevent the flush from reaching my face. I didn't want to act embarrassed, but maybe it would make the whole exchange appear more real.

Uther winced and cleared his throat. "She must be nervous about the wedding tomorrow. Why don't we just go into the bathroom and fix the issue? Let's go...see what we're up against."

"That's one way of putting it." Ladon cringed. "Dude, you may want to grab some Poo-Pourri, a mask, or *something* to protect you from the smell."

I hunched over. "My poop doesn't stink," I said through clenched teeth. Would he just leave us the hell alone, or was this some sick karma attacking me because I'd lied?

Ladon dry heaved and stumbled down the hallway, and I swore he was holding his breath.

Good to know that he couldn't stand talking about bowel movements. Who would've thought a trained warrior who'd killed and had blood splattered on him would be squeamish about poo?

"Let's get you taken care of." Uther grinned as he entered the bedroom.

I shut the door behind me and dropped the act. Luckily, Eva was in the bathroom and wouldn't hear anything. I murmured, "I'm glad he fell for it."

"You're something else." His irises twinkled before his face became stern again. "But *he* couldn't get here himself to get Thorn's number. Drake has been watching everyone who tries to get close to you, including his father."

That wasn't surprising, especially since his mom had expressed displeasure with him choosing a breeder, as well as a wife. "Why should I trust you?"

Uther lifted a brow. "Do you have any other options? You won't make it out of here, and Thorn will be captured if you don't accept our help."

My body turned to ice. I hated that he was right, and I'd been trying to deny the inevitable, but that was hard to do when someone smacked you in the face with it. "What exactly are you asking me for?" My chest tingled as I stopped trying to sense whether he was on my side. He already knew enough to take us down if he wanted to.

"Thorn's number." He pulled a cell phone from his back pocket.

I laughed. I had no clue what it was. Thorn had kidnapped me, and then we'd mated. I'd never needed his number, which I hadn't realized until now.

Uther tilted his head and observed me. He asked, "What's so funny?"

"Let me connect with him to get it." I opened myself up to Thorn and said, *The king sent a guard here to ask for your number.*

Our connection warmed immediately. *Be careful. It could be a trick,* Thorn replied.

My heart ached, the pain damn near debilitating. What I wouldn't do to be with him. If it hadn't been for Eva, I would've tried to break out of here again, to hell with the consequences, but I couldn't leave her behind. I couldn't break that promise to Mom.

Rubbing my chest where it hurt, I tried to focus on the conversation and not on how much I needed him. *I know. He knew I was expecting to hear from King Arman, and he's seemed trustworthy so far. What do we have to lose?*

Thorn's frustration increased, and my limbs shook harder. He replied, *Not much, but I hate the idea of talking to the king. I still don't believe he was behind saving my parents and Saphira.*

Has Saphira tried calling her dad? The last I'd heard, she hadn't wanted to. She didn't want to make her father more of a target than he already was just by being her blood.

We decided it was too risky, he replied, and I sensed no malice through our bond. His parents had been kidnapped, and he knew getting family more involved was a lot to ask of anyone. They were probably monitoring Saphira's parents in the hopes she would reach out to them.

Though I didn't want to push him, we didn't have a ton of time. The shower turned off in the bathroom. Eva would be joining us soon. *If we're going to give him your number, we need to do it. Uther can't stay in the bedroom with me much longer without making Ladon more suspicious.*

Thorn's dragon snarled as he asked, *A guard is with you in a bedroom?*

Maybe that hadn't been the best detail to include. *Ladon was watching us, so I pretended that my stomach hurt and said I'd stopped up the toilet. It chased him off so I could talk to Uther alone.*

My stomach tickled from the humor swirling through the bond.

He replied, *Gods, I needed that. I miss you and your crazy stories so damn much.*

"You're mated to him?" Uther whispered as the bathroom door opened, and Eva stalked out.

When her gaze landed on Uther, she froze, and her mouth opened. "What is *he* doing in here?"

Uther stiffened. "I'm just about to leave." He held out his phone to me.

Babe, I connected. *Do you mind giving me a number in case the king calls? This might be our best bet. What is there to lose? They already know you're coming.* Last night, I'd even begged him to stay at the cabin and rescue me later, but he wouldn't budge. He didn't want Drake forcing me to do anything.

Fine. He huffed. *It's not like Falkor doesn't have it already.*

That was true. When his parents were being held captive, Falkor had called Thorn to inform him and give him timelines.

He rattled off the number, and I quickly typed it into the phone as footsteps headed toward us. I handed the phone back to Uther, and the warrior placed it back in his pocket just as the bedroom door opened.

I hunched over again and shuffled toward Eva. Her eyes widened as I placed a hand on her shoulder and whimpered, "It's not any better."

She blinked in confusion. As Ladon stepped inside.

"Are you going to be all right?" Eva asked, her face lined with concern.

"I... I don't know." My face burned, and I wanted to bury it in Eva's chest, so I didn't have to look at all their faces. "I'm just glad Uther unclogged the toilet."

Coughing, Uther rubbed his nose. "Uh...yeah. I'm glad I could help." He pivoted toward Ladon and strolled past the older warrior into the hallway.

"Just...try not to do it again." Ladon inched backward, too, and searched the area around me, like he expected a huge gas cloud to emerge. "And get a handle on your issues before the wedding. You can't be doing *that*," he said and gestured to my butt, "during the ceremony. Drake won't allow it."

My dragon hissed, but laughter bubbled in my throat. I was a mixture of emotions and wasn't sure which one I'd settle on when all was said and done, but laughter was *way* better than crying.

When the bedroom door shut, Ladon muttered, "What the *hell* is Drake thinking?"

That sent me over the edge. I clapped my hands over my mouth to keep my chuckles silent. If I'd truly been in this much agony, I wouldn't have been giggling uncontrollably.

"Everly, what is *wrong* with you?" Eva asked as she placed her hands on my shoulders. "You're acting like we aren't trapped, constantly watched, and being forced to have some demented relationship with an egotistical asshole who also happens to be a dragon prince."

The shaking in my chest changed to uncontrollable sobs. My smile vanished as tears poured down my face. We were screwed, and if the king couldn't find a way to save us, I'd be married off to Drake tomorrow and forced to spend my nights beside him.

Lifting her hands, Eva stepped back. "Okay, forget I said anything. I prefer laughter over this."

But there was no going back. A shiver ran through me, and I wrapped my arms around myself to get warm.

"Hey, I'm sorry," Eva whispered as she touched my arm. She crawled into the center of the bed and opened her arms.

That was exactly what Mom used to do when we were hurting. The pain of losing her weakened my legs. I clambered onto the bed and scooted over to Eva. I faced the door and pressed my back to her chest as she wrapped her arms around me.

"Cry it out." Eva squeezed me gently.

She left out the other part of what Mom would say—*Things will look better in the morning.*

My connection with Thorn warmed, and his voice popped into

my mind, *Did that guard do something?* Cold tendrils of fear wafted into me, tightening my chest.

No, it's just... I'm not going to get out of here, I answered, not bothering to pretend I wasn't broken. *I'm going to be married to that prick tomorrow, and not you. I don't know if I can handle that. I want to be your wife and have children with you.*

A lump choked me when I realized what I'd said. We'd been mated less than a week, and I'd spent most of that time stuck with Drake. It would be a miracle if I didn't scare Thorn away.

We're going to have that, Thorn vowed. *You're more than my wife already because we've completed the fated-mate connection. A wedding would be a formality and a way to celebrate the merging of our souls with everyone since I'm pretty sure you wouldn't have wanted them in the bedroom when we forged the bond.*

Some of the pain in my chest ebbed, but not enough to allow me to laugh. *No, and I'm glad that telling you I wanted to marry you and have babies didn't scare you away.*

Fuck no, he snarled. *That made me ecstatic. I feel the same way. You were human for so long that I didn't want to make you feel trapped or uncomfortable. But you are never getting rid of me, and I will get you out of that wedding tomorrow. Vlad is talking to Arman now.*

Do you have a plan?

Not yet, but we're working on it. He paused and pushed warmth into me. *What I need you to do is get some rest and trust me when I say I will find my way to you. Always and forever.*

I didn't doubt his words, but sometimes, promises couldn't be kept, even those made with the best of intentions. *You can't know that. And Thorn, what's my freedom worth if you get caught?*

Fate didn't put us together to have some Romeo and Juliet ending. His determination made my worries vanish. *I will do whatever it takes to get you back here with me. Please, trust me.*

Okay. I'd walk through fire with him as long as I was at his side.

I closed my eyes and pictured Thorn's face, tracing my finger along the sheets, imagining they were a paintbrush. The small, calming motion was enough to ease my soul.

As my eyelids drooped and closed, Eva continued to hold me.

Before I drifted off to sleep, Thorn connected with me again. *Ev, we've got a plan. You'll see me soon. We'll sneak you out before the wedding preparations begin. I love you. Get your rest because, once you get home, you won't be going back to sleep until I get my fill of you.*

My chest lightened, and I smiled. *I love you. I can't wait.* Then I drifted off to sleep.

SOMETHING SHOOK MY BODY, stirring me awake. My heart leaped.

Thorn was here. Eva and I were finally getting out of this hellhole.

I opened my eyes, and harsh reality crashed over me.

CHAPTER NINE

I'D BEEN HOPING to find Thorn standing at the foot of the bed, but instead, it was Queen Mira. She wore emerald satin pajamas, and her hair was pulled into a low ponytail.

My heart clenched, and my blood turned to ice. Thorn hadn't come. *Please tell me you're okay.*

I glanced out the window across the room and noted that the sky held the pinks and oranges of the rising sun. It had to be around seven thirty, but I felt as if I'd had only a few hours of sleep.

I'm not okay, Thorn replied, his dragon snarling. *We ran into an issue. The king said he'd open an entrance for us that only he knows about, and the damn door isn't open.*

Maybe the king hadn't meant to help free us after all. Could his real plan have been to ensure his oldest son's safety but also allow Drake to get what he wanted—Eva and me? *What are you going to do?*

I'm not sure. Thorn paused. *We're brainstorming the next best strategy.*

The queen smiled sadly. "It's okay to be nervous. I thought you might be and hoped the three of us could get ready together."

Though I wanted to tell her no, that wasn't an option. If Drake found out I'd turned his mother away, there would be hell to pay, but more than that, I didn't want to hurt her feelings. Planning the wedding with her had been horrible, but she was the only reason I'd made it through. Mira was kind and considerate...everything that Thorn was, and Drake wasn't. Eva had been quiet, I guessed because of the way Drake had treated her that morning, and Mira had noted our discomfort and planned most everything. I probably shouldn't have let her, but I didn't have the ability to plan this wedding.

"Yeah, of course." I threw off the covers and sat up. I stilled for a second to get my bearings. Everything inside me screamed to cut loose and get the hell out of here, but I knew, without a doubt, that every warrior was working today.

She pressed her lips into a hard line and placed her hands on my shoulders. "I know the circumstances are less than ideal and Drake makes it challenging to love him."

I choked. There was no question—I *didn't* love him. My stepdad was an *angel* compared to Drake, and that was saying something. My stepdad was indifferent and cruel when I got in his way; Drake was a power-hungry egomaniac. If there was a person I hated in this world, it was *him*. But I couldn't tell her that, so I posed a safer question. "What makes you say that?"

"What woman doesn't want to plan their wedding?" Queen Mira arched a brow. "And I see the way you look at him. He chose your sister as his breeder, which—having a breeder is a tradition I'm not fond of. But that's how Drake is. He pushes people brutally far to find out if they love him."

I forced my mouth to remain closed. This was clearly how the king and queen justified Drake's actions, saying he did horrible things to test how much others loved him. But that wasn't right. Drake thought he owned the world, that he could do whatever he wanted, without consequences, not to prove their love.

Not only had the king's decision changed Thorn's life but their own, too, and for the worse.

I chose my next words carefully. "And when does he stop pushing?"

Her face turned stony, any trace of warmth gone. "Never."

This proved that some parents refused to see their children for what they were.

She scoffed and rolled her eyes. "But...there are times when I see hints of the young boy underneath. Like early this morning when Drake showed up, needing his father." Her eyes glistened as she blinked. "But that's enough of that sort of talk. Today is a happy day. My son is getting married, one step closer to taking over the throne, and I get a *daughter*."

I wanted to tell her that I was already her daughter but informing her that I was mated to her other son wouldn't be the smartest move. I wondered why she didn't know I was mated to Thorn because King Arman had realized it quickly. But she *had* given me an important clue. *I think the king still plans to help us.*

What makes you say that? Thorn connected.

Because Queen Mira informed me that Drake showed up early this morning, needing his father. I wanted to ask the queen more questions, but I didn't want to make her suspicious or risk a nearby warrior overhearing us. So, I bit my tongue, hoping to ask questions sporadically and not alert her. "Well, he's probably nervous about the wedding, too. It's a huge commitment that no one should take lightly."

"Exactly." Queen Mira's attention flicked to Eva, who was still sound asleep.

That action alone was telling.

"Anyway." She quietly clapped her hands and took a few steps back. "Why don't you wake your sister while I get a maid to bring us some coffee and breakfast? My servants will bring the dresses and makeup to you. We can get ready here to ensure Drake doesn't see you before you march down the aisle."

Nausea churned within. There was no way in hell I could eat, but a cup of coffee would be amazing. "Okay." I should have said more—she was trying to be kind—but I couldn't. I did *not* want to get dressed and dolled up for... I couldn't even finish that thought.

Of course. He's watching the king because he probably hasn't determined how Vlad, Cassidy, and Saphira escaped. Thorn growled. *We're trying to figure out another way in in case the king doesn't show up soon. The back terraces are crawling with guards, so we need to wait until some guests arrive so we can blend in.*

The queen hurried away to get things rolling...which meant my ass would be getting dressed. Last night, I'd banked on not having to deal with the whole preparation part of the wedding, but that had been wishful thinking.

Everly, you will not marry him, Thorn vowed. *I don't care what it takes. I won't allow it to happen. You won't be forced to be with someone you can't stand.*

My hands clenched. *It's you or no one.* No one could ever replace Thorn, and I wanted to ensure he was clear about my feelings.

Warmth wafted through our bond as he replied, *I love you.*

Damn straight you do. I lifted my chin as if he could see me. *And I love you, too. You're stuck with me forever. I'm like a fungus you can't get rid of. I've set up camp in a part of you, a part you can't remove me from, and I'll keep coming back.*

I never liked fungus...until now, he teased.

My cheeks hurt, and I realized I was smiling.

Eva groaned. "Have you lost your mind? You're grinning like a fool. We aren't safe, and you're about to marry Drake!"

That was like a splash of ice-cold water. My skin itched, and I leaned toward her and murmured, "I was talking to Thorn."

"That telepathic thing?" Eva rolled toward me and propped her head on her hand. "That's still wild, but I guess it's helpful, given our situation."

Being able to talk with Thorn and having Eva here were the only reasons I hadn't completely lost it. "Yeah, but they ran into a snag this morning and are sorting it out."

Eva's eyes brightened. "But they're still coming, right?"

I nodded and rubbed the spot where the bond connection warmed. "We have to play along so we don't raise suspicions."

She saluted me. "I can do that."

The bedroom door opened, and Queen Mira rushed in with three servants behind her. It was time to get ready.

DRINKING COFFEE HAD BEEN A MISTAKE—SOMETHING I *never* imagined I'd say. But as I stood in the bathroom, taking in my appearance, the acid churned, adding to my upset stomach. I wanted to puke, but I couldn't risk getting the gown dirty.

Thorn, Saphira, and his parents were trying to find a way in, but every time they peeked out of the entrance hidden in the woods, a warrior flew over. If they stepped out, the warrior's dragon would sense them immediately. There were more guards than expected, which meant Drake must have pulled some in from nearby thunders. If Thorn and the others hadn't gotten there several hours before dawn, they wouldn't have made it into the tunnel. As it was, they were stuck and planning to move at the last possible second, when everyone's guard would be at its lowest.

My long blonde hair cascaded over my shoulders in loose curls, and my makeup was done in earth tones with brown eyeshadow, blush with a golden sheen, and a warm brown lipstick that I wouldn't have been able to pull off before becoming a dragon.

The dress had been unexpected—all gold, no white. It was a sleeveless one-shoulder sheath with ruffled beading throughout. The sweeping train gave it an elegant flare but didn't go on for miles like those in the royal weddings. The sweetheart neckline emphasized my cleavage, and the slit on the left side of the skirt ended just shy of my hip, offering glimpses of my leg. The dress was gorgeous... royal and my style.

The look was completed by glittery silver high heels that clasped around the ankle. Queen Mira had given me an elegant diamond necklace to wear and large silver diamond earrings in the shape of a dragon. I reached for the bracelet Mom had given me, but all I touched was skin. My heart dropped, and I wished I had a token to remember her by, but I'd left it behind for Thorn.

The queen had picked out everything perfectly, just for the wrong son. My insides tore to shreds as I stared at my reflection.

High heels clacked toward me over the wood floor, and Eva entered the bathroom and stood beside me. She looked beautiful with her straight, dark brown hair and smoky eye makeup that made her steel-blue eyes pop, her lips a nude shade that appeared completely natural. Her dress was simple and elegant compared to mine. It was a matte silver with cap sleeves and a similar sweetheart neckline. The top was lace, and the long skirt was made of soft tulle with detailed ruching. She wore gold shoes but no jewelry.

"You look beautiful, Everly," she said softly and frowned.

She didn't have to explain. I knew what she was thinking—*you look great, but I wish you didn't since it's almost time for your farce of a wedding.*

I swallowed to keep down the vomit and turned toward her. "You look gorgeous, too." Not only was my life changing, but hers was, too. I suspected this was the beginning of the end for us if Thorn didn't get us out of here.

"Thanks." She averted her gaze and crossed her arms.

Any updates? I hated harassing him, but our time was almost up. If he was going to rescue me, I kinda needed him to do it now.

We're at the tunnel's opening, waiting for the guard hovering over us to leave. Then, I'll make my way out and blend in with the guests, he replied.

I choked and placed my hands on the counter, trying to breathe slowly. *They're looking out for you. You're going to get caught.*

They're expecting me to blaze in like a crazed fated-mate monster, he replied, determination flowing through, *not someone who tries to blend in with the crowd. No one besides Falkor, Ladon, and Brenton knows what I look like, so I'll stay away from them and keep my head down. It's my best chance at getting to you. I just have to keep my cool. I'm coming for you, Ev.*

"Everly," the queen called from the bedroom. "It's almost time."

I looked back at my reflection in the mirror. I'd always been the girl who tried to make peace and not cause problems and look at where that had gotten me. I'd been hoping that Thorn would save me, but maybe I needed to save myself.

First things first. I needed something I could use to defend myself.

Eva's brows furrowed. "What's wrong?"

"Everything," I scoffed as I scanned the bathroom for something, anything, I could use as a weapon.

She followed my gaze and tilted her head. "Did you lose something?"

"No, I think I finally found something." I was done being a pushover.

Queen Mira joined us, looking every bit the royal she was. Her dark hair was styled in an elegant French twist, and her makeup was perfect. A huge diamond necklace hung between her breasts, and her strapless tulle dress featured a diamond-beaded belt that contrasted with the royal purple color of the garment.

Her smile was breathtaking. "It's time to head to the back door. Some warriors are waiting to escort us. It's eleven forty-five."

The time had arrived.

Panic clawed my insides, and my heart raced. *Are you heading to the terrace?* I hoped he'd forgotten to inform me and was already moving into place.

The damn guard isn't leaving, he replied, his anger slamming through me.

I flinched at the internal assault, but I was more perplexed as to why I hadn't felt his turmoil before now, as if he'd hidden his emotions from me.

We're about to begin, I informed him.

I'm on my way. Nobody will stop me, he replied.

A stabbing pain assaulted my heart. *Thorn, no. The guard will alert everyone, and they'll catch you.*

He didn't respond, and the anger tamped down once more.

Dear goodness. What had he done?

More determined than ever, I forced a smile and lifted my chin, despite my knees weakening. "Okay, give me a second. I'll meet you and Eva in the living room. I need a moment to myself."

Queen Mira placed a hand on my arm. "Of course, my dear. Just don't be too long." She looped her arm through Eva's and led her out the bedroom door.

Eva glanced back at me, her face twisted with worry.

I waited until their footsteps had reached the living room, then took the hairbrush from the counter and butted the end against one corner of the mirror. It took a few solid hits, but a large section splintered off, and a crack zagged across the entire mirror. I didn't have it in me to care.

The largest chunk of glass was about three inches long and two inches wide—big enough to use as a weapon but small enough to fit in my bra. I snatched the hand towel hanging to my left, ripped the material in half, then grabbed the piece of glass, careful not to cut my hands. I wrapped it in the cloth and delicately placed it in my cleavage, low enough that neither the white cloth nor the glass could be seen.

A strangled sensation wafted through the fated-mate bond. Breathing rapidly, I linked, *Are you hurt?*

It felt like forever before he responded.

TIME STOOD STILL as I waited for Thorn to respond. My pulse pounded in my ears, and I prepared myself to go find him.

Damn Drake and everyone else.

I wouldn't allow my mate to be harmed.

I'm fine, he replied, but his dragon hissed. *The warrior swooped down and attacked me. My magic responded...and I took his dragon.*

He was outside, and anyone who passed through could recognize him. *Thorn, don't risk yourself for me. I'll find a way out of here.* I placed my hands on the counter and lifted my head, staring at myself. My fierce determination made me look like a different person.

There's no way in hell I will wait here while you take on the royals and the warriors on your own, he replied. *I'm coming for you, Everly.*

My heart swelled. A nagging part had lost hope that there was a way out of this, but his words made my determination more desperate to prove it wrong.

"Everly," the queen called as the bedroom door opened. "It's time. We really do have to leave."

I jerked upright and tensed. She couldn't come in here and see what I'd done to the mirror. I had to go.

Taking a deep breath, I strolled into the bedroom and met her. I couldn't walk too quickly or let my panic show; otherwise, the warriors might think I was up to something. I needed to act like the broken girl they expected.

"Sorry. I just—" I forced my bottom lip to quiver, and my dragon snarled at how pathetic I looked.

"Oh, darling." Queen Mira mashed her lips together and hurried to me, placing her hands on my shoulders. "I promise, this isn't as bad as it seems. As part of the royal family, you will never want for anything."

I snorted then coughed to hide my laugh. My shoulders shook, so I hunched over, pretending to sob. Her statement was so ironic. I might have all the luxuries of living in a fancy house with servants, but I didn't want that. I wanted Thorn, my freedom, and a life with him where we didn't have to hide. None of that would happen if this marriage with Drake took place.

She kissed my forehead and murmured, "You'll be happy. You'll see. We can spend time together, figuring out ways we can help our people."

Help.

That was the one thing I'd aspired to do in my life and the whole reason I'd finished a premed degree at UHC. Mom had died of cancer, and I didn't want another child to have to experience the loss of a parent to that monstrous disease.

Though that dream might have been squashed, a new one emerged.

I could help the dragons by eliminating the biggest threat to them.

Drake.

"You're right." I lifted my head and smiled sadly. "I *can* help the dragons."

Her irises sparkled as she lowered her arms. "I knew you would be the perfect daughter-in-law."

My throat ached. She was so happy, and I planned on eliminating her child. I liked her, and I hated to do that to her, but Drake should never be in power.

Footsteps pounded down the hallway. Based on the stride, they belonged to Ladon.

"If you don't come out of there now, I'll *force* you out," Ladon threatened as he appeared in the doorway.

Queen Mira arched a brow. "You dare speak to the future queen in such a manner?"

"I serve the king and the prince." Ladon straightened. "If you want kindness, Everly needs to get moving. *Now*."

"We were heading out just as you got here." Queen Mira lifted her chin and stared down her nose. "I'm sure Arman will be intrigued by the way you're talking to us."

Ladon smirked but didn't respond.

Huffing, the queen looped her arm through mine and led me down the hallway. In the living room, I found Eva flanked by Uther and Jessie. She glanced up and exhaled loudly.

I wanted to kick myself. I'd spent too long back there, planning my vengeance.

"It's about damn time," Jessie said as she wrinkled her nose. "Drake was about to come in here."

Oh, I'd bet he was. That would've made the situation more complicated.

Hurt and trepidation coursed through my connection with Thorn.

My heart stopped, and my knees shook. *Thorn, are you hurt?*

"Whoa," Queen Mira murmured and wrapped an arm around my waist, pulling me against her. "Don't lock your knees—you'll pass out."

If only that was my problem.

Thorn replied, *I'm fine. I'm back in the tunnel. Arman finally appeared, and he's guiding us.*

Able to stand again, I smiled and steadied myself. "Thank you, and I'll try to remember that." I then asked him, *Where is he taking you?*

I don't know, Thorn replied, a turmoil of emotions rising like a tsunami. *I'm hoping it's not a trap.*

Ladon marched to the back door and opened it. To the right of the terrace, the servants had built a temporary white wall to prevent the guests and wedding party from seeing me. It was about eight feet high, so not even my guards could be seen, which might help me when I escaped.

I looked to my left...and my heart sank. Twenty warriors were posted at the tree line, but I couldn't bank on that number. Drake knew I was mated to Thorn, which meant I could be relaying numbers and people's positions. There was no telling how many were hiding in the trees, and I couldn't see them since I was in human form and not dragon.

The sun shone as it inched higher over the treetops, and the temperature had to be in the high sixties. The day was gorgeous with fluffy white clouds in the sky.

Queen Mira stood on my right as Eva appeared on my left. The three of us carefully walked forward, and our high heels sank into the grassy ground. I kept my balance, but Eva clutched my arm, nearly falling over.

"Watch it," Jessie snarled at my sister from beside the queen. "If you mess up her dress, Drake won't be happy."

I wanted to punch the warrior in the face. For a human, Eva was handling this well. I would've already fallen on my ass if I hadn't been a shifter.

With her free arm, she lifted her long skirt and focused on her feet. "Sorry. I didn't mean to grab you like that."

"It's fine." I cut my eyes to Jessie, daring her to say something else. "You can hold on to me. I can take it."

"I don't see how you two aren't falling..." Then she huffed. "That's right. You're dragons."

Queen Mira chuckled, the sound like music. "I may be a dragon, but I've had my share of falls. Being a dragon shifter doesn't make you graceful."

My arms itched to hug her. She was down-to-earth and easy to get along with. She looked every inch a queen.

My insides hardened. This had to be an act. She and the king had tried to kill Thorn. How could a kind and generous person do that? Maybe Drake was just like her. Maybe her charismatic personality hid the evil underneath.

But that didn't make sense, either. Why hide it when she was the queen?

The one motivation that explained their actions was that she and the king believed Thorn was dangerous to their people. Yet Drake was out of control and power-hungry, and they accepted him without issue.

There was no point in focusing on that. I could try to rationalize the actions of others all day, like I'd done with my stepdad for the past six years, and never understand their reasons for treating others badly.

As we reached the end of the yard, the white wall curved, ending at the edge of a royal purple carpet where a maid stood, holding a lavish bouquet of dark purple and lavender irises and baby's breath.

My nose wrinkled, but I forced myself to smooth my expression. I'd expected this wedding to be over the top but come *on*. A *carpet* outside?

With each step we took, my heart raced harder. The faint grape-soda-like scent of the flowers filled my nose, and my throat constricted. If Thorn had been waiting for me down the aisle, I'd have raced to the finish line...but he wasn't. Losing everything was all that waited for me.

Please tell me you guys are in position. I hated to pressure him, but I was almost to the aisle. I needed him to get me the hell out of here, pronto.

We're still in the damn tunnel, Thorn answered with a growl. *Arman promised that Drake won't start the wedding without him.*

I snorted, and both the queen and Eva glanced at me.

"Sorry," I whispered. "Just nerves." That wasn't a lie, unfortunately.

I'm about to walk down the aisle. I became lightheaded and had to concentrate on moving my legs forward. I had to remember I had a weapon between my boobs if it came down to that.

Thorn's dragon snarled. *Arman says we're almost there.*

The maid was close to my age, her ash-brown hair pulled into a messy bun. She held out the flowers to me and smiled sweetly. "You look beautiful, my lady."

My head tilted back. I'd never been called that before, and I was certain I never wanted to hear it again. But that wasn't her fault—she was doing what she'd been trained to do.

I took the flowers and said, "Thank you."

She curtsied to the queen and me, then headed back the way we'd come.

"This is where we part ways," Queen Mira murmured and stopped. "Eva and I will walk down the aisle, and when the piano and violin play the bridal march, that'll be your cue."

I didn't want to wish misfortune on anyone, but if the entire symphony got a sudden stomach bug, I'd be a fan. Anything that would get me out of *this.*

"You go first, dear." The queen gestured for Eva to precede her, then smiled as a man my age, who I'd never seen before, appeared.

He wore a black tux with a white shirt and a black tie. When he held out his arm for Eva to take, his lips curled, and his cedar-brown eyes darkened with disgust.

Eva inhaled sharply, and Queen Mira *tsked.* She patted the man's arm. "Come now, Daniel. If you didn't look so threatening, she wouldn't be as uncomfortable."

"Yes, my queen." He bowed his head slightly, and his gelled, mousy-brown hair didn't move an inch. "I'm just disappointed that Drake didn't want a best man."

"You know how Drake is. He doesn't like to share the stage with anyone." The queen's chuckled held an edge. "Now, go on, Eva. He won't bite."

Releasing my arm, Eva inched toward Daniel, trying not to fall on the grass. Once she'd woven her arm through his, the two of them headed down the aisle. Before she disappeared from sight, she glanced back at me, her bottom lip trembling.

She was scared, and I couldn't do a damn thing about it.

"That is Drake's best friend," Queen Mira murmured as they vanished around the corner. "I'm sure you'll be seeing a lot of him, once things calm. He lives on the property to the left of the chateau."

No wonder the guy seemed like a jackass. He was friends with Drake.

All too quickly, Daniel came back and retrieved the queen, leaving me with Jessie, Uther, and Ladon.

Chills ran through me, and they had nothing to do with the slightly cool weather. I had to hang on to the fact that King Arman wasn't there, which meant Drake would have to wait.

Then a piano began to play the beginning of the "Here Comes the Bride" song, and a violin's soothing strokes intertwined with the notes.

My breath caught. This was not supposed to be happening. *Are you here?* I glanced at the sky, expecting to see a dragon. When I didn't, I glanced around the yard for Thorn. But he was nowhere.

We're hurrying, he replied.

"You need to go," Ladon growled from behind me and pushed my shoulder forward.

I had no choice. If I didn't go willingly, they would force me, and I didn't want to risk something terrible happening if Drake saw them dragging me down the aisle.

I gripped the bottom of my bouquet hard and took a step onto the rug. *I need you to move faster. I'm walking down the aisle.*

White-hot rage slammed into me. *That bastard.*

As I pivoted toward the terrace, I saw a hundred guests on their feet, facing me. I almost choked. With such short notice, I'd hoped no one would come.

Each chair was covered in a white cloth with a sizable royal purple ribbon tied around it. At the other end of the carpet stood a man I'd never seen before. Drake was at his side. Irises covered the terrace, and a white sheet hung behind the man and Drake, blocking the house from view.

Drake gestured for me to come to him, and I forced myself to move forward and not away. Every cell in my body screamed at me to run, but that wouldn't solve anything. When I struck, the timing had to be perfect.

As I walked past the seated guests, the hairs on my neck lifted. I'd never given much thought about the attention a bride received on her wedding day, but I felt as if the stares might crush me.

An empty chair sat in the front row next to the aisle, with Queen Mira sitting in the next seat. Eva sat beside the queen, and her eyes glistened as they locked on mine.

The empty chair had to be King Arman's.

I took the last few steps onto the terrace's wood floor and didn't look at Drake. Instead, I focused on the man standing before me.

His bronze skin was the same shade as Saphira's, and his chocolate-brown eyes examined me. Unlike Daniel, his short, dark brown hair ruffled in the wind, giving him a more natural look. He seemed familiar, and after a second, I realized why. This was Saphira's dad.

Drake straightened his shoulders. "Let's begin, Errol."

The older man's brows furrowed. "But the king—"

"Is late," Drake said forcefully. "Let's *begin*."

My breathing quickened, and I tried to control it so Drake wouldn't notice. *He's pushing to begin now.*

We're almost at another door, Thorn said.

Almost didn't cut it. Hell, there was even a song written about it.

Errol spoke, but I couldn't make out the words. It was as if I were underwater, similar to the shock I'd felt the day Thorn had kidnapped me and I'd learned about dragons.

My knees nearly gave out, and I realized fear was controlling me. I lifted my chin and focused on the piece of glass between my breasts.

I'd have to use it.

Drake turned toward me, and I realized I'd lost track of time. I'd been up here way too long—the vows or claiming would be happening soon.

"Everly?" Errol said, and I jerked my gaze to him.

I swallowed hard and cleared my throat, not wanting to sound broken. That would only make Drake feel more powerful. "Yes?"

"It's time to exchange vows. I need you to look at Prince Drake," he said with a sad smile.

He knew something was wrong.

It's time, I connected with Thorn. *Where are you?*

I'm in the chateau, he replied. *Almost there. Delay them however you can.*

Drake gripped my arms and forced me to turn to him. He smiled, but his eyes were devoid of warmth. He was playing the part he wanted the attendees to see. "Hey, I'm right here with you. No need to be nervous."

Then Errol said the words I'd been dreading. The very words I hoped he'd never get to. "Do you, my prince..." He trailed off, giving me the chance to act *now*. If I didn't, everything would be over.

CHAPTER ELEVEN

THE NEXT WORDS came too fast from Errol's mouth. "Do you, my prince, take Everly to be your wedded wife?"

My heart raced as Drake's mouth opened. I dropped the bouquet, ready to attack, just as he said, "I—"

Glass shattered behind the white curtain, and I kneed Drake in the crotch. Eyes bulging, he inhaled sharply and grabbed his junk.

Drake dropped to his knees, and the guests broke out into startled murmurs. Just as Drake opened his mouth again, the white sheet behind Errol ripped away, revealing the chateau and Thorn.

I froze, unable to look away, afraid he was a mirage.

Thorn was gorgeous, determined, and worthy of being painted. He wore his typical jeans, Timberlands, and a black shirt that hugged his body. I could see every curve of muscle, and my mouth puddled. His shaggy dark hair was a little longer, hanging in his sky blue eyes, and his teeth were clenched, emphasizing his strong jaw.

He was here, as promised, to save me.

He raced to Drake and punched him. Then he declared loudly, "As the first-born prince, I do take Everly to be *my wife.*" He turned to me and pulled me into his arms.

My skin jolted, electrified by our fated-mate connection, and I inhaled his scent, minty amber with a faint hint of brimstone, which indicated he was a dragon shifter. I was home, but if we didn't get moving, I wouldn't be for much longer.

I pulled back and searched those around us. Four guards stood on the terrace, their tranq guns aimed at Thorn, and two dragons were flying toward us.

"Uh..." Errol's mouth hung open as more warriors barreled down the aisle.

A broken gasp from Queen Mira had me glancing behind me.

"Thorn?" Her face twisted in agony. "Is that really you?"

He tensed but didn't take his eyes off me.

Drake got back onto his feet, though he stayed hunched over. He snarled, "Kill him *now*. Then I'll take Everly as my wife."

Thorn's roar rattled the ground and the terrace. His pupils elongated. "You will *not* have what is *mine*. She is my *fated mate*."

"What?" the queen whispered, sounding shocked, but now wasn't the time to contend with her emotions.

The tallest warrior in the back aimed his tranq rifle at Thorn just as an arrow shot across the clearing and pierced the warrior's neck. The arrows kept coming as someone launched an attack from above. The four warriors with tranqs were taken down in seconds, and whoever was on our side turned their attention to the rest.

It had to be Vlad. He had trained Thorn.

Leaning toward me, Thorn connected, *Get your sister, and take her inside the chateau. Top floor, the bedroom all the way to the left as you're facing the house now. When you get there, let me know, and I'll come after you.*

My heart thumped. I didn't want to leave him, but he wouldn't budge until I was safe.

Gunfire came from the bedroom as bullets pelted the area below. Guests jumped to their feet, screaming, and raced toward the guest home, moving away from the shots.

Chaos was a good thing.

I pivoted and jumped onto the grass. Eva and Queen Mira were standing by their seats, immobile.

I hurried to Eva, twisting my ankle mid-stride in the damn high heels. What sort of dumbass wore heels on a lawn? Me. I was that dumbass. I bent down and removed them. "Eva, take your shoes off. We have to run."

Thorn snarled, and I glanced over as two airborne dragons swooped down at him. He bared his teeth as the earth-brown dragon extended its claws and the charcoal dragon opened its mouth. My heart lurched into my throat. But as I took one step toward him, the earth-brown dragon swiped at Thorn. Thorn's hands glowed as he dodged the talons and ran to touch its tail just as the dragon lifted back into the sky.

His hand brightened, and the dragon roared louder. Then, with each second, the dragon's roar weakened, and its body shrank. It was as if the dragon were stuck and couldn't fly away. Soon, its scales faded.

My breathing quickened as I watched Thorn's magic at work. I'd never seen anything like this before, but the pure rage on his face told me he wasn't fully in control. The magic was controlling him.

Gunfire blasted from the bedroom upstairs, but not soon enough. The charcoal dragon's talons dug into Thorn's shoulders, and it flapped its wings, lifting him off the ground.

"Thorn!" I tried to scream but choked on the sound.

Thorn released the former earth-brown dragon, and a naked man landed on the terrace. The man, perhaps in his fifties, sobbed, not bothering to get up.

A hand clutched my arm, and I turned to see Daniel.

His jaw dropped as he took in what had happened. "The monster took the warrior's dragon!" he yelled, ensuring everyone could hear him with their supernatural ears, despite the chaos.

I yanked my arm out of his grip and rushed toward Eva, but Daniel grabbed my arm again.

I'm coming, I connected with Thorn. I didn't want him to think I'd abandoned him.

Don't, he replied, the bond between us sizzling. *Get out of here.*

A strangled cry rang over the grass, and I turned to see Thorn's glowing hands on the dragon's legs. The dragon was already shrinking, but blood dripped from my mate's shoulders.

"You're coming with me," Daniel snarled, and he jerked me toward the guest wing.

I wasn't going anywhere with this douche canoe. With my free hand, I clutched the side of my dress to prevent myself from tripping. Then I spun around and kicked Daniel in the stomach with as much force as possible.

He sailed backward and smashed into an aisle chair in the third row. His head hit the back of the chair and smacked onto the ground.

Babe, I need you to go, Thorn connected, his anger and worry flooding me, squeezing my chest like a vise. *More warriors will come, and we need to get out of here. They'll run out of bullets soon. I'm sure Vlad already ran out of arrows.*

We. He was right. *We* needed to leave. I had to focus on that.

"Eva, come on," I commanded and found her with her high heels off. Good girl. She'd listened to me without arguing, for once in her life.

She nodded, ready to move.

I took her hand and glanced at Queen Mira. She stood unmoving, watching Thorn with one hand over her heart and fear etched onto her face, her expression both relieved and scared.

She was a good woman but misguided, and that had unfortunately destroyed my mate's childhood. I paused in front of her and said, "Drake made him do the very thing you and your husband feared. Thorn was in hiding until the son who could do no wrong kidnapped people, including a human he forced here to be his breeder, and tried to force a woman who is mated to another to marry him. Think on *that* next time you think there's any good in Drake."

Having said my piece, I turned to the house. The warriors were closing in now that the panicked guests were mostly out of the way, but the gunfire was still holding them off.

Eva and I hurried to the side of the terrace and up the steps just as a swirling noise swooshed toward us. A sickening impact had me jerking my head around.

First, I saw my mate. He was back down on his feet, hurrying toward me. Then a familiar scream lodged in my ears.

Saphira.

"Everly, please help my father!" she cried.

My chest tightened as my gaze landed on Errol. He was standing where Thorn had been a moment before, a tranq dart lodged in his abdomen. He must have shielded Thorn.

I clenched my hands. I wasn't sure I could carry a dragon a foot taller than me and a hundred and fifty pounds heavier, but Saphira had sacrificed herself for me, so I had to try.

Just go. I'll get him and be right behind you, Thorn connected as he rushed to the older man.

I gritted my teeth until my jaw ached. *Your shoulders.*

I'm fine. I promise, he connected as he bent and threw Errol over one shoulder.

"Errol!" the queen yelped, springing into action.

Things were escalating. As I turned back toward the house, an arm wrapped around my waist and yanked me against a chest.

The leather smell that hurt my head invaded my senses. Of *course,* it'd be Drake.

"Let her go," Eva snapped and stepped toward me.

Drake's chest shook with laughter, and I twisted my head back and saw a sinister smile on his face. He said, "Never. She's mine."

He's going to die, Thorn bellowed from ten feet away and moved toward me despite carrying Errol.

The time had come. I reached inside my bra and removed the glass. The sharp edges cut my hand, but I didn't give a damn. I was going to kill this sick asshole.

I stabbed him in the chest, and vomit rose in my throat. I'd never wanted to kill someone, but Drake's death would solve the majority of our problems.

A metallic stench swirled around me as something warm trickled down my hand.

Blood.

Drake jerked back, and his nostrils flared. "You *bitch!* You're going to pay—"

I punched him in the nose. "I will *never* be yours. I'd rather die than see your face ever again."

Blood gushed from his nose, and his black suit had a wet stain from where I'd stabbed him. Unfortunately, I'd missed his heart, but the wound should slow him down.

Everly, Thorn said.

Right. We had to go. Kicking Drake's ass felt good, but I'd rather get out of here.

"Stop her!" Drake shouted as he pinched his nose.

I grabbed Eva's hand and was dragging her to the door when a tranq came flying at me. Trusting my gut, I stopped in my tracks, yanking Eva behind me just as the dart whizzed past.

They'd expected me to keep moving and had aimed with that in mind.

Thorn opened the back glass door, and Eva and I ran toward it. More tranqs shot at us, and when I was half a foot from running inside, one of them hit Eva in the arm.

She yelped, and I spun, lifted her up like she was a baby, and raced inside the doors. She felt as light as a child. *Heck yeah.*

I was surprised to find no guards inside. How was this possible?

"Leave me here," Eva said slowly, the drugs taking hold.

"Shh." That would never happen.

Gunfire continued to burst out back as we ran through the large living room. The light gray walls reflected the sunlight with slightly darker, luxurious couches centering a large tiled chimney. The same dark cherry wood floors ran throughout this side of the house, including the gigantic curved stairway. With each hurried step we took, the bronze chandelier swung as if it sensed impending doom.

Taking the stairs two steps at a time, we reached the top floor. Thorn turned left, heading to the bedroom he'd indicated earlier. The hallway was long and had the same light gray paint, but large crystal chandeliers hung every ten feet. We passed by a few mammoth, black cherry wood doors, but I didn't have to question where we were heading.

It had to be the door at the end of the hallway, the very one King Arman stood in front of with a lit candle.

His gaze landed on Errol, and he frowned.

Great. He wouldn't allow us to leave with his advisor. What else could go wrong?

He opened the door and waved us in. As soon as Thorn and I entered the room, he shut and locked the door behind us. The candle held a strong scent—French vanilla—and it diluted the smell around us.

This had to be the king and queen's bedroom. It was massive, taking up the entire side of the house. Windows overlooked the back, facing the terrace where Vlad and Saphira stood, shooting guns, and the front of the house, where Cassidy was firing.

Saphira's long, curly, dark brown hair was swept back in a low ponytail, and her mocha-brown eyes squinted as she fired the weapon. Her skin was back to its normal gorgeous bronze color. Vlad stood beside her with a rifle. His wavy, caramel hair was no longer greasy, and his cornflower-blue eyes were locked on the fighters below. His ivory skin looked almost ghostly next to Saphira but was alluring in its own right.

Cassidy's dark gold-brown hair hung in her face, but her hazel-green eyes were focused outside. Her light tan complexion was closest to Thorn's.

They each wore a black shirt and jeans.

None of the guards had been stationed inside the chateau. They hadn't expected a threat to come from inside.

Like the rest of the house, the same wood accents were present, but that was where the similarities ended. A gigantic bed with a gold frame sat against the far wall. A royal purple blanket sat folded on the end of the bed, on top of a white comforter. Above the bed, a circular section of the ceiling was cut out, platter style, and painted a royal purple in the center where a bronze chandelier hung. To the right, a spectacular gold-framed painting took up the entire wall, with two purple chairs that had been pushed against the bed in front of it. On the other side were an enormous black cherry wood desk, a sectional, and a table where a huge sunset puzzle that had only been partially put together.

My heart hammered, and despite my new dragon strength, my sister was getting heavier...enough to make me winded. I'd hoped that my days of forcing myself to exercise were behind me, but even as a dragon shifter, I would have to work out.

King Arman hung his head, then glanced at Thorn, Errol, Eva, me, and back to Thorn. Gesturing to everyone in the room, he said, "I hope you realize how much I'm giving up and betraying by helping you."

My eyes widened. He had to be kidding. *That* was what he'd wanted to say when Thorn would be leaving again and never returning?

"That's worse than trying to have your own son killed and then guilting him when you're trying to set something right for him?" I lifted my chin despite the sweat beading on my face from how damn heavy my sister was. "Please, spare us the theatrics. You wouldn't be in this situation if it wasn't for Drake."

Saphira snorted.

I was so sick and tired of the royals' attitude. They'd tried to kill Thorn, then had given him up, while Drake—the epitome of a douchebag—could do no wrong. Something was messed up in their heads, and I was done tolerating their stupidity.

"Now listen here—" King Arman started, but then a loud groan echoed through the room.

CHAPTER TWELVE

MY HEAD WHIPPED toward Vlad and Saphira, and my ears thundered. Vlad stumbled back with a tranq dart in his arm. He gripped the tranq and tossed it to the floor, swaying on his feet.

He was going to black out at any second.

"You have to *leave* now, before you can't." King Arman rushed to the huge painting and slipped his hand behind the bottom right corner of the gold frame.

Saphira wrapped an arm around Vlad, tossed him over her shoulder, and ran from the window. Tranqs pelted the area where the two of them had been standing seconds ago, and I realized that another round of warriors was in place.

Feet pounded below as the painting and frame slid sideways.

"Go." Arman pointed at the passage he'd revealed. "I've arranged for someone to pick you up at the other end, but it'll be several hours from now, so stay in the tunnel until I can divert the warriors and you can get out unseen. Do *not* fly. They'll be searching for your scents. Go south. My contact will meet you on the main road a few miles beyond the dragon lands."

Cassidy was the first to move. She rushed to the king and lifted a brow. "They won't believe we didn't harm you."

"Fine," he snarled as he placed the candle on the nightstand and broke the window next to the bed so it would appear as if we'd escaped. He came back to stand in front of her. "I deserve it, so do it."

A deep growl emanated from Thorn, and he handed Errol off to Cassidy. "Let me."

Hurt and anger swirled inside me from him, and I wanted to tell him not to strike the king. But if I ever got a chance to knock out my stepdad, I'd do it without hesitation. He'd been awful to me, but not nearly as bad as King Arman had been to his son.

Nodding, Cassidy adjusted Errol in her arms and took off into the hidden passage with Saphira right behind her, carrying Vlad.

More warriors clambered up the stairs.

Air sawed through my lungs, and I moved to the opening and waited for Thorn. I wouldn't leave without him. I'd lay Eva down and close the door before I allowed it to come to that.

"You saw the button I used earlier to open the passage. It'll close it as well." The king lifted his chin. "Do it and *run*."

Something hard slammed into the bedroom door. The guards were almost upon us.

Thorn punched the king in the back of the head, and the king's eyes rolled back as his body lurched to the left...landing right on the bed.

My heart warmed as I entered the passage with Thorn right behind me. He spun around and pressed the button just as the bedroom door cracked, and the secret door slid shut, cutting off the noise.

A stale scent replaced the sweet smell from the bedroom.

Thank goodness the king locked the bedroom door, I connected as some weight fell from my shoulders.

We still need to be quiet in case the guards can hear us, Thorn replied. He turned carefully toward Cassidy and Saphira, who stood a few feet away, and held out his arms to take Errol back from his mother. Saphira then handed Vlad over to Cassidy.

The tunnel was about ten feet wide and twelve feet tall with cobwebs hanging throughout the area. Thorn appeared more massive in the small space.

There was no light, but that wasn't a problem with my dragon eyes. If Eva woke up, she'd be spooked. *Is there a place with more light?* I cradled my sister close to me. My brow creased. She'd been tranqed with the same drugs as Errol and Vlad, and she was a small human.

Yeah, there's light at the other end of this tunnel where we need to wait, he replied and held out his free arm. *Let me take your sister. I can tell how uncomfortable you are.*

Could I hide anything from him anymore? Even when I'd left to give myself up, thinking his parents, Saphira, and Eva would be released, I hadn't managed to hide that I'd sneaked out for long. He'd sensed me and awoken before I'd reached Drake.

I shook my head. *I've got her. You're already carrying Errol. If you're going to take a second person, get Vlad. He's significantly heavier.* If anyone needed a reprieve, it was Cassidy.

I want to help my mate. He frowned, and his disappointment swirled through me.

My cheeks hurt from the huge smile that spread across my lips. *If my sister wakes up, she'll be more comfortable if I'm holding her. Let me be there for her. Please? After all, she was captured because of me. This is the least I can do.* My shoulders slumped. Her life was forever changed because I hadn't done enough to protect her.

His irises darkened. *You do realize she would've been his breeder anyway if you hadn't interfered, and you wouldn't have gotten caught up in this if you hadn't been so selfless. If it's anyone's fault that you two got dragged into this, it's mine. I kidnapped and changed you.*

I exhaled and tried to be logical. He and my siblings were the only three things that hindered my pragmatic side. When I faced any other problem, I could separate my feelings from my actions...but not when it came to them. Never them. *It's the king, queen, and Drake's fault. Your biological parents for being closed-minded assholes, and Drake for being a narcissist who believes he owns the world.*

He brushed his fingers along my cheek, the jolt sizzling between us. I closed my eyes and damn near moaned from his touch. I'd missed him so much that it physically hurt.

Saphira quietly cleared her throat.

My gaze flicked to hers. She arched a brow and nodded in the direction of the tunnel we needed to be heading down.

We better move, I connected, staring into his gorgeous eyes, which reminded me of my favorite shade to use for painting the sky.

The lines around his eyes tightened. *You're right. I can't risk them finding you.* He stepped around me, and I wished that Eva hadn't been a barrier, so I could've felt his muscles brush my breasts as he passed. But we'd have time to reconnect later.

"Let me take Vlad, too," he murmured and reached out his hands.

Cassidy smiled but shook her head.

She wanted to take care of her mate. I could respect that. She was taller than me, so his huge frame didn't overpower her like Thorn's would've done mine.

Saphira took the lead and headed toward the exit. Her pace was slow and methodical, instead of relieved and carefree. We weren't out of the woods yet, literally, or figuratively. Cassidy was between Thorn and Saphira, and I took up the rear.

Being in the back was so worth it. I got to watch Thorn's ass the entire way and admire how his back muscles rippled from carrying Errol. I normally stuck to painting landscapes and faces, but there was a time and a place for exceptions, and the next time I got my hands on brushes, paints, and a canvas, his entire body would be one of them. Although...I would leave out certain delectable places. I didn't want anyone else to ever see them. Those parts were all *mine.*

My body warmed just remembering him naked.

Warmth flooded through our connection as Thorn connected, *Do you like what you see? I can smell your arousal.*

My face flamed. Not because he could smell it but because that meant Cassidy and Saphira could, too. I hadn't even officially met Cassidy, and *this* would be the way I was introduced to her. If we hadn't been in such a dangerous situation, I'd have run away and hidden. *Your mom is going to hate me.*

What? He slowed and glanced over his shoulder.

Shock pulsed through our bond, and my breath caught.

His brows furrowed. *Why would you say that?*

Because I'm ogling her son, and she can smell what he does to me. I closed my eyes for a second. *Why else?*

He grinned and winked. *Oh, she understands. I've smelled many things I'd rather not have been privy to while growing up with those two, and they're fated mates, too.* His nose wrinkled at what I assumed were those memories.

Maybe we could all pretend that no one had smelled anything. I was downwind from them.

"Oh, gods," Saphira groaned. "They're not together ten minutes, and it smells like a brothel."

Then again, maybe not. Though I loved Saphira, I would have no problem killing her at this moment. Too bad I hadn't dislodged the glass from Drake's chest so I could stab *her* with it.

Thorn chuckled, his happiness wafting through the bond. "What I'm more intrigued by is why you know what a brothel smells like. Did you visit, or did you work there?"

"Thorn Wight," Cassidy exclaimed and turned around, careful not to bump Vlad into the wall.

There was no doubt about it—she was his mother. The mom tone was unmistakable, and my heart ached from remembering my own mom.

His shoulders shook. "I'm twenty-seven years old. I can give Saphira hell when she's making my mate feel uncomfortable."

I wanted to bury my face in Thorn's back for many reasons, but mainly so Cassidy couldn't see me. Instead, I lifted my chin, faking that the banter and attention didn't bother me. "I don't know what you're talking about. I'm in the very back. You can't smell anything."

Saphira twisted to look at me. She placed a hand on her hip and arched a brow. "You wanna bet? I wouldn't be surprised if the warriors tracked us down. That's how strong it is."

I narrowed my eyes just as a deep moan echoed in the tunnel.

"Please, for the love of the gods, stop talking about my son and his mate," Vlad grumbled as he rubbed a hand over his forehead. "My head hurts, and there are things better left unsaid."

I could get behind that sentiment. We should drop it and not address the elephant in the secret passageway...or the dragon that ate the elephant...or whatever.

We all paused, and Cassidy squatted as Vlad stood and leaned against the side of the tunnel, blocking Saphira from view. I had to wonder if he'd done that on purpose, but some tension left my shoulders.

"At least, the king came through for us." He yawned and stretched his shoulders.

I glanced at Eva, then at Errol hanging over Thorn's shoulder. I bit my lip. "How come you woke up before Errol?" I understood why Eva remained unconscious. She was human and had a slower metabolism, but Errol had been shot first.

"I removed the dart before all the liquid leaked out." He pointed at Errol and my sister. "If those two still have the dart lodged in them, we need to remove them. The darts have a slow-release mechanism to keep people asleep longer."

That would've been nice to know a while ago. I kneeled and dropped Eva's legs to pull the dart from her arm. I was already worried about the dose she'd gotten, but to know more had been trickling in made me panic. I hadn't thought about pulling it out while we'd been running for our lives.

"How did I not know that?" Thorn grumbled. Using his free arm, he felt Errol's side and yanked out the dart.

Vlad shook his head. "I learned about the upgrade when we were kidnapped."

My heart sank. All of us had suffered so much.

"Do you think she'll be okay?" I couldn't hide the worry in my voice. "She's human."

"Yeah, it'll knock her out longer." Vlad stood, though his legs wobbled under him. He glanced up and down the tunnel. "How much longer until we reach the exit?"

Saphira was back in view, and she pushed a stray curl from her face. "We're halfway."

"Let's keep pushing." Vlad smacked his cheeks to wake himself up. "We need to listen so we know when we can risk leaving."

The king had said he would handle the warriors, but if Drake had his way, he would go behind his dad's back and force them to keep watch in large numbers. We could hope, but there was no guarantee we would make it out of here tonight. I only hoped that whoever was coming for us wouldn't give up.

I kept hold of the dart, careful not to stab myself with it. I wanted to get an idea of how the contraption worked and what sort of anesthetic they'd used to subdue us.

The time for lightheartedness was gone, and even though our moment of levity had been at my expense, it had given us a reprieve from the tension. Vlad was right. We needed to get into position so we could meet our next contact.

The five of us walked, though a little slower since Vlad was still impacted by the drugs. I focused on Eva's breathing and heartbeat, ensuring it didn't slow enough to cause alarm.

Something skittered past my feet, startling me. *Rats.* My skin crawled. They were gross disease carriers, especially the ones that lived underground.

Light shone at the end of the tunnel, but there was no obvious exit, just a dead end.

A lump formed in my throat until I noticed the light was coming from above.

How odd.

The closer we got, the clearer the exit became. It was over the tunnel. When we reached the end, I looked up and saw tiny holes that allowed us to see outside.

Something caused the light to vanish, and a scream lodged in my throat.

Thorn turned and placed a hand on my arm. He connected, *It's a guard walking past the rocky edge. They blocked the sun. No one has found us.*

Forcing myself to breathe steadily, I tried to focus. His touch grounded me, and I turned and rested my head on his arm. I needed his touch after being separated for so long.

He wrapped his free arm around me, and the jolt thrummed between us as the five of us who were awake stood in silence.

When there was no noise from outside, Vlad's jaw twitched. He exhaled and glanced at the two people still passed out in our arms. "I know this isn't ideal, but we need to get out of here after the next round of warriors passes."

My brows furrowed. "But the king said we should wait." We couldn't risk getting caught again. Darkness would give us more coverage.

Concern wafted from Thorn as he and his dad locked gazes.

He was keeping something from me.

I swallowed hard and narrowed my eyes. "What aren't you telling me?"

Thorn hung his head while Vlad crossed his arms. Vlad said, "If you don't tell her, I will. Waiting will only cause us to have to fight the warriors again."

"Just tell me," I gritted out.

Saphira rolled her eyes. "I'll do it."

She turned her attention to me...and winced.

CHAPTER THIRTEEN

THE ONLY THINGS that kept me grounded were Thorn's arm around me and holding Eva to my chest. I was about to scream at them to tell me, but if I was too loud, a warrior might overhear me.

"Drake will take matters into his own hands and use every possible resource against us." Saphira bit her bottom lip.

Nausea churned within. "Elliott and Peter." Drake would target my brother—Eva's twin—and my stepdad. Though I didn't truly care about Peter, my siblings did. He was their last remaining parent, and I would do anything to ensure they didn't lose him.

I sagged against Thorn, wanting to punch something. I hadn't thought of that, which infuriated me, but I knew Drake would never stop looking for someone to use against us. People like Drake couldn't let anything go. He would always hunt us.

Babe, I'm so sorry, Thorn connected, and his face twisted. *I wish—*

It's not your fault. We wouldn't have this conversation again. *We'll find a way out of this.* I should've killed Drake when I'd had the chance, but I'd missed his heart. Part of me was relieved that I had—I didn't want to kill *anybody*—but if I'd succeeded, we might not be in such a dire situation.

My blood cooled, and I arched a brow at Saphira. "You do realize that also goes for Brenton and Tyson, right? You're officially lumped in with us if they realize you helped attack the warriors back there."

Saphira hung her head as if she hadn't thought of that.

Cassidy growled softly. "I wish our thunder link worked the same as a wolf pack. Saphira could find out what's going on with the search and what their plans are."

I blinked, trying to understand. "How would she know that?"

"Wolves can communicate with everyone in their pack." Vlad tapped his forehead. "Just like you can with Thorn but with everyone. If our bonds worked the same as a wolf bond, and since you're part of our thunder now, the four of us could mindspeak to one another."

That would have been handy, especially with the whole wedding debacle.

"Ugh," Errol moaned, and his foot jerked.

Saphira exhaled, and her shoulders relaxed. "Dad?" she whispered and squeezed between Cassidy and Vlad.

Releasing me, Thorn kneeled and gently set Errol on the ground, propping him against the wall.

Be careful. There are rats, I connected with him. *Do you think that's smart?*

They're more afraid of us than we are of them. Thorn looked at me with a smile, then studied my face. *Or...maybe not?*

I hugged Eva closer and squinted. *Do you know how many diseases they carry? Hundreds. And several of them are deadly.*

Remember, we're dragon shifters, not humans. We don't get sick, but don't put Eva on the ground, he replied and stood. *That's a different story.*

I grimaced. There was no way I'd risk my sister like that.

The sound of flapping wings had me holding my breath. I understood that warriors were searching for us, and I feared we would give ourselves away if we weren't careful. I exhaled slowly then inhaled deeply to calm my racing heart.

Errol's eyes fluttered open, and he glanced around the tunnel. "Where are we?"

"In a secret passageway," Saphira answered as she squatted in front of him. "We're waiting for the warriors to pass so we can get away."

He locked his attention on her and leaned his head back against the cement. He whispered, "Saphy, thank gods you're here."

"I'm sorry you got involved in this." Her eyes glistened as she touched his arm. "I had hoped it wouldn't come to this, but with what Drake has been doing, I couldn't stand back and pretend not to notice."

"None of us can any longer," he said as he patted her arm. "I was supposed to go with you all, anyway. The king pulled me aside last night and informed me of his plans."

His heartbeat remained slow, but it could have been calm due to the drug still coursing through his blood, so I couldn't tell if he was lying.

I hated to be *that* person, but we couldn't blindly trust anyone... not after Saphira's uncle, Brenton, betrayed us. "You officiated the wedding. You almost married me to that asshole."

Rubbing his forehead, he sighed. "I know. I'm sorry. The king and I didn't expect him to start the wedding without Arman in attendance. It was unprecedented. Then again, we assumed he had a sense of honor for our traditions. Clearly, that is not the case."

Errol had pointed out that King Arman wasn't there, and Drake had pushed him to start, putting him in a dangerous position.

He frowned, his irises darkening. "At least, you married the right person."

My head jerked back, and my heart ached. "Wait. That counted?"

Hurt wafted through our bond, Thorn's feelings adding to my

shock. Indigestion burned, but it wasn't from the coffee this morning; it was from the guilt over how I'd made Thorn feel.

"Yes. He is a prince—even though people thought he was dead. That was why I worded the question the way I did...so that any prince could speak up." Errol exhaled and sat upright. "I hoped Thorn would do what he did."

I'm sorry if you didn't— Thorn started.

No, I want to be married to you, I interjected. I couldn't fathom hearing the words I knew he was going to say. *I was just hoping it wouldn't be at a wedding someone else planned, and I wanted both of us to be able to say an 'I do.' Not only that but to also commit to each other among the people we wanted as guests, not random strangers watching in the hopes of getting on the good side of King Arman and Drake.*

He sighed and pushed a piece of hair behind my ear. He connected, *I didn't think of it like that. Just that I couldn't let Drake have you.*

Our buzz zinged, and I closed my eyes, treasuring the moment. It had been far too long since we'd been together, and my dragon was growing restless. She wanted to connect with him, but here and now was *not* appropriate. *I know. You have nothing to feel bad about.*

Footsteps pounded above us, and dirt sifted through the holes and landed in Vlad's and Cassidy's hair.

Vlad placed a finger to his lips, and all of us went quiet.

I could only hope Eva stayed silent in her sleep.

Instead of focusing on the noise above, I listened to her heartbeat and breathing. Neither had slowed more, but I wished she would wake up soon. She was getting heavy.

Let me have her, Thorn connected as he gently took my sister from me and cradled her in his arms the way I had. *She's my sister, too.*

My heart warmed, and I stared into his eyes. I thought him touching my sister might bother me, but it didn't. There was no doubt he was all mine, and he was helping her to take care of me. *I love you.*

His eyes twinkled, stealing my breath, and my heart skipped a beat. *I love you, too.*

Every time warriors passed by, the light was blocked for a few seconds. Their footsteps were strong and steady, and more dragons flew overhead. There were a few minutes between the warriors, and as soon as the next group ran past, we would have to make our move.

We had to get to Elliott and Peter before Drake did, or we'd be right back in the situation I'd just escaped. And next time, Drake wouldn't wait to get what he wanted. He'd kill Thorn, marry me, and make Eva his breeder.

Eva turned her head, and I held my breath. Of course, *now* she'd stir. Hopefully, it was just from being jostled.

When we move, I need you to promise that you'll keep going, no matter what, Thorn connected, his determination flaring through our bond.

I placed my hands on my hips as my blood heated. *What the hell does that mean? I'm staying beside you the entire time.* I was done splitting up. The past several days had been horrible, and I refused to go through that again. *Just because I did something stupid doesn't mean it's your turn.*

He pressed his lips into a line, but his shoulders shook gently. *I meant if I need to handle one of the dragons.*

With my sister in your arms? I scowled, allowing myself to get annoyed with his quiet laughter. At least, he was wise enough to attempt to hide it.

Fair point. I may have to hand her off to Vlad. Carefully, so that my sister wasn't bothered, he leaned over and kissed my forehead. *We all have to get to safety, me, included. If Drake captures me, he'll use me against you, and that is something I will never allow.*

My lungs worked a little easier. He wasn't planning to sacrifice himself.

The footsteps above quieted, and Vlad moved to the right side of the hole. He placed his feet into the small cement slots I hadn't noticed and climbed up. He touched the top of the covering and paused, looking down at us. "Is everyone ready?"

We glanced at one another.

Cassidy bit her bottom lip. "Errol, can you climb and run, or do you need more time to let the drugs wear off?"

"I'll be fine." Errol stood and placed his feet shoulder-width apart, then lifted his hands, stretching side to side.

That was one of my favorite moves in yoga.

"Wait." Saphira clenched her hands. "What about Brenton and Tyson? I know Brenton betrayed us, but not Tyson."

"Don't worry about them," Errol said as he gestured for Vlad to open the lid. "We've handled it."

My brows furrowed, but Vlad opened the lid before we could ask more questions.

He stepped out, and Cassidy hurried up and climbed out behind him. Once Saphira and Errol were out, I scurried up the small makeshift ladder. The cement was jagged, likely from not being used much, and my bare feet ached as I climbed.

Thank goodness I hadn't worn my high heels, or there was no way I would've made it.

At the top, I placed my feet on the mulchy ground. I turned to help Thorn out, but he was already gracefully climbing up the awkward cutouts, carrying my sister.

It was a good thing he'd taken her from me. I wasn't sure I could've done that.

Vlad shut the lid, the top looking just like a rock on a slight incline. I never would've guessed it wasn't natural.

Out of the corner of my eye, I noticed movement.

Warriors.

They were heading this way. More must have joined the search. We'd wasted too much time, and now we were vulnerable.

Cassidy murmured, "Come on." Grabbing Saphira, they took off running.

Pointing at me and Thorn, Vlad indicated for us to head out.

I pivoted to run but stilled when I noticed Thorn not budging.

"Errol and I are still impacted by the tranq. We'll slow you down if we take the lead," Vlad rasped. "Go, before we lose Saphira and Cass. You have the human girl."

Thorn growled but took off, running at a pace I could keep up with. Vlad and Errol hurried behind us, and we dodged and wove through the trees.

As I ran, my dress caught on twigs and branches, slowing me down. The warriors hadn't noticed us, but they'd pick up our scents once they reached the spot where we'd come above ground.

The constant breeze would help. I could only hope we would be far enough away before anyone caught our scents. *How far is it to the dragon territory border?*

Four miles, Thorn replied. *If we keep up this pace, we should be out of this area in thirty minutes.*

Thirty minutes. My legs were already stinging from scratches, and we'd gone maybe a quarter of a mile. With each passing minute, I hated this dress more and more.

Saphira and Cassidy slowed down, and we soon caught up with them. The six of us ran in rhythm, and I kept my eyes locked in front of me to make sure I didn't get injured more and wind up not being able to run on my own. We were already carrying one too many people, but Eva wouldn't have been able to run as fast as the rest of us.

A few squirrels and a skunk scurried away, and I tensed every time. I kept expecting someone to jump out from behind a tree and tranq one of us. *Where are all the warriors?*

Probably still close to the chateau, but they'll spread out soon since they haven't found us, Thorn answered. *They didn't expect us to get very far, or we would've already been spotted. King Arman didn't lie when he said no one knew about the secret passage.*

At least, there was that.

Errol grunted from behind. "Tell Cassidy to go slightly right, so we'll run into the road."

"Absolutely not," Vlad snapped. "That's taking us toward the houses."

"That's where Arman left a vehicle for us," he huffed, out of breath. "If we go down first and then right, it'll take more time."

Vlad sighed but didn't respond.

Cassidy veered right, pushing Saphira that way, confirming Vlad had relayed the message, after all.

We picked up the pace, and if someone had asked, I would've said we'd been running for hours. My feet were raw from the rocks and twigs I jogged over. Soon, a road appeared, and I spotted a black SUV.

Saphira stopped. "You've got to be kidding me. He'll take us straight back to Drake."

My attention landed on Brenton, and my blood froze. She was right. We couldn't trust him.

As I opened my mouth to agree, the sound of flapping wings caught my attention. I spun around to find three dragons flying toward us, their eyes locked on me.

Just when I'd hoped we might get away, we now had *two* problems.

Thorn handed me Eva and turned toward the dragons. He raised his hands, making his intentions clear, while Vlad removed a pistol from around his ankle. The two of them stood side by side, ready to fight.

I spun around to find Cassidy with a gun, rushing toward Vlad and Thorn, while Saphira marched directly to her uncle, her hands clenched at her sides.

"Saphira," Errol rasped as he rushed forward, intending to be involved in whatever was going on with his brother.

My chest constricted. I didn't know what to do: help my mate or get into the car so I could hide my sister from the battle.

The dragons roared louder as they reached us.

There was only one thing I could do.

CHAPTER FOURTEEN

TRUSTING MY GUT, I forced my legs forward. My dragon roared as my chest clenched since I wasn't standing beside my mate, fighting, but I had to get my sister to safety first.

My lungs burned. I thought to my dragon, *I'm coming back to him. But what do you think will happen if I try to help and become an easy target because I'm holding my sister? The dragons know we're mates. They'll use me against him. I'm protecting him better this way.*

Some rage ebbed, so I continued toward the SUV. *I'm not happy about this, either.*

Just like when I'd handed myself over to Drake, my dragon begrudgingly relented. She was all about protecting Thorn too, but her instinct was more animalistic. She wanted to fight everyone that threatened him.

I connected with Thorn, *I'll be right back. I'm just going to put my sister in whatever getaway vehicle King Arman arranged for us.*

Stay safe, Thorn replied. *The three of us can handle them, and I can focus better if you're not in danger, especially after being apart for so long.*

My heart panged. He hadn't meant to hurt me, but we'd been

apart because I'd been foolish enough to trust Drake. Granted, I wasn't sure what would've happened if I hadn't snuck away. For all I knew, things could have been worse, but they might have been better.

At least I'd learned we couldn't trust Drake, even when it came to dragon law. He'd confirmed that he thought himself above it, by word and deed, and he'd intended to keep or kill all five of us despite what he'd promised.

Saphira reached Brenton and shoved him in the chest.

His emerald eyes widened as he stumbled back, and the sun reflected off his dark brown complected head. He straightened, rubbing his hand through his black goatee. "Clearly, you haven't been informed who the getaway driver is."

She laughed bitterly as her irises darkened. "Like I'd ever trust *you* again."

"Saphy, he's telling the truth," Errol murmured. "The king asked him to wait for us here. In the tunnels, you even mentioned needing to protect him and Tyson, and this is why I said not to worry about it."

The sounds of dragons roaring and swooping filled the air, adding to the tension. I didn't care that Brenton had betrayed us, because Thorn could take his dragon if he led us back into danger.

"I didn't mean to betray you that night." Brenton tensed. "I was followed, and I only became aware of it a few minutes before you three showed up. You arrived just as they got into position. I had no way to tell you."

I reached the SUV, a black Nissan Pathfinder. Someone was in the passenger seat, but the windows were dark enough that I couldn't make out their face. "Who's in the car?"

"What?" Saphira gasped and rushed to the driver's side window. "You brought Tyson into this?"

"Like I said"—Brenton's nostrils flared—"we're going with you. We aren't coming back."

I'd have been more worried if Tyson hadn't been in the vehicle. That would mean Brenton did plan to come back. "If we take their phones, any electronics, and switch cars at the first opportunity, we can ensure they don't contact Drake." I nodded to the empty road. "Unless you can make another car appear out of thin air?"

Saphira fisted her hands as Errol placed a hand on his daughter's shoulder. "Brenton is telling the truth. Drake overheard my conversation with him and was suspicious. He assigned guards to watch him, and I couldn't warn him because Drake forced me to stay with him."

Her face was lined with worry, but I didn't have time to stand here while their drama unfolded. I adjusted Eva in my arms and opened the back driver's side door. I gently placed Eva in the seat and spun back around in time to see Cassidy fire the first shot.

The navy dragon that had been attacking her flew back, but I didn't see the bullet pierce its skin. There was no blood or injury, as if the bullet had bounced off its scales, making it flinch back.

Thorn's hands glowed as he held a hunter-green dragon's lower jaw, forcing its head up. The dragon's mouth was open, trying to bite Thorn, but its body was shrinking.

Our bond sizzled like before when he'd taken the dragons of the warriors at the wedding. It was different from our fated-mate jolt, and I guessed I was sensing his magic.

To my mate's left, Vlad held both a gun and a knife. He slashed at the talons of the lemon-yellow dragon trying to lift him.

Though things appeared under control, that could change in a moment. "Saphira, please keep an eye on my sister." I took off running toward my mate and his parents.

"Yeah, sure," Saphira deadpanned. "Not that you gave me a choice."

Under normal circumstances, I'd have grinned, but not when my mate was being attacked.

I had to get to him.

Thorn's attacker's scales were vanishing, and the dragon was human size again. Blonde hair appeared, as well as a human female's face. She was naked. He wasn't doing anything wrong, but my dragon didn't care, and a deep growl rumbled in my chest.

The female warrior dropped, her head smashing into the ground. Her eyes rolled back as she passed out on impact.

The navy dragon swooped down, and Cassidy turned, aiming her gun, but when she pulled the trigger, it didn't fire.

It was jammed.

The navy dragon's gigantic mouth opened to bite her, but Thorn spun around and punched the dragon in the eye, seconds before it could lock down on Cassidy's arm.

Head jerking back, the dragon snarled, its teeth grazing Cassidy's upper arm. Blood oozed from the scratches.

Now that Thorn was helping her, I'd help Vlad.

Turning my attention back to him, I watched as the lemon dragon circled the clearing and barreled back toward Vlad. Vlad raised the knife in his hand, not the gun, and I wanted to scream at him to shoot the dragon. When Cassidy had, it had slowed the dragon down for a minute.

The lemon dragon had all four sets of talons extended. Smoke trickled out of its nose as it homed in on Vlad. He crouched, and I realized the dragon's strategy would work.

When I was less than ten feet from Vlad's back, the lemon dragon struck him as the swirl of Thorn's magic surged through our connection—Thorn was taking the navy dragon's dragon.

Vlad swiped at the lemon dragon's front talons as the back ones dug into his sides. The dragon flapped its wings, lifting Vlad off the ground.

Vlad groaned and dropped his weapons. The knife fell at my feet, missing my big toe by a foot, and the gun fell farther away from me.

I bent, swiped up the closest weapon—the knife—and jumped, barely catching Vlad's feet.

Warm liquid hit my face as Vlad grunted from carrying my weight. I hated to make his injury worse, but I didn't know what else to do. I didn't feel comfortable shooting a gun and didn't want to risk hitting Vlad accidentally. The knife had seemed like the smartest choice. Now I was having second thoughts.

"I'm sorry," I said and tried to climb Vlad's body.

My dress flapped in the breeze, tangling around my legs, and I couldn't use my hands to climb him because of the damn knife. Every second, we lifted higher, my dress tangling around me even more.

Instead of helping, I was making matters worse, and we were about ten feet off the ground.

Everly! Thorn connected below, the cold tendrils of his fear gripping me. *What are you doing?*

Trying to save Vlad, I replied as the wind hit my face, splattering Vlad's blood all over me. *But it's not going so well.*

I see that, Thorn growled. "Cassidy, get to the car."

I had no idea what was going on down there. Vlad gritted his teeth as he leaned down, face twisted in agony, and extended a hand to me. I turned the knife so the blade rested in my palm and gripped the handle so I could hand it to him without stabbing him.

The lemon dragon roared and rocked forward, heading toward the ground. My body lurched as our momentum changed, giving me enough of a boost to use my arms. I got the butt of the knife into Vlad's hand.

The sound of additional wings weighed my limbs. *Thorn!*

It's just me, Thorn replied as his plum scales came into view. His front talons gently grabbed my sides as the lemon dragon jerked and shrieked.

Thorn's talon's dug into my side a little as he connected, *Release Vlad. I've got you.*

Sides protesting, I obeyed, trusting my mate. Thorn lifted me to one shoulder, where I grabbed onto his scales and hoisted myself onto his back. My skin buzzed from our touch despite us being in two different forms.

The lemon dragon flew upward to get away.

Thorn flapped his wings, soaring toward the dragon as Vlad shoved the knife into one of the talons that held him. The dragon shrieked and threw its head back in agony. The talons retracted from Vlad's side, and blood poured from the wound. I wouldn't have known he was injured if I'd been watching him, because Vlad didn't pause as he sliced into the other talon.

The dragon dropped him just as Thorn swooped below, catching Vlad in his talons. The lemon dragon soared away. Backup would be here soon.

I didn't even think about shifting. I should've shifted at the first sign of an attack, but I'd dumbly stayed in human form.

We were all trying to stay in human form so we could use our weapons and get to the vehicle quickly, and it was going fine, until it wasn't. Are you hurt? he asked, flying toward the waiting vehicle.

I smiled tenderly, and my chest expanded so much it hurt. *I'm fine.* Just a little banged up but better off than Vlad and Thorn.

He landed softly and placed Vlad on his feet. Cassidy stood by the car and helped Vlad get into the vehicle as I climbed down Thorn's back and glanced behind.

The two warriors whose dragons Thorn had taken were out cold. The man had landed awkwardly on his knees, making him appear to be in the child's pose with his naked butt facing us. Unfortunately, I learned a very uncomfortable fact about this stranger—he had a caterpillar butt crack. It was so damn hairy.

"Everly!" Saphira shouted from the SUV.

Thankfully, that yanked my gaze away from the sight I'd never be able to unsee. *That* vision was one I would never put on a canvas.

Cloth hit my face, and I grabbed a pair of large jeans and a shirt.

"I understand he's not bad looking, but the last thing I want is him butt-naked in the car with us, rubbing all over you after being separated for so long." She jumped back in the car and climbed into the backseat.

Thank goodness for this. I didn't want anyone seeing Thorn naked for longer than necessary.

I turned to find him already back in his gorgeous muscular human form, and I drank in the sight, even as I tossed him the clothes. He grabbed them and quickly dressed, connecting, *Get into the vehicle. I'm going to grab my phone real quick.*

As I stuck my head in the door, I noticed Brenton was already behind the wheel and Errol was in the front passenger seat. Eva was propped against the passenger side window with Saphira in the middle next to her and a teenage boy, who had to be Tyson, was in the seat on the other end. Luckily, the middle row was also a three-seater, but four of us needed a spot.

I bit my lip. I could sit on the floorboards once the others got settled.

Cassidy slid in first and scooted across to the spot behind Errol. Vlad settled into the middle seat. Strong arms wrapped around me as Thorn picked me up like a princess and arranged me on his lap in the final seat. He slammed the door, and Brenton peeled away without missing a beat.

Thorn tightened his arms around me, and I breathed in his scent as the jolt surged between us. The car swerved as Brenton desperately drove away, but as usual, Thorn protected me from any discomfort.

"We've got to get to Everly's family home quickly. Drake will send people there as soon as that yellow dragon tells him we got away," Thorn said, his chest vibrating against mine.

I purred before I realized what I was doing. Being somewhat safe in his arms was the most comforting thing I'd felt in forever.

He tilted my face toward his and kissed me. The jolt between us sizzled, and my breathing caught as my body flamed. Kissing him was like a drink of water after being stuck in the desert. My dragon roared with his as his tongue brushed my lips.

"You weren't kidding, Saph," Tyson said from behind us. "Not even a minute in the car, and they're making out, while she sounds like a cat."

And that was enough to remind me we had an audience, two of whom were Thorn's parents, so I pulled myself away.

"Do I ever exaggerate?" Saphira quipped.

Errol chuckled. "Don't answer that, anyone. It's a trap."

Face burning, I looked behind me and took in Tyson. His skin was a shade darker than Saphira's, and his eyes were a warm olive. His midnight black hair was cut short, and he was smaller than Thorn and Vlad, but still muscular. His attention was on his cousin, his face filled with adoration.

Saphira had mentioned they were close, and the way he looked at her confirmed it.

Though they were trying to lighten the mood, I couldn't joke around, not until Elliott and Peter were with us and Eva was awake.

We hit a bump, and Vlad grunted, grimacing in pain.

"Babe..." Cassidy said with concern.

"I'm fine." Vlad forced a smile. "Just a little beat up. After a good night's rest, I'll be better."

No one responded, the lighthearted atmosphere gone.

Once Brenton had the address, the vehicle descended into silence, and I laid my head against Thorn's chest, listening to the one noise that trumped the sound of a paintbrush on canvas—his heartbeat.

WE PULLED up in front of the two-story robin-egg-blue house. My skin crawled. There were no strange vehicles in sight, and Drake wouldn't risk flying here in dragon form, especially during the day. But there was no telling how far behind us he was or how Peter would react.

The only good thing was that my white Audi A4 was still in the driveway, in the cutout section to the left of the white garage.

Thorn opened the door and helped me out. "Just Everly and I will go in. That way, there will be fewer people to get situated if someone arrives."

No one questioned him; the leader he was meant to be shone through, but I paused. "What about Eva?"

"She'll recognize me. It's fine." Saphira nodded and gestured to the door. "We don't have time to wait."

I swallowed. *Why don't they go on? It's not like we can fit Elliott and Peter in the car with us. We'll take my Audi.* I hated to do that, but if Drake showed up, I didn't want all of us to get caught.

I'll tell them. Go on inside and get them ready.

I turned and rushed to the door, bending to retrieve the key under the mat. I slipped it into the lock and opened the door, then jerked back, surprised at what I found.

Peter was pacing behind the black leather sofa, and Elliott sat on the couch in his normal spot. They turned their heads toward me as Peter scowled. His chestnut-brown eyes hardened, and his light brown hair was messy on top like he'd been running his hands through it, the gray on the sides adding to the troubled look. His brown suit jacket was thrown over the back of the couch.

He took a hurried step toward me, stabbing his finger at me. "Drake just called. He told me you'd be coming here. What the hell have you done?"

"Dad," Elliott murmured. He looked identical to Eva; the only differences were that he was taller, and his hair was significantly shorter. "He's not a good dude. He took Eva in the middle of the night."

"Because *she*"—he shook his finger again—"didn't follow through."

My submissive side wanted to placate him, but my dragon roared. We didn't have time to waste. I lifted my chin. "Grab a few things, and let's go. We have to get away before Drake gets here."

Elliott jumped to his feet, but Peter lifted a hand and said, "We aren't going anywhere. We're going to hand you back to him and get Eva back."

My body jolted as Thorn entered the house and stepped up beside me. He growled, "The hell you will."

UNABLE TO STOP MYSELF, I leaned on my mate. For the past six years, I'd had no one on my side when it came to dealing with my stepdad and siblings, but not anymore. My throat thickened as my love for Thorn overwhelmed me.

Peter's nose wrinkled. "Who the *hell* are you?"

Slipping his arm around my waist, Thorn lifted his chin. "Her husband."

Even though the wedding hadn't been a joyous occasion, I *really* liked hearing him say that word. It wasn't as if he could throw the word *mate* around yet. Unfortunately, Elliott and Peter would be learning about the dragon world, soon enough.

"What?" Elliott gaped. His eyes were so wide I feared they might pop out of their sockets. His attention settled on me. "Is that true?"

I beamed, unable to keep a neutral expression. "It is." I leaned my head against Thorn's shoulder.

Peter took a menacing step forward. "You'll have to annul it so we can get Eva back from Drake. You said you would take her place. Then you run off and *marry* him? I knew you were a piece of—"

"You better stop right there," Thorn warned as he released me and marched over to Peter. He grabbed Peter by the collar of his button-down shirt and lifted him. "One insult thrown her way, and your life will be a lot worse than anything Drake can do to you. Do you *understand?*"

Sniffing, Peter blanched. "Yes."

"Good," Thorn snarled and dropped him. "We've got to leave *now*."

I glanced out the door, expecting Drake to be here, but found Brenton pulling out of the driveway and heading toward downtown. At least, that group would be out of harm's way. We needed to be right behind them.

"Uh..." Elliott raced to the television and unplugged the gaming system.

Out of *all* the items he could focus on bringing, it would be that. I almost told him to forget it, but Eva could use a sense of normalcy and comfort. Playing games with her twin would give her some semblance of being back home.

"I should get stuff from my bedroom." Peter headed toward me to climb up the stairs, which were in front of the door.

We can't let either of them out of our sight, Thorn connected as he followed Peter. *And we need to go. Warriors will be here any second.*

I stepped in front of Peter, blocking the stairs. "We have spare clothes. You two will be fine." I connected, *Can you come here? He'll try to go upstairs as soon as I move to get my keys.*

Peter's hands clenched. "Get out of my way, Everly. This is *my* house, and I'll do as I want."

"Can't you trust me?" Every time we got near each other, he treated me as if he resented my presence. It wasn't enough to prevent me from coming around, though, since the twins were my half-siblings. He did seem to care about them, but ever since Mom had gotten sick, he'd channeled his malice toward me. Whenever I'd visit to keep my promise to Mom about taking care of my siblings, I'd avoid my stepdad as much as possible. Inevitably, he'd treat me like I was scum he merely tolerated. "We're trying to keep Eva safe."

He snorted. "You're trying to keep her safe? Then where the hell were you when Drake came for her? You left to protect her, yet she was taken anyway. You're selfish, even if you pretend you aren't."

His words stung because they were true. I had failed my mom and Eva, but not on purpose. But I sure as hell wouldn't fail them again.

Our connection grew uncomfortably hot from Thorn's rage. Hands fisted, he marched over to Peter and growled, "Clearly, you didn't understand, and I will not tolerate your disrespect."

"You listen—" Peter started and spun back toward the living room in time for Thorn to punch him in the side of the head.

Peter hit the back of his head on the stair rail and dropped, crumpling onto his side. Elliott yelped.

I blinked, trying to comprehend what had happened. Then a deep, hearty laugh shook my shoulders. "That's one way to shut him up."

No one talks to my wife and mate that way. Thorn's eyes softened. *You deserve the world, and I intend to give it to you and beat anyone who hurts you or stands in your way. That asshole was doing both. He's lucky that's the worst he got.*

Though Thorn and I had met under less-than-ideal circumstances, I wouldn't change it for the world. It had gotten us *here*, and if I died today, it would be while knowing what it felt like to be truly loved and accepted and what loving someone unconditionally felt like. Many people didn't get to experience that in an entire lifetime. *I love you.* Even those words didn't seem momentous enough for how strong my emotions for him were.

And I love you. He smiled. *We'll have to continue this discussion when we get back to the cabin.*

I winced. Here I was, standing around like a lovesick schoolgirl, when our enemy would be beating down the door at any second.

Enemy.

Wow.

If someone told me a month ago that I'd be in the middle of a supernatural drama, I would've taken them to seek help.

"I'm ready." Elliott lifted the gaming system and controllers. "As long as I've got these, I'll survive. Just don't punch me like dad."

The sad thing was, he meant it. "Don't run your mouth like him, and we won't have a problem. Besides, we'll ensure you have deodorant, soap, shampoo, and a toothbrush. Basic hygiene is a must."

He tilted his head and held out the gaming system to me. "Says the sister who's standing in the house with blood in her hair and running down her face and splashed all over some gaudy gold dress while barefoot."

I jerked back. He had me there. I touched my face, and sure enough, I felt dried blood. Vomit inched up my throat, but my dragon hissed at my human theatrics.

Where are your keys? Thorn asked as he lifted Peter and tossed him over his shoulder. His muscles rippled, and my body warmed.

Right. Keys.

I shook my head, refocusing on the threat and not my mate's tantalizing body, and hurried past the sofa into the kitchen and grabbed my keys from the basket on the counter.

My chest ached. This might be the last time I saw the kitchen that Mom and I had decorated shortly after she'd been diagnosed with cancer, but I pushed the memories away. I dangled the keys from my finger. "Let's roll."

Opening the door, Thorn rushed outside. I waved Elliott on, wanting to take up the rear. I pressed the unlock button, so Thorn could get Peter situated in the vehicle, while the two of us were slower coming out.

With each step Elliott took, parts of his gaming system jostled, causing him to slow even more. I bit the inside of my cheek to prevent myself from snapping at him. Maybe allowing him to bring the system hadn't been smart. If we got caught because he was too slow, my good intentions would lead to disaster.

When we stepped onto the long porch, Thorn was shutting the

back passenger side door of the Audi. Elliott shuffled down the stairs, and I locked the door and replaced the key under the mat. Though I doubted it would make much difference, I didn't want whoever came by to think we were frantically on the run, even though we were.

Thorn slid into the driver's seat, which somehow didn't annoy me. I liked to be in control, but with him, being a passenger didn't bother me.

Ten years later, we finally reached the car. Yes, I was being dramatic, but damn, it sure felt as if it had taken that long. I opened the back driver's side door, trying to get Elliott to hurry, and as soon as he swung his feet into the car, I slammed the door shut and ran around to the front passenger seat.

Thorn pressed the button to start the car, and as soon as the engine turned, he backed out of the driveway.

I buckled my seatbelt and took deep breaths like I learned in yoga. It wasn't as effective, since I couldn't do the stretch that went along with them inside a moving car.

Elliot sighed and fidgeted behind me, trying to get situated. "You said you were trying to keep Eva safe? What did you mean by that? Isn't she with Drake?" Though he was trying to control his voice, it grew thick with emotion.

As Thorn drove down the street, I turned in my seat and smiled sadly. "Actually, I was with her. She and I escaped, but she was tranqed, and some of our friends and Thorn's parents are taking her to the same place we're heading. You'll see her soon."

Eyes glistening, Elliott let out a shaky breath. "She's not with him, either." He leaned his head back against the headrest and stiffened. "Wait. She was *tranqed*?"

Tires squealed, and I jerked my head forward. Several large black Suburbans turned the upcoming corner and barreled toward us.

There was no doubt who they were.

Warriors.

A lump formed in my throat. At least, we weren't at the house. I could only hope they were so focused on getting there that they didn't notice us, especially with my tinted windows.

When the third and final SUV passed us, the vehicle slammed on its brakes.

No. This couldn't be happening. *Thorn, I connected.*

"I know," he rasped as he pressed the gas pedal, taking a turn at a much faster speed than I was comfortable with. He expertly maneuvered the car as tires screeched and the SUVs cut hard, spinning in our direction.

Thorn glanced in the rearview mirror as we approached the main road leading to downtown. "Elliott, it's going to get rough, so hold on."

"Is that them?" Elliott breathed, watching them out the back window.

I gripped the black leather center console and the door handle, my gut heaving as Thorn turned onto the main road. A car blared its horn behind us as we cut them off, but Thorn didn't ease off the gas.

My mid-size sedan was significantly smaller than the Suburbans, so we were able to swerve through vehicles efficiently.

The Suburbans raced behind us, honking their horns, and weaving through the traffic after us, but we were gaining distance.

My heart hammered, and I grimaced as Thorn cut another person off. The car slammed on its brakes, honking, and the lead Suburban slammed into the back of the car.

The car flipped around from the impact and wrapped around a telephone pole.

My hands shook. *Thorn, I need your cell phone.*

His brows furrowed, but he fidgeted in his pocket and handed it to me.

I expected him to take the next left that would lead us away from downtown, but he remained on the main road.

Dialing 911, I connected with Thorn, *Why are we going downtown?*

If we take the main road, we won't be able to lose them, he replied as his hands gripped the steering wheel.

The 911 operator came on the line, and I informed them of the accident and that the person who'd run into the smaller car was chasing us. I then mentioned two more Suburbans were still pursuing us. After telling her where we were heading, she told us that police officers would intercept us.

As soon as I hung up, Thorn connected, *That's actually a smart plan.*

Just make sure they don't catch up to us before the police arrive. I rolled down my window and chucked the phone.

Ev, what the hell? Thorn connected, surprise flickering through him. *Dad or Mom may try to call us.*

I winced. I hadn't considered that. *Sorry, but I had to toss it, so the cops don't follow us.*

He nodded. *Right. We'll just need to tell them when we can.*

The traffic light turned yellow, and Thorn punched the gas. My car lurched forward, and Elliott grunted as his knees hit the back of my seat. My kidneys complained.

We sailed underneath the light just as it turned red, and I glanced in the side mirror.

I'd hoped that the Suburbans would stop, but they swung into the opposite lane and swerved past the handful of vehicles between us.

Luckily, traffic wasn't heavy, and another wreck didn't unfold.

Thorn's knuckles turned white, and soon, sirens sounded. Two cop cars rushed past us toward the Suburbans and blocked the lane, preventing them from following us.

My head fell against the headrest.

Now, we have to get to the cabin before another car finds us, Thorn said as he took the next left and headed out of the city.

As soon as the long, winding roads with less traffic surrounded us, I relaxed. We were heading in the opposite direction from the dragon lands, which meant we shouldn't pass any guards.

Thorn took my hand, the jolt thrumming between us. He connected, *Lay your head back, and get some rest. We're safe now.*

After the torturous week, a nap sounded fabulous. I placed my head on his shoulder and breathed in his scent. I needed to touch him, and even in the slightly uncomfortable position, I was out fast.

EVERLY, Thorn's voice popped into my head, and my eyes fluttered. *We're at the cabin. Do you need me to carry you in?*

The offer was tempting, but with Elliott and Eva around, I needed to be strong. I lifted my head, my neck aching from the position I'd slept in. *No, I'm fine. You deal with Peter.*

He nodded, his gorgeous eyes locked on me. *That's what I thought you'd say. Let's get you inside. I've been waiting for this moment for far too long.*

"What is this place?" Elliott asked from behind.

I opened my door and climbed out. "Your home for the foreseeable future."

He followed my lead. Standing outside the car, he leaned back inside to gather his gaming system. "And Eva is in there?"

Glancing to the right, I noticed the black SUV parked there. "She should be inside."

Thorn tossed Peter over his shoulder, and as we walked up to the one-story log cabin, the front door opened, revealing Eva in a pair of brown sweatpants and a white T-shirt. She rushed into my arms.

I stiffened, having expected her to run to Elliott.

"Thank goodness, you're okay. They told me you were, but I needed to see it with my own eyes." She leaned back, touching her chest.

My eyes burned, but I forced a smile. "We made it, and we brought Elliott and your dad here."

Her attention flicked to Elliott, and a huge smile lit her face. She took a step toward him, her arms outstretched.

Elliott shook his head. "Dude, you just hugged her, and she's all bloody. I know I love my game character like that, but that's pretend. So, like—"

Eva didn't hesitate and threw her arms around him. She whispered, "You brought our game."

He scoffed, "Of course, I did."

Thorn walked into the hallway, and I followed him. We found Saphira, Errol, and Brenton in the den, sitting on one of the black futon couches, and Vlad, Cassidy, and Tyson on the other. The charcoal walls didn't seem so dark this time around, likely because I'd spent time in actual Hell. My gaze landed on the white back door and continued out the square window to the woods.

"Thank gods, you two made it back." Cassidy sighed. "I was just about to call you to see if everything was okay."

Saphira snorted. "I take it Peter wasn't the most agreeable."

"He was an ass," Thorn growled as Eva and Elliott entered the cabin and shut the door. Then the two of them joined us in the den.

"I'll take him into the Wolfram Dwinn room and lock him up." Thorn nodded back toward the hallway. "Then I need a minute alone with Everly so we can talk and clean up."

That was the room he'd put Saphira in when he'd first brought us here. The tungsten had been forged with Thorn's own royal dragon fire, and not even dragon shifters could break through the metal or shift when surrounded by it. Peter would be very securely locked in.

I inhaled swiftly. There was no telling what Thorn wanted to say, but I deserved to hear whatever he needed to get off his chest.

"Sounds like a plan." Cassidy went into the kitchen as she continued, "Vlad needs to clean up too, and I'll cook us something to eat. Everly has to be starving."

Food sounded amazing, but *after* I cleaned up. I wanted the blood off me.

I turned to the twins. "Will you two be okay for a bit?"

Eva pointed at the gaming system. "Hell yeah. I've been jonesing to play."

The two of them hurried to the television and started setting everything up.

As Thorn and I turned down the hallway toward the bedrooms, Saphira muttered, "Just keep it down. We all have good ears."

We reached the first door on the right, and Thorn nodded at it. "Go ahead and get in the shower. I'll be right there."

He probably wanted me to get clean before we talked, and I couldn't blame him.

I entered the bedroom and breathed in his minty-amber scent. The stark off-white walls and the queen bed with the same purple sheets we'd made love in for the first time now felt like home.

I walked past the bed and the dresser to the bathroom and turned on the shower. As the water warmed, I bent to grab a towel from under the sink. I tossed the white towel over the shower rod and heard the bedroom door shut. When I glanced up, Thorn was leaning against the bathroom door frame.

Turning to him, I rubbed my arms.

Then he gestured for me to come to him, an unreadable expression on his face.

My heart nearly stopped. What did he want?

CHAPTER SIXTEEN

I STRAIGHTENED, trying to find some sort of calm. This was the first time we'd been alone since I'd snuck out in a poor-ass attempt to save Thorn's parents, Saphira, and Eva. If he wanted to yell at me, I deserved it.

My feet moved toward him without me giving it much thought. We'd been apart for too long, and at least, I'd get to be near him when he told me whatever he had to say.

Inhaling, I had to get something off my chest. "Before you say anything, I just want to say again how sorry I am. I know I fu—"

He kissed me, cutting off my words, and connected, *None of that matters. I just need you.* His tongue brushed my lips, begging for entrance.

My body thrummed as our dragons purred together inside our minds. I hadn't expected this, but it was a more than welcome surprise. We were mates and had been apart too long. We needed to connect again.

To be one...even for a few moments. One soul, one body, one everything. The way we were meant to be.

His minty scent engulfed me, making me dizzy. I opened my

mouth to him...and my skin cracked as something that had dried on my face stretched.

Blood.

Ew. He was kissing me while I was covered in blood—though it was mostly Vlad's. I took a step back.

Thorn's forehead lined, and he tilted his head. "Did I do something wrong?" His concern wafted through me.

"*No*," I said forcefully. I glanced down at my chest and the splotches of blood. "I *want* to kiss you and—" My face burned as I cut off and waved at his body. "You know." I cleared my throat.

He grinned wickedly. "Nope. Not a clue. You'll have to spell it out for me."

I stuck out my tongue, well aware this was the happiest I'd been since the last time I'd seen him. "Well, some would say that leaving you guessing works in my favor." I scrunched my nose and sighed. "But can we hold off until *after* my shower? I'm covered in blood and want to wash off the stench of the chateau."

Pursing his lips, he closed the distance between us and slid his hands around my waist. He connected, *Actually, I've got an idea I think we and our dragons will approve of.* He unzipped my dress and tugged it, so it fell to the laminate floor, leaving me in nothing but my white strapless bra and black panties.

His gorgeous blue eyes glowed, and his pupils slitted as he ogled me. My breath caught, and my body flamed with desire.

Even covered in blood, you're the most gorgeous woman I've ever known. He growled as he unhooked my bra and tossed it aside. His fingers slid underneath the line of my panties and pushed them to the floor. *Pure perfection.*

Sliding the curtain to the side, he nodded toward the tub. *You should get clean.*

I nodded, my body humming. I damn near tumbled into the tub, and he laughed, deep and sexy. "Don't get hurt. I need you in top form."

My body blazed hotter than ever as he shut the curtain.

I stepped underneath the hot water, enjoying the way it splashed over me. Pink water puddled around my feet as the blood rinsed off.

Thorn moved around outside the curtain as I scrubbed my fingers through my hair and down my face, removing the dried blood that tried to stay behind.

The curtain opened again, and Thorn stepped into the tub.

Need bloomed heavily within me as I ogled him from head to toe. Every inch of him was more chiseled, muscular, and huge than I remembered, perfection compared to the statues of gods that people had sculpted so many centuries ago.

He leaned toward me and moved to my right, snatching the shampoo bottle from the side of the tub. I huffed in frustration, and he smiled.

"Turn around," he murmured, and I didn't hesitate.

The warm water hit my front as he worked up a lather in my hair. His fingers dug into my scalp as the berry smell of the shampoo swirled around us. My stomach clenched with need, even as he relaxed me.

His hand touched my waist, turning me around. I leaned back into the spray, rinsing the shampoo from my hair and body.

Leaning over again, he squirted conditioner in one hand and took a bar of soap in the other. When I turned around, he worked the conditioner into the ends of my hair while his other hand rubbed the bar of soap over my body.

After a minute, he used both hands to clean my body and placed the soap back on its shelf. I turned to rinse off, but he shook his head and connected, *I'm not done yet.*

His left hand cupped my breast, rubbing suds across my nipple, while the other one slipped between my legs. Unable to stand, I leaned against the back wall of the tub, allowing the water to wash over my body, but he didn't relent. His thumb rolled over my nipple as his fingers circled within my folds. Tension built, and my breathing turned erratic. As ecstasy coursed through me, I moaned, and Thorn kissed me, swallowing the noise.

After my body stopped quivering, I pushed him off and smiled wickedly. I arched a brow. "My turn."

Just like he'd taken care of me, I washed his hair, and my fingers grazed the mark that haunted him at the base of his neck. I hadn't gotten a chance to study it because of all the drama. It looked more like a tattoo than a birthmark, showing a detailed image of a dragon. I was lingering, my hand itching to trace the outline, when he stiffened and turned around to rinse the shampoo from his head. A twinge of discomfort swirled between us.

I didn't want to make him feel awkward, so I moved on to do what I'd been looking forward to most—cleaning his body. I followed every curve of muscle and slid my hand downward to find him hard.

His body shuddered as I stroked him, trying to make him feel like he'd made me feel. His hips swiveled, increasing the rhythm, and he leaned toward me, capturing my lips.

Safety and happiness meant being with the one person who was made for you in a way that couldn't be replicated.

He pulled away from my lips and kissed down my neck. When he reached the base, he nipped like he had the night we'd claimed one another. He grabbed my hand, removing it from his body.

I moaned, wanting to keep going, but he lifted me, placing my back against the wall as he slid inside me. Our dragons roared as he slowly slid in and out, and I wrapped my arms around his body.

I wanted to pleasure you, like you did me, I connected, but I was already matching his pace, spreading my legs to feel him deeper.

Oh, you will. Don't worry. He snarled as he nipped at my throat and quickened the tempo. *This is the only way I want my ending— with me deep inside you.*

His words urged my dragon on, and I dug my fingers into his back, needing to mark him in the way he was marking me. He groaned as his fingers dug deeper into my skin.

Our love for each other mixed with our growing euphoria. Releasing his hold, he took my hands and pinned them against the wall as he kissed me again.

We orgasmed at the same time, our pleasure blending. I wasn't sure how long our bodies thrummed from the high, but when we finally came down, the water was cooling.

Guiding me back under the stream, he rinsed us off. A loud knock sounded on the bedroom door.

"I hate to, uh...interrupt," Cassidy called out, "but dinner is ready, and it's going to get cold."

My stomach growled, and Thorn laughed. The sound was carefree and warmed my heart so much it could burst.

"We're getting out," he called back as he turned off the water. "But you guys don't have to wait on us. Eat."

Part of me didn't want to get out of the shower despite the chill. That meant my mate would get dressed—a true tragedy. I'd been more worried than I'd let on about not seeing him again, and I hated for any part of him to be covered. But it was better than everyone seeing him naked.

He wrapped the towel around me and kissed the top of my head. He connected, *We need to get you fed.*

I pouted. "But we could stay here and have sex again."

"There's no question about that." He winked as he snatched another towel from underneath the sink and dried himself. "As soon as you eat and we handle Peter, I'm bringing your sexy ass right back in here to make love all over again."

Batting my eyes, I dropped the towel lower, exposing the top of my breasts. "Or we could go for round two now."

Behave. Though I want to ravish you, one thing is more important —making sure you're taken care of, which means eating. He strolled out the door, dropping the towel so I could see his tight ass walking away. *Besides, it's selfish. If you don't eat, you won't have the energy to have sex all night. So, a small break is winning.*

All night.

I liked the sound of that. I hurried and got dressed, not wanting to be left behind.

Dinner went better than I'd imagined. I'd thought it would be awkward, but Cassidy, Vlad, Thorn, and I sat around the dinner table, while Tyson, Eva, and Elliott played a shooting game. Saphira, Brenton, and Errol sat on one of the futons, watching them play, while poking fun at Tyson whenever he died.

It was almost as if we'd known one another a lot longer than we had.

Cassidy had cooked steaks and potatoes and made a salad. I hadn't had a good home-cooked meal since Mom had died, so the moment was bittersweet but delicious. The only thing nagging at me was my stepdad, who must have still been passed out since he wasn't making noise from the back room.

I lifted a bite of steak to my mouth just as Saphira strolled into the kitchen.

"So..." She leaned against the window in front of me, grinning wickedly as she crossed her arms. "Eva told me you were in over your head with Falkor."

Inhaling, I dropped my fork, and it hit the plate with a loud clank. A sour taste filled my mouth as I glanced from her to my sister.

Eva paused the game.

Elliott jumped from the floor and spun toward her, scowling. He rasped, "What the *hell?* Cheater! I was winning."

"You still will be. Chill." She turned around to watch the exchange between Saphira and me.

My jaw dropped. "You *didn't.*" She'd *told* Saphira. The little traitor.

"I hope your mouth didn't do that when you were hanging around there." Saphira smiled devilishly. "Unless you're a biter." Her attention homed in on Thorn. "Is she a biter?"

I wanted to die. That was a moment I didn't want to relive *ever* again.

Thorn placed his arms against the table and frowned. "What does Everly being a biter have to do with Falkor?" His irises darkened as he glanced at me.

"We're missing something." Cassidy wiped her mouth with a napkin and set it down. "Does anyone want to enlighten us?"

"No!" I yelled at the same time Saphira replied, "Yes."

Everly, what's going on? The concern wafting from Thorn had my nerves jumping.

"It was something that happened the first night Eva and I were *there*," I replied, wishing Saphira hadn't brought the story up.

Vlad's jaw clenched. "Did Falkor do something to you?"

Smoke trickled from Thorn's nose, and I realized Elliott didn't know about dragons yet. I glared at Saphira and said, "She's making it sound worse..." I paused. The whole situation had been horrible. It couldn't have gotten much worse. "More..." I didn't know what to say to diffuse the situation.

Thorn slammed his hand on the table, cracking it. I was reminded of King Arman.

"Dude!" Elliott's eyes bulged. "You broke that huge-ass table. I need to work out with you. The ladies would be flocking to me like moths to a flame."

Thorn wasn't calming down.

"I tried to escape the first night we got there, and Falkor grabbed me and threw me over his shoulder, my face to his chest. I had what I thought was a bright idea." I closed my eyes and rubbed my forehead, not wanting to see anyone's reaction. "If I pantsed him, he wouldn't be able to walk without stumbling, and Eva and I would have time to run away."

Relaxing, Thorn rolled his shoulders. "So why is she insinuating—"

I had to get it out before I couldn't. "Because I didn't consider where my head was in relation to his..." I twisted my face as the food inched back up.

"Junk." Saphira snorted. "His junk was in her face. She went balls deep."

My eyes flew back open to see Saphira beaming as she studied

Thorn and me. She was enjoying watching me squirm and Thorn's fated-mate reaction.

Brat.

"Whoa." Elliott lifted a hand. "You gave a dude a blow job to escape?"

"*What?*" I glared at him. "Of course not. Why would you think that?"

He gestured at Saphira. "She said 'balls deep.'"

This was getting worse. My face heated. I did not want to be discussing *this* at all, but especially not with my twin siblings. "She thinks she's being cute and clever."

"Oh, she's *not*," Thorn growled, his pupils slitting.

Cassidy clapped her hands. "Well, this has been fun." She mashed her lips together, but the corners of her mouth tipped upward.

"Though the execution didn't go as planned, her strategy makes sense." Vlad nodded. "When you're in a bad situation, you might have to try unusual methods to get out of it." He patted Thorn's arm. "You have a very smart mate."

"Mate?" Elliott's face was lined with confusion. "You mean wife, right?"

"Yes, wife." Thorn placed an arm on the back of my chair. "And Saphira, if you bring that up again, I won't hesitate to lock you in the back with Peter." He grinned so wide he showed his bottom teeth.

Her face fell, and she crossed her arms. "Fine. I've been locked in a horrible room for far too long and unable to shi—"

I glared at her, cutting her off.

Her mouth dropped, and she cleared her throat a little too loudly. "Shit. Unable to shit." Her cheeks turned red as she realized what she'd said.

I laughed wholeheartedly. That was what she got for giving *me* shit. The thought made me laugh even harder because the saying had the word *shit* in it. I was losing my shi—mind.

Elliott flinched and stepped back. He whispered to Eva, "These people are weird and make me uncomfortable. When Dad wakes up, I hope he'll push for some answers."

I tensed. I wished there was a way I could shield him from this world, but it was impossible. Drake was making sure of that.

Everly, he'll be fine. Look at Eva. She's already adjusting to everything, even though she's human, Thorn connected and leaned over to kiss my cheek. *They're your family and love you far more than you know.*

I wasn't sure that was the case. Both Elliott and Eva had always seemed indifferent to me.

A loud bang came on the door as Peter shouted, "Help! Someone help me!"

Lovely, the asshole was awake. Elliott was about to get his wish because Peter had to understand what we were up against. If he didn't cooperate, he could make our lives a whole lot harder.

Thorn and I stood and marched down the hall with Elliott, Eva, Cassidy, and Vlad right behind us.

It was time to face the devil that had haunted me for so long.

AS I APPROACHED the bedroom to confront Peter, my body coiled tighter. This man had been indifferent to me for the fourteen years I'd lived with him, and after Mom had passed, if I'd stayed in his presence too long, he'd become cruel. To keep my promise to Mom to protect my siblings, I'd had to lie low and not push him so he would allow me back into *his* home.

Avoiding him was ingrained in me.

But to keep that promise to Mom, I had to face him. If I let him push me around, Eva's life would become worse than death, and Elliott would likely die.

I turned left to continue down the hallway, passing the door to Thorn's room and the second bedroom, which Thorn had originally placed me in when he'd kidnapped me on my way to the chateau.

Outside the door to the bedroom that held Peter, I stood still and tried to gather my wits. My racing heart wasn't helping matters; instead of slowing to help my calm settle in, it was going faster.

You don't have to do this, Thorn connected and placed a hand on my shoulder. *You can go back to the living room, and I'll handle him. It would be my pleasure and honor.*

His anger thrummed through our connection, and I came close to smiling. Who would've thought that having a man who was willing to protect me at all costs would be this damn thrilling? Before Thorn, the thought of anyone taking care of me had sat uneasily with me. I didn't want to wind up like Mom, whose husband had essentially turned his back on her in the months before her death. I wanted to be independent and self-reliant, but now I realized I could be those things with a strong man beside me, which meant I had to be part of this conversation. "It's something I have to do."

Elliott fidgeted and asked, "Uh...who are you talking to? No one said anything."

I flinched. I'd been so focused on Peter that I'd answered Thorn out loud. My carelessness would make Elliott more uneasy, so the truth had to come out.

I glanced at Eva, who nodded as if she already knew what I was thinking.

Peter banged on the door again, yelling, "Somebody, please help me!"

Let's just do this, I connected with Thorn. I'd learned a long time ago that dragging out something you didn't want to do only made the anxiety worse. Elliott's uneasy glances were already making my skin crawl.

Okay. Thorn removed the key from his pocket and unlocked the door. As soon as it clicked, Peter gasped and stumbled back from the door.

I snorted. I couldn't help it. He'd begged for help, but when someone came, he clearly regretted it.

The door swung open, and Peter came into view. He rubbed his head where Thorn had punched him, and his irises were dark, like he was in pain.

"Headache?" I asked, strolling into the metal-lined room.

The dark metal reminded me of aluminum foil, and it covered the entire space from floor to ceiling. The room was set up similarly to the other two bedrooms with a bed against the outside wall, a barred window to the left, and a small dresser in the far-right corner. A door on the left led to a tiny bathroom, which was covered in metal, as well.

He scowled. "Yes! Your *husband* knocked me out and locked me in a room. Wait until I get out of here."

Thorn entered and stood next to me, and Peter cowered.

"Dad?" Elliott rushed inside the room and stopped a foot away, his worried eyes scanning his father. "Are you okay?"

"No, I'm not *okay*." Peter dropped his hands and glared at Thorn and me as Eva, Cassidy, and Vlad tensed. My stepdad continued, "They forced us to leave against our will, and now they've dragged Eva into this. Drake will have my head."

Eva shook her head. "They didn't *drag* me into this. They got me out of it. You have no idea what Drake is like."

"Please." Peter wrinkled his nose. "If Everly hadn't run off with this walking steroid-induced muscle freak, she'd be with Drake, taking your spot as she promised, and *you* wouldn't be involved."

Head tilting back, Elliott looked at me, brows furrowed.

"Do *not* talk about my son that way," Cassidy hissed between her teeth, stalking forward, her pupils slitting. "He's a better man than you by leaps and bounds."

Vlad caught her wrist and tugged her back into him.

This was what Peter did. He tried to control the situation with harsh words and manipulation. I was so over the entire thing. "Maybe if you hadn't embezzled money from the Hales, neither I nor Eva would be involved."

"What?" Eva gasped. "You embezzled money from them?"

Not wanting him to change the subject, I told her, "That's why you were initially promised...as payment. I found out and took your place, but things went awry. If Peter hadn't stolen money, this would be a non-issue." Although, I couldn't get too upset about it. It had led me to Thorn.

Nostrils flaring, Peter stepped around Elliott to get closer to me. "If it weren't for Kelly, I wouldn't have had to embezzle money. Her sickness damn near ruined our family."

A cold realization washed over me. "Is that why you were so cruel to her in the end? Because treating her cancer was putting a strain on you financially?" I'd always wondered what had changed him from a caring husband and father to someone who ignored us to the best of his ability.

"Yes, she was going to die. Why stay in the hospital and rack up all those bills?"

My vision turned cloudy, and my eyes burned. "Because she was in intense pain and didn't want to die in our house, where Eva and Elliott would have had to watch her dead body be carried out. She didn't want those memories to haunt them."

"So, she wanted to be a burden?" Peter snorted darkly. "*My* burden, which forced me to deal with *you.*"

Though I'd always known he felt that way, hearing it was worse than I'd anticipated. At least, it was out there—the elephant that had been shadowing our relationship if you could call it that.

Thorn snarled and stepped in front of me.

But Cassie was the one who spoke in a deep rasp. "Listen here. The day you chose to marry Kelly was the day you took on the responsibility of not only being a father to the twins but to Everly, too. If you didn't want that responsibility, why marry her?"

"Because she got pregnant." Peter ran his hands through his hair. "I wanted an heir for the family company, so I asked her to marry me. When she was healthy, it was tolerable. She handled all the children, but when she got sick—" He took a step back toward the wall.

Hurt was etched onto Elliott's and Eva's faces. Eva whimpered, "I always told myself it was because you were dealing with losing her, but that wasn't it." She stomped her foot and clenched her hands. "Then you were willingly going to hand me over to a dragon shifter prince to be his *breeder?*"

Peter huffed and rolled his eyes. "Don't be dramatic. The Hales may be strong and powerful, but dragons and being a breeder? Come on!"

"She's not being dramatic." It was time for Peter to understand what he'd done, though I doubted he'd care. "They are dragon shifters, and he had no intention of making Eva his wife."

"Wait." Elliott stumbled back a few steps. "Is that why your eyes do weird things, and you were talking about shifting to get away?" He bit his bottom lip and glanced at me. "But you...you're not one. How could you be with him?" He gestured to Thorn.

I licked my lips and stepped around Thorn to see my brother better. Thorn placed a hand on my arm, the jolt thrumming through my body. His action, and the way his feelings swirled through our bond, told me everything I needed to know without him saying a word—he was right here with me.

"That's the thing." I inhaled, trying to keep my voice level. "I am one. Now."

His jaw dropped, and his attention flicked between Thorn and me. Finally, he asked, "Did he bite you?"

Saphira laughed from the living room, confirming everyone in there was eavesdropping on the conversation.

Damn dragon hearing.

"He turned me, but not with a bite." We were getting off-topic, but Elliott had a right to some answers. "I fell and would've died if he hadn't used his abilities to change me so I could heal faster."

Elliott inched away, his legs hitting the footboard of the bed.

Sighing, Thorn lifted his hand slowly. "Don't worry. I won't change you."

His shoulders relaxed marginally.

"Don't be an idiot," Peter scoffed and smacked Elliott on the back of his head. "You're completely gullible if you believe that."

A low snarl emanated from my chest as I stepped toward Peter. It was one thing when he treated me that way, but I would not tolerate him treating my siblings like that. "Touch him again, and what Thorn did to you will be a walk in a park compared to what I will do."

Peter scowled.

"Dad, it *is* true." Eva moved to stand between Peter and me. "I saw people shift right in front of my eyes. Dragons are real, and Drake wants to use me as a breeder."

"Why?" Peter tilted his head back and winced as if the movement hurt. "If they're dragon shifters, why would they need a human to have kids with? Seems like it would weaken the genetic line, especially with someone like her." He waved his hand at me.

"Clearly, you didn't learn what happens when you insult my mate." Thorn sneered and tugged me behind him again.

Vlad cut his son off. "Though tactless, Peter asked a fair question. In general, we live to be around five hundred. Because of our long-life expectancy, our women don't reproduce very often. Normally, each couple is successful with one child, two if they're lucky. Over the last two centuries, more dragons have died than have been born, so our numbers are getting dangerously low. Drake thinks the solution is to attempt to have multiple children with a human, while also having a wife to bear a true heir."

"He's operating under the assumption that dragon magic is strong enough that any child born will be a dragon." Cassidy rubbed her forehead. "Though, no one I know can prove that. For all we know, the human could die."

Elliott wrung his hands together. "Let me get this straight. Drake is a dragon prince who wants to screw both my sisters, and we're hiding from him to ensure that it doesn't happen?"

I nodded and leaned into Thorn's side, needing his support depending on how my brother reacted.

Eyes bulging, Elliott beamed. "That's *badass*. Dude. I should've played *Spyro* when it came out on the PS. I could've prepped on how to fight dragons!"

I rolled my eyes. Everything led back to video games with him.

Eva chuckled. "Really? Badass? Not what I was going for, but I was Drake's prisoner when I found out. But I'm sure our daily battles in *Demon's Souls* will suit us just as well."

Peter's attention homed in on me. Disbelief poured from him, but I didn't give a damn. He'd soon learn we weren't lying.

"I'll take my chances." Peter lifted his chin, though he moved his head slowly. "Release me, before I call the cops."

"How will you do that?" Thorn bared his teeth. "I took your phone, but you should already know that."

Peter harrumphed. "When I don't show up to work tomorrow, people will search for me. If you let me out now, I'll blame it on *her*." He pointed at me.

Lovely. He was willing to let his own stepdaughter go to jail without batting an eye.

"That's a risk every single one of us is willing to take." Vlad nodded to the door.

He wanted us to leave, and I was more than willing.

Cassidy walked out the door first and paused at the frame. "I'll bring you some dinner, but it's best if you stay in here."

"What?" Peter hissed. "You're going to lock me alone in here where I can't watch over my own kids?"

Now he was playing the doting parent?

"It's fine. Elliott and I can stay in here with him." Eva gestured to the door and flicked her gaze to me. "I'm tired anyway, after the crazy afternoon."

"But the game!" Elliott pouted. When Eva gave him a look, he exhaled and said, "Can wait 'til morning."

I hated to leave them in here with Peter, but something told me Eva had her own agenda. I followed Vlad out the door but paused and said over my shoulder, "If you need anything, just holler. I'll hear." Then I continued without looking back, not wanting to see Peter again.

Thorn shut the door behind us and locked it. "Dad, here." He reached around me to give Vlad the key. "Everly needs to rest after everything that happened today. I'm going to put her to bed."

His father smiled. "That sounds like a good plan. We won't be too far behind you. My wounds are healing, but rest will speed up the process. Cassidy and Saphira were already talking about sleeping arrangements, so we can take it from here."

After learning why Peter resented Mom and me and everything in between, the day had caught up to me. I hadn't gotten back to Thorn a moment too soon because I wasn't sure I could've gotten through this alone.

Thorn placed a hand on the middle of my back, guiding me to our bedroom. "Oh, and Everly," Vlad called out. "Welcome to the family. I look forward to spending more time with you when we're all better rested."

At his sincerity, the pain swirling through me ebbed, and I smiled in return. "I look forward to the same and to being part of a family."

As Vlad turned back to the living room, Thorn and I stepped into our bedroom. I crawled into bed as he shut the door and quickly joined me. I snuggled against his chest, listening to his breathing and heartbeat. There was no sound more beautiful.

My body thrummed from having his arms around me.

He kissed my forehead, his lips so warm and firm. *Ev, get some sleep.*

What happened to all the sex? I teased, but my eyes were shut and unable to open.

His chest shook with quiet laughter. *Oh, it'll happen, but we have tomorrow and every day after. I won't lose you again. Rest now because you'll need your stamina.*

My cheeks hurt from smiling as I drifted off to sleep.

The smell of bacon, eggs, and pancakes hit my senses, and my eyes cracked open. The comforting jolt of Thorn still buzzed across my skin, and I glanced up to find him watching me.

His sky-blue irises sparkled, and a tender smile filled his face. *You are somehow more gorgeous while you sleep. I hadn't gotten a chance to watch you sleep before now.*

I winced. Though he hadn't meant it maliciously, guilt still weighed on me. After all, I'd snuck out on him after our first night together, after we'd completed our bond.

My stomach grumbled, and my mouth watered. I wasn't sure how I could be this hungry.

Untangling from me, Thorn stood and gestured to the door. "Your food awaits, my lady."

I rolled my eyes just as Cassidy called from the kitchen, "Everyone, come and get it before it gets cold."

I crawled out of bed and ran my fingers through my hair to tame the beast on top of my head then quickly grabbed one of my outfits from the duffel bag. I put on a pair of black shorts and a flowy, olive-green top, while Thorn dressed in jeans and a navy shirt.

We held hands as we walked into the kitchen, where every seat was already taken, even one of the futon chairs with Tyson, Saphira, and Brenton.

Peter, Eva, and Elliott were sitting at the table between Vlad and Erroll. Though Peter wasn't handcuffed, I wasn't concerned with Vlad and Cassie nearby. They could handle him.

Thorn and I filled our plates and hurried to the vacant futon to eat breakfast.

I enjoyed sitting next to my mate while hearing chatter about normal topics around the kitchen. Peter was silent, but everyone else discussed the weather, hiking, and what we should do today. Of course, Elliott was hell-bent on playing video games.

Saphira and Tyson were trying to one-up each other with some sort of roasting. I caught that Saphira had a mouth bigger than the Eiffel Tower. In many ways, those two reminded me more of siblings than cousins.

You're happy, Thorn connected as he set his plate on the coffee table in front of us.

There was no point in denying it. *It just seems normal, which is amazing after going through hell. Let's go on the hike with Vlad, Cassidy, and Errol.* I used to hate hiking but getting out into nature after being trapped in the chateau for so long sounded perfect...and being away from Peter made it even more appealing.

Just no sliding down any hills, Thorn teased and kissed my cheek.

A cell phone rang, breaking the moment.

I glanced over my shoulder and saw Vlad remove his phone from his back pocket. His jaw tensed. "It's the king."

"King?" Elliott echoed. "Wait. Is that Arman?"

"Elliott, what did we talk about last night?" Peter snapped. "They're just messing with us, and for some reason, your sister has agreed to go along with it."

"I told you it's all *true.*" Eva huffed as the phone rang a third time. "And it was pure hell being there."

Neither of us wanted to go back.

Cassidy pointed to the phone. "You better answer."

Standing, Errol moved behind Peter and placed a hand over my stepdad's mouth. Peter grunted and tried to move his head, but Errol didn't budge.

With Peter contained, Vlad answered, "Hello?"

My dragon ears could hear it all. King Arman said, "Run. Now. They've found you, and a huge group of warriors is heading your way."

Vlad hung up, and the room went silent, except for Peter's mumbles.

My blood turned cold. Just when I'd felt safe enough to want to hike, this happened.

"How did they find us?" Brenton's hands shook.

I should've realized this last night. "Didn't you say he had a phone?"

Thorn nodded. "Why?"

"His biggest client is the Hales. They gave him a phone to ensure they could reach him at all times." And it was in the house with us. We should've thrown it out last night.

Peter laughed, and as soon as Errol removed his hand, he said, "I told you last night that, if you let me go, I'd blame it on her. But no."

That was why he'd been so cocky.

"Drake tracked us with it." Vlad groaned as he jumped to his feet. "I took the phone away from him last night while you were showering, but I didn't think about them tracking it."

"We've gotta get out of here." Errol glanced at Saphira, his eyes wide with fear. "They'll be here in less than thirty minutes. Is there another place we can go?"

"No." Vlad pinched the bridge of his nose. "Since we lived in Atlanta, I sold my backup houses because the city was so expensive. I only kept this one because it was close by."

"It doesn't matter where we're heading as long as we get Everly away from *here*." Thorn climbed to his feet so fast he damn near blurred. "We can shift and get out of here."

"Shifting will help them track us. Our scents could linger in the air." Vlad licked his lips. "We'll have a better chance at getting away by vehicle." He glanced at the phone. "There is a place we can go, but we should rent two cars, so they won't be able to spot us easily when we're farther from the city."

Thorn and Eva had to get out of here. Drake would take Eva to be his breeder and kill Thorn. Neither was going to happen.

Elliott blanched but ran toward the television and began unplugging the gaming system. Instead of asking about shifting and scents, he'd decided to use the extra time to salvage his games...again. A reaction I would never understand.

"Mom and Dad, take the truck keys on the key chain by the front door. We can't risk leaving the truck behind in case they can glean information about the full name I go by now," Thorn instructed and turned to me, placing his hands on my shoulders. "Eva, Elliott, Peter, Everly, and I will take her Audi. Everyone else, get into Brenton's vehicle. We've got to go."

Everyone dispersed. Elliott strode out of the cabin, balancing the gaming system, with Eva right behind him. I snatched the keys from the hook by the door and unlocked the car, climbing into the passenger seat.

That was when I realized Thorn and Peter hadn't come out. Thorn wouldn't delay unless something had gone wrong.

Peter had to be up to something.

"Stay here," I instructed and opened the car door in time to hear a loud crash from inside the cabin.

CHAPTER EIGHTEEN

I SHOULDN'T HAVE RUN out without making sure Peter was following. I should've known he'd try something, but instead, I'd left Thorn to handle my stepdad alone. Of course, Thorn knew he couldn't be trusted.

Anger flared through our connection, and my blood boiled. Whatever Peter was doing had pissed off my mate.

The front door was still open, so I breezed into the living room in time to watch Thorn punch Peter in the head. His eyes rolled back as his body crumpled. Thorn didn't even try to catch him. He let Peter's body hit the wooden floor between the kitchen and living room.

"What did he do?" I breathed as I reached Thorn's side.

A metallic stench hit me. I looked at his upper arm, which had a deep cut. My jaw clenched.

"I'm fine." He bent and tossed Peter over his shoulder. "He snatched a knife when we were all dispersing and used it on me when I tried to force him to leave."

My chest constricted. "I'm sorry."

"For what? Your mom marrying a douchebag?" He took my hand

and tugged me to the door. "It's not your fault. Stop taking on that responsibility."

His words were like a slap to the face. I often apologized for things that weren't my fault, but in this instance, I felt like it was. *If it wasn't for me, Peter wouldn't be here cutting you.*

Having you in my life has made me the happiest I've ever been, he replied as we stepped back outside. *I'd happily let him cut me every day if that was the price of finding you.*

My chest ached from the way it expanded. I'd never felt so happy, even when Mom was alive.

Mom.

I froze. "I need my bracelet." Mom had given me the bracelet after getting diagnosed with cancer. I'd left it behind with Thorn when I'd run off to hand myself over to Drake. I'd wanted to leave a piece of myself behind for him, and it was the one item I truly valued.

He squeezed my hand and replied, "That's what I was getting when Peter grabbed the knife." He patted his jeans pocket. "It's in here. I'll give it to you once we get into the car. I know how much it means to you and didn't want to leave it behind. We might not be able to come back."

Tears burned my eyes. Of course he'd done that for me. In the short time we'd been together, he'd come to know me better than I knew myself—in some ways, anticipating my needs before I did.

Vlad backed up the white, beat-up pickup truck and rolled down the window. "Follow me. I have an idea where we can go."

Nodding, Thorn rushed to my Audi and tossed Peter in the back driver's side seat. Eva resettled in the center as I hurried to the front passenger door. I was all for Thorn driving, especially if the dragons arrived before we got away. I didn't want to try to outmaneuver them, and I suspected Thorn was more than capable of doing it.

As soon as I shut the door, Vlad pulled out, and Brenton followed right behind him.

Thorn slid behind the wheel and started the engine.

When he put on his seat belt, he winced, reminding me of the cut on his arm.

My shoulders drooped. *I can drive if it's uncomfortable for you.*

I'm fine. He put the car in reverse.

Vlad and Brenton took off, driving faster than normal, and unease settled over me. In one swoop, Thorn had put the car in drive and caught up.

The dirt road jarred us as we ran over branches and pebbles.

Eva sighed. "Did you have to knock him out?"

I glanced over my shoulder to see Peter slumped against her.

"He stabbed me, so be thankful that's the worst he got." Thorn tightened his hands on the wheel. "No promises if he's rude to Everly again. I don't care if it's just a scowl. I will do more than knock his ass out."

My dragon purred, and my heart skipped a beat.

"Uh...is that noise coming from Everly?" Elliott asked from behind me. "Because I'm certain there's no cat in here."

My face flamed. Thank goodness Saphira wasn't here, or she'd start in on the cat jokes again.

Do not be ashamed. Thorn reached over and took my hand. *A dragon purring means they are happy and feel loved. The sound is dead sexy.*

I bit my lower lip, and some of my spirits dampened—I'd never heard Thorn purr when he was with me. But now, while we were trying to get away from impending warriors, wasn't the time to discuss that.

Glancing at the sky, I exhaled when I didn't see any dragons. The woods thickened around us as the three vehicles hurried down the dirt road. We were still in danger because we hadn't passed another house, and if the dragons got close, they'd know it was us.

"Seriously." Elliott cleared his throat. "Is that a dragon thing? Purring?"

He wouldn't let it go.

"No clue." Eva groaned. "She never did it back at the prison." Something thumped in the back seat, and I assumed it was Peter hitting the door, but I didn't care enough to look.

"Wait!" Elliott squeaked. "Drake put you two in *prison?* No fucking way."

Thorn fisted his hands. *You didn't tell me that. I thought you were in the guest house.*

"She meant it metaphorically. Neither of us wanted to be there, and warriors were watching us constantly."

"Everly even had to pretend she had stomach issues to try to talk to one of the warriors alone," Eva snorted.

Every rash decision I'd made would haunt me for the rest of my life. Even if I managed to forget for a while, Eva and Saphira would constantly remind me of every ridiculous thing I'd done. I was surprised the twins hadn't brought up the time when I was sixteen and Mom had asked me to mail her and Peter's tax returns, and I'd bought a penny stamp to send it. I'd been so confused about why anyone would buy more expensive stamps when they sold some for a penny. When Mom had explained, she'd exclaimed that, for someone so smart, I did some pretty silly things. Not that I would dare bring up that story to any of them.

"Oh." Elliott leaned forward. "What kind of stomach issues? Like the explosive kind, the cramping kind, or the scent-alone-could-kill-everyone-who-came-into-contact kind?"

I sighed. My siblings had never been interested in what was going on in my life...until now.

The corners of Thorn's mouth tipped up, and he glanced at me. "That's a valid question."

Traitor. I squinched my nose at him.

"Everything with you is either poop or blood." Eva huffed.

"Yeah. The two best things in life," Elliott scoffed. "You need blood to get the oxygen to your organs, and you need to poop to get rid of the stuff your body doesn't need."

Unfortunately, he wasn't wrong.

Elliott grasped the headrest as he leaned forward. "So, which poop issue did you pretend to have?"

The best thing I could do was answer and hope we moved on. "The kind that clogs the toilet, but despite it being pretend, I'd rather not talk about it."

"Mad respect." His hands disappeared as he sat back in his seat. "A total twofer. Cramping *and* smell."

The main road came into view, and some tension left my body. If we could blend in with the traffic, we might be home free.

We turned west. *Where are we heading?*

No clue. Thorn flicked his attention to the sky. *Dad has figured something out. I'm sure we'll stop somewhere soon to rent some vehicles. The last thing we need is for Drake and the warriors to be searching for your and Brenton's vehicles. Drake could issue an alert on the Dragonnet, and dragon shifters would be watching for us.*

Dragonnet? There were so many things I still had to learn.

He nodded. *It's an intranet for dragons. They post announcements, news, and any speeches the royals desire to deliver. It's the one-stop space for all dragon happenings, activities of other thunders, and all other relevant information.*

Now I remembered that he'd mentioned it before.

Out of the corner of my eye, something moved high in the sky. I turned my head...and my breath caught. Forty warriors were flying so high that no humans would be able to make them out...but I knew they had dragon sight.

We'd barely missed them, and luckily, there were now several vehicles on the road. They didn't expect us to know they were coming.

Thank goodness King Arman had warned us.

Thorn, I connected.

I see them, he replied and took my hand. *We'll be out of here before they realize we're gone, and they won't be able to track us down by scent.*

That didn't mean they wouldn't scour the area. My pulse quickened, but I forced myself not to tense. I didn't want to alert Elliott or Eva that something was amiss.

"Oh, hey." Thorn released my hand and reached into his pocket. He removed my bracelet and placed it into my hand.

The white gold was warm, and I ran my fingers across the interlinking small hearts and diamonds that clasped in the back. With my other hand, I touched the two white gold hearts hanging down. The first heart was inscribed with *Everly* and the other with *The love between a mother and daughter is forever.* A lump formed in my throat as my heart swirled with emotions. I'd do anything to have her here with me, but at the same time, it was also best that she wasn't here now. She'd be another pawn for Drake to use against me, and he had enough of those.

I put the bracelet on and took Thorn's hand again, enjoying the jolt of our connection and the smooth metal against my skin.

Lean your head back and get some rest, he said and squeezed my hand comfortingly.

I arched a brow. *Really? We just woke up.*

He cut his eyes to me. *At least, try to relax. Or I'll get Elliott talking about poop again.*

Who are you? My mate or Saphira? I leaned my head back, pretending I was upset. *You look like Thorn but sound like her. I'm all sorts of confused over here.*

If we weren't in a hurry to get away, and if your siblings weren't in the back seat, I'd make sure to alleviate all of your confusion. He winked.

Heat swarmed through my body, and he grinned wickedly.

Tease, I connected.

His look stole my breath. He was so damn handsome in every way. I couldn't wait to paint him one day. I had to; he was a masterpiece.

Using the buttons on the steering wheel, he turned on the radio and scanned the stations. I fidgeted and got comfortable, staring out the window as "Blackhole Sun" by Soundgarden played, thankful that I had Thorn in my life.

———

Two hours later, we were pulling out of an Enterprise Rent-A-Car in two Suburbans. Apparently, Vlad was a man of many talents and had fake IDs for himself and Cassidy, so they'd put the cars under their aliases and opted for the company's rental insurance.

We parked the other vehicles across town in a motel lot. If the warriors found them, they wouldn't automatically realize we had rented cars.

Everyone from my Audi climbed into the Suburban that Cassidy was driving, while everyone else climbed into the one with Vlad. We put Peter in the passenger seat so we could keep an eye on him. He sat silently pouting, which I was all about. It was just as good as him being unconscious.

Thorn sat behind Cassidy, and I opted to take the seat behind Peter, since I had shorter legs, which left Elliott and Eva in the far back. Elliott had pulled out a Nintendo Switch, which he and Eva were playing. I swore the boy had a game stowed away everywhere.

As soon as we got on the interstate, heading northwest again, Thorn tapped his hands on his leg. "There's only one place I can think of in this direction, but Vlad would never take us there."

My mouth went dry. That sounded ominous. *What are you talking about?*

"His family thunder." The area around Thorn's eyes tightened. "He hasn't been back there or even spoken to anyone, including his parents, since we hid away in Atlanta."

"Desperate times call for even more desperate measures." Cassidy glanced in the rearview mirror. "We have nowhere else to go."

"What about a hotel?" The last thing I wanted to do was put more people in danger.

"We don't have unlimited funds, and Drake will have dragon shifters searching for us. They know what we all look like." Cassidy watched the road. "We can't get jobs and risk them finding us, we can't go back home to Atlanta, and the cabin has been compromised. We literally have nowhere else to go. I tried talking him out of it, but we're out of options."

My leg bounced. *Maybe I should go back. If he has me—*

Thorn's pupils slitted, and he growled so loudly that the car shook. "That is *not* an option, Everly. If you so much as think that again, I will not let you out of my sight...*ever.*"

"Whoa," Elliott gasped from behind me. "That's badass, but I *never* want to get on his bad side."

"It took *this* for you to realize that?" Eva sighed. "Not him punching out Dad twice?"

"Eh. Dad's an ass." Elliott's tone held some anger.

Peter glared over his seat at his son, but surprisingly, he remained silent.

If Thorn hadn't been so angry with me, I would've pushed the topic more.

"I'm not trying to upset you but look at how many of us are on the run. Going to another thunder could add more people to that number," I said and took his hand, but he didn't squeeze back like normal.

"What Thorn is trying to say, not so eloquently, is that there is one thing Drake wants more than you." Cassidy changed lanes, following Vlad. "Thorn. Even if you handed yourself over, he won't stop looking for us. Vlad and I were captured before you were promised to Drake."

I hung my head. Regret surged through me. "You're right. I wasn't thinking." I stared at the floorboard and removed my hand from Thorn's.

At the last second, he snatched it back. *I know you're trying to help, but I just got you back, and you're already considering doing the same damn thing all over again.*

You're right. Why did I keep wanting to sacrifice myself? I wasn't a martyr, nor did I want to be. I just wanted *him* and my siblings safe...no matter the cost. But they were right. Even if I turned myself in, that wouldn't be enough...not for Drake. *I'm sorry.*

I need to know you won't ever do something like that again. He clutched my hand tighter.

I promise. I don't know what I was thinking. I wanted to kick myself for even considering it.

Some of his worry eased. *Good, because otherwise, I might have to give you a spanking.* A twinkle returned to his eye as his playfulness swirled inside me.

The vehicle fell back into a comfortable silence.

———

AN HOUR LATER, we passed through the small, quaint town of Mount Airy, North Carolina. Several miles past that, we turned onto a gravel road.

The Suburban bumped and jolted as we passed a few ranches and drove deeper into the woods. The houses were spread a few miles apart, and I was surprised the dirt road continued for so long. This had to be the thunder neighborhood.

Fifteen miles from the last paved road, Vlad pulled into a driveway. Before the vehicles were turned off, the front door of the white ranch house had opened, and an older man and woman rushed onto the wooden porch.

Vlad got out of the Suburban. "Mom. Dad. We need your help."

"You're alive," the man said, his voice quivering. He was close to seven feet tall with gray hair and a matching beard with a few hints of brown. He took a step toward Vlad but stopped when Thorn climbed out of the car.

"My baby boy." The woman's voice shook as tears trickled from her slate-gray eyes. Her hair was ashy blonde, several shades lighter than her son's. As she passed her husband, Vlad's father grabbed her arm.

The warmth vanished from his cobalt eyes. He glared at Thorn then flicked his attention to Vlad. "What have you done?"

MY HEART STOPPED. Vlad's parents recognized Thorn...but how? He'd been in hiding since he was six, and the only reason the royals knew what he looked like was because he'd shown up to save me.

"I can explain." Vlad lifted a hand. "But it would be better if you let us into the house before others see us."

His dad's body coiled, but his mom rushed over and hugged Vlad.

A lump formed in my throat. There was no way he was going to let us in. I clenched my hands, jumped out of the Suburban, then marched around the hood, ready to aid Vlad.

"Aiden." Vlad's mother pulled back and placed a hand on his father's forearm. "He's our son, and we've both missed him dearly. We can at least hear him out."

Huffing, Aiden scanned the area behind us. Pain flashed in his eyes. "Fine." He patted his mate's arm before dropping his hand and schooling his face into a stern expression. "But all of you get in here. The last thing we need is someone from the thunder seeing you without warning."

"Agreed." Vlad swirled a finger around, indicating we needed to move.

As Thorn hurried past me, his arm brushed mine, and the jolt surged through my body. Every touch from him was like a high I never wanted to come down from.

My siblings climbed out of the car, and my attention landed on Elliott. As expected, the Nintendo Switch bulged from his pocket. No wonder he wore baggy jeans. How else could he carry around his electronics?

I snapped my fingers and gestured to the game. "Leave it in the car."

"What?" Elliott lurched back and stuck out his bottom lip. "But they'll be talking, and I'll get bored."

Sometimes, it was hard to remember he was considered an adult. I lifted my head. "Boredom helps creativity. It's healthy to be bored from time to time." Mom had often told me that whenever I'd complain. One day, when I was a toddler, I'd gotten so bored that I must have driven her to her breaking point. At the time, we'd been tight on money, so she'd decided to splurge and buy some finger paints, starting my love of painting.

Elliott and Eva never learned that love because Peter had bought them all kinds of gadgets to keep them entertained.

His irises darkened with hurt. "Now you sound like Mom."

My heart panged, and I smiled sadly. "I'll take that as a compliment."

"Hurry up," Aiden rasped as he held open the front door.

I couldn't blame him for his uneasiness. If he knew who Thorn was, he knew he was inviting trouble into his home.

Vlad held out his hand, and Cassidy hurried to him as Thorn dashed to the driver's side back door to monitor Peter. My stepfather climbed out, and they glared at each other as we headed to the house.

Head hanging, Aiden sighed. "Dammit, Alina. They also brought humans. I should've listened to my gut."

"You did." Alina brushed a hand over his shoulder before stepping into the house. "You just needed me to guide you."

Vlad and Cassidy paused in front of the door, and Aiden blew a raspberry as he stepped to the side, allowing our group to enter.

One by one, we walked into the house, Thorn and I taking up the rear.

We stepped into the living room. It was large enough to hold all thirteen of us, but only two hunter green couches faced each other in the middle of the room. A black coffee table sat in the center with an open laptop on it. The walls were off-white, and a beige carpet ran everywhere I could see. The house must have been built in the eighties because it had popcorn ceilings.

Thorn walked behind a couch, and Peter went to a corner of the room. I stopped close by, so I could keep an eye on him.

Aiden's mom smiled as she strolled to Cassidy. "You're mated to my son."

"I am." Cassidy beamed. "I'm so glad to finally meet you."

Saphira snorted and plopped onto a couch. "Someone stand in front of the door. We don't need this one getting away." She gestured to Peter.

"Man." Elliott shuddered as he strolled over and sat next to her. "Let me tell you, even if he did get out, his sense of direction's crap. Dad can't find anything in Asheville, and he's lived there his entire life."

Good to know, Thorn connected as he moved beside me and took my hand. *Your brother is a wealth of information.*

He is. I hadn't even known that about Peter. This was the most talkative Elliot had ever been. It was like meeting a new person.

"Well, maybe we should let him go, then." Tyson sat across from Saphira, his brown eyes sparkling with interest. "He's been a pain."

"Even when the cops told him to come to my friend's house, he got lost." Elliott snickered.

Peter scowled. "Let's not bring up that night. No one wants to relive the phone call from the cops informing me that they found my *son* at a party with his pants down."

Saphira's brows furrowed. "Why were your pants down?"

"Of course, someone would ask." Eva grimaced. She knew the story.

"Senior prom." Elliott pounded his chest. "Me and some of the guys drank a lot and wanted to see how fast we could extinguish the bonfire."

Eva closed her eyes as if something were haunting her. "They decided to do it in front of us girls. Let's just say Dad was pissed when he didn't get the deposit back for Elliott's tux. Pee on a bonfire is one of the worst smells I've ever experienced in my whole life."

Errol took the spot on the other end of the couch Tyson was sitting on. The older man leaned back and murmured, "Thank gods I had a daughter."

"Oh, don't worry, Uncle Errol. Saphira has done—" Tyson started.

Saphira pointed at him and snarled, "Do *not* finish that sentence."

Chuckling, Brenton took the middle spot between his son and brother. "Yes, son. Don't."

"Is this why you came?" Aiden asked as he crossed his arms and glared at Vlad, who stood next to him. "To talk about peeing on bonfires? We don't hear anything from you for twenty-one years, and then you pull up with *him*"—he pointed at Thorn—"and three humans who aren't supposed to know about our existence."

Cassidy bristled but didn't say anything...at least out loud.

"No. They just *talk*. Incessantly." Vlad rubbed his hands together. "And I didn't reach out for the past twenty-one years to protect you."

"From what?" Aiden spread his arms. "Because it sure seems like you brought a shitstorm to our door."

"We thought you were dead." Alina stepped between Vlad and Aiden and placed a shaky hand on her son's arm. "We knew if you were alive, you wouldn't just disappear without a word, but it's apparent we were wrong."

Vlad ran his hands through his hair. "Remember the last job I left to do?"

Aiden's brows furrowed. "You mean the one you refused to tell us about? Something about the king and our security?"

"Yes," Vlad answered as he took Cassidy's hand. "The king hired me to kill someone who posed a threat to the dragon nation."

"Badass." Elliott bobbed his head, his eyes wide. "That's epic."

"It wasn't." Vlad cut his gaze to my brother. "I soon learned that the mission was to kill the six-year-old prince and his nanny."

Tyson sneered. "I knew the king was no good, especially with how he caters to his jackass son." He flinched and glanced at Thorn. "No offense."

Muscles tensing, Thorn shrugged. "Doesn't offend me. Vlad's my dad in all the ways that matter."

"Wait!" Elliott jumped to his feet. "You're a prince, too." His mouth dropped. "And you married my sister. Holy shit. I'm royalty!"

"I don't think that's how it works, E." Eva shook her head.

Errol chuckled. "That's definitely not how it works."

"Aw. Man." My brother sat back down like the world had treated him cruelly.

Patting his leg, Saphira winked. "Royalty is just a state of mind. If you think it, you can become it."

"Fuck, yeah." Elliott's entire body bobbed.

"Let me get this straight." Aiden rubbed the back of his neck. "The king hired you to do a job, and not only did you not follow through, but you also hid your targets from him?"

"He was a six-year-old *boy*," Cassidy snarled and turned to Aiden. "You'd be okay doing that if it was *your* job? And might I add, Thorn is an amazing, sweet, and loyal person. He doesn't deserve any of this."

"Sweet and loyal?" Aiden parroted and motioned to Peter. "We saw the video of the wedding where he kidnapped *her*." He gestured to me. "He stole people's dragons!"

Hurt, guilt, and love swirled from Thorn as he watched the situation unfold. I hated that he had to go through this, and I wouldn't let Cassidy and Vlad defend him alone. I lifted my chin. "Yes, he came to save me from being forced to marry a man I didn't want. And he, along with Vlad and Cassidy, *saved* my sister from becoming Drake's human breeder. He took those dragons, but we were outnumbered, and they were attacking us."

Aiden deflated. "They were forcing you to marry Prince Drake?"

I nodded.

"There's a more pressing question." Alina glanced from me to Eva. "Your sister is human? How is that possible?"

"I changed her." Thorn placed his hands on my shoulders. "And by doing so, I created my fated mate, who Drake tried to take away from me, after kidnapping Vlad and Cassidy."

My skin buzzed from his touch, and I leaned back against his large chest.

"The humans are here because Drake wants the one girl as his breeder and would use the other two to get you to turn yourself in." Aiden rubbed his temples and looked at Vlad. "You sure got yourself into a difficult situation."

"One I would gladly get into all over again if given the opportunity." Vlad focused on his parents. "When I attacked Thorn and Cassidy that day, twenty-one years ago, that little boy—the one the king was so desperate to kill—was more concerned about saving his nanny than himself. Yesterday, he walked into fire, knowing he was risking his life, to save his mate and her sister. In the twenty-one years in between, no one knew Thorn was alive. Everyone thought he was dead, and did he do anything to cause problems?"

Silence was the answer.

"You know he didn't, or it would've been all over the Dragonnet, like the wedding is now." Vlad clasped his hands together. "We have nowhere else to go."

"I hate to interrupt and ruin this moment." Errol stood and placed his hands in the pockets of his dark slacks. "But won't this be the first place Drake looks for us?"

"Not the first." Vlad rubbed his mouth. "But they will come eventually. We need to make a plan instead of rushing everywhere."

I sighed. This was only a short-term solution.

Hey, it'll be okay, Thorn connected and wrapped his arms around me. *No matter what, they won't get you or Eva again. As soon as we get settled, I'll get us fake IDs, so we can get the hell out of here.*

I turned and stared into his gorgeous eyes. *Eva and I aren't the only ones I'm worried about. I don't want anything bad to happen to any of us.*

He brushed his fingers across my cheek and rested his forehead against mine. *We'll make sure they're all set up before we go.*

Why did he keep mentioning leaving? My throat went dry, but I didn't want to get into that discussion right now.

"Over twenty years ago, they were watching this location like a hawk, and Vlad never made so much as a phone call to us." Aiden's voice thickened. "They'll probably search wherever they tracked you to before checking here again. But they *will* come, and it will be sooner, rather than later. You can't stay here."

My limbs trembled, and my pulse pounded in my ears. My attention flicked to Vlad, whose face had gone white and stony.

He'd expected his parents to help us.

"Fine." Vlad lifted his chin. "I get it. But for what it's worth, I wasn't trying to hurt you."

"No. It's *not* fine." Cassidy stepped around him and stared both his parents down. "Do you know how hard he struggled with not reaching out to you? Every holiday, every birthday, hell, even on your anniversary, Vlad fell apart, wishing we were part of your lives and part of the thunder he grew up with. He sacrificed his world to protect Thorn, me, and *all* of you. He didn't want to burden you with the knowledge that would make you a target for the king's abuse and maliciousness. But now we're here, asking for the help you're so upset he didn't ask for twenty-one years ago, and you're turning us away? Why? For vengeance? To get back at him for protecting us?"

Even if Thorn hadn't told me, I would have known they were fated mates by the way they defended each other. Cassidy wouldn't let Vlad's parents hurt him without having her say.

"Why did he decide to stop protecting us?" Aiden lifted a brow. "Are we no longer worthy?"

Cassidy laughed bitterly. "That's not it, at all. He finally found a reason to come home. He's been hoping for one every day for the past twenty-one years, but nothing could justify it. Now, there *is* a reason, and your son needs your help. This was why I tried talking him out of coming here to begin with."

"That's what people do when given a chance." Thorn released me and took my hand, tugging me to follow him as he stepped up beside Vlad. "They disappoint you. All these years, Vlad talked about what an amazing man you are, but you're no better than the king. Let's go. We've wasted too much time here."

Thorn let go of me and forced Peter toward the door. Saphira and the others stood from the couches, and our group moved to leave.

When Vlad touched the doorknob, Alina called out, "Wait. Please don't leave. Not yet."

Aiden growled. "Alina."

I turned around to see the older woman glaring at him as she said, "You had your say. Now it's *my* turn to get stuff off my chest."

CHAPTER TWENTY

I HOPED whatever she was about to say would be in our favor. So far, in the face of Vlad's sudden resurrection, she'd been the more level-headed of the two.

Vlad didn't turn. He continued to face the door, his hand on the knob. Cassidy stood close, ready to defend her mate.

"Your father has made it clear where he stands, but as soon as you walk out the door and leave, he'll regret it." Alina flexed her fingers at her sides. "And, even if he doesn't, I won't stand here and turn my back on my son, even if Aiden is the leader of our thunder."

"Alina," Aiden growled, but the older woman ignored him.

"Unfortunately, I do agree it's too risky for you to stay here. Not just for us but for our thunder. The royals could be on their way here now. I can give you cash so you can rent rooms at a hotel the next town over, and I'll make some calls to find a place for you to stay in the near future."

My lungs inflated more freely again. I'd thought we were doomed, and his mother was helping us, although mainly for Vlad's benefit.

Grimacing, Vlad slowly turned and looked at his mother.

The rest of us shuffled to the side so we weren't blocking their view of each other.

"Thank you," he rasped, his eyes glistening.

Though I hadn't been around him long, I already knew he was a strong, smart man, yet his parents had so much influence over him. From what I'd seen, parents didn't understand the lasting impact they had on their children until random moments of clarity like this.

My heart ached, and my fingers caressed the pendants of the bracelet Mom had given me. Even six years later, her loss still gaped inside me, especially when something good or bad happened, and I reached for the phone to call her, only to remember that was impossible.

Thorn pushed warm love and comfort through our connection, knowing exactly what I needed. Though I no longer had Mom, I had him, and that meant more to me than the world.

"Of course." Her body shook harder. When she stopped in front of him, a tear trickled down her cheek. "But it comes with one stipulation."

I tensed. I'd thought this had been going so well. Had that been an illusion?

Vlad huffed. "Which is?"

"You *can't* disappear on us again," she murmured and hugged him. "I can't survive it a second time."

His face crumpled, and Cassidy glanced at Thorn, then flicked her eyes toward the door.

She wanted us to leave, so I wasn't surprised when Thorn said, "Let's give Vlad a moment with his parents. Everyone, get in the Suburbans. We'll leave as soon as he's ready." He walked over to Peter, standing close, not willing to risk my stepdad trying to run.

Saphira nodded. Gently nudging Alina and Vlad out of the way, she opened the door. We walked to the vehicles and climbed into the ones we'd ridden in here. Thorn put Peter back in the front passenger seat and got into the seat behind him to keep watch. He didn't trust Peter to sit behind us since he seemed to be trying to find a way to

There was a garage, but we parked both vehicles in the driveway, facing the road in case we needed to exit quickly. Ten steps led to a front porch with four teal Adirondack chairs angled invitingly toward each other. Behind the chairs was a large wooden door with a glass storm door in front of it.

As soon as the engine turned off, Peter sighed.

I wondered if there was anything like dragon metal that we could use to put him into a deep slumber until we got things settled. If dragons were real, then maybe Maleficent existed too, and she could spell something for him to prick his finger on and sleep for a hundred years.

One could hope, but Thorn had mentioned only wolf and bear shifters. I hadn't asked about vampires, witches, demons, or angels.

My heart thudded, and my skin crawled. The idea of vampires wigged me out more than the others. I rubbed my neck where my pulse pounded under my skin.

Thorn glanced at me and linked, *I won't let him be rude to you. I'll knock him out in a split second if that will make you feel less uneasy.*

That's not it. My throat constricted with how much I felt for him. *I was wondering if vampires, witches, angels, and demons are real. I'm a dragon shifter, but I don't know anything about the supernatural world.*

His gaze softened. *Vampires and witches are real. Angels and demons are not. We won't run into vampires out here. They live in cities where their food source is all around. The bigger the city, the more vampires live there. Witches tend to live out in the woods and keep to themselves. Out here, we're more likely to run into witches than vampires, but even that's unlikely. Witches can sense energy, and they'd know we're here. They wouldn't come near us unless they needed something for themselves.*

Everyone got out of the vehicle, and Thorn connected as he stayed close by Peter, *The code is 4181210 to get in the house.*

I walked up the steps, opened the storm door, then punched the code into the device above the doorknob. There was a click, and I pushed the door open. We entered a large den with wood paneling and maple hardwood floors. Two black couches sat across from each other with two large black ottomans between them and centered in front of a large flat-screen television. In the back of the room was a fully equipped pool table.

Across the room from the front entrance, a double sliding glass door overlooked a flowing river. If I'd had a canvas and paints, this would've made for a perfect landscape to paint.

We piled into the house, and Thorn gestured to the wooden stairs on the right. "There are two bedrooms upstairs. A second master, which I thought Vlad and Cassidy could have, and another room with twin bunk beds and a full-size bed."

"Maybe I should go lie down." Peter crossed his arms. "I have a headache due to some menacing dragon hovering over me."

Thorn beamed. "Take the one upstairs with the bunk beds."

"I'll watch him," Saphira offered with a smirk. "I've wanted to have a *chat* with him since the first time I heard him speak to Everly."

"Saphy," Errol gasped and nodded toward the twins.

"Nah, it's fine." Elliott waved a hand. "Just knock Dad out, and I'll watch him. He's easier to be around when he's asleep."

My eyes widened. Peter had never been very involved with the twins, but he wasn't rude to them like he was to me. I'd thought he didn't interact with them much because I was around, but maybe I'd been wrong.

I stopped breathing. Maybe I'd broken my promise to Mom before I even realized it.

Thorn turned to Peter. "All it'll take is one hateful tone, word, or attack, and I *will* knock your ass out again." He took my hand. "If you even look at my *wife* with a hateful expression, I will end you."

The jolt sizzled between us, and my heart doubled in size. Mom had always been in my corner, but not even she could match his devotion. I wasn't sure what I'd done to deserve such a sexy and amazing person, but I wouldn't complain. With Thorn, I was happier than I'd ever been, even when dealing with constant threats.

Jaw twitching, Peter closed his eyes as his Adam's apple bobbed. "I got it."

Saphira snorted. "Are you sure? Because you said that earlier and got knocked out again. I don't even know why." She pouted and glanced at Thorn. "What did he do?"

Turning to the side, Thorn lifted his shirt to reveal where Peter had cut him. The cut was just a scab thanks to shifter healing. That healing speed was the only reason I'd survived the fall in the woods when I'd cracked my skull. If Thorn hadn't accidentally changed me, I would've died.

Seeing his injury had my blood boiling. "If he does anything to Thorn again, I'll kick his ass."

A huge smile crossed Cassidy's face. "I'm so glad Thorn found you."

"I'm not," Peter grumbled so low he had to think we couldn't hear him. "If he hadn't gotten involved, Everly would be with Drake, and none of this would've happened. Once again, it's all *her* fault."

A snarl rattled Thorn's chest, but I tugged him back and wrapped my arms around him—well, as far as they would go. Though Peter was a jerk, he hadn't meant for us to hear him. When my arms touched Thorn, some of his anger eased as our connection thrummed at full speed.

"Just so you know," Tyson said as he sat on the couch close to the back door. "Every one of us heard you. Dragons have excellent hearing. Everly is the only reason you didn't get knocked out again."

Face blanching, Peter suddenly found the floor very interesting.

"I'm going out for some fresh air." Eva walked across the den.

Before she could reach the back door, Cassidy shook her head. "I'm sorry, but we all need to stay inside. A dragon could fly overhead, and if the wedding was broadcast, they'll know your face. I'll order us pizza, but we are stuck inside."

"Then it's a good thing we have this to keep us entertained."

Brenton strolled to the pool table and grabbed a stick. "Come on, Errol. I bet I can still kick your ass."

Elliott and Eva sat on the couch next to Tyson, and Elliott pulled out the Switch and gave one of the controllers to Eva. Tyson settled in to watch them play, while Cassidy removed her phone from her pocket and headed to a door on the left that led to the kitchen.

"I've been sitting enough," Peter grumbled as he moved to the corner of the room farthest from everyone. "I'll just stay here."

"Fine with me." Saphira sat on the couch closest to us and patted the middle seat. "Come watch something with me, Everly."

Not wanting to stand around, I led Thorn over and sat down, and Saphira searched for something on TV. I snuggled up with Thorn, relieved to be with him and not in danger. For this moment, the two of us could just be.

The next morning, my body thrummed, and my eyes fluttered open. My body felt rested despite barely having any room on the full-size bed. Thorn took up almost all the space due to his size, but that meant I'd been wrapped in his arms all night.

Last night had been rough. Thorn and I had wound up in the room upstairs with Peter and Elliott, with Cassidy and Vlad in the master bedroom close by. Saphira and Eva had taken the master bedroom downstairs, and Tyson, Brenton, and Errol had stayed in the other room downstairs with a bunk bed and a twin.

After spending some time with his parents, making things right with his dad, Vlad had arrived in better spirits.

A large, warm hand slipped under my shirt and rested on my stomach. My body warmed, and I bit my inner lip, trying to keep my head on straight. Peter and Elliott were right across from us in the bunk bed.

But that didn't stop the desire from knotting in my stomach. Thorn's lips were on my neck, and I'd begun to forget why this was a bad idea when there was a loud knock on the front door.

Thorn's arm tensed around me. Then he released me and jumped to his feet.

Peter and Elliott were still snoring loudly across the room, but even that couldn't block the noise from downstairs.

After a second, another series of loud knocks pounded on the door, and my lungs seized.

Thorn threw open our door just as Vlad and Cassidy ran past, heading down the stairs. By the time I made it out of the room, Vlad was opening the front door with Cassidy beside him and Thorn halfway down the stairs.

"Mom?" Vlad asked breathlessly. "What's wrong? I thought Dad was supposed to come."

My heart pounded as I reached the bottom step and stopped next to Thorn.

Alina stood in the doorway, eyes wide and cheeks pink. She glanced around, as if expecting someone to show up, then put a piece of paper in Vlad's hand. "Go there. Now. The warriors are at our thunder."

CHAPTER TWENTY-ONE

"WHAT?" Vlad stiffened. "How did you get out of there?"

"I'd already left the house this morning to help set up the booth at the local farmer's market with some of the thunder women." Alina rubbed her hands together, her head haloed by faint pink and dark purple clouds that indicated the sun was about to rise. "Luckily, we usually do go to the market together, so it wasn't out of the ordinary. Aiden linked, telling me they were on their way and to come here and let you know." She hugged her son as she rasped, "I've got to get back. They're demanding everyone return. Go there." She pointed at the paper. "The leader of the thunder can be trusted, but he's not happy about getting involved. He's doing it for your father. Make sure the human man behaves."

I froze. Everything kept getting worse instead of better.

Thorn wrapped an arm around my waist, and I leaned into his side, both of us experiencing the sadness of watching Vlad and his mom say goodbye again. They'd already lost twenty-one years together because of the king, and now they would lose even more time.

Alina pulled away and glanced at Cassidy. Alina placed her

hands on the younger woman's shoulders and gave her a heart-breaking smile. "One day, I hope I get to know you. From everything Vlad told us about you, I know you're an amazing woman, and you already feel like the daughter we always wanted. Keep him safe."

Cassidy's eyes glistened. "I promise. I'll do anything in my power to protect him."

"I know." Alina turned to Thorn, and her lips mashed into a line. "I'm sorry for the hell you've gone through. We need you to prove to the world that our king and prince are wrong in how they lead. It's your destiny."

My dragon inched forward, brushing against my mind. She agreed with everything Alina had said, and my human side did too. The king had allowed fear to govern his decisions, and Drake was an asshole. Thorn was a good man who understood the struggles of living like no other royal could.

"Screw destiny." Thorn's eyes glinted. "I'm not interested in helping the very people who turned their backs on me without a moment's hesitation. There are only three people I'm concerned with keeping safe—Everly, Cassidy, and Vlad. They've never betrayed me, not even when the opportunity presented itself."

His fingers tensed, digging into my skin. The jolt shot through me, giving me a feeling of peace only he could provide, but part of me ached for him. Though I agreed with Alina, I understood where he was coming from. Even Saphira hadn't wanted to believe or help him at first, and she would've turned her back on him if not for me.

Alina winced and opened her mouth, but her eyes glowed, and she exhaled. "I've got to go, and you all need to get out of here. They're already spreading out to search the area, so it won't be long until they come here." A tear trickled down her face as she scanned the four of us again before turning around. She darted to her vehicle before she paused and glanced over her shoulder. "Like I told Vlad growing up, fear forces people to do stupid things, and sometimes, you've got to be the bigger person to prove to everyone they're wrong."

Her words washed over me. If what the king had said about Thorn's grandfather was true, there was a reason people feared Thorn's magic. Though they were wrong, they had no way of knowing they were associating one person's horrible actions with Thorn.

Vlad cleared his throat. "Just...please, you and Dad be careful, and if you need help, you have my cell phone number."

"I love all of you. Be safe." She got into the car and drove away.

We stood in silence until her headlights blended in with the trees. I hadn't been up for ten minutes, and already we'd found ourselves in yet another threatening situation.

Thorn's anger wafted through our bond, and I wrapped my arms around his waist to calm him, before the stress of fleeing again added more strain to the tension running thick within him.

He kissed my forehead, the jolt zinging to my core. He connected, *I'm fine. I promise.*

My head tilted back. *Are you sure? And how did you know I was worried?*

The corners of his mouth tipped upward. *With you here beside me, I can get through anything. And I can feel your worry.* His anger faded into warmth and the same emotion he usually emanated toward me—love.

I hated to ruin the moment, but we had no time to waste. "Let's get packed."

We split up to inform the others that we had to leave, and I headed to the bedroom on the main level where Eva and Saphira were rooming together.

Within five minutes, we were loaded up in the vehicles and heading toward the main road. Like last time, Vlad drove one vehicle and Cassidy the other. If something were to happen, the two of them could use their fated mate link to communicate without a phone.

This time, Eva rode in the front passenger seat next to Cassidy, with Thorn and me in the middle row, and Peter and Elliott in the back. At first, Eva had complained about not sitting with Elliott so they could play a game, but Peter wanted to sit in the back, so she'd jumped into the front seat willingly.

She'd grown up a lot during the past week, and the fact was bittersweet. She'd needed a little bit of grounding. Eva and Elliott usually retreated into video games and each other, instead of dealing with their problems, but I *hated* that her wake-up call had come through Drake. The man could have stripped her innocence away at a time of his choosing, a thought that had my blood run cold. I had to hold on to the fact that she hadn't actually experienced that.

The address Alina had given us was over an hour and a half away, near the small town of Abingdon, Virginia. Elliott grumbled and groaned in the backseat, while Peter breathed loudly as he sat behind me on the passenger side.

Thorn had fetched Elliott and Peter, and when my stepdad had come downstairs to join us, he'd been pale and visibly shaking. Obviously, Thorn had said something to get him to cooperate, but I hadn't asked Thorn what. As long as Peter behaved, I didn't give a damn. Peter deserved whatever he got, and I knew Thorn wouldn't actually kill him because of me and my love for my siblings.

When the GPS alerted us that we were twenty minutes away, Eva fidgeted in her seat. "What are the people helping us like?"

Cassidy stared straight ahead as we drove through a charming downtown. Brick buildings stood to our right, and to our left was a small community park with a water fountain in the middle. She answered, "I have no idea, and neither does Vlad."

A hateful snort came from Peter. "Figures. You kidnap me and Elliott and take us to people you don't even know. How do we know we aren't walking into a trap?"

My dragon snarled as my breathing quickened. He always had to be negative and patronizing, and I couldn't let it roll off me like I had so many times before.

"Technically, I'm here willingly." Elliott lowered his Switch. "Which means it's not kidnapping."

Turning around in my seat, I narrowed my eyes. "You'd rather have stayed home so Drake could use you to force Eva to return to be his human breeder? Is that what you're saying?"

"If you—" he started.

Thorn's growl was so loud that my ears rang. He rasped, "If the next words out of your mouth insult my wife in any way, I will *end* you. I'm sick and tired of the way you treat her."

My dragon purred. The Everly from a month ago would've been appalled and considered his threat a red flag, but not this version. I wanted to rub my body all over him to show my appreciation for how much he loved me.

Peter huffed and leaned back in his seat, and I faced forward. Thorn's pupils turned to slits as he scanned me. My body warmed, needing him in a way that was very inappropriate while in a car, surrounded by other people and headed into unknown territory.

The bond between us sizzled.

I bit my bottom lip, trying to force some sanity back into myself. *I love you,* I connected with him. Those were the three best words I could come up with to start expressing the extent of my feelings for him.

You own me, he replied, the spicy scent of his arousal surging between us.

Those words had a desperate need building within, stronger than before. Every cell burned, and I had the overwhelming urge to unbuckle and straddle him.

"We're fifteen minutes out," Cassidy said a little too loudly, and my face burned.

She must have smelled my desire, which would have been awkward enough without her being my mother-in-law.

My heart pattered. Thorn was my mate and husband. I couldn't get over that. Though the wedding had been forced and I would've preferred something Thorn and I had planned together, I'd already known he'd be my husband someday. I wished it had been about the two of us and not Drake and me.

We turned onto a road that took us deeper into a thickly wooded area, away from downtown, which I would've loved to visit if Drake hadn't been hunting us.

Thorn chuckled, the sound warm and sexy. *Don't be embarrassed. We're fated mates. New ones at that. Our reaction to each other is expected and normal.*

Maybe. I suspected my emotions for him would never change, and that was both terrifying and thrilling. *But she's your mom.*

Remember, you'll smell her and Vlad for the same reason. He winked.

My body felt light and carefree. He made me so damn happy, and I couldn't figure out how I'd lasted twenty-two years without him.

The remainder of the ride passed quickly as the two of us enjoyed each other's company. When we hadn't passed anyone for several miles, Cassidy turned onto a dirt road that we would've likely missed if the GPS hadn't given us a hundred-foot warning.

The road curved as the white and chestnut oaks and loblolly pines thickened. The area seemed more remote than Thorn's cabin and Vlad's parents' thunder. We continued along the curving dirt road with nothing but woods thickening around us.

"Y'all, I hate to agree with Dad, but am I the only one who has ever watched a horror movie?" Elliott grumbled. "I mean, come on. I say we turn the fuck around."

"El, chill." Eva turned toward us and rolled her eyes. "You know I've watched them. I was sitting right next to you every damn time, holding your hand so you wouldn't cry."

"Gah, don't *lie*," he scoffed. "I told you, I had something in my eye."

She tilted her head. "Every time someone jumped out with an ax or machete?"

"I admit, the timing wasn't the best, but my eyelashes clearly have a mind of their own," he retorted. "Yes, it sounds suspicious, but dammit, you'll just have to trust me."

Does he really cry during horror movies? Thorn connected as he smirked, stealing my breath away.

Just one little move, and he turned me into complete mush. *I don't know. They didn't include me in all things twinning.*

His brows bunched together. *Twinning?*

That's what they call their one-on-one time—or when they say things at the same time. I realized they hadn't used the phrase in the past day or two, probably because Eva still wasn't quite herself. This moment right here was the closest she'd been to the Eva I was used to.

"Will you two stop it?" Peter snapped. "I don't know what's worse. Hearing you babble back and forth or being stuck around—"

Thorn's head jerked toward Peter, and my stepdad blanched.

"Woods," Peter finally said. "There's no telling what kind of wild creatures are out here."

Laughter bubbled in my chest, and I bit the corner of my mouth to prevent it from spilling out. My humor died, though, when we rolled over a hill and the woods opened to reveal a modern white barn. A red truck with an extended cab was parked next to it, and a sizable man around Vlad's father's age leaned against the wall by the large wooden door.

As we descended, the side of the barn came into view. This place was the size of a large house. There were two windows in the front and two on the visible side, and they were covered by some sort of barrier, likely wood, which prevented me from seeing inside.

When we all got out of the vehicles, Thorn marched over to stand between Peter and me and took my hand. He cut his gaze to Peter, who stiffened.

Good.

The older man's gray hair was styled back, and his muscles bulged from under his polo shirt. His warm tanned skin gave his six-and-a-half-foot frame a healthy glow.

His rich brown eyes narrowed as he lifted his chin and settled his gaze on Thorn. "I'd hoped that Aiden was wrong, but the resurrected dragon prince who steals other shifters' dragons is, in fact, part of the group he asked me to hide."

"My father wouldn't lie." Vlad stepped forward, blocking Thorn partially from the man's view. "And here I thought you were his oldest friend, Theron."

Theron snarled and arched a brow. "I am, but that doesn't mean I couldn't hope he was mistaken."

Uncomfortable heat emanated through my connection with Thorn. His hand tightened on mine as he rasped, "If you didn't want to chance me being here, you should've said no."

"You're right. I wasn't thinking clearly, especially since you've come here seeking shelter and are speaking that way to the very person who's risking so much by taking you in." Theron sneered. "Your presence here puts my entire thunder at risk, especially my son."

Especially his son? That was an odd thing to add.

"If you don't want us here—" Cassidy started.

Theron lifted a hand. "I *don't* want you here. Alerting the warriors to your presence would be the smart thing to do."

Thorn tensed, and my heart stopped.

"But Aiden has never asked me for a favor, so I'm doing this for *him*. Make no mistake—if anything goes awry, you *will* leave without putting up a fight. If you can't promise that, I won't give you access to the hiding spot." The man's face was lined with worry, and his voice grew thick with emotion. "Sol is already on Drake's radar, and I can't make him more of a target. He's already lost too much."

His heartbreak called to me. His tone was so familiar, reminding me of when I'd had to tell people that my mom had cancer.

The words were rough against my throat, but I asked the one question I'd hoped to ask when I was a doctor. "What's wrong with your son? Why is Drake a danger to him?"

Theron's head jerked back, and he inhaled sharply. "Drake is hunting him, too."

CHAPTER TWENTY-TWO

I WAITED WITH BATED BREATH, but I wasn't sure I wanted to know the answer. That was the thing about knowledge. Once you had it, there were no takebacks. Knowledge was power, but sometimes, it had the power to destroy you.

Theron's face twisted as if he smelled something horrid. "Is this a joke? You're the royals' advisor."

"No, I'm the *king's* advisor." Errol winced. "Or I was. Pretty sure I can't do that when I'm on the run."

"What's the difference?" Theron snapped, his nostrils flaring, "They're one and the same."

Everyone was focusing on the wrong thing. I took a step forward. "Can you humor us?" I waved my free hand between me and the others. "I have no inkling of what you're referring to."

"I'm with her." Saphira placed her hands on her hips and stared him down. "Drake shouldn't be *doing* anything. He's just the prince, not the king."

Theron's brows furrowed as he studied us. Then his jaw slackened. "You really don't know?"

"I just learned about the existence of dragons, so..." Elliott quipped from behind me, where Thorn and I had positioned ourselves to keep the humans from Theron's attention.

Thorn closed his eyes as if he'd already learned there was no stopping my brother.

That was probably true, but I'd at least try. I gave him a stern look over my shoulder.

"Hey, you may be my older sister, but you don't get to *mom* me." Elliott moved so he could see Theron. "There should be no surprise about my lack of knowledge. I just wanted to be upfront and clear."

Eva groaned. "El, for goodness' sake, I'm with Everly on this one."

"I'd rather never have learned about dragons or been forced to come here," Peter complained. He glared at Thorn in challenge, the very thing Thorn had told him not to do.

Hot rage boiled through our bond, and his dragon roared, hurting my ears. But that had been my stepdad's point.

Babe, he wants you to blow up and give this man a reason to call Drake, I connected. I understood how Thorn felt, but Peter was intelligent. He knew exactly what he was doing. *If you want to teach him a lesson later, fine. Just not now.*

The heat cooled marginally, informing me I'd gotten through to him.

"And humans? Really? Harboring the prince and the runaway fiancée wasn't enough?" Theron hung his head, but then his gaze jerked back up to me. "Wait. They're your family?"

He didn't have to say more. I understood the unasked question. "Yes. Thorn changed me, which is why Drake took Eva, my sister, to become his human breeder and wanted me as his..."

Thorn fisted his hand.

Yeah, I couldn't force myself to say *wife,* so I could only imagine how he felt thinking I might say it.

"He's a prick." Tyson sneered, his body shaking with such rage. "He ruins everything he touches."

"Son," Brenton warned. Then he bit his bottom lip.

"Dad, we aren't back *there*." Tyson spread out his arms and glanced at the sun, which had risen high in the sky, indicating it was close to noon. "Theron has his own grievances with Prince Drake, which I still want to hear."

"So do I." Errol rubbed the back of his neck. "Do you mind sharing?"

Theron pushed away from the barn and strolled past the edge of the group and onto the dirt driveway. He kicked at the ground, raising a small dust cloud, which the faint, cool breeze blew away from us toward the trees.

"The past few years, Drake has made an unofficial decree." Theron placed his hands behind his back and stared into the trees. "I only learned of it this past year. He's been eradicating the weak, and with every week, he's been searching closer and closer to here."

Eradicating.

The word hovered around us, making the air so heavy I couldn't breathe.

Inhaling sharply, Brenton placed a hand on his son's shoulder and asked, "What do you mean by 'weak' and 'eradicating'?"

"The weak—as in any dragon who isn't at their peak." Theron straightened his shoulders. "The old, the weak, and especially the handful of dragons with some sort of disability...like my son. And you know what 'eradicate' means."

I grew lightheaded, and Thorn's shock ran through our bond, adding to my turbulent emotions.

"Are you saying Drake is *killing* dragons?" Saphira clutched her chest. "His own people?"

Theron nodded, his face flushed. A vein bulged between his eyes. "It's been happening for the past three years, apparently, but we just learned of the trauma when a thunder in Utah alerted us a year ago. Forty dragons were killed, leaving the thunder at a total of fifty."

The numbers didn't make sense. "Wait. I thought you said only the old, weak, and disabled. Forty out of ninety is an awfully large number." That was almost a fifty percent death rate in one attack.

That much of the population couldn't be old, and weak, and disabled dragons appeared to be rare. Hell, even though Theron and Aiden had to be in their sixties, they didn't look that old, except for the gray hair. They were just as muscular and strong as Vlad and Thorn, which made sense, given dragons lived for about five hundred years.

"They also killed any thunder member who didn't agree with the man Drake designated as the new leader. A friend of mine who left our thunder to join his mate's thunder gave me a heads-up because he knows about my son. Otherwise, we'd have been clueless until they attacked."

Vlad rubbed a hand down his face. "Drake needs people who won't revolt against him or rat him out to the king."

Theron laughed humorlessly. "You're still sticking with the king not knowing that his son—his heir—is doing these things?"

"He does *not*." Errol's jaw tensed. "I would've overheard something if he did, and I'm still confused about how it would be possible."

"I believe King Arman is clueless." Tyson's lips curved. "Drake injured me, lied to his dad, and drove us to live on the outskirts of town. He blamed me for it. He's a jackass, and he intends to finish the job of killing me."

Drake was a psychopathic narcissist. The very worst kind in the world.

I turned to Peter and arched a brow. "You still want to go home?"

He scowled but didn't respond.

"That's why it's a huge risk to have you here." Theron scrubbed his hands through his hair. "Because of the potential attack, I bought this land in case Sol and I had to leave fast and go into hiding for a while. We're an hour's flight from my thunder, so the risk is a lot less than having you at our location. As long as you stay put so there's no risk of anyone seeing you, everything should be fine. I stocked the kitchen while you were on your way here."

"We understand." Errol stepped forward, a warm smile on his face. "We appreciate the shelter you're providing."

"Wait." Saphira eyed the barn warily. "We're staying *here?*"

"Won't be much different from how you smell now," Tyson quipped, bumping her arm. "Maybe it'll be an improvement."

"Absolutely not." Peter shook his head. "*This* is where we're expected to stay? Hell no. You all need to take me home. This is the final straw. I'd rather take my chances with Drake."

Thorn snarled. "You won't make it that far because your death will happen before you make it five feet from me. I will not allow Drake to capture you and use you as leverage against Eva and Everly."

Recoiling, Theron pressed his lips into a line.

He wasn't happy with how Thorn was handling things, and my heart sank.

I was done having the same conversation repeatedly. I lifted my chin and glared at my stepdad. "Peter. There are two ways this can go down. One, you behave and understand that the *only* reason you're here is because you're Eva and Elliott's dad and we're trying to protect you and your children. Or two, we can gag you and tie you to a chair so you can't eat, pee, or get a drink of water without permission. I refuse to let you keep pushing everyone's buttons, and the sound of your voice is getting on my nerves. One more negative thing, and you will have made your choice...permanently."

Peter's eyes darkened and sweat sprouted above his lip.

Apparently, my threat had been more effective than Thorn's, which surprised me, but I'd take it.

Theron squared his shoulders. "I'm serious. *One* more thing to make me regret allowing all of you here, and I will evict you, and you can become someone else's problem. Do I make myself clear?" He glared at each of us. "I've got backup measures in place. If I disappear or show up late, I've instructed several members of my pack to notify Drake. I can use my fated-mate bond to give my wife the barn's location if Drake comes, and if I don't return, she can bring the warriors here."

"Having Drake show up is a risk to your son." Cassidy ran her hands along her stomach. "Surely, you wouldn't contact him."

"First off, my son wouldn't be there when they arrived, so it's not an issue." Theron crossed his arms. "And second, Drake has made a video stating that anyone with information on Thorn and Everly that results in their capture will be owed a great debt. That would come in handy if he ever does learn about my son."

I wanted to tell him that Drake was lying, but he wouldn't believe me. I could see the determination in his eyes. He believed that, since Drake had said it on the Dragonnet, he couldn't go back on his word. Explaining Drake's treachery would just be another strike against us.

Theron glanced at the sky. "I've got to return home before they get nervous." Then he focused on Vlad and walked over, handing him keys while saying, "I'm trusting this group because of your father. Don't let me down."

"We won't." Vlad took the keys. "I promise. We want to remain hidden until we figure out what to do."

"Don't go into town. We can't risk exposing you and this place." Theron headed toward the tree line. "I'll be back tomorrow to check in and make sure there isn't something you're lacking. There are clothes inside, though I'm not sure they'll fit all of you. What's here is yours, just as long as you take good care of things."

"Thank you." I nodded at him, and some of the weight of the world disappeared from my shoulders. This man seemed like a good guy, and I hoped we'd have a few days to regroup.

He darted into the tree line to shift and go back to his thunder.

The eleven of us remained quiet, and soon we heard the faint noises of limbs cracking, indicating Theron was in his dragon form. In animal form, he'd be able to sense us, even that far away.

My dragon grumbled, and the urge to shift damn near overtook me. It'd been almost a week since I'd shifted, and she was growing restless. *Do you think the two of us could go flying tonight?*

Thorn grimaced, and guilt squeezed our bond. *Of course. I should've thought of that before now.*

My shoulders sagged. I hadn't meant to make him feel guilty. *It's not your fault. We've been on the run. But yes, my dragon is urging me to shift.*

We'll take care of that, he promised. He placed a hand on the small of my back just as Vlad slid the key into the lock and opened the door.

"Oh, thank gods." Saphira marched inside. "It's not actually a barn."

We entered a large open area that reminded me of Peter's basement back in Asheville where his home office was located. The floor was concrete, and although there wasn't a large desk inside, there were four plastic benches that each seated four. To the left was an island bar that had a few bottles of wine and whiskey, and there was even a black telescope in the corner. A loft overlooked the room, and I wondered where the stairs were to reach it.

On the far side of the room, two white walls divided up more living areas. Each wall had a door midway down.

Saphira hurried to the left side and flung open a door, revealing a hallway. She wandered in as Tyson and Eva hurried over.

Let's check out the other side, Thorn linked as he led me to the right side.

We walked through that door. Inside was a long hallway with the same concrete floor. The first door to the left opened to a bedroom with a queen mattress and cream walls. The mattress lay on the floor, but there were gray sheets and a comforter on top. There was no furniture, paintings, or anything personal, but this was a safe house.

On the far side of the bed, a sliding glass door led out back to a fire pit. On the other side of the room, I spotted sliding closet doors and a bathroom. I wandered over and peered in. The tub was standard size with a marbled shower wall. A toilet sat between the shower and the sink, and the cabinet under the sink was small. The bathroom wasn't tiny, but it wasn't roomy, either.

We headed back out and found a half bath at the end of the hall and, to the right, a den with a big flat-screen TV and an L-shaped, brown couch. Walking through the den, we located a small laundry room to the left and a sizable white kitchen to the right. The stove, refrigerator, and dishwasher were silver, and all the cabinets were white with a gray laminate countertop. On the right side of the room was a round, white, wooden table that seated eight.

Peter, Elliott, Vlad, and Cassidy strolled into the kitchen behind us with Saphira and the others only steps behind.

We fanned out, and Saphira, Eva, Elliott, and Peter sat at the table.

"This place is large enough for us." Cassidy sighed as she brushed past us toward the stove. "I was worried for a second."

"There's only one bedroom over here." Thorn pulled me against the wall beside the dishwasher.

"Yeah, but there're three bedrooms on the other side, as well as three full bathrooms. The one bedroom with a black couch and bunk beds also has the stairway to the loft, which has another bunk bed and a full-size mattress. So technically, there are five bedrooms in total." Saphira ran a hand over the cream wall and wrinkled her nose. "They could have chosen a better color. It's so bright."

That was the least of my worries. "Are there enough beds for all of us?"

"The second bedroom has two double beds, and the last one is a bigger room with a queen, like on this side." Brenton gestured to where we'd come from. "With two fated-mate couples, that works out perfectly."

I didn't know how we'd gotten so lucky, but after all the shit luck we'd had, I was more than willing to take it.

Cassidy opened the refrigerator, and Theron hadn't been lying. The entire fridge was full with no space to spare. He'd made sure we wouldn't need to leave for anything, but with our metabolisms as dragon shifters, I was certain the food wouldn't last long. There were steaks, vegetables, milk, cheeses, hamburger meat, chicken—pretty much anything we could want. We owed this man so much money.

My stomach grumbled. I'd gone way too long without food. We'd run out of the house this morning without eating.

Tyson laughed. "I'm glad that was someone else and not me."

My face burned, and I turned into Thorn's chest. When I tilted my head up, Thorn beamed at me with adoration in his eyes. He kissed my forehead and said, "Let me go make my baby something to eat."

"Nope, I can handle that," Cassidy said, shooing him away. "Besides, Vlad has other plans for the rest of you."

Thorn narrowed his eyes. "Like what?"

"Training." Vlad rubbed his hands together. "Errol, Saphira, Brenton, and Tyson have led sheltered lives. They need to be able to hold their own when the warriors inevitably find us, and Everly is a brand-new dragon."

"It's a waste of time," Thorn said, his hand tensing. "We won't be here for long. We'll leave the country. If we go somewhere remote, we should be able to hide. There's no need to learn how to fight if there's no battle."

"Uh, I have a family business." Peter scowled, but he kept his tone from its usual cruel cadence. "I can't just leave."

His company wasn't our problem, but what Thorn wanted to do was. My heart ached, and I murmured, "You want to run away?"

"Not run away." Thorn faced me, giving me his full attention. "Protect you and everyone we love. Here, we'll be in constant danger."

"Honey, do you really think Drake will stop hunting you?" Cassidy shut the refrigerator door. "You're a threat to him and the throne."

She was right. Drake wouldn't stop looking, especially with Eva and me involved. "And what about your people? We just learned that Drake is hunting and killing some of them." I swallowed hard as I placed a hand on his chest.

"We've gone through this." Thorn brushed his fingers against my face. "As long as you and my family are safe, that's all that matters. The other dragons will figure out their problems on their own."

The jolt penetrated my soul, encouraging me to take a step closer. King Arman had done a number on him, and I could only try to undo the damage. I opened my mouth to speak but couldn't.

"Uh...where do I fit into this picture?" Saphira jutted out a hip. "I'm not your family or Everly's. Are you just going to throw me and *my family* to the warriors and get away?"

Tyson stood, his face twisting in anger. "Figures. You can't take the jackass out of the royal blood."

Thorn's rage slammed into me like a raging inferno. He rasped, "Do not lump me in with them *ever* again."

If I didn't interject, this confrontation would go too far. But with the hurt swirling from Thorn, I feared everyone would know the pain he usually tried to hide.

CHAPTER TWENTY-THREE

MY HEART CLENCHED at the pain and anger roiling through my mate. The resentment he'd built up over the years was so strong it stole my breath. Whatever issues I had with Peter didn't even come close to Thorn's level of devastation. I'd known my mate had deep-rooted issues, but it was worse than I'd realized. He might be stronger because of it, but that didn't mean he wasn't wounded to his very core.

His own parents had tried to have him killed because they feared him.

Thorn took a menacing step toward Tyson, and I jumped in front of him. I placed my hands on his chest and locked eyes with my mate. *Just like you have issues with the royals*—I was careful not to say family—*so does he. Remember what Saphira told us. Drake injured his dragon, leaving him disabled, and now he's learned that Drake is killing people like him. He's got his own baggage, and he's lashing out. Please, be the man I know you are. Understanding, kind, and strong.*

He exhaled, his minty breath hitting my face, and his irises came close to returning to their gorgeous color—just a tad darker. *Only for you. Only because I want to be the man you deserve.*

My heart skipped a beat. Even when he was hurt and angry, his love for me shone through. I couldn't help but fall in love with him more.

As my dragon grumbled, I turned toward the kitchen table. Brenton and Saphira had stood up and flanked Tyson. They were ready to protect their family, and that reinforced my trust in them.

I lifted my hands to diffuse the situation, but I had to stand up for my mate. "Look, that was a low blow. Thorn didn't have anything to do with what Drake did to you or the way the king protected his son. In fact, the king—his own father—tried to kill him. Or did you forget that?"

Tyson closed his eyes.

"I'll be honest. When I met Thorn, I didn't trust him." Saphira remained tense and on alert. "I thought he was full of shit, though I could tell you were taken with him. Now, I understand why—he's your soulmate, and when he turned you, he created his fated mate. Because of that connection, I saw the truth. Drake is much worse than I realized, and Thorn wasn't lying at all. But what Tyson said holds true. Thorn admitted to only caring about protecting the people he loves."

"Yes, that's exactly what I said," Thorn added.

If anyone were to hurt Thorn, I'd defend him, but the urge to smack the shit out of him surged through me. I was trying to calm the tension, and he'd reinforced the words that had brewed up the tension in the first place. I knew he was smart, but he wasn't showing any common sense, allowing his emotions to get the best of him.

"Then why the hell are we here?" Peter spat, his body rigid.

For once, I couldn't blame my stepdad, but I knew Thorn. He had to be talking out of his ass, or I'd make sure to beat some sense into him...maybe while pleasuring him sexually.

Whoa. Where had that thought come from?

"Because if any of you are captured, the people I love will be at risk." Thorn pulled at the roots of his hair. "That's why I tried not to forge connections—because the more people you let in, the more people are at risk." Thorn gestured to Peter. "I can't stand you, but your kids love you. If Drake threatened you, Eva or Elliott would be desperate to save you, which then puts Everly at risk. The same thing goes for Saphira. So yeah, maybe you aren't the ones I'm most concerned with, but that doesn't matter. I care about your safety because that's how I protect Everly."

I winced. That sounded somewhat better, but it still wasn't the most reassuring thing he could've said.

I was surprised when Brenton relaxed.

Straightening, Brenton nodded. "When it comes to someone taking care of their fated mate, we have nothing to worry about. You'll protect us just as valiantly as her."

Saphira lifted a finger. "I allowed myself to get captured to save you, and I don't even make it into the somewhat-loved category?" She tilted her head back. "I'm offended." But humor glimmered in her eyes.

"Well, I like you now if that's any consolation." Thorn chuckled as he placed his hands on my shoulders and tugged me close, so that my back was pressed against his chest. "And Everly loves you, so there's that."

That was true, even though I hadn't gotten around to telling her that.

"Uh..." Elliott raised a hand. "May I ask a question?"

"Technically, you just did." Eva stuck out her tongue.

Peter rolled his eyes, giving me pause. I'd always thought he did that only to me, but my suspicions about his indifference to the twins seemed more and more like a certainty. He didn't treat them as poorly as he treated me, but I could see why they relied more on each other than their dad.

"What is it, dear?" Cassidy asked with a smile. "And you never need to ask permission. There are no silly questions."

Rubbing her hands together, Saphira waggled her brows.

I didn't want to know where she was heading, so I added, "No silly ones, but there are some that could be deemed inappropriate and won't get an answer."

She frowned, closed her mouth, and pouted.

That was what I'd been afraid of.

"What's a fated mate?" Elliott pursed his lips as he looked at me and Thorn. "Because these two moved super quick."

A line of worry creased Elliott's forehead, and my chest expanded. Was he worried about me?

"Fated mates have become rarer among our kind as our numbers dwindle." Errol smiled sadly. "They're an intense version of soulmates. It happens when a soul has been split between two people. When two human soulmates meet, their urgent connection can be confused for lust. The emotions and attraction are immediate, and when it happens between two supernaturals, their magic calls to them and intensifies the connection. Fate intervenes to ensure the two halves find each other. They are destined to be together, and if one dies, it's like a part of the other is lost for eternity."

He spoke as if he understood the loss. "Was Saphira's mother your fated?"

He pressed a hand to his stomach. "She was. Brenton's and my fated mates were leaving to shift, but they weren't careful, and hunters accidentally shot them before they could change into their dragons. It happened sixteen years ago." His voice cracked and died away, the emotions too much.

So both Saphira and Tyson had been young when they'd lost their mothers. No wonder Saphira hadn't mentioned hers during our time together.

"It was an accident. They didn't wear bright clothes, and they blended in with the landscape. The hunters called the police and waited at the edge of the dragon lands, a spot that had become inundated by humans." Brenton picked up the story. "They were let off the hook because we didn't want more attention drawn to our lands, and they hadn't killed them on purpose. If it hadn't been for Tyson,

Saphira, and the king, I'm pretty sure both Errol and I would've done something stupid that we would've regretted."

Now it made sense why Saphira had been so opposed to viewing the king poorly. He'd helped her dad and her uncle during a painful time. That was why Brenton held so much resentment toward Drake but not the king—he felt he owed the king a debt.

"Wow." Elliott's jaw dropped. "Having a fated mate sounds intense."

"It is," Vlad added, standing beside Cassidy. "Which is why we *all* need training, including Everly."

A panicked sensation surged through our bond as Thorn's hands trembled on my shoulders. He rasped, "No. We need to think of a way out of the country and not distract ourselves with something she won't ever need."

Saphira bobbed her head. "So, you're fine with her getting another faceful of someone else's penis? Good to know."

A guttural growl emanated from Thorn's chest, and my dragon purred. I didn't know why, but him almost losing control over that comment had me wanting to claim him all over again. His possessiveness turned me on.

Yes, I'd become that girl...and I wouldn't change it for the world.

But I had to stay levelheaded until he and I were alone. "I'm not asking for permission. I *will* train with Vlad. This is something I have to do. Hell, it's something we all need to do, including Eva, Elliott, and Peter."

"Dude, I can totally buy *Spyro*." Elliott removed his Nintendo Switch from his pocket. "I don't even know why I haven't yet, but that ends now."

Vlad blinked. "Does he really think a video game will teach him how to hold his own against dragons?"

"He's human." Thorn's forehead creased. "It's not like going outside and practicing hand-to-hand combat will make a difference when the time comes to fight. That's why we need to focus on finding a way out of the country, instead of wasting time training them."

I wouldn't say this out loud, at least not yet, but I connected with Thorn, *What if you change them like you changed me? If they agree to it.* I wanted it to be clear that I didn't want them forced into it.

His hands went still. *Maybe. Not Peter—he's a fucking prick—but your siblings, I wouldn't be opposed to. That might make things easier. But even if they agreed to it, I'm not sure I can.*

You took away several dragons back at the chateau. He had done it with ease, so I wasn't sure why that would change now.

I didn't mean to. My dragon and I were fighting to save you. Thorn lowered his hands and stared at them. *I wasn't in control. The magic took over.*

The same had happened when he'd changed me into a dragon shifter. I'd been dying, and he'd reacted. He hadn't meant to do it, but I was so thankful he had. *Okay. That's fine. It was just a suggestion.*

He turned me to face him as if we were the only two in the room. *Talk to them alone, not with Peter around. If they want me to try, we can, but tell them no promises.*

I pushed my love for him through our connection. I wanted him to know how much I appreciated and adored him.

"Uh..." Elliott cleared his throat. "What happened here? He was arguing, and now the two of them are looking at each other in a way that's making me very uncomfortable."

"It's call eye-fucking." Saphira blew out a breath. "And they've been doing that since day one, when I thought she'd lost her mind for looking at our kidnapper that way. I'm glad it's because they're fated and he turned out to be a good guy, or there would be hell to pay."

"Good guy?" Peter scoffed. "That's what you call it?"

"He is to her," Eva said softly. "That's all that matters to me."

That was one way to ruin our moment, but we were with nine other people, so we probably shouldn't be looking at each other this way. Now that I had Thorn's attention and he wasn't being obstinate, I figured now was a good time to try again. "The dragons won't expect humans to be trained. That could buy us more time to reach them if they need help, and I need to know how to fight now that I have a dragon."

"We could train them with guns and arrows." Vlad steepled his fingers. "Even if we wind up leaving the country, we can't right now. Every dragon shifter is on high alert and so scared that they won't think twice about reporting us. It won't hurt to train everyone, and that way, we'll keep up our strength. Dragons live around the world, so there will always be a risk."

Thorn huffed, and I placed a hand on his chest and gave him a small smile. *I want to train, and my dragon is restless with all the running and sitting around we've been doing. What's the harm in me learning how to defend myself?*

"Fine. You're right. It wouldn't hurt for all of us to be more prepared and for me not to become rusty." He mashed his lips together. *I can never say no to you.*

My pulse quickened, and the jolt of the electricity between us only added to the sensation.

"Then go." Cassidy shooed us out. "Let me cook while you all train. Lunch will be ready in a few hours. The protein bars you ate earlier won't sustain you for much longer."

Our group stood, and even Peter begrudgingly obeyed.

THE REST of the day passed in a blur, including our all-too-brief lunch break when we devoured the delicious meal Cassidy had prepared.

Saphira and I teamed up as sparring partners, and though she wasn't formally trained to fight, she still had more experience than me, and she kicked my ass over and over.

Tyson and Eva partnered up, leaving Peter with Elliott, and Brenton with Errol. Thorn had wanted to work with Saphira and me, but Vlad had intercepted. I was glad because, if Thorn had trained us, any time I got hurt, he'd have been tempted to end the training.

After lunch, Vlad took Errol, Brenton, Saphira, and me deeper into the woods and away from Thorn's watchful eye. We practiced fighting in our human forms, and I caught way too many blows. My ribs and sides throbbed from how many times Saphira had hit me.

"This is our last round before we call it a day," Vlad informed us from beside a white oak at the edge of the small clearing we'd found.

Sweat glistened all over my body. Though I ached all over, muscles burning from my efforts, it felt amazing to be sore.

Saphira lifted her hands and smirked. "Ready for another beating?"

She was as competitive as I was, and unfortunately, she was also way better at this.

I was determined that, before long, I'd beat her.

Raising my hands caused my ribs to protest, but I pushed the discomfort from my mind. I didn't need Thorn homing in on it—he'd already shown up twice to get me to stop.

"Go!" Vlad shouted.

Bouncing on her feet, Saphira watched me, ready for me to strike. I'd been playing offense the whole time, and it hadn't worked, so this time, I'd make her move first.

She snickered. "That won't change the outcome." She stepped forward and shifted her weight to her left side.

Vlad kept reminding us to watch for our opponent's tells, and this was the first time I'd picked up on a clue. I spun to my left just as she kicked. She hit air, and momentum kept her moving.

I spun back around and punched her in the stomach, bringing her to her knees. My dragon surged forward, urging me to kick Saphira in the face, but I aimed for her side. She caught my foot, lifting it upward.

The leg holding me up wobbled. I pushed off it before I lost my balance and made contact with her side.

She stumbled, releasing my foot, but I couldn't right myself, so I landed on my back, pain surging through my body.

Everly, Thorn connected, his worry swirling through.

I didn't have time to respond. He knew we were sparring. I jumped up just as Saphira caught her balance, her cocky smirk gone.

"I see someone finally learned something," she spat. "It's about time."

She was trying to mess with my mind, but I wouldn't let her. Instead, I lifted my hands, ready for her to attack.

Rushing toward me, she leaned to her left side again, but she didn't put all her weight on that foot like last time. Instead, her right fist surged toward me. I ducked, then punched her in the stomach again.

As she stumbled back, I righted myself and pretended I was going to kick her in the stomach again. She lifted her hands to catch my foot, but I aimed for her ribs, like she'd done to me so many times. She didn't have time to correct as I nailed her in the midsection, and she crumpled to the ground. She hissed as she stood and shook herself, ready to continue the fight, but electricity pulsed through the air.

"That's it," Thorn said, stepping from between two red cedars. His jaw was clenched, and his attention was locked on me. "Cassidy wants us back for dinner." Our bond filled with rage.

"Fine." Saphira sighed but winced. "I could use a break."

I puffed out my chest. This was the first time I'd seen Saphira winded.

"Yeah, yeah." She rolled her eyes but smiled. "You're a quick study, but don't get too arrogant. I'll be kicking your ass again tomorrow."

Vlad came over and patted my arm. "Everly did fantastic today. You progressed a lot faster than I expected. You're a natural fighter, as if you were meant to be one of us."

I beamed. Other than Mom, I'd never received praise from a family member, and that was what Vlad was quickly becoming.

Brenton and Errol both had black eyes, but they had smiles on their faces. Apparently, dragon shifters enjoyed a good brawl.

As the five of us started back toward the barn, Thorn gently caught my arm, holding me in place. He connected, *We aren't going back. I can't. Not right now. Not after what I saw.*

I lifted my chin, refusing to cower. *We agreed I would train. There's no reason for you to be angry.*

"We'll be back shortly," he informed the others. At Vlad's nod, he took my hand and led me deeper into the woods.

The connection between us sizzled as we picked up our pace. Luckily, my body was already healing, a nice side effect of being a shifter, and I didn't struggle to keep up.

As the sounds of the others vanished, Thorn kept moving forward. After a few miles, he stopped and turned to me, his pupils slitting. He stepped toward me, gently pushing me against a tree trunk.

He growled, "I need to inspect you for injuries."

CHAPTER TWENTY-FOUR

THE BARK CUT into the back of my arms, and a knot of desire twisted in my stomach. First, we needed to address the tension hanging between us. "Why are you mad at me?"

"I'm not mad," Thorn murmured as he leaned closer to me. *I was concerned when I felt your pain, but then I saw the end of your fight with Saphira. My dragon and I approve.*

He placed his hands on the trunk, trapping me, and focused on my lips. The sweet scent of his desire mixed with his usual minty amber, hiding the hint of sulfur. My breathing quickened as I stared at his strong jawline and full lips.

I became hyperaware that I was covered in sweat and reeked of body odor. I placed my hands on his chest, holding him back, the jolt of our connection pulling at my soul. I connected, *I need a shower. I stink.*

Smirking, he lowered his head. *It's fucking hot, and in a second, you'll be sweating even more.*

But the food... I tried to be sensible, but my dragon inched forward, and my body thrummed, needing the relief only he could bring. Still, if we didn't show up, everyone would know why.

Food can wait, he interjected and kissed me.

His lips were soft and urgent, and he threaded his fingers into my hair.

The sweet pressure and gentle tug had me coming unglued. I opened my mouth, and his tongue swooped inside. His minty taste consumed me, and I responded to each stroke with eagerness. I slipped my hands inside his shirt, tracing the curves of his muscles. He shuddered and cupped my neck, drawing us closer together.

Each line of his abs was part of a masterpiece. I would have to do a nude painting of him as soon as I had some place to hide it for my eyes only.

He groaned, and my cells sizzled as his hand swooped down and moved under my shirt, then my bra. He caressed my nipple, and I leaned my head back against the trunk as warmth spread through me.

Trailing a hand lower, I unfastened his jeans and pushed them and his boxers down so I could touch his hardness. I stroked him, and he hissed between his teeth.

He whispered, "Gods, you feel so good." Then he unfastened my bra, lifted my shirt, and bent down, replacing his fingers with his mouth.

I gasped and closed my eyes, reveling in the sensations building inside me. His hips swiveled, keeping pace with my hand, as his tongue worked his magic over me.

You're better than mint chocolate chip, he connected, unbuttoning my pants, then moved his fingers underneath my panties and between my legs. He circled and pressed in perfect rhythm, causing me to move faster.

With my eyes closed, the sensations took over, and the sounds of the breeze rustling through the branches and animals in the underbrush emphasized we were alone out here, desperate for each other.

The friction built, pushing me close to the edge, but I needed him inside me. I wanted him to find his pleasure at the same time I did.

I let go of him and opened my eyes. Watching him had my body

to ever feel like you can't talk to me about anything. Your well-being, both emotionally and physically, is my top concern. And I *am* happy. Happier than I ever thought I'd be, and I'm sorry I made you doubt that even for a minute."

His sincerity washed through me and settled comfortingly in my chest. There was no reason to hide anything from him. He accepted me for who I was, flaws and all.

"You know what?" he whispered against my earlobe, sending goose bumps all over my body. "I know what we should do."

I warmed for round two. If I had to choose between sex and food, sex with him would win every time. As long as I died while orgasming, I'd count it as a win. I bit my lower lip and whispered, "I haven't got a clue. Why don't you tell me?"

He grinned wickedly. "Well, we're both naked..." He winced and glanced down at his pants and boxers pooled around his ankles. "For the most part."

I laughed as my body tingled. I'd never imagined I could be this happy. "Sorry about that. I kinda got desperate, and that helped me get what I wanted faster."

He winked. "I approve of the strategy."

I trailed a finger down his chest, enjoying how his pecs quivered under my touch. "So...what is this idea of yours?"

"You, my love, have a one-track mind," he growled as he peppered kisses over my cheek. "But I was thinking we should shift and go for a flight."

My heart clenched while I also shuffled my feet. Two conflicting emotions mingled: disappointment that he wasn't speaking of sex and eagerness to take to the sky.

Gods, I love you. He beamed. *You look like a pouting puppy dog that has a treat dangling in front of her.*

I shrugged. *I was hoping for more sex but flying sounds nice, too.*

Then you shall have both. He booped me on the nose and kicked off his shoes. *But your dragon is restless, and it'll cause problems if you don't shift. Let's fly, then have another round of sex before heading back to the barn.*

I leaned against the trunk and watched my sexy mate peel the rest of the clothes from his body. His muscles flexed, and my stomach somersaulted all over the place.

He took a few steps back, so we'd have room to shift. Faint purple splotches appeared on his tanned skin as he transitioned into his dragon. With each second, his scales became more pronounced and darkened to his gorgeous silvery-plum color.

My dragon brushed against my mind, eager to follow suit. I thought to her, *Let's do this,* and she didn't hesitate. She surged forward, melding with my mind. Our thoughts had already begun to merge, but when we were in dragon form, we were truly one.

The ground got farther away as my bones altered me into my dragon form. Within seconds, my feet and hands became silver-scaled limbs ending in talons, completing my transition.

I turned my head toward Thorn, who had been watching me. His sky-blue irises shimmered in the darkness, and he flapped his wings, lifting off the ground.

Allowing my dragon to take over, I followed Thorn, and we rushed into the sky. The wind blew past my scales, giving me a sense of freedom, and I enjoyed watching my mate in his strong dragon form. We were close to four times our human size, which meant my mate was over thirty feet of pure muscle.

With my dragon-heightened senses, I noticed a group of foxes running underneath us and several owls flying about two miles away. Most importantly, nothing out here could harm us.

The sky was clear, and we were high enough that no humans could see us. I stared into the true night sky, which I was finally able to see with my dragon eyes. The dark blue was peppered throughout the atmosphere with green and yellow splotches and spots of cobalt and pink swirls from the center of the Milky Way. It was second on my list to paint once I finished my masterpiece of Thorn.

Settling into a rhythm next to my mate, I reveled in the sense of peace swirling through me, and the two of us enjoyed our time together.

A WEEK PASSED, and Theron came back every few days to check in, update us with news, and take a grocery order.

Thorn had hoped that the hunt for us would die down, but Drake had increased the number of warriors searching for us. In a way, I was thankful. Thorn was determined our group should leave the country, and I'd been trying to talk him out of it.

Training had been going well. Saphira and I were now on equal footing, and Vlad had promised that tomorrow we would switch partners so I could spar with Errol. He said fighting different people would strengthen our strategy.

My skin buzzed from holding hands with Thorn. We'd finished our nightly routine of sex, flying, and more sex. Since Vlad and Cassidy had taken the isolated master bedroom, I didn't want Saphira, Tyson, Errol, and Brenton to hear Thorn and me in ours. Besides, I liked having sex outside. Being a dragon had changed me so much, and I was beginning to like myself.

We broke through the tree line behind the barn and found Eva and Elliott by the unlit firepit, sitting in two of the Adirondack chairs.

Neither of them noticed us as we strolled closer.

"I wish there was internet out here." Elliott gazed at the stars. "I miss my gamer friends, especially since you've become a stick in the mud, and Tyson is in the house, pouting."

Eva scowled. "First off, I'm not a stick in the mud. I just don't want to be in a position where I can't defend myself again. As for Tyson, he wants to train with the dragons, but he's too weak and stuck with us humans. He isn't pouting. He's depressed. He reminds me of Mom those first months after she was diagnosed with cancer."

My feet stilled as the memory sprang into my mind. She'd been so upset that she'd become suicidal and would've tried to end her life if we hadn't intervened and gotten her some help.

What's wrong? Thorn connected and scanned the area for a threat.

Tyson. I turned toward him, my vision blurring. *I didn't realize he was struggling that badly.*

Thorn winced. *Yeah, I didn't want to worry you, but I get it. When your dragon is injured and you can barely fly, it makes things difficult.*

That was why Saphira, Tyson, Brenton, and Errol shifted together at different times from us. Vlad and Cassidy would go out later, after Thorn and I got back, but those four always flew at midday while we were eating lunch, and they weren't usually gone for long. It had to be because Tyson couldn't handle a longer flight.

I strode forward, wanting to be part of the conversation. "Do you think he might harm himself?" If there was a chance, we needed to watch him more closely.

Eva yelped, and Elliott's head snapped around.

His eyes bulged as he pointed. "What the *hell?* How did you sneak up on us?"

"We didn't." Thorn lifted a brow. "Remember, listening at all times is something we're supposed to be working on."

"This is why I'm a *stick in the mud.*" Eva lifted a hand. "Because dragon shifters are strong, fast, and quiet."

"There's one easy solution." Elliott waggled his brows and smiled so wide it was creepy. "Our brother-in-law can *change* us."

My mouth went dry. Thorn and I had talked about offering to change my siblings, but we hadn't gotten around to it yet. We'd been focused on so many other things, and Thorn hadn't seemed eager to treat my siblings as guinea pigs.

When neither Thorn nor I responded, Elliott's jaw damn near touched the ground. "Wait." My brother jumped to his feet. "Is that an option?"

You can offer it to them, Thorn said as he squeezed my hand comfortingly. *If they want to, I can try. It would make things easier if they were strong as dragons.*

We stopped across the firepit from them, and I inhaled, searching for the right words. "Thorn has offered to *try* to change you...*if* you want. He can't guarantee it, and it's not a requirement."

"Fuck yeah." Elliott lifted a fist.

Eva's brows furrowed as if she were perplexed.

"Really?" Thorn's head tilted back. "When you first came to the cabin, you asked if I would change you as if you didn't want it."

I'd forgotten about that, and Elliott's quick yes now made me uneasy.

Elliott bobbed his head. "Well, yeah. At first, I was like, uh...no. But now that I've had time to acclimate...I've decided it'd be badass. So, fuck yeah, I'm down. Where the hell do I sign?"

I wasn't expecting that level of enthusiasm, Thorn connected, apprehension swirling through our connection.

Same. He hadn't taken the time to think it through. He was just gung ho. "What about you, Eva?" I wanted to see how she reacted.

"The thought has merit, but it's a huge change." She rubbed her arms. "Even though you're growing more comfortable with yourself, that only happened recently. I... I need to think about it."

Now *that* was rational. "How about you both think it through? It's not like the offer is now or never. It doesn't expire. Besides, Thorn isn't even sure he can do it. This would be a whole life change. You'd have another being inside you that was never there before, and you'd see and hear things that don't make sense. It's not an easy transition, so at least, take a night to decide."

Elliott pouted and rolled his eyes. "Fine. I'll take the night, but my answer will still be yes tomorrow."

He reminded me so much of a young child.

"I'll try, then." Thorn mashed his lips together, trying not to smile.

"Wait." Eva's face lit up, and her attention landed on my mate. "Is that something you can do for Tyson to fix his dragon?"

"No. He's already a dragon..." Thorn spoke slowly, speaking to her delicately. "I can't give him another one."

My stomach swooped alarmingly. She'd made me think of something I hadn't before.

Something that might prevent everything Drake was killing for.

CHAPTER TWENTY-FIVE

IF I HADN'T KNOWN any better, I would have thought I was floating as my breath stuck in my chest. "You said you took Arman's dragon and gave it back, right?"

Thorn faced me with furrowed brows and nodded.

I didn't want to jump right to the end, needing to think every-thing through before I got ahead of myself. "And you mentioned you can use your magic to pull the energy of past dragons from the air to create a new dragon shifter, like you did for me, right?"

He scratched his head. "Yes. I don't know how, but when that magic pulses from me, I can feel the essence of dragons who've passed and the energy of the dragon inside the person as well. They feel the same, just...one is inside a living person."

That information enthralled me, but that was a discussion for a later time. "Hypothetically, what if you took Tyson's dragon and gave it back? Maybe whatever injured his dragon could be replenished from the surrounding essences. Maybe you could heal his dragon's injury."

Eva smiled, her irises lightening with hope. "Do you think that could work?"

"I... I don't know." Thorn rubbed his hands together, his face lined with worry. "My magic is a curse. I don't see how it could do something good like that."

My heart panged. I didn't believe that, but Thorn did. Why wouldn't he, after his own father tried to kill him for having this ability? If healing Tyson worked, it could convince other dragon shifters that Thorn wasn't a threat, and he would see the good he could do for his people. "If Tyson is willing, what's the worst that could happen?"

"I'll go get him." Elliott jumped to his feet and jogged to the house. "I'm sick and tired of seeing him mope around."

I frowned. He sounded similar to Peter with his lack of empathy, but I had to remember he was young, and he'd been raised by his father for the past six years with me visiting only intermittently.

When Elliott went into the barn, Thorn kicked at the grass. *I'm not sure this is a good idea. What if I mess him up further?* His trepidation weighed on our connection.

Moving closer to him, I placed my hand on his arm and looked into his eyes. I pushed all my love toward him and connected, *We'll be honest with him about the risks, and if he says yes, it won't be your fault. We warned him. Babe, you changed me, and you've taken the king's dragon and given it back. I don't think there's much at risk here, since you'll be learning to connect with your magic, and potentially relieving a dragon shifter of something that is impacting him.*

His sky-blue irises locked on me, and I reveled in them, memorizing each diamond fleck. The next words flowed out before I could even think about them. *I believe in you.*

His eyes widened, and his breath hitched. Something nebulous crossed his face before strong emotions swirled between us. The sensation was both heartbreaking and joyful.

He wrapped his arms around me, pulled me close, and kissed me.

You don't know how much that means to me, he connected as his tongue brushed against my lips.

"Uh..." Eva cleared her throat. "I know I'm not usually the

mouthy one, but no one else is here to say anything, so it's on me. I'm pretty sure I just got pregnant watching you two."

I laughed and took a step back, enjoying the moment. This was what normal felt like: being in love with an amazing man and having my little sister there to rag on me about it. I could only hope there were many more moments like these in our future.

The back door opened, and Saphira, Brenton, Tyson, Cassidy, and Elliott came out. Saphira had an eyebrow arched, while Tyson's eyes were downcast. Brenton had a curious gaze, and Cassidy scanned the surroundings as if looking for answers. Elliott's body language was the most unique. He had a bounce in his step and a grin on his face.

When they reached the firepit, Saphira stood behind the chair across from me and crossed her arms. "What exactly do you want to talk to Tyson about?"

At least, Elliott hadn't run his mouth. There was no telling what would've come out. I'd imagined something like, *You want a new fucking dragon?* or an equally blunt question.

"Well, I—" Thorn bit his lip, our bond cooling as his insecurities filled it.

"I wanted to run something by Tyson." I'd take the blame so if it didn't work out, everyone would be mad at me and not Thorn. I refused to let Thorn carry a mistake on his shoulders, when it would be my fault for suggesting we heal Tyson in the first place.

Tyson pursed his lips. "Let me guess. You want me to hide if there's a fight since I'll only cause more problems." The agony on his face broke my heart.

They hadn't exaggerated the pain he was enduring.

"No, not at all." I stepped forward, wanting to be seen as the leader. "I was wondering if you'd be open to Thorn attempting to remove your dragon and give it back to you. It might reverse the injury Drake gave you that day in the clearing when you stood up for Saphira against him."

"Wait." Brenton lifted his hands. "Thorn can fix him?"

Tyson flinched.

"Not that you're broken." Brenton huffed and pinched the bridge of his nose. "I didn't mean it like that."

"How else could you mean it?" Tyson glared at his father, his eyes glistening.

Drake had caused so much strife in people's lives. He'd hurt Tyson, forcing him to feel inadequate.

"Sometimes, people phrase things ignorantly or make mistakes." Eva rubbed her arms and glanced at me. "They might say the wrong thing or say nothing at all—which could be worse—and act distant because that's all they've known since someone important passed away."

My breath caught. Was that her way of addressing what our relationship had been like during the last six years since Mom passed?

"What are the risks?" Cassidy asked, changing the direction of the conversation.

That was probably the safest bet.

"The biggest one is that I don't know what I'm doing." Thorn's shoulders were hunched slightly. "I changed Everly from human to dragon shifter, and when I was six, I took King Arman's dragon and gave it back to him immediately. Other than those two instances, I've only recently taken dragons, and that was mainly fueled by my need to save Everly. After making her a dragon shifter by accident, I tried to take her dragon away, and it didn't work. The risk is that I might not be able to take your dragon if I'm not being fueled by emotion, or I might take it away and not be able to give it back, making you human permanently."

"Do it," Tyson said without hesitation. "I'm good with you trying whatever."

"Hell yeah." Elliott pumped his fist. "That's what I'm talking about."

Saphira scowled and growled, "Let's not encourage him to act irrationally."

"I'm with Saphira," Brenton said as he placed a hand on Tyson's shoulder. "We need time to think it through."

"No, *we* don't need time." Tyson glanced from Brenton to Saphira. "Maybe you two do, but that doesn't matter. I'm a legal adult now, and I want Thorn to try. I'd rather try and become a human forever than be scared and never have a way to truly fly like I should be able to. At least, if I'm human, there'll be a reason I'm not like the two of you, and I won't have a dragon going stir-crazy. I want to try, and that's my choice."

Saphira rubbed her chest as Brenton rubbed his temples.

Cassidy exhaled. "I'm not trying to push my opinion, but I've had to come to grips with Thorn and his magic. One of the hardest things about caring for someone is knowing when to let go and when to push back. This is a choice between Tyson and his dragon, just as it's up to Thorn whether he tries to use his magic."

My vision blurred. I hadn't considered that Thorn using his magic might impact Cassidy. Maybe this was something he and I should've discussed with her. She had given up everything to protect him. "I'm so sorry. I didn't think about what I was suggesting."

"No reason to apologize, dear," Cassidy assured me with a sad smile. "You didn't do anything wrong. If Thorn can use his powers for good, that would be beyond amazing."

That was the point. I believed that if Thorn got over his fear of using his magic, it could be a blessing and something that could help dragons if they wanted it.

"She's right." Brenton clasped his hands. "If Thorn and Tyson want to try this, knowing all the facts, who am I to try to stop them?"

"His dad." Saphira lifted her hands. "Even if Tyson becomes human, Drake will still hunt him. It's not like that's his get-out-of-jail-free card."

"Why does that sound familiar?" Elliott tapped his chin. "What video game did you take that from?" He snapped his fingers. "It's from *A Way Out,* isn't it?"

"No, dumbass." Eva shook her head. "It's from *Monopoly.* We used to play it with Mom and Everly on board game night."

His mouth dropped open. "Oh, yeah. Back when we were heathens and didn't own electronics." He shivered. "Those were hard times."

"Seriously?" Saphira lifted a brow. "You're derailing a serious conversation."

"Saphy, you know I love you." Tyson gave her puppy-dog eyes. "But if Dad can get behind this, why can't you? Either way, Thorn is going to try. I'm asking for your blessing, but it's not required."

She scoffed, then took a deep breath. "Fine, but only because I love you and you got injured protecting me. I guess it's the least I can do."

The dread and fear rolling off Thorn increased, and our connection became heavy and cold.

"When do we try?" Tyson lifted his chin and focused on my mate.

"Whenever you want?" Thorn swallowed, his Adam's apple bobbing. "Now, tomorrow, a week from today."

"Now." Tyson took an eager step forward. "If you *can* heal me, I want time to train with Vlad and the others. I need to be as strong and healthy as possible to hold my own if something happens."

Thorn stiffened but nodded. "Remember, you might turn human."

"It's a risk worth taking." Tyson surveyed the area. "Where do you want me?"

"Wait." Elliott bounced on his feet. "Do we need candles or to chant something to help with the magic?"

"What?" Thorn stared at him as if he had two heads.

Sometimes, I wondered about my brother. "He's not hosting a seance. He's tapping into the magic he has naturally. There's no need for blood or sacrifices." Wait. I didn't actually know that for sure. When he'd changed me, I'd been bleeding, and when he took the warriors' dragons, the people had been left human. *Or do we need a sacrifice?*

Thorn sighed. *Technically, pulling the essence from the air means a sacrifice has already been made—the human part of the shifter has already died for it to be released. Even though I'm not a witch, all magic comes at a cost.*

Good to know, I replied as I looped my arm through his. As expected, some of his anxiety ebbed at my touch, making me feel treasured.

Thorn chuckled dryly. "Though I don't need a witchy setup, I would prefer it if everyone but Everly and Tyson would go inside."

"No candles and chants, and now I can't even watch." Elliott hung his head. "This is sorely disappointing."

"Elliott, sometimes, it's not about you." Eva rolled her eyes. She took her brother's arm and tugged him toward the barn. "Let's go kill some people."

"Okay. Those five words are my most favorite to hear, and they make this sting a lot less." He picked up his pace. "I'm going to kick your ass."

"Your brother." Cassidy snickered and shook her head. "That's what I thought raising a teen boy would be like, but Thorn wasn't like that, so I thought I'd been misguided. Now I'm learning Thorn was the exception and not the norm."

My brother didn't have the same background as Thorn, but I didn't want to mention that. No one needed that reminder. "Thorn is the exception to every rule." I glanced at my mate, the warmth of his love spreading through my body, even reaching my toes.

"I was about to argue about staying out here, but I'm afraid if I do, I might vomit." Saphira gagged, her face scrunching. "I thought those two were bad before. Oh boy, I was wrong."

That was the second comment like that in the past hour. I should have been offended, but I was more than pleased.

Cassidy winked at Thorn and me before nodding to the barn. "Let's get you inside before you throw up your dinner."

Brenton wrung his hands. "I'll stay close to the door. Just shout if you need me."

That was what a good parent did for their child—worried.

"Of course," I breathed.

Saphira, Cassidy, and Brenton went inside. Once the back door closed, Thorn took a deep breath and said, "Maybe you should sit down."

Hurrying to the chair in front of Thorn, Tyson sat, facing the firepit. "I'm ready."

I wish I were, Thorn replied as he rubbed his fingers.

My chest tightened. *If you don't want to try this, don't. I wasn't trying to push.*

I'm willing to try. This way, I'll know if I can actually change your siblings. Thorn placed his hands on Tyson's shoulders. *I need you next to me, but not touching me. I don't want to mess with your dragon by mistake.*

That I could do. *I'll always be at your side.*

He smiled. *I know. There's no doubt in my mind.* He closed his eyes, and his jaw clenched.

A few minutes passed, but neither he nor Tyson reacted or made a noise beyond breathing.

I can't do this, Thorn connected. *I don't feel anything.* Frustration wafted from him.

Remember what it was like when you felt the magic at the chateau and when you changed me? That was all that I could think of to help. *Remember the emotion and hold on to it.*

Okay, he replied as he closed his eyes tighter.

A strangling emotion surged through me, reminding me of when he'd been desperate to reach me. His hands glowed as his magic swirled inside him. My eyes widened.

Tyson gasped as the connection between Thorn and me grew hot and vibrant. Something swirled between us, a sensation that I'd felt once before, as if I could feel the brush of Thorn's magic.

The intensity increased, and Tyson whimpered, "It's gone."

"Give me a second," Thorn rasped as his eyes opened and focused on me.

The air around us buzzed. Not quite like the connection of our fated-mate bond but more like a warm hug brushing over my skin.

Pupils slitting, Thorn stared into me, and something inside me tugged as if he could see my soul—which wasn't far-fetched, given he was my other half. Air sawed through my lungs as my body thrummed and warmed in ways that had never happened simultaneously.

That night, when I saw you fall down the incline and hit your head, I was devastated and crazed, he connected, and a shiver ran down my spine. *Now I understand why. My dragon recognized you despite you being human. He refused to allow you to die and, by doing so, created our fated mate. When I made you a dragon shifter, there was so much blood I feared I couldn't save you. But you are strong— the strongest person I've ever known—and I'm so damn glad you decided not to reject me as your mate. I doubt I could've survived that hurt.*

I could never reject you. I inched closer, needing to be next to him. *Even when I was human, I didn't want anything bad to happen to you. Hell, even the night I first saw you in your car outside Drake's bar, your eyes captivated me.*

When you marched into that bar, I almost raced after you, wanting to protect you from him, he confessed. His hands dimmed, and the strange buzzing in our connection lessened.

For a minute, Thorn and I couldn't peel our eyes off each other.

Finally, my mind cleared. *What was that for?*

You said to recreate what I felt the night I changed you, so that's what I did. He smiled shyly. *And I think it worked.* Pride swirled through our bond, and my chest puffed out for him.

I gulped as my body tingled. Now we'd find out if Thorn could heal dragons that were impeded. "Tyson, how do you feel?"

He jumped to his feet and faced Thorn and me.

I expected him to show joy and relief, but his face was a shade paler than normal. He whispered, "Something's not right."

CHAPTER TWENTY-SIX

MY HEART THUDDED against my rib cage, and Thorn frowned. Our connection became frenetic as concern replaced the pride he'd felt.

"What do you mean something's not right?" I asked, touching Thorn's arm. This time, my touch didn't have as much of a calming effect. He barely relaxed.

I winced. I was the reason for this, but I couldn't take it back. *Before we panic, we have to hear the facts.*

It's been the same since I was a child—I'm cursed. No good can come from my magic, he replied as our bond heated with his anger. *This was a mistake. I shouldn't have tried. I should've known better.*

The urge to hang my head and close my eyes surged through me. Instead, I forced myself to stand tall. If I crumbled, I suspected Thorn would only struggle more.

Tyson stared at his hands as if they would reveal the answer. With each second that ticked by without an answer, Thorn's emotions became more turbulent.

"Please, Tyson," I said softly and leaned toward him. "Your explanation doesn't have to be perfect. Just tell us how you feel."

"Different." He dropped his hands, and his forehead wrinkled. "It's like it's *my* dragon, but not."

I tilted my head. "Does it feel different or react differently to you?" At least, he had a dragon that was somewhat familiar.

"It's *mostly* the same, but I don't recognize it completely. It feels weird." Tyson rubbed his hands together. "Like when you get bandaged or something."

"Gods, Tyson." Thorn's voice broke, and his shoulders sagged. "I'm so sorry. I should've known better." Heartache penetrated our bond, and I damn near collapsed to my knees.

Thorn was letting his emotions get the best of him, and I refused to allow it. "Before we assume the worst, maybe you should shift and see what's different."

If he can shift, Thorn connected but thankfully had enough clarity not to say it out loud. *I might have made his situation worse. Maybe the king was right, and I shouldn't be around other dragons. All I do is harm them.*

I clenched my free hand, allowing my fingernails to bite into my palms. I would not let the king ruin this amazing man. He was spiraling, and it was my fault. I hadn't realized he'd take it this hard if it didn't pan out, especially when we'd warned Tyson that we didn't know whether it would work, and the young man had agreed to try anyway. *Thorn, none of this is your fault. Let's see what happens.*

"Yeah, I can do that." Tyson rolled his shoulders and inhaled. He called toward the house, "Dad, wanna go on a flight with me?"

Part of me wanted to go with him, but I bit my tongue. He hadn't been comfortable before when he'd known his dragon had issues. The last thing he probably wanted was Thorn and me hovering around, inspecting his dragon. Some insecurities were hard to get over.

The back door opened, and Brenton hurried toward us. His face was tight, and his eyes narrowed as he inspected his son. "Of course. Are you all right?"

"I'm not sure." Tyson nodded toward the tree line. "But I guess we're about to find out."

Brenton nodded. "Let's go."

"We'll be back soon." Tyson exhaled. "I won't leave you two hanging."

The two of them headed off, leaving Thorn and me alone. My mate paced the open grassy area between the barn and the firepit. He ran his hands through his shaggy hair and kept his gaze cast downward.

I'd never seen him like this. "I'm sorry, Thorn." I took a step toward him and stopped. He might not want me close after what I'd encouraged him to do. Maybe that was why my touch hadn't calmed him as much as normal. "I understand why you're upset with me."

He stopped and turned to me. His face twisted. "I'm not upset with *you*. I have no reason to be. You wanted to do something good for someone. That's one of the reasons I love you—you truly care about others." He lifted his arms. "And I want to be able to do that *for you*, but almost every time I use my magic, bad things happen." He hurried a few steps closer to me. "I'm afraid of what might happen when you realize that, and I'm afraid something bad might happen to you because of me."

My breath caught, and I didn't hesitate. I closed the distance between us and touched his cheek, enjoying the jolt that thrummed under my hand. "Was changing me a bad thing?"

He flinched. "Of course not, but at first, you weren't happy about it."

"I was caught off guard, and there was all the crap with Drake and Eva." I caressed his skin. "But I wouldn't change it for the world. I'm happy now, all because of you. You need to see that. You need to see that nothing bad has happened because of *you*. Drake was already targeting my family, and I was already *promised* to him. The only detail that changed was that I would be his wife, instead of his breeder, which wasn't that much of a difference."

A low growl emanated from his chest. *I hate hearing about that, and one day, we will get the hell out of here so he can't breathe down our necks.*

If we leave and don't fight, he'll always be hunting us. I understood he wanted to believe there was somewhere safe we all could go, but a place like that didn't exist. Not with someone like Drake, a powerful royal whose ego was more important to him than anything else. We'd embarrassed him in front of his people; he wouldn't let that go. If anything, every day that hate and resentment festered inside him made the danger worse.

But there were more pressing matters, so I pivoted. *You said your magic is a curse, but you made me into a dragon.* We stared at each other. *I don't feel cursed. I, for once in my life, feel complete and like I belong.*

He leaned down and pressed his forehead against mine. *Of course, I don't feel like changing you into a dragon was a curse, but I did it without your permission. It's like, whenever I want to do something the right way, I mess up. Remember, you wanted me to take your dragon away, and I couldn't.*

I had forgotten about that. I couldn't imagine being human again and giving up the amazing connection I had with him. There was nothing in the world more important, not even my promise to Mom. *Maybe you couldn't because we're fated mates. You took Tyson's from him, and you gave it back. Maybe your magic changed me because, as you said, your dragon recognized what I was.*

Brows furrowing, he straightened. *I hadn't thought of it like that. It would go against everything within me to turn you back to human, but still, you asked, and I couldn't deliver.*

And I'm so damn thankful for it. I tugged at our connection, pushing the magnitude of my feelings toward him. *Then we wouldn't have this, and I will never give it up.*

His irises lightened, and some of his turmoil lifted from our bond. Though the feelings were still there, they weren't as strong.

The back door opened, and Saphira, Vlad, and Cassidy joined us in the backyard.

Saphira chewed on her lip and scanned the trees behind us. "Is Tyson okay? I heard Brenton come out but was trying to give them a few minutes before I barged in to check on him."

I lifted a brow. "I didn't realize you were capable of such self-restraint." I tried schooling my expression because I was teasing her. If she didn't have self-restraint, she would've ratted Thorn out to the cops who had come by the cabin before we'd learned everything.

She scrunched her nose. "I have my moments, and I know how Tyson is struggling. I didn't want to make things worse for him." Her lips tipped downward.

Thorn placed an arm around my waist. "We aren't sure. I took his dragon away and gave it back, but he said something didn't feel right. He and Brenton went for a flight to see what happened."

Wings flapped overhead, and our group glanced skyward. Two dragons came into view, flying over the treetops, barreling toward us. They were similar in size, but the one on the left was cream-colored and the other was maroon. Both were flying without issue.

Thorn's arm tensed around me.

"Is that them?" Vlad's cornflower-blue eyes reflected the rising moonlight, now that darkness surrounded us.

"Yes, but Tyson's reddish color is lighter than it was." Saphira's eyes narrowed. "Like a shade lighter. And he isn't flying wobbly like before."

The two dragons descended and landed in the open area beside us.

Tyson flapped his wings and threw his head back, roaring faintly before taking to the sky again.

"You did it, Thorn." Cassidy beamed, her attention locked on Tyson. "I'm so proud of you."

I'd expected the pride to return to Thorn, but the bond constricted in a way that stunned me.

He said he felt different, and his color has changed. Thorn's breathing turned ragged. *I don't know what that means.*

You had to use some of the ancestors' essence to make his dragon whole. Maybe that's the result. I burrowed into his side, placing my head on his shoulder. *It makes sense that it would no longer be exactly the same magic, and he did say it felt mostly the same, just a little odd. Maybe that's why. To heal him, you had to change him a little. But the point is, you did heal him, Thorn. I needed him to focus on the miracle. No one but you could've done that. Now he won't be in danger, like before.*

A happy lightness filled our bond, and when he smiled, my heart skipped a beat. The anger disappeared as he watched Tyson fly high into the sky.

This was what he'd needed. A true win. Maybe...just maybe... he'd stop seeing the magic as a curse and understand the possibilities it could open for his people—the safety he could provide.

***

THE NEXT FEW days were rewarding. I was competent enough to hold my own, and Tyson joined the dragons' training. His enthusiasm was better than anything else to make the atmosphere feel less threatening. He'd acclimated to his dragon, which he found to be more similar to his original dragon than he'd feared. All he'd needed to do was shift and fly with it for them to settle in with each other.

Eva still hadn't decided whether she wanted to become a dragon, and I was thankful she wasn't rushing into anything. It wasn't a decision to take lightly. Thorn had agreed to turn Elliott, but only after Eva had made her final decision, regardless of what she landed on.

Saphira and I were in the middle of a fight. She stood in front of me, waiting for me to make a move. Despite the chill of the late May breeze, our bodies were slick with sweat.

Not wanting to disappoint, I glanced at her stomach to make her think I was going to kick. When she shifted her weight to protect that area, I lifted my leg to continue the ruse and tapped her jaw. We'd agreed on no hard hits to the face.

She frowned and gritted her teeth. "Dammit! That's the second time I've fallen for that!" She settled back into a fighter's pose.

"That's good," Vlad called from his corner where he was sparring with Tyson. "You're learning your weak spots. Keep it up."

He was an excellent teacher. Tough when needed but also encouraging when someone felt discouraged.

I prepared myself. The one thing I'd learned about Saphira was that, when she was emotional, she tended to be rash.

Ev, Theron is here, Thorn connected with me from his spot with Eva, Elliott, and Peter in front of the barn. *I thought you might want to know.*

Hearing his voice, I was slow to notice Saphira's kick and pain exploded in my stomach, and I doubled over, falling to the ground.

"Whoa!" Saphira squealed. "Everly, I'm so sorry. I thought you'd block it."

Eyes burning and blurring, I hissed through my teeth. I had let Thorn distract me, and now I was paying the price.

Everly, what happened? Thorn's voice popped into my head. *I'm on my way.*

My thoughts were scrambled, but I knew he needed to stay there with Peter. There was no telling what he'd say or do around Theron if one of us wasn't with them. *I'm fine. Stay with Peter and Theron. I'll be there soon. Saphira kicked my ass. That's all.*

His dragon roared.

It was my fault, not hers. Unable to see the world around me through my unshed tears, I watched a blurry form hurry over to me and place a hand on my shoulder. A musky cinnamon scent wafted around me.

Vlad.

"Hey, you okay?" he asked, concern thick in each word.

My skin prickled, indicating that everyone was watching me. I hadn't gotten hurt like this before, meaning I'd royally screwed up. I gritted, "Yeah. Thorn connected with me and said Theron is here."

"Ah, you were distracted," he said and patted my arm. "Though it's a hard lesson to learn, it was one best served here. Even when your fated mate talks to you, you have to pay attention to your surroundings and not get lost in your bond."

"Believe me." I gasped, but the pain began to recede. "I learned."

"I'm so—" Saphira started.

I lifted my hand. "We were sparring. You didn't do it on purpose."

"I wouldn't be so sure about that." Tyson snorted.

"Hey! No one was talking to you," Saphira snapped.

I blinked, a few tears trailing down my cheeks.

Brenton and Errol shook their heads at each other, and Errol said, "And I thought these two were done acting like siblings."

"Come on. I'll help you up." Vlad held out his hand.

I took it, my sides screaming as I straightened. It was a damn good thing I was a dragon shifter. I'd bet this would have taken days to heal if I'd been human.

"Cassidy said lunch will be ready in thirty. Let's take a break and head in." Vlad waved toward the barn but stayed next to me.

Tyson, Errol, and Brenton led the way, trying to get Tyson away from Saphira before he riled her up more. Saphira had a deep scowl on her face, feeling guilty for what she'd done.

"I promise. I'm fine." I smiled. "Like Vlad said, it was better for me to learn this now instead of in battle. This way, I have time to lick my wounds before getting even with you later."

Her mocha irises twinkled. "Oh, you think you're going to get even? Please. Next time, I'll kick your ass and not feel bad about it."

Now *there* was the Saphira I knew and loved.

"Let's see what updates Theron has." I headed for the barn, knowing the two of them would follow me.

Within minutes, we stepped into the clearing and found solemn faces...except Peter's. He smiled as if he'd won the lottery.

"What's going on?" I asked, picking up the pace.

"The warriors." Theron placed a hand on his stomach. "Aiden alerted us that they're at his location, which means my thunder is next. You need to leave, so I can bring my son here."

"But he can stay here with us," Thorn rasped as his neck corded. "I don't understand why we need to leave."

Theron bared his teeth. "If my son finds out about you, that will put him in more danger. I'd hoped the warriors would bypass us, but they're getting closer, and I have to protect my son. I'm sorry, but you all need to leave."

Theron and Thorn were reacting emotionally and not thinking clearly.

"If your son isn't there when they arrive, they'll ask questions." Vlad lifted his hands. "I get the need to protect your son, but if the warriors realize something is amiss, you'll only reveal to them that you have something to hide. I'm not saying I don't sympathize, but that alone could place a target on his back."

"There's something that could protect both groups," I said and glanced at Thorn. He'd healed Tyson's dragon—maybe he could do the same for Theron's son.

Theron laughed harshly. "Like what? It's like you think I haven't tried to find a solution."

Everly, no, Thorn connected. *I did that for Tyson to help us.*

You're going to let a dragon shifter get marked for murder when there's something you can do to save him? I asked, lifting a brow. *Thorn, you can't mean that.*

Thorn flinched, my words hitting their mark.

Before he and I could finish our conversation, Tyson stood tall. "I had an injured wing, and Thorn healed me. I no longer have that issue."

Mouth dropping open, Theron glanced from Tyson to Thorn. Then his face went red as he growled, "Oh, *hell* no. He's not touching my son. I saw what he did to those warriors. Your group needs to leave."

Thorn's hurt slammed into me, and I marched forward. No one made my mate feel that way.

I'd bring Theron to his knees.

CHAPTER TWENTY-SEVEN

HURT AND ANGER rolled from Thorn, adding to my rage. Even when Thorn proved his magic could be used for good, some scared dickhead made him feel as if that wasn't good enough.

I strode to Theron and pressed my finger into his chest. The older man blinked several times.

"You want to condemn Drake for hurting the weak, but you're as bad as he is." I lifted my chin as my dragon inched forward. "You're letting the opinions of others, and what you *thought* you saw, paint a picture of my *mate*, a man who's a million times better than you, because you're allowing your fear to control you."

Theron's pupils slitted as his dragon peered through. I couldn't blame him; I was being aggressive, so naturally, his dragon would sneak out.

He sneered. "They've replayed the wedding several times, and you can't say he didn't steal those warriors' dragons."

Everly, let it go, Thorn connected, warmth spreading through our connection. *We need to leave before the warriors get closer.*

If he thought I'd let this asshole say what he had without putting him in his place, Thorn would soon learn better. I continued. "Of course, he did! Because Drake manipulated me into giving myself up, supposedly to save my sister, Saphira, and Thorn's parents. Drake wanted me to be his breeder, but instead, when he realized Thorn and I had completed our fated-mate bond, he decided to make me his wife so Thorn would expose himself to save me. What would *you* do if your mate was taken against her will and forced to be with someone else?"

"I know I'd be going crazy," Vlad interjected from behind me. "And I would've done worse than Thorn. He didn't kill the warriors. He just took the dragon of anyone who attacked him when he was trying to get to his mate."

Something unreadable passed through our connection, but I didn't have time to focus on what Thorn was feeling. I had a threat to put in his place.

Theron looked over my shoulder at the group behind me.

"If it's any help, I didn't trust or like Thorn at first," Saphira said and moved to my side. "But after a short time, I realized he wasn't what the king and Drake had portrayed. I'm the daughter of the king's most trusted advisor, and Drake threw me in a jail cell because I'd sided with Thorn. He promised Everly, in front of me, that if she handed herself over, he'd release the four of us, but when she did, he went back on his word. He said he was above the law. After seeing what a difference Thorn made to my cousin"—she gestured to Tyson—"if I were you, I would let him help your son. That's the only sure way to protect him."

Theron yanked on his hair. "I... How do I know you're telling the truth?"

"The king asked me to help his son, Thorn, to save his fated mate before Drake could force her to marry him." Errol strolled to Saphira's other side. "He trusted me, especially after what Drake did to my daughter. I wouldn't be here if I believed Thorn was the real threat to the kingdom. I willingly left the king's side to protect my daughter and obey the king's command. You have a son. You should understand this completely."

"And you know my dad," Vlad added.

Theron sighed. "Let's say maybe I was overreacting, and I'm open to the possibility of Thorn helping my son." He turned to my mate. "Is that something you're willing to try and can do?"

I swallowed, waiting for the inevitable no from Thorn.

Our bond fluttered, and Thorn replied, "Yes, on both counts."

My chest expanded, and I looked at him and asked, *Really? I thought you didn't want to.*

I don't, but you're right. If I don't help, we're sentencing an innocent dragon shifter to death just because he's different. And after Vlad, Saphira, Tyson, and Errol backed me, I don't really have a choice. Thorn winked as our connection heated. *And you telling him off was hot. Besides, if I help his son, we can stay here longer. Then we'll have more time for lovemaking, which I desperately need.*

I smiled. *I'm always open to sneaking away to spend time alone with you.* As long as he'd decided to help on his own, I was here for it. Obviously, he did care; he was just jaded, and I couldn't blame him for that. I believed that with each positive thing he accomplished with his magic, he would see things differently.

His pupils slitted, and my dragon purred. Thankfully, only internally.

"Okay." Theron exhaled and nodded. His irises glowed. "My wife will find Sol and tell him to meet us at the edge of our thunder's territory. It'll be best if only Thorn comes, so we can remain undetected."

"I need to come too." The thought of Thorn heading to a thunder alone, when the warriors were nearby, didn't sit well with me. Theron's focus would be on protecting Sol, not my mate.

"And me." Vlad tensed. "If the warriors come, we can't leave Thorn there by himself, and he is *my son.*"

"Fine, but no more." Theron rubbed a hand down his face. "I'm only agreeing because I understand those bonds, but we need to move. We have a couple more days before the warriors appear, but I'd rather try it now, while it's less risky."

Why don't you stay here? Thorn frowned. *It would be safer.*

If I were heading off somewhere, would you stay behind? I arched a brow. I already knew the answer, but I needed to hear him say it.

He surprised me when he sighed. *Fine, but at the first sign of anything suspicious, you leave, even if I can't yet.*

In other words, if he hadn't finished replacing Sol's dragon. *Fine.* Hopefully, we wouldn't get into that situation.

The front door opened, and Cassidy strolled out. Her face was lined with worry. Vlad had been keeping her apprised of what was going on.

She rubbed her hands down her pants and jerked her chin toward the barn. "Lunch is ready."

My stomach growled, but food would have to wait. We needed to act, not only due to the threat the warriors posed, but also because Theron could change his mind.

Vlad must have had the same thought. He said, "Will you put aside plates for Thorn, Everly, and me so we can eat once we return?"

"I'd think twice before letting my stepdaughter go with you." Peter scowled, his beady eyes darker than normal. "She causes more problems than she's worth."

When Thorn took a menacing step toward him, realization washed over me. That was the exact response my stepdad wanted. He wanted to make Thorn look bad in front of Theron.

Don't, I connected, my urgency filling our bond. *He's manipulating you.*

Thorn halted just as Eva crossed her arms and said, "Dad, the only person who causes problems is *you.* You embezzled money from the Hales, which is the only reason Everly and I got involved. So go look in the mirror to find the person who's to blame, and stop trying to drive a wedge between Everly, me, and Elliott."

My gut tightened. Was he the reason Elliott and Eva had treated me with so much indifference for so long? Since the Hale situation had arisen, the twins had been treating me differently. They actually felt more like siblings than mere acquaintances, and I'd seen a side of them that had disappeared when Mom died.

Theron's forehead creased, and I wasn't sure if it was from confusion, concern, or both. Either way, leaving before Peter got more riled up was our best option. I should've known he would pull something like this, but he'd been playing along the past few days, so I hadn't thought twice about it.

"We can finish this conversation later," Cassidy said, glaring at Peter. "Thorn, Everly, and Vlad need to go." She went straight to Vlad and hugged him. Their eyes glowed, and she pulled away and patted Thorn and me on the arm. "Go on. Brenton, Errol, and I have it from here."

"Hey!" Saphira placed her hands on her hips. "Don't play the old-people card on me. I'll help watch Peter and his sniveling ways."

Vlad nodded. "Let's go. I don't want to drag this out."

Theron hesitated, and my stomach sank. Then the older dragon glanced at Tyson, and something firmed in his expression. "Yes, let's go." He spun on his heel and marched toward the tree line, and Thorn, Vlad, and I followed.

Suddenly, I paused. "Wait. We need to pack a bag, so we have clothes to change into."

"It'll be fine," Theron replied, not breaking his stride. "My mate will bring things for you to wear while you're there. You won't be staying long, just enough to do...whatever Thorn does."

That would work. And anyway, the clothes he'd stocked here were slightly too large for my human size, and I'd learned that wearing shorts was my best option. I had to wash my panties and bras each night because none of the extras here fit me.

"Let's shift, and you all can follow me." Theron turned toward us. "Let me be clear. I'm not comfortable taking you this close to the thunder, but Sol can't travel far in his dragon form. If something goes south, I will do anything to protect my thunder."

He didn't need to spell out what he meant—he would tell Drake where we were. Even if we ran, the dragons would know where we'd started.

Aggravation swirled from Thorn, and he growled.

But I understood both men. Theron was helping us as a favor to a friend but didn't fully trust us. And Thorn didn't like being threatened, especially when I was involved.

"We understand. You've already made that clear. But know that when someone is helping you, they don't want to hear the same threat again." I tried to keep a level tone. We were all highly emotional. *Thorn, remember, he's taking us to his mate and son. How would you feel if someone you didn't trust was about to meet me? Try to see it from his perspective.* That was a trick I'd picked up over the years when dealing with Peter.

"I agree with Everly." Vlad smiled, and there was pride in his eyes.

"All right." Theron marched into the tree line. "Let's take flight."

Within a few minutes, the four of us were flying skyward, higher than we did at night, since the sun was out, and we needed to stay away from human eyes.

Theron's Carolina-blue dragon took the lead. Thorn and Vlad flanked me, Thorn's gorgeous plum dragon on my left and Vlad's olive-green dragon on my right. Among such colorful dragons, my dark silver color didn't seem as vibrant.

Peter better be damn glad that Theron was there, and you stopped me. I could've easily killed him, Thorn connected, his sky-blue eyes locking on me. *He wanted Theron to force us to leave so Drake would have a better chance of finding us.*

Which is why you didn't act impulsively, I reminded him as I brushed the tip of my wing against his. *You need to let that go and enjoy the moment. We can worry about him when we return. You need to focus on your magic.*

I didn't react because you were there as my voice of reason. He focused forward. *But you're right. We'll deal with him on our return.*

For forty-five minutes, Thorn and I enjoyed our flight. We hadn't ventured far from the barn, so traveling faster and farther away was amazing.

All too soon, Theron began a descent into a thick section of trees. We'd reached our destination.

Using my dragon senses, I searched the area. I detected rabbits hopping below, a few elk roaming, and other woodland creatures enjoying the wilderness.

Two human forms waited as well.

That had to be Sol and Theron's mate.

Not sensing anything threatening, our group swooped down. Thorn and Vlad did their own assessment.

Stay close to me, Thorn connected. *Though I think he's trustworthy, we can't be too careful.*

I have no intention of wandering away from you, I assured him. My time of trying to sneak away and act on my own was over. Drake had cured me of that.

We landed where the two people stood waiting. Theron's mate was shorter than six feet tall, with shoulder-length ash-blonde hair and forest-green eyes. She looked to be in her forties, though there was no telling how old she truly was.

A man in his mid-twenties stood next to her. If he had a dragon injury, I never would have guessed. He was close to six and a half feet tall and looked strong, like his father, with dark blond hair, chestnut eyes, and a light brown goatee that was neatly trimmed.

I'd expected Theron's son to be closer to Vlad's age than mine, but Theron's wife was younger than her mate, so maybe that explained it.

"Here are your clothes," Theron's mate said, gesturing to the four outfits laid out in front of us. "Go shift. People in our thunder saw Sol and me head this way alone after searching for Theron all morning."

Great, now there was even more urgency around our plans.

After carefully grabbing the clothes, we dispersed into the trees. Thorn and I stayed together and shifted into our human forms. We dressed quickly and headed back out to join the others.

When they saw Thorn, neither of them flinched. Theron must have warned them.

Theron's mate took an eager step toward Thorn and asked, "Is what you told Theron true? Can you heal Sol?"

My skin itched from the nervousness swirling through my bond with Thorn.

"I'll try," Thorn replied as he took my hand. "I healed someone in a similar situation a few days ago, but there is one thing I have to prepare you for."

"What?" Theron scowled. "You didn't imply there was anything my son had to worry about."

Vlad lifted a hand. "Hear him out, please."

My mouth went dry, but I needed to contribute. "It'll make sense if you do."

"Honey, they're right." Theron's mate touched his arm. "We can always decide not to let him do it."

Theron sighed and leaned into his mate. "You're right, Hydra. I just worry."

"Please, tell me everything." Sol leaned forward, his eyes wide.

Fidgeting, Thorn launched into what we'd learned from Tyson about his dragon changing slightly.

When he was done, Sol nodded. "I'm in."

Unease prickled through our bond, and I squeezed Thorn's hand tighter, silently telling him I was right there. I connected, *You've already done this once, and I'll be right here beside you.*

That's the only reason I can go on, he replied, and my heart missed a beat.

"Are you two okay with it?" Vlad added as he moved to Thorn's other side. "We don't want anyone to get upset over whatever happens."

Hydra smiled sadly. "If it's what our son wants, we won't stop him."

"What do we do?" Sol crossed his arms.

A quick look around confirmed there was no seating like back at the barn. Instead, Thorn stepped in front of Sol. "I need to touch you. Remember, I'll have to take the dragon away first, and you'll feel the loss."

Sol nodded.

Thorn released me and placed his hands on the younger man's shoulders. He inhaled deeply, and the flutter in our bond started.

He was nervous, and having Theron and Hydra watching wasn't helping matters. But I doubted they'd be willing to leave. *You've got this. I believe in you.*

I hope you're right, he replied as he closed his eyes. *Remember not to get too close.*

A long moment passed, and nothing happened.

Theron and Hydra glanced at each other, and Sol shuffled his feet.

Panic swirled through our bond as Thorn struggled with his magic.

Remember what it felt like when the warriors attacked you at the chateau? I almost reached out to him but stopped short. *Take your time.*

Thorn inhaled again, and after another moment, his hands glowed. Hydra's, Theron's, and Vlad's eyes widened.

None of them had seen Thorn use his magic before.

The same strange feeling soared through our bond, the vibrations warm and consuming. As soon as it started, the sensation vanished.

"It's gone." Sol sounded startled.

"I warned you." Thorn closed his eyes tighter. "Now, I'll give it back to you." His face twisted in agony for a moment before his hands sparked and the thrumming filled our connection. His magic tugged at our bond, and his hands glowed brighter.

Hydra gasped.

When Thorn's hands dimmed, Sol gasped as well.

"Did it work?" Theron asked as he rushed to his son.

Sol nodded. "I feel my dragon, and like he said, it feels different."

"All you need to do is fly, and you'll settle into each other." I smiled, seeing the joy light up Sol's face. "That's what helped Tyson."

"Thank you so much." Theron scratched the back of his neck. "I know I was cynical, but this—"

Vlad lifted a hand. "Don't. You've already helped us more than we can ever repay."

A branch snapped several yards away, and the six of us tensed.

Someone was spying on us.

CHAPTER TWENTY-EIGHT

THORN TURNED toward the noise and stepped in front of me, partially blocking me from view.

I wanted to yank him behind me, especially if the threat was a warrior, but I understood he was acting on the same instinct to protect me.

My lungs seized. If it was a warrior, they would've already notified the others that we were here.

Theron hurried toward the noise, racing between a yellow poplar and an oak tree, and disappeared from view.

"Dad," Sol whispered loud enough that Theron could hear.

When there wasn't an immediate response, Sol took a few steps forward, but Hydra clutched his arm and murmured, "You're not acclimated to your dragon yet. You need to stay put. Besides, he found the person watching. It's Wyvern."

My lungs started working better. The name seemed familiar. "Who's that?"

"Theron's righthand man." Hydra dropped her hands to her sides. "Ever since we learned the warriors were near, everyone's been on edge. Wyvern noticed us hurrying away, and he couldn't find Theron. He must have been making sure everything was okay."

The sounds of footsteps drew closer, and both Theron and Wyvern stepped into view.

Vlad and Thorn went rigid. If I hadn't known better, I would've thought a warrior was here, but maybe their wariness had to do with the frown on Theron's face.

Wyvern was shirtless, which didn't help matters for Thorn with me here. The new dragon was muscular, his warm, medium-brown complexion enhancing the curves of his muscles. He placed a cell phone in his back jeans pocket and folded his arms over his broad chest. His dark eyes assessed Thorn and me, and I noticed his eyes had a fold in the upper eyelid in the inside corner.

"Why are *they* here?" Wyvern asked, rubbing a hand across a scruffy goatee. He sneered at me like he thought his look of disgust would impact me.

A laugh bubbled in my chest, but I held it in. Laughing wouldn't help, but seriously, Drake had the menacing look down pat. Compared to him, Wyvern looked as threatening as a kitten.

"The less you know, the better," Theron rasped and pointed behind them. "Why don't you head back to the thunder?"

"Are you serious?" Wyvern jerked his head back. "Why have you allowed them here?" He paused, his cheeks reddening. "Wait. Are they blackmailing you? Is that why you've been disappearing so much lately?"

Thorn shook his head and bared his teeth. *This is why I didn't want to help them. I get accused of horrible stuff, even when I do something good. It's not worth putting us at risk.*

My heart ached. Every time he felt good about something, something else came along to ruin it. My hands clenched. "No, we aren't blackmailing him." I lifted my chin, refusing to cower, and flanked Thorn. "My *mate* just healed Sol so when the warriors do come, he won't be targeted."

Wyvern's brows furrowed. He looked at Thorn. "Why would you do that?"

"Because Thorn is a good person," Vlad interjected as he stepped up beside Thorn.

It was clear we would protect Thorn, no matter the cost.

"How did you..." Wyvern's eyes bulged. He turned back to Theron. "Have you been *helping* them?"

Jaw ticking, Theron glanced at us and said, "You three, go on. I'll handle things from here."

Thorn's nostrils flared. "Gladly."

The three of us spread apart, readying to shift.

Sol hurried to Thorn and touched his arm.

My mate tensed, not meeting his eyes.

"I just wanted to say thank you again." Sol dropped his hand. "You saved my life, and I will *never* forget that."

"The same goes for me." Hydra smiled but stayed several feet away. "Your secret is safe with us."

Wyvern frowned. "We can't let them go. The prince is searching for them, and we all saw on the Dragonnet that this asshole stripped those shifters of their dragons." He scoffed. "I can't believe you allowed him to touch Sol!"

A deep growl emanated from Thorn's throat. Hot anger and cold tendrils of fear swirled through our bond. A hot fudge brownie with ice cream was an amazing combination of the two temperature extremes, but *this* sensation was far from comforting. It was unnerving. If Thorn felt I was under threat, who knew what he'd do?

I grabbed his arm. Some of his turmoil ebbed, but not as much as I'd hoped.

"You will let us go," Thorn rasped. "The only reason those warriors lost their dragons was that they were keeping me from my *mate*." He wrapped an arm around my shoulders and pulled me to his side. "Drake and the warriors tried to force my mate to marry *him*, despite her being mated to *me*. So I did what I had to do to save her."

He lowered his arm. "Let me be clear. If you prevent us from leaving or put my mate in harm's way, I won't hesitate to do the same to you."

There was no question Thorn loved me and would do anything for me, and I treasured that. But I wasn't sure if threats were the right route to go with Wyvern.

Wyvern's jaw dropped as he stared at Theron and asked, "Did you hear him? He said he would take my dragon!"

"Because he senses you're putting his mate at risk," Theron growled and gestured at me. "If I had that power, I'd do the same if you talked like that about Hydra, especially if the person hunting her wanted to make her his wife."

"By helping them, you've put the whole thunder at risk." Wyvern shook his head. "What do you think will happen if Drake finds out? Hell, they knocked out the king!"

Vlad touched Thorn and me and murmured, "We need to go."

He was right. Wyvern was distracted, arguing with Theron. If we gave them time to calm down, we could be stuck here, especially if Wyvern had a fated mate, or if he'd texted someone in the thunder to alert them about us.

Taking Thorn's hand, I guided him into the trees as Sol and Hydra moved to stand between us and Wyvern.

"Hey!" Wyvern shouted. "You're not going anywhere!"

Thorn tensed, but I tugged him deeper into the woods after Vlad. There was no doubt the three of us could get out of here with Hydra, Theron, and Sol there to protect us.

"Yes, they are," Theron replied. "I'm the leader of this thunder, and I'm telling you to let them go. He healed Sol. Do you understand? Or do I need to remind you why I'm in charge?"

There was a moment of silence before Wyvern sighed. "Fine."

Thorn relaxed as the three of us continued into the woods at a quick pace.

"Let's shift." Vlad stopped in his tracks and turned toward us. His skin took on a green hue. He'd already called his dragon forward.

Moving far enough away from Thorn and Vlad, I did the same.

As my dragon surged forward, my vision sharpened, and my hearing amplified. My body expanded, and I found myself in my dragon form.

When Thorn completed his shift, the three of us took off, soaring back to the barn, but a chill still ran through me.

THE REST of the day passed. We filled everyone in on what had happened back at Theron's thunder, and soon, dinner was ready. The scent of meaty lasagna filled the house, and my stomach grumbled.

Though I wanted only the pasta, Eva, Elliott, and Peter enjoyed a salad with their main course. My appetite for greens had vanished since I'd become a shifter, but I craved meat and carbs all the time. Thorn had explained that needing more calories, carbs, and protein was a side effect of being a dragon.

Thorn, Vlad, Cassidy, Saphira, and I headed outside to the firepit to eat. I sat between Saphira and Thorn. I tilted my head up to stare at the night sky and enjoyed all the new colors and views I hadn't been able to see as a human.

"So... Sol and Wyvern." Saphira twirled a piece of hair around one finger. "Were they attractive? The only dragon males I've met are the ones who live around the chateau or Drake's friends, who, let's be real, are pompous and unappealing."

Putting his fork on his plate, Thorn glared at Saphira.

"What?" Saphira stuck out her tongue. "Just because she's mated doesn't mean she can't find other men attractive. She's taken, not blind."

I smirked. Since I'd met Thorn, all other men had paled in comparison. Someone I would've found attractive a month ago, I wouldn't even glance at today.

Cassidy leaned over the arm of her chair and patted Thorn's leg. "I bet their looks didn't even register on Everly's radar, now that she has you."

"Oh, come on." Saphira rolled her eyes. "There's no doubt Everly is devoted to him." She mouthed to me, *You can tell me later.*

Thorn snarled.

I took his hand as I answered, "I won't have a different answer." We were concluding this conversation now. "Thorn is hands down way more attractive than either one of them. It's like comparing a kid's fingerpainting to *The Starry Night.*"

"Uh..." Saphira glanced up at the sky.

"The painting *The Starry Night* by Vincent van Gogh. Not the actual sky." Sometimes, I forgot that many people didn't love paintings the way Mom and I did.

Vlad nodded. "That is a gorgeous painting."

Okay, at least *someone* was cultured.

"To put it more bluntly, once you find your fated mate or complete a bond with a chosen mate, you inherently don't notice anyone else in that way." Vlad shrugged and smiled at Cassidy adoringly. "And I wouldn't want it any other way. She is the sun, moon, and stars to me."

Saphira's face twisted in confusion, and she blew out a breath as she stabbed a large bite of her food. "Forget I asked."

"I'm more than happy to do that." Thorn took another bite.

Something dinged. Vlad leaned over in his seat, removing his phone. "Dad texted me. That's odd." After he swiped the phone and read the message, he jumped to his feet, his plate crashing to the ground.

Thorn was a second behind him. "What's wrong?"

I swallowed the bite I'd just taken, the food almost lodging in my throat. I climbed to my feet too, putting my half-eaten plate on the seat.

Vlad answered, "Dad received a text from Theron. Theron wants us to run. The warriors are there, and they're picking up our trail from a few hours ago."

My stomach heaved, and it wasn't because of the food. "They can't do that, right?"

"If they know we were there earlier today, they'll assume we're close." Thorn assessed the area as if he expected Drake or the warriors to pop out at any second. "They'll eventually find us here. We need to flee *now*."

Chest constricting, I shook my head. "What if Theron and Hydra are in trouble? They helped us. We can't turn our backs on them." I understood wanting to get away from danger, but running would mean abandoning our allies.

He turned to me and placed his hands on my shoulders. He lowered his forehead to mine and said, "I helped them, Ev. I healed Sol. We've done our part to give back. All I care about is keeping you safe."

We always came back to the same conversation. "Running won't keep us safe. The only way we become safe is by facing the threat together, which means we can't abandon the people who could be our allies."

"You heard Wyvern." Thorn lifted his head, his determination wafting through me. "He had no interest in giving me a chance, despite Sol, Hydra, and Theron telling him I helped Sol. He was ready to hand us over to Drake. Staying here will only lead to our capture. I can't lose you again. I can't survive that." His fear and agony crashed through me.

My insides knotted, and my dragon whimpered. I'd hurt him so much when I'd handed myself over to Drake. It didn't matter if my intentions had been good; we'd come so close to losing each other.

But if I hadn't tried to do the exchange and someone had died, I would've had to live with that regret my entire life. "These are *your* people. Drake is hunting down the weak and old and slaughtering them. I understand you feel abandoned and betrayed, but Theron didn't turn his back on you...and that was before he knew you could help Sol."

"She's right." Cassidy set her plate on the grass. "Thorn, the dragon shifters never turned their backs on you. Your parents did. And they feared you because they haven't been given a reason not to.

We will *never* be safe. Isn't it better to go there and help—which Drake and the warriors won't expect—than let them attack us when they're prepared?"

Thorn cut the air with a hand. "The thunder isn't under attack. The warriors are looking for *us*."

"Oh, please." Saphira crossed her legs and finished chewing her bite. "We *all* know Drake will be with the warriors. He wants to be there when you get captured. He'll hurt some, if not all, of the thunder to make sure no one knows your real location. Theron may have told you to run, but that doesn't mean they're safe. He just feels indebted to you."

Thorn closed his eyes, chest heaving. I could sense how much he wanted to leave, but he was in the minority.

Sometimes, the hardest part of life is doing the right thing when you don't want to, I connected to him and squeezed his hand. *And you're the type of man who knows right from wrong. If we run, you'll regret it. Maybe not today or tomorrow, but eventually, it will catch up to you.*

Something strange passed between us, and his voice popped into my head. *I'm not that guy, Everly. The world could burn to the ground, and I wouldn't care as long as you were safe.* When he opened his eyes, his pupils had slitted.

My traitorous body warmed as my dragon purred. His overwhelming love for me was intoxicating.

I also want to be the man you deserve, which means I'm willing to do this...for you. He brushed his fingers along my cheeks, leaving them flush in their wake. *But at the first sign of something going wrong, we leave. I will not allow Drake to capture you again and force you into something you're unwilling to do. Keeping you away from him matters most to me.*

Of course. The same for you. Though I wanted to help Theron and his thunder, I couldn't watch Thorn be taken. If they caught him, they'd kill him. *But Vlad is right. They won't expect us. This could be our best chance to end this.*

"We'll go." Thorn took my hand and moved to face everyone else. "But if the warriors aren't harming or threatening the thunder, we leave.

Vlad and Cassidy nodded, while Saphira arched a brow.

"We better get going." Saphira took her last bite, chewed, and swallowed. "If Drake is involved, as I suspect, it's probably already bad."

The five of us headed into the barn and found the others in the kitchen and den. We informed them of what was going on, and everyone was on the same page as Vlad, Cassidy, and me. Brenton and Errol were especially determined to help. They couldn't stand idly by while Drake acted the tyrant, and Tyson hated Drake even more after learning that Drake had been targeting people with injuries like his.

We also decided that Eva, Elliott, and Peter needed to stay. It would be too risky to take three humans into battle.

As everyone got ready, Thorn found some rope and tied Peter to a chair in the kitchen. We didn't trust him enough to leave him free to roam.

Everyone headed outside with Thorn and me in the rear. As we left, I heard Elliott mumble, "If he'd changed me, they would've had another dragon on their side."

I smiled. Several days had passed, and he hadn't changed his stance about becoming a dragon, so maybe when we got back, Thorn could change him.

Soon, all eight of us were flying toward the thunder. We were lucky we'd gone there earlier, or we wouldn't have known the way.

Even flying couldn't calm my frazzled nerves.

Keep an eye out, Thorn connected as he flew close to me. Each time we flapped our wings, they brushed together.

Vlad led the way, and Thorn and I stayed at the back so the dragons wouldn't see us first.

As we approached, I became aware of a group of people down

where we'd landed earlier. None were in their dragon form, so we weren't at risk yet.

"If you don't tell us who the abomination was meeting with, I'll cut the throat of a thunder member of our choosing. The person who informed us of Thorn's presence here and the leader of the thunder know what's going on." Drake's cold voice echoed up from the spot. "Maybe I should kill someone now so you can see I mean it."

My heart raced, and I flapped my wings harder.

There was a scuffling sound, and Theron cried out, "No, not my son!"

CHAPTER TWENTY-NINE

EVERLY, Thorn connected as he easily caught up to me. I remained focused on the area where Drake and the others were below. *We can't rush in. We need to be smart.*

Maybe that was true, but someone important to the man who'd helped us so much was in danger. There were only ten others there, besides Theron, Wyvern, Sol, and Drake. We wouldn't be grossly outnumbered. I suspected Sol and Theron wouldn't attack us, especially if we handled Drake. It wasn't like we were rushing into a fight with fifty warriors.

Vlad flew faster, which was good, seeing as he was in front of the group. If anyone was going to reach them first, it would be him. And Thorn couldn't connect with him like he could with me.

We are being smart. We agreed to come here and help if this thunder was in danger, and there are only ten warriors down there. I kept up my quick pace as our group plunged toward the thunder. *They're under threat. I promise, if I get in harm's way, I'll let you know, and you do the same for me.*

The clearing we'd landed in earlier came into view just as a warrior grabbed Sol by the neck. The sound of our wings must have finally registered because Drake's beady eyes turned upward and focused on Thorn.

A cruel smirk spread across the ugly prince's face, and I was ashamed I'd ever found him physically attractive. His onyx eyes seemed even darker, and his dark brown hair was still styled perfectly in spikes. "Here they come, proving how stupid the abomination and his disciples are. They willingly enter the dragon's lair."

Please, whatever you do, don't let them capture you, Thorn begged as his trepidation weighed down my wings.

Then it clicked. Thorn was terrified of losing me because he was petrified of the royal family. He wanted only to keep those he loved safe, but not because he didn't care about his people. It was because, since he was six, he'd been hiding from the king. The fear he'd felt as a little boy had grown as he'd gotten older, and he was merely trying to survive.

My heart ripped in two. I hated that I hadn't seen it before.

I pushed the warmth of my love and confidence toward him. *You don't need to fear them. You're a force to be reckoned with. They should cower before your strength and determination. Only you can end Drake's plans. You're the firstborn heir to the throne, and you can take his dragon. Do that. Reverse the roles. Make him quake at the sight of you.*

The warriors raised their weapons, and my heart constricted. They had tranq guns, which meant they planned on capturing us instead of killing us.

Drake wanted to put on a show.

"Shoot!" Falkor commanded from his position next to Drake. "Remember, we don't kill them...yet."

Ladon rushed to flank the ugly prince's other side to protect him, and the other eight guards fired.

I stopped moving my wings, ending my forward progression, and Vlad, Cassidy, and Thorn did the same.

Saphira, Errol, Brenton, and Tyson didn't. The four of them

changed their trajectory, but they weren't in danger, since all eight guards had been aiming for Thorn and Vlad.

Of course, the guards recognized the four of us in dragon form. Not only that, but they knew Thorn was the plum dragon, and six of the darts had been aimed at him.

As they reloaded their weapons, Thorn flew forward. His strength shone through as he sped past everyone and darted downward.

My heart clenched. Okay, I'd wanted to inspire him, but I hadn't meant for him to do *that*. I couldn't take it back now, or I might distract him and cause him harm. But that didn't mean I would leave him alone to take on all the warriors. He was strong, but he needed help.

The seven of us charged forward as Thorn swooped down. The warriors aimed their rifles at him, not focused on the rest of us. They viewed Thorn as the real threat.

I'd never seen anyone fly as fast as Thorn, and as the guards fired at him, each shot missed by mere inches.

Thorn spread out his talons and snatched the tranq rifles from the hands of two guards then barreled into the last four, who had their tranq guns trained on him.

Gunfire exploded as I surged to the head of our group, adrenaline making me faster than ever before.

I had to get to him. If he got tranqed, I'd need to carry him away quickly.

A loud, guttural roar came from deep within as I reached the treetops. Vlad and Cassidy were a few feet behind me, almost as desperate to reach their son as I was.

"Falkor! Ladon!" Drake barked. "Get him *now!*"

That settled my target. Eliminating Drake would also end most of our other problems. King Arman would let Thorn live as long as he didn't make waves.

My blood boiled with rage, and my stomach heated as flames

scorched my insides. Drake was a tyrant and weirdly obsessed with getting his way, feeling entitled to whatever he wanted.

Several guards screamed, and Thorn jerked his head up. The sensation of his magic took hold, telling me what he was doing—stripping the warriors of their dragon.

Falkor and Ladon aimed their rifles at Thorn, but Vlad, Cassidy, and I had caught up. Vlad stopped short, shielding Thorn from a shot as he attacked a guard close to him.

Cassidy took Ladon, while I expelled flames on Falkor. Of course, I'd be stuck with him, as if Fate were giving me hell for dropping his drawers. My flames licked his skin as the rest of the group reached Thorn and Vlad to help fight the remaining three warriors, who were readying to aim their tranq rifles at Thorn and Vlad again.

Grimacing, Falkor stood strong as my flames engulfed him. His skin turned pink from the burns, and he didn't move. My flames were having an impact on him, but unfortunately, it wasn't as much as I'd hoped, probably because he was a dragon. Something was better than nothing. I still had so much to learn about dragons.

All too soon, I didn't have any flames left, and my fire thinned as my lungs burned for oxygen.

Falkor narrowed his eyes and swiveled his tranq gun at me.

Too little too late. I chomped on the arm holding the rifle. The metallic taste of blood filled my mouth as he grunted. Vomit inched up my throat. I'd never tasted blood like this before. The idea of having human fluids in my mouth didn't sit well with me. I'd cut up all sorts of things in my premed classes, and I hadn't expected to have *this* much of an issue.

With his other hand, he punched me in the nose. Pain exploded in my snout and shot into my head. Tears burned my eyes, and I jerked back as my jaw went slack, but I'd managed to keep a firm enough grip that my teeth ripped his skin. Despite the damage, he still held on to the rifle.

My dragon roared, loud and angry. She was upset that I'd allowed myself to get distracted by something so silly as the taste of blood. Despite all the training back at the barn, I hadn't been fully prepared for an actual battle in dragon form. But failure wasn't an option.

"Make sure you don't permanently hurt Everly," Drake commanded as he stumbled back, spun on his heels, then raced toward Theron's thunder.

He was a scaredy-cat or whatever the equivalent was for dragons who lacked courage. Maybe he should put *himself* on his list of weak dragons for deserting his men.

Falkor swung at me again, but I was prepared. I caught his arm with my left talon, digging my claws into his wrist. I wanted to injure both his arms so he couldn't use any weapons on us. He was one of the strongest fighters. Putting him out of action would hurt their cause, especially if he was injured enough that he couldn't command the others.

Drake's getting away, I connected with Thorn. The only thing keeping me going was the magic thrumming through our connection. As long as he was using it, he was alive and well enough to function.

We all saw his cowardly ass scurry away, Thorn replied.

A loud snarl sounded behind me, and out of the corner of my eye, I watched as Tyson lifted himself into the air and chased after Drake.

Thank goodness. Someone needed to go after him, and I was glad it was Tyson. It would serve Drake right if Tyson took him down.

Falkor kicked at my back talons, trying to knock them out from underneath me, then swung the arm with the rifle at me, but it didn't get far. I wondered if it was broken.

Even though his kicks hurt, my legs didn't give out. With my right talon, I swiped the rifle away and pushed him backward. He tumbled down and landed on his back, his eyes bulging.

Sol appeared at my side and swiped up the rifle. He straightened and fired it, lodging a tranq right into Falkor's stomach.

Blood oozed from Falkor's arms and dripped into the grass as he snarled, "None of you will get away with this." His eyelids lowered slowly then closed as the dart knocked him out.

Sol pivoted to where Ladon and Cassidy were fighting. I turned toward them in time to see Ladon lodge a dagger into Cassidy's left side. Cassidy drew her head back and snarled just as Sol fired the gun. The tranq hit Ladon in the neck.

The strange magical feeling from Thorn ebbed, and my breath caught. Something might be wrong...but as I focused on the bond, I didn't feel any further discomfort coming through.

As Ladon collapsed, Cassidy grabbed for the dagger with her talons, but blood coated the edge, and her scaly skin slipped off the blade.

"I've got it," Theron said. He rushed past Sol and me to her side, then yanked the dagger out as Vlad reached his mate.

Are you okay? Thorn connected. The ground shook as he raced toward me.

I took in the area. All eight guards were lying on the ground, out cold. All of our people seemed all right, but Saphira's gaze was fixed on something just beyond me.

I jerked in that direction. Wyvern stood there, equally still. He was focused on Saphira as if nothing else in the world mattered.

Clearly, Saphira had found one answer she'd been so desperate for earlier—whether Wyvern and Sol were handsome. Apparently, she approved of Wyvern, judging by the tangy smell of arousal wafting off her.

Now was *not* the time for this.

Thorn roared, rushing toward Wyvern. Though he was in dragon form, it was clear that Thorn was beyond pissed. Wyvern was obviously the one who'd ratted us out to Drake.

The threat was enough to snap Wyvern out of his daze.

"I'm sorry." Wyvern lifted his hands. "I thought I was protecting the thunder! I didn't know he'd come here and torture us."

Smoke trickled from Thorn's nose.

In fairness, no one understood that the prince is that horrible. I'd hoped that no leader could be that cruel, but Drake was obviously a product of his grandfather, the former marked dragon who'd used his magic to force people to do his will. *At least, they hoped he wouldn't be.* I touched Thorn's arm to send him some calm.

"Look, I know Wyvern messed up, but we have a more pressing issue." Theron rubbed the back of his neck. "There are forty more warriors back with the thunder. Drake left the majority there to ensure no one slipped away. If he makes it back, he'll send them here, and your scent won't have time to dissipate if you leave now."

My pulse thundered. We should've expected more warriors. Of course, Drake would bring a large number with him after what had happened at the wedding.

Worse, we couldn't fly away, not after Sol had nearly died at Drake's hands.

Shit. Tyson, Thorn connected.

I couldn't swallow. Tyson had flown after Drake.

A gunshot rang out. Something horrible was going down.

Brenton took off toward the noise with Saphira and Errol on his tail.

Even though Tyson wasn't blood, he'd become my family. When I flew after them, I expected Thorn to argue, but he and his parents followed as well. We all raced toward the threat.

As we rose higher, I saw twenty dragons winging toward us in the distance with just as many in human form on foot below.

Drake had mobilized his troops.

Thorn, I connected. *You need to go.* This was all about catching and killing him. I couldn't risk that.

There's no way in hell I'm leaving you, Thorn replied, his own stress seeping through. *Even if I run, they'll chase after me. It would be hard to get away with numbers like this.*

I looked at the ground and noted two figures closer to us than the oncoming warriors. Drake and Tyson. Tyson was naked and passed out on the ground. Drake squatted next to him, one hand gripping Tyson's hair to keep his head up. He held a dagger at Tyson's throat, and blood trickled down his neck.

Despite my being airborne, the world shifted around me.

CHAPTER THIRTY

DRAKE LIFTED HIS HEAD, a victorious sneer on his face.

Leaving to save Thorn wasn't an option. Neither was allowing Drake to cut Tyson's throat.

Throwing his head back, Brenton let out a thunderous roar.

"Stay back," Drake spat. "Or I'll slit his throat."

He won't, I connected with Thorn. Unfortunately, he was the only one I could communicate with in dragon form. *He needs Tyson alive to ensure he survives.*

Don't be so sure, Thorn replied as his mistrust thrummed through our connection. *He only cares about control, and the warriors will be here in seconds.*

My stomach hardened. Drake only needed to hold off for another minute and he'd have plenty of backup. *You need to go.*

I'm not going anywhere without you, and he won't allow either of us to get away. He'll kill Tyson as soon as we try to leave. Thorn's fear chilled our connection.

And this is why we had to come here. Sol would be dead if not for us. If we turned our backs on people we could help, we'd be no better than Drake. I needed Thorn to realize that.

"*All* of you are going to shift back into human form now." Drake tightened his grip on Tyson's hair, pulling at the scalp.

Even unconscious, Tyson moaned in agony.

All of us paused. Since we'd come in dragon form, we hadn't brought any weapons. If we changed into our human forms, we'd be defenseless against the warriors, who were armed with guns.

The seven of us glanced at one another as if we were all thinking the same thing.

Drake's face reddened. "Now! Or I'll slit his throat this instant!"

The first of the warriors came through, and I recognized two of them—Jessie and Uther. Uther's face was scrunched with discomfort, while Jessie's eyes homed in on Thorn and me.

The rest of the warriors filed in behind Drake. There was no way we were getting out of this.

Errol, Brenton, and Saphira landed first and shifted back into human form. A few of the warriors watched them, but most were focused on Thorn, Vlad, Cassidy, and me.

They thought we were the biggest threat, perhaps because they knew Thorn cared about the three of us, but they thought he might not see Tyson as family, and therefore, might not care about his death as much.

They were wrong.

The four of us landed behind Errol, Saphira, and Brenton and pulled our dragons back. I hated being trapped like this. Before long, I'd be exposed to Drake and his men in ways I'd never wanted to be. My mouth filled with saliva.

My body shrank as my dragon begrudgingly separated from my mind.

"Let him go," Saphira cried. "We've all landed and shifted as you demanded."

Drake pouted. "I'd hoped that Thorn and Everly would need more convincing." He chuckled and removed the dagger from Tyson's neck, replacing it in the sheath at his side. "But the abomination is a coward. He's all big and bad when he catches us off guard, but as soon as my warriors and I are prepared, he cowers. And *this* was the son my father feared."

I took a hurried step forward and pointed my finger at the dickhead. "He's not *afraid*. He cares about Tyson. One would think you'd feel the same way, seeing as he used to live next door to you."

"Ah...Everly." Drake scanned me, making my blood turn cold. "With a body like yours, maybe I won't need a breeder after all. You are quite delicious, in both dragon and human form."

A menacing rumble shook the ground as a strong arm wrapped around my body. My skin caught fire.

Thorn.

He tugged me behind him, chest heaving with each breath. "Do *not* look at her. She is my mate and wife, and I will *kill* you for everything you've done to her."

I wanted to step around Thorn and tell Drake exactly where he could go, but Thorn's hatred and anger flooded our connection. He didn't want anyone ever seeing me this way, especially not *him*.

I couldn't blame him. If someone had been trying to force Thorn to be her husband and lover, I didn't think I'd have been keeping it together as well as Thorn was.

Drake laughed, the noise like sandpaper to my ears. I winced but refused to cover them, not wanting to show a hint that he had influence over me.

"You really think you're going to make it out alive?" Drake glanced over his shoulder at the warriors. "He's delusional. Though he may be the firstborn, I'm the true heir. Everyone sees him as an abomination."

My patience snapped. I poked my head from behind Thorn's back and said, "Just because you keep throwing that word around doesn't make it true. Thorn is the one trying to save dragons you're determined to kill. That's why he attacked the chateau—you were forcing me to marry you against my will."

"Don't forget, *love*." Drake tilted his head as he released his hold on Tyson. The unconscious man dropped to the ground. "You're the one who hunted me down in the bar that night. You *asked* me to choose you. Don't make this into something it isn't."

I flinched. I *hated* that he had me there. "You were planning to take my little sister, who'd just turned eighteen."

"None of this matters." Vlad lifted his chin. "Like Thorn said, you won't be taking Everly or hurting my son. Give Tyson back, and we'll leave. No one needs to get injured."

Jessie snorted. Her black helmet had pushed her bleach-blonde bangs into her cinnamon eyes. "There are forty of us to your seven. You're in human form with no weapons. Do you really think that's how this is going down?" She aimed her rifle at Vlad.

Sol, Theron, and Wyvern weren't here. I wondered briefly why they hadn't shifted into dragon form.

"What would King Arman say about this?" Errol hung his head. "Your father is a good man. He didn't raise you to threaten your people and kill your brother."

The sound of more people approaching made me freeze. Theron had said there were forty warriors. Who were these newcomers? Maybe it was Theron's thunder, but that wouldn't make things better. They would follow their prince to protect their thunder from harm.

"My father is *weak*," Drake snarled and bared his teeth. He spun around to the warriors. "Surround them and take them back to the thunder."

"Wait." Uther frowned. "We aren't going to kill Thorn here?"

"No," Drake's snarled, "We need to get it on video so all dragons can see. After what he did at my wedding, they need to know I won't tolerate actions like that."

We can't go with them, Thorn connected. *We need to grab Tyson and get the hell out of here. Everly, if the warriors detain us, our chances of escaping will be low. I won't lose you. I'll make them all pay for the hell they've caused.*

My vision blurred as the warriors closest to us removed hand-cuffs from their belts. The dark shiny metal was distinctive—

Wolfram Dwinn. If they put those on us, we wouldn't be able to shift back into dragons, and Thorn wouldn't be able to access his magic.

"Jessie," Cassidy said in a broken voice. "We were friends. You don't have to do this."

I started. As a former royal nanny, Cassidy would know many of the warriors.

"We *were* friends, but when you took off with the prince and protected him, everything changed." Jessie kept her gun trained on Thorn. "You won't get any help or sympathy from me."

That was the thing. Drake owned his warriors. *Even the ones who don't agree with him, like Uther, will follow because he's threatened their families.*

Thorn hissed, his pupils slitting. *That's exactly what my grandfather did when he was king.*

More warriors raced out of the trees and surrounded us. Thirty of them kept their guns trained on us, while ten moved closer, ready to handcuff us.

I spun and pressed my back to Thorn's.

When I tell you to run, go, Thorn's voice popped into my head. *As soon as the warriors with the handcuffs get close enough, I'll steal their dragons.*

That would cause chaos, if only for a moment.

I tried to breathe slowly, needing a clear head. If shit hit the fan—er...the flames hit the scales—I didn't want to be caught with my pants down, like Falkor. Granted, I was already buck naked. But still.

The ten guards split up. Four headed toward Thorn. Their hands shook as they got closer, as if they knew he planned on using his magic.

A woman warrior was in front, her jaw trembling harder with each step. "Now, don't do anything stupid. There are thirty guards with weapons aimed at all of you." Her voice quivered.

"If you're going to handcuff me, just do it," Saphira gritted out, her irises glowing as her dragon showed through. "Don't be timid...

unless the only warriors Drake could get on his side were those too weak to go against him."

"Get them *now*," Drake bellowed. "And knock them out, if that's the only way to get them to stop talking."

I couldn't see him, but I pictured him stomping like a toddler.

Uther appeared in front of me, his face twisted with regret. He opened the handcuffs and lifted both hands so I could see what he was holding. His gaze remained on my face and didn't travel down my naked body.

Drake had forced him into this.

When the woman reached Thorn, a white light glowed around them, brighter than the midday sun.

Thorn was channeling his magic.

"Merigold!" the male warrior behind her shouted.

The warning came too late. Thorn touched the woman, and magic thrummed through our bond.

"Grab a warrior!" Vlad exclaimed, and thanks to our training, none of us hesitated.

I jumped toward Uther as he pivoted to catch me. His intention was clear, but at the last second, I switched direction and grabbed his arms.

Gunfire erupted, and my dragon jerked forward, tapping partially into my mind, which she'd never done before. I sensed a tranq barreling toward me. I dropped to my knees, and the dart passed over my head by mere millimeters and lodged in Uther's chest.

"Shit," he rasped, but the damage was done.

Another warrior aimed his rifle at me, and I gripped Uther's arms, forcing him to turn toward the warrior as the tranq flew toward us. The tranq hit Uther, just an inch away from where my hand held him.

The warriors were taking into account what I was doing.

A thud sounded to the left, and Saphira yelped, "Uncle Brenton!"

He must have gotten hit.

Screams came from near Thorn, and I saw four warriors positioned deeper in the trees to my right, training their rifles on him. I had to do something.

Uther's body grew heavy as the drugs took effect. I wished I'd been dragon born so I'd be stronger. I released him, and he dropped like a brick as I moved toward my mate.

They're shooting— I started as Theron, Sol, and Wyvern appeared from behind a tree and jumped on three of the warriors. One fired a shot.

"No!" Cassidy shouted as she lunged in front of Thorn, taking the dart to protect her son.

Theron knocked out the fourth warrior, and the three of them ran back into the shadows of the woods. They were helping us while staying out of sight. Drake and his warriors remained focused on Thorn.

The rest of the warriors raced toward us, rifles ready.

We couldn't escape. There was no way.

A loud, familiar voice broke through the chaos. "Stop this. *Now!*"

Everyone froze. The warriors lowered their weapons, and I spun around to find King Arman and ten more guards stepping through a thick section of trees.

"Father," Drake gasped. "What are you doing here?"

"I heard Thorn might have been found." King Arman's neck corded. "I told you I wanted to go with you when he was located. Why did you not alert me?"

Oh, I knew that answer, but I figured I didn't need to say anything. From the expression on King Arman's face, he already knew as well.

"I want to prove what I'm capable of, Father." Drake's warmer persona slipped on like the slimy skin of an actor on stage. "Isn't that why you put me in charge of the family business, so I could prove I'm fit to lead?"

Saphira laughed, not bothering to cover it up. "You're not fit to breathe the same air as us."

Drake's eyes flashed, and the monster within snuck out for a second. "Say that again, and I'll—"

"You'll *what*?" King Arman snapped. "Threaten her like you have the thunder here when they called and informed you that they'd seen Thorn? And now you have an entire group, including my *royal advisor*, standing here naked in their human forms without weapons, while warriors attack them?"

"Oh, please." Drake rolled his eyes, unable to maintain his fake persona. "They're all traitors, and every one of them will die...except my darling Everly."

Thorn snarled and took a menacing step toward Drake.

Jessie aimed her rifle at my mate again.

"Remember not to kill him." Drake rocked back on his heels. "That's what he'll get when we arrive home, along with everyone here...including Errol."

"No." King Arman marched to his son. "You will let these people go. For the past twenty-one years, Thorn has stayed hidden, causing no problems or harm. He's no threat to us."

Drake straightened and glared at the king. "Yeah, I learned that when I found his address in your desk a few years ago. You allowed him to live, risking *my* claim to the throne. When I asked Falkor what he knew about Thorn, he told me everything, and we made a plan to eliminate him."

That was why Falkor had told the king he needed to protect Drake all that time ago.

"You're just as bad as my father," King Arman spat. "Thorn posed no harm, and now you've hurt others in our thunder because you're fixated on him and Everly."

Drake pounded his chest. "I'm doing what's needed to ensure the dragons survive. That's what a king does. You're content to let us die off."

"He's killing injured dragons, sire," Errol murmured and gestured at Tyson, who was passed out on the ground. "That's what we learned here. But Thorn healed Tyson. He can fly and fully connect with his dragon again."

King Arman's attention swung to Thorn. "You healed an injured dragon?"

"Not just one," I interjected. "Two. He mended them both, and he changed me. His magic has far more potential than just stealing someone's dragon or forcing people to change for his own selfish gain."

The king strolled across the clearing to Thorn. He placed his hand on his son's shoulders and stared into his eyes. He whispered, "You're not like my father after all. I'm so sorry that it's taken me so long to see that."

Our bond filled with uncertainty. Maybe we'd survive this. The king was finally supporting his son.

"Father, he's an abomination," Drake spat. "He took four dragons here, and eight more not too far from here. Maybe even Falkor's and Ladon's since they're not here."

The king's eyes flashed with anger, and he kept a hand on Thorn's arm as he turned to address his other son. "No, *you're* the abomination. You forced him into doing that to protect the people he loves. I see it now. You, Drake Hale, are *not* fit to lead." He dropped his hand and stepped toward Drake. "I denounce you as the official heir to the throne."

"Thank gods," Saphira rasped.

"You can't do that," Drake snarled. "He wasn't even raised royal. No one will follow him, not after what they've seen him do."

"In time, everyone will see what he is like, just as I see who you've become." The king turned back to Thorn, his shoulders slumped. "Son, I'm so sorry. If you'll give me a chance—"

Before he could finish, Drake removed the dagger from its sheath.

I charged forward, pushing past Thorn. "King Arm—"

Before I could reach him or warn him, Drake had stabbed King Arman in the back.

His words were cut off, and his eyes widened. He turned slowly and blinked at his son. "What...have...you...done?"

The positioning of the dagger was so precise, and I knew from my time at university exactly where Drake had hit the king. His heart. My hope that we would soon be free lessened with each strangled breath King Arman took.

No matter who you were, even if you were royalty, doing the right thing could result in someone closest to you stabbing you in the back.

The world tilted as the king stumbled, his lavender shirt turning crimson. His heartbeat stuttered. Even as my mate's warmth pressed into my back with that comforting buzz, I knew.

Drake had won.

USA TODAY BESTSELLING AUTHOR
JEN L. GREY

HIDDEN FATE
THE MARKED DRAGON PRINCE TRILOGY
3

CHAPTER ONE

BLOOD TRICKLED from the mouth of the dragon king, and his legs wobbled. When he stumbled, two warriors grabbed his arms and helped him regain his balance.

A dagger protruded from his back.

"How could you?" his deep voice rasped as he gaped at his younger son. His blood soaked the bottom half of his lavender shirt, turning it crimson. His midnight-black irises lightened as death drew closer.

A mix of emotions swirled through Thorn's and my fated-mate bond as he watched his estranged father fade in front of his eyes, mortally wounded by none other than Thorn's younger brother, Drake.

Drake was born soon after his parents had tried to kill Thorn at the tender age of six. They'd nurtured the very son who'd grown into the exact thing they'd feared Thorn would become—evil. Not only had Drake stabbed his father, but he'd also hunted Thorn to kill him, and he'd tried to force me to marry him, even though Thorn and I were fated mates.

The cool breeze of late May from the Blue Ridge Mountains

shifted the tree branches in the small clearing and brushed across my naked skin, bringing the metallic stench of blood to my nose. I stepped closer to Thorn, needing his body heat and the jolt of our fated-mate connection. Our group was all naked. Drake had forced us to shift into our human forms, or else he would've hurt Tyson, who lay unconscious at his feet, naked with a tranq lodged in his side.

Drake's nose wrinkled as he lifted his head. "You're trying to prevent me from taking the throne...from making our race strong. You criticized me for choosing a wife and a breeder. I'm doing what's necessary to ensure our race doesn't die out."

Because his father had denounced his narcissistic ass as the true heir to the throne. This confrontation, though, was limited to the warriors here and our group, which no other thunder would trust, not yet. That had to be why Drake had stabbed his father.

To my right, Saphira straightened. The front section of her long, curly, dark brown hair cascaded over her shoulders, covering her breasts, and the other half fell to her mid-back. The color emphasized her gorgeous bronze skin. She narrowed her mocha eyes as she spat, "Like killing all the injured and old dragons? And forcing a human to be your breeder even though she might die?"

"I am keeping our bloodline pure." Drake clenched his hands. "If our race wants to survive and thrive, someone has to do the hard things." He waved a hand at his father. "*He* wasn't up to the task. He was going to hand over the throne to an *abomination*."

I snorted, unable to stay silent. I'd done that for too long with my stepdad, accepting the poor way he treated me, and I'd recently learned that he'd treated my brother and sister similarly while I'd been gone. "That's complete bullshit. Thorn is not an abomination. He's strong, caring, and can heal the injured. Having a permanent injury doesn't make anyone weak." Anyone who'd ever had to persevere and learn how to survive through adversities was stronger than Drake and all his loyal warriors combined. He was an entitled jerk who'd never had to struggle.

Drake's ice-cold ebony eyes drilled into me.

Bristling, Thorn fidgeted so that his naked body blocked most of mine from Drake's view. Thorn snarled, his anger palpable. Everyone must have felt it.

"Everly. Dear fiancée..." Drake sneered at me. Despite the breeze, his dark brown hair remained in perfect small spikes. "That is your *one* slip. Once we are married—"

Body shaking, Thorn stepped forward. My eyes locked on his mark, the very thing that had instigated this entire mess almost two decades ago. Spread over the base of his neck to the top of his back, the mark resembled a dragon tattoo. It denoted that he possessed magic, the kind that petrified the king and all the other dragons. Thorn could create new dragon shifters. He could also take a dragon shifter's magic away—a power Thorn's grandfather had possessed and abused for evil.

"She is *my mate* and *wife!*" Thorn bellowed. He tensed, every muscle in his back pronounced. He stepped over one of the ten unconscious warriors as the other forty surrounding us remained frozen in place. Everyone, including Vlad, Cassidy, Saphira, Tyson, Errol, and Brenton, was still reeling from what we'd witnessed— Drake stabbing his father, King Arman, in the back.

Drake laughed loudly. "Maybe now, but not for much longer. Once we get you back to the château, we'll record all of your deaths... except hers." He pointed at me. "Of course."

"Son, this isn't you." King Arman's voice came out garbled. Blood ran down his chin and onto the front of his shirt. "We raised you better than this."

The few times I'd met the king, power had radiated from him, enhanced by his dragon and his tall, muscular build. His salt-and-pepper hair and the crow's feet around his eyes gave him a wise air, although he'd made the foolish mistake of driving his older son—my mate—away. Now, even with two warriors attempting to hold him up, he dropped to his knees.

"Your Highness." Errol's face twisted with agony, and his chocolate-brown eyes darkened as he raced past his daughter, Saphira, and his brother, Brenton, toward his king. His short, dark brown hair ruffled as he squatted next to his friend and ruler. "Maybe Thorn can heal you."

"No!" Drake exclaimed. "There will be no healing him unless you want to rush your death. I have no problem killing you here if you push me."

My heartbeat quickened, and I moved closer to Thorn. He was now several feet in front of me, but as I stepped between Cassidy and Vlad, they each gripped my arms.

"Don't make yourself more of a target," Vlad murmured. His wavy caramel hair was wild, and I refused to look any lower than his cornflower blue eyes because he was as naked as I was.

"If Drake focuses on you again, Thorn might lose his ability to think straight," Cassidy added, her hazel eyes focused on Thorn, Drake, and the king. "We could get away if we time it perfectly."

My chest expanded. I hadn't considered trying to escape. Drake's warriors were distracted, but we couldn't walk away, not if Thorn could help his biological father. *Can you heal him?*

"I...I can't," he answered aloud, then connected with me, *It's a mortal wound.* Hurt and guilt slammed into me. *Your head wound was a slow bleed, not like this. There's no way to save him.*

Evil mirth darkened Drake's irises as he stepped toward his father on the side opposite Errol. Drake bent and chuckled menacingly while staring into King Arman's eyes. "What does it feel like, learning that the son you cast away and tried to bring back can't help you? Do you like knowing that even as you die, neither of your children can stand you?"

Thorn punched his brother in the face as a tear ran down King Arman's cheek. Drake stumbled back several feet, blood pouring from his nose.

The king's going to fall, I connected, as my lungs seized.

Drake wasn't focused on his father as he pinched his nose to get the bleeding to stop.

Agony ripped through Thorn, and he kneeled in front of King

Arman and pulled the man into his arms. The blood from the king's mouth smeared across my mate's stomach, though everything inside me screamed at me to go to him, Cassidy and Vlad tightened their hold on my arms, keeping me back.

Drake snarled as blood trickled into his mouth, making my blood run cold. Thorn's back was turned to the asshole.

I yanked out of Cassidy's and Vlad's grip and rushed between Thorn and Drake, positioning myself so I could see both men.

"I'm...so...sorry." King Arman's words were nearly inaudible, even with my new dragon hearing. "I...was...wrong."

Thorn moved the king onto his side to look into his eyes.

I touched Thorn's arm, our jolt sizzling. I needed him to know I was there. At one time, the king had been a loving father to him.

"I forgive you," Thorn whispered, taking in a ragged breath.

A sad smile spread across the king's face. Then his already faint heartbeat stopped. The world seemed eerily quiet. The breeze slowed, and the only sounds were of everyone's pulse and breathing.

Two things the king would never experience again, all because of Drake.

Anger boiled inside me. I'd never held such rage before. Even though the king had done something horrible, he hadn't truly wanted Thorn to die. All of *this* was on Drake.

Drake wanted Thorn dead and me as his wife, so he'd ordered his warriors and all the other dragons to hunt us down.

Theron, Vlad's father's friend, had hidden us in his safe house near his thunder, and Thorn had healed his son to thank him because Drake was also hunting and killing injured dragons. Theron's second in command, Wyvern, had seen Thorn do it and, without knowing the true situation, alerted Drake to Thorn's presence. Drake had come here, willing to kill as many of Theron's thunder as needed to draw Thorn out. And now Drake had killed King Arman because the king had finally been poised to do what was right.

It all led back to the arrogant prince.

Tears trailed down my mate's face, stirring up that anger and hatred inside me. No one hurt my mate.

Errol, Saphira, and several warriors sniffled as they watched their king die. Every sound fed my hate.

Something moved in the corner of my vision, and I turned to see Drake pulling a tranq gun from a male warrior's side.

I jumped to my feet as Drake pointed the gun at Thorn's neck. There was no way in hell I'd allow him to shoot my mate. I connected, *Thorn, duck!*

My dragon surged forward in my mind, helping me move faster than normal. In a flash, I leapt the five feet to Drake and tackled him.

As I slammed into his chest, his arm lifted. I tried to stop my forward momentum, but Drake fell backward, and I tumbled right after him. At least he'd dropped the tranq gun.

A moment before my body would have pressed against Drake's, a strong arm wrapped around me and yanked me back against a hard, muscular chest. My skin buzzed.

Thorn.

Warm wetness hit the center of my back, and a lump formed in my throat.

I knew exactly what it was.

King Arman's blood.

White-hot fury blazed, but when Thorn's fingers pressed into my skin, I realized his anger was exacerbating mine.

"You will pay for *everything*," Thorn snarled, as he gently set me aside. "I'm going to tear you limb from limb."

"I'd like to see you try," Drake hissed as he stood. "I'm the acting king now that my father is dead."

That confirmed my worst fear. "King Arman said the throne doesn't go to you," I spat.

"He *never* said that. I don't know what you're talking about." Drake moved closer to me, and Thorn stepped back to keep the same amount of distance between us and him.

Drake smirked at me. "You'll be my wife and queen, especially with a body like that. I'll forgive that you allowed the abomination to touch you...just for *him*."

"You son of a bitch." Thorn pulled me behind him, blocking Drake's view, and connected, *Get out of the way.*

"Shoot him and detain the others!" Drake commanded his warriors. "We need to hurry back to the château. There are several executions to record and a coronation to plan."

Saliva filled my mouth. This time, we weren't getting out of this.

When none of the warriors moved, Thorn punched Drake in the jaw. Drake stumbled back, tripping over Tyson's unconscious body, which lay near five of Drake's guards.

Thorn rushed Drake again, but Drake snarled, "You know what will happen if you disobey."

The female warrior lifted her rifle with shaky hands, aiming it at Thorn.

No! Not this again.

As her finger touched the trigger, I connected with Thorn, *Get down!*

He dropped, and for a split second, my heartbeat steadied...until the dart barreled toward me. I ducked, too, and the dart sailed an inch over my head.

Thank goodness Thorn had over two feet on me, or that would've gone sideways.

Thorn stood, and one of the king's warriors lifted his weapon. His hands were steady as he fired...and the tranq soared past Thorn and into the woman who'd shot at my mate.

The warrior shouted, "Thorn is the future king! Protect him!"

Drake's eyes bulged, and his face reddened. "Take down anyone who's against me, or your families will be *killed*."

Several of Drake's guards pivoted and aimed their guns at Thorn.

My breath caught, and I wasn't sure what to do.

"Protect Thorn!" another warrior yelled from the back, and two who were aiming at Thorn were hit with darts and fell to the ground.

Thorn, get out of the crossfire, I connected. Now that the warriors had moved back several feet, I rushed to Tyson and tossed the young shifter over my shoulder. Unfortunately, his penis hit my arm, but there was nothing I could do about it. We were all naked for this fight.

When I turned, Thorn was running, heading toward Theron's settlement, chasing after Drake.

A gentle hand touched my shoulder. I spun around, ready to defend myself and Tyson as best I could with one arm, but Cassidy's familiar face made me pause. She whispered, "We've got to leave. Get Thorn to listen. You're the only one who can do it." She took Tyson from me and ran back the way we'd come from, toward the safe house. Vlad helped Errol get away, and they rushed after her.

Glancing back, I marked Thorn as he was about to slip through the tree line after Drake. I connected to him with the only thing I could think of and prayed it would work.

Thorn, I need you!

<h1 style="text-align:center">CHAPTER TWO</h1>

CONCERN WASHED over me as Thorn responded, *What's wrong? Are you hurt?* Regret and guilt weighed down our bond as he spun around, his eyes narrowing.

The knot in my chest loosened. I hadn't been sure I could reach him, but thank goodness, his concern for me outweighed his hate for Drake. About a third of the king's warriors were fighting those loyal to Drake...though I wasn't sure if *loyal* was the right word since he'd threatened their families. Regardless, the outcome was the same. Eventually, they'd overtake the king's warriors and capture us. *We need to leave before—*

That asshole won't touch you. His irises darkened to cobalt. His pain and anger rushed through our connection. *Run. I'll get King Arman and be right behind you.*

My heart squeezed so tightly that it throbbed. I understood what losing a parent was like, but this had to be worse for him. This parent had abandoned him and tried to make things right moments before he died.

I stayed put, needing to make sure he wouldn't let his hate and anger take over again. Chaos unfolded around us. The guards were focused on each other, and the ones who'd fought to protect Thorn were fleeing.

Luckily, Drake's guards were chasing them, leaving us alone, but they wouldn't for long.

Thorn lifted the king and rushed toward me.

Ev, go, he connected, his face twisted with concern.

A few of the remaining warriors paused, and a woman called, "Thorn and the girl are getting away!"

Tap into your dragon, Thorn connected and ran even faster. In a second, he caught up to me.

With no time to lose, I replicated what I'd done earlier. My dragon surged forward and connected with me, lending my legs extra strength.

My skin tingled as we rushed toward the thick line of oaks and red cedars.

Something whistled behind me. My breathing quickened, and I braced for the prick of the dart. My dragon surged, guiding me to zigzag instead of continuing in a straight line.

Fear squeezed my chest and the bond as my emotions and Thorn's melded together. He was moving in the same pattern, and neither of us was hit.

Footsteps sounded to our right, heading toward the clearing. Probably more warriors.

My knees wanted to buckle, but my dragon roared. If we fell, Thorn and I would be captured. I gritted my teeth and pushed through the discomfort.

The footsteps stopped.

Falkor asked, "What in the *hell* is going on?"

"Where is everyone?" Ladon piped in.

The two guards were awake. It felt like a lifetime ago since we'd knocked their asses out back where we'd found them with Theron, Sol, and Wyvern.

"Uh...the king is dead, and the warriors are fighting each other over who should be king," one answered quickly. "We're going after the girl and Thorn."

"What do you mean, warriors are fighting against Drake?" Falkor bellowed, a hint of hysteria in his tone.

Of course he wasn't focused on the king's death but on people acting against Drake. I wondered if that was because he was Drake's guard now or if there was more behind it.

We were gaining distance from them, and I was more than okay with that. Let Falkor and Ladon distract our pursuers.

Their voices grew fainter, and I almost cried with relief when Falkor commanded, "We can worry about the girl and Thorn later. With the king gone, it'll be easier to catch them. We have to make sure no one hurts Drake. *He* is the *future* and protecting him is our priority."

He was right. With the king deceased, there was no one left to keep Drake in check. All the injured and old dragons would be openly hunted, the same as we were. But that was a problem for later. Right now, we needed to get away.

Something was brewing in Thorn, but as the scents of Saphira, Errol, Brenton, Tyson, Vlad, Cassidy, Sol, Wyvern, and Theron thickened in the air, I didn't have time to decipher it. We were close.

A few minutes later, we ran around an oak tree and found them with Hydra. As soon as we came into view, Cassidy and Saphira let out huge breaths, their shoulders relaxing.

Cassidy murmured, "Thank gods. We were about to come looking for you."

Brenton held Tyson in his arms, and Saphira and Errol flanked him.

"Sorry," Thorn murmured as we stopped in front of the others. That emotion I'd sensed had morphed into guilt and disgust, weighing heavily on our connection. He was struggling, and I *hated* that I wasn't sure how to help him. I didn't want to pry while we were still in danger.

I studied my mate for the first time since he'd picked up King Arman. Blood from the king's wound drizzled down his bare, muscular chest and streaked his body. Bile churned in my gut. Carrying his father's body was something he shouldn't have had to do.

Saphira looked toward my mate, and a growl emanated from my throat before I could stop myself. Her gaze was firmly on the king, but it was still way too close to my mate's naked body. I hated that he was exposed to another young, attractive, and very *unmated* female.

Surprisingly, Wyvern snarled as well, and Saphira glared at him.

We were all experiencing heightened emotions, and we needed clothes, *stat*.

"Let's leave." Vlad cleared his throat and glanced at the area behind Thorn, avoiding looking at me.

I kept my gaze set from everyone's shoulders up. There were some things you could never erase from your mind—like seeing your in-laws naked.

"I can't leave my thunder." Theron shook his head and turned to his mate and son. "You two go with Wyvern, and I'll meet up with you when I can."

My chest burned. Because of Drake, more people were being forced to run. This had to end.

"That's a bad idea." Wyvern raised his hands. Unlike us, Wyvern, Hydra, Sol, and Theron were dressed because they hadn't flown to get here. "I'm the one who reached out to Drake. He'll trust me more than you. Besides, you need to be with your family, and you might need to use your *resources* to find another safe location."

What is he talking about? I didn't want to ask out loud and delay us further, but I also wanted answers.

Thorn shook his head as he turned around, facing the direction we'd come from. *No clue.*

"Dad, he's right." Sol pursed his lips. "I'm pretty sure Drake knew we were lying."

"Yeah, but Wyvern attacked the warriors when the warriors were attacking them." Theron gestured at our naked group. "If something were to happen..."

Saphira nodded and stepped forward. "I agree. We can't risk Wyvern staying here. He needs to come with us."

"Dear." Errol touched her arm. "We shouldn't interfere with thunder politics. Unlike the king, they haven't asked for an advisor."

Wyvern smiled at Saphira. "Don't worry. I'll be fine, and I promise you'll see me soon. I can't stay away from you for long."

Yeah, they were definitely attracted to each other.

"If Theron and Wyvern know what they're doing, we *need* to go. Our scents need time to dilute." Vlad steepled his fingers. "Time is truly of the essence."

"We must bury the king," Brenton added, frowning deeply.

"Seriously, go." Wyvern gestured at the sky. "We were hidden by trees, so no one saw us attack the warriors. I'll keep you updated on everything I learn."

Huffing, Theron nodded and patted Wyvern on the arm. "You and Sol are the two I trust the most to lead the thunder in my absence. Just make sure you aren't in danger, and if something happens to you or the thunder—"

Wyvern lifted a hand. "We'll let you know. I get that I fucked up by informing Drake that Thorn was here, but that was before I learned what he'd done for Sol. I'm sorry I caused this problem, not only for our thunder but for Thorn and the others as well." He nodded to us.

I nodded back. He had messed up, but I understood. I would've done the same thing if I'd thought people I loved were in danger. Hell, I'd handed myself over to Drake to save my sister, Eva, from a fate that happened anyway.

"Let's shift." Vlad stepped back, getting more room for his dragon form. "And Thorn, I'll carry the king from here. You've done enough." The last sentence was filled with emotion.

Everything was settled.

"Okay," I said. "We've all had enough naked time."

Everyone nodded, and we spread apart. Soon, every one of us, minus Wyvern, the king, and Tyson, was in dragon form. Theron gingerly grabbed his clothes, and I was confused until I noticed the lump of a cell phone in his back pocket. He'd need it to communicate with Wyvern.

"Go on." Wyvern waved us away, his gaze locked on Saphira. "I'll hold them off. Be safe."

I was certain those last two words were mainly directed at her. The butterscotch scales on her cheeks reddened, proving that dragons could blush.

Since it was still bright out, we bolted high into the sky, with Vlad carrying the king and Brenton carrying his son in their talons. I focused on our surroundings, making sure no aircraft were nearby. We flew as high as we could, and then Cassidy gestured in all different directions.

She's suggesting we split up, Thorn connected. *Let's go right. We can fly around the long way.*

I was more than okay with that. After the battle, I needed a release, and now wasn't the time to get it sexually from Thorn for so many reasons, so flying would have to do the trick.

The two of us peeled off, flying east with the sun at our backs. Summer was approaching, and the air was warm, even all the way up here. We flew in tandem, and I glanced back to see the others break off into groups. Sol stuck with Brenton and Tyson, leaving Hydra and Theron together.

After several long minutes, I couldn't take the silence. *I love you, and I'm here.*

Guilt and shame swirled inside him, and my dragon whimpered. Something strange was definitely going on with him.

I love you, too, and I'm so damn sorry, he replied, staring at me with those gorgeous eyes that matched the sky around us.

Something stirred inside me, making my scales crawl. *What do you mean?* I tried to keep my voice level, but I was confused.

When Drake killed my fath—King Arman, all I saw was red. He hung his head as we turned slightly, easing our way back toward the barn. *And I put you in danger.*

You didn't. He must have forgotten why we'd been there. It had been my influence, my suggestion, and now he felt awful about it? My lungs couldn't fill completely. *Remember, you didn't want to go. If I'd known—* I stopped. I didn't know what to say that wouldn't make it worse. No matter what we'd done, people would have died.

You were right to push us to go. Now we have someone Drake trusts who will alert us if something seems suspicious. We need more allies like that. But when King Arman died, I was so angry and fixated on Drake and everything he'd done that I left you behind. His eyes glistened. *Next time, that could easily be you. I wanted to stop him. I wanted to protect you, but instead, I left you exposed and vulnerable.*

My chest expanded so much that it hurt. I hated that I had put such a heavy burden on him. *You did* nothing *wrong. Your father died right in front of you while weapons were trained on us.*

Yeah, that sucked. Smoke trickled from his nose. *But if something had happened to you because I ran off to kill Drake, I wouldn't have survived that. Hell, I almost didn't survive you being stuck in that château with him. I sure couldn't handle not having you on this earth any longer.*

I've been training to protect myself. Remember? My heart skipped. Even through everything, his biggest concern had been me. I'd never had someone love me this much. He felt bad because he thought he'd abandoned me, though he'd chased after a threat to protect me. It would have been comical if it didn't burden him so much. *You have nothing to feel bad about. As soon as I said I needed you, you didn't hesitate. You came back to me.*

His dragon smiled. It was big, toothy, funny, and sexy all at the same time. *I've always been chasing after you. It started that night at the bar, the first time I saw you. I followed you home that night, albeit not with the best intentions, but I was drawn to you even when I thought I shouldn't be.*

The memory of that night crashed over me. I'd hunted Drake

down to ask him to take me instead of Eva as payment for my stepfather's crime—before I'd learned about *all this*. It was the best bad decision I'd ever made and one I would never want to change. Yes, it had gotten me into this situation with Drake, but it had also led me to Thorn. *I remember seeing your eyes in the car from underneath the bill of your hat. I felt the pull, too.*

That was what we were—destined to be together. Fated mates.

All too soon, our flight came to an end. After looking around to make sure no one had followed us, we began our descent. The others dropped into the trees and started to shift back into human form, but before Thorn and I landed, I noticed something scrambling underneath us—something larger than the usual small forest animals. *Do you see that?*

Yeah, Thorn replied, and hot anger flared between us.

He swooped down, and I followed on his tail. A section of branches thinned, giving me a glimpse of what—no, *who* it was.

My stepfather. Peter.

And he was running for his life.

CHAPTER THREE

THE MOMENT he heard our wings, Peter's chestnut eyes narrowed as he scanned the area for something...most likely a place to hide.

His eyes widened, and he scurried toward some low brush between two sizable oaks and crawled under the branches. He clearly didn't think we could see him. His gray stood out starkly among the browns and greens shrouding his body.

Maybe this was comical, but not now. Not when there was so much at stake and with a man who thought only of himself, even over his own children.

Thorn didn't waste time. He landed and stuck his forelegs into the bush, then yanked my stepdad from his spot. Peter's face blanched as Thorn lifted him. In Thorn's talons, he looked tiny, despite standing at five-ten.

All dragons were gigantic, around four times the size of their human form, and Thorn was already huge for a human, coming in at seven and a half feet tall. Smoke flowed out of his nose as his chest heaved. The anger emanating from my mate was stronger than ever before. He needed time to decompress and mourn, but we didn't have that luxury.

"I...I'm sorry." Peter's bottom lip quivered. "I...I didn't—"

Part of me wanted to stand back and let Thorn do whatever he wanted, but if today had reminded me of anything, it was that I needed to protect my siblings. He was *their* father, and if something happened to him, they would be parentless...like me. *Babe, I know he's an asshole, but we have to remember Elliott and Eva. It would hurt them to lose him, even if he is a bad father.*

None of the anger ebbed, but Thorn replied, *I know. You don't want me to kill him. That's the only reason he's still breathing, but we can't trust the twins to watch him again. And if he doesn't stop putting you in danger, I don't know how long I can hold back.* He turned to me, his eyes full of concern.

The world tilted.

My siblings.

Peter must have done something to them to escape, and dammit, I couldn't ask him in this form. I had to get to them.

Thorn and I took off, flying over the treetops. The barn was in view, so we were isolated from any humans. We'd kept an eye out for hikers and campers before landing. None were around, which wasn't surprising. Theron's land was private property.

As we drew closer to the barn, Elliott and Eva ran out of the house with stony expressions.

They had to be looking for Peter.

The moment they noticed Thorn and me, shock registered on Elliott's face. His steel blue eyes widened as we landed in front of them. Thorn released Peter, who fell with a loud thud.

Peter winced and groaned as he reached behind to rub his tailbone.

"What the *hell?*" Elliott asked as he stalked to his father. "You ran away without bothering to tell your *kids?*"

Hissing, Peter jerked his head up. "Yes, I did. Because my *kids* are fine hanging around with fire-breathing dragons who knock out their only living parent!"

Elliott shrugged. "Can you blame us? If Thorn had tied you to that chair *and* knocked you out, you wouldn't have gotten away. If you're going to get mad at anyone, get mad at yourself. It's not our fault you're more pleasant when you're unconscious."

Your brother is strange, but he's growing on me, Thorn connected as he moved to stand beside me.

Brushing a loose strand of her dark brown hair from her face, Eva huffed. "El, I'm not sure you're helping."

Seeing them standing side by side in the sunlight reminded me of how similar they looked. The same shade of eyes and hair, the same nose and mouth, and the same fair skin tone. The only differences were that Elliott was taller and his hair was cut much shorter but long enough for his bangs to hang permanently in his eyes.

"Me?" Elliott puffed his chest. "I'm not the idiot who ran away, thinking I could get past badass dragons." His attention flicked to Thorn, and he rubbed his hands together. "Though that's about to change, since I'm ready to be one myself."

I sighed, and the sound was more dramatic in dragon form. We'd promised that Thorn would change him when we got back. We had a lot more problems now than when we'd left, so I'd completely forgotten.

Is he expecting me to do it now? Thorn connected, humor and annoyance washing away some of his anger. *While in dragon form and with Peter sitting right in front of me after he tried to escape?*

Yes. My brother had a one-track mind that I firmly blamed on video games. He couldn't focus on anything other than what he wanted most in the moment, and right now, that was to become one of us. His need for instant gratification was why I'd forced him to take a few days to think about it.

The sounds of human footsteps caught my attention, and I glanced over my shoulder to find Saphira, Cassidy, Vlad, and Errol approaching. The others must still be shifting, but these four would want to know what was going on.

Vlad took in Peter as he slowly climbed to his feet, and then he looked at Thorn and me. "What happened?"

"Dear old Dad tried to run away." Elliott rolled his eyes. "I should've known he didn't actually want to watch Eva and me play video games. He's never wanted to before."

"You get engrossed in them." Peter scowled. "Both of you."

At least he hadn't done something horrible to them, such as knock them out, like I'd feared.

"You two go ahead and shift." Cassidy gestured toward the tree line where we'd shifted earlier. Our clothes would still be there. "We'll keep an eye on him."

Errol headed to the front door and glanced back. "I'll grab Sol, Theron, and Hydra some clothes while you three handle this."

"Maybe we could do more than just watch Peter." Saphira smacked the back of her hand against her palm. "I could do what Thorn's had the pleasure of doing several times now."

Peter grimaced. "My head just stopped hurting a few days ago. No need to knock me out again."

"Oh, but I think there is." She grinned, showing every one of her teeth. Saphira was a gorgeous and scary woman, and I loved seeing Peter shiver underneath her gaze.

Come on, Ev, Thorn connected, his wing brushing mine.

My head spun as our fated-mate bond thrummed between us. The bond was intense in both forms since we were two parts of the same soul.

As we headed for the trees, Brenton and Tyson stepped from between a red cedar and a sweetgum. My talons almost gave out when I saw that the younger dragon shifter was awake. His warm olive eyes locked on me, and he slurred faintly, "I heard that you picked up my ass and got me away from Drake." Dark circles lined his eyes, showing that the tranq was still affecting him.

My heart skipped a beat. I hadn't expected a thank you. I would have done that for anyone because it was the *right* thing to do. The fact that I liked him had made the risk more worth it. I blew out a breath, seeing as I couldn't speak in this form.

Brenton beamed, his emerald irises sparkling. "Come on, son.

Let's go get you something to eat and drink to help you recover from the tranquilizer."

Thorn and I flew over the trees a little ways to where we'd left our clothes. We landed and pulled back our dragons, and I heard Errol giving Theron, Hydra, and Sol their clothes.

As soon as Thorn and I were dressed, he pulled me into his hard chest. His lips were on my neck, and he breathed me in deeply. My temperature rose.

I spun around in his arms and stared into his face. *Are you okay?*

Now I am. He lowered his forehead to mine, brushing a finger across my cheek. *For a second back there, I didn't think we were getting out.*

In truth, I hadn't thought so, either. If King Arman hadn't shown up, we would probably be on our way back to the château, and not voluntarily. Cold tendrils of fear curled into my chest, and his eyes darkened as he sensed my emotions. I forced a smile to ease the tension in my body. "But we did." That was what we had to focus on. "And because of the king."

Pain lined his face, twisting a knife into my heart. Thorn had endured more than enough pain to last a lifetime.

"It was." He nodded and kissed me.

My lips sizzled from his touch, and I leaned into him. After what we'd gone through, I needed this moment as much as he did...alone and together.

"And for that, I'll have to let go of some of my hate. Because of him, I didn't lose you, and though I'd love to sneak away with you, we can't. We need to determine where to head next. It won't be safe here for much longer, and that's the only reason I can pull away right now." He moved back, frowning.

Heart racing, I wanted to change his mind, but that would be careless and stupid. "I fully plan to take you up on that offer once we finally get some alone time." I pouted and kissed him again.

His tongue slipped into my mouth, making my brain fuzzy as his faint vanilla taste and minty amber scent overloaded my senses. This man looked like a god and tasted like happiness. I didn't know what I'd done to deserve him, but I would be thankful for him each and every day.

Eagerly, I responded to him, my hands fisting in his shirt. The urge to rip it from his body almost overwhelmed me, but then footsteps belonging to Theron, Hydra, and Sol filtered through my haze. I groaned and forced myself to pull away. Glancing into Thorn's eyes, I found his pupils were slits from his dragon peeking through. He smiled and kissed the top of my head before intertwining our fingers and pulling me back toward the barn and everyone else.

With each step closer to the barn house, I remembered how dire our situation was. Hydra, Theron, and Sol were about five hundred feet ahead of us, so Thorn and I picked up our pace and caught up to them as we stepped out of the tree line.

Everyone was outside, with Peter on the edge of the group between Cassidy and Saphira. Tyson was eating a sandwich and drinking a soda, while Vlad, Errol, and Brenton had found shovels and were digging a hole next to where the king lay underneath a beautiful dogwood. I could hear Saphira filling Elliott and Eva in on what had transpired back at Theron's thunder, but when Thorn's agony swirled into me, I focused on my mate.

He was staring at the king.

King Arman had been powerful, but he wasn't anymore. Though we couldn't see the wound where Drake had stabbed his father in the back, the king's lavender shirt was stained crimson except at the very top near his neck. His skin had been a dark olive, but now it was almost white—like the vampires I'd seen on television. The power he'd radiated was gone...extinguished, just like his soul.

Thorn squeezed my hand gently before releasing it and jogging to the grave. I wanted to go with him, but he needed time to grieve without me hovering. When he needed to lean on me, I'd be there.

The four of us reached Saphira, Elliott, Eva, Cassidy, and Peter just as Thorn took the shovel from Vlad and said, "Why don't you go be part of that conversation, and I'll finish this?"

"Of course." Vlad nodded, the corners of his mouth tipping downward. Instead of saying anything more, he walked over to join us, giving Thorn the space he needed as he worked with Errol and Brenton.

Pulling my attention away from my mate was excruciating, but I turned so I could take part in the conversation.

Out of the corner of my eye, Eva stiffened. A chill ran through me as I followed her gaze, which had landed on Sol.

My muscles relaxed. From the way she'd reacted, I'd expected a warrior to be behind us, ready to attack. Still, her reaction was strange.

Sol tilted his head and took a hesitant step forward before stopping and swaying as if he were being tugged toward her.

Something curious stirred inside me. Could they be soulmates? Surely not. That would be too coincidental. From what I'd gathered, fated mates had been commonplace at one time, but as the dragon shifter population had plummeted, so had the number of fated-mate bond connections. What Thorn and I had was rare and must have been even more so since I'd been born human. I had to be reading the situation wrong.

Vlad jumped right in, addressing Theron. "Wyvern thinks you might have a connection that could hide us. Is that the case?"

Fidgeting, Theron rolled his shoulders. "It's possible. But it'll take time to set up. I have to make a post." He removed his phone from his back pocket, the one he'd taken the time to pick up gently in dragon form to bring with him.

I sucked in a breath. "Wait. No. You can't post that on the Dragonnet. Drake will track us."

"Wait." Elliott lifted a hand, his face radiating joy. "Did you fucking say *Dragonnet*? I don't know *what* that is, but it sounds *badass*, and I want to play it. I'm totally in!"

Sol's brows furrowed, and Hydra stepped back, placing a hand on her chest.

Of course Elliott had assumed it was a video game. "It's an

intranet for all dragon shifter communications and where the royals can send out information and video speeches or whatever to their subjects." I still wasn't one hundred percent sure about that.

"Oh, don't forget weddings." Saphira wrinkled her nose. "They like to broadcast those as well."

If Thorn's parents hadn't been there, I would have given her the middle finger.

She smirked. "That's what you get for that comment back there."

She meant the brothel comment about her and Wyvern. I wanted to mouth off in return, but now wasn't the time. We had serious things to focus on. I'd get the brat later.

Scratching his head, Theron tried to regroup. "This isn't Dragonnet. It's a network for the thunders that have injured or differently abled dragons. It's a communication board on a private server that you have to be screened to enter. That's why I had to make sure I brought my phone."

"If you're sure Drake won't find out, then sure." Vlad lifted his hands. "It's not like we have many options."

"Okay." Theron swiped his screen and typed out a message.

After he was done, Errol rubbed his hands together. Our group turned in time to watch Thorn lift the king and carefully place him in the grave.

"I thought we might have a moment of silence to say our goodbyes before we finish the burial." Errol placed his shovel on the ground and rubbed his hands together. "We won't be able to take him back to the château where all the royals are usually buried. Mira can't even be here for the burial of her mate, but his loss is still felt here by all of us."

As Thorn stood, he wiped the dirt from his hands onto his jeans and reached out to me. He connected, *Will you come stand beside me?*

You never have to ask, I replied as I moved to his side. He wrapped an arm around me, using me as an anchor. His sadness, guilt, and resentment washed into me as he mourned the man who had at one time been his father and had become one again just moments before his death.

Our group surrounded the hole, each person deathly silent—even Eva, Elliott, and Peter. The birds chirped, and the breeze picked up as if the world wanted to say its goodbyes as well.

I wasn't sure how long we stood there, but the sky had darkened to twilight, and tears still fell.

Then Theron's phone dinged.

He pulled it out, and everyone tensed. I'd forgotten that he'd put out that message a while ago.

"Did you find someone?" Saphira asked breathlessly.

Theron rolled his shoulders. "Yes...but there's a catch."

CHAPTER FOUR

"OF COURSE THERE'S A CATCH." Elliott nodded, a slight smirk on his face. "This is like a motherfucking *movie*, and this is the sort of shit that happens. Let me guess...a battle to the death, and winner takes all?"

Sol's brows lifted, and Eva shook her head.

I hadn't seen Elliott this animated since before Mom got sick. It was odd that something like *this* was getting him back to being the spunky, weird kid I knew.

Thorn's annoyance flared through our bond.

"No." Theron shook his head. "It's—"

"Wait! Don't tell me." Elliott bounced on his feet. "Let me guess. How about—"

"Oh!" Tyson pointed both pointer fingers to the sky. "A race. Fastest dragon wins protection for a night."

"Fuck yeah!" Elliott bobbed his head. "That would require a nightly race. It would be nonstop preparation and adrenaline. Will we have shelter for another night? Who knows? Will Thorn mother-fucking—" He paused and blinked. "Holy shit. What *is* your last name? I don't even know my sister's name anymore."

Does he even realize we're in danger? Thorn connected, his hand tightening on my waist.

There was no way to respond that wouldn't infuriate him further, so I kept my thoughts to myself.

"It's Hale," Tyson answered and patted Elliot on the arm.

I grimaced, my stomach roiling.

"Thanks, bruh," Elliott responded, and fist-bumped Tyson. "Will motherfuckin' Thorn Hale win us safety for yet—"

"Stop right there with this nonsense," Thorn growled. "And Everly's and my last name is *not* Hale."

My heart skipped, and my belly fluttered. I still thought of myself as Everly Woods, but we *were* married.

"Oh, gods." Saphira huffed. "Now they're at *bruh* level."

"What are you talking about?" Elliott lifted his chin, strolled to Tyson, then threw an arm around his shoulder. "He's been my bruh for *a week*. Between the video games and training, we already forged that bond."

Tyson snorted and winked at his cousin. "It's a true bruh-mance."

"Don't," Saphira deadpanned and lifted a hand. "I can't handle this."

Growling, Thorn stepped away from the king's grave and toward Theron, tugging me along beside him. He gritted out, "Ignore them and tell us grownups what's going on."

"Gladly." Theron tore his glare from the two young men and glanced around at everyone else. "A woman in the network offered shelter for a few days, but only if Thorn agrees to heal her daughter."

"What?" Thorn's pupils slitted. "You told them about *me*?" Our bond heated, and it wasn't in the pleasant way that indicated desire.

Trying to ease my mate's mind, I squeezed his hands and connected, *If they trust one another, I can see why he wanted to be forthright about what they'd be getting into.*

He should've asked us first, he replied, tugging me against his side. *I'll be damned if I take you somewhere that warriors might be waiting to pounce on us.*

"I *had* to." Theron bit his bottom lip and stepped away from Hydra. "I can't just show up with you, and with Sol healed, they'd know. They're more willing to accept the risk by knowing their injured child or thunder member can be healed. Don't you understand how much we all *hate* Drake and what he stands for?"

He had a point. Anywhere we stayed, the thunder would eventually know we were there. Maybe it was better to give them a heads-up so they wouldn't feel tricked into helping us. But we were screwed in our current situation.

"Look, I told them that Drake killed the king and is putting his plans into action without any barriers. I also told them how you helped us instead of running off like you could have." Theron bit his bottom lip. "The king's death is making everyone panic. This particular thunder that reached out is in the Midwest. It's a two-hour flight from here."

That was farther away from Asheville and the royal dragon lands. The warriors would be focused on the internal uprising, and then they'd focus their efforts on looking for us here first, knowing we'd taken the king with us and wouldn't get far.

Vlad crossed his arms. "How do you know they won't make a deal with the guards? My dad vouched for you—that's why we came here. What assurances do we have that this woman is trustworthy?"

"Everyone in this network knows that Drake is killing our people and is not to be trusted. Today's events solidified that decision for all of us. If Thorn is willing to heal the injured thunder members of the people who are willing to risk hiding us, then we have a better chance of resolving this situation." Theron placed a hand on his chest. "I would not be taking Sol and Hydra to a place with people I didn't trust. Drake now associates *us* with *you*. There's no getting out of that, and you all know it. If I'm willing to risk the lives of the two people I love most, I think I deserve the benefit of the doubt."

"Unless you allied with them to bring us in as a way to make up for *betraying* Drake." Errol rubbed his chin. "That's also an option."

"We know that wouldn't work even if we wanted it to." Hydra

stood tall next to Theron. "Unlike my mate, I'm not afraid to admit that the thought crossed my mind, but to Drake, we're traitors. There's no way he'd forgive us even if he said he would."

Brenton kicked at the dirt left over from digging the grave. "If there is an injured dragon network, why didn't I know about it? Tyson would have benefited from that."

"We all found each other in passing, and one thing led to another." Sol shrugged, flicking his attention to Eva every chance he had. "We didn't know about Tyson. No one had seen him around."

Tyson's face fell. "That's because I barely ever left the house."

I swallowed around the lump in my throat and shivered, reminded of what it'd been like to be constrained. The panic of knowing I couldn't connect with my dragon had been damn near overwhelming.

"That doesn't matter." Thorn tapped his fingers against his leg. "We need to make a decision and move. If a few warriors aren't already searching for us, they will be soon, and more will join them. We need to leave while we can."

The sky was darkening, too, which would hide us from humans and aircraft.

I sighed. The hardest decision I'd had to make before all this was whether to go home after exams or work an extra shift at the coffee shop instead of studying. Now I and everyone I loved was being hunted.

"I don't think we have an option." I turned against Thorn's chest to look him in the eye. He was the one who would ultimately decide. "Theron has been on our side, even if begrudgingly, since we got here. If he trusts this woman, I say we should as well."

Peter sneered and glared at me. "Everly's always putting her nose in places—"

"Someone shut him up, or I'll do it myself." Thorn's jaw clenched, and his nostrils flared. "If I trusted myself not to cause permanent damage, I'd knock his ass out, but if he insults my mate and wife one more time, I won't care about the outcome."

Mouth snapping shut, Peter swallowed. Apparently, he didn't like to learn, but he remembered enough to know better.

A smile tugged at my lips, and I tried to keep my face neutral.

"My mate is *right*." He paused, shooting eye daggers at Peter. "We don't have much of a choice, so if everyone is agreed, we should pack some supplies and go."

Sol's shoulders drooped. "I promise Edna and Mindy are solid. Mindy's dad died in the car crash that injured her five years ago."

This was the first time I'd heard of a dragon suffering a permanent injury while in human form.

"Let's split up and move." Vlad stared at the sky. "Get the bare essentials and load up the cars."

Hydra stilled. "We're not flying?"

"It's too risky." Vlad hurried to the door of the white barn house. "A warrior could come across our scents, and they'll have eyes in the sky. Traveling in vehicles will help us blend in better."

Raising a hand, Eva waved. "Let's not forget about the humans who can't fly."

"Or!" Elliott lifted a hand. "Just hear me out. You could change us, and *then* we could fly."

"Elliott Abbot," Peter rasped. "Shut your *mouth* right now and speak for yourself. I don't want to become *that*." He gestured at me.

Out of everyone here, he'd targeted me. At one time, that would've hurt, but now I rolled my eyes. He tried to blame me for anything he disliked.

Thorn released me, marched over to Peter, and got in his face. My stepdad stumbled back until he slammed into the side of the house. Thorn's face was red, and smoke trickled from his nose as Peter blanched.

Thorn punched him in the jaw.

My stepfather's head snapped back and bounced off the siding. His eyes watered, and he quickly covered the spot where he'd been hit.

"Clearly, you needed a reminder." Thorn's neck corded as he remained in my stepdad's space.

Eva and Elliott winced and closed their eyes. Even though Peter was difficult, he was still their dad, and I hated that this kept happening. However, Thorn couldn't handle his toxicity...especially toward me. I couldn't blame my mate. I'd be the same way, too.

"Just shut up," Elliott snarled. "For your own sake."

Wrapping an arm around Saphira and me, Cassidy nudged us toward Hydra, Theron, and Sol. She led most of us inside to get ready, while Vlad, Thorn, and Peter remained outside.

I wasn't sure what they were doing, but it wasn't my problem. I had Thorn to protect me, and even though I was certain I could do it myself, I no longer had to. I hurried inside to grab some things for both of us, leaving my stepdad to figure a way out of his own mess.

Luckily, we still had the two Suburbans, and Theron had his sizable older red truck, so we had enough vehicles to travel somewhat comfortably. We'd all packed a bag each, enough to have a few changes of clothes and toiletries to get us by.

Thorn drove one of the rentals, and I sat next to him on the passenger side. Eva sat right behind me in the middle row, with Saphira next to her. The two of them had been flipping through magazines they'd brought from the barn. In the very back, Peter sat behind Eva so Thorn could keep an eye on him in the rearview mirror, while Elliott sat in the center with Tyson beside him, the boys playing on Elliott's Switch. Every few minutes, one of the boys would yelp, and eventually, Eva drifted off to sleep.

Everyone else in our group was in the other Suburban in front of us, which Vlad was driving behind Theron's truck.

We'd been in the vehicle for over eight hours, and Thorn and I were struggling to stay awake. It was nearly four in the morning.

Thorn yawned, and I reached across the center console and held his hand.

Do you need me to drive? I asked. We were in Indiana, and the surrounding woods gave my dragon a sense of peace. A reddish sign came into view with a drawing of a man sitting cross-legged that said, ***Welcome Nashville Pioneer Art Colony Est. 1872***.

Glancing at me, Thorn smiled. *It looks like we're here.*

"You're going to die, asshole," Elliott snickered from the back of the Suburban.

Those two had been playing that game the entire time, and I wasn't sure how. I struggled to keep my eyes open, but they hadn't lost their enthusiasm.

The only things stopping me from falling asleep were keeping Thorn company and the odd emotion swirling through our bond. It was a strange mixture, and I wasn't sure what it meant, so I'd stayed awake, singing along to Soundgarden as we drove.

Soon, we were driving through downtown. There were several buildings side by side that weren't connected, and each one looked well-maintained. They weren't uniform in appearance, though, and the effect was welcoming. A few brick buildings mixed with aluminum-sided ones in various shades of yellow, green, and white made the place homey. Brown benches sat in front of a few shops, and one establishment's small porch was covered in birdhouses. It declared itself the General Store and Bakery.

This place would be so fun to paint, and I tried to burn each detail into memory so that I might be able to recreate it on a canvas one day. Mom would've loved to paint the picture with me like we had of the Asheville skyline in my attic room. Out of habit, I reached for the bracelet she'd given me before she died, but I came up empty-handed.

My throat dried. I had to remind myself it was in my bag, safe and sound. I'd stopped wearing it because of training and never knowing when I'd need to shift.

Hey. Thorn's mouth tightened. *What's wrong?*

Nothing.

He arched a brow and narrowed his eyes at me. He wouldn't let it go.

It's just…I was thinking about how Mom would've loved to paint a picture of this town with me, and then I reached for my bracelet… Emotion crowded uncomfortably in my chest. The last thing I wanted to do was cry, especially in front of Peter.

One day, you'll be able to wear it again. He nodded as if that settled everything, but my weird mix of emotions intensified, and I realized what it was: grief and a desperate need for calm. *I will make it safe for you to paint to your heart's content and wear whatever jewelry you want without hesitation ever again.*

Some of the discomfort ebbed as my heart fluttered. *Will that, by chance, include a wedding ring as well?*

His irises darkened. *Damn straight it will, and an engagement ring. I'll make everything right as soon as I kill Drake.*

Well, that had escalated quickly. Even though I preferred this version of Thorn, I was certain he hadn't thought of what it would mean if he followed through on that plan—that people would be looking to *him* as the new king.

I wouldn't bring that up until later, when we were closer to shutting Drake down.

We left the little downtown area and turned onto a dirt road that led us deeper into the woods. It seemed like a perfect dragon location with privacy and space away from humans.

The moon was descending, and thick, fluffy clouds floated in the dark sky. After several miles, a red, one-lane covered bridge came into view. Luckily, with how early it was, we didn't have to worry about traffic. We slowed for each vehicle to cross alone, and then Theron picked up speed, leading us to our destination.

As we followed the dirt road, a shadow flew overhead, too large to be a bird.

My stomach clenched as my heart stopped. I connected, *Dragon.*

"SHIT," Thorn rasped, as he slammed on the brakes. The abrupt stop stirred up dust around us.

The large ebony dragon easily flew over the vehicles and landed on the road in front of Theron's truck. It opened its wings, making it appear larger. The road was too narrow to turn around.

I scanned the sky as my heart thundered. I expected to find more dragons rushing toward us, but none were visible from where I sat.

Thorn's and my connection squeezed tightly, melding our fear.

Slamming the Suburban into reverse, Thorn backed up hurriedly, just as Theron jumped from his truck.

What the *hell* was he doing? Did he have a death wish? Other warriors could arrive at any second, and he'd climbed out of his vehicle willingly. None of this added up.

Something dropped in the back seat, and Elliott yelped. Eva and Saphira groaned and stirred as the vehicle jerked and dramatically reversed.

"Wait," Theron shouted, turning toward us with his back to the enemy. "It's Edna. I recognize the dragon. It's not the *others*."

Others.

Warriors.

I exhaled, and my shoulders slumped. I'd been so sure that the enemy had found us. Why would Edna do this when she knew we were coming to her house? Was this a warning or scare tactic to ensure we knew she was in control? As if we weren't already aware. That was the only possibility I could fathom.

Some of the tension in our connection ebbed, relieving the pressure in my chest. Thorn's scowl was firmly in place, and he swung his door open, marching past the hood of our vehicle right toward them.

We were all tired and stressed, and this scare had pushed Thorn over the edge. I hopped out, then looked back at Saphira.

She yawned and blinked, trying to get her bearings. "What happened?"

That was the question of the hour...literally. "Not sure. But I need to go with Thorn. Keep an eye on Peter, and make sure he doesn't do anything stupid."

Peter *hmph*ed, and I didn't need to see him to picture the scowl on his face.

"Dad, *come on*," Elliott chastised. "You've been knocked out twice, threatened more than I can count, and just got punched in the jaw. I'm with Everly. The possibility of you doing something stupid is high, and you accuse *me* of losing my short-term memory. All it would've taken was one punch for me to learn my lesson."

Mashing her lips together, Eva smiled timidly.

"I'll handle him." Saphira nodded, giving me the go-ahead to leave.

Pivoting on my heels, I hurried to catch up to Thorn. Vlad was beside him, and they both reached Theron.

"What the *hell* was that?" Thorn's chest heaved. "I thought the warriors had found us. Is this a sick game she's playing?"

Theron put his hands in his jeans pockets. "I'm sure it's not. She must have her reasons." He glanced at the dragon.

I followed his gaze, having to tilt my head all the way up to see her face. My eyes locked with her intelligent stormy gray ones. I paused by the passenger door of Vlad's Suburban. Her attention was on me, not Thorn.

A chill ran down my spine, and unease filtered through our bond as Thorn noticed.

Get back in the vehicle, he connected as he moved in front of me, blocking me from the dragon's view. His back pressed against my chest, and my skin sizzled.

I placed a hand against his back and replied, *No, we're in this together*.

His muscles tensed, but before he could say anything, Edna tapped the end of her long wing against her scaly chest, then flicked her head in the direction of the bridge.

"What?" Theron removed his cell phone from his back pocket and glanced at the screen. "I plugged in the address you gave me."

If he was expecting an answer, he'd be sorely disappointed. She was in dragon form. I opened my mouth to say that, then shut it. That comment was something Elliott would say, which meant I would be taken as a smartass. Now wasn't the time for that.

She fluttered her wings and flipped one back in that direction again.

"You do *trust* her, right?" Vlad raised his eyebrows. "I just want to confirm. I'm with Thorn—this doesn't feel right."

Edna growled low and bared her teeth.

"That's not helping matters." Thorn puffed out his chest and reached behind him to place a hand on my waist.

Cursing, Theron put his phone back into his pocket. "Yes, I trust her. There has to be a reason for this."

The dragon nodded and hovered off the ground.

Everyone went back to their vehicles. Thorn and I buckled in, and he put the vehicle into reverse again.

Eva leaned forward and asked, "What's going on?"

"We aren't sure." Thorn clenched his jaw. "Saphira, Tyson, and Everly, I need you three to tap into your dragons and see if you sense any danger. This whole situation feels off."

Soon, we found an outlet to the dirt road with enough room for us to turn around. Thorn did so, the wheels squealing despite the dirt from how fast he was driving. My body jerked from side to side until we were heading back the way we'd come. Vlad and Theron followed suit, and I realized what had happened.

Thorn and I were in the lead. If there was an attack, we'd be the first ones hit. My stomach soured, and Thorn's hands tightened on the wheel, blanching his knuckles.

Nothing will happen to you, he connected and darted a look at me just as the red covered bridge came into view. *I swear. I'll die before I let anything happen.*

That's the problem. I was his weak spot, and I hated that. *I know you would, and just as much as you don't want something to happen to me, I feel the exact same way about you.* We would both gladly give our lives for each other. This was the sort of love that so many people coveted, but there was a reason I hadn't felt the sensations as strongly when I was human. I hadn't been strong enough to handle them. I was barely able to in dragon form. It was agonizing at times.

How about this? We stick beside each other and make sure neither of us gets into trouble.

My heart skipped a beat. Times like this reminded me that he saw us as equals. He was so protective because I was his fated mate and so precious to him. *I like the sound of that.*

He winked, though the usual warmth in his gorgeous eyes was missing. *Me, too.*

Edna took a right over the treetops just as a gravel road appeared.

Thorn slowed and coasted into the turn. "Do you sense anything?" His pupils slitted as his dragon surged forward.

My chest burned as my dragon surfaced and brushed against my mind. Though I couldn't sense things as well as when I was in full dragon form, my vision was enhanced. A mile away, a fox ran through the trees, and nearby, some bunnies were stirring. The only large things I could sense were Edna and a house two miles in the distance. "Nothing out of the ordinary."

"Same," Saphira answered.

"I do." Tyson coughed, and Thorn and I tensed. Tyson continued, "Elliott just farted, and it smells like rotten eggs."

The horrible stench hit me, and it was so strong, I could taste it. I gagged.

"Holy shit," Elliott gasped. "I swear, you smelled it before it even completely left my butthole. That is so fucking cool."

"Can I just say that I, for one, am glad I'm not a drag—" Eva started, but then she wheezed. "Oh, my God. Let me roll my window down, *please.*"

Thorn growled as he pressed the child lock release button on the door handle. Both Saphira's and Eva's windows lowered, and they hung their heads out.

"Tyson, for the love of the gods," Thorn bit out as he glanced in the rearview mirror. "You know better than to pull that shit. I thought you saw something. You do realize, if this goes wrong, we're all going to be in danger?"

Begrudgingly, I rolled my window down as well. This car needed to air out, pronto.

A loud huff came from the backseat, and I didn't need to turn around to know who it was.

Peter.

I think something crawled up into your brother and died. Still scanning the area, Thorn lowered his window as well.

I mashed my lips together, but a small laugh escaped. Leave it to my brother to cause chaos when it was least convenient.

"This smells great." Elliott sniffed. "I don't know what your problem is."

"And you wonder why I didn't want you helping out with the company," Peter grumbled.

"El, I don't know how many times I have to tell you." Eva pinched her nose shut. "No one likes the smell, so just *stop.*"

Neck cording, Thorn gritted out, "Everyone focus. We'll be there soon."

That sobered everyone up, and I refocused on connecting with my dragon. I didn't sense anything other than the normal animals in the woods, which was a good thing. None of them sensed any danger.

A two-story light green house stood before us with a beige stone chimney and a dark green slanted roof. The house sat in the center of a half acre of cleared land surrounded by thick trees.

We pulled right up to the red wooden front porch as Edna landed in the middle of the yard. Her eyes flicked to us before she turned and slid into the trees to shift back into human form.

Everyone climbed out of the vehicles and stood in front of the house. Three wicker chairs and a red wooden bench were placed in the yard, but as we'd been driving for so long, none of us sat.

"What is this place?" Thorn asked as he came around and took my hand, tugging me between Vlad and himself. He scanned our surroundings, his pupils slitting as he looked for something out of the norm.

Eva stood on Thorn's other side. Sol strolled up to take the spot beside her. Elliott and Tyson were between Sol and Saphira, but for once, they were silent. Errol and Brenton flanked Peter. Theron stood closest to where Edna had disappeared, with Hydra next to him.

"I don't know." Theron swiped his phone screen. "It's a thirty-minute drive from the main thunder, where we were heading."

Other than Edna flying at us out of nowhere, nothing seemed off.

"She's heading back, so we're about to find out." Cassidy faced the direction Edna had disappeared into the woods.

Silence descended.

Edna stepped into the yard, and my jaw almost dropped at her appearance. The same smoky gray eyes took in our entire group as she smiled warmly. Her hair was a caramel brown that hit a few inches past her shoulders, and she was only a few inches taller than me, coming in around six feet. The impression I'd gotten from the dragon was nothing like the kind woman standing before us.

She tugged her cyan button-down shirt over her jeans. "I'm so sorry I alarmed you. I'd planned on you all staying with Mindy and me, but the closer you got, the more restless I felt, so I went for a flight. Then I doubted my decision, but you guys were already close. The best option was to bring you here, a backup location I have for Mindy and a few of the older members in case..."

She didn't have to finish her sentence. Every single one of us knew what she meant: in case Drake came looking to kill her.

Thorn's jaw unclenched. "I'd rather your thunder not know we're here." He then connected, *We saw how well that went with Wyvern.*

Fair point. And Theron hadn't been very willing to help us until Thorn had healed Sol. Trust had to be earned, but hopefully, since Theron trusted us and the two of them had a connection, this would go more easily.

"Listen, I'm not comfortable hiding things from my thunder." She bit her bottom lip. "It doesn't feel right. They do know about this place, but we all avoid it so no one will tie us to it. Until I see that Thorn will follow through on his promise, I'm most comfortable with you staying here."

"Of course, Edna," Theron said and wrapped an arm around Hydra.

Edna took a moment to study each of us and frowned when her gaze landed on Peter, Eva, and Elliott. Her lips pursed. "And why did you bring humans? It's bad enough to have the marked one and Drake's missing fian—"

A menacing growl emanated from Thorn. "Do *not* finish that sentence. Everly is my fated mate and *wife*. Drake took her, knowing she was *mine* and kidnapped her family to force her to surrender. That's why there are humans with us."

My heart skipped a beat at the word *mine*. I loved when he claimed me in front of others *and* behind closed doors.

Her eyes bulged. "Wait. Are you saying the humans with you are her family? That she was human and became your fated mate?"

He nodded, pulling me more tightly against him. "She was."

Edna stepped back and clutched her stomach.

She looked afraid, prompting me to say, "He did it to save me. I was going to die—it wasn't malicious. And I'm so glad he did." I glanced up lovingly at my mate.

Tilting her head, Edna observed me, and after a moment, her hands dropped to her sides. "That's good to know. But how is that possible? Mending a dragon doesn't make complete sense to me, but to create a new one from thin air?"

That was a good question and one that had a simple but complicated answer.

"When a dragon shifter dies, their magic is released and stays around us." Thorn narrowed his eyes as if he could see the magic hovering. "Healing and creating a dragon are pretty much the same. To heal a dragon's magic, I must remove the magic from its body and infuse it with our ancestors' magic to mend it. When I turned Everly, I filled her body with the magic of our ancestors, and it created her own unique dragon."

Edna tilted her head. "That's actually beautiful and makes sense."

I yawned. I couldn't help it. I'd been struggling to stay awake, and now the adrenaline from potentially being in danger had vanished, along with every last bit of energy I'd had.

Elliott snorted. "I've been up just as long as you, and I'm not falling over."

"That's because you're used to playing video games all night long." Eva placed a hand on her hip and shot him a glare. "And Everly fought the warriors."

Edna walked past our group and up the stairs to the front porch. She removed a key from her pants pocket and unlocked the front door. "I need to get back before the thunder wakes, and you all should get some rest." She opened the door wide. It almost hit the back of a heather-gray cloth couch in the living room.

"There are six bedrooms," she informed us as she handed the key to Thorn. "A master and another downstairs across the house from each other, three upstairs, and one in the attic. The attic bedroom actually has three full-size beds and a queen, so there should be plenty of room."

I waited for her to go inside, but she remained at the door and continued, "You all go in and get some rest. I'll bring Mindy by later today after lunch. If you need anything, feel free to call me. Just don't come to the thunder." She paused, glancing at all of us.

I forced a smile and murmured, "Thank you."

Wincing, she sighed. "I wish I could say I was doing this for you, but honestly, this is for Mindy. If Thorn can heal her, it'll be worth it."

Our bond pulsed with Thorn's trepidation. Each time he needed to use his magic, he grew uneasy. But his nervousness didn't seem as bad as before. I hoped he was beginning to realize that his abilities might not be a curse.

"It will be." Sol beamed as his arm brushed Eva's. "He made a difference for me."

"Good." Edna strolled past us, heading back toward the woods where she'd shifted.

She must have had clothes stowed away for when they came here, especially since she'd flown all this way, and it was at least a forty-five-minute drive back to the thunder.

Let's go inside, Thorn connected. His large hand pressed against the small of my back, buzzing against my skin and urging me in. A combination of grief and needing peace simmered in our bond.

I walked around the huge couch, which looked like two L-shaped pieces pushed together to form a U shape. There was a matching footstool in the center and a fireplace in front. A TV was perched over the mantel.

"We need to assign everyone a room," Vlad said as he entered the house after Thorn.

After a few seconds, we'd all crammed inside. Elliott flopped on the couch. If I sat down, I'd be asleep in seconds.

Saphira pointed at the couch. "I'll sleep here in front of the door.

I'm tired of bunking with people." With a lifted brow, she glared at Elliott.

He rolled his eyes but moved down the couch, clearing a spot for Saphira. "Just wait until I'm a dragon."

"Everly and Thorn should have some privacy for at least a night, so Vlad and I can room with Peter." Cassidy walked over to the doorframe on the right. A hallway left of the stairs led to a bedroom. The stairs were directly in front of us, with some sort of table to the right, but the wall cut off most of my view.

"I guess that means Eva, Dad, and I are rooming with Cassidy and Vlad in the attic." Elliott pouted.

Sol bounced on his feet. "If you don't want to stay in a room with them, I can."

Cheeks flaming, Eva stared at the wooden floor but smiled shyly.

"What?" Theron shook his head. "No. They're family. They should stick together."

"Yeah, man." Elliott scowled and crossed his arms. "You sleeping in the same room as my sister? Not happening."

"We'll take a room down here," Thorn said and guided me to the hallway. "You all can figure out the rest. I need sleep." The pressing heat swirled harder between us, a desperate emotion taking hold.

The rest of the group continued to talk, but I couldn't focus on them. Thorn was struggling.

We headed down the hallway to the first door and stepped into the master bedroom. The wooden floor and beige color scheme matched the rest of the house, and a king-size bed sat against the far wall. Thorn locked the door and placed his head against the wood as those emotions he'd been holding back burst through him.

I stepped toward him and wrapped my arms around his waist. It was my turn to take care of him in whatever way he needed. *Just know I'm here.*

He spun around in my arms, his eyes darkening. *I know.* His lips touched mine as his tongue begged for entrance.

And just like that...all my exhaustion was gone.

CHAPTER SIX

AS HIS TONGUE stroked into my mouth, my body warmed. It had been over twenty-four hours since we'd had sex, which felt like forever. My stomach clenched with need, but I pushed it aside...for now.

My dragon roared in protest as I pulled back, breathless. Thorn countered my move to eliminate the distance I'd put between us.

Hands on his chest, I pushed him back hard enough for his eyes to open, allowing me to see his gorgeous sky blue irises. I'd already memorized every diamond fleck in them. They were one of my favorite parts of him and the first thing I'd noticed, even at night in a car.

His brow furrowed. *What's wrong?*

You're upset, and I want to make sure you're all right before we go further. I cupped his cheek, noticing his long lashes framing those eyes. *Don't get me wrong. I'm all for sex, but I don't want you to use that as a remedy to ignore what's going on inside you.*

Blowing out a breath, he frowned and clenched his jaw. *That's the last thing I'd ever want you to think I was doing.* He lowered his forehead to mine and wrapped an arm around my waist, pulling me close.

In fairness, I didn't think it was intentional. I smiled sadly. *But you did just lose your biological father, and you've been a mess of emotions since we left the barn.* I kissed his cheek. *I don't want to push, but I also don't want to taint our bond, even accidentally.*

He nodded and took my hand, leading me to the bed. We sat on the mattress, my hand running along the gray paisley comforter as we scooted up to lie back on the two oversized pillows.

Lifting our joined hands, Thorn stared at the wood-paneled ceiling. "You're right. I've been struggling. I hated him for *so long*, and then for him to denounce Drake and apologize to me, only to die right after..." His pain and guilt flared through our bond. "I...I don't know how to feel. On the one hand, I'm still angry. It took all of *this* for him to finally see the truth? But then I feel guilty for being mad." His voice cracked, and I turned to him as his eyes glistened.

"You have *every* right to be hurt, angry, and confused. The king screwed you over, and even after he realized what he'd done was wrong, he wasn't willing to stand up to Drake...until it was too late. He doesn't get a pass just because he's dead."

The thing was, I understood how Thorn felt...somewhat. My heart clenched over the loss we shared. "Mom was an amazing mother to me, but when she died, not only did I lose her, but I got left with Peter. I was so angry about it, but I didn't have anywhere else to go or anyone else to help me. Though I wasn't mad *at her*, I felt guilty about being angry at all because she was gone. It took me a while to realize it's okay to be upset and that sometimes, life hands us crap, and we have to figure out a way to move on."

"I'm so damn sorry you had to go through that." Thorn's face twisted in agony. "I wish I could've been there to help you. That you could've leaned on me."

"I've come to believe that everything happens for a reason." A tear trickled down my cheek, my vision clouding. "But the point is, I felt guilty for being mad. If she hadn't married Peter, Elliott and Eva wouldn't be here, and though we weren't close then, I still loved them and couldn't imagine a world without them."

A smile tugged at the corners of his mouth. "I could've gone without smelling your brother's fart tonight. It was pretty rank."

I giggled, my chest expanding. I'd never told anyone how I'd felt when Mom died, and I was glad I'd told Thorn. He knew exactly what to say. "True, but—" I placed a hand over his heart. "I want you to know that I believe your biological parents loved you, and at least King Arman realized his mistake and was able to apologize. If he hadn't, you'd have gone on thinking he never loved you. And Thorn, I think that could've hurt the man I know you're going to become. So grieve, scream, and flip off the world all you need, but know that through it all, I will be standing right beside you."

Warmth soared through me, and Thorn purred, the sound enthralling.

"With you by my side, I know we'll conquer the world." He scanned my face and whispered, "You own me."

My breath caught, and desire pooled inside me, causing a deep ache in my core. I needed him so desperately, but I had to make sure he was okay.

When his lips landed on mine, I had to say something else before I lost myself in him. Unable to speak, I connected, *Maybe we should sleep.*

In a little while. His hand slipped under my shirt, and he unbuttoned my jeans. *I promise, I just want to make love to you, my mate. There is nothing else on my mind other than wanting to merge with you and show you exactly how I feel.*

As his hand slid under my panties, all I could focus on was his touch, his scent, and my longing to taste him again.

His fingers circled between my lips, and he lowered his head, kissing me again. This time, I had no thoughts of stopping. His emotions were searing hot from his love for me, confirming I was the *only* thing on his mind.

Our tongues collided, and his faint minty taste turned me on even more.

Desperate, I clutched his shirt, pulling him on top of me. His hands didn't miss a beat, shifting the pressure that had my head arching back. His lips moved down my face to my neck, and when his teeth grazed my skin, ecstasy exploded within me as he took me over the edge.

He raised his head, watching me melt into him. *So damn beautiful*, he connected as his irises darkened to cobalt.

Crazed, I yanked at his shirt, and he chuckled. The dark, throaty sound had need soaring through me again. His fingers weren't enough. I needed him inside me.

Removing his hands, he rolled to the side and tossed his shirt to the floor as I lifted, stripping my shirt and bra off. Within seconds, we were naked and ogling each other.

I took in every curve of his muscles. My favorite part was the V that pointed down the one part of him that could satisfy me. Though I hadn't touched him, he was ready.

When I reached for him, he caught my wrist and held it by my head as he settled between my legs. He whispered, "If you touch me, we might not get to do this. I'm already close. You're so damn sexy."

"Well, that would be a shame," I breathed, loving how he'd restrained me. A shiver of anticipation ran through me.

He entered me slowly, our gazes locked. His pupils slitted, fueling me further. I bucked my hips underneath him, and with his free hand, he grabbed my waist.

Sex with him before had always been mind-blowing. In fact, each time we came together, it was better than the time before. But this time was completely different.

Lips on mine, he moved at a slow pace, slipping deeper inside me than ever. The emotions between us were intense, the build of sensation slow and powerful. My body arched against his, and he groaned.

Nipping my ear, he connected, *You're driving me crazy.*

The words made me feel loved and sexy. Our connection opened wider, each of us feeling the other's emotions. I treasured the moment as we pleasured each other, and our souls merged like they'd been meant to do.

Sweat slicked our bodies, and the friction increased until I couldn't contain myself. I pushed on his shoulder and moved on top of him. I was tired of him having all the control, and he didn't resist.

I grabbed the headboard as his hands cupped my breasts, fingers gently rolling my nipples. Somehow, I kept the pace slow, and then I glanced down at his body. His muscles flexed as he thrust into me in sync with my movements, his eyes dark and heavy with desire.

His beauty and the love he had for me made my chest ache painfully. He was perfect for me. *You own me, too,* I connected, because sometimes, *I love you* just didn't cut it.

His dragon roared, and an orgasm ripped between us. His pleasure merged with mine, and his hands continued to do delicious things to my body. Our bodies convulsed, and I grew dizzy.

I wasn't sure how long the ecstasy lasted, but when I crumpled onto him, fatigue hit me hard. He turned, curling his body around me, and within seconds, I fell asleep, content and happy in the best place in the world—his arms.

AN ALARM BEEPED, and my eyes fluttered open. Sun shone through the closed blinds of the window next to my bed, the light hitting Thorn's arm, which was threaded underneath my head. His other heavy, warm arm was slung over me, and my body buzzed intensely. It took me a second to realize that we'd fallen asleep naked after having mind-blowing scx. My dragon purred at the memory, and heat flared between my legs again.

The only thing dampening my desire was the buzzing of the damn alarm.

I groaned. "When did you set that?"

He grumbled. "I didn't. It's coming from down the hall."

Footsteps approached from down the hallway.

Where we were and why flooded back into me. "What time is it?"

"Time for you assholes to get up," Saphira said from the other side of the door. "Edna will be here within the hour, and we need to be ready."

I exhaled and snuggled deeper into Thorn's chest. I called out, "Just a little more sleep." Though I had no intention of sleeping. My body was ready for round two.

"Uh, no. Get out here." Saphira gagged. "I can smell your intent, and hearing the two of you last night was more than enough. You kept my ass up for an hour while you *violated* each other."

Thorn chuckled and propped himself up on his elbow. He nuzzled my neck, a hand brushing down my body. "We did not violate each other. However, if that's what you want to hear, we can do that—" His hand slipped between my legs, and I gasped as that familiar clench of desire slammed into me.

"Ew. No." Saphira banged on the door. "If you start, I'll make sure to get Cassidy and Vlad down here immediately. I know Everly would *really* appreciate that."

That was the equivalent of a cold shower, and I scooted away from Thorn, already missing the touch of his hands.

"That was low," Thorn hissed, but he smirked. "But don't worry. I can make her forget that she cares."

"Oh, really?" Saphira bit out. "We'll see about that. The *brothel* smell is already cut in half. I'm assuming what's left is from Thorn."

I snarled. The idea of her purposely smelling him almost made my dragon come unglued.

"Girl, I was teasing," Saphira said warily. "For all I know, it's you. Believe me, I don't want to sniff your man. I have someone else I'd much rather be sniffing."

Wyvern.

Something had jolted between them when they'd seen each other while confronting the warriors. I hadn't had the opportunity to ask her about it. Some of my anger ebbed, allowing me to think rationally again.

"Don't listen to her." A wicked glint sparkled in Thorn's eye. "You should ravish me to make sure Saphira knows I'm yours. Maybe even stake your claim against my neck again."

My dragon roared, urging me to do just that. Damn the consequences.

"That's it. I'm going. Just remember, someone's coming who could rat us out or kick us out on our asses." Saphira stomped away, and as promised, she clomped up the stairs.

Inching closer to him again, I kissed him, lingering on his lips. I connected, *Though I love seeing you smile, we do have to get ready. We need to grab something to eat so you can focus on healing Mindy.*

His smile fell, and I hated that I was the reason for it. He nodded. *You're right in every way. If we want to be able to be like this always*—he gestured to the room and how we were lying naked together—*we have to eliminate the threat. I'm just not sure how we do that.*

My body sagged against his. I'd been pushing him to do the right thing. I knew his reluctance wasn't because he didn't want to but because he'd been through so much trauma. Though I wished the king hadn't died, maybe his death wouldn't be in vain if Thorn finally saw the light. I just wished it hadn't taken losing his biological father to accept himself. But I couldn't deny that being on the same page as my mate was nice. *We start out by helping whoever we can, finding allies, and training them. With everyone's help, we'll figure out the rest from there.*

He pecked my lips and climbed out of bed.

I scanned his naked body. Every inch of him was hard and solid... every single one. My body flared back to life.

Grinning, he grabbed his jeans. *Too bad you turned me down.*

Damn shame. I licked my lips and forced myself to get up. My dragon spurred me on, knowing he'd let me devour him if I insisted, but my logical side screamed at me to stay the course. If we wanted a life where we didn't have to worry and could just be together, we had to stay focused...at least during the day, when we had things to accomplish.

With every ounce of willpower I had, I strutted past him, copping a feel along the way. His sensual groan turned into one of frustration when I moved my hand away. I scooped up my clothes and dressed quickly while he watched.

He shook his head and laughed. "That was just dirty. You'll pay for that tonight."

Just like that, he had a knot forming in my stomach all over again.

EDNA AND MINDY would be here any minute. Elliott, Peter, Tyson, and Brenton stayed in the house, while the rest of our group stood in the front yard, waiting for their arrival.

Sol and Eva sat on the red bench swing, talking about some game that Eva liked. They leaned in closely to each other as if the world around them had ceased to exist.

The rest of us stood in a semicircle. I looped my arm through Thorn's and laid my head on his shoulder as Saphira stepped forward beside me to look at Theron on Thorn's other side. She asked, "Have you heard anything from Wyvern? Is he—er—the thunder doing okay?"

My eyebrows quirked. That was more than normal interest. I had to talk to her sooner rather than later about what was going on between them.

Nodding, Theron pressed his lips into a line. "I talked to him a little while ago. The thunder is fine. Drake threatened them, but as Wyvern suspected, the thunder was left to him to rule since he showed loyalty by alerting Drake to us. He's supposed to notify Drake if he hears or sees us again."

At least that hadn't blown up in our faces.

"Wyvern asked about you," Hydra said, placing a hand on her mate's arm. "He wanted to make sure you, specifically, were okay."

Saphira's face reddened, and she beamed.

"Why would he..." Errol's words died as he studied his daughter. His forehead lined, and his mouth gaped.

An engine that had been rumbling faintly in the background grew louder.

"Are they coming by vehicle?" Vlad moved further into the yard and near the dirt driveway.

Staying close to her mate, Cassidy followed. "It would make sense if they did, in case warriors are searching the area."

"She didn't say either way." Theron crossed his arms. "But we're about to find out."

Our group fell silent as a burnt orange Mazda CX-5 pulled up. In the driver's seat was none other than Edna.

The woman in the passenger seat was a few years younger than me, close to Eva and Elliott's age. Her hair was a little shorter than her mother's and dyed a vibrant burgundy that made her chardonnay-gold eyes glow. As soon as the car was parked, Mindy opened her door and got out. Her eyes immediately focused on Thorn.

They hurried toward us, Edna rubbing her hands together.

Mindy just smiled at Thorn like he held all the answers. "I hear you're going to heal me."

Our fated-mate bond constricted from the pressure she'd put on him.

Thorn rolled his shoulders, and his body tensed. "I'll try."

Her expression faltered, but Theron stepped in and introduced everyone to Mindy.

"We don't have long." Edna glanced at her car. "The news of the king's death hit the Dragonnet, as did the warriors' preparations to search for your group. Our thunder is concerned. Mindy isn't the only one at risk, so we'd like to bring some of the older members here for safety. I need to tell them about you before that can happen. Fear has a way of causing chaos, and I need to head back and get things moving...if only for their peace of mind."

The anxiety rolling off Thorn amped up even higher.

You've done this twice, now. You've got this. I squeezed his arm comfortingly.

Thorn nodded. "Okay. Where is your injury located?"

I remembered she'd been injured while in human form.

"My back," she whispered.

He turned to me, kissed my cheek, and connected, *I can't risk you touching me.*

Let me know if you need me. I stepped far enough away to give him the space to not feel like he'd impact me accidentally.

Theron and the others followed suit.

Now I have an audience, Thorn connected as he placed his hands on Mindy's shoulders. "I'm going to channel magic inside you. If I can fill in the missing magic, your dragon will feel a little different until you shift and fly."

Mindy bit her bottom lip as Sol stood on the porch and called out, "He's right. After flying, you'll reconnect with your slightly different dragon. It'll be okay."

I asked, *Do you want me to ask them to go inside?*

No, it'll make everyone uncomfortable. He closed his eyes. *I'll be okay.*

"I'm going to remove your dragon for a moment and give it back," he informed her as his hands glowed. "Don't be afraid."

The magic churned through him, and I watched as everyone's mouths dropped open. Only Theron, Hydra, and I had seen him use the magic before, and it was amazing.

His hands lit up the area around him despite the sun shining high in the sky.

I smiled as my chest swelled. He hadn't even hesitated or needed my help. He was getting control of his magic and not struggling to connect with it anymore.

As the friction vibrated through our bond, I knew he was already working. The moment he took her dragon, Mindy whimpered, "It's gone."

Then a different tension filled our bond...an emotion I'd felt from him only one another time—when he'd realized Drake had captured me.

Terror.

I can't heal her, he connected. *Her dragon isn't injured.*

Fear strangled me. If he couldn't heal Mindy, we weren't safe anymore.

CHAPTER SEVEN

MY MOUTH SOURED as his words replayed in my mind. Our group was in horrible trouble. The deal had been clear: Edna would help hide us if we healed her daughter. If Thorn couldn't heal Mindy, she might inform Drake that we were here.

Mindy whimpered, I assumed due to her missing dragon. From the friction swirling through our bond, I knew Thorn was holding on to it.

His fear strangled our bond, making it seem half its normal size. The warmth of our usual connection cooled in my chest.

I'm going to give it back to her, he connected. *Her dragon is about to dissipate. I can feel it.*

Do it. He needed to hear me say it. *The only thing worse than not healing her would be taking her dragon away.*

Tension roiled from his body. I didn't have to be connected to him to sense it. Out of the corner of my eye, I saw Vlad inch toward Cassidy. His jaw clenched. He sensed something was amiss. Of course they could read Thorn. He was their son, after all.

The friction in our connection intensified as Thorn gave Mindy her dragon back. The moment the transfer was complete, our bond returned to normal. His hands stopped glowing, and he removed them from her shoulders.

Mindy gasped and opened her eyes.

"Well?" Edna asked as she scurried over to her daughter. "How do you feel?"

She bent down toward her toes...and groaned. "My back still hurts. It doesn't feel any different."

"What?" Theron shook his head. "That's impossible. He healed Sol and Tyson."

"The agreement was that he heal her." Edna's eyes hardened. "And he didn't." She turned to my mate and scowled. "Why? Is it because she's a female?"

My mate's jaw slackened. "What? Gods, no. That has nothing to do with it."

Anger sparked through me, and my hands fisted. I didn't like her insinuation. He'd risked his life for my sister and me.

My breath caught, and my attention settled back on Mindy. "Wait. You were hurt in human form, right?"

She arched a brow but nodded.

"Sol and Tyson *weren't*. They were injured in *dragon* form." I bit the inside of my cheek, letting my hypothesis settle over me. I was premed, so though I didn't understand magic, I understood the human body. "When you were injured, did you go to the hospital for care?"

Edna scoffed. "Of course not. It's forbidden. Her dragon healing kicked in within a day, and we were focused on burying my mate— her father."

That was the answer. "She might have healed, but her back wasn't in proper alignment. Just like a broken bone, it has to be set in a brace so the bones can heal *properly*. It's not an issue with her dragon."

"She's right." Errol stepped forward. "Thorn's power is to create or take a dragon. He can fill in gaps in their magic, which is how he healed Tyson and Sol. Mindy's magic isn't missing anything, so he can't heal her. It's impossible."

Mindy hung her head, a tear trailing down her face. "So...I'll always be broken."

My heart ached. Drake had made these people feel as if there was something wrong with them, as if they weren't whole, just because they were different. The same thing had happened to Mom when the disease had been killing her.

What they didn't see was that they were stronger than the rest of us. They kept moving forward when others might have given up. "You are not *broken*," I insisted. "You are strong. Stronger than Drake and his idiotic notions. Do not let someone like *him* define how you see yourself."

Flicking her gaze to me, Mindy sniffed. "You don't know anything about me. You don't know if I'm strong or not."

"I don't have to know you to see your strength." That was the thing about being broken the way I had been for so long. There was something in a person's gaze...a lifelessness that she, Sol, and Tyson hadn't shown. I gestured to Edna. "And there's no way her daughter wouldn't be as strong as she is. She wouldn't allow it."

Mindy snorted and wiped away a tear. "Okay. You've got me there." She blew out a breath and placed a hand on her stomach. Her gaze went over my shoulder to my mate. "Thank you for trying."

Some of the tension in our connection eased as Thorn came to me and placed an arm around my waist. He murmured, "I'm sorry I couldn't heal you, but my mate is right—don't let a douchebag like Drake define you. If I'd done that, I'd have handed myself over to him for execution, believing I didn't deserve to live because of my powers."

Pride swelled in my chest. That was exactly what Mindy needed to hear. "And I would've been mar—"

Fingers digging into my side, Thorn snarled. The white-hot anger seared through our bond, eliminating the fear from moments ago. "Do *not* finish that sentence, *please*."

I shut my mouth. *Sorry. I was trying to help.*

Remorse floated through as he connected, *I know. You have nothing to be sorry for, but remembering that and knowing he's hunting you...I just want to rip his throat out. The only reason I haven't rushed off to do it is because you're here beside me, keeping me grounded.*

My heart ached from how much I loved him.

Cassidy cleared her throat. "We'll pack up and leave. Please at least let us get out of here before you notify Drake."

"I'll pack our things," Hydra said and turned toward the house.

The swing squeaked as Eva's feet hit the wooden porch. She'd been listening in the whole time. I glanced over my shoulder to see Sol easing in front of her, blocking her from Mindy's and Edna's view.

"Will you hold off until we leave?" Vlad asked as Cassidy and Hydra rushed through the front door.

"Yes, of course." Edna's face crumpled. "I don't want harm to come to any of you. I just need to protect my daughter and thunder the best way I can."

"That's bullshit," Saphira snapped and marched over to stand beside me. She placed her hands on her hips.

"Honey..." Errol warned. I didn't have to turn around to know he was trying to rein Saphira in.

"This isn't fair. Thorn tried." Saphira waved a hand at my mate.

"Saphy," Brenton hissed.

Saphira didn't flinch, her attention on Edna and Mindy. "We held up our end of the bargain. It's not Thorn's fault that she can't be healed. He *tried*."

But that wasn't how it worked. Life wasn't fair. I'd learned that six years ago when Mom died, and Thorn had learned that at the tender age of six. Shit happened, and we had to deal with it. Having a meltdown would accomplish nothing...other than, perhaps, Edna not waiting until we were gone to contact Drake.

I placed a hand on Saphira's arm, and her breathing calmed. "We need to get ready and leave. This is their decision, and it's final."

She huffed, some smoke trickling from her nose. I tugged on her arm and almost cried when she relented. I'd expected her to fight more.

Thorn's hand fell from my waist, and I was surprised that he didn't follow us—until he said softly and full of regret, "I'm sorry I couldn't help. I wish there was something I could do to keep you off Drake's radar, but my mate's right. Do not let one person define you when everyone else sees who you really are."

"Mom, maybe—" Mindy started.

"They have to go," Edna said firmly. "They *have* to. If Drake and his warriors come here and learn about your back issues, that will be bad enough, but if they find *them* here as well, he'll kill us. We can't risk it."

Saphira spun around, lurching toward the two women, but I held tightly to her arm and dragged her up the stairs.

I got that leaving wasn't ideal, but we had no other choice. "If we force them to allow us to stay, we'll be no better than *him*."

That knocked the wind out of Saphira and gave Errol and Brenton a chance to reach us and take her from me.

A moment of silence descended before Theron rubbed his hands together. "How long do we have until you warn Drake and the warriors?"

"I'll give you one more night." Edna sighed. "Like Saphira said, Thorn tried, and the reason he couldn't heal her makes sense. I don't think you guys are lying, but our people have to come here and hide, and I don't have a good enough reason for you all to be here, putting them more in danger. I wish things were different, but that's not our world. Not anymore. I need you out by dawn."

Dawn.

That was more time than I'd expected. That would give us a night to figure out where to go.

"Thank you." I held each woman's gaze. "For giving us shelter, even for two nights."

Frowning, Edna nodded. "I truly wish I could do more. If the warriors come through and we're certain they won't come back, I'll message Theron."

As the two of them headed back to their car, Thorn marched toward me, a scowl on his face and his shoulders hunched. Vlad and Theron stayed put, watching the two women pull away.

You did the right thing, I connected. I needed him to know how much he meant to me. When he reached me, I cupped his cheeks with both hands. *You own me.*

He smiled sadly. *You make me into the sort of man I never expected to become,* he replied, the warmth of his love spreading through the bond. *I wish I could save you from all of this, because you know you own me, too.*

I pressed a soft kiss against his lips. *As long as you and I are together, that's all I need.*

Intertwining our fingers, Thorn tugged me to the porch just as Saphira, Errol, Brenton, and Sol went inside. We would figure out our next steps and survive. We had to.

There was no other option.

That night, we all hung out in the living room in silence. Elliott and Tyson didn't even play video games.

No one had volunteered to let us into the injured dragon network, as I was calling it. After learning that Thorn couldn't help Mindy, everyone feared allowing us near.

That wasn't the main problem. Even though Cassidy, Vlad, and Thorn had saved money in case of an emergency, it wasn't that much. We could find a place to rent somewhere, but we'd have to find a source of income, which was a huge problem since a dragon shifter could pass by at any second and give away our location to Drake. We also couldn't go too far—not if we wanted to stop Drake from hurting more people.

One thing at a time. I thought about painting for money, but I couldn't risk going back into Asheville to sell my work through the gallery, and I didn't have a client list of my own to contact.

"The safest bet would be allowing me to get back to my *job*," Peter grumbled from where he stood in the corner of the room, a deep sneer on his face.

No one responded. Vlad sat on the far end of the couch, searching on his phone for a house to rent, and Theron swiped his phone every few seconds from where he sat between his mate and son. Of course, Eva was crammed in beside Sol, next to Cassidy. Saphira sat on the other end of the couch, with Errol between her and Brenton. Elliott and Tyson sat on the footstool in the center.

Thorn and I leaned against the wall perpendicular to Peter, too restless to sit down. He didn't want to wait until the morning to leave in case Edna decided to call Drake early.

When Theron glanced at his phone, he blanched.

I wasn't the only one who'd noticed, because Sol asked, "Dad, what's wrong?"

"Just got a text from Wyvern." Theron closed his eyes and lowered his head. "There's a huge problem."

Saphira's head jerked toward him so quickly I feared it might fall off. She rasped, "Is he okay?" Her mocha eyes darkened as she jumped to her feet like she was prepared to leave.

"Yes, he's fine." Theron looked at Peter, Eva, Elliott, then me as he said, "We've got another issue."

Stomach souring, I asked, "What now?"

"You four have been reported missing." Theron dropped his phone into his lap. "Every dragon shifter will now link Everly's family to us. We aren't just hiding from dragon shifters anymore—humans will be able to recognize us as well."

My breathing seized. This had Drake's name all over it.

Peter snickered. "I told you that you should've left Elliott and me out of this. I figured this would happen."

"Yes, because if we had, you'd have been far better off in Drake's *prison*." In a way, I wished we had left Peter there, but we'd be in a worse situation if we had. Eva and Elliott would have been beside themselves, and Drake would have made sure to hurt him to get the reaction he wanted from them. This way, the four of us were safe.

Thorn wrapped an arm around my waist and glowered at Peter. "You should be thankful you're here with us, especially since Drake already hates you."

A phone rang, and Theron cursed. "It's Edna."

Something heavy weighed my limbs. If the news was out nationwide, that had to be the reason she was calling.

"Answer it." Hydra pressed her lips into a line. "There's no point in holding off. She might tell you that the warriors are on their way."

"Tell her I found a place and I'm about to book it." Vlad removed his wallet from his back pocket and pulled out a credit card.

Theron answered the phone. "I know why you're calling. Vlad's booking—"

"We need Thorn." Edna sounded desperate.

I leaned into Thorn's side as my heart hammered. Something was wrong.

No one responded. I looked up at my mate.

"If he doesn't come here, someone will die." She sighed. "I'm not sure if he can save her, but he's here. I hope he's willing to try."

Everyone stared at Thorn, waiting for his answer.

This could be a trap, he connected, pivoting toward me.

It could. We couldn't be foolish. Edna might turn us over to the warriors to protect her daughter, especially since you couldn't tell Mindy was injured by glancing at her. But there was one issue. *What if it's not?* Could we let someone die because we let fear dictate our response?

"If this is a trick, I will take every one of your dragons," Thorn rasped, his pupils slanting.

"Understood," she replied. "Theron, I'll send you the address so you can come straight to the house. Please hurry." She hung up, and a second later, his phone dinged.

Vlad and Theron jumped to their feet as Thorn and I headed for the door. When I reached the edge of the couch, Thorn spun around to face me and said, "Stay here. This could be a trap. I can't risk you going."

I laughed. The idea of staying behind was absurd. I glared at him and prepared for war.

HURT SWIRLED THROUGH ME, stealing my breath. I knew he didn't want me to go out of fear and not because he thought I couldn't handle myself, but that didn't lessen the sting. "I'm going."

He huffed and touched my arms as he rasped, "Please. Stay. If something were to happen to you—"

"Oh, *hell*, no." I stabbed my finger into his chest, hitting rock-hard muscle. "If *I* were leaving, there would be no way you'd stay behind. That goes the same way for *both* of us."

"If it were the other way around, there's no way I'd allow you to leave." Thorn's jaw clenched.

Elliott snorted, and Saphira muttered, "And here I was beginning to believe he wasn't stupid."

"Stay out of it," Thorn barked as his nostrils flared, but his gaze didn't leave mine.

"Thorn..." Cassidy's voice held warning. "You're in the wrong, and we don't have time for this. Hydra and I are staying for our own reasons, but you're the true heir, and Everly is your mate."

"That's my point." Thorn lifted his chin, his irises darkening. "That's why Everly needs to stay here with you and Hydra."

He listed the two other mated women, making his point clear—they weren't demanding to go, so why was I?

I swallowed my anger. If I didn't calm down, we'd fight each other even longer. All my years of swallowing my anger around Peter were coming in handy. *I get that you want to protect me, but you didn't want to go in the first place. You're going because of me, and I need to be there. I trust Edna. They seem like good people. So if this is a trap, it's because they're in trouble, and I couldn't live with myself or you if something happened and you made me stay here alone. Remember how you felt when I left you to turn myself over to Drake?*

He lowered his head, touching his forehead to mine. I could feel the change in our connection. *Thinking something could happen to you makes me damn crazy.*

I feel the same about you, but other than my stupid moment when we first connected, I haven't asked something like that of you. I leaned back and softly kissed his lips. *Please don't keep doing the same to me.*

You fight dirty. He frowned, but defeat darkened his gorgeous sky blue eyes.

I chuckled and laid my palm against his chest. *I don't mean to, but it's only fair that we respect each other. I want us to be a team, and this is something we should do together.*

You're right. He huffed. *I'm sorry.* He took my hand and tugged me toward the door.

"It's a damn good thing he came to his senses, or I'd be helping Everly with the smackdown." Saphira stood and marched to the door. "I'm going with you four."

Errol's mouth opened, and he turned around in his seat. "Saphy, no."

"I have to. This is getting worse because people like me ignored Drake's horribleness and let it get out of control." Saphira crossed her arms. "You can stay here and plan our next steps while I go with my bestie."

I grinned. She'd called me her best friend. No one had called me that before, and I realized I felt the same way about her. Even when I'd met her when she'd come to take me to Drake, something about her had been comforting.

"We'll watch her." Vlad nodded. "But we've got to get going."

"Be safe." Errol frowned as he watched us walk out the door.

The five of us were in the yard. My dragon stirred inside, ready to fly. It hadn't been terribly long, but I'd learned that anytime I got anxious, she inched forward, wanting to help. "Saph, let me run in and get a duffel bag so we can carry our clothes there in dragon form."

"No." Theron removed the keys to his truck. "We can't risk it. If the warriors are on their way, they could be nearby. The last thing we need is our scents in the air."

Thorn stopped in his tracks, pulling me to stand beside him. Vlad and Saphira paused, following his lead. Thorn said, "You're right, but before we pull into their neighborhood, we need to get out of the vehicle and make sure we don't sense anything strange. Since we won't be in our dragon forms, it'll be harder to detect threats."

"That's fine." Theron didn't break stride to his vehicle.

The rest of us hurried toward the car again. Theron was already inside with the engine started when the four of us reached it. Vlad took the front passenger seat as Thorn climbed in behind Theron. Of course, I got stuck in the middle, with Saphira scooting in next to me a second after I was settled.

As soon as the last door closed, Theron reversed and quickly turned the car around, then barreled away from the safe house. He tossed his phone to Vlad. "Can you plug in the address? I think she put in the exact house. I have a general idea of how to get to where Edna cut us off."

"Yeah." Vlad swiped the phone and tapped.

Thorn's unease swirled between us, and I took his hand. I understood what was going on. He didn't want to do this, but for a different reason this time. It wasn't about wanting to run. Rather, he was petrified that this was a trap and Drake was taking advantage of our good nature. I couldn't blame him, but Edna didn't strike me as a dishonest person.

"I hate to agree with Thorn's attitude toward Everly, but he has a point." Saphira sighed. "Theron, are you sure she wouldn't lead us into a trap to save her daughter? Think about you and Sol. We need to be on the same page, and I feel like you're the one who's rushing in blindly...and you're driving the truck."

I loved how she'd put all that out there. She clearly had grown up watching her father, the advisor to the king.

"That's fair." Theron's hands tightened on the steering wheel. "But every parent on the injured network cares about the others. It's not just about saving their family members but everyone. If this were a trap, I firmly believe she would've warned me somehow. I get that you're all suspicious. I would be, too, if I hadn't been involved in this network for the past year. We take risks to get resources to other people's hiding spots and address needs such as financing and contacts. A few of us have shared our addresses with other families in the network when they were compromised and warriors were getting close to them. If one of us betrayed another, it would ruin everything our network stands for."

The tightening sensation lessened from Thorn, but his body was still tense, and he kept a death grip on my hand.

"I got the same read from her." Vlad turned toward us. "That's the only reason I didn't push not going. But that doesn't mean we just throw caution to the wind. Someone could be pressuring her and watching her so she can't warn us."

That was true. If warriors were there, they'd be watching her every move. But I still believed she would try to notify us somehow.

The GPS started talking in that horrible nasally voice, and the truck became silent. We drove over the red covered bridge again and past where Edna had stopped us. With each mile, my heart pounded harder as we kept watch, tapping into our dragons.

"Roll down the windows," Vlad said, lowering his.

All four windows went down, and the cool night wind of early June swirled around us. We could hear and smell everything this way.

I asked my dragon to amplify my hearing and vision, not enough to begin the shift but better than my normal human form. Though I couldn't sense the surroundings from miles away like I could as a complete dragon, I could sense things nearby, which wasn't much. Just a few foxes and some raccoons scurrying around in search of food. Between them being out and the lack of dragon scents, my lungs worked more easily.

A few minutes later, some houses peeked through the tree branches. The GPS began talking, guiding us toward the area. Several two-story buildings came into view, the bottoms in brick and the top halves sided in various colors. Each house sat on an acre of land that backed up to the woods. Of course, if an entire thunder lived here, they wouldn't need more room since they wouldn't have to constantly hide their existence from their neighbors.

Theron stopped on the right edge of the dirt road and turned off the vehicle. None of us climbed out, remaining quiet and listening.

A door opened, and a man ran out into the yard of the fifth house down on the left. "Mindy! Your mom said she needs you." His voice broke. "Emily needs CPR!" The guy dropped to his knees. "I can't...I just can't see her that way."

There was no way this was a setup.

"We need to go." Pain ripped through my chest as memories of Mom's death swirled around me. I touched my wrist but came up empty. The bracelet was still safely in our bag.

No one moved, and I gritted my teeth, ready to explode.

"You heard my mate. Now go." Thorn wrapped his arms around me, pulling me to his chest. *Baby, what's wrong?*

That heartbreak. A tear rolled down my cheek. *Someone he loves is dying.*

Theron punched the gas, and as we pulled up in front of the dark gray house with the man on the ground, Mindy rushed toward us from across the street.

My medical training surged through my mind, and I reached past Thorn and shoved the door open, then rolled over him and onto my feet. I knew CPR, and I had to get in there to help.

"Thank gods you're here." Mindy ran toward us. "We need you to come inside."

"I heard CPR is needed." I rushed to the door. "I can help with that."

Mindy's eyes bulged, and her shoulders sagged. "Good, because I have no clue what to do, and she's gotten worse."

The man straightened when he saw Thorn and me. He appeared to be in his thirties, with short dark blond hair and olive skin. His slate gray eyes narrowed. "What are *they* doing here? Will he take the baby's dragon? Will that even save her?"

I flinched, but I was pretty sure I was caught up. "Someone is having complications from having a baby?" There were so many scenarios running through my brain. She could be having a heart attack, which Thorn couldn't fix.

"She's human." Mindy wrung her hands and glanced at Thorn. "We were hoping he could change her."

"Mindy!" Edna screamed from inside.

We were running out of time.

Mindy raced to the door and waved us in.

"Wait." The man pointed at Thorn. "He can make someone into a dragon shifter? All I saw on the wedding footage was him taking dragons."

Thorn growled. The man wasn't helping his wife, friend, or lover by delaying Thorn.

"Yes! He changed me," I answered and took Thorn's arm. "Let's go. If her heart stops, we won't have much chance of keeping her alive."

The man paled. "Then go! Help her. *Please.* Save my wife and our baby."

"Theron and I will stay out here and keep watch," Vlad said and pointed at Saphira. "Go inside and help. I'm thinking your style of help will be better than ours."

"That's for sure." Saphira didn't hesitate, rushing after us.

The stairwell split the foyer. Mindy ran up the dark beige carpeted stairs to the top level. A flimsy plastic gate sat to the right of the top floor, blocking the opening to the stairway. A navy cloth couch butted up against it, with a flatscreen TV on a stand across from it, but when someone screamed in pure agony, the surroundings blurred, and that became the only thing I could focus on. We turned left, rushing down a hallway into the first bedroom.

Then the nightmare truly began. A woman I assumed was Emily lay in a king bed on what had once been white sheets. Half of the fitted sheet was now stained crimson. Her heart was barely a flutter, telling more of the story. Her body was wearing out.

The little bit of training I had kicked into gear as soon as I saw Edna standing helplessly between Emily's legs. The baby's head wasn't showing, and Emily's legs hung lifelessly. The baby couldn't get out that way.

This was bad. *Really* bad.

I jumped into action.

"Oh, my gods," Mindy squeaked. "She's far worse than when I left."

That didn't help matters. "Saphira and Mindy, lift her legs the way you have to when you go to a gynecologist appointment." I examined Emily. "Thorn, if you can, change her. We need shifter healing to kick in. Her body is overstressed."

Mindy and Saphira ran to the woman's legs on either side of Edna, but they just stood there, staring at each other. Mindy murmured, "Do you have any idea what she's talking about?"

"No dragon shifter I know goes to a gynecologist."

Ugh. Of course they didn't. They wouldn't want a human doctor working on them.

Thorn went to Emily's shoulders and placed his hands on her. I felt the moment he tapped into his magic. The thrumming started in our connection, and his hands glowed.

I was again in awe of his growing confidence in his magic, and I was certain he hadn't noticed that he was getting attuned to it.

Emily's heart sputtered, and I moved from between her legs and rushed around Mindy to her other side, across from Thorn. His magic pulsed into her, and as I watched, her pale, blotchy skin smoothed into a beautiful complexion, but the color didn't darken. The thrumming stopped, and he removed his hands. Her heart still fluttered, and she was gasping for air.

Next came the hard part. I'd have to monitor her and be ready to administer CPR since the baby was still coming and her new magic couldn't focus only on healing. I pivoted and snatched one of Emily's legs, bending it up toward her chest. "This is what you need to do." I nodded to the leg by Saphira.

To her credit, she didn't hesitate and followed my example.

"Mindy, take my spot."

The young shifter listened, but when she took the leg, her face twisted in agony.

Shit. Her back.

"Here, I'll do it." I took the leg.

She hung her head.

I didn't need to be able to mind speak to know what she was thinking. I hadn't meant to make her feel inadequate, but I didn't want her in pain. However, this was probably for the best. "She knows you, so she'll be more comfortable if you're next to her head, talking and guiding her through the process."

Mindy's face lifted, some of the pain easing from her eyes. "Oh, yeah. That makes sense."

"See if you can wake her up," I suggested, pulling the leg back.

"I see the head," Edna said with relief. "Finally. I was worried."

That had to be partly due to Emily's new dragon growing stronger.

"Uh..." Thorn cleared his throat and stared across the room at the window, making sure to keep his head north of her stomach. "What do you need me to do?"

If Emily hadn't been so close to death, I would've laughed at him. Such a typical male. "Go keep an eye out with Vlad and Theron."

"And leave you?" His brows pulled together, and he flinched.

"You'll be on the other side of this wall." I smiled reassuringly. "I'll let you know if I need you. Ask her husband to come back in."

"Okay," he said and eagerly left the room.

Saphira laughed. "He couldn't get out of here fast enough."

"Can you blame him?" Mindy quipped and placed a hand against the woman's face. "Emily. Can you hear me?"

She moaned quietly in response, and that was enough to make me feel better. Emily was coming around. Now we had to focus on the task at hand.

I wasn't sure how long we were in the bedroom, but eventually, the guys came inside the house and waited in the living room. About thirty minutes ago, Emily had given birth to a boy, and I'd stayed with her longer to make sure she didn't go into cardiac arrest. During that time, her heartbeat had grown stronger, her dragon magic swirling inside and healing her. Even though she was healing, her husband had scooted a chair next to the bed, where Emily could see the baby while he held him.

That had been one hard labor.

The front door opened and shut, and Thorn's discomfort flowed into our bond. Someone must have come in.

Glancing at Emily and her mate, whose name I'd learned was Mikah, I said, "I'm going to check on things out there."

Before they could respond, a woman shouted, "What in the *hell* are they doing here, Edna?"

Thorn connected, *We've got to go. Now.*

Dazed, I hurried out the bedroom door, the irony not lost on me.

Even when you did something nice, sometimes...it didn't matter.

CHAPTER NINE

AS I STEPPED into the hallway, I found a middle-aged man and woman standing at the top of the stairs, their attention on the living room. The woman's indigo eyes were locked on my mate, who was standing in front of the television, with Vlad and Theron flanking him and Saphira moving to stand in front of him.

The woman's reddish-brown hair was pulled into a haphazard bun with several tendrils curling around her face. Her white shirt was wrinkled, and her jeans had a coffee stain on them despite the early hour.

The man beside her was similarly disheveled. His ice-blue eyes had dark circles under them, and his dark blond hair was unkempt. Though the woman was the one who'd asked the question, the man seemed even unhappier.

Edna strolled out of the kitchen and squeezed past the couple into the living room. She lifted her hands. "Katla, I need you and Volos to calm down. If it weren't—"

"Calm *down*?" Katla scoffed, a vein bulging in her neck. "You have the very man who steals dragons in this house with my son and his wife! How the hell am I not supposed to be frightened? My sweet daughter-in-law is in there, near death after giving birth. We came here to check on her, and we find this instead?" Her voice trembled.

Theron and Vlad inched closer to Thorn protectively.

No one had updated them. Maybe telling Katla that everyone was okay would calm her. I said, "The baby was born safely, and Emily's going to be okay."

Volos and Katla jerked their heads toward me, the man's face blanching further. He rasped, "That's the king's heir's kidnapped fiancée. She's here with the dragon thief?"

Thorn snarled, his jaw clenching. "She is *not* his." His anger soared between us, so powerful that it was palpable to everyone.

Yeah, that plan hadn't worked. If anything, I'd made the situation worse.

"You took all the dragons and kidnapped her because you wanted her for your own." Katla shook her head, taking a few steps away from Thorn and bumping into her mate. "And now you're going to take all our dragons."

Smoke trickled from Thorn's nose as his pupils slitted.

"Son," Vlad whispered, placing a hand on his shoulder. "You have to remember that Drake will twist the story in his favor and pit others against you."

"Not everyone is privy to what you did for my son," Theron added, trying to ease the tension.

Saphira snorted and rolled her eyes, not bothering to hide her disgust. "If that were the case, do you think he would've been sitting here in the living room when you arrived? Or standing here now, letting you run your mouth? Seriously?"

I mashed my lips together to hold in my laugh. Leave it to her to spell out their stupidity.

"Maybe he just got here." Katla crossed her arms, but her words lacked conviction. "He hasn't started."

"Thorn and Everly"—Edna gestured at us—"are the only reason that Emily and your grandson are alive."

Some of Thorn's anger ebbed. *Though Edna is backing us, you need to be ready to go. We can't risk someone bringing the warriors here. Not after everything we've been through.*

I hated that he was right. I wanted to keep an eye on Emily a little while longer, but we'd already stayed too long, especially since Edna had informed us that the warriors were heading this way. Further, Edna had set the strict condition yesterday that we needed to leave by dawn.

"Grandson?" Katla whispered dreamily.

Beaming, Edna nodded. "Yes. You have a *grandson.*"

Glancing at Volos, Katla touched her chest. "How did they prevent a different story from happening?"

Mindy appeared at the threshold between the kitchen and the hallway. "Thorn changed Emily. She's a dragon now, and because of that, her body could handle the birth."

"As things were, Emily was struggling with the labor. Everly came in, knowing what needed to be done." Edna smiled and rubbed a hand down her face. "I've helped deliver a baby before, but I've never handled a birth with such complications. Things would have ended differently if they hadn't answered my desperate call...even after I told them they couldn't stay in the safe house."

Surprise filtered through our connection.

"Wait." Volos's face scrunched. "Is that the real reason you ran us out of here earlier? Emily was near death, and you asked these people to come and didn't tell us anything until it was over?"

"No." Edna cut a hand in the air. "When I asked you to leave, it was before Emily took a turn for the worse. Emily said she needed silence so she could concentrate. She was in so much pain, and her labor wasn't progressing. It wasn't until her body started to shut down that I called Theron and begged for Thorn to come."

Katla's bottom lip quivered. "We heard Mikah yelling last night, and we tried calling so many times. No one answered, but thankfully, Mikah texted us, saying the labor was progressing and Emily was doing better. We waited as long as we could stand before coming here. We were so scared that something horrible happened and that's why we weren't hearing from anyone."

"That's my fault." I could tell the past several hours had been hard on them. "I wanted to monitor Emily's heartbeat. Even though she was changed into a dragon shifter, her pulse wasn't strong. I didn't want her to be more stimulated until I was comfortable she was out of danger."

Volos's breath caught. "Is she still in danger?"

In a way, this was my dream—to be the person who told family members that their loved one was all right and going to survive. It had been the message I'd prayed to hear about my mom so many times, and though it had never come, the doctors had been amazing until the end. But this was the kind of news every doctor hoped to give. "She's fine and going to make a full recovery."

The couple hugged each other as Katla whimpered, "Oh, thank gods."

Something warm coursed through our bond, and I glanced at Thorn to find a proud grin on his face. He connected, *You really are meant to be a doctor. You're glowing.* Then something dampened the warmth. *And because of me, you might never get to become one.*

I despised how he always put the burden on his shoulders and never anyone else's. *No, it's because of Drake, remember? And being with you, well...life has changed, and new priorities have emerged.* I opened myself up more to our connection, wanting him to feel the magnitude of my truth.

"*None* of this was Everly's fault. I took the coward's way out, not wanting to call and tell you not to come." Edna frowned. "If that had been Mindy, there's no way in hell I wouldn't have headed over. I just thought it might be easier to inform you after Everly gave me the okay. That was the wrong call. I should've realized you would've heard Mikah last night and needed a good update. I was so preoccupied that the thought didn't occur to me, and I'm sorry for that."

The door to the bedroom creaked open, and Mikah stuck his head into the hallway. My heart pounded until I noticed his smile and the baby swaddled in blankets in his arms. He tiptoed out and quietly shut the door behind him.

All the hurt and anger vanished from Katla's and Volos's eyes, which twinkled with excitement. Even Thorn's emotions became light and happy as all of us focused on the new life.

Katla took a tentative step forward. "Is that *him?*"

My cheeks hurt, and I realized I was smiling. I'd never been part of something like this before, and my heart felt full to bursting. Moments like these were why I'd wanted to become a doctor—knowing that in some small way, I'd made a positive impact in someone's life. And the icing on the cake was that Thorn was here, seeing what his magic had done. *Yes, I may have helped with the labor, but if it wasn't for your magic—what only you can do—Emily and the baby would've died. If that's not proof that your magic isn't a curse, I don't know what is.* None of us had surgical experience, and many people didn't realize there was an art to a C-section. You had to cut precisely in order for the child to survive.

"It is." Mikah hurried next to me to stand before his parents and pulled the blanket down from the sweet baby's face. "I'd like for you two to meet your grandson, Thorn."

My heart ached with such happiness. My attention drifted to my mate, whose mouth had dropped open. He moved toward the hallway, his arms wrapped around his body as a mixture of emotions swirled through him. *You're right. My magic can be used for good. It can be used to help people instead of hurting them.*

A sob built in my chest, but not from sadness. I was so damn glad he was finally seeing himself in a different light.

Vlad and Theron were right behind him, and Saphira remained in place. The corners of her mouth tipped upward as she rocked back on her heels. "Seriously, you're going to give the guy a big head, and it doesn't need to get any bigger."

I gave her a look of warning as I watched my mate experience something unique.

"You don't have to name him that." Thorn's voice was deep and emotional.

"I know we don't." Mikah stared at his son in his arms. "But we want to. My wife and child wouldn't be here if it wasn't for you and Everly. It was a no-brainer which name to choose when we realized he was a boy. Emily and I agreed it would be one of your names for doing what you did for us, especially when you didn't have to."

"Hey!" Saphira winked. "I held one of her legs, so you should've considered naming the baby Saphira, even for a moment."

Everyone chuckled, and for an instant, Thorn and I felt content... as if we truly belonged.

Then Theron cleared his throat. "I hate to ruin this, but our group should get going. The sun is rising, and we need to get back to the others so we can head out."

That reminder had my stomach hardening. Even when we felt like we belonged, we didn't. Not only that, but the warriors could show up at any time without any notice.

Vlad nodded. "Congratulations on your new addition. Having a child, especially now, is truly a gift."

"It'll be best for Emily to shift into her dragon when she can," I said. I remembered how disconnected I'd been with my dragon until we'd merged. "She shouldn't rush it, but if she starts feeling antsy, that will help her connect with her dragon."

Come on, babe. Thorn reached a hand toward me, waiting for me on the steps.

"Let me go check on Emily one last time." I pivoted back to the room. "I just need a sec." I quietly opened the bedroom door and heard that Emily's heartbeat was stronger. She was asleep, lying on the bed with a fresh, clean white comforter surrounding her. She was going to be fine.

I shut the door again and made my way to my mate. As we got ready to leave, Mikah, baby Thorn, Katla, and Volos sat on the couch in the living room.

When I took Thorn's hand, Edna said, "Don't leave. Head back to the house and stay. After what you've done for us, that's the least we can do to repay you."

Hope sprang to life in my chest. We didn't have anywhere to go. Allowing us to stay would help us more than she realized.

"Are you sure?" Theron asked carefully. "We don't want you to do something you aren't comfortable with."

"Not only that, but the later we leave, the more thunder members will see us." Vlad chewed on his lip. "We can't risk word getting back to Drake and the warriors."

"No one should be up if you leave now, but that will change soon." Edna patted Theron's arm. "But after we learned what happened to your thunder, no one will be tempted to say anything. We don't want the warriors here. Though most people know we have a safe house, they have no clue where it is. I did tell them it exists because fear for Mindy and two older couples was taking hold of our thunder. When I confirmed we had a backup in place, some semblance of control replaced the fear. They won't risk our thunder, not after Mikah, Mindy, and I tell them everything you've done. They'll want you to stay, and it's my call."

"And we'll back them." Katla now had the baby in her arms. "I'm so sorry for the way we reacted. But Mikah, Mindy, and Edna wouldn't lie, and because of you, we have a grandbaby."

Vlad and Thorn looked at each other, uncertainty lining their faces.

"If anything seems off, I'll let you know." Edna placed a hand on her heart. "Please trust me like I trusted your group when I opened our safe house to you."

She had us there. Though she trusted Theron, we could've been forcing him to use his resources. Having us here was a leap of faith.

I think we should trust her, I connected with Thorn. *I believe she would tell us if something didn't seem right. Besides, can we risk not having a safe place to stay? Leaving could be worse.*

Thorn pursed his lips. "Okay. But if even one person isn't behind it..."

"We'll let you know." Edna crossed her heart. "I promise. Our community is tight, and I can read my people. I just need to sleep after being up all night. Then I'll talk to them before bringing over the couples and Mindy to stay with you."

The house would be full, but it was worth the crowd if we got to stay. I smiled. "Thank you."

"Now go on, before more people get up." Edna pointed at the front door. "I'll visit you later, after the conversation happens."

That was all we needed.

As we walked down the stairs, Mikah popped up, looking over the banister. "Thank you all again. It was an honor to meet you, Your Highness."

"You're welcome," Thorn growled, though surprise swirled between us as we hurried outside and climbed back into the truck.

As soon as the truck pulled away from the neighborhood, my eyelids grew heavy. I laid my head on Thorn's shoulder, and he wrapped his muscular arm around me. I closed my eyes, enjoying the sounds of his breath and heartbeat while his scent hung around me.

You know...after we handle Drake and save our people, maybe you and I can live near your university so you can get back to school and become a doctor. Watching you tonight was damn sexy, and you made me so proud. His fingers stroked my arm, and both my skin and heart tingled.

I lifted my head as the world tilted. *Wait. No more running away? You actually want to stay?*

Let's just say I finally see that you're right. He kissed my forehead. *Our people don't deserve to live in fear and under constant threat. They deserve to have full lives, happiness, and a leader who will fight for them. If we run, it wouldn't be right. All these dragons are being killed because Drake doesn't understand their worth. We have to fix this, for them and for the two of us to have the kind of life we deserve with each other.*

I cupped his face, afraid my chest might crack open from all the happiness swirling through me. My mate was amazing, and he was finally seeing his worth and what was right for us all. Plus, combining my dreams would be fantastic. I nestled back into his side. *I'd like that future. You could rub my feet as I studied all night.*

I'd do more than rub your feet. His chest rumbled with desire.

I smiled.

"Ew," Saphira gasped. "I don't know what you two are saying, but quit it. I can smell the effect. You are not *alone* in the backseat."

I laughed, but it cut off as I fell asleep quickly.

DARKNESS DESCENDED with no word from Edna. None of us knew how to take it, and Theron had sent several text messages that had gone unanswered.

I was worried that something had changed with Emily, but I believed Mindy or Edna would've contacted us by now. We'd all been exhausted, but Thorn and I had woken up a couple of hours ago, hungry and horny, and not necessarily in that order.

Thorn, Vlad, Theron, Hydra, Sol, Eva, Cassidy, Errol, Brenton, and I were sitting in the den. Tyson and Elliott were upstairs in the room with Peter, playing their video game, while Saphira was still sleeping.

Errol sat on the far end of the couch next to his brother. "If you keep helping dragons, word will get around."

Brenton scowled. "But so will our location. We all know how Drake is about that."

"Has your thunder heard anything?" Cassidy asked Theron from her spot between Brenton and Vlad.

"Nothing." Theron blew out a breath from his spot on the far end of the couch, opposite Errol. "They haven't even heard from Drake since it all went down."

"That's because the warriors are focusing on those who oppose him." Vlad rubbed his forehead, his elbow brushing me. "Which is good. That's one reason they haven't gotten further with their search, but Drake will want to solidify his hold on the throne as quickly as possible."

Eva's forehead lined as she asked, "How would he do that?"

"The coronation." Sol slid an arm over the back of the couch behind her.

"This is insane." Hydra pouted, but her irises twinkled at what her son had done to Eva. "I don't know how we're going to fight this."

"It'd be a whole lot easier if we had someone on the inside," Thorn said as he placed a hand on my thigh.

Theron's phone beeped. He glanced at the screen and raised his eyebrows. "Well, this just got interesting."

My lungs seized. Who could be messaging him now?

CHAPTER TEN

I RUBBED my hands on my legs, trying to calm the ringing in my ears. We always seemed to be running toward or away from something, but Theron's body language was one of puzzlement, not danger.

Thorn tensed, his jaw twitching. "What's going on?"

"I just received a text from Wyvern." Theron swiped his finger over the phone again.

Saphira's head snapped toward him, her eyes bright.

Chuckling, Sol rolled his eyes. "That's not interesting. You two message each other constantly. I'm surprised Mom hasn't gotten jealous yet. You run to your phone every time it dings, wondering if it's him."

"Not all the time." Hydra wrinkled her nose at her son. "When it matters, his attention doesn't stray, so I'm not worried."

His smile disappeared as he grimaced. "I don't want to hear stuff like that."

"Oh, I'm pretty sure I'll be hearing and smelling stuff like that from you soon enough." Hydra's smile was blinding.

Eva dropped her head, her cheeks reddening, and her hair fell across her face as she used it as a barrier.

I wasn't the only one who'd noticed how they revolved around each other, but I understood my sister was more on the private side and didn't like the attention. I could relate to that, though I'd overcome it recently. "What was interesting about the text?"

"A warrior is at our thunder, asking Wyvern to contact us on his behalf. Apparently, he's been talking to Vlad's parents as well, and there's no telling who else." Theron placed the phone on his lap. "He wants to schedule a time and place for all of us to meet."

My head tilted back, and a lump formed in my throat. I hadn't expected *that*.

"Obviously, that's not going to happen." Cassidy chuckled hard. "I get that there were warriors fighting against Drake when the king died, but we know he's putting them in their place. We can't trust anyone."

She had a point, but I still believed that most people wanted to do the right thing. Of course, there were exceptions—there always were—but I couldn't bring myself to think most people were bad. That was too black and white when the world was full of gray. Everyone was a villain in someone else's story. By teaching me my love of painting, my mom had also helped me to understand that the world was more complex than right and wrong, and to capture an image perfectly, you had to see it from all angles.

"Who is it?" I doubted I knew them, but I had to ask.

"A warrior named Uther." Theron mashed his lips into a line.

Uther? Now my head really jerked back. Out of every warrior possible, it would be him.

"I don't know him," Theron continued. "But he's been poking around. Vlad's parents informed Wyvern that someone was asking about us discreetly, and now this person is doing the same thing. It can't be a coincidence."

"I heard of him recently." Errol leaned forward, resting his elbows on his knees. "He moved to the château grounds the week

Everly was taken, but he wasn't assigned to the king and me, so I'm sure his allegiance is with Drake. I wouldn't trust him."

Drake had hand-picked him, and I wondered where he'd pulled Uther from.

I swallowed to get rid of the uneasy feeling. "I wouldn't be so sure about that."

Vlad's attention landed on me. "What makes you say that?"

"He was one of the guards assigned to watch over Eva and me while we were there."

A menacing growl vibrated deep within Thorn's chest as his anger boiled through our connection.

I placed a hand on his arm, hoping to provide comfort. "He was nice—kind and regretful. Drake made it clear on multiple occasions that if Uther did something he didn't like, his young daughter would pay the price. Despite that, Uther treated us kindly and looked out for us the best he could. Even when we were at Theron's thunder and the warriors attacked, he didn't want to hurt us."

"Which means Drake could be using Uther's daughter against him now to set us up." Thorn's body quivered. "For all we know, Drake told him to be like that to earn some level of trust."

The urge to pull away from Thorn surged through me, but I remained still. He was upset, and his words held merit. If I were him, I would possibly be thinking the same thing.

I took his hand and squeezed it, pushing down the frustration fluttering inside me. "I get it, but you weren't there."

His face twisted in agony. "You don't have to remind me. I was living each one of those hellacious moments away from you and losing my damn mind the entire time."

"Thorn," Vlad warned. "That was hard on her as well. You need to remember that."

We didn't need to keep rehashing this. We *all* knew it had been a horrible time for everyone. But I was surprised when Eva spoke up.

"It was a horrible time for Everly, too. Despite her puking all night and tossing and turning, she protected me every step of the way.

And Uther *is* kind. Whenever Everly was forced to go with Drake, he'd stay behind to make sure another guard wasn't cruel to me."

A deep scowl settled over Sol's face. Though he hadn't been around when all this had gone down, he obviously didn't like hearing about the time the woman he had a crush on had been forced into captivity and mistreated.

I was beginning to think my hunch that he and Eva were soulmates, like Thorn and I had been before he'd changed me, wasn't so far off after all.

Still, I had to focus on what she'd said, and that information was good to hear. I'd suspected that Uther had protected her since Eva had never fallen apart while I'd been gone. But Thorn was still a bundle of nerves beside me.

"Look, I'm not saying we trust him completely." I couldn't be blind to Thorn's point. Drake could have realized that Uther had an amicable relationship with us and be exploiting his daughter. "But I think it's worth considering."

"And let me add"—Brenton patted his chest—"when someone threatens your kid, it doesn't leave you feeling warm and fuzzy toward them. Based on what Everly and Eva are saying, this isn't something he'd *want* to do, which could be to our advantage."

Hydra leaned into her mate. "What did Wyvern think? Did they talk on the phone?"

"No, he showed up at the thunder with a handful of other guards. They said they came back to see if they'd missed any clues, but after they split up to search the area, Uther circled back." Theron ran a hand through his hair. "He said he didn't have a lot of time but that Drake was settings things in motion, and if we wanted to stop them, we had to act soon. He also said he needed to get in touch with us and asked if Wyvern knew of a way. Of course, Wyvern said no, but he asked us if we needed him to say something else."

"Are they still there?" Vlad asked as he and Cassidy met each other's eyes, using their fated-mate connection to communicate.

I don't like this, Thorn connected, his grip tightening on me.

There are so many ways meeting him could go wrong. It's not worth the risk.

I inhaled, trying to think clearly. *What if he's sincere? What if we could have someone on the inside? You want to fight Drake, and I agree. We should. We have to. But right now, we're running and hiding without many allies. This could swing things in our favor.*

"They are." Theron crossed his arms. "But I'm not sure for how long. They came at nightfall so they could fly over the area without worrying about humans seeing them as easily."

Thorn sighed and leaned his head back on the couch.

We were all tired...so damn tired.

Standing, Vlad paced around the footstool in front of the television. "Everly and Eva know him better than any of us. He wasn't the king's hire, so Drake would have something to leverage over Uther to force him to remain loyal. Maybe he wants to be free, and we should meet him."

Releasing my hand, Thorn straightened. "Dad, you can't be serious. If it's a trap, we'll be handing ourselves over to them!"

Arching a brow, Vlad leveled his gaze on Thorn. "You should know I wouldn't go in blindly. Nor do I think Everly and Eva would. We'd have to assume it *is* a trap."

"That's good." Errol bobbed his head. "We'll need to make sure no one is hiding at the meeting place and that he's not followed."

"We need to set up a location where we don't plan on staying." Vlad rubbed his hands together. "We'll be ready at the real location and watch when he arrives. There'll be no chance for others to get into position ahead of us."

Thorn rolled his shoulders. "I could get behind that plan."

"Wait." They were missing something, or I'd lost my mind and wasn't following. "We have one problem to figure out before we can get to the meeting logistics."

Narrowing his eyes, Brenton focused on me. Then he snapped, "How to get the meeting scheduled without putting Wyvern and the thunder at risk."

Exactly. "Even though I trust Uther, you all are right. Drake could be pulling his strings, so if Wyvern schedules the meeting, it'll prove that he's in contact with us, putting them all in danger."

"Shit," Thorn growled, and lowered his head. "You're right. It doesn't even matter if he's trustworthy. We can't risk it, which is more than fine with me. I didn't like the thought to begin with."

There had to be a way to fix this. "Errol, Brenton. Do you have any friends you trust at the château?"

"I do." Errol rubbed a hand along his chin. "A maid who cleans my house, the château, and the house the guards live in on the grounds. I've known her since she was a child, and when her parents passed, I got her a job on the premises. I made sure she was provided for as best I could, and I know the type of person she is. She told me Drake was up to no good, but she refused to tell me specifics, and I thought it was his usual shenanigans like when he was younger. When I realized what Drake had done to Saphira, her warnings made more sense, but it was too late. Then the king asked me for help, and I knew it would get me back to my daughter. There was no question where my priorities lie."

"Is there a way she could leave a message for Uther that no one else would find?" That might be impossible, but it could work.

Some of the worry ebbed from the connection as Thorn connected, *You're brilliant. Have I ever told you that?*

My face heated. He actually hadn't, but he'd complimented me several other ways.

Taking my hand, Thorn leaned toward me and said, "When I lived in the château, I remember the guards having their own lockers in the house where they log their weapons upon returning them into inventory. While the other maids are working, she should be able to slip a note into his locker undetected. Then they wouldn't be able to guess who left the note. We just need a way of communicating with her."

"Errol and I can drive several towns over and find a phone to call her." Vlad grabbed a set of keys. "If they trace the call, it won't compromise our location, and if they somehow get wind of the meeting, we'll have it set up in a way that doesn't lead them here."

The plan was shaky at best, but it was the only option I could think of to get a message to Uther. We couldn't risk giving away our location or proximity to Edna's thunder.

"Now?" Errol's mouth dropped. "I thought we were waiting on Edna."

"We should leave the message as soon as possible if Drake has imminent plans we need to know about." Vlad headed to the door. "The good thing is they won't be sure who is connected to us, which will give the warriors pause before the meeting. We'll schedule something for tomorrow night so they don't have too much time to get things ready." As he opened the door, I heard the faint sound of engines.

Someone was headed this way. It had to be Edna and the others they were bringing.

We headed into the yard as Vlad and Errol reached one of the Suburbans.

Edna's car and a Ford Escape SUV pulled in a few yards back so Vlad and Errol could leave.

Edna climbed out of the car, frowning. "What's going on?"

"We received some news, and Errol and I are going to drive several towns over to make a phone call." Vlad opened the front door. "I promise we'll go far enough that it won't be traced back here."

Edna's forehead wrinkled, but all she did was nod as two older couples got out of the Ford, and Mindy shut the passenger door. The two older men stepped to the back and removed a pair of large suitcases as Mindy reached into the back seat and pulled out a duffel bag. This was the group who'd come to stay here.

The two women stared at us. The taller of them had thick gray streaks in her black hair and crow's feet set deep around her pale brown eyes. She was about Saphira's height, so she had several inches on me. The other lady was all gray, but her face was less wrinkled. Her baby blue eyes had a layer of white over the top like cataracts.

The shorter one smiled as her gaze settled on my mate. "Belinda, that's him. The prince who saved Emily and our precious new baby."

Belinda beamed. "Tia, he's nothing like the angry man we saw on the net of dragons." She hurried toward us and threw her arms around my mate, hugging him tightly.

For a split second, Thorn stiffened, and his shock pummeled through our connection before he relaxed and wrapped his arms around the woman, giving her a small hug in return. The emotions rolling off him had tears burning my eyes. He was moved by the gesture.

Mindy snorted. "Belinda, it's called Dragonnet. How many times do we have to tell you?"

"Eh." She waved a dismissive hand. "Close enough."

"Honey…" The man with short white hair chuckled as he carried their bag. "Leave the poor prince alone. You can't just go hugging everybody. Besides, he's young and muscular. Don't make my dragon more jealous, especially when I know you'll be lying next to my feeble old body tonight." His emerald eyes twinkling, the man's smile didn't break as he marched to his mate. When she pulled back, he patted Thorn on the shoulder.

"Oh, please, Merlin. There is nothing feeble about that body." She winked and nestled into his side.

Heart swelling, I didn't want to look away from this lovely couple. Maybe having them around wouldn't be as awkward as Thorn had feared.

"See, Tia knows better than to go hug on a young'un." The other man laughed as he came near. He and Merlin were about the same height, coming in at around seven feet. This man had salt-and-pepper hair, though it was more salt than pepper, and a matching beard. His dark brown eyes held a similar twinkle of mischief.

Tia placed her hands on her hips. "Maybe I should just so you don't think I'm fully trained, Ryu."

At least now we knew their names.

"I bet when I said two older couples, you thought you'd need to behave for their sake," Edna said. She laughed and patted Ryu on the back. "You'll soon learn they're worse than teenagers." She launched into introductions.

We gave them our background and story along with why we had humans with us. They handled everything with grace and seemed genuine in their desire to share the house.

When it was clear everything would be fine, Edna left, and our group headed inside, minus Vlad and Errol.

As soon as the front door shut, Brenton called out, "Tyson, Elliott, Peter, and Saphira, come on down so you can meet our new roommates."

"Oh, great. More dragons," Peter ground out as they thumped downstairs.

"I take it that's the disgruntled human we can't trust." Tia waggled her brows. "This will be fun. Being old gives me an excuse to run my mouth without apology."

Elliott led the way downstairs, pouting—until he glanced at our group. His eyes bulged, and he missed a step and tumbled down the rest of the stairs. He landed at the bottom, his head smacking the floor with a sickening thud.

I rushed to him, fearing the worst.

CHAPTER ELEVEN

AS SOON AS I kneeled by Elliott, Thorn was across from me, assessing the situation. The bottom half of Elliott's body lay on the stairs, while his torso was on the ground. He was lying face down, but I could hear his heart beating wildly.

"Elliott," I whispered brokenly. If I lost him, I didn't know what I'd do. I wanted to flip him over, but I had to fight the instinct. It could make his injury worse.

He groaned and groggily said, "What the *fuck* happened? I saw an angel. Then all of a sudden, I was falling. I think it was for her."

I had no clue what he was talking about. "There's no angel here."

Thorn snickered. "Speak for yourself."

Cutting my eyes at Thorn, I couldn't help but grin. Elliott wasn't necessarily okay, but talking coherently was a good sign.

"Is he all right?" Mindy asked, and I noticed she'd pushed through the group to kneel at his head. Her forehead creased as her attention locked on Elliott.

The entire group wore similar expressions...except Peter, who shook his head with a scowl.

Wow. He was showing some real fatherly concern.

"I don't know yet." I touched his legs. "El, can you feel my touch?"

"Dude! That tickles." He jerked and winced. "Stop."

A laugh bubbled out of me. "Okay, I knew you were ticklish as a toddler, but I thought you would've grown out of it *some*."

Tyson nodded while pumping a fist. "Heck, yeah. Next all-night marathon, I'm going to use that to my advantage."

"Oh, *hell*, no." Elliott lifted himself off the floor and glared at Tyson. "That's cheating. And only losers cheat. You just don't like that I can beat your ass, but suck it! You're a fucking dragon. You aren't getting any sympathy from me."

Belinda *tsked*. "Language."

Usually, I'd agree, but his choice of words was not my concern right now. "Elliott, stay still. We need to make sure nothing's wrong, or you could hurt yourself worse." One side effect of a brain injury was loss of balance.

"Uh, sorry." He swung his head toward Belinda but stopped short when his gaze settled on Mindy. His body jerked as his mouth dropped. "She's really here."

I was so confused. "What are you talking about?"

"The angel," he said simply, then clamped his hands over his mouth as his cheeks turned red.

"Oh, I think our little human here has a crush on Mindy." Tia chuckled.

"Uh...I mean, she's cute." Elliott glanced at Mindy. "You're cute." He looked away and shrugged, though his face was the same shade as a tomato. He tugged on his borrowed navy shirt, which was two sizes too big on him. Our options here were limited, and he was stuck wearing dragon-sized clothing.

Tyson hung his head. "Not smooth, and can you move? I'm trapped on these stairs, and I swear, your dad is literally breathing down my neck."

I didn't want Elliott to move more, but when I noticed he wasn't struggling more than usual and had control of his limbs, some of my worry eased.

He's okay, Thorn connected and took my hand, pulling me into the living room beside him.

The comforting buzz of our connection washed away the rest of my concern.

"I'll get him some ice," Mindy said, and she hurried past the stairs to the kitchen.

When she returned, Saphira joined us, and while Elliott iced his face, we hung around the living room and chatted. We'd learned that both couples were close to five hundred years old, which was pushing the older end of a dragon's lifespan. They'd been born in this thunder, had lived here most of their lives, and had all been best friends since birth. They told us about Edna's conversation with the others and how the thunder had unanimously voted to allow our group to stay here.

In return, we answered their questions. What I hadn't expected was the information they provided about Thorn's grandfather.

As Thorn listened, his brows pulled together. Taking after Vlad, he paced in front of the television. His apprehension blanketed me, making my skin crawl. I also had to stand, but I leaned against the wall, knowing he needed to expend his nervous energy.

"You knew my grandfather personally?" Thorn wrung his hands.

"I wouldn't say *personally*." Merlin shook his head and placed an arm around his mate. They were sitting on one end of the long couch. "Back then, we didn't have the..." His face wrinkled.

Mindy chuckled. "Dragonnet."

"Oh," Elliott mumbled next to her, and Mindy focused on him, adjusting the position of the ice on his head.

Biting her thumb, Saphira blinked from her spot on the stairs. She'd missed the debacle, and she'd been side-eyeing them since she'd come down.

"Dude, that's so sad." Tyson snorted and shook his head.

Luckily, Cassidy and Hydra were sitting between him and Elliott, or Elliott probably would've elbowed him in the side.

My gaze landed on Eva and Sol, who were sitting on the footstool in the middle of the room. I couldn't help but notice they were now holding hands. Their relationship had started off with a reaction similar to Mindy's and Elliott's, and I wondered if it was coincidence or if all three of us were destined to be with dragons. But that was impossible.

"Let the lad get the attention the only way he knows how." Tia giggled.

Merlin patted her leg. "Now, honey. Behave."

"Ha. You know better than to waste your breath telling *her* that." Belinda wiggled a finger.

Thorn's anxiety was palpable, and Brenton must have noticed, because he pushed off the wall on the other side of the room where he'd been standing next to Peter, close to the front door, and spoke.

"From what I remember, before the internet, every ten to fifteen years, the king would make rounds to visit the thunders and update them personally." Brenton steepled his fingers. "Each year, the king focused on a different region, and if there was an announcement everyone needed to hear at once, he would have warriors help spread the message worldwide. The more thunders heard the news, the faster it traveled."

Sort of like the rumor mill of the modern world for things people didn't want documented. The more people who knew, the quicker word spread.

Merlin scowled. "The last time we saw your grandfather was near the end of his life. His health was failing, which made him even angrier. The last time he visited our thunder, our leader told us all to stay inside. We'd heard stories of his cruelty and how just looking at him the wrong way could make him strip you of your dragon. When the king came and saw none of us waiting for his arrival, he assumed we were hiding something. He stripped our leader of his dragon, killing him. He was close to four hundred—too old for a human to survive. Then he stripped several more of the oldest members of their dragons. After someone finally confessed to why we hadn't greeted him, he began to calm down, but then he took ten more dragons to be sure."

"Of course he did." Thorn rubbed the back of his neck, where his mark lay, and grimaced. Discomfort and shame coursed through our bond as they always did when anyone talked about his mark and its history. He did everything he could to hide the mark, even from me, and it had taken me seeing the birthmark while we were naked and vulnerable in front of Drake to realize it. Even when we showered together, he kept his front side turned to me.

You are not him, I connected, pushing my love toward him. His father had destroyed the way Thorn saw himself, and though he was getting more comfortable with his magic, the baggage wasn't gone. I had faith it would go—he just needed time to process everything.

I wondered if his grandfather had been mentally ill. "Something must have caused him to become like that."

"Abusing his power did." Belinda frowned and shook her head. "When a person from the royal line is blessed with the magic, it's intended to restore the balance of dragonkind."

That stopped Thorn in his tracks. "What do you mean?"

"You don't know?" Tia tilted her head, examining him.

"Would I be asking if I did?" Thorn countered gruffly. He crossed his arms, which molded his white shirt to his muscular chest more than normal.

My body warmed, and saliva pooled in my mouth while my dragon inched forward. He was so damn sexy, and for a moment, I forgot where we were.

"Thorn Wight," Cassidy scolded. "I taught you better than that."

And that was exactly what I'd needed to get my head on straight. This moment, this conversation, was not the time for me to want to pleasure our bodies. My dragon huffed as she settled back inside me.

"No, I deserved that." Tia crossed her legs, nestling into Merlin.

"I did ask a stupid question. I get on to young'uns for doing that, but here I am, doing the same damn thing."

"Hey!" Elliott shook a finger at her. "Language."

An adoring expression crossed Merlin's face as he stared at his mate. "You have a knack for doing the exact thing you scold others for."

"I'm old." She tapped her head. "I can't be held liable for my actions."

"Please." Belinda snickered as she smacked Tia's arm. "Your memory is fit as a fiddle. Don't let her fool you."

I was pretty sure we'd all figured that out. But Thorn needed answers. Since he was no longer pacing, I moved beside him and took his hand. He squeezed my hand tightly.

I cleared my throat, hoping they'd get the message.

Bowing his head slightly, Merlin answered, "It makes sense that you don't know. Most everyone around now is too young to remember the stories from before your grandfather's reign, and he left a mark. Fear has a way of molding the present and concealing the good others did previously."

"You're talking about other royals who had the same gift." Hydra's brows furrowed. "Now that I think about it, I do remember hearing some of the history. The mark is associated with King Arthur."

"King Arthur?" I hadn't heard that name before.

"Arthur was my grandfather's name." Thorn swallowed.

"I've never heard him called that before." Now that I thought about it, that was strange.

Eva inched closer to Sol. "It's like Lord Voldemort from *Harry Potter*. No one wants to say his name."

"Huh. If he's the villain in the movies, it's a good comparison." Sol wrapped an arm around her.

Eva's mouth dropped. "You've never seen the movies?"

Sol scratched his head. "I don't watch much television."

Elliott moaned, and Mindy dropped the ice and gently touched the knot on his forehead. "Are you okay?"

"No!" Elliott shook his head hard, proving he was milking his injury for her attention, and gestured at Sol. "I'm not okay. He doesn't play video games, and he hasn't watched the *Harry Potter* movies? The next thing we'll learn is that he doesn't like *Star Wars!*"

Sol flinched.

"Oh, my God." Elliott turned back to Mindy. "I'm feeling faint again. This can't be real life. The guy my sister likes doesn't know *anything.*"

Face scrunching, Mindy blew out a breath. "I don't, either, so maybe you don't want my help after all."

Elliott's eyes bulged out of his head. He whipped around to look at Tyson. "Dude, please, if our bruh-mance is going to survive, tell me you aren't like them. They get a pass, but for you, dude, there's no coming back from that."

Tyson scoffed. "Please. Do I look like some uncultured swine?" Then *he* flinched and glanced at Mindy and Sol. "No offense."

Lifting both hands, Sol tipped his head back. "Offense taken."

"Don't worry." Elliott waved him off. "He'll be fine. But apologize to Mindy."

"Fine. Sorry, Mindy." Tyson placed a hand over his heart. "I didn't intend for my truth bomb to be taken so harshly, but being the bigger person, I'm willing to help you out for my bruh. We can watch *all* the things."

Peter grunted from his place against the wall. "I thought the two of them were bad, and now it's like they're multiplying."

This conversation had been completely derailed. There was only one solution. "Go upstairs, take Peter, and watch *Star Wars,*" I ordered. "Educate these underprivileged individuals so they'll be on your level."

Snapping, Elliott pointed at me. "Now you're talking my jam. I get the gist of the story. King Arthur was bad and made people think his power was bad, and Thorn here is going to remind them that it's not the case. Noted and filed." He stood and pulled Mindy to her feet. "And I have my friend Jared's password to his Disney+ account, so *Star Wars* marathon, here we come!"

"He's going to kill you." Eva laughed as she and Sol stood with them.

"Eh, he's human, and we'll probably never see him again," Elliott answered as he grabbed his father's hand and tugged him toward the stairs. "We're going to be dragon shifters soon!"

They continued talking as they clomped up the stairs, and when the door shut, Thorn connected, *Finally. I love our brother and sister, but damn, sometimes, they make things so convoluted. I have a feeling that tomorrow, Elliott will go back to harassing me to change him.*

My stomach cartwheeled. I loved the fact he'd called them *our* siblings. He thought of them like family. *Yes, he will.*

"To be young and falling in love." Tia snorted and laid her head on Merlin's chest.

"You were saying?" Thorn prompted, guiding the conversation back to his grandfather.

"Before King Arthur, two other royals had the same magic. From what I heard as a little boy, they were the ones who saved dragonkind when our numbers were dwindling." Ryu yawned. "But King Arthur destroyed their memories and instilled fear in his people, which is what you have to overcome."

Something swirled inside my mate—warring emotions of hope and dread.

"Listen, I hate to end this chat, but we're up later than normal." Belinda stretched. "I'm about to fall asleep over here."

Brenton grabbed the new couples' luggage, and Cassidy jumped to her feet. She said, "There's a room upstairs with two queen beds, if that's okay."

"That's more than perfect." Tia stood. "We can do the old sock on the doorknob thing when one of us is busy. I saw that on some show a while back."

Saphira laughed loudly. "Oh, gods. I needed that."

As the others meandered away, Saphira sat next to Hydra. The two of them began talking about Wyvern and things going on back at Hydra and Theron's thunder.

Thorn led me toward our room. When the door shut behind us, he pulled me into his arms, and a mixture of his emotions overwhelmed me. I wasn't sure what to do other than hold him.

An emotion settled over him as if he'd made a decision. He pulled back, and I saw something in his expression that I hadn't expected.

I froze.

CHAPTER TWELVE

THE ENTIRE TIME I'd been with Thorn, a heaviness had shrouded him, even when he was happy. Over the past week, that sensation had lightened, but not by much. I'd come to realize what it was—scars. Scars from his magic, his past, and his family. I was pretty sure that ever since I'd rolled into the picture, I'd made it worse because now he feared losing me. Granted, running off while he'd slept to turn myself over to Drake, thinking it would save our loved ones, hadn't helped.

Now, a look and lightness like hope filled him and stole my breath. His sky blue irises were brighter, the flecks of diamond standing out more, and his face didn't show the lines of worry that were usually there unless we were making love.

My heart expanded. He'd always been gorgeous, but this version of him was transcendent. "What's going on? I've never seen you like this." My smile was reflected in my voice.

"I..." He blew out a breath, grinning. "I understand what you've been trying to tell me. That this magic isn't a curse. That was only how I'd been taught to feel about it."

"Really?" I arched a brow, my heart fluttering. I didn't care how he'd gotten here, just that he had. I could only hope that his eyes were truly opening to the amazing man he was and was still becoming. "Just *now?*"

He snickered and tucked a piece of hair behind my ear, the sizzle of our connection thrumming between us. He murmured, "I know. I should've believed you, since what you think is most important to me. In fairness, it's the only reason I've come as far as I have." His smile drooped. "But to hear the history that people either didn't bother to tell me or didn't know confirmed what you were saying all along. My magic *is* a gift, and it's about keeping the balance and ensuring our race doesn't die off. Helping to heal injured dragons and create new ones so they don't have to endure what Emily did is also a blessing."

Balance. Sacrifice. Two words that always seemed to circle magic. "Well, the bad always seems to outweigh the good and instill fear."

"It does. It has." He settled his hands on my hips. "And I have a mate standing beside me who never knew about my past, yet she still tried to convince me that my magic could be used for good."

His love poured into the bond, and I felt as if I could combust from happiness. I cupped his cheek and connected, *It's because I know you. Even before we became what we are now, when everything indicated I shouldn't trust you, I knew you weren't bad. You are a pure soul who was misunderstood for far too long, and a fundamental change won't happen overnight. You have to believe that yourself—I can only get you so far. And I'm happy that the conversation tonight changed that for you. You deserve to be happy and not hate your reflection in the mirror or the mark on your back.*

You own me, Everly Woods. His pupils slitted as his dragon peeked through. *You have my heart, my body, my soul, and my trust. I don't know what I did to deserve you, but I won't give you up. No matter what, I need you by my side.*

Warmth flooded me, and my stomach clenched with desire. *You own me, too. No matter what. When things settle, I plan to have Errol sign our marriage certificate so I can take your last name.*

That would make me so happy, he replied and kissed me hungrily.

His tongue swooped into my mouth, and I answered each stroke with my own pent-up desire. I bit his lower lip. Growling, he placed his hands on my ass and lifted me to settle against him. He was already hardening as I wrapped my legs around his waist.

He moved forward, his hands kneading my cheeks, and had me tumbling back onto the bed. My hair fanned out around me as he leaned over and paused.

"So damn beautiful," he murmured, and his lips landed back on mine.

My hands slipped under his shirt, tracing the curves of his hard muscles. His stomach quivered with each brush, showing the power I had over him.

His hands moved under my shirt and slid underneath my bra, caressing my nipples. I moaned, not even trying to hide the effect he had on me. His deep, sexy chuckle had me writhing inside.

Pulling away from my lips, he whispered, "I love how you respond to me."

"I feel the same way." I winked and dropped my hand to his crotch, touching his hard outline.

He growled as he kissed his way down my neck, his teeth scraping the skin where my pulse pounded. My dragon roared inside, thrilled by the attention. I unfastened his jeans, tired of the barrier between him and my hands, as he continued to suck on my neck.

His jeans dropped on the floor, and he shifted his weight as he continued to stroke my breast. With his other hand, he pushed his boxers down, giving me the best view of the entire day. The only way it would be better was if he were shirtless, too.

My hand wrapped around him, and I stroked him. He groaned as he dropped to his side and removed his hand, leaving me bereft. Within seconds, he was removing my jeans and panties. Then he lifted up, pointing to my shirt, and grinned. "That's kind of in the way."

I bit my bottom lip. "Oh, is it?"

"Very much so," he responded as his hand slid between my legs. I sucked in a breath, eager for him to continue. But his hand disappeared.

My eyes popped open, and I glared. *What the hell?*

Shirt and bra off. He narrowed his eyes. *If you want me to continue.*

The spicy scent of arousal swirled between us. I loved it when he got bossy. He was never over the top with me, just the right amount without being disrespectful. *Only if you do the same.* I quirked a brow.

He beamed and quickly removed his shirt, then tossed it to the floor. *Your turn.*

I laughed. His eagerness was so endearing and made me feel desperately wanted. As I rose to remove my shirt and bra, I took in his body. Hard and tanned, it was better than any painting I'd ever seen, which was saying something. Just looking at him had me pulsing with a need that wouldn't be satisfied until he was inside me.

His eyes reflected the same hunger, and the world tilted. From what I'd heard through my school acquaintances, the undying love you felt for someone and the thirsty need for their body faded with time, but so far, that wasn't the case with us. In fact, it was the opposite. Every day, every touch, and every time we had sex had me jonesing for my next hit of Thorn. The thought of having any sort of life that didn't include him next to me was so devastating, I couldn't consider it.

Hand sliding back between my legs, Thorn moved his mouth to my breast. His tongue rolled over my nipple as he teased the spot that already had friction building inside me. My hand circled him again, and I stroked in time with what he was doing to my body.

Pleasure washed over me as we opened our bond to each other. There was no doubt he loved me as much as I did him, but love didn't fully express what we felt for each other. It was otherworldly, something that couldn't be explained...all-encompassing.

As I neared ecstasy, I pulled away.

He reached for me again, frowning. "Uh...where the hell do you think you're going?"

But there was one thing I needed to do before we connected. Something I'd been wanting to do our entire time together. "Turn over."

His irises sparkled as he flopped onto his back, and he held his hands out to his sides, ready to grasp my legs when I straddled him. He grinned wickedly, and I laughed. I couldn't help it. "Now turn around."

Face falling, he tilted his head. "Uh...what?" He glanced at the mattress as if that would explain everything.

"Turn around?" I laughed and swirled my finger.

He mashed his lips together. "I'm down for almost anything you want to try." He moved as if to see if I had something behind my back. "But I'd like to discuss it first, especially if it might involve my exit."

I smacked his leg, chuckling. "I am all about every inch of your body, except that one place. So don't worry. Nothing will get near your butthole unless we discuss it first."

"Just so we're clear." He rolled onto his stomach.

Once he was settled, I crawled up the bed next to him and ran a hand over his back to the bottom edge of his mark. He tensed, sensing where my fingers stilled.

I waited for a second. If he told me to stop, I would, but when he didn't say anything, I traced the outline of the dragon's body, its wings extended. A shiver coursed through him, and his dragon purred as I traced the image from the top of the wing to the dragon's head. I connected, *It's gorgeous. With the level of detail, it's hard to believe it's not a tattoo.*

Believe it or not, it's like I can feel you touching my dragon. I'm exposed to you. It's so intimate. His breath caught, and something shifted between us, drawing us closer.

You don't have to hide from me. I continued to trace it, my dragon inching forward. She was as excited as I was to finally touch his entire body, and more need pooled between my legs. *I would rather die than hurt you.* The truth of my words had the air whooshing out of me. But it was true. Everything inside me lived to keep him safe and happy.

A deep purr escaped my man as well. *I know that, and I can't take it anymore.*

He flipped over, and I almost complained until I saw the expression on his face. His eyes darkened with desire as he grabbed my waist and pulled me onto his lap. He placed a hand on the back of my neck and brought my head down so he could kiss me.

Our mouths melded together, and I shifted my hips while he guided himself inside me. As he filled me, my body rocked ever so slowly against his. The movement was sensual and all-consuming.

I pulled my mouth from his, wanting him deeper so I could ride him. He groaned as his hands cupped my breasts, his fingers caressing my nipples. He rocked underneath me, and our bodies moved in sync.

Pleasure soared through me as we quickened our pace. Our emotions intermingled, both of us feeling the other person completely. As my ecstasy increased, his did in tandem, proving our souls were interconnected.

He thrust underneath me, and I swiveled my hips, sensation taking over my body.

Sitting up, he repositioned me on his lap, grabbing my waist while his mouth covered my breast. As his fingers dug into my skin, I moved faster, both of us desperately racing toward our climax.

I cupped his head, pulling him away from my breast, and kissed him again. I wanted to taste, smell, and feel him. As his tongue swept into my mouth, my orgasm rocked through my body. I responded eagerly to the kiss, and he shuddered through his own climax.

After who-knew-how long, our bodies stilled, both of us completely satiated. I rolled off him and cuddled into his arms.

As my eyes began to close, a knock sounded at our door. Cassidy called out, "They were able to get hold of the woman, and she's going to deliver the message. They're on their way back. I just wanted to let you know all is well so you two can get some sleep. We can talk more in the morning. Good night."

Any remaining tension ebbed from Thorn, and we fell fast asleep in each other's arms.

THE NEXT MORNING, Thorn's weight left the bed, stirring me. I opened my eyes to find him dressing his gorgeous body.

I pouted. *What are you doing? You're taking away my eye candy.*

His brows lifted. *There's still some eye candy left.* He gestured to his face and tilted his head.

Sure. I rolled my eyes, fighting to keep the corners of my mouth from tipping upward. *I'll pretend to agree.*

His mouth dropped open, and he patted his chest. *Are you saying you only find my body attractive?*

Your face isn't bad. The smile broke through. *I mean...it'll do.*

It'll do? He gasped and jumped on the bed, his fingers digging into my sides.

I giggled, jerking away. My sides were the ticklish part of my body. He straddled me, locking me in place.

Tears streamed down my face from my laughter. *Please stop. I can't take much more.*

Just like that, he stilled. "I guess, but just so you know, I won't be putting out for a while. Not until you begin appreciating this face."

"Lies." I squinched my nose. "You can't hold out on me." I lowered my hand and grabbed his crotch, which was already hard from him being on top of me.

"Fine," he scoffed, then kissed me. "But I'll have you know I love every part of you, including your foul breath."

I slapped my hands over my mouth, my face burning. I blew out and sniffed. "*Fine,* I'll go brush my teeth."

"I was just teasing." Chuckling, he pulled my hands away from my face and kissed me again. *I had to get you back somehow.*

Unable to refuse, I kissed him. *And I was teasing, too. Your eyes were the first thing that drew me to you.*

He winked. *I know.*

"Where were you sneaking off to?" I wiggled out from underneath him. Though he was aroused, he had something else on his mind.

"To find Vlad and Errol and learn the details." He stood and helped me out of the bed. "I felt bad not waiting up, but having time with you was more important."

My heart swelled. "Let me go with you." I hurried to my feet, threw on my clothes, and ran my fingers through my hair. "I'm hungry, anyway."

Taking my hand, he led me into the kitchen. The cheery shamrock cabinets greeted me. The kitchen was spotless, but the smell of bacon and eggs lingered, indicating Cassidy had already cooked and cleaned up breakfast. I glanced at the time and noticed it was after ten.

"They're finally awake." Elliott sighed and placed a hand to his forehead. "It's been days."

"Are you having a *Gone with the Wind* moment?" I teased as I opened the refrigerator in search of something for Thorn and me to eat.

"Sis, I didn't fart." Elliott dropped his hand on the wooden table. "I would own it if I did."

Thorn broke into a fit of laughter. *Your brother doesn't know much beyond video games and random gross facts, like peeing on fires.*

Don't remind me. I grabbed some bacon and two cold biscuits.

"She meant the movie, dumbass," Eva deadpanned. "I swear, I love video games as much as you do, but I still know the romance classics."

"Says the person who thought *Super Mario Kart* was the best game ever." Elliott crossed his arms. "So I don't take offense."

"I was *six*." She grabbed a napkin from the middle of the table and tossed it at him. "You thought *Donkey Kong* was an epic game!"

"Fuck, it *is* epic." He lifted a hand. "Two badass gorillas or some stupid cart that slides on bananas. Please, you make me sick."

Where were Sol and Mindy? I needed them to distract Eva and Elliott from their bickering. "Where is everyone?"

"Outside, training with the oldies." Elliott smirked.

"Elliot!" I slammed the door shut and glared. "They are your elders."

"Please. Tia is an instigator, and Belinda pretends to be offended but eggs her on. Let's not even talk about Merlin and Ryu. Those two are worse than me. They took over my gaming system this morning until Vlad and Theron came upstairs and told them they needed to train with the others." Elliott rubbed his hands together. "And calling them oldies riles Tia up, which serves her right for telling Mindy I was staring at her all morning."

Oh, dear goodness. I opened a cabinet and pulled out two plates, which I covered with biscuits and tons of bacon.

"Why aren't you two with them, and where's Peter?" Thorn asked as he placed a hand on my back, our connection buzzing.

"Vlad and Theron made Peter go with them, and El and I stayed behind because we wanted to talk to you." Eva stood, running her hands down her legs. "I've made my decision about becoming a dragon."

My heart hammered. This was it. And I wasn't sure whether I wanted her to say yes or no.

<h1 style="text-align:center">CHAPTER THIRTEEN</h1>

THORN BRUSHED his fingers against my back. A *zing* flowed through me, and calm settled into my heart, slowing it to a normal pace. No matter what she decided, I'd respect it as long as she was making the decision for the right reasons.

"Oh, my gosh," Elliot gritted out. "Just come out with it. She wants to change, so, like, let's do this thing." He stood and patted her shoulders while waggling his brows. "Thorn, lay your glowy hands on me. I've been ready for weeks."

"Uh..." Thorn's nose wrinkled. "I don't even know how to respond to that. For one, I'm certain you're trying to make this pervy. And two, I'm not changing you until your sister gives me the final okay, and we'll do it *outside*. I have a feeling that as soon as you feel your dragon, you'll try to shift, and we're not messing up this house."

Leave it to Elliott to speak on Eva's behalf. I rolled my eyes and focused on my sister. Before I could say anything, Elliott started up again. He placed a hand on his heart, and his bottom lip shook way too hard, like he was being overly dramatic. "I must say, I thought Everly and I shared *everything*."

I groaned, while Thorn's mouth dropped open. I was certain

Thorn hadn't thought Elliott would take this further, but my brother loved pushing the envelope.

Wanting to save my mate, I pointed a finger at my brother and popped our biscuits into the microwave. "Sure. I'll share everything with you once I play a round under your profile on the PS."

"You bish." His eyes bulged. "You wouldn't."

"Sharing everything would also include your gamer profile and stats so I can play the higher levels I can't get to on my own." I pressed the buttons on the microwave and hit start, my stomach grumbling for breakfast.

You play dirty, Thorn connected as his humor wafted between us. *I love it. Don't ever change...not even with me.* He walked behind me, wrapped his arms around my waist, and kissed the tender spot on my neck, causing goosebumps to rush over me.

"Fine." Elliott scoffed. "Just take me outside and change me. I was teasing, but Everly ruined *all* my fun."

With Elliott deflated, I'd chat with Eva before he started back up again. One thing about my brother—he rebounded quickly. "Is it true?" Needing to see my sister, I begrudgingly pulled away from Thorn. Every tic, every eye flicker, every...well...everything.

She rubbed her lips and nodded. "Yeah, I've decided to become a dragon. I just wanted to think everything through."

Smart. That was what I'd wanted them to do, but I had to make sure she wanted to change for the right reasons. "May I ask why?"

"It would be easier." She spread out her arms and gestured around the room. "We can help you fight, and we won't need as much protection."

Those were good reasons but temporary ones. Something must have triggered her to take the plunge. The microwave beeped, and I opened the door and handed Thorn the plate while I grabbed the other biscuit. *I'm going to talk to her alone. I need to make sure Elliott isn't pressuring her into this.* I didn't think my brother would, not on purpose, but his enthusiasm could be overwhelming.

I'll keep him entertained, but you owe me. I'll take payment in sexual favors, he replied and kissed my cheek before speaking out loud. "I don't know, man. I was thinking *Super Mario Kart* is a pretty badass game. You race other people and get a trophy at the end of it."

Elliott's jaw almost hit the table. "Are you *fucking* serious? If you are, there is something fundamentally wrong with you." He proceeded to launch into a dissertation about why my mate was horribly wrong about everything in life, how the games he viewed as badass hindered his ability to think through other things properly and he needed to fix the error of his ways.

I took a bite out of my biscuit, wanting to do something other than laugh and make this situation worse. I glanced at Eva, who rubbed her temples as if Elliott were giving her a headache. When I caught her eye, I nodded toward the door leading out back. She stood and hurried to the door. As we walked outside, I glanced over my shoulder and saw Elliott gesturing everywhere and Thorn's eyes glazing over.

Yeah, I owed him for this, but I had to admit, I was surprised he knew as much as he did about *Super Mario Kart*. There was still so much I didn't know about him, even though I felt like we'd never been apart.

Outside, we could see the group about two hundred yards away in the open field, training. Eva's eyes darted to Sol immediately. Everyone had paired off, including Vlad with Peter. They were all sparring in human form.

Eva must have felt me watching her because she cleared her throat and put her hands in her jeans pockets. "Is something wrong?"

That was a loaded question. An easier question would be what was right. "I wanted to talk to you where Elliott couldn't answer on your behalf." I took another bite of my biscuit and went to lean against the trunk of a white dogwood tree. "I want to make sure you really do want to change. Once you get a dragon, Thorn might not be able to take it back. He couldn't with me." Which still didn't make sense, since he had no trouble removing a born dragon shifter's magic. Maybe he couldn't remove a dragon he'd created.

"Yeah, I'm sure." She nodded. "This is right for me."

"What made you change your mind?" I wondered if it was because of a certain dragon shifter. If they weren't fated mates, he could stumble upon his and crush Eva. From what Thorn had said, fated mates were rare and something to be treasured, but given the people around us, I was beginning to think they were less rare than anyone thought.

Her cheeks reddened, giving me the answer without her saying anything.

"Look, I get you think Sol is cute, but changing for *him* isn't the answer." My appetite vanished. I didn't want to discourage her, but I had to protect her. "We've all seen how you hold hands, look at each other, and sneak away, and that's all fine. I want to see you smile, but if you take it to the next level, and you two don't work out, I don't want to see you hurt."

"I know." She closed her eyes, then opened them and focused on me. "I get it. That's one reason I didn't say yes right away when I met Sol—I still took time to think about it. Maybe it's not a good reason, but Ev, each day I'm around him, something inside me becomes more desperate for him. Hell, the first time I saw him, his eyes captivated me. It's like he can see right into my soul."

I froze. That was *exactly* how I'd felt when I'd first seen Thorn. "Eva—"

"Let me finish," she said forcibly, then winced. "Please."

That was why we'd come outside—for me to listen. I nodded and forced myself to eat.

She huffed, pushing her long hair over her shoulders. "I get your concern, and I'll be the first to admit that if this were you, I'd be asking the same questions. But I don't want to lie. Yes, a major reason is Sol. He helped me get there. I don't want to have a life he isn't in, but it's more than that. I knew the answer wasn't a flat yes or no even before I met Sol." She wrung her hands as grunts from the group's training sounded in the background. "When Drake took us, I'd never felt so helpless, even more so than when Mom died. Not only could I not save you, but I couldn't even help myself."

She shivered, and though I itched to hug her, I forced myself to remain in place, knowing she needed to get it all out.

"I didn't say yes immediately like Elliott did because that level of change scares me. Will I even recognize myself afterward? That question keeps circling my head, despite everything else screaming I should do it. But as I've watched you become a stronger, more confident version of yourself, and after Sol came into the picture, that question lost its impact. So, am I saying yes today because of Sol? Maybe. But I *swear* I've known for a while that my answer would be yes all along. I needed time to accept it. He just got me there faster."

I exhaled. "Okay. I just need you to understand that even if you change, there's no guarantee the two of you will wind up together." Until she turned into a dragon, we wouldn't know if they were fated mates. I didn't want to make any false promises just because I suspected the answer was yes.

She wrapped her arms around herself. "Is that even close to what it was like between you and Thorn when you were human?"

"Yes." I wouldn't lie to her. I couldn't. That wouldn't be right. "It was like I could sense the type of person he was, even though he'd kidnapped Saphira and me. I wanted to be around him even while fearing him at the same time. I thought I was getting Stockholm syndrome, but it was our souls reaching out to each other. But Eva, that's supposed to be rare, so I don't want to get your hopes up in case—"

"In case it's not." She exhaled and dropped her arms. "I get that, and thank you for not lying. I promise I would've come to this decision regardless. I wouldn't do it just for a man."

I took the last bite of my biscuit and pulled her into a hug. "I believe you." My eyes burned as my vision clouded. I was going to cry if I didn't pull myself together, and that was the last thing I wanted to do. I was happy she'd confided in me, something I didn't think she would've done before Drake took us. "We'd better get in there and save Thorn. He was distracting Elliott so we could talk."

"Oh, yes. That man is a saint." Eva's irises twinkled. "Just for the record, I'm so glad he's my brother-in-law. He is completely in love with you, and that's why he puts up with Elliott. He deserves a medal."

Laughing hard, I said, "Maybe, but he did call you and Elliott his family earlier, and he meant it. So yeah, he's a keeper."

Before going in, I scanned the group again and grinned when I saw Peter sitting on the ground, refusing to stand and continue to fight. For some reason, our decision not to change him brought me comfort. At least I knew what to expect from him.

The two of us entered the house to find Elliott still talking. Thorn was staring at the table, his empty plate and two steaming cups of coffee in front of him.

My heart fluttered. *Is one of those for me?* I desperately needed a cup.

Yes. Although I'm contemplating drinking it if you don't hurry. He took a sip from his blue mug, leaving the purple one for me. *Your brother has almost put me back to sleep.*

I know one way to distract him—if you're willing to change them while the others are preoccupied. I grabbed my cup.

Let's do it. Thorn nodded. *Honestly, I'll be more comfortable when they're dragons. And they'll need time to acclimate.*

Another good point. They'd need to learn how to fly and get comfortable with their dragons. "Who wants to change into a dragon first?"

Elliott's head snapped up so fast, I wasn't sure how it hadn't fallen off. "Uh...*me.*" He pounded the table. "I said yes the moment it was offered, so you'd better change me before *her.*" He gestured to his sister.

We'd better do this before Peter gets back. If what I'd seen outside was any indication, he'd be plodding in here shortly now that everyone knew Thorn and I were up. I almost asked if Peter was aware of their decision, but I stopped myself. It didn't matter. They were legal adults, and with the danger we were in, it was smart to change them so they could better protect themselves.

Elliott rushed through the kitchen to the front of the house. "Let's go out this way so Dad won't know what's going on. Better to ask for forgiveness than permission."

Unfortunately, that was my answer.

We hurried outside, and Thorn had no problem changing either of my siblings. It was strange because his hands glowed, and the friction still wafted through our bond, but not like before. I sensed he was no longer afraid to use his magic.

"Okay, both of you are done." Thorn dropped his hands from Eva's shoulders.

I wouldn't have known they were changed if he hadn't announced it. But then Elliott clutched his head and groaned, "It's like something's inside me, trying to control me."

"It's your dragon." I remembered how unsettling it had been to feel a new being inside my body, like the dragon and I had two different sets of thoughts. "You can spend time acclimating to it later. We need to see if Mindy and Sol are your fated mates. If they are, they can help you shift more easily."

Thorn ran a hand down his face. "I need to fly, too. My dragon is getting restless, but we'll have to keep a close watch so any nearby warriors don't see us."

The sound of footsteps approached from behind me. Vlad's group was heading back, likely for lunch, though Thorn and I had just eaten breakfast.

Sol and Mindy glanced our way and stopped in their tracks. Behind me, Elliott and Eva gasped, and hope flared in my chest.

Were both sets of them soulmates?

When they rushed past Thorn and me with a desperate look in their eyes, I knew without question: my siblings had fated mates.

Thorn took my hand and led me to the house. I almost wanted to stay and watch, but I relented. They deserved time alone with each other. Who knew what would happen when we met Uther?

On that note, Thorn and I headed inside to learn what would happen next.

THE NEXT DAY, our group drove four hours south of Nashville, Indiana, to Nashville, Tennessee, where Vlad and Errol had decided to meet Uther. It was a large city and a public place where we could monitor our surroundings and ensure no dragon would be flying overhead, watching us or setting a trap. Once we met Uther, we'd tell him to follow us west to Kingston Springs, Tennessee, where Theron, Sol, Mindy, Hydra, Eva, Elliott, Saphira, Brenton, and Tyson were guarding the backup meeting spot.

I'd thought that Eva and Elliott might argue to stay with me, but they were too excited about flying. Elliott was determined to fly so fast that he could go back in time to harass his past self. They also wanted to stay with their mates, even though neither had completed their bond...yet.

Peter was staying at the house with Tia, Belinda, Merlin, and Ryu. We didn't want him learning who our allies might be and figuring out another way to cause problems, especially since his, my, Eva's, and Elliott's faces were splashed on the news everywhere. The new additions to the group had offered to watch him. Tia liked to remind Peter that both his kids were now dragons. She enjoyed his extreme displeasure.

That left Vlad, Cassidy, Errol, Thorn, and me. We'd split up into the two Suburbans. I'd wanted to be part of the meet and greet, but we couldn't risk someone recognizing me from the news. So Thorn, Cassidy, and I were in a separate Suburban parked beside a Target, where we could watch the whole thing.

Errol and Vlad stood by one of the large red concrete balls outside the store, waiting for Uther. The idea was to get him out of his car, drive by like we were pulling out of the lot, and make sure no one was in his vehicle while he was distracted.

Cassidy was in the driver's seat with Thorn and me in the middle row. Of the three of us, Uther would be least likely to notice her.

I glanced at the time. It was approaching eight o'clock, and the sun was setting. He should be here any second. I fidgeted in my seat, and Thorn placed a hand on my arm.

"Everything will be fine," he assured me.

Vlad had parked their rented white Honda Civic nearby. We'd leased it under another name, so if this was a trap, our Suburbans would be safe. If something went sideways, the plan was simple: we'd meet a few miles south, the two of them would jump into a Suburban, and we'd head out. Cassidy and Vlad would use their fated-mate connection to communicate where to go.

A black four-door sedan pulled into the lot a little too quickly. My eyes narrowed in on the driver, and my breath caught. It was Uther, and there was a black Tahoe right behind him.

My heart dropped. I'd hoped this wasn't a trap. We needed his help. But the presence of a second vehicle couldn't be a coincidence.

CHAPTER FOURTEEN

A KNOT FORMED in my stomach as my lungs struggled to work. "He's here, but another car is tailing him."

I'd hoped I wasn't wrong about Uther. I'd seen the side of him that didn't like what Drake was doing, but I also understood that people would do anything to protect their own flesh and blood. I would've bet that he would try to warn us. Maybe he had and we'd missed it.

"I'm letting Vlad know." Cassidy hung her head. "I'd wished this would work out, and now we have to get away."

"No." Thorn shook his head. "We keep the plan the same. If they follow us, that'll give us more people to question—as long as more don't follow them. Be on the lookout. I'll call Theron to give them a heads up when we're heading that way."

My belly gurgled uncomfortably. "That's risky." Everyone I loved was part of our group, and some of us, if not all, could get hurt.

Thorn looked at me and chuckled dryly. "The tables have turned."

My brows furrowed. "What?" As far as I knew, we were in the same situation, one we'd attempted to prepare for.

"Normally, it's you trying to convince me to take a risk." He turned back to keep watch over the situation. "That's all."

I crossed my arms, too scared to take my attention away from Uther and the trailing vehicle. I doubted they would take a stand here, but the warriors could have guns. I forced myself to breathe. "Do you care to elaborate?"

"I was just getting ready to." He chuckled again, but the sound was tense. "We have no leads on Drake. No idea what his next move will be. All we have are vague ideas. That's why we risked coming here, and that shouldn't change now. They don't know our numbers, and this is the smallest group they'll send to remain incognito so we don't see the trap coming."

That was a good point, but there could be more vehicles nearby. If Uther left for our secondary location, we'd get a good idea of numbers by following him to see if anyone pulled in behind him. Worst case, we could abort the plan and find an opportunity for Vlad and Errol to get away.

"They could call in where they're heading, or they could have trackers." Cassidy's hand remained on the wheel.

With that many eyes on us, we couldn't risk driving by. Their windows were tinted as well, so it wasn't like we could get an accurate head count. My gaze remained glued on the parking lot entrance, looking for other vehicles that could be holding warriors.

"I know. That's why we have to move fast when we reach the others. Even if we just grab one of them and take off." Thorn tensed. "This isn't ideal, but it's the best chance we have to fight Drake. We won't win unless we get on level footing with him, and even then, it might not work. He has limitless resources and a way to control the message that gets out to the thunders. *All* the power is in his hands, and we need to take some from him or skew it our way."

His words were like a blast of cold water. I'd known we were at a disadvantage, but he'd spelled it out so blatantly that there was no way we were going to win unless we took risks. Worse, if we lost, we'd run out of places to hide. This was potentially our one shot. "He's right." Denying it would be like blow-drying an oil painting—futile and messy.

I could see his smirk out of the corner of my eye. He was eating this up.

Bite me, I connected, pushing my humor and annoyance toward him.

Gladly, but when we get home. I don't mind showing affection in front of Mom, but we have warriors in our midst. Even I have boundaries. He glanced back out the window.

Two could play this game. Though I knew nothing would happen, I couldn't let him say something like that and drop it.

Uther was strolling up to Errol and Vlad, and we were safe—for now—so I leaned over, keeping my gaze on the entrance behind us, and brushed his crotch ever so subtly.

He growled faintly. *Then again, maybe I don't.*

I snickered, surprised I could be somewhat happy in this moment, but I shouldn't have been. Thorn made everything better. I moved my hand, knowing we didn't need more distractions.

You were gloating, so I had to give you hell. Some of the tension uncurled in my stomach. So far, no other suspicious vehicles had entered the lot. That didn't mean we were safe, but at least they hadn't come barreling in, trying to force Errol and Vlad into a car.

The humor between us ebbed as he connected, *Sorry if it came off that way. It just felt nice, needing to convince you of something for a change. I love you even more for being able to admit I was right.*

My heart ached. He'd been dealing with emotions that I'd never fully understand, and he was working through them and seeing things I couldn't. *And I love you for wanting to protect us and your people.*

It just took me time to come around and understand you were right. Thorn leaned forward, toward the passenger front seat. *With Drake in charge, we'll never be safe.* Unease filtered through the bond, and I turned forward to see that Uther had his arms crossed and was frowning.

"What's going on?" Thorn asked.

Cassidy glanced over her shoulder. "Uther isn't thrilled about following us to another location. Apparently, he had a plan of his own, but he conceded."

I grimaced. "Did he say anything about the other vehicle?"

"No." Cassidy tapped her fingers on the steering wheel. "We're all hiding stuff."

Neither side trusted the other. I understood that Uther might feel conflicted about meeting with us, but hell, he was the one who'd contacted us.

Errol and Vlad headed to the new rental car, while Uther went back to his sedan. Vlad pulled out of the spot and headed toward the exit.

We had to be on alert to ensure no one else was following us. My gut churned. What if I didn't pick up on someone following us and we got hurt?

What's wrong? Thorn connected, his gorgeous eyes scanning me, and my heart skipped a beat. *Do you see something?* His concern added to mine, and my chest constricted.

I had to get a hold of myself, or I'd have a panic attack. The last time I was close to feeling like this was when I'd been struggling with Mom's death. Knowing that if this meeting went wrong, everyone I loved would be at risk had the helpless feeling swirling inside me all over again. *Just worried I might miss something.*

This is a group effort, he replied, taking my hand in his. *If something goes wrong, it's all our fault, not just yours.*

That didn't make me feel better, but if I didn't get control of my emotions, I would miss things because they were ruling me and not my logic. I forced the agonizing sensation away. *You're right.*

Vlad, Errol, and Uther drove past us in their respective cars with our group leading the way. Neither Vlad nor Errol glanced at us, and Uther was too focused on staring in his rearview to notice us.

That was good.

A minute later, the Tahoe pulled out of its spot and trailed behind them, keeping fifty yards between themselves and Uther.

Cassidy followed the same protocol and stayed back the same distance, and I could only pray the Tahoe didn't notice us. We didn't have to keep up with them to learn where we were going, but we had to stay kind of close to see if anyone was also following them.

I gripped Thorn's hand more tightly, realizing this was harder for me than anything else before. I felt helpless sitting in the back seat of a vehicle, waiting and watching. In every other tense situation, we'd been moving or fighting. I'd had the illusion of control, or at least my mind had been preoccupied.

Pressing buttons on the dashboard, Cassidy called Theron on the Suburban's Bluetooth. It rang once before Theron answered. She filled him in as Thorn and I watched the cars between us and the Tahoe. If more people joined them, they wouldn't expect us to be behind them, so they would fill in between Uther's vehicle and ours, likely behind the Tahoe.

The two of them hung up with a plan. Hydra would stay near the vehicles with Theron's phone in case someone saw anything or we needed to call with an update while the rest of them shifted and scouted out the area. Either way, Hydra could use her fated-mate connection with Theron to get the messages across.

Twilight was upon us, which meant humans would have a harder time making out the dragons and hopefully think they were a flock of birds.

A maroon Ford Explorer pulled into the lane beside us and slowed, merging as we got onto the interstate heading west. The woman in the vehicle was taller than average and had long, silky blonde hair. Could she be a warrior? Judging by how quickly she'd rushed up, I had to at least consider it.

We turned onto the interstate, and Cassidy sped up. Breaking my gaze from the Explorer, I noted that we'd fallen behind and she was trying to catch up.

The woman beside us did the same and glanced at me. I jerked my head down, trying to hide—not that it would do any good. The windows were tinted. It wasn't like she could make me out, even with dragon eyesight.

What's wrong? Thorn connected. *Do you see something?*

I don't know yet. There's a woman in the car next to us, but I'm not sure if she's following them. I bit my bottom lip, trying to calm my raging nerves. *Do you?*

He shook his head. *Not yet.*

At least that was something.

The Explorer dropped behind us, the woman focusing forward, and we barreled toward a split in the highway.

Which vehicle is it? Thorn leaned over the space between our two captain's chairs to look out my window.

Just as he did, the interstate split, and the woman turned east, opposite where we were headed.

My body sagged as anxiety melted away. Although we weren't out of danger, I was relieved that another warrior wasn't following us. *She went east instead of west. It was a false alarm.*

More restlessness swirled through our connection.

Do you see something? I asked, anxiety clawing in my chest again. Wow, that peace had been short-lived. Thorn didn't freak out unless he thought we were under direct threat.

No, he answered as he released my hand and rubbed his legs. *That's the problem. I'd expected us to spot at least one more car by now.*

I scanned the interstate again. A white truck and a blue SUV caught my attention. They'd been near us for a while and had split west with us, but nothing seemed suspicious about the vehicles.

He clucked his tongue. *Maybe we're being followed, but they have a tracker on Uther's vehicle so they're staying far behind. They might suspect we have our own backup.*

That was something I hadn't considered, and the strategy had *Drake* written all over it. Luckily, we were leading them into a public section of woods. *We need to call Hydra so she knows what we're up against.*

Thorn nodded and filled in Cassidy. Once again, she called Hydra, and Thorn voiced his concerns. When the call ended, we settled into silence.

―――

ALL TOO SOON, we neared the parking lot in the woods where we'd planned to meet. If dragons came, we'd have the forest to cover us since there was no overnight camping in the area.

Hydra had called ten minutes ago to confirm the parking lot was empty, now that darkness was thick around us. Theron and Brenton had taken the Suburban and Mindy's car to a nearby parking area hidden by the numerous red maples and cypress trees that were lush and green in the late spring.

Each moment we'd gotten closer, Thorn had grown twitchier, putting me on edge from our shared bond. I tried to practice my yoga breathing, but it was futile. I was too focused on watching every damn car that passed us. Yoga wasn't just a physical technique. Emotional health was equally important, and I couldn't find my center.

We turned down a road and switched off our headlights as Vlad and Errol's car disappeared into the parking lot with Uther on their tail. The Tahoe slowed to a stop twenty feet away from the turn, allowing the trees to hide us, and turned off its engine, likely so that Vlad and Errol wouldn't hear or see the vehicle.

My stomach bunched until I swore a tourniquet had been tied around it, cutting off the blood flow. They were trying to hide their presence, and what terrified me was that it might have worked if we hadn't followed them.

"Let's sneak up on them." Cassidy turned off our vehicle. "Stay in the woods and hurry. We need to get there before they get out, or they could hear us." She opened the glove box. We'd stashed three guns inside. She pulled out two and passed them back to us.

Hands shaking, I took the weapon. I didn't know how to shoot a gun, but I could point and pull the trigger. I knew that much. When we got home, I'd need Thorn or Vlad to teach me how to shoot for real.

Cassidy and I climbed out, with Thorn following me. He murmured, "Don't shut the door in case they opened theirs at the same time. They can't see the open-door light, but they could hear the door shut."

Good idea. And if we needed to rush back to the Suburban, we could jump right in without pause.

We hit the woods to the left of the Tahoe, stepping in deeply enough that the lush branches would hide us for as long as the occupants stayed in human form.

With each step I took, my heart pounded louder in my ears, and the cold metal of the gun had my skin crawling. I kept expecting them to open their doors and try to sneak behind Errol and Vlad, but no one had made a move...yet.

A few owls hooted in the distance, and a flying squirrel jumped from branch to branch right above us. When we reached the side of the Tahoe, we all took a tentative step forward, but we couldn't make out anything through the tinted windows.

There was no telling how many warriors were in the car.

Thorn's jaw twitched, and his anxiety peaked. My blood whooshed through me.

The driver's door opened.

Thorn whispered so low I almost didn't hear him, "Surprising them is our best option. On the count of three, we run and surround them."

Another door opened, and Thorn lifted a hand, raising one finger...then two...and three.

I took off, my lungs seizing, desperate to get there before I froze.

CHAPTER FIFTEEN

HAND SHAKING, I kept the gun at my side. Holding it felt so unnatural that lifting it before I had to could be disastrous.

Out of the corner of my eye, I noticed Cassidy run around the back of the Tahoe to the other side. I remained focused on the side closest to me.

Thorn stayed beside me, and I knew why. He could feel my emotions. He knew I didn't feel comfortable doing this...at all.

Wings flapped overhead, and I could make out two distinct sets. I didn't risk looking up to see who the dragons were, but they were currently my favorite people.

When the driver stepped out of the vehicle, Thorn pointed his gun at him.

"Drop your weapons. Now," Thorn growled. "How many of you are there?"

"Shit," the driver rasped. "This isn't how it's supposed to go down."

"Yeah, we know. You wanted to get the jump on us instead." Thorn's jaw clenched, and his eyes flicked to the woman in the front passenger seat. "Answer me. How many people are in this vehicle?"

Saphira's butterscotch dragon landed in front of the Tahoe, and Tyson's maroon dragon landed behind Thorn and me. With the vehicle too close to the trees, there was no room to land on the other side next to Cassidy.

Footsteps from the parking lot ran toward us, and I heard Uther yell, "Wait! Don't hurt them."

He might as well not have said anything. Thorn, Cassidy, Saphira, Tyson, and I were on high alert. If the warriors had been hoping to surprise us, their attempt had been futile, and this was what they'd say.

"How many?" Thorn asked again. "This is the last time I'll ask you."

The back passenger door in front of me swung open, and the driver growled, "Chandra, close the door *now*."

I grabbed the edge of the door, yanked it all the way open, and lifted my gun. My hands shook so hard, I was surprised I didn't drop it.

The woman froze. Her cognac-brown eyes widened.

"Hands up," I said, barely above a whisper. The words rubbed my throat raw. This felt *wrong*.

She immediately lifted her hands. A strand of her auburn hair fell out of her ponytail and into her face, and her bottom lip quivered.

This woman didn't look like a warrior. She was tall, which was the dragon norm, but her face held a softness that most warriors lacked, like she was still innocent. Hell, even my face didn't have that innocence anymore, and I'd been fighting for a month, if that.

"Listen. This is one big misunderstanding," Chandra said.

Then the driver cut in, "We're here because we need your help."

There was no doubt that the driver and front passenger were warriors. The guy had a square-cut jaw and muscular arms, and the way his charcoal eyes scanned the area for more of us screamed experience. His confident stance, despite having a gun pointed at him, sealed the deal.

The female warrior had the same sort of composure. Her long, straight, dark brown hair was pulled into a low ponytail, and her dark chocolate eyes looked flat and emotionless, like she was assessing every possible scenario.

Behind me, Tyson snarled, but I wasn't sure if it was from curiosity or a threat.

Uther rounded the edge of the woods on the road that led into the parking lot. Vlad and Errol were on his tail as they reached us.

Smoke trickling from her nostrils, Saphira prepared for a fight.

"Oh, gods," Chandra groaned, pulling my attention back to her. I caught a flash of long golden hair in the back seat of the car. A child called out, "Are they going to hurt us?"

A lump formed in my throat, and suddenly, I was looking into cobalt irises surrounded by thick black eyelashes. A girl no older than six stared right back at me from behind Chandra. I lowered my weapon. I couldn't put a child through this.

Cassidy gasped. "Why do you have a little girl back there?" She swung her gun toward the warrior woman sitting in the front passenger seat.

"Wait. *Please*." Uther's face twisted in agony. Errol and Vlad now had his arms restrained.

The little girl's eyes stayed locked on me. She scooted forward as a middle-aged woman in the middle row on the passenger side grabbed her hand. This woman also had long, straight, dark brown hair and dark brown eyes. She was almost an exact replica of the woman in the front passenger seat, like they were twins, but her features weren't as harsh as those of her clone.

"Are you Everly?" the child asked, and tried to wiggle out of the middle-aged woman's arms to reach me. "You have to help my daddy. Listen to him, *please*."

I forgot how to breathe. "Are you Uther's daughter?"

She nodded, and when I glanced at Uther, a tear trickled down her face. "Yes, I'm Reece. He said we needed to come here and meet you. That you reminded him of my momma and that you would protect me."

My heart broke, and Thorn's tumult of emotions swirled between us.

"What is she talking about?" Thorn asked while he kept his gun trained on the driver.

Uther dropped to his knees. "We aren't here to attack you. I should have known you guys would be wary, but I wanted to make sure you were willing to listen to me before I brought up the others."

Thorn lowered his gun a few inches but not enough that if they made a move, he couldn't still shoot. "Yeah, you should've. This could be a trap."

"It's not." Uther hung his head. "I wouldn't risk my daughter's life like that."

Saphira turned and hissed in Uther's face.

She didn't trust him, that much was clear. Even Thorn's distrust floated into me, but Uther's words tugged at me, making me hesitate.

I'd heard how much he loved his kid. "You might not have a choice. This might be the only way you can save her—by turning us in."

"Uther isn't the only one Drake has leverage over. He's threatening all of us with people we love," the woman in the front seat said as she lifted her hands, too.

They were making sure we knew they weren't armed...that they weren't a threat. Something inside me already trusted them, but the others weren't convinced yet.

I took a step toward the vehicle, and Tyson edged a wing in front of me.

"I handled this poorly. I see that now." Uther's remorse sounded sincere. "I should've been forthright when we got to Target, but I didn't see you, Everly. You're the only one I know I can trust, and I didn't want to risk Reece. So...I asked where you were, and when Vlad and Errol insisted I come here, I assumed it was because you and Thorn were waiting to talk with me. I...I knew you would have people watching us, but I thought you'd be part of the party we were meeting with here. Now we look like we can't be trusted, but I did this because our time here is very limited. Our vehicles are being tracked."

I clenched my teeth so hard, my jaw ached. His story made sense, and it wasn't like he could've told me this over the phone since we'd used Errol's contact to send him the location.

"Why should we believe a word you say?" Thorn growled. "Talk to me, not my mate. You're pulling on her heartstrings, and it doesn't take more than a minute in her presence to realize what a kind, sympathetic woman she is."

"Fine." Uther straightened his shoulders as if he weren't being gripped on both sides. "I protected your mate more than you realize when she was captured. Drake put the fear of the gods into us, saying that if we treated Everly with too much kindness—or even *looked* at her kindly—and if any of us showed her any warmth, there would be hell to pay. But even with those threats, I protected her the best I could by deflecting Falkor and Ladon when they wanted to harass her through Eva or enter the room while they were sleeping. I did all I could while keeping my daughter safe, but I want to do more. That's why Jerry, Gemma, and I brought our family here. Drake is trying to use them against us."

Vlad tilted his head. "You want to leave them with us." He wasn't asking a question but stating a fact.

"Yes." Uther nodded toward the Tahoe, and his gaze met Thorn's before he continued, "Jerry and Gemma"—he pointed at the man and woman in the front seats—"brought them here so they can stay with you. We're asking you to protect them and hide them with you. They can't protect themselves—that's why Drake's leverage is so effective."

Saphira shook her head and huffed.

Cassidy crossed her arms. "You can teach them to fight. You don't need us for that. For gods' sake, you three are warriors."

"Training won't help." Gemma closed her eyes. "If Kari could handle it, I would've trained her alongside me."

Then it clicked. "They're injured." My gaze swooped to the back seat, looking for signs. Narrowing my eyes, I saw how Reece had gotten out of Kari's grasp—Kari had a deformed hand. I didn't see anything different about Reece or Chandra, though.

"In the womb, you took most of the nutrients, and that's why Kari has that injury." All my premed classes were churning in my mind, highlighting info about twin pregnancies.

Gemma frowned. "Yes." Then she opened the car door and stood.

"That's not surprising, especially since it's hard for dragons to get pregnant. We definitely aren't built to carry twins." Cassidy lowered her gun. "In fact, I've never heard of twins before."

Neither had I, but that wasn't saying much.

"Chandra—my mate—her tail was injured when she first shifted by one of her thunder members. It was an accident." Jerry glanced over his shoulder adoringly. "She's fine unless she needs to move quickly."

This was heartbreaking. Just because these people were a little different, Drake considered them to be disposable and insignificant.

My attention kept slipping back to the little girl with the kind eyes and gorgeous blond hair that made her irises brighter. "What about Reece?"

Uther sighed. "She has a limp."

She was so young. Now my brain flicked through medical reasons for an uneven gait. Unless someone had done something to hurt her. My blood heated at the thought.

Uther bit his bottom lip. "Her mother, my *wife*, was human. Tashya struggled throughout the pregnancy and died giving birth. We had to cut Reece from her womb."

My mind flashed to Emily and baby Thorn. If my mate hadn't changed Emily and the baby had survived, he might have been in a similar state. "I'm so sorry." Reece had been so right when she'd said that her mom had protected her. Her mom had given up her life for Reece.

"But you aren't from the kingdom's lands." Errol released his hands and paced a few feet away. "How did you get involved with Drake?"

"It happened when he turned eighteen and started visiting the thunders." Uther rolled his shoulders, his attention flicking to his daughter, whom he could see through the front windshield. "He had an ulterior motive—he was trying to get an idea of the region-wide average age of our population to see if there were other weak dragons like"—he lifted his hands to do air quotes—"a 'useless' dragon who lived near the château. Unfortunately, we didn't know that, so when Reece ran out with her limp, we thought nothing of it. But he took notice immediately. When he told a warrior to grab her for questioning, I interceded and took the guard down. That was when he made the deal with me: come work for him, and Reece would be safe."

Tyson snarled, fire trickling from his mouth.

What Uther had said was horrible on so many levels. The "useless" dragon Drake had referred to must have been Tyson. And to consider killing a child? That was even more unforgivable. I hadn't thought I could think worse of Drake, but I'd been proven wrong...again.

"Similar story happened to us." Gemma leaned against the hood of the Tahoe. "Drake zeroed in on Kari's hand like it was a beacon."

That wasn't abnormal. People tended to focus on things that were different.

I believe them, I connected. I needed to know where Thorn was with this decision. His emotions were all over the place. He wasn't as angry anymore, but he hadn't put away his gun, either.

Me, too. Finally, he lowered his arms and scanned the group.

Tyson and Saphira both seemed more relaxed, but they weren't budging, and I was thankful to have them here in dragon form. If something happened, they'd be extremely helpful.

Now we needed to see if Uther would deliver on his promise. "You said you had information for us?" I pressed.

Even though Vlad had let Uther go, he hadn't moved away, and his gaze kept flicking around the group, searching for any signs of dishonesty or threat. I'd learned that about Vlad—he was always on guard. I suspected Cassidy getting kidnapped had stripped him of any sense of comfort he developed over the years.

"I do...*we do.*" Uther gestured at himself and the others. "But we need you to promise you'll protect our loved ones first. That they can go with you."

Our group glanced at one another. This was less than ideal, seeing as we couldn't talk about it before committing. This was a big ask. We'd be taking in three more people, and we were already struggling to stay hidden.

Vlad cleared his throat. "Isn't Drake watching your loved ones? He'll notice they're missing."

"If we work together, he won't know they're gone before we execute our plan." Uther's neck corded. "Reece lives at our old thunder home, and everyone wants her safe. These two live on the château grounds, but they're reclusive and stay in their house because Drake has made it clear he doesn't want them near him. As long as we don't give him a reason to suspect us, he shouldn't find out. But if he does...well, that's why we need them to stay with you—for protection."

What do you think? I needed to hear Thorn's thoughts before I shared mine.

We have no choice, Thorn answered and turned his head toward me. His irises lightened with all his emotions. *We have to take them in. We need Uther's help, and these three deserve a safe home where they'll be welcome.*

Vision blurring, I nodded. *I agree. They wouldn't hand them over willingly if Drake was involved. If Drake attacked, they'd be stuck in the crosshairs.*

Thorn glanced at his mom, who nodded and turned to Errol and Vlad. When they didn't counter, Thorn straightened his shoulders. "Fine. We'll keep them with us as long as we can check them and anything they brought for trackers."

Jerry exhaled, the lines on his face smoothing out. "Thank gods. I can't keep living with the worry that today will be the day when Drake snaps and kills her."

That was what I needed to hear. The genuine relief was justified and not something Drake would have wanted them to say. He didn't like people speaking ill of him.

"Let them out. Errol, Cassidy, and I will check them and their bags before taking them to our vehicle." Vlad marched to the back door of the Tahoe.

That meant Thorn and I would be staying behind to chat with the warriors. Gemma, Jerry, Uther, Thorn, and I moved to the front of the Tahoe so we wouldn't be in the way.

Uther removed a cell phone from his back pocket and handed it to Thorn. "I was told to give this to you. It's a burner phone that can't be traced. The numbers you need are already programmed into it. And Drake's coronation is in two weeks. If it happens, he'll have all the power he wants. For now, he has to work through red tape to get thunders to support his claim to the throne. Two weeks is all we have to make a plan and execute it. We don't have time for mistakes."

Two weeks.

That wasn't enough time.

"We've already stayed in this location too long." Jerry fidgeted. "If someone is watching us, they'll have questions. We need to go."

"Let's say a quick goodbye first," Uther replied and locked eyes with me. "Please make sure Reece is all right."

I placed my hand over my heart. "I promise."

"Okay, your first message is already on the phone. Now I'm going to say goodbye to my daughter."

Chandra, Kari, and Reece hurried toward the Suburban while Thorn swiped the phone.

My breath caught when I saw the name of the person who'd messaged. Maybe this was a trap after all.

CHAPTER SIXTEEN

I LOOKED AT THORN, feeling every ounce of his disbelief, anger, and longing. His face was twisted in the most heartbreaking combination of those three emotions, his eyes wide and his jaw clenched. He brushed a finger along the message like it was a life force.

The message was simple.

A Devastated Mother: I'm sorry for everything. Words can't express the depth of my regret and the love I've always had for you, but we don't have time for that. I'd rather say it in person, but what I have to say is that your father and I were so wrong about you. I know Drake killed Arman, and it's time for us to work together to ensure he doesn't lead our people. That right belongs to you. Let me know when you get this.

He must have longed for a message like this as a boy, and it was almost a slap in the face for him to receive it now.

I placed one hand on his arm, wanting him to know I was here for him in all ways...the ways that mattered. "Babe, we've got to move. If someone has pinged the spot, there's no telling where the warriors are. Some could be close. We can't risk staying any longer."

My heart squeezed uncomfortably. But I'd felt worse, and so had Thorn, and unfortunately, that had been because of *my* bad decision. The one where I'd sneaked away from him after completing our fated-mate bond to turn myself over to his brother.

That thought crushed my heart further. If not for the sound of my heartbeat, I'd have believed it had stopped.

Every bad thing that had happened since Thorn's parents abandoned him was because of Drake. Their parents had been content to let Thorn live in hiding, despite knowing where he was...until Drake had learned about him.

He sighed and put the phone in his back jeans pocket. "You're right. Let's move. We can figure out what to do about her."

My heart filled again. We were truly one, and we both knew it.

Hand in hand, we rushed toward the Suburban. Halfway to the vehicle, Uther, Jerry, and Gemma stepped into view, heading back to their own vehicles. Uther's eyes were glassy with unshed tears, and that vise tightened once more.

Uther stopped in front of me. He stared into my eyes as a tear trickled down his cheek. "Everly, please take good care of her. She's going to cling to you."

He didn't have to explain; his daughter already had. "I will. I promise." Not only would I protect her but every person Drake threatened.

"And that's the only reason I can walk away from her again." He wiped the tear as Jerry and Gemma continued to their Tahoe. "This has to end. I need to be with my daughter...to watch her grow up without worrying *he* might kill her. I need to be her father. She's already lost too much."

Thorn placed a hand on Uther's shoulder. "Everly and I will ensure she's always watched over. You have my word. You protected my mate, and I'll protect your daughter."

Taking a shaky breath, Uther turned to Thorn. He squinted as if Thorn were a puzzle, but then he nodded. "Tashya made me a better man, despite her not being a dragon. The two of us revolved around each other as if we *were* fated to be one. If she could do that to me, I can only imagine how a fated mate could influence someone else. I know the emotions and feelings are supposed to be stronger, though I don't know how that could be possible. But it has to be because the man standing before me isn't the same one who saved Everly from the château. It's a man I wouldn't mind following after all."

"That's the thing, though—I don't want to be *followed*. I just don't want Drake to destroy our kind...like my grandfather did." Thorn dropped his hand and scowled.

"Fair enough." Uther huffed and glanced back at the Suburban hidden by some trees. "Sometimes, it's the one who doesn't want to lead who makes the best leader. I'll call you later after we visit a thunder near here to see if they know anything about you. At least with the location you chose, there's one close enough to justify an excursion out here."

"Be safe." I'd always been fond of him, but now he was truly putting his neck on the line. I wasn't foolish to think it was for me; it was for his daughter and the future he wanted her to have, but he was still risking everything to better the lives of all the shifters. "If something goes sideways, let us know. We'll try to help you."

"I'm assuming the queen gave you the phone." Thorn's hope and trepidation swirled through our connection. "Do you believe we can trust her? Or is Drake putting her up to this? From the Dragonnet, it seems she's backing him."

"That's something you'll have to ask her." Uther lifted his hands. "Drake hasn't been hiding his nastiness since King Arman died, and everyone is at his mercy, trying to survive."

That made the situation worse. I didn't know why, but I'd foolishly hoped that wasn't the case. I'd hoped he would be kinder to those in his employ, given they were potentially loyal to him, but maybe his meanness was just the way he was. He felt entitled to everyone's loyalty, regardless of how he treated them, and he took what he wanted by force—boy, had I learned that the hard way.

"Be safe, Uther. And feel free to call us on a burner phone to check in with Reece. I'm sure she would love to talk to you," I said as I tugged Thorn toward the Suburban.

"You be careful, too, and I do have a burner phone. I saved the number on yours," Uther replied as Jerry and Gemma climbed into the Tahoe and shut their doors. The engine started.

That was good to know. We wouldn't be answering any calls we couldn't identify, and maybe not even all of those. We had to be careful about who we trusted. Even taking this burner phone was a huge risk, but if Uther, Jerry, and Gemma trusted the queen enough to bring it here and hand over their loved ones, that was enough for me.

Saphira and Tyson stood near the Suburban. Their bodies weren't as tense, but they were still being watchful.

My human ears picked up a few faint wing flaps, which meant dragons were flying overhead. I looked up and made out their forms high in the sky. If I'd been only human, I wouldn't have heard or seen them.

Cassidy was back behind the wheel with the engine running. Kari, Reece, and Chandra sat in the back row, the little girl sitting in the middle with Chandra on the passenger side and Kari on the driver's side. The trunk was open while Vlad and Errol searched their bags for trackers or whatever else could be used for locating our home base.

Thorn and I strolled to the back, and I said, "I'm assuming the three of them are clear."

"We checked them first." Vlad zipped up the bag and tossed it in the corner. "And the two bags I checked don't have anything they can use to track us."

"This one doesn't, either." Errol closed the dark purple bag and placed it on the other side. "As long as we can trust that they won't track the phone they just gave us, we're good to go."

It all came back to trusting the three warriors. Every time, I came to the same conclusion—we could—but a little fear still sat hard on my stomach, mainly because the queen was involved. But I'd seen how she'd reacted when she'd learned Thorn was alive. She'd been happy, so that was the only reason I was willing to continue with the plan.

Thorn placed an arm around my waist, anchoring me to him, and connected, *If you want us to change our minds about trusting them, we can.*

He was having similar thoughts. *I think they're all being honest... even the queen. I just worry about her loyalties remaining steady if she realizes Uther wants to kill Drake.* I hadn't put that piece together until he'd forced me to discuss it.

I agree, but I believe she doesn't want him as king. I remember the love she and King Arman had for each other. They were fated, one of the last few pairs to find each other back then...so I believe she's upset with him. Something like hope spread from my mate. *I think we do trust them, but we don't let our guard down completely. We schedule watches among the thunders so that if warriors come at us, we'll have a warning.*

You're right. This is our best chance, but that doesn't mean we can't take precautions. A plan like that did make me feel better.

"We continue on as planned," Thorn instructed. "But we'll make sure that two of us are always on watch, and we'll rotate the schedule."

"Good." Vlad shut the trunk. "I agree, but caution saves lives. Worst case, it gives us time to work on our observation skills, which we'll need when we attack the coronation."

A humorless laugh bubbled out of me unexpectedly. "First a wedding and now a coronation. He'll be more prepared this time around."

"Yes, he'll be paranoid." Errol nodded. "We can strategize back at the house."

House. Not *home.* The word choice didn't go unnoticed, but in fairness, the place didn't feel like home, either, other than when I was in Thorn's arms, especially with Peter always hovering nearby with a scowl on his face like he was trying to overhear everything.

Turning me toward the back door, Thorn said, "Saphira and Tyson, tell the others it's time to leave."

The two dragons nodded and took off just as the Tahoe turned onto the road, passing us. Uther's black sedan was right behind them.

I glanced skyward in time to see the hint of Elliott's hunter green dragon and Eva's olive green dragon high in the sky.

Just like before, Thorn and I sat in the middle row, where we couldn't be easily identified if a dragon happened to look through the windshield.

"Thank goodness we planned on keeping the car overnight." Cassidy glanced into the rearview mirror. "Otherwise, we wouldn't have had room for everyone."

We'd been torn initially, thinking we should drop the rental car off after the meeting so we wouldn't have to pay for another full day, but we'd realized that we wouldn't be able to get it back before the rental office closed. That was a blessing now.

I didn't want to say it was good luck in case jinxing was an actual thing. I hadn't believed in superstitions growing up—I was all about science and logic—but after learning about an entire supernatural world, I now questioned everything.

Cassidy put the car into drive and slowly turned around, heading back toward the interstate.

"Shouldn't we wait on the others?" I rubbed my hands on my shorts, trying to work out my jitters.

Shaking her head, Cassidy kept her focus on the road. "Vlad said to go on so we can get our new charges settled. We'll be rolling in around two in the morning."

We needed to get these women to their temporary home.

I looked into the back seat, and my lungs froze.

Chandra had her arms wrapped around herself with her legs folded up on the seat against her chest. She was staring at the holes in her jeans like she was in another world.

Beside Reece, Kari stared out the window. Her shoulders were hunched as if the weight of the world were pressing down on her, which it probably was. Every single person in our group had a target on their back, and the same man was hunting us all.

Then there was Reece. Her demeanor was slightly different. Instead of retreating into herself, she was staring right at me. Her eyes glistened, making her irises appear more navy, but there was something mixed in with the sadness...something like hope.

I tried to swallow unsuccessfully.

Thorn's forehead creased with concern, and he followed my gaze. "Are you okay?" A soft warmness swirled through our bond as he examined the girl.

"I am now." Reece nodded eagerly. "I mean, I miss Daddy. Every time I see him, we aren't together long, but I know Everly will fix it so we don't have to be apart anymore."

My head tilted back, and my breathing quickened. "I'll try my best. And one of the best ways to protect you and your daddy is to keep his identity a secret. We need to say we found you and that you needed help. If people recognize you and know who you're related to, it could put us all at risk." I wouldn't promise something I couldn't deliver. I'd never been a fan of lying and did it only when I felt the truth would hurt someone over something pointless, or by omitting something when I thought it would save the lives of people I loved.

"Okay, I trust you." The little girl nodded so confidently that her blonde hair bobbed around her. "Because if you remind my daddy of Momma, that means you're a good person, and you'll protect me just like she did."

A sob swelled in my chest, and holding it back was damn near impossible, but I managed. I wanted Drake gone more desperately than before, and it had everything to do with this little girl. I didn't want to disappoint her. Our plan had to succeed, not only for her but for everyone I loved.

I promise we'll figure this out, Thorn connected and took my hand. *We will all be able to live without fear, and you won't disappoint this little girl. Together, we can take on the world.*

As usual, he'd said what I needed to hear, and his emotions

backed up the words. He wasn't saying them just to appease me. I squeezed his hand back and turned toward the window, ready to keep an eye on the vehicles around us. As we'd said, we needed to be cautious.

THE NEXT MORNING, I woke up late. Tia and Ryu had taken the night watch in their dragon form. They'd stayed far enough away that if they sensed a dragon, they would have time to warn us, but were close enough that someone would have to be looking for us to be there. I'd learned that thunders tended to stay away from other thunders, so the likelihood of a random dragon flying by was low.

The three new additions had claimed the couch as their bed. Unfortunately, all the other rooms were taken, but the couch was comfortable and large enough to fit all three of them.

A strong arm circled my waist and pulled me against a thick, strong chest. Thorn's breath hit my ear, and my body warmed. We hadn't had sex last night, and I was more than eager to make up for lost time.

I turned to him and smiled as I took in his soft expression. His love and arousal swirled between us.

Then there was a loud knock on the door, and Theron called out, "You two need to come out here and see this."

The urgency had us jumping from the bed and rushing to the door.

That was when I heard the queen's voice. I paused and turned around the bedroom, seeking the source. The burner phone lay on the end table next to Thorn's side of the bed. Her voice wasn't coming from there. So where was she?

Thorn and I raced into the living room, where Elliott had his laptop hooked up to the television so everyone could see what was going on.

The queen stood next to Drake, looking seriously into the

camera. Her expression was full of sorrow, but she patted Drake's arm lovingly as she said, "I know some are concerned about Drake taking over too quickly, but the circumstances are unprecedented. The king died before the prince was officially crowned as his heir. But please know we're doing exactly what King Arman wanted, and we must make sure that things continue to go as King Arman planned by crowning my son to fulfill his legacy."

"That *bitch*!" Elliott yelled, as Thorn's feeling of betrayal prickled in my veins.

I blinked, hoping this was another nightmare. If it wasn't, we could be attacked at any second.

CHAPTER SEVENTEEN

EVERYONE WAS HERE except for Peter, who must have been pouting upstairs in his room. The living room was silent as each person took in the severity of the situation. The queen had given a burner phone to Thorn via Uther. Either Uther had been in on it—which I doubted with his daughter here—or she'd screwed him over as well.

My stomach roiled. The queen was helping Drake weed out all the traitors, and we were *all* in danger.

Betrayal, hurt, and anger—the conflicting emotions that swirled through Thorn whenever it came to his biological parents—overwhelmed our bond. All I could do was push my love toward him and take his hand, reminding him I was there.

The queen dropped her arm from Drake and stepped forward, staring straight into the camera. "I ask for you all to trust the process because my mate—your king—and I always strove to do the most important thing in our lives: protect our people." A sad smile took over her face. "Please, be patient as we make the necessary changes to secure a better future for us all."

Drake beamed in the background, the charismatic persona he

somehow managed to achieve emanating from the screen. I hated this confident look more than his smug real one. Many people out there would fall for this persona and willingly trust him. Sometimes, a confident face or essence was all people needed to get behind someone without bothering to look under the surface.

"Thank you for listening." The queen stepped back, returning to her place beside Drake.

"The queen looks nice," Reece sighed from her spot on the couch. She was sitting with her rainbow-colored blanket over her legs. "It would be amazing to meet her one day. Maybe I could dress up like a *princess*."

I pressed my lips together, trying to keep the scowl from my face. Obviously, Uther and his thunder hadn't told her everything. She was so young, but it also scared me. She was unaware of the threat the queen posed, and it broke my heart. It wasn't my place to tell Uther how to handle his child, but that didn't mean I wouldn't discuss it with him when he called...if he were ever able to again.

Drake glided to the forefront of the screen. His face contorted with what viewers would assume was worry and despair, and he placed a hand over his heart. "You heard my mother, the queen. These are unprecedented times, and we need to move quickly, especially with my brother at large. I must secure the throne before he attacks again and strips more people of their dragons." He straightened his shoulders, looking straight into the camera like the queen had done. "I vow that I will hunt him down and take care of him and anyone who aids him. I miss my dear, sweet fiancée terribly and hope she'll be returned home safely. Until then, I'll remember every kiss we shared and believe there will be many more in our future."

The memory of the one time he'd forced me to kiss him in front of the king and queen slammed into my brain, and I fought the urge to gag. I clutched my stomach, hoping the bile wouldn't burn my throat. I'd tried to erase that horrible memory for so many reasons.

Thorn shivered with rage. His jaw clenched, and he rasped, "That prick is going to die."

Reece's eyes bulged, and she wrapped her arms around her stomach and shrank back on the couch. Kari and Chandra were beside her, and they scooted closer to her.

We weren't used to having a small child here. *Babe, you're scaring Reece.*

He flinched and pulled his attention away from the television and toward the little girl. He connected, *It's so damn hard to keep my head on straight when he talks about you like that.* His neck corded. *I want to jump through the television and kill him.*

I leaned my head on his arm. *That's what he wants and why I need you to stay focused.*

Does he think I don't know about that kiss? And he's still calling you his fucking fiancée? Thorn snarled, and Reece glanced fearfully in our direction again.

"Reece, that's the man your daddy has to work for to protect you." Kari bent so she was at eye level with the little girl. She continued to talk, but I had to calm Thorn down. Drake had pushed his buttons, which he'd likely intended in case we were watching.

I tugged my mate toward the front door. Saphira hurriedly opened it, guessing my intent. Thorn had a level head on his shoulders when it came to everything but me.

"We'll be right back," I informed everyone.

The late morning sun hovered about three-quarters of the way up in the sky. I faced my mate, cupping his cheek with my hand. "I want to forget that it happened, but Thorn, it did, and he will do anything he can to get a reaction from you. He wants you to act irrationally."

His nostrils flared, but his breathing slowed at my touch. His face contorted with heartbreak. "I know, but that's the thing. It works. How would you feel if another woman was acting that way about me? Claiming me in front of the world and making it clear I'd soon be hers?"

My stomach clenched, and my blood boiled. That would be worse than a nightmare. He wasn't trying to be a possessive, jealous asshole, but we were mates, two parts of one soul, and hearing someone act like one half of us belonged to someone else was maddening. "Babe, I know. I'm not saying this is easy, and I hope you'd be having the same conversation with me if the roles were reversed." I wasn't judging him, but we didn't have the luxury of reacting to emotion if we wanted to win.

Some of the tension released from his shoulders, and he pressed his forehead to mine. He chuckled humorlessly. "I would be."

"Exactly." I smiled softly. "Anytime he talks like that, ignore him. Otherwise, we're giving him what he wants. Do you want to make Drake happy?"

"Fuck, no," he growled as he wrapped his arms around my waist, pulling me against his body. "I want him to be the angry one when he realizes we've won."

I tapped his forehead with my fingers. "You do realize that winning means you might be the one taking over the throne, and the queen might be working with Drake. We could be in a whole lot of trouble right now." The only reason I wasn't completely freaking out was because Belinda and Merlin were out there keeping watch.

He exhaled, the anger ebbing, replaced by uncertainty. "I've been thinking about that, and I don't want to rule. I've made that clear, but if Drake isn't an option, what if I'm the only choice?"

"We'll cross that bridge when we get there." I didn't want him to feel pressured into making a decision that didn't need to be made now, but I did agree with him. He might not have much of a choice, and I also believed he was the most fit to lead. He'd be the type of leader people would be willing to die for. "But when the bridge comes and you're torn about whether to cross it, don't take my needs into account." Because he would. He would prioritize my wants and needs over his people. I was his weakness and, in some ways, his fatal flaw.

"Of course I will. That's just as important as any other piece," he whispered vehemently as he placed a finger under my chin and tilted my head up so I was staring into his eyes. He pressed, "Your happiness is the most important thing to me. Damn the consequences."

His emotions soared between us, reinforcing every word. Even without a fated-mate connection, I'd have believed him. He didn't lie or sugarcoat truths to make others happy.

"I wanted to be a doctor to help people. To heal the sick or, in some cases, help them toward their end with peace and as much grace and dignity as they can keep." I'd seen what had happened to my mom during her cancer treatment. The denial, the depression, and her body breaking down on her. Through it all, she hadn't found peace until I'd told her she could leave. That I'd be fine on my own. That she could stop fighting for me. Within minutes, she'd faded away.

He nodded, his sky blue eyes darkening a shade, and the diamond flecks in his irises stole my breath. He connected, *I know. That's why you becoming a doctor is a priority.*

"Let me finish." I took his hands and squeezed. "What I'm trying to say is, if *you* want to become king, I'll still be fulfilling my dream."

Tilting his head, he furrowed his brows. "I'm not following."

"Maybe it's not the dream I envisioned six years ago, but I'll still be helping others." I clasped my hands. "We'd be making sure that dragons who are different or elderly aren't persecuted. Think about Reece's situation, all because a dragon shifter fell for a human and no one could help them. If you're king, we can help people the way we helped Emily and baby Thorn." My heart raced thinking about all the good we could do. "We could help those down on their luck in a way that wouldn't be insulting because we can relate to them better than can royals who were raised privileged. We could—"

He laughed, the sound refreshing, deep, and sexy. "I get it." His irises twinkled. "You still get to fulfill your dream if I choose to take on the responsibility of leading our people."

"Yeah." I smiled, surprising myself. That really was the case. I hadn't realized it until now, but Thorn ruling the dragons would protect a lot more people, along with our actual future.

"I don't know how I got so damn lucky to have you be mine, but I will cherish you always," he vowed and kissed me. My stomach knotted with the familiar urgent need, but now was not the time or place.

Two seconds was all I gave myself to enjoy the kiss before pulling away. I licked my lips, relishing his minty taste. "We need to go back in and determine our next steps if the queen is working with Drake." All my hope from the night before had left me raw.

Thorn flinched and tightened his hold on me. "I know it was foolish, but I was kind of hoping she meant what she said, which shows that hope doesn't change anything."

"Hope is one of the most powerful motivators. Hope for a better future keeps underdogs fighting." He couldn't give up or become defeated. That was exactly what Drake wanted. "It's what motivates our group to take Drake down, and when nurtured correctly, that hope can turn into a flame of passion. That's what we're going to do." I pointed at the door. "Head in there and spread those flames."

"Okay." He smiled adoringly at me. "Let's go inside and do that. And I have a little girl I need to make up with."

When we entered the house again, not much had changed. Reece, Chandra, and Kari sat in the center section of the couch, with Elliott and Mindy on the ottoman. Sol, Eva, and Hydra were on the left side of the couch, and Tia, Ryu, and Tyson were on the other. Theron, Brenton, Vlad, and Errol paced behind the couch. The sound of pots and pans clanging informed me that Cassidy was in the kitchen, odd for this hour.

One person was missing. "Is Peter still upstairs?"

"Yeah, he went up after dinner." Elliott rolled his eyes. "He said he needed space where there wasn't as much drama."

That sounded like Peter. He wanted Drake to win—I could feel it. "He can't know that people are helping us from the inside."

"Reece, I could use your help," Cassidy sing-songed from the kitchen.

Ah, that must be why she was making something at such an odd hour. She was using it as a way to distract the little girl while we discussed strategy.

When Reece's feet hit the floor, Thorn strolled over and squatted in front of her. He hung his head and murmured, "I'm sorry if I upset you earlier. The prince was saying a lot of stuff about my Everly, and I didn't like it. However, I shouldn't have spouted off like that. It was wrong."

Reece's smile was blinding. "It's okay. Daddy gets upset, too, when he thinks about how he and I can't be together." She threw her arms around Thorn's neck, pulling him in for a tight hug.

This time, when my eyes burned, it was from happy tears. She was a bright light that we needed so desperately in our world right now.

Standing, Chandra pushed a piece of hair behind her ear. "We should go help."

"Yeah." Kari climbed to her feet. "Let us know if you need us for anything."

My heart ached as the two grown women also hurried away. They were more than welcome to talk strategy with us, but it was clear they either didn't feel comfortable or wanted to stay with Reece. Either way, I wouldn't push them.

Vlad rubbed the back of his neck. "If the queen is working with Drake, they could already have our location."

"I don't know." Errol strolled around the couch and leaned against the edge of the fireplace. He pursed his lips. "If I hadn't seen the broadcast, I never would have believed it. Though giving up Thorn caused problems in their relationship, King Arman and Queen Mira loved each other very much. They were truly fated. I don't see her supporting Drake, knowing he killed his father, her mate. I don't care if he is her son...so maybe she doesn't know or doesn't believe it."

Saphira and Brenton took the spots on the couch our newcomers had vacated. Saphira crossed her legs and leaned forward, placing an elbow on her knee. "Maybe she doesn't think the dragons will support Thorn as king."

"I swear." Tia rolled her eyes and crossed her arms. "The king and queen didn't know what their people would do. Let's be real—most of the time, they stayed holed up in their big, fancy mansion and did shit like this to inform us heathens of their decrees. It's insulting. Even if Thorn didn't have a lick of power, I, for one, would want someone like *him* ruling. He understands not having money and the struggles that we-the-people actually go through. I don't need that scoundrel prick or the spoiled queen making decisions for me."

"Dear." Merlin placed an arm over his mate's shoulders and pulled her close. "Sometimes, it's best if you don't say *everything* that's on your mind."

Elliott shook his head. "Don't listen to him. Say it. I love hearing it." He glanced at Mindy and shook his head. "Babe, it's a good thing she's taken, or you'd have some serious competition."

Giggling, Tia blushed. "Oh, that boy makes me feel young."

Instead of getting growly, Merlin chuckled. "It's a damn good thing I know you would never stray, or I'd be teaching this young man here a lesson or two."

"Oh, I'd be helping you." Mindy placed her hands on her hips and narrowed her eyes at Elliott. Unlike the older man, she wasn't teasing. They weren't fully mated yet, so there was no doubt super-heightened emotions were swirling through her.

Tyson snorted. "Dude, you're in trouble."

Luckily, that wised Elliott up. He lifted his hands. "Babe, I was kidding. You know I love you." Then his face blanched, and his mouth dropped open.

I don't think your brother has said the L-word to her before, Thorn connected, mashing his lips together.

Mindy's breath caught. She blinked several times. When she opened her mouth, a phone rang.

The ring had come from Thorn's and my bedroom.

That broke the moment, and utter silence fell, even in the kitchen. It was the burner phone that Uther had given Thorn.

When it rang a second time, Thorn sprang into action and raced to the bedroom. Vlad and I were hot on his heels, with Theron and Saphira right behind us.

He snatched the phone from the end table, swiped it, and put it on speaker. He snarled, "Are you calling to gloat and inform us that warriors are on their way?"

It was the queen. I shouldn't have been surprised, but the pain etched into Thorn's face tore me in two.

No matter what, I'd make sure this woman never made him feel like this again.

CHAPTER EIGHTEEN

THORN'S ADRENALINE spiked as my throat constricted. I hadn't realized I'd put so much hope in all of this panning out so we'd have a chance to beat Drake at his own game. My heart felt obliterated.

Finally, the queen sighed on the other end of the line. "I shouldn't expect your trust. I haven't earned it."

Thorn laughed cruelly. "Well, we did just watch you say that you're backing Drake as the king, so forgive my problematic attitude."

"You heard me say I would back my son—the one I know will continue on his father's course. I won't lie. Part of me wishes it were Drake. It would make things easier. But there was a reason I didn't use his name."

Thorn's hurt sliced through our bond, stealing my breath with his agony.

I placed a hand on his shoulder. "Stop the games. You can't keep playing both sides."

"Everly, I'm assuming that's you." The queen wasn't asking. She knew.

I didn't humor her with a confirmation.

After a pause, she huffed. "You saw my shock the day I learned Thorn was alive. I couldn't fake that. Then I saw him at the wed—"

Thorn snarled so loudly the sound hurt my ears.

"Do *not* finish that word," he seethed. "You were going to let that arrogant *douche* marry my fated mate."

"I didn't *know*." The pain in her voice was evident. "I didn't have a clue."

I was tired of everyone's bullshit. "When Drake forced me to meet you two at breakfast, you thought you caught a whiff of Thorn's scent as I sat down. You reacted so strongly that the table almost toppled over."

Errol and Vlad moved closer, coming to stand on our other side so we could all see one another. I could smell Saphira and Tyson and hear them breathing at the threshold of the door.

"If that was the case, Mira," Errol said, frowning, "you would've known she was mated to Thorn."

"I couldn't believe it." Her voice sounded so sad...so weak. "First, I learned that the son I thought was dead had been alive all this time, and then the son I did know brought home a fiancée who reminded me of the son I thought was dead, and things just spiraled out of control. I didn't want to face what any of it could mean."

She'd been in denial. Gods, I understood that. I'd seen what Mom went through when her entire life changed. Though this situation wasn't a terminal illness, it was still life-altering. Sometimes it was easier to turn a blind eye to something that could change things fundamentally than it was to deal with it...until you had to.

Some of my anger fizzled, but Thorn's didn't. He hadn't gone through anything like this before, not really.

"That's why you kept the announcement generic." Vlad rubbed the scruff on his face. "You didn't mean Drake when you were saying that. You meant Thorn the entire time."

"Yes. I will *not* betray Thorn...not again." Her voice shook as if she were suppressing a sob. "Drake went too far in killing Arman, but he threatened to injure more people I care about if I didn't partake in the video and make it look like I supported him. I...I can't...handle causing more pain through my decisions and indiscretions."

Errol clenched his jaw. "He's threatening you?"

"No, but he will if I don't play the doting mother. He isn't aware that I know he killed Arman. He told me it was Thorn, and that opened my eyes to what's been happening all along. Thinking back, Arman and I ignored so many signs. We focused everything on him because of our guilt and grief over what we'd done to Thorn."

That all-too-familiar stream of emotions swirled between my mate and me. Again, Thorn felt hurt, sad, and betrayed, but with hope also blending in. The sensation was so intense that my body weakened. Even the buzz of our connection didn't ease what he was going through, and I wished I could do something beyond just standing next to him. I wanted to fix the problem...but it was something only time could heal.

"How did you find out?" he asked roughly.

There was a pause. "I can't tell you. I promised them."

It sounded like someone the queen trusted had told her everything. *Do you trust her?* I connected with Thorn, needing to hear his unbiased opinion before the inevitable group conversation.

He glanced at me and took my hand. *I do, which makes this harder.*

Just like the king's death had taken a bigger toll on him than he wanted to address, I could sense his sadness. It was easier to think of his biological parents as bad people than as flawed beings who had made a terrible mistake. *Me, too.*

He nodded.

"What's your plan, Mira?" Errol covered his mouth with his hands.

She sighed in relief. "Someone in Drake's inner circle is feeding me information. I can tell you where Drake's going and what his plans are so you can save the people he's trying to..."

The silence was thick, and the four of us glanced at one another. None of us spoke up to finish her sentence. If she was saying what I thought she was, then I needed to hear *her* acknowledge it, and we needed to find out how much she knew.

"That he's trying to k-kill." Her voice broke on the last word, but she'd said it solidly enough for us to understand.

She knew everything.

"I can't get over that. The way he's been manipulating us while hurting our people." She sniffed. "And my poor, sweet Arman paid the cost for our obliviousness. But no more. This has to end."

"That information will help us save our people, but to stop the coronation, we need to know more than the locations Drake plans to attack or search," Thorn said, tugging me to his side so our bodies pressed together.

The sizzle of our connection exploded, but I couldn't enjoy it in the current situation.

Queen Mira exhaled. "I'm figuring that part out, but we need allies. I need you to help thunders and find the guards who fought for you. That's your first assignment. A dragon shifter flying near Pilot Mountain in North Carolina noticed a group of ten warriors in the woods. They think the guards are loyal to *you*, Thorn. Drake is preparing to send fifty warriors there tonight to kill them. You need to get to them first."

Our group became silent. This was a huge risk, one that would surely send us into a trap if she was working with Drake. But if she was telling the truth, we would have ten trained men fighting alongside us. That would be a huge increase to our extremely low numbers.

"Okay." Vlad nodded. "That's close to Mount Airy, so it makes sense they'd be near Theron's thunder because they couldn't risk flying for too long. They didn't venture too far, which the warriors wouldn't expect, but moved farther from the king's lands in case they had to run away. Also, it's near the mountain from which the town got its name, and the location is a draw for human hikers, so Drake's warriors can't search the area easily in dragon form."

A knock came from the other end of the phone, followed by a

woman's voice calling out, "Queen Mira, Prince Drake has requested you come to the office. He wants to chat with you."

"Of course," Queen Mira responded with a strong voice that sounded significantly different from the one she was using with us. "Tell him I'm changing and will be down in a few minutes."

"Yes, ma'am." Then the sound of the maid's footsteps receded.

There was a shuffling noise, and the queen's more urgent voice came over the phone. "I've got to go. Text me when you have the warriors, and hurry. Drake won't sit on this knowledge for long. He'll want to attack when it's dark to hide from the humans. I won't have my cell phone on me. I can't chance Drake finding it, or all of this will be ruined, but I'll check it periodically, especially at night when I retire."

At least, Drake was determined to keep dragons a secret from humans...for now. There was no telling what Drake might be planning for the future. Knowing him, ruling the dragons wouldn't be enough. He craved power, and the only way to satisfy that craving was to conquer more.

"You all be safe, and Thorn...I love you," she breathed. "I'm sorry it's taken me so long to see the truth."

A burning sensation slammed into me, and it felt as if I'd been stabbed in my chest near the core of our connection. If I hadn't known better, I would've thought I'd been stabbed in the heart just like King Arman, but this was emotional suffering, not physical.

"You stay safe, too." His voice was a deep rumble. "Bye." He hung up the phone, not waiting for her to hang up first.

The silence was heavy for a few beats.

I moved where I could see Saphira and Tyson. We all wore varying expressions of dread. Whatever choice we made would be risky. This could be a trap, though I doubted it, and if it wasn't, where the hell were we going to put ten more people? We were already out of rooms, and the couch was taken.

"It's about damn time people realize who Drake truly is." Tyson sneered. "Seriously, if they hadn't overlooked his shit, maybe the king would still be alive."

Thorn grunted so lightly I almost didn't hear him, but the sadness and regret emanating from him whenever he thought of or talked about his biological father pierced between us. Errol's mouth tugged into a frown.

Taking a ragged breath, I gritted out, "That may be true, but people here have ties to the king, and those words were hurtful. Though Arman acted like a coward by ignoring signs of the person Drake was becoming, he didn't do those things, and he died trying to do the right thing. At least Queen Mira is still trying to fix the problem. Don't waste your energy being mad at the wrong people."

Flinching, Tyson stepped back. "You seem so nice most of the time, then *bam*. You're the scariest one of us all."

"Dude, try being her brother," Elliott called from his spot in the den.

All of them, especially Elliott, had been listening to the entire conversation.

"One day, when I was ten, I hit a beehive with a stick to see how much it would take for the hornets to spew out and attack me," Elliott continued, confident we all wanted to hear how his story tragically ended. "Let me tell you, it didn't take much. As I was running in the front yard for my *life*, I saw Everly standing on the front porch, just watching me. *Watching me.* She yelled at me to run faster and opened the door for me to run inside. I got stung five times, and she rolled her eyes as she took care of me. She told me if that didn't fix my curiosity, nothing would. She gave me no sympathy and definitely didn't kiss my boo-boos."

Out of all the things he could have brought up, that was the story he'd chosen to tell? I rolled my eyes. "A *swarm* of hornets was chasing you. What did you expect me to do? We would've both wound up stung. And I'd told you the day before not to bother the hive! You had it coming."

"Exactly! Siblings are supposed to stick together, but no, you stayed safe and sting-free on the porch, watching me."

I pressed my head into Thorn's shoulder. "You'd *just* started running. You make it sound like I was watching you run in circles, laughing maniacally in the background. I was about to yell at you to come in when you saw me." Sometimes, it was exhausting to be around him. I'd forgotten that over the past six years since the twins had retreated into themselves.

"That's the version in *my* head," he countered.

"This is why the invention of video games was so horrible." Tia sounded disgusted. "These young'uns don't know reality from fiction."

"I thought I did," Elliott retorted. "Then I learned that dragons, wolves, and who knows what else are real! It's all fair game now."

"Despite the usefulness of this conversation, we should focus on the ten warriors we need to rescue." Vlad smirked slightly and leaned against the wall between the end table and the bathroom door. "It's a five-hour drive. We need as much time as possible between when we get there and when Drake's team arrives so our scents won't be in the air. They won't be able to piece together that the men are with us."

The lightness Elliott and Tia had provided was gone. Vlad had a good point. "What are we thinking? Do we know for sure it's not a trap?"

"I don't think it is." Errol paced in the open area of the bedroom. "But I'd hate to not be wary. For all we know, Drake bugged the queen's room and can hear everything she plans."

"Which means we need to be careful. Luckily we have the rentals cars under various aliases of Vlad and Cassidy." Thorn tossed the burner phone on the bed. "We'll need both Suburbans to bring the ten new additions back with us. So, two of us in each vehicle—the driver and a passenger in front."

"Fated mates will make the best teams so everyone can communicate quickly without worrying about dead spots." Vlad pursed his lips. "Cassidy can stay back with the group here so we can keep each other updated, and Everly can ride with me in one of the Suburbans."

My stomach knotted. Vlad had been nothing but great to me, but we hadn't spent a ton of time alone. Sitting in the car with him for five hours might be uncomfortable, but his plan had merit.

"Theron can ride with me, and Hydra, Errol, and two others can ride in the rental car." Thorn licked his bottom lip.

"I'm going." Saphira wagged a finger. "I may not have a fated-mate connection, but I want to be involved. These people know me, and more familiar faces will be helpful."

I hadn't thought of that. The guards the king had brought had likely worked with him for years.

"Brenton should go as well. He'll know some of them, too." Errol strolled to the door to leave the bedroom.

Tyson blocked it. "Why shouldn't I go? Is it because I used to be injured?"

"What?" Errol shook his head hard. "That's not it at all. It's because you were more of a recluse, and Brenton was an advisor to the king for almost as long as I was. People will recognize him, especially since he's older."

Tyson's head hung, and his cheeks burned. "Oh, yeah. That makes sense."

My chest hurt. Even though he was healed, the way he'd been treated still affected him. I hated that Drake had made him feel like less of a person when he was just as whole as any of us.

"We've got a plan." Vlad clapped his hands. "Now it's time to execute it. Everly had a good point earlier—do *not* mention anything to Peter about who our source is. If asked, we saw someone mention this on the Dragonnet. Don't trust him."

Our group dispersed to get ready to head out for another long day.

THE CAR RIDE with Vlad wasn't as awkward as I'd feared.

I wore one of Thorn's baseball caps, keeping it pulled low over my face in case we passed anyone we knew. Thorn had done the same, and I learned he kept caps around for when he wanted to hide half his face.

Cassidy had packed us some lunch and snacks so we wouldn't have to stop often on the way there or back. We also brought large coolers filled with sandwiches. There was no telling when these ten guards had last eaten. For all we knew, they were living off the land.

I learned that Vlad had similar tastes in music to Thorn, and I realized Vlad had probably influenced Thorn's taste growing up. We talked about our hobbies and interests, and when he learned that I loved to paint, his eyes glowed. Though Vlad wasn't a painter, he'd loved collecting paintings...until his life had changed twenty-one years ago.

As we pulled into our destination parking lot, I stared at a mountain of rocks surrounded by trees. We jumped from our vehicles, ready to search the area for any signs that Drake's warriors were already here, but as the queen had promised, they weren't here since darkness hadn't fallen.

We trooped into the thick black gum, eastern red cedar, and tulip trees. The air was warm, around eighty, and a herd of elk roamed nearby.

Thorn came to my side as we walked deeper into the woods. None of us spoke, afraid we might scare the warriors or miss the sound of a threat. We tried to keep our steps light...feeble.

Vlad and Theron led our group, with Thorn and me right behind them. Hydra and Brenton took the rear, with Saphira and Errol between us.

I found myself enjoying the sun on my skin and being part of nature—something I'd despised as a human. My dragon inched forward, the animal side of me reveling in being free and unbound.

We must have been walking for over an hour when something

startled us to our right. It was too large to be an elk and too small to be a bear.

Our group turned and tiptoed toward the sound. I stifled a gasp when I saw one of the king's warriors who'd been at Theron's thunder.

One of us kicked a rock. At the rattling sound, the warrior jerked his head around, right toward Hydra.

Someone he didn't recognize. He spun and ran away as quickly as possible, forcing us to chase him.

The man yelled, "They're here! Run! They've found us."

"Wait!" Thorn shouted, but that only made them run faster.

They didn't recognize his voice, which wasn't surprising. They hadn't heard him speak much before. Between seeing Hydra and hearing an unfamiliar voice, their panic took over.

Shit. We had to stop them before they disappeared...or Drake's warriors found us.

CHAPTER NINETEEN

I RAN AS FAST as I could. Our only saving grace was that human hikers could be in the area, and this site could easily be seen, so the men weren't likely to shift into dragon form unless they were super desperate and afraid. But these were the king's warriors, and they were loyal—keeping the secret of the existence of dragons even while in danger would be important to them out of respect for their former leader.

We could hear more hurried footsteps now. The other warriors were running, too, but that was a blessing. At least they'd stayed close together.

We all must have tapped into our dragons, because our group picked up its pace, and so did the man running ahead of us.

Thorn, don't hold back. They need to see you before they scatter, I connected. Though he hadn't been feeling anything other than determination, I also knew he didn't want to leave me behind, which would slow him down. *If I get into trouble, I'll let you know.*

He tensed as he ran past the other side of a red cedar and then past me. Finally, he replied, *Are you sure?*

Yes. Now go. That was the whole point of coming here, but I knew he needed to hear me say so.

He picked up his pace and flew by everyone, confirming what I already knew. He was the strongest of us all...hell, probably out of all the dragons. No one had told me this outright, but there was a reason the royal line ruled—they emanated power. Thorn had the same raw power as his father. He was strong, and with his mark, he could be unstoppable, which was how his grandfather had terrorized their world. To me, Thorn's situation was different because he was my mate. Even though I knew he was powerful, that power didn't affect me. Not in the same way I saw it affect others until they got to know him and saw the man he was.

Theron and Vlad surged forward, leaving Brenton, Errol, Saphira, Hydra, and me behind. They weren't as fast as Thorn, but they were stronger than the rest of us.

The warrior was pulling away, but I could still see the back of his head. I had to split my attention between him and dodging the trees in front of me. He was smaller than the other warriors I'd met, but with each pump of his arms, his triceps bulged. I was certain that even though I'd become a dragon, the loose skin of my underarms still wobbled every time I moved my arms—though with all the training we'd done, I hoped I was getting more toned.

Thorn was gaining speed, and his frustration swirled through me.

I noticed the other footsteps had gone silent...like they'd stopped running. *Thorn, something's up.*

Before I could say more, a clearing came into view. The other nine warriors stood waiting, rifles pointed right at us.

Bile burned in my throat. Out of all the possible scenarios, I hadn't considered *this*. Maybe the warriors regretted their decision and had turned on us. That would be the best way to gain Drake's forgiveness if they wanted to rejoin what could be the winning side, especially with our limited resources.

The man who was running blew past the two tallest men in the center of the group. A gigantic, ripped, deep-bronze complected man whose braids of ebony hair were pulled into a bun on top of his head had locked his graphite eyes on Vlad, while a fair-skinned male with dark blond hair styled upward, who was only a few inches shorter and not quite as buff but could still take on an ox, had his sapphire eyes on Theron.

"Stop where you are and raise your hands," the bigger man snarled, his voice as deep and menacing as his muscles.

We all slowed, even Thorn, and his fear peaked within our bond. I knew exactly why. He wasn't afraid for himself—he was freaking out because he was fifteen feet away from me and not able to protect me.

We weren't as prepared as we'd thought, and I feared we'd walked into a horrible trap.

The guards at either end of their line, both women, were focused on my mate, while the remaining five focused on the rest of us. I recognized them vaguely from our brief time together in chaos.

"Wait." The tan-complected woman on our left with dark brown hair lowered her rifle a few inches. The skin around her midnight-black eyes tightened as she let out a deep breath. She lifted a hand and tilted her head. "Who are you?"

Thorn straightened his shoulders and lifted his chin. "Thorn Wight."

"No way." The female warrior on the other end snarled. She still had her rifle trained on my mate, her cinnamon irises glowing with anger. "This is a trick. Maybe witch magic? Thorn wouldn't be able to find us. He's in hiding and doesn't have the resources." She jerked her head back, the ends of her golden brown ponytail swishing over her shoulder.

"It *is* him." Errol pivoted around me and came into view. "Drake has learned where you are. A dragon shifter saw you and reported it. His warriors will be here tonight to eliminate you."

The guy who'd been running from us gaped. "Errol? Is that really you? Prove it."

"First off, witches don't interact with dragons, and second, I was there when the king asked you to become part of his inner circle. He told you that he'd noticed your passion for doing the right thing, and he needed you at his side."

He sucked in a breath and nodded. "It is you."

"And this *is* Thorn. There's no deception involved." Errol gestured to my mate.

Tragedy had a way of messing with details, and when they'd last seen us, we'd been naked. My dragon snarled at the thought of the others—especially the women—seeing my mate unclothed. It was a good thing they weren't certain they recognized him, or I might have had to kill them for that reason alone.

"This isn't a trick," Errol finished. "We have a source inside the château who notified us that you were hiding in this area."

I appreciated that he didn't divulge who the informant was, but it wasn't surprising. He was the king's advisor, after all. Though these warriors were loyal to the late king, that didn't mean we could trust them yet.

The ten scanned each other, and Runner Guy nodded. "Lower your weapons."

I was surprised Runner was the leader of the group. He was the scrawniest man in the mix, but if the two who flanked him hadn't been so huge, he probably would've appeared much stronger. He did appear older, so maybe that had something to do with it.

Everyone listened without hesitation. It was clear this group trusted Runner, which was good for us.

Doubt crept through our bond from Thorn. He wasn't sure how to handle this situation.

"I'm sorry we startled you." I walked over to Thorn, the warriors watching me the entire way, and took my mate's hand. "That wasn't our intention."

"Wait," the third and final female guard said from the other side of the dark bronze, muscled man. She lifted a hand. "You're the one Drake is determined to marry."

Thorn snarled, his pupils slitting. "She is *my mate* and *wife*."

Tension filled the air as the warriors' expressions turned to various levels of wariness. They didn't trust Thorn yet, despite the king's dying wishes. Unfortunately, they'd hit the sorest subject possible when it came to him.

Squeezing his hand comfortingly, I rolled my eyes and pushed my calm toward him, trying to keep the situation from escalating again. Though they'd promised their allegiance to Thorn, it had been on King Arman's say-so. We didn't need to scare them away. We needed their help.

"Drake proclaimed he'd make me his wife when he realized Thorn and I had completed our fated-mate bond." I smiled sadly.

"And he goes cuckoo where she's concerned because of that." Saphira snorted as she sidled over beside me. "Hell, even when she was human, those two circled each other like they might combust."

The jaw of the fiery pale girl on the end dropped. "You were *human?*"

You need to step in, I connected. He had to be seen as our leader. We needed them to be confident about King Arman's decision. *These people will follow you. Just focus on our goal—where Drake isn't around to terrorize us anymore.*

Inhaling, Thorn stepped closer to me and said, "Yes, she was. She got hurt, and I had to change her, or she would've died. I had no idea I was changing the woman who would become my fated mate."

The fiery girl smiled dreamily. "That's romantic."

I hadn't thought about our situation like that, but she was right. No one else had a story like it.

"I'm not trying to be rude, but what Errol said is true. We came to bring you back with us." Thorn flinched, then added quickly, "*If you're willing.*"

That addition wasn't needed, but that made me fall for him more. It was another reminder of the type of man he was—kind, considerate, caring, and the ultimate leader who would let someone choose what was best for them as long as it didn't hurt others. And he was all mine.

The ten warriors glanced at one another again, like they were talking telepathically, though it wasn't possible.

"Actually, we would *really* appreciate that." Runner stepped forward, all sense of wariness removed, as if they'd decided something. "We're starving, and we've been too afraid to go inland. We've been staying out here to avoid hikers, though not well enough." He shook his head and pointed at himself. "My name is Arrow." He nodded at the others.

"I'm Echo," the gorgeous dark-bronze freight truck added.

The woman beside him lifted her hand, her warm smile reflecting in her amber eyes. She was about a foot shorter than Echo, and her dark brown hair was pulled into a tight ponytail as well. There was dirt smeared on her cheek, contrasting with her deep tan complexion. "I'm Opal."

"And I'm Fury," the fiery girl at the end added bluntly.

The other huge guy flanking Echo introduced himself. "Smokey."

Putting his rifle through the loop and on his shoulder, the man next to Smokey lifted his chin, his dark brown eyes hesitant. Somehow, his black hair was still spiked, even though he'd been out here for weeks, and his ebony scruff was thick. He was almost as short as Arrow but stouter, and his medium-brown complexion glowed. "Blaze here."

Beside him was a man with gorgeous tan skin. He had dark, unruly, curly hair and mesmerizing carob-brown eyes. He was only an inch taller than Blaze, but there was something happy about his presence. "Most people call me Amazing, but I also go by Owen."

"That's the Prince Heir, and you're pulling that shit?" The next warrior rolled his pine green eyes. Though he wasn't as ripped as Echo and Smokey, he was pretty damn close. Light auburn hair hung in his face, and he had black smudges, like war paint, across his cheeks, making his lighter complexion look ghostly compared to everyone else's.

"He's Rex," the woman on the other end added while glaring at the guys. "And I'm Sydney."

I was hoping I could remember each name.

Thorn stepped in and introduced our group one by one. Once introductions were done, the mood changed. The warriors began to fidget, eager to get away. I didn't blame them. Though I didn't mind nature anymore, if I'd stayed out here for as long as they had, my human side would've been ready for a shower and clean clothes immediately. They were still wearing their black warrior outfits, and while that had likely helped them blend in, especially at night, it was long past time to do some laundry.

"Follow us," Theron said, and he started back toward the vehicles, Hydra walking next to him.

Saphira and Brenton followed, with Errol and Vlad next. Thorn and I fell in behind them, and Opal and Arrow followed us. The rest of the warriors broke into pairs, but I didn't glance back. I wanted to get the hell away from here before Drake and his warriors arrived. They could fly, which meant their travel time would be significantly less than ours, but they would have to wait until it was dark to land. It was getting close to five, so we might hit traffic on the way back to the house. That was fine. I just wanted time for our scents to dissipate.

Our trek was quiet, and though the warriors' footsteps were steady, something uncomfortable nudged at me. I couldn't place what it was, but the hairs on my neck rose.

With each step, the sensation of being watched intensified, and a cold warning coursed down my spine. Thorn didn't appear to be affected, and no one else did, either. Maybe my anxiety was getting the best of me.

What's wrong? Thorn connected, sensing my unease through our mate bond. He stiffened beside me, tugging me closer to him.

I know this sounds weird, but I feel like we're being watched. A shiver ran down my spine. I couldn't kick the sinking suspicion.

Thorn scanned the area, and his breath caught. *Something is following us on your side and slightly behind us. I hadn't noticed it.*

I glanced over my shoulder, frowning.

The warriors had stern expressions like there was a threat nearby. They sensed whatever it was, too.

"The wolves," Arrow said tensely. "They came across us the first day we settled here and talked with us. We're technically in wolf territory. When they heard what happened, they were fine with us hiding here. Other shifters told them about what Drake's been up to. They think he'll come after the wolves once he conquers the dragons, and they don't want him in charge."

The wolves surrounded us, and my heart thundered. They were tense, as if they might attack. When the group in front of us stopped, Thorn hissed beside me.

Since I was shorter, I couldn't see what was happening, but then a deep voice sounded from in front of us. "What's going on here?"

When Thorn wedged us between Vlad and Errol and released my hand, my heart ached. This was the first time he'd ever left me behind without me urging him to.

"We came to take Arrow and the others to safety." Thorn continued to push forward, and when Theron and Hydra parted, I caught a glimpse of the action.

A naked older man blocked our path. He had short gray hair and a matching goatee. His arms were bulging without him flexing. At one time, he would've been the buffest man I'd ever seen...but now I'd met dragons. Despite being older, nothing on him was sagging, and unfortunately, that was yet again something I couldn't unsee.

"I didn't realize we were on wolf territory, and I'm sorry we didn't alert you to our presence." Thorn looked over his shoulder and scowled when he saw I had a clear view of the naked man. He moved to block the older man from my view.

Thank you for that, I connected. I had no desire to see anyone naked but him, and it unsettled me that this man had no problem standing in front of us completely nude.

"Why didn't you know this is wolf land?" the older man pressed, his voice turning gritty.

"Because I haven't been involved in the supernatural world for over twenty-one years. I've only recently acclimated again." Thorn lowered his head, but not in submission—in respect.

It was strange how I picked up on things like that now.

"You're the prince the warriors here are so desperate to protect." The older man's voice softened. "You're the true heir to the dragon throne?"

I couldn't breathe. Whatever Thorn said now would set the course for our future, and I was grateful we'd talked about it earlier.

"Yes, I am." Thorn nodded, and something shifted in our bond...acceptance.

"Good." His answer was so simple. "My name is Lowell."

"I'm Thorn."

A wolf howled in the distance, and the sound was chilling.

"Nice to meet you, Thorn," the wolfer shifter replied. "Are you expecting more of your people?"

I sensed the warriors behind me tensing, and Vlad's neck corded.

Thorn shook his head. "No. Why?"

"Because twenty more dragon shifters are entering the woods two miles west of here."

CHAPTER TWENTY

MY LEGS ALMOST GAVE OUT. We'd expected Drake to send people here after sunset, but they were already here, and we were outnumbered. I feared we were about to find out how badly our warriors were suffering from malnutrition.

Considering how well things had been going today, we should've been prepared for this. Our luck always ran out, a fact I tried not to focus on too often. So far, we'd scraped by, but that particular silver lining could vanish at any time. It was too scary to consider because I could lose Thorn...forever.

Overwhelming sensations surged through our connection. Thorn felt the same way that I did...and adding that to the emotions rolling off the dragon shifters surrounding me only made things worse. Like I was drowning on land.

When Thorn stopped blocking my view of Lowell, allowing me to see the older man's naked form again, that was the icing on the proverbial cake. He was so worried that he didn't care about my view of the naked older man anymore.

"Those are *not* our people. They're loyal to Drake." Thorn

tensed. "But thanks for the warning. We need to move before they find us."

"It won't be long." The older man stepped aside into the thick brush. "But I can buy you some time."

"Don't." Thorn jerked his head toward the vehicles, indicating he wanted us to move. "I'd hate to drag the wolves into this mess. It's bad enough with dragons suffering. We don't need more of our brethren species getting involved."

Lifting a brow, Lowell scanned my mate again, seeing him in a new light.

Saphira and Brenton took off toward our vehicles with renewed vigor.

Thorn gestured for Theron and Hydra to move next, but no one budged, and even Saphira and Brenton paused when they realized no one was coming behind them. I went to my mate, refusing to leave him. The warriors followed suit, remaining right behind me.

"I'll take up the back." Thorn gestured more urgently while leveling a heavy gaze on me. "And make sure I don't see anything."

I'll be in the back with you. I pushed my determination toward him and planted my feet on the earth. He needed to know I was unyielding on this.

"No, Your Highness." Arrow shook his head and crossed his arms. "We are here to protect you, not the other way around. And I'm certain I'm talking for everyone here and not just us warriors."

Nodding curtly as if he'd come to a decision, Lowell clapped my mate on his arm and said, "If you hurry, you'll make it out of here. I can buy you time with little risk since they're on wolf lands. Drake might not like it, but it won't seem like we're aiding you. So go. Now. For the sake of all supernaturals, we need you to take the throne."

I smiled and took Thorn's hand in mine. I was certain that Lowell was the alpha of this pack and had made a decision about Thorn. Best of all, he approved of my mate. We needed any help we could muster.

Surprise filtered through our bond, and Thorn's heartbeat quickened slightly, but my mate's face remained a mask of indifference.

"Thank you. But please don't cause problems for yourself and your pack."

"We appreciate your concern." Lowell stepped into the trees, his hunter green eyes glowing. His voice changed into one that sounded half human, half animal. "Now go."

Bones cracked, and fur matching his hair color sprouted over his arms. I'd never seen a wolf shifter before, let alone one shifting, and I was intrigued, but we didn't have time to loiter.

Everyone watched Thorn and me, waiting for us to make the first move, as if they were afraid to run in case we lagged behind.

Instead of arguing, Thorn took my hand, and we moved in unison. Appeased, Brenton and Saphira spun on their heels and took off again, this time with Theron and Hydra. Vlad and Errol paused and settled in behind us and in front of the warriors, likely so Vlad could keep an eye on Thorn and make sure he didn't do something noble to save us. There was no guarantee that Lowell's plan would work.

As we picked up our pace, I heard the wolves running away on our left. At least Drake's warriors hadn't parked in the same lot we had. There must be one on the other side of the mountain.

Each breath I took was harder than the last, mainly because I was listening for any signs of someone approaching. With the adrenaline coursing through my veins and fear's cold claws digging into my chest, my hearing seemed better than usual, even being tapped into my dragon. But all I could hear were the wolves running away and the sound of our footsteps, along with some squirrels scurrying through the trees. Between that and the scents of dragon shifters, trees, and sunshine, I wasn't losing my mind.

Well, maybe I was. I *smelled* sunshine, which I'd never noticed before, but with the warmth on my skin and the fresh smell surrounding it, there was no denying it.

The tree line came into view, the parking lot peeking between outstretched branches. We were close, but I didn't want to get my hopes up, not with the warriors laboring to breathe behind us.

Hints of their hunger bled through, weakening their magic and their endurance. It wasn't drastic, and they were keeping up, but if we had to engage in a fight, there was no telling how long they could hold up against other well-trained warriors who hadn't been suffering like they had.

Noises came from the left, and my heart stuttered. *Do you hear that?* The source wasn't small like a wolf; it was more human-sized but moving too quickly.

Yes, I do. Thorn kept his attention focused forward. *Keep running. If we start scanning the area, it'll slow us down. They're far enough away that we should be able to get to the car without trouble.*

The warriors behind us stiffened, their movements not quite as quiet, confirming they were also straining and on high alert. Everyone's footsteps remained strong and steady.

When Saphira and Brenton broke through the trees, part of me felt relieved, but I locked that down. We weren't out of the woods yet, and I didn't mean literally. Until we were in the vehicles, driving away with no one following us, we could still be attacked.

My dragon roared, inching forward and ready to be released for battle. I could see a few cars with humans hanging around them close to our vehicles. Shifting would not be possible, but at least Drake's warriors would have to be careful around the prying eyes.

A few seconds later, Thorn and I were on the dirt path to the parking lot.

I could hear feet pounding from about a mile away.

We'd get out of here, but not without Drake learning we had the ten warriors and that Theron and Hydra were part of our crew. I only hoped that didn't mean something worse for their thunder, but we'd discuss that once we were on our way out.

Brenton jumped into the driver's seat of the rental car, while Saphira took the front passenger side. The rest of us split up, heading to the vehicles we'd ridden in to get here.

Over his shoulder, Thorn told the warriors, "Five in each Suburban."

As we jogged past two families getting hiking gear together to head into the woods, they all stared at us. We were running, maybe in an obvious hurry, but not so fast that we screamed supernatural...at least, I didn't think we did.

I realized that wasn't what had caught their attention. It was the ten warriors with rifles on their backs.

"Honey," a middle-aged mother said as she scurried to her two preteen kids. "We need to go."

The father nodded abruptly and ran to the driver's side door to unlock their vehicle.

I hated that we'd scared them, but there wasn't much we could do. I ran to the Suburban parked closest to the road and jumped into the front passenger seat. I wanted to ride with Thorn, but using our fated-mate connection could be beneficial. Caution would help us in this situation.

Echo, Blaze, Fury, Owen, and Opal climbed in the back of my vehicle, and as soon as the door shut, Vlad put the car in reverse and peeled out of the lot.

I turned around in my seat, searching for the enemy dragon shifters. One of the human families that had been squatting when we'd run by had stayed, while the other family had piled into their car. The warriors chasing us must have split off, casing the area outside of the woods. They couldn't move too quickly and were still three-quarters of a mile away. Luckily, the other cars in the lot blocked our tags, so all they'd see were the types of vehicles we were driving.

Thorn and Brenton backed their vehicles out, and the three cars raced to the road. I could hear seatbelts buckling in the back as the warriors settled in. Fury sat in the middle of the far back row, with Opal and Echo flanking her. I was surprised that of three men in the car, the largest one had gotten shoved into the far back until Echo placed an arm around Fury's shoulders. They must be together, but they had distinct scents, meaning they weren't bonded yet.

"I need you to keep an eye out and make sure no one is following us," Vlad said as he stepped on the gas, going fifteen miles over the speed limit.

I wanted to tell him to go faster, but that would be reckless. We could get pulled over, and that would only cause more problems.

"We're on it," Blaze said from his spot behind me.

My head rolled back as the world spun. I forced out a breath I hadn't realized I was holding, then filled my lungs to capacity.

All the vehicles were moving, and we were making headway back to the safe house. Even better, trained warriors were keeping an eye out in case someone was following us. That hadn't gone over so well with me last time, so I focused on calming down.

I'd give anything to be in that vehicle with you, Thorn connected in my head, his nerves still frazzled.

Unlike me, he didn't show them, and since we were going to rule over the dragons once we took Drake down, I'd better develop a poker face of my own. With Peter, I'd managed to hide my emotions because he'd always been indifferent and mean to me. That was easier to take than people I loved being in danger. I was damn sure they could see every emotion rolling across my face.

Me, too. I turned to stare into the side mirror. I wanted to do my part, even with warriors in the vehicle, but I did feel better that I wasn't the only one watching for tails, or I'd think *every* car was following us.

After twenty minutes of no one saying anything, some of the tension eased. I told the warriors there was a cooler in the back with sandwiches, and Fury immediately leaned over the back seat and dug in.

When they passed me a sandwich, I settled back and continued to keep watch...just to make sure. I suspected it would feel like a much longer ride back.

THE NEXT MORNING, Arrow, Echo, Errol, Vlad, Theron, Cassidy, Thorn, and I were in the kitchen after breakfast. Despite Peter's protests, Elliott and Eva had dragged him outside to train with the others, saying that even though he was the only human, he had to learn to defend himself.

We'd gotten back late and hadn't discussed our situation because the warriors had been exhausted. We'd found extra sheets and pillows, and they'd camped on the floor of the den, promising it was the most comfortable they'd been in weeks.

The table had been cleared of dishes, and everyone but Errol was sitting around it with cups of coffee, the scent of bacon still lingering.

Cassidy placed her teal coffee mug on the table. "So, they know these warriors are with us. We wanted to have that be a secret advantage."

"There was nothing we could do." Thorn leaned back in his seat across from her. "They arrived. If those wolves hadn't warned us, they might have chased after us and caught us." He leaned over and took my hand resting on top of the table.

Vlad ran a hand through his thickening scruff and placed his elbows on the table. He didn't say anything, but his forehead was lined with worry.

"We need more allies," Errol stated as he paced behind us. "But how can we achieve that while we hide?"

Arrow rubbed a finger against his bottom lip. He was sitting at the end of the table between Thorn and Cassidy. "One thing we can do is train *everybody* like the warriors. We'll teach them the way we... er, the enemy thinks. They'll surprise Drake's people and have a better chance of escaping them."

Excellent. This reminded me of something from a few days ago. "We should train them with weapons. I had to hold a gun the other night, and I was uncomfortable. I need to learn to shoot."

"Why did you need a gun here?" Echo scowled and examined the room like it held answers.

"It wasn't here," Theron said from his spot near the back door, a few feet away from Arrow and Cassidy. He'd been watching the others train outside. "It was when we met with Uther, Gemma, and Jerry, and they gave us a burner phone and asked us to take in their family members, who Drake was using as leverage to force their loyalty."

We filled the warriors in on everything that had happened to date.

"Those three are good people." Arrow took a sip of his drink. "I can think of several others who would ally with us, but it's too risky to reach out to them."

"There might be another way for us to gain more allies." Thorn cleared his throat as something brimmed through our bond: anticipation.

Hope sparked inside me. He had a plan. "What?"

"Theron, you still have access to the injured dragons' network, don't you?" Thorn winked as a warm feeling spread between us.

I tilted my head. I had no idea where he was heading with this. "Do you want us to move again?" I asked. The bouncing around was hard, but if they thought we might be at risk, I was willing to do whatever was necessary.

"That's not what I'm getting at. What if we coordinate meetings so I can heal more injured dragons?" He gestured at me. "And Everly could help with those who were injured in human form and give them some relief."

My heart leapt. "That won't guarantee us allies."

He shrugged. "Doesn't matter. It's the right thing to do—as long as we know our meeting location will be secure."

"I'm telling you, the people in this network—they aren't like that." Theron turned to the table, his eyes lighter than I'd seen in days. "Just the fact that you're willing to help would make a world of difference to so many."

"And word will spread, and other thunders won't be afraid of you." Errol grinned. "Some will want to ally with you just because of the good you're doing for the community, and that will make it easier for others to follow you two."

Us two? "You mean him," I said.

"The king is only as strong as the queen beside him." Errol smiled kindly. "Mira is capable of so much, but none of you had the opportunity to see it because all the light was on King Arman."

Echo chuckled. "That lady is as strong as they come. I've seen it with my own two eyes—when she walked into a room and spoke, King Arman listened. Their love was inspiring."

His words dampened my mate's spirit, and I understood why. He hadn't gotten the chance to notice it...not as a man. He could remember it only through a little boy's eyes.

I glanced out the window and saw Peter scowling with his arms crossed on the sidelines. He'd been a constant pain in the butt, and ever since Elliott and Eva had been changed, he'd become sulky and silent, dragging us down.

Reece was outside, despite not training like the rest, and stood next to Peter, trying to talk to him, but he ignored her just as he'd done to me when I was her age...at least, when my mother wasn't around.

Something clicked, and a lightness filled my body. "I know what we can do to completely derail Drake and solve another problem."

CHAPTER TWENTY-ONE

ALL SEVEN PAIRS of eyes pinned me. The idea had rushed at me so quickly. We'd have to work out logistics, but I believed it could *work.*

Thorn quirked an eyebrow. *Are you adding to the suspense?*

Bite me, I replied as I lifted my hands, getting ready to talk.

Gladly. He inched forward. *I didn't get the opportunity this morning, so I have no qualms about doing it right here at the table in front of everyone.*

Heat flooded my body, and my dragon surged forward. Never would I have believed I'd be the type of girl who'd love a man this possessive and unafraid of public affection, but here we were. I hoped it never changed.

"What if we use Peter for something useful?" I rubbed my hands together, focusing back on what I'd been planning.

Thorn thumped a hand on the table like a drum. "Sold. I don't need to know anything more. Let's get rid of the man who keeps glaring hatefully at my mate *before* I lose control and kill him."

I laughed, surprising myself. Thorn had a way of making me smile, no matter the circumstance.

"Though I want to agree with Thorn, Peter knows too much about us." Vlad's shoulders sagged. "And I'm not sure how he can be useful."

"Hear me out." I lifted a hand. "Obviously, we'd have to get Edna and the thunder on board, but what if we can find a place where we can all work together to tend to the injured, but we paint a different story for Peter and let him sneak away?"

Errol paused mid-step but said nothing.

"What do you mean by 'paint a different story'?" Theron squinted as if he were trying to see the bigger picture.

"We tell him Edna freaked out and said we needed to find another place on our own to hide." I started tossing out ideas without thinking any of them through. "And then make it sound like the warriors abandoned us so Drake thinks we're on our own again, with no place to go."

"I mean, they're training the others outside." Arrow gestured to the door. "Why would we be training you if we planned on leaving?"

Cassidy chewed on her fingernail. "No, wait. This could work. You all hid, and when they came to bring you back with us, you realized your location had been compromised."

"We can say we were tired and hungry, man." Echo smirked. "We took a chance to get out of there and get some food. Then we'll let slip that when Edna kicks Thorn and the others out and they have no place to go, their usefulness is over. After all, King Arman is dead, and there's no way Thorn and Everly can win."

I hated how that sounded and almost regretted bringing up the idea. Maybe the warriors would realize they were invested in a sinking ship.

"So we cut our losses." Arrow winced. "That sounds awful, but it would make sense. If they had nowhere to go, we would separate so we only had to worry about ourselves...the ones best trained for the situation. Some might not buy it, but hell, we just need Drake to."

"And he would." Vlad snorted humorlessly. "He only looks out for himself. His focus will be on finding Thorn before the coronation to ensure nothing goes wrong, and he'll believe that you warriors would know that and try to save yourselves."

He was right. Though none of us were like that, Drake was. That sort of rationale would make sense to him because that was what he'd do—cut his losses and save his own ass.

"Edna would have to be willing to leave with her thunder," Thorn said as he placed a hand on my thigh. "Even if we have her pretend to send us away, Drake wouldn't let her go unpunished."

"We would have to take her with us." Theron nodded. "And it wouldn't be ideal. I'm not even sure where we *could* go. They have a thunder of over one hundred people. We can't all cram into one house."

Unfortunately, that was a good point. "We'll have to split up, if you think we can find enough safe locations."

"If we first help the injured dragons to those who hide us, I think we can find a handful of people who can take us all in." Theron removed his phone from his back pocket. "That would also allow us to spread apart and be harder to locate."

"We have Uther and Queen Mira to warn us if Drake and his warriors are coming to our location." Thorn shrugged. "Uther calls us every night to talk to Reece, anyway, but we aren't making that public knowledge because of the human hanging around. He'd rat us out in a heartbeat."

That was true. Uther called often, and the queen had helped us yesterday. They were coordinating who could get a hold of us best.

"It all comes down to whether Edna will agree." Cassidy ran a finger along the edge of her coffee cup. "Do we think she will?" She glanced at Theron.

"There's only one way to find out." Theron swiped on his phone. "But I suspect she will. Why don't you all head out there and train while I talk to her?"

Thorn's hand tensed on my leg, and he connected, *Don't get me wrong. I like you being able to defend yourself and find you training sexy as hell, but I hate it when you get hurt. It's worse than when I do.*

To his credit, he rarely got hurt, even when he trained with Vlad. Thorn was the strongest out there by far, and when he, Vlad, and Cassidy had been living in hiding, he'd worked construction jobs so he could get paid under the table. He was fit, tough, and all dragon—then add in his strong alpha royal genes, and he was a beast. With the warriors we had in tow now, he might struggle a little, but not like the rest of us.

I know, but it's good for me. I turned and brushed my hand over his cheek. Just like Vlad, he had a little scruff on his face, and it scratched my fingertips. *And I don't get hurt as often anymore.* I was about on par with the others now. Though I was smaller and not built as sturdily since I wasn't born a dragon, I could get out of tight spots more easily due to my size. It helped me as often as it hurt me. That was one thing Vlad and Theron were trying to focus on with me: using my differences to my advantage.

After a quick kiss, I stood and flicked my gaze between Echo and Arrow. "Will one of you teach me to shoot a gun? I'd like to be more confident if I ever need to use one again."

"You have a very smart wife and mate, Your Highness," Arrow said as he smiled at me.

"Thorn." Thorn cleared his throat uncomfortably. "Just Thorn, and I know. I'm one lucky man."

Vlad climbed to his feet. "I'll run out to get some weapons and meet you in the back."

Our group dispersed, and even Cassidy joined us outside. Though she was trained, we all had to be in top shape for what came next. And that was exactly what we were going to do.

***

THAT NIGHT, our plan was in place. Edna had agreed. She'd said she would feel better at another location, anyway, in case the warriors learned that Emily had been changed or caught hints of Tia, Ryu, Merlin, and Belinda and their age. After all, the two empty houses had clearly been occupied. It would lead to questions. Apparently, she hadn't been sleeping well, worried about the situation as it was.

After Edna talked to the thunder and they all agreed, she and Theron reached out to other thunders in their network. Though it was less than ideal, we were looking for places farther from Asheville so we'd be centrally located for the thunders that wanted to bring their injured there for Thorn to heal.

The plan was in place—we were doing this tonight. The sooner, the better, so it would be more believable that Edna was kicking us out for bringing the warriors here. Arrow had discussed the plan with the nine warriors so they'd all play along, but we didn't inform anyone else since we needed the others to react accordingly.

We were all eating dinner—a quick, simple meal of hamburgers, steaks, and veggies that was easy to pick up, but nothing out of the ordinary for us—when there was a pounding on the front door. Mindy, Elliott, Cassidy, Vlad, Eva, Sol, Reece, Chandra, and Kari were crammed around the table with the extra chairs we'd added.

Five of the new warriors, plus Errol, Theron, Hydra, Belinda, Tia, Merlin, and Ryu, had gone outside to eat on the front porch, and Arrow, Echo, Sydney, Fury, Rex, Saphira, Tyson, Brenton, and Peter were sitting on the couch. Thorn and I sat on the ottoman facing the door, trying to appear relaxed, but it was so damn hard. We had a plan, but I worried something would go wrong. Something *always* went wrong.

Another knock sounded, and Peter's eyes widened, either from fear or hope. I doubted he'd be upset if Drake found us and came swooping in. That was why he needed to go.

"Edna, what did you expect us to do?" Theron asked more loudly than necessary so Peter could hear everything, too. Thorn set his plate of food down just as the door opened.

Edna's face was pink, her hands clenched at her sides. "It was *one* thing when it was just you all. I still wasn't thrilled with that, remember? You had your bags packed to leave. But now you've brought

Drake's warriors here as well? There's only so much risk I'm willing to take!"

I placed my empty plate on the floor, and Thorn and I stood, needing to appear concerned and on edge.

Following our lead, Arrow placed his plate on the couch where he'd been sitting. He'd picked the side of the couch closest to the door and quickly pivoted around it to stand before Edna. He lifted his hands in surrender. "We aren't Drake's warriors. We turned against him when he killed the king—after the king decreed he wasn't the true heir to the throne."

"You're smart, but that doesn't change things." Edna karate-chopped the air. "The more of you here, the more mouths I have to feed and the greater the worry that you'll be spotted. I have my own thunder to think of. You all need to leave. I'm sorry, but Tia, Belinda, Merlin, Ryu, and Mindy are the only ones who can stay."

Chairs scraped against the floor in the kitchen. Then footsteps hurried toward us.

Vlad marched in. "Edna, look. We should've talked to you about it. We're sorry. You're right, that was inconsiderate. But there was a tip on Dragonnet about them, and they'd protected us at Theron's thunder when Drake and his warriors had been ready to capture us. We owed it to them to help."

"That's fine." Edna spread out her arms. "I'm all for acts of kindness. That's why I've let you stay here for as long as you have. But even kindness has a limit, and mine has been reached. You need to pack up and leave, *tonight.*"

"Mom, you can't be serious." Mindy pushed past Vlad and hurried into the living room. Her eyes were wide, and her mouth trembled. "You want to split me up from my *fated mate.* This has to be a sick joke. These people are part of our *family* now."

Edna flinched, her face twisting in agony. "I'm sorry, honey. Elliott can stay, too."

My stomach dropped. *We should've told those two.*

Brushing his arm against mine, Thorn responded, *They'll understand later. Their reaction is genuine.*

He was right, but seeing the hurt and anger on my brother's and his fated mate's faces tugged at me. I knew how I'd be feeling if this were happening to Thorn and me.

"Can you give us one more night to get our things together?" Thorn clasped his hands in front of his chest. "I understand you don't want us here, but just give us a night's rest, and we'll leave first thing in the morning."

"That's the right thing to do, Edna." Tia *tsked* from the front porch.

I didn't need to see the older lady to know she had a disapproving look on her face. That was one thing I loved about her. She didn't have a problem speaking her mind, similar to Elliott and Saphira. The only difference was she was old enough to use her age as an excuse, though we *all* knew better.

"Fine." Edna's jaw clenched. "But that's it. At dawn, you must go. No do-overs this time. And until then, you need to stay in the house unless it's to load your vehicles. I mean it."

Mindy stomped, then winced like she'd done it too forcefully and hurt her back. Her voice was laced with pain as she rasped, "I'm going with them. I can't ask Elliott to leave his sisters and father behind when people are *hunting* them."

"Babe, it'd be safer if you stayed—" Elliott started.

Mindy spun on her heels, her pupils slitting as she waved a finger in his face and sneered, "Do *not* finish that sentence. I may have a bad back, but I'll find a way to kick your ass if you do. There is no way we're splitting up. It's you and me together, just like your sister and Thorn. Got it?"

He winked. "I may need you to take me to any room that will give us some privacy so you can show me *exactly* what you'd do to me, but you know, in a more fun way that results in us—"

"*Nope*," Eva said, uncharacteristically forcibly. "I'm stopping you right there. You're my *twin*, and there are some things I *never* want to hear."

"And I'm Mindy's mom." Edna leveled a dark gaze at him. "I know what fated mates do, and we don't need any visuals."

Peter huffed and rolled his eyes, unhappy with this situation. Frankly, I didn't care. I was glad he was the one on the short end of things, for once.

"Dawn. That's it," Edna said and hugged Mindy. "And you do what you have to do. I understand." She headed to her car.

"Well, she woke up on the wrong side of the bed," Tia muttered from outside, loudly enough for Edna to hear. "She usually keeps a level head, but she's gone off the wall."

"Hun," Ryu warned.

Belinda didn't hold back. "She can still hear you. You aren't as quiet as you think you are."

"Damn being old," Tia muttered, and Merlin chuckled.

The people on the front porch entered the house and shut the door behind them while everyone in the kitchen joined us in the living room. It was standing room only, and everyone was on edge.

Good. That was what we needed.

"What are we going to do?" Tyson asked from his spot between Saphira and Opal.

Thorn stood up straight, but the emotion coursing through the bond made my skin itch. Shame. "I know I was thinking we could fight Drake, but if we have nowhere to go, there is only one option—the one I thought was best from the very beginning. We need to leave the country. It'll be harder for him to search for us outside of the States, and yeah, we may have to hide, but it won't be as dangerous as staying here."

Now I had my part to play. "But he won't stop hunting us...ever." This was a conversation we'd had over and over, which was why we'd thought it would be believable if he pitched it.

"And my business is here." A vein in Peter's neck throbbed. "I've already been gone too long. I've got to get back. People count on me."

And we wanted to make Peter desperate.

"You mean *Drake* counts on you. He's your biggest client. Do I have to knock you out again?" Thorn snarled, turning the disgust he had with himself on Peter. "I've been itching to do that again for a while, now."

Vlad ran a hand through his hair. "I hate to say it, but we might need to leave until we can figure out a more permanent solution."

Reece whimpered and buried her face in Chandra's shirt. My heart hurt again for not letting everyone know.

"There's no way in hell I'm leaving the country." Arrow shook his head. "Besides, there aren't enough vehicles, so the warriors and I will go our separate way. It'll be best for all of us."

"What?" Saphira's jaw dropped. "You've got to be kidding. Splitting up is the worst thing we can do. That's the worst excuse I've ever heard."

"Just say what you mean, man." Echo looked down his nose at us. "Arrow doesn't want to tell you the truth. The truth is, we don't want to be here. We were loyal to the *king*, and there's no way in hell Thorn can take the crown from Drake. He doesn't even have a place to sleep starting tomorrow night. The best thing we can do is cut our losses—and that's all of you."

A few of the other warriors nodded uncomfortably.

"But we saved you from Drake." Errol shook his head. "And now that we don't have shelter for you, you're bailing?"

Sydney shrugged. "We made a mistake, but putting more cards in with your losing hand will only worsen our problems."

"You guys are assholes." Elliott wrinkled his nose and spat on the floor.

Of course he would actually spit on the floor. That was my brother. In fairness, he was mad at the warriors and Edna, and this was *her* house.

"There's no point in fighting." It was still light outside, and Peter needed to feel comfortable enough to run. He was a coward and wouldn't leave in the dark, so we had to speed this along. "We all need to clean up and pack. We have to be out of here in less than twelve hours."

Everyone stood, looking at each other, then scattered to pack. The thing was, we *did* need to pack. We needed to leave as soon as possible so we could put as many miles between here and ourselves whenever Peter made it back to Drake.

I watched as Elliott and Eva headed upstairs, and Peter slowly got off the couch to join them. He had a huge scowl on his face.

Thorn and I strolled into the hallway...and then his footsteps paused.

Arrow made his move and tapped Peter on the shoulder. This was the plan we were banking on—he was supposed to get Peter outside while we were all "distracted" and tell him to leave so Peter could tell Drake they'd aided him, hoping that Drake would partially forgive them.

But Peter ignored him, turning back toward the stairs as we turned left to head down the hallway. He wasn't going outside to talk to Arrow.

We needed him to go so we could tell the others what was really going on and he could "escape."

If he didn't leave now, our entire plan would be ruined.

CHAPTER TWENTY-TWO

MY BREATH LODGED as I tried to figure out what the hell to do. Thorn and I kept walking down the hallway because we *had* to. Otherwise, Peter would know we were watching.

"Hey," Arrow whispered.

He lowered his voice. It wasn't nearly as quiet as it needed to be for Thorn and me not to hear him; however, he had to be loud enough so Peter would with his human ears.

"What?" Peter snapped. "I've got to pack before my *son-in-law* knocks my ass out for, like, the tenth time."

Thorn's amusement wafted through our bond, and a giggle built in my chest. I swallowed to hold it down, afraid it might be too loud if the noise escaped.

I sort of wish I could go knock his ass out now, Thorn teased and tugged me to his chest. His sky blue irises lightened, almost matching the diamond flecks in the center. His eyes were my favorite thing about him—the color of the cloudless sky—with his plum silvery dragon wings being second, a color I favored when I painted the night sky. Both colors represented details I enjoyed most when painting any scene.

Our connection sprang to life, but I couldn't focus on it. Not with everything going on.

"Outside, *now*," Arrow whispered urgently. "You'll want to hear this."

"Fine." Peter scoffed. "But only for a minute."

Some tension eased from my body, but I wasn't sure I could trust my gut. What if he didn't leave?

When the front door shut, Thorn and I crept into the living room. Though Edna wasn't truly kicking us out, once Peter got loose, Drake would send his warriors here as quickly as possible. I wasn't foolish enough to think that Peter couldn't locate us. Yes, we were on a ton of land, but there was a mailbox with numbers in the front of the house. He could give them precise enough instructions to get here.

"They're busy. You should leave them," Arrow said on the porch outside the door.

He must have been blocking it so Peter couldn't come in.

"I *want* to." Peter huffed. "I've tried, but they caught me sneaking away, and I don't want to piss off that unstable jackass and have him punch me *again*."

My hands fisted. He didn't get to talk like that about Thorn...my *mate*. I reached for the doorknob, my dragon snarling in agreement, our anger blending as one, when Thorn caught my hand.

He beamed, the happiness lighting his face breathtaking. *I love this side of you. I mean...really happy Everly, aroused Everly, and possessive Everly are all three tied as top contenders, but we want him to leave. Remember?*

Next time, I will punch him. Hell, I was getting comfortable with a gun. Maybe I could shoot him in the leg. Nothing that would cause serious injury, just pain, which would only be a small piece of what he'd exposed me to during the past six years.

Let's add badass Everly to that list of top-four contenders. He waggled his brows. *Seriously, all versions of you are my favorite... except when you're mad at me. I don't like that version.*

I rolled my eyes. *Neither do I.* Just like I didn't like it when I hurt him. That was the worst feeling in the entire world.

"Go. Tell Drake that we're not on their team and that we let you go so you can tell him what's going on." Arrow's voice deepened. "Echo will help you get out of here while they're preoccupied with packing. The rest of us can distract them until he returns."

"Seriously?" Peter asked warily.

"How else are we going to get a message to Drake?" Sydney gritted out. "It's not like we can say, 'Hey, we made a mistake.' The only way we can apologize is to get someone he's open to trusting out of here to let him know we're turning against them *and* they have nowhere to go. If Drake's warriors rush here, they should be able to track them."

He paused, and my heart raced. I'd expected him to jump at the opportunity. What the *hell* was going on?

Peter huffed. "This could be a trap."

"We're splitting up from *them*." Rex snorted drily. "We made it clear we don't want to be on the losing side, but whatever. Suit yourself. Go back in like a good little human and get ready. I'm sure your company will be fine without you indefinitely."

I held my breath, waiting for his response. I'd thought he'd be halfway down the road by now, but he was still standing on the porch.

Crap.

"*Fine.*" Peter's voice grew higher in excitement or fear...maybe a combination. He wasn't out of the woods yet. "I'll tell him. Just get me the hell out of here. They'll be looking for me any second. I can't even go to the bathroom without someone knocking on the door."

As if he had summoned Elliott and Eva, they headed down the stairs, their eyes wide. Their mates were following them, their faces blanched.

"Dad—" Elliott started, but I placed a finger to my lips.

I didn't want Peter to get startled and be too scared to leave. Elliott's brows furrowed as Eva scanned the living room.

"Let's go. You can't get your stuff or tell your kids goodbye." Echo's voice grew louder, as if he were reaching for the door, too.

Eva's head tilted back, her pupils slitting. A snarl came out of her throat, and smoke trickled from her nose. She was angry, and she'd shift if she didn't stop it.

Mauve scales peeked through her pale skin. We had no time. I ran to the threshold of the door and whispered loudly enough so they could hear, "This is what we want. Please, calm down."

"What?" she breathed, a puff of smoke hitting my face. "You *want* him to leave?"

I waved a hand in front of my face, dissipating the smoke. Thank goodness we'd cut all the fire alarms, or they'd be ringing. "Yes, the whole thing is staged."

I'd been worried about Elliott running his mouth when I should've been more concerned with Eva taking action. She was always quiet, making her easy to overlook, but her time as Drake's captive had changed her. She'd been training with vigor, and she'd become a woman of action.

Mom would've been just as proud as I was.

Sol took the last few steps and stood right behind Eva, scratching his head. He asked, "So...we aren't leaving?"

Thorn wrapped an arm around my waist, making it clear we were in this together. He said, "We have to go. Peter can help them find this place. Edna and the others are leaving as well, but the warriors are staying with us."

Sighing, Mindy's body sagged. "Oh, thank gods. I couldn't believe Mom would do that to you after the way you helped Emily and considering that Elliott and I would be split up."

"Unfortunately, you'll still have to choose." Thorn frowned. "We can't all go to the same place—there are too many of us—but you're more than welcome to stay with us if you prefer."

He didn't put pressure on them, and I understood why. Elliott was my brother, but I refused to be like Peter and not allow him to make his own choice. "Or if Elliott wants to leave with your family, that's fine, too. You two are fated, and being apart would be difficult."

"Uh..." Elliott gawked at Eva and me. "It's just, you two are family, and..."

Tears burned my eyes. Before all of this had gone down, he wouldn't have included me in the equation. Now he didn't want to be apart from Eva *and me*. Something finally clicked into place—we truly were family.

"It's fine," Mindy said. "Mom has her entire thunder to look after, and you all need as many people to help as possible. Besides, you guys are my family, too, and I'm learning how to defend myself in ways my body can handle, despite the wreck." Mindy leaned forward and kissed Elliott's cheek. "So don't worry. I won't try to talk you into splitting from our sisters."

Thorn squeezed my side, and a tear fell from my eye. I hadn't realized how badly I needed this moment.

The front door opened, and all the warriors except Echo headed inside. Thorn and I glanced over our shoulders as Fury nodded.

"Echo should be back in a few minutes. He's carrying Peter to the side road." Arrow bent down and grabbed the blankets he'd slept in. "The countdown is on."

"Mindy and Elliott, are you two packed?" Thorn took my hand and tugged me back toward the room we'd been sleeping in.

Elliott pursed his lips. "I've got to get the gaming system and a few other things. When we realized Dad never made it upstairs, we stopped what we were doing."

"Can you finish up and get Mindy to ask Tia, Belinda, Ryu, and Merlin to gather their things?" Thorn opened the door to the bedroom. "They're leaving, too."

Mindy turned back on her heels. "Sure can. They're in their room. I'll go tell them now."

This time, we all dispersed, getting ready to leave the place that had been home for the last few weeks.

Around eight the next morning, our group—minus the older

dragon shifters, who'd stayed with Edna—rolled into the place we would call our new home.

We were all exhausted after heartfelt thank-yous and goodbyes and a ten-hour overnight drive. Sleeping in a loaded vehicle while fearing that someone might notice our tag had everyone on edge. We hadn't wanted to risk swapping put the vehicles but planned to do so as soon as we got settled.

Theron led the way in his oversized red truck, while I rode in the SUV with Cassidy, Reece, Kari, Chandra, Echo, and Fury. The warriors sat in the middle row, with Echo behind my seat and the two women and Reece in the far back. We'd split up in the best way possible for fated-mate communication, so Thorn and I were riding separately again.

My dragon surged forward, making my skin crawl even more. Between retrieving the warriors and now this, we'd been split up a lot during the past twenty-four hours, with only a couple of hours at the house together in between but with everyone around. I needed alone time with him horribly, even if it was just cuddling, and I couldn't fathom how I'd managed to not try to run and escape to get back to him when I'd been separated from him at the château.

His dragon grumbled through our bond, and his voice popped into my head. *When we get there, I'll need you in my arms. It's been ages since I've touched you.*

I chuckled. I shouldn't have been surprised we were going through the same withdrawal. We were so in sync it wasn't even funny, and our connection grew more and more each day. *No one will be able to pry me away from you.*

We'd just passed through Steelville, a small Missouri town, and were following a stream into the woods. Steelville was quaint, with a small downtown area of brick buildings lining both sides of the main street, and I was learning that most dragon shifters preferred to live in these types of isolated places.

Several miles from the center of downtown, we turned onto a dirt road into the thickening trees. After a few more miles, we turned right onto another dirt road that took us closer to huge, rolling mountains. As we rounded a bend, three small cabins surrounding a pond came into view. Each cabin was identical, with hunter green siding that blended in with the trees and a lighter green porch with steps that led to a white wooden front door.

A man close to Thorn's age was leaning against the first one, and we pulled into that driveway. I knew better than to think we were staying with the thunder, since we couldn't risk our enemy seeing us if they dropped in.

We stopped in a line, and soon, each vehicle was unloading.

The man leaning against the stair rail, looking every inch the warrior, pushed off and strolled toward us. His dark auburn hair was styled upward, and his face was clean-shaven, revealing a sun-kissed complexion. His peridot eyes focused on Theron.

"Spike." Theron strolled over to the man and held out a hand.

The younger man took it. "You must be Theron."

"I am." Theron yawned and winced. "I'm so sorry. It's been a long night."

Thorn strode up to me and took my hand as he said, "Thank you for letting us stay here. I know it puts you out."

"If this helps you take down Drake after what he did to my dad, I'm all for it." Spike's jaw clenched. "He should still be in charge of this thunder—he was only three hundred years old—but Drake made sure that didn't happen. Not with his injured talon. Between my dad and the five older dragons that his warriors slaughtered, let's just say it's been a hell of a year for deaths at Drake's hands, and the pain is as fresh as if it had happened yesterday."

His anger and pain broke my heart. "I'm so sorry for what he did to you." Those words weren't enough, I knew. I still missed Mom so much; I'd give anything to hear her voice one more time...to smell her honeysuckle scent I was so damn close to forgetting.

"Me, too. But I'll tell you now, this is your home until you don't need it. We don't have injured or old dragons that need hiding anymore, and I knew one day we might need to help another thunder and shouldn't give up the land." He scanned us, taking in our various conditions. Then his attention landed on Reece as she limped to my other side. "Obviously, I made the right decision. You all need rest. I'll come back later when you're better able to talk, but I want you to know right here and now that my thunder will fight alongside you. We don't have huge numbers, only forty able bodies to fight, but we're yours."

Relief poured from Thorn. "That's forty more than we had just a minute ago. Thank you."

"I know you said you have twenty-seven. Each house will hold nine, but it'll be tight." He patted the wall. "There are two bedrooms in each—a queen bed in one and a double mattress bunk bed in the other. There's also a sofa in the living room that has a queen-size pull-out mattress. Other than that, there's a kitchen and one full bathroom." He gestured between the first and second cabin. "That way, there's a building with four showers and more restrooms. Dad built this place in case we had to take others in, so if there's an emergency, you can use those, too. I went ahead and pulled out the sofa beds in each house, and all the sheets are clean. I haven't been able to run to the store, but I'll do that before I come back later tonight so you'll have plenty to eat."

While on the run, I'd seen more kindness than I ever had before. All these people were taking us in and providing food and electricity. Though I wished Drake wasn't a threat, sometimes the horribleness in one person revealed the goodness in others. Despite Drake hunting us, these dragons had formed a network to support and take care of one another, and it was more beautiful than a painting could ever be.

"Thank you," Reece said softly as she took my hand.

"Doors are unlocked, with the key on the kitchen table." He strolled into the woods, heading toward a motorcycle leaning against a cypress tree. "You know how to get a hold of me if you need anything."

The groups formed pretty easily. The warriors wanted to make sure there were at least two in every house, so our cabin wound up consisting of Thorn, me, Reece, Chandra, Kari, Eva, Sol, Echo, and Fury. Vlad, Cassidy, Theron, Hydra, Saphira, Tyson, Rex, and Opal went to the center cabin, with the rest of the group heading to the third. We wanted to keep a mix of groups in each house so we could all get to know one another.

Owen and Asher took guard duty while the rest of us got some sleep. Like before, we would take shifts to keep watch. Not that we didn't trust Spike, but there was just no telling when a threat might fly overhead since people would be scouting the area for us.

Our cabin was smaller than I'd realized. We entered the living room, and the hide-a-bed was pulled out as promised, the end of the mattress reaching just in front of the white refrigerator. To the left was a stove, a small sink, and a large cabinet that served as the pantry, with a square table that sat four in front of it. To the right of the living room and across from the couch was a door that opened into a bathroom, and a door to the far right opened to one bedroom. I could see a queen-size bed with no other furniture inside. As I peered further left, I could see that the other door opened to the room with the bunk beds. This place was so small that everyone would hear every noise we made.

The group insisted that Thorn and I take the queen room while Reece and the other two women took the couch, and the rest went to sleep in the bunk beds.

I crawled into the lumpy bed. Thorn shut the door and slipped in next to me, then pulled me into his arms. As the comforting buzz of our connection took over, he pressed a soft kiss on top of my head, and I fell quickly asleep.

A ringing noise went off, stirring me awake. I blinked my eyes open only to be blinded by the morning sun reflecting off the wall. We hadn't been asleep for long.

The ringing kept going, and Thorn mumbled as he pulled me back into his arms.

Thorn, a phone is going off. I sat up, pulling myself from his arms to get my bearings.

It's the burner. He reached under his pillow, removing it. There was a missed call.

As he opened the phone, a text message came through.

Theron's thunder is in trouble. Warriors on the way.

My heart leapt into my throat. Peter knew Theron had been talking to Wyvern, and we'd all forgotten. He must have reached Drake.

CHAPTER TWENTY-THREE

I READ THE TEXT MESSAGE, willing my exhausted brain to catch up. There was so much fog, I couldn't function. All I knew was that I needed to do something.

Finally, on the third read-through, I noted it was from Uther. Adrenaline pounded through my body, fully waking my brain.

Thorn tensed beside me before removing his arm from underneath me and jumping to his feet. He typed out something on the phone as I followed his lead.

Standing beside him, I glanced at his reply: **When did they leave?**

I opened the door to the living room and rushed past the sofa bed, trying not to wake the girls.

We didn't need to wait for Uther's reply. Either way, we needed to get to Theron quickly so he could contact Wyvern. I wanted to kick myself that we hadn't contemplated that Peter would tell Drake *everything.*

As we hurried out the front door, Kari groaned. "What's going on?"

Answering her would take precious time that Wyvern and the

others might not have. *Go. I'll be right behind you*, I connected to Thorn.

He hesitated, then nodded and jogged toward the next cabin over. I turned back to Kari, who was sitting on the bed, her face tense. In all the chaos, Chandra was awake as well, her attention locked on me. The two warriors were standing in the doorway, rifles in hand. I was thankful that Reece was still asleep. The last thing that sweet little girl needed was more turmoil.

"Do we need to get to the vehicles?" Kari tossed the covers off her legs.

"No." I lifted a hand. "Drake is on his way to attack another thunder, and we're sending word to them. We're fine here. Go back to sleep."

Chandra frowned. "Is there anything we can do?"

The reality of the situation sank in. "No, there's not. We all need our rest for training and what comes next. If something changes, I'll wake you and let you know."

Kari yawned. "Thank gods." She covered herself up and lay gently back on the bed, trying not to wake Reece.

"Do you want us to go with you?" Echo asked and stepped into the room, hitting the side of the table. He was huge and took up all the space between the pantry and the table.

"Stay here with them, please, in case something happens here." I scurried to the door and paused as I grabbed the handle. "I'm running next door."

Fury walked onto the porch with me. "I want to stay out here for a bit. I thought something was wrong, and I needed a moment to calm down before going back to bed."

I couldn't blame her. Most of the time lately, I was running on adrenaline. I had a feeling that whenever things calmed for us, I would crash for a month to catch up on sleep and everything I'd neglected physically.

Tapping into my dragon, I ran to the edge of the porch opposite the stairs and jumped over the railing. I dropped, my feet hitting the grass, and took off running.

The hairs on the nape of my neck rose as I considered what might happen next. The front door was open, and I could hear shuffling in the house.

"We've got to *go*," Saphira said loudly as I took the stairs two at a time. "They're going to hurt Wyvern!" The last word took on a hysterical edge.

"Saphira—" Thorn said slowly as I stepped into the doorway.

"No!" Saphira stood in front of the sofa bed, shoving Thorn into the kitchen table behind him. The table groaned across the wood floor and slammed the wall, shaking it. "You don't get to *Saphira* me. We're getting in the car and going *now*."

Vlad and Cassidy stood between the table and the stove. They grabbed the table, trying to hold it in place, blocking Rex and Opal from coming into the room. They were stuck at the door.

Grunting, Saphira grabbed Thorn's arms. Pain prickled through our fated-mate connection, and my dragon roared.

I barreled toward her, grabbed her arm, then yanked her away from my mate. Every cell in me was on fire, wanting to teach her a lesson, but the part that loved her like a sister surged forward and asked me how I'd feel if Thorn were in a similar situation.

I'd done many stupid things in the name of protecting him, and as much as I wanted to rip her head off for hurting my mate, she was going through the same thing trying to get to hers.

Her pupils were slitted, and her hands shook as she kept her hold on Thorn. I'd suspected that Wyvern was her mate by the way they responded to each other, and this confirmed it.

"Saphira, do *not* touch my mate like that again, or you won't be able to walk to the car," I snarled, my dragon leaking through. What I wanted to do to her was way worse than this, so I counted my blessings for the control I had.

Her irises blazed with anger. "It's easy for you to say when everyone you love is here and *safe*."

I'm fine, Thorn connected. *I promise. It's just the stress catching up to all of us. If you were in danger, I would do far worse than what she just did to me.*

With his reassurance and having him back on both feet, some of my anger ebbed. My throat constricted. "Saphira, you're like family to me, and so are Theron, Hydra, and Sol. Their thunder is important to me, just as much as everyone here."

She took in a shaky breath and unclenched her hands. I heard the faint sound of a phone ringing on the other end of a call Theron was making. "You're right. I'm sorry." She hung her head.

I pulled my attention away from Saphira to take in our surroundings. Just like Spike had said, this place was identical to ours, right down to the sheets. Tyson sat on the sofa bed, his hair messy and his mouth open. The vacant spot beside him smelled like Saphira, which meant she had probably opened the door to let Thorn in.

"Hello?" Wyvern's voice replaced the ringing.

My gaze settled on Theron and Hydra. They were standing in the doorway of the bedroom on the right with the queen bed.

"Gather the thunder and get the hell out of there," Theron barked, the skin around his eyes tight. "You've been compromised. They know you've been talking to me."

"What?" Wyvern asked in disbelief. "How? We've been so careful."

Rubbing a hand down his face, Theron grimaced. "Someone who's been around us got back to Drake, and I didn't realize he knew you and I were still in touch. I'm sorry. I should've figured that out."

Another phone alert went off, and Thorn glanced at the message. "It's Uther. They're leaving the château, but there are five warriors an hour closer, and they'll be flying. They need to grab some things and leave. He said the warriors are coming from the south, so if the thunder flies north, they should be able to get out undetected."

Theron sighed. "Your best bet is to grab what you need and be ready to leave in ten. I'll reach out and see if anyone else can take you in."

"Okay. I'll call you back soon." Wyvern hung up, and the room filled with silence.

Theron was already typing out a message on what had to be the network system, looking for another location that could provide aid.

We were putting so many thunders at risk, and I feared we might have used every resource available.

"When they leave, they need to separate into groups." Vlad tapped his fingers against his leg.

My dragon stirred, and an uneasy feeling coursed down my spine. I watched Saphira, noting how she was wringing her hands. That was a safer way to work out her concern rather than on my mate, so I stepped outside onto the porch. The wide-open space eased my dragon and me.

Joining me, Thorn led me to the side that overlooked the pond. Now that we were out of there, more people were able to fit in the front room. We'd left the door open.

"That will make it harder for them to decide who to track." That was Rex. "They won't know who all's involved, and since Wyvern is the acting alpha while you're gone, they'll focus on him. They'll blame him for the breach, even if he didn't make contact."

This had to end. We had about eleven days to get a plan in place, including an army, before Drake officially took control of the dragons. We had to begin thinking offensively and get ahead of them.

Theron joined us on the front porch, his phone in his hands. "There are a few thunders around Memphis that can take in the majority of my people. They're about an hour's flight time apart, but they're close enough. We still need a place for about twenty of them."

I understood the predicament. Once shifted, they needed to know where to head. They couldn't risk stopping and someone seeing them along the way. It was best for them to fly high and stay away from planes and other dragons. "What about here?" Especially for Saphira, it would be best if Wyvern came here, but I didn't want to make that decision. That was Theron's place.

Leaning against the railing, Thorn tugged me so my back pressed against his chest. He wrapped his arms around my waist, the sizzle of his touch nearly taking my breath.

"We have an extra building with bathrooms. We can take turns sleeping outside, or we can make space on the floor," Thorn added.

"It would be nice to have Wyvern here so he can be part of the training and the upcoming attack." Theron stared out at the pond. "Drake will be hunting him since he's been in charge. It's not like we have a ton of options."

"It's settled." Thorn nodded. *And maybe Saphira will calm down.*

I mashed my lips together, trying not to smile. I glanced back inside to find Saphira sitting at the kitchen table with her head in her hands, looking worse than I'd ever seen her...which was saying something since she'd been Drake's prisoner for a while.

When Theron's phone rang, her head snapped up. As Theron told Wyvern everything we'd discussed, I headed to my friend and hugged her. I murmured, "Wyvern will be here soon."

Her breath caught, and she shook. "Thank gods."

I had to believe Theron's thunder would be all right. And there was one thing we could do to distract ourselves until they got here: train.

So that was exactly what Vlad, Tyson, Cassidy, Thorn, Saphira, Theron, Hydra, and I did as we waited for Wyvern and the others to arrive.

My body was slick with sweat as Cassidy and I sparred. We'd been out here for over three hours, and the hot Missouri sun was beating down on us.

Any time we took a break, restlessness would seep back in.

The others were slowly waking and joining us. The warriors were training Kari, Chandra, Saphira, and Errol on firearms across the pond so they wouldn't risk hitting anyone, while Vlad and Thorn taught Mindy, Eva, Elliott, and Tyson how to shoot with arrows about a hundred yards within the thick trees. The rest of us sparred. Part of the strategy we'd decided on was that we needed to use different tactics on the warriors: dragons, gunfire, arrows, daggers, and whatever else we could get our hands on. That would force them to split their response against different groups, based on how we were fighting, versus them employing a straight strategy across the board.

My stomach growled, eager for the pizzas we'd ordered to get here pronto, but I didn't dare take my eyes off Cassidy to search the road. I would hear the vehicle coming, anyway. Rex and Opal had left thirty minutes ago to get the food, and I was hoping they'd be back any minute.

Cassidy swung her fist at me, and I ducked, avoiding that blow, but her left fist swung upward and nailed me on the chin. My neck jerked back. Pain exploded through my jaw, and I stumbled a few steps.

A loud roar rang in my head, and it wasn't my dragon. It was Thorn's. His concern wafted through me, but I pushed it away.

The last time he'd distracted me, I'd gotten hurt, and I refused to take another blow like that. A groan slipped from me, but I pushed through the pain as I bounded over to Cassidy. She raised her hands, an arrogant smirk on her face, and I almost questioned my next move.

I faked a punch with my right arm, and she went to block it while keeping an eye on my other hand. Making sure my arms didn't move, I placed my weight on my left leg and kicked her in the stomach.

Her eyes widened, and she stumbled back several feet, more than I had. She hunched over and wrapped an arm around her stomach just as Thorn reached my side.

"Are you okay?" he asked, pulling me into his arms. His mesmerizing scent was even better with the musk of his sweat laced through it. My stomach clenched with need.

"I...think..." Cassidy gasped, then chuckled painfully. "She's more than fine."

My eyes flicked to Vlad, who was staring at Cassidy with concern.

"I'm sorry—" I started.

"No, it's my fault." She stood straight. "Vlad has been telling me to come out and train with you instead of cooking all the time. I didn't realize I was quite this rusty."

I moved my jaw from side to side, pain flaring back to life. "You got a good hit in yourself."

Thorn's hands gently touched my jaw as he examined it.

My chest swelled with how much I loved him. *I'm fine. I'll be healed in a few hours.*

He scowled. *That doesn't make me feel better.*

The sound of an engine purred, and my heart quickened. Food!

Should I be jealous that the sound of food arriving has your heart racing more than when I pulled you into my arms? he teased, his eyes lightening.

You have me warm in a whole different way I plan on showing you later, I connected and kissed him.

Theron's red truck appeared with Rex behind the steering wheel. We smiled and waved, but Rex didn't respond, and all Opal did was lift her hand and nod curtly.

When Thorn and I reached the vehicle, Rex climbed out and said, "We shouldn't have let Peter go."

What had my stepdad done now?

CHAPTER TWENTY-FOUR

THORN'S BODY TURNED RIGID, and the world shifted under my feet. With all the bad things that had happened to us, I thought I'd have been used to the anxiety, but I stumbled a step.

A large, warm hand grabbed my arm, anchoring me in more ways than one. Without Thorn, I wouldn't have been able to get through this with my sanity intact. He was my foundation...my home.

"What happened?" Thorn gritted.

"Breaking news came on." Rex smacked his lips like he'd tasted something bad.

Opal leaned against the hood of the truck and crossed her arms. "Next thing we knew, *Peter* was on the screen."

I leaned my head against Thorn's shoulder and winced from the pain that flashed through my jaw. I'd almost forgotten that Cassidy had hurt me—it didn't compare to the agony ripping through my heart. Although I knew Peter had never *loved* me, I'd hoped he wouldn't cause more problems for us, especially with the twins involved.

"He informed the world that he got away from his kidnappers, but his beloved children and stepdaughter couldn't break free," Opal ran her fingers through the end of her ponytail. "A menacing man by the name of Thorn Wight still has them, and he needs everyone to watch for them since the police didn't find them at the last known place they were being held. Then they showed a recent photo of Thorn they'd somehow obtained."

Not only were Eva's, Elliott's, and my faces plastered all over news outlets for every human and supernatural to see, but Thorn's was, too. It was a smart strategy. "We were being cautious, anyway, so it doesn't change much."

"Other than Peter being a bigger annoyance, which isn't surprising. I only wish I'd punched him a few more times before he left." Thorn exhaled, and his neck corded. "If I didn't love Everly so much, I would've already killed him."

"Oh. *That's* why he's still alive." Rex opened the truck's back door. "We've been wondering. He's worthless. Though he did allude to you traveling north and potentially leaving the country, so at least he's splitting Drake's focus to a larger area, and fewer warriors will be concentrated close by."

The aroma of pizza drifting from the back seat had my stomach gurgling again. I could smell the sausage, pepperoni, and cheesy goodness that needed to be in my stomach *right now*. Although the news they'd revealed was less than stellar, it wasn't detrimental. If we got out of the more immediate danger, we'd deal with the kidnapping charge.

Right now, we were hidden, so Peter's public announcement didn't change our strategy. "For Eva's and Elliott's sakes, I don't want him dead. I know what it's like not to have a living parent—it sucks. Better to have a self-centered one than none at all. He does stuff for them...occasionally." Maybe not as much as I'd thought, but I didn't want Thorn or me to be the reason he died. Regardless of his spitefulness, he was their family.

"Hey, I'm not one to judge." Rex shrugged and reached into the back seat, snatching up ten pizza boxes. We'd put in a gigantic order for the twenty-seven of us, plus the twenty who would be here any second. One hundred pizzas should get us by until Spike brought more supplies.

We headed to the large clearing where everyone had been training. There was a sizable wire table with eight chairs. As we set out the food, the sound of wings beating overhead caught our attention.

Glancing skyward, I tapped into my dragon and spotted numerous dragons descending quickly toward us. My heartbeat picked up a notch. Though we knew Wyvern and the others were coming, I wasn't sure what they looked like in their dragon form, so they could be friends or enemies.

Thorn's trepidation washed over me, then disappeared as the group drew closer. He connected, *Theron, Hydra, and Sol aren't worried. It's them.*

My shoulders relaxed, and I noted the duffel bags hanging from their talons. Relieved that they were here, I turned my attention to organizing the pizzas into ten piles. Each of us would get one whole pizza, and I expected the men to eat at least half of another.

The twenty dragons landed within the tree line. They'd shift and join us soon. Saphira, Hydra, Theron, Sol, and Eva hurried to the thick stands of cypress and oak trees to wait on the new thunder while everyone else hurried to grab their food.

When everyone had gone through the line, Thorn and I grabbed a box each of our own and headed toward Theron and the others. We sat against a tree trunk just as Wyvern and his thunder members came out to join us.

As soon as Saphira saw him, she ran right into his arms. He picked her up and kissed her as if they'd always been together.

We watched as the new arrivals hugged their thunder members and met Eva. The group was mainly comprised of men and a few women who appeared to range in age from their twenties to fifties, all fit and muscular. They must have been selected to come here so they could fight alongside us, and that made me like Wyvern even more.

When the last people hugged, Thorn cleared his throat and smiled. "Please, come eat. Then it's time to discuss what we'll do for several days to prepare for the final battle with Drake while we heal as many injured dragons as possible."

THE NEXT NINE days blurred together. We were on the go nonstop, breaking only for sleep. The fated-mate couples completed their bonds, which wasn't surprising, given the looming threat. Why waste time not being connected when the end could be near, even if we didn't want to admit it?

Spike kept us informed about what was going on with dragon politics since we didn't have access to the internet. Drake appeared on the Dragonnet daily to inform the shifters that we were causing more chaos, trying to pit us against one another and reemphasizing that anyone helping traitors would face death. He didn't allude to the uprising, giving the illusion of control.

But there *was* dissent brewing. Thorn and I had been traveling nonstop, meeting shifters halfway between their thunders and where we were staying in various wooded areas while the warriors watched out for any threats while we were busy.

Thorn had healed over fifty dragon shifters, and word was spreading through the injured dragon network like wildfire. That number alone was three-quarters of the known healable injuries in the U.S. Additionally, he'd changed twenty humans who were in relationships with dragon shifters into dragons.

Even though Thorn couldn't heal dragons who had sustained injuries while in human form, I was able to help with rehab exercises to alleviate some ailments, such as back and neck injuries from car wrecks or other accidents. One thing I'd discovered while working with shifters who couldn't fully recover was that many of them had birth conditions from being born to a human whose body wasn't strong enough to birth them. The result was often permanent injury, if not dying along with the mother.

Errol had heard rumors that dragons were taking humans as

mates because our numbers were dwindling, which was how Drake had gotten the idea of having a human breeder. But in every situation we'd found, the dragon shifter said they'd felt an undeniable tug toward the human—like Thorn and I had to each other.

Between ten birth conditions and twenty humans that Thorn had changed, our group had developed a theory. Since dragons were dying out, their destined mates were being born human, and that was why dragons were finding connections with humans.

The same people who had started off wary about helping Thorn and me now supported us. Thorn had shown them the great man he was, giving people hope that there could be a better future if he ruled the dragons.

Uther and the queen had been in constant touch. Since Theron's and Edna's thunders had scattered and Drake's people had found their safe houses, they believed Peter's information was true. Five warriors had altered their search for us to the north, near the Canadian border, which made it easier for other dragon shifters to visit Thorn for healing, but even those five were heading home to protect Drake during the coronation.

We'd considered attacking ahead of time, but with only five warriors away, we'd determined it would be safer to keep training while Thorn and I helped as many dragon shifters as possible in case the future didn't pan out like we hoped.

Spike and nine of his thunder members were grilling hamburgers, steaks, pork chops, and hot dogs. Vlad, Thorn, Theron, Wyvern, Saphira, Errol, Cassidy, and I had pulled the table next to the grill Spike was manning and sat down to talk strategy.

Scooting his seat closer to mine, Thorn placed an arm around my shoulders despite the sweltering heat. Unease swirled through our connection, and I wanted to climb out of my skin.

Tomorrow morning, we'd make the ten-hour drive to the dragon lands. We planned to leave by eight in the morning so we'd have time to get acclimated before we moved on the château after nightfall.

Dragons could see well at night, and it would be easier to cloak ourselves in darkness.

Vlad sighed beside Thorn. "Let's go over numbers."

I flinched. Everyone had been avoiding this part of the conversation. We all knew we would be greatly outnumbered.

Leaning into Thorn, I tried to focus on the sizzle of our bond and the comfort he provided.

"They'll have about three hundred warriors on guard at the coronation." Errol sat across from me, the faint crow's feet around his eyes deepening. "There'll be a minimum of one hundred on guard already. I assume that half will be on guard tomorrow night with the coronation so close. We'll have a little time before the remaining warriors descend."

A lump formed in my throat, and I couldn't speak.

Thorn jumped in. "The queen told me there are five hundred warriors in total. Drake has been recruiting extensively, offering hefty signing bonuses for people who come work for him as long as they pass the screening."

Which wouldn't be hard. Dragons were fit, and there were over one hundred thousand of us in the U.S. That they'd found an additional two hundred who could reasonably step into warrior shoes wasn't that surprising.

Saphira wrinkled her nose. She took Wyvern's hand and looked at her father, then spat, "Oh, I'm sure there was more than cash involved. Drake likes to have control, so something more caused two hundred dragons to magically come on board less than three weeks after his father's death, especially with how his warriors have been getting around, checking on the thunders."

"They tried talking me into becoming one of them, but I told them no way." Wyvern's face twisted in disgust. "I told them we were already down a leader, and they let it go. I'm sure others weren't so lucky."

Theron tapped a finger on his lips. "Maybe because Uther was involved with your thunder."

"You're probably right. Another warrior approached me first, but Uther intervened after I made that comment."

I was thankful I'd been at the château to meet Uther. Not because of Drake or betraying Thorn but because we wouldn't have any inside allies if it hadn't been for Eva's and my time there.

Biting her bottom lip, Hydra leaned back in her chair and glanced at her mate beside her. "That's almost double the numbers we were expecting."

"What about our side?" Cassidy countered from across Hydra and next to Vlad. "We have fifty-six here, not counting Reece."

Reece had pouted about not being part of the fight, but she was six. We wouldn't risk bringing her with us, and Spike had offered for his thunder to take care of her.

"And twenty from my thunder, including me." Spike lifted his tongs at the grill a few feet away from Errol and me. "From what I'm hearing on the injured network, that's not all."

My heart stopped. "What do you mean?" To hear others that might be willing to fight alongside us was amazing, but we didn't want too many people to know our plan. Though I didn't doubt these people were loyal and wouldn't betray us, secrets had a way of snow-balling when too many people were aware.

"Don't worry." Spike flipped a steak over. "They don't know the details. Those weren't mine to share. But in the network, people are asking how they can help Thorn secure the crown. They want Thorn and Everly as their king and queen. Not only do you two want to help everyone, but you also understand the lives we lead. That's something we've never had in any other king and queen."

To hear my name connected with Thorn's as if I could do the same amazing things as he could blew my mind. Thorn had changed lives, whereas I was just doing what I could to help. "He'll make an amazing king." I turned toward my mate, smiling so widely, my cheeks hurt.

"I never would've gotten here if it weren't for you," he replied, raising my hand to his lips and kissing the top. "You're the real prize they're getting."

Saphira gagged and shook her head. "I thought that once I found my fated mate, they wouldn't gross me out any more. But looky there, I was wrong."

"Oh, stop it." Wyvern chuckled and kissed her cheek. "We're just as bad as they are."

Errol cleared his throat uncomfortably but grinned. "Is there anyone on the network who would be willing to join us and can hold their own?"

Spike shrugged. "A few, but I didn't say anything since we hadn't talked about it."

The more Spike hung around, the more I liked him. He didn't push his own agenda and said over and over that all dragons, regardless of age or ability, were strong in their own right. He wanted a king who understood that.

The rest of our group strolled out of the trees, where they'd been training with the warriors with bows, daggers, and guns. Arrow headed straight to our table and joined the conversation. Vlad quickly filled him in on what we'd discussed.

Arrow nodded. "We need numbers, but not too many unknown variables. It could cause chaos since they haven't trained with us. We also want to surprise Drake. Yes, he may have five hundred warriors, but a third of them won't want to harm anyone. A lot of the warriors don't like Drake and were there for the king. If Drake has forced people to join him, and if they see we're winning or making headway, they won't be out to kill, only to draw blood to cover their asses."

It made sense.

"We don't need to attack them at the château." Vlad rubbed his hands together. "We draw them out so Drake will be less protected and go in through the secret tunnel." Only the king had known of the passage, and with his untimely death, that secret was ours alone. "Wait," said Vlad, pausing with a frown. "I thought you had to wait for him to let you in last time."

"There's a hidden button he pushed when he came and got us. It's low to the ground and blends in with the cement—we would've never found it without him." Some of Thorn's tension eased. "If we can pull the warriors away and slip in via the bedroom undetected, it could work."

"That's our tentative plan, but you should talk to the queen tonight." Cassidy frowned. "See where Drake is staying and where she thinks he might go."

"Do you want me to call in some people to help us?" Spike lifted a brow as he removed the meat from the grill and put it on a large plate.

We glanced at one another, and finally, Thorn said, "Only those you fully trust and know are great fighters. We don't need weak fighters who will result in casualties just for numbers. Give brief details about a possible confrontation and tell them to gather near the royal dragon lands outside of Asheville."

Spike grinned. "I can do that." He glanced at the people working the other grills. "Is everyone finished cooking?"

He didn't need an answer because some were already carrying plates of food to the table, while a few others were removing the meat from the grill.

"Let's eat up." Spike beamed. "Get stuffed. We'll need the calories tomorrow."

"Thank gods!" Elliott groaned as he leaned against his mate. "I'm withering away over here."

Just like that, the tension was gone...at least while we were eating.

THE EVENING WAS ENJOYABLE, with all of us hanging around talking, knowing that tomorrow, everything would change for the better or worse. We took the moment to enjoy one another's presence. Elliott and Tyson complained about missing video games and how they had so much time to make up for, while the rest of us poked fun at one another over little things we'd learned from training.

Thorn and I were leaning against the trunk of a cypress, talking with Saphira, Wyvern, Eva, and Sol, when Spike sauntered over. He patted Thorn on the shoulder and slid what looked like a small box into his hand.

What's that? I asked, more curious about how Spike was trying to be sneaky.

Nothing. Thorn put whatever it was into his pocket with an evil smirk.

I arched a brow, not paying attention to the others. *Uh...are you keeping something from me?*

He laughed, his irises lightening. *Not at all. I just want to ask you something.*

I tilted my head back, my stomach squirming. *What's going on? Just ask.*

"Guys, I need time alone with Everly." Thorn took my hand and led me toward the woods.

Saphira called out, "Wyvern and I will need time for that, too, before the night's over."

I rolled my eyes. "We'll make sure to stay in the area. I don't want to chance smelling your brothel."

"You're just jealous you aren't the only two who smell that way now!" she shouted as we stepped into the thick woods.

I used to think she was horrible, but your brother has taken over that spot, Thorn connected as we leisurely strolled away from the others. *Now I find her slightly amusing.*

Elliott's large personality has a way of making others' seem less... aggravating. I leaned against his arm and listened to raccoons stirring, now that the sky was darkening. *What's going on?*

Patience, he said, and nervousness trickled between us. My mouth dried.

We hadn't been nervous around each other since we'd formed our mate bond, so this was throwing major red flags around. Wariness weighed on my limbs, and I didn't push any longer. Part of me was afraid of what came next.

We came to a clearing where wildflowers bloomed around a grassy knoll. He turned toward me, taking a deep breath. "I want to apologize for something. Something that was stolen from us that I can't fix."

I took a step back, wanting to retreat, but the intensity of his stare froze me in place. I asked the question because I didn't have any other choice: "What do you mean?"

CHAPTER TWENTY-FIVE

THE NERVES FLOWING into me through our connection had my stomach in knots. Add in the way Thorn's heartbeat increased, and my pulse thundered in my ears.

The battle was tomorrow, but why did I feel as if it might be right now?

"Hey." He smiled sadly and touched my arm. "You're not the one who's supposed to be nervous."

I laughed humorlessly. "Kind of hard when I can sense everything you're going through. What's wrong? Whatever it is, we can figure it out together." I needed him to confide in me, not leave me in the dark. This was worse than fighting an enemy.

"Ugh, I'm doing this all wrong." He dropped his hands, rubbing his palms against his jeans. Then he removed the box from his pocket and got down on one knee right in front of me.

I couldn't breathe. The anxiety coursing through us turned into something else...but I wasn't sure what. My heart squeezed as if it'd tripled in size and was about to explode from my chest.

"I know we're mated and married." He beamed, but sadness dark-

by both human and dragon standards, but our marriage was forced... taken out of our control."

Guilt settled hard. We'd gotten married to keep Drake from claiming me as his wife according to dragon law. I'd been upset, not because I didn't want to be married to Thorn but because someone else had planned the wedding on their timetable. It wasn't something Thorn and I had planned and celebrated ourselves, and we hadn't had a chance to argue about what font to use on the invitation or what Eva and I would pick out as my dress. Someone else had selected everything to their own tastes, and it was nothing we would've selected. "It's fine. I'm not upset about it anymore. You aren't responsible for *any* of that."

"No, but that doesn't mean I don't want to fix what I can—because *you're* worth it." He huffed and settled the box in the palm of one hand. "*We're* worth it."

He opened the box, and I saw three rings nestled inside. One was a diamond engagement ring that was simple and elegant, everything that represented us. It appeared to be a two-carat square-cut diamond with tungsten bands wrapped around one another. The band on top was covered with small diamonds, making it the same width as the central diamond before narrowing into a normal-sized band. The other two rings matched each other, with one slightly smaller that had to be mine. Both bands were tungsten with etchings that resembled dragon scales.

"Thorn," I breathed, a sob lodging in my chest.

"Most dragons don't give each other engagement rings, only wedding bands, but I wanted to do this for you. Though we'll take it off when we shift, in human form this feels right—to symbolize how we met but also to respect that for most of your life, you were human."

He removed the engagement ring, and I lifted my left hand so he could slip it on. Faint scales appeared as he slipped the ring on my finger, and a tear trickled down my cheek as I realized this ring was perfect for me. I connected, unable to speak, *I love it.*

Thank gods. He sighed and climbed back to his feet, removing the two bands and putting the box back into his pocket. "The wedding bands are to symbolize our dragon sides uniting as one."

My hands shook as he slipped the ring on.

"There. Perfect." He smiled as he came closer, the scales disappearing into his unblemished human skin, and he turned the ring to the side so I could see the engraving.

You Own Me

Unable to hold the sobs in any longer, I let go, my shoulders shaking and more tears trickling down my face. This moment was perfect, and even better, we were alone. No wedding could come close to this.

He'd moved to slip my wedding band on my finger when I croaked out, "Wait."

His alarm slammed into me, and his jaw clenched.

It was his turn to sweat, but only long enough for me to remove the engagement ring. I said, "The wedding band goes on first, then the engagement ring on top." He probably hadn't realized that since he was a dragon...and a man.

Relief flooded him, and he chuckled as he slid the wedding band onto my finger. "I was nervous there for a second."

I put the engagement ring back on, and the two rings perfectly nestled together. "You shouldn't be. You own me, too. And now it's *my* turn." I snatched his band from him, and my body tingled when I saw he'd put the same engraving on his.

I slid the ring on his finger and connected, *I do.* Dragon law could go fuck itself, for all I cared. I wanted to claim him as mine the same way he'd claimed me at the château.

You don't know how badly I needed to hear you say that. He leaned his forehead against mine, pulling me into his arms. *Hell, I didn't even realize I needed it.*

That was the thing about us. We knew what the other person needed, even if we were clueless. *Thank you for this. This means so much to me, and it's more perfect than any wedding ever could be. You and me alone, together, and having this sacred moment is more precious than any ceremony.*

You deserve it all. Adoration filled his face as he gazed into my eyes. *Every day, I need you to know you're more important to me than anything else. Even if we wind up running the kingdom, your happiness and your safety will always be my priority. Maybe it shouldn't be that way, but I wouldn't change it for the world.*

It might be selfish, but I wouldn't, either. *I feel the same way about you. I will always be on your side...against all odds.*

Oh, I'm clear on that. You wouldn't still be here if that weren't the case. He ran his fingers through my hair. *Tomorrow, when we take the throne, I want it to be clear that we belong to each other in every way possible. That we're a package deal. I'm not just taking over as king, but we're leading together to help our people and make things right in this world.*

My body heated at his touch and his words. I didn't know what I'd done to deserve Thorn, but I would never give him up. He valued me in all the ways that mattered: heart, body, soul, and mind. *I could be happy anywhere in the world as long as I'm next to you.*

He kissed me, the warmth of his love pouring into me. My tongue brushed his lips, eager to taste him. Groaning, he opened his mouth, and our tongues collided. He matched my every stroke, and his hand fisted the hair at the back of my neck, deepening our kiss.

But it wasn't enough.

I needed all of him.

Slipping my hand under his shirt, I traced the curves of his muscles. With each brush of my fingers, the sizzle between us increased as his abs constricted, driving me wild. The rest of the world disappeared, along with all the anxiety and drama. He was my drug, and I was addicted, needing him more than I'd ever needed anything in my life.

He tore his mouth from mine and kissed down my jawline and neck. I leaned my head back, giving him better access. He paused at the juncture of my throat and collarbone, right where my pulse pounded against my neck, grazing his teeth along it.

My dragon roared as my head spun. Though we'd already claimed each other, solidifying our bond, there was something so possessive in that action that I became a puddle in his arms. Mind fuzzy, I lowered my hands, fumbling to unfasten his jeans, *needing* to touch him.

He chuckled, low and throaty, feeling every ounce of my desperation. He moved me backward a few steps until the thick trunk of a tree pressed against my back, giving me balance.

Finally, I unbuttoned his pants and pushed them and his boxers down. He sprang free, and I wrapped my hand around him.

Gods, you drive me crazy when you get like this, he purred as he leaned back and removed the shirt from my body.

I moaned in protest until he covered me again. His hand slipped around my back and unfastened my bra in one quick motion. He tossed it so it landed close to my shirt, and I moved my hand, stroking him.

He hissed, his body shivering. My dragon growled in approval as I slowed my pace to drive him wild.

He lowered his head, his mouth capturing my nipple as he grabbed the band of my elastic-waist shorts and pushed them and my panties down. His tongue rolled across my nipple, and I leaned my head back just as his fingers slipped between my legs, circling.

The sizzle of our connection and the way his mouth and hands worked my body had pleasure swirling through me. He teased and tormented me until my stomach clenched, and I quickened the pace of my hand on him, wanting to work him into a frenzy.

He groaned and opened his connection to me further. I reciprocated, and our emotions and sensations merged, becoming one. The friction built in me, bringing me to the edge. His fingers quickened, and ecstasy slammed into me and our bond. My body shook as he didn't slow, freezing me in place and holding me at the mercy of his touch.

When the pleasure ebbed, a more desperate hunger took its place. That wasn't all I needed.

Clutching his shirt, I spun around and slammed him against the tree. I didn't try to be careful, just ripped the shirt off him. As the material revealed his perfectly toned chest, my body demanded another release, but with him.

I climbed him, wrapping my legs around his waist, and he sank right into me.

"You own me, Everly," he whispered, a hand cupping my cheek as he moved inside me. "All of me. Forever."

Rocking against him, I held eye contact. "I love you so much it hurts at times, and I'm so thankful I'm a dragon so I can experience every single one of those emotions."

He pressed his hips into me and rolled, forcing me to lean back, but I wanted to watch him as we made love.

Taking our time, we enjoyed the slow buildup. We'd done it slowly before, but this was extra special. Not only had we claimed each other, but we had rings that signified our bond. A piece to carry with us even when we weren't beside each other.

With locked gazes, we moved in sync, the friction building in us. I wrapped my arms around his neck, and we pressed our foreheads together, keeping our eyes on each other the entire time.

One of his hands cupped my breast as the buildup promised to explode, and when he gently ran a finger over my nipple, the orgasm rocked me. My body shivered as pleasure flooded between us, and the area around his eyes tightened. His mouth opened as his release joined mine.

Our breaths mingled as we watched each other come undone. The pleasure was constant and never-ending. We stayed that way, breathless, until our pulses calmed.

Then he kissed me...and I was ready to go again.

It was close to ten before we managed to stop touching each other. We'd had sex four more times, each time better than the last, but we had to get back and see what else our allies might have learned.

Begrudgingly, I put my clothes and shoes back on, and Thorn found his pants ten feet away in some brush. I wasn't sure how that had happened, but we'd had sex in a different position every time, so...yeah.

Thorn nodded toward the cabins, indicating he was ready to return, but all I could do was growl.

His brows furrowed. "What?"

"You're shirtless." I pouted. I didn't like the idea of anyone else—especially the women—seeing him like that.

Chuckling, he pulled me against his chest and kissed my forehead. "That's your fault. You ripped my shirt apart."

I extended my bottom lip out further, trying to prevent a laugh from escaping. It had been my fault after all. "Seemed like a good idea at the time...now I'm not so sure."

"Oh, it was a very, *very* good idea," he said as he nipped my bottom lip. "And sexy as hell. I like you that desperate."

My face flamed, but I didn't try to hide. Not with him. "Well, you, my dear, have a way of making me that way, and I'm pretty sure it won't ever change."

"Good." He sucked on my lip. "Because I need to work on my endurance. Five times just wasn't enough. I think one night, we need to see how many rounds we can go."

I moaned, already wanting to have sex again. "You'd better stop, or we'll be having another go right now."

His fingers dug into my hips. "Then let's—"

"You know we need to contact the queen," I interjected. If he finished that sentence, I would be naked again in seconds.

"Fine." He released me and took my hand instead. He connected, *Only because we need to make sure we're prepared for tomorrow so we can sex it up again.*

I laughed, knowing this moment of no stress would dissipate the closer we got back to camp. "Deal."

Hand in hand, we headed back, and when we reached the cabin grounds, everyone was still in the same area, but there were no smiles or laughter anymore, only serious and stern faces.

Saphira arched a brow. "You guys were gone longer than any of us, which is sad since you two were the first to leave." Then her eyes landed on my hand. "Oh, my gods. Did you exchange rings?"

Everyone turned to look at Thorn's and my hands, and Eva, Saphira, Cassidy, Hydra, Mindy, Kari, Chandra, and Reece hurried over and gushed. Normally, I wasn't one for attention, but in this instance, it didn't bother me. This was yet another way Thorn and I had claimed each other.

Let me go grab a shirt, Thorn connected as he sneaked away, happiness brightening his face.

When Thorn came back, we got serious.

Thorn informed us that the queen had answered. Drake had taken over the royal bedroom. She was staying in the bedroom all the way down the hall. Theron and Spike alerted us that they had reached out to the thunders they knew had fighting experience in the injured network to see if they would help. Many had said they'd try, but with such short notice, they weren't sure how many could come.

We'd done everything we could for tomorrow. The only thing left to do was get the best night of sleep possible.

We all went to bed, but even though I was cuddled in Thorn's strong, comforting arms, sleep eluded me.

I focused on closing my eyes...and enjoying his touch.

<hr>

My heart hammered. We were walking through the woods toward the royal dragon lands, having parked about twenty miles from the edge of the property in a public area humans used.

There were a hundred of us. Spike and Theron had hoped for

more, but we were running out of time, so they'd messaged their contacts, telling them where we were going in case more could come, though I wasn't hopeful. We had more than I'd expected, so I'd count that as a blessing.

Uther had said three hundred guards were watching the territory at all times and that Drake would be increasing that number by morning. Essentially, the closer to the coronation he got, the more guards he put on duty, but that was a good thing. That meant most of them wouldn't be well rested.

We'd split up to travel to avoid detection and had chosen a meeting place a mile outside of dragon lands. We needed to reach the edge of the property around midnight.

Thorn, Elliott, Mindy, Eva, Sol, Saphira, Tyson, Wyvern, Arrow, and I were traveling together. We walked in silence, trying not to rush. Drake's warriors would be watching for us in dragon form. Arrow had informed us that humans didn't come close to the dragon lands, likely deterred by the dragons' presence, but we had to be careful. These woods weren't technically part of the dragon lands.

As we neared our destination, trepidation surged through our group. Even when I thought about something else or concentrated on the feel of Thorn's hand in mine, my limbs grew heavier. We were heading into a fight against trained people who outnumbered us, but there wasn't a better option.

Though it'd been hours, it felt like we reached the meeting location in minutes. None of us dared to speak.

I laid my head against Thorn's chest, and his arms wrapped around me as we waited for our allies to arrive. Even Elliott didn't speak, his face pale, knowing what we were about to do. Not only that, but their father was likely with Drake.

Opal, Echo, and Fury would lead Kari, Chandra, Hydra, Errol, and Brenton. They'd take the right side of the château. Cassidy, Rex, Blaze, and Owen were in charge of the group that would attack from the left, which included Mindy, Eva, Sol, Elliott, and Tyson. Both groups would use a combination of bows and firearms. It would make it harder for the warriors to counter any of them since they'd have to deal with both bullets and arrows. The rest of us would attack down the center so they could follow and surround the château, hopefully catching Drake's warriors by surprise. We had daggers and would be fighting by hand or in dragon form. The few of us who'd trained regularly with firearms each carried a gun as well, including Vlad, Theron, Spike, a few others in his thunder, and me—just enough to throw Drake's warriors off balance.

Our warriors and Spike's group would be in dragon form to start, while the rest of us would stay in human form until we knew what we were up against. There was one hard rule: Thorn, Vlad, Theron, Saphira, Wyvern, and I would stay in human form to enter the château through the secret passage, which couldn't be done in beast form.

We got organized in silence since, this had all been agreed on before now.

Thorn and I took our position front and center. It had been a point of contention with the others, but we'd stood our ground. How could we expect any of them to participate in this fight if we weren't willing to lead the charge? It didn't seem ethical.

Are you ready? Thorn asked, taking my hand. We each held a dagger in our other hand. His anxiety mixed with mine, and I knew it had more to do with the possibility of me getting injured than the fight itself.

I needed to counter him with confidence. *Let's do this.*

Our group moved quickly and a lot less quietly. The dragons would know we were coming, so we needed to use surprise to our advantage.

We hurried onto the dragon lands, crossing the road that marked the territory. I could hear our people shifting into their dragons behind us, but from what I could tell, this area was clear.

Our group stood in the clearing, waiting for Drake's warriors. That was the plan—lure the warriors out so we could fight them here.

Time ticked by, and Vlad groaned. "They aren't coming," he

sneered. "They're making us come to them so they have the upper hand."

My heart sank. Of course Drake wouldn't let his warriors leave his side. He wouldn't want to risk his life, knowing we'd be desperate to get to *him*. But he hadn't accounted for one thing. Something that would bring him to his knees.

I turned around and scanned the group. "Who has a phone I can use to connect to the Dragonnet? I have an idea."

CHAPTER TWENTY-SIX

DRAKE'S EGO was his ultimate weakness, and I planned on using it against him. He had enough advantages over us—we needed to force him to send the warriors here.

"I do." Spike held out his phone. "I'm already logged in."

What are you thinking? Thorn asked and squinted at me like he was trying to see inside my mind.

You're going live on Dragonnet to tell the world we're at the château, about to attack, and that you're going to be king as your father decreed moments before death. I turned to him and looked into his eyes. I'd just called the king his father.

He flinched but recovered quickly enough, so I continued, *Ramble, do whatever it takes, but stick with that story. Make Drake lose his shit and want to shut you up, even if that means the warriors leave him to come here.*

His eyes twinkled. *You're brilliant and downright scary. Remind me never to get on your bad side.*

You'd better not. I arched a brow, enjoying his teasing. *Or you'll have more at risk than losing the crown.*

Before taking the phone from Spike, I lifted a hand. "This could put your whole thunder at risk. I want to make sure you've considered that."

"My presence here already does that," Spike countered, placing the phone in my hand. "It won't make a difference."

I took the phone, not having a rebuttal. That was true and one reason I didn't blame other dragon shifters for not showing up. If we lost, they, and potentially their thunders, would die for allying with us. They had just as much at stake as Thorn and I did.

I nodded because my throat was thick with too many emotions to express. These people believed in us, and all I could do was hope we didn't let them down. I reached for Mom's bracelet and our rings, none of which, of course, were there. They were all safely back at Spike's cabins so I wouldn't lose them during the battle. One day, I'd be able to wear all my precious jewelry without fearing I'd need to fight or shift.

Thorn took my hand and squeezed it comfortingly. *Let's do this together. If we make it through this, it'll be you and me leading our people.*

Part of me wanted to say no, that he was the one they needed to see, but it would infuriate Drake more if the woman he'd proclaimed as his was standing by his brother's side where she was always meant to be.

"Actually..." I handed the phone right back to Spike. "Will you record us?"

"You've got it." He lifted the phone. "Just tell me when you're ready. I'll use the king announcements hashtag to get the live stream on Drake's radar quickly."

"Use all you need." Thorn placed an arm around my waist, pulling me against his side.

We should've dressed differently for this, but we'd come here assuming the warriors would be eager to attack us. The possibility of us going live hadn't occurred to us, so we were wearing dirty jeans and black shirts to blend in with the shadows.

Even so, Thorn always held an air of power. His dragon was so damn strong, far stronger than Drake's, and that couldn't be ignored, even without being physically in Thorn's presence. His chiseled face was entrancing, and add in the light scruff that emphasized his strong features, and he was a highly arresting man... and all *mine.*

I, however, was a prime example of a hot mess. My hair was pulled into a low ponytail so it wouldn't get in my face when fighting, and I wore no makeup. Why would I for a war?

None of that mattered; this was something we had to do. Otherwise, we'd be walking into a slaughter.

Ready? Thorn connected and looked at me.

I was sure our height difference was comical, with him having almost two feet on me, but I loved how my head fit right at his chest. *As ready as I'll ever be.*

This was your idea. His chest shook. "All right, let's do this."

I inhaled to calm the stampede dancing on my heart. I'd been nervous going into battle, but not *this* badly, and I wasn't sure what that said about me.

"Rolling," Spike said as he pointed at us. All the others who'd followed us there moved back as if making sure they weren't in the frame. Those already in dragon form stayed on the road, waiting for instructions.

Sweat beaded on my forehead, and my heart pounded in my ears. Even deep breathing wasn't helping me.

Luckily, Thorn didn't miss a beat. "Most of you probably don't recognize me in my human form since my bro—" He stopped and connected, *I can't call him that.*

You only need to refer to King Arman and Queen Mira as your parents, I assured him. It didn't matter that he and Drake were related—it mattered that he was Arman and Mira's firstborn son. *And remind everyone that you're older.*

His unease ebbed. He cleared his throat. "Drake has played on repeat the time when I removed some of his warriors' dragons while desperate to save my *fated mate* from being forced to marry *him.*"

Anger roiled into our connection, and Thorn's breathing turned ragged.

I nestled my head against his arm to show the world I did so without being forced. I stepped in while Thorn recovered. "The only reason Drake wanted to *marry* me was that he knew Thorn and I were fated. He wanted Thorn to try to save me so he could capture and kill him. He wanted to put fear inside *you* so you would be easier to control."

Thorn found his voice again. "All of you thought I was dead. The truth is I went into hiding when I was six because of the fear that surrounded my powers. I stayed in hiding for the past twenty-one years, not bothering anyone until Drake had my adoptive parents kidnapped to force me to return." Thorn paused, letting the meaning of what he'd said settle over everyone. "I believe he did that because he knows I'm older, stronger, and the rightful heir to the dragon throne. I threatened his position."

A dragon roared miles away, from the direction of the château. The tension that had coiled in my stomach unraveled. Drake was watching. Now we had to get the warriors here.

"King Arman realized his error when he witnessed Thorn protecting a thunder that Drake was attacking," I continued. Now that we had Drake's attention, we needed to clinch it. "The king came to stop the attack and found us there. He realized Drake does not have the temperament to take over. He apologized to Thorn for allowing his fear to control him when it came to his own son, and he announced that Thorn was the rightful heir to the throne." I paused. "Drake killed his father on the spot."

More roars came from behind us, and the sound of wings flapping became louder.

The warriors were coming.

Thank gods. I hadn't been sure it would work.

"That's why my *mate* and I are here." Thorn gestured to our surroundings. "We're outside the royal dragon lands, ready to face my brother." An icy feeling of disgust swirled through our bond at that word, but he continued without missing a beat. "I'm here to fight for Everly's and my freedom, and for every single one of you. One of the last things my father said was for me to take the throne, and I will do everything in my power to respect that wish."

Though my back was turned to the approaching dragons, I knew the moment they arrived. There was a shift in the people behind Spike, who tore their gazes away from us and into the sky.

Vlad lifted a dagger as the dragons on our side flapped their wings and ascended.

It was time to fight.

"No matter what happens tonight"—Thorn's jaw clenched —"know that being different doesn't make anyone inferior. Protect one another, stay loyal, and remember to love one another."

Our dragons flew overhead, racing toward the oncoming warriors. Thorn and I turned to see what we were up against.

At least fifty dragons flew toward us. They hadn't bothered to come in human form, which meant more of our people needed to shift. Our arrows and bullets wouldn't severely injure them, although they would annoy them. We'd planned for this, knowing most of us would need to shift at some point.

Come on, Thorn connected to me, tugging me toward the woods. *Let's move.*

I glanced over my shoulder, searching for Vlad, Saphira, Wyvern, and Theron. They were supposed to come with us. Everywhere I looked, I saw humans shifting into dragons, blocking my view.

I can't find our team, I replied as I tried to keep up, despite glancing behind us.

Saphira and Vlad know where the rock is. Thorn kept pushing forward. *They'll be rushing there, the same as us.*

That was one thing we'd agreed on. It was inevitable that the groups would split up, and we were to move forward as planned. I hated the thought of only a handful of us running together in case of an attack, but we needed to take advantage of the smaller warrior numbers.

We jogged through the clearing as a burnt orange–scaled dragon swooped down, going for Thorn. My mate released my hand to battle the dragon, and I noticed four others peel away from the herd and fly toward us.

They'd wasted no time locating Thorn, which was why I'd wanted the others with us.

Get to the secret passage, Thorn connected, as the burnt orange dragon expelled flames at him.

Although I knew the flames wouldn't hurt him, acid churned in my stomach as this asshole went after my mate. *You thinking I'll leave makes me wonder how well you know me.*

With my right hand, I pulled my gun from its holster, and with my left, I gripped my dagger. I didn't hesitate; I aimed the gun at the burnt orange dragon's closer eye and fired. The bullet hit its mark, and the dragon's fire fizzled out immediately as its body dropped to the ground.

Our warriors had taught us three spots to aim for on a dragon: the eyes, the nose, and the small area where its jaw and neck connected. The eyes and nose were a dragon's most vulnerable points, and striking them would cause actual damage. The small area between their mouth and throat would sting but wouldn't take them down. Everywhere else would feel like a bug hitting them—annoying, but it wouldn't hurt.

Thorn moved closer to the dragon, his skin flushed from the flames, but the other four were almost upon us.

I'll take the navy and scarlet dragons. Swinging my gun toward the larger scarlet one, I shot at its nose. Thankfully, my aim was good, and the scarlet dragon let out a horrifying screech as it plummeted.

The oncoming attackers took note, and I knew without a doubt that I wouldn't have such an easy time taking them down.

Gunfire erupted behind us, along with the sound of arrows whistling through the air. As more wings flapped, my jaw clenched more tightly. Both sides were engaged, and we were officially at war.

I kept my eyes locked on the approaching navy dragon, who'd been joined by a mustard dragon and a violet dragon.

I lifted my gun, and the dragons zigzagged so I couldn't get a clear shot. They weaved around each other, making their pattern random. I didn't want to waste bullets and miss my mark, so I held my fire.

The violet dragon cawed—a sound I'd only heard from a bird before—and the three of them straightened and dropped.

All three targeted my mate as if I were of no consequence. I'd show them they shouldn't underestimate me.

Extending its talons, the violet dragon went for Thorn's shoulders, while the other two aimed for opposite sides of him with their huge mouths wide open. Drool dripped from their sharp, jagged teeth as if they were looking at their all-time favorite snack.

I focused on the navy dragon first.

Thorn's magic thrummed through our bond, and his hands glowed. He planned to strip the violet one of his dragon by grabbing its talons. He'd done it before.

Running away from him, I stretched out my arms, keeping them steady. I aimed for the navy dragon's soft spot near the throat, going with my gut and firing. The bullet went into the dragon's mouth and hit the back of its throat. Its mouth clamped shut, and it whimpered. Unlike the other two, it pulled away and flew back toward the château.

Pivoting, I was about to shoot the mustard dragon when a dark brown dragon hurtled in front of me a second before I pulled the trigger, steamrolling the violet dragon deep into the woods.

Thorn forward rolled, his body disappearing a second before the mustard dragon's teeth gnashed right where his torso had been.

That was too damn close for comfort.

An arrow whizzed across the clearing and lodged in that vulnerable spot near the mouth and throat of the mustard dragon. It threw its head back, roaring, but Thorn and I didn't waste time watching to see what would happen.

We took off running.

More dragons would be coming, which was what we wanted, but our people wouldn't last forever. We needed to get to the château, find Drake, and kill him.

As we reached the first stand of thick red cedar and oak trees, Thorn and I turned around.

The fight was brutal, despite our having greater numbers. Obviously, Drake's warriors were better trained, but so far, we were holding our own.

More are coming, Thorn connected, pulling me back to the present.

Now that he mentioned it, I could make out the sound of dragons flying this way. I forced myself to turn around and take off deeper into the woods, with Thorn keeping pace beside me.

Even in the woods, the dragons would sense us, but they wouldn't know who we were until they reached us. Hopefully, most would assume Thorn and I were with the others.

We picked up our pace, and for once, I didn't feel completely winded. All that training was paying off because it didn't use to take much for me to get a cramp in my side. My lungs filled easily, but I wouldn't celebrate my new fitness achievements until this was over.

Two dragons darted toward us from between the treetops. They must have peeled off from the main group to deal with us. The magenta dragon had its gaze on me, but it shifted its attention to Thorn, as did its lavender dragon friend. Why were they ignoring me? The likely reason had a chill running down my spine.

Drake didn't want me hurt. He still wanted me by his side.

Keep running, Thorn connected, taking my arm and pulling me along beside him. *The entrance is just up ahead.*

He was right. With two dragons chasing us, maybe no one else would join them. If we could drive them off, we could safely hide away.

I tapped into my dragon, and she pushed me forward. In the distance, the hill with the fake rock entrance came into view, and I pushed harder. The sound of the wings was right behind us.

Spinning, I raised my gun and aimed at the dragon's nose, but as soon as I pulled the trigger, the dragon lifted higher, and the bullet hit its neck and bounced off. The dragon scoffed.

The magenta dragon turned its creepy white eyes on me, suddenly deciding to attack. It made a clucking noise, and then the lavender one focused on me as well.

They sped across the last remaining feet toward me, and Thorn snarled at my side. As I readied myself, he jumped in front of me.

No! He didn't have time to fight them off, either.

He was going to die.

THORN'S MAGIC flared through our connection as his hands glowed, but they were on us. He reached for the dragons, and they jerked back out of reach. They darted into the air, preparing to descend on him again.

Wheezing, I gripped my dagger, ready to cut an asshole, when the magenta dragon's head jerked toward where the rest of the fighters were.

The lavender one darted over Thorn's head toward me. I held my dagger close to my side so the dragon wouldn't see it. I would wait until the last possible second to reveal my hand after stumbling and making it think I was frozen in fear.

Unfortunately, I didn't have to act. This entire battle scared the shit out of me. There was so much more to lose than just our lives. The future of our people was at stake.

Thorn snarled as the dragon floated just out of reach of his white-glowing hands and dipped down, its talons extended toward me. Then I realized what was going on.

They were going to take me to Drake.

I'd rather die than be back at his side.

Get down, Thorn connected.

Gunfire pelted the magenta dragon, and rushing footsteps came closer. It had to be someone we were waiting on.

Sharp nails dug into my shoulders, and I swung my dagger, ignoring the agonizing pain. Thorn spun around, but the mark was made. The dragon flapped its wings, jerking me backward.

My dragon roared inside as I slammed my dagger into the top of the lavender dragon's talon. It shrieked but maintained its hold on me with its uninjured talons, lifting me higher. I drew my gun and leaned back, aiming for where the jaw connected with its neck. If it released me and I fell on my back, it might hurt, but I'd be out of its grip.

I fired, hitting the spot, and the dragon screeched.

The dragon and I dropped.

I closed my eyes, bracing for impact, but something hard slammed into me, and soon, I was hugged against a strong, masculine chest as someone ran with me in his arms.

Between the scent and the buzz, I knew without a doubt who my savior was—Thorn.

Something crashed, and over Thorn's shoulder, I saw a large lavender tail barreling toward us.

Watch— I started, but that was all I got out.

The tail slammed into Thorn. His upper body crashed on top of my left side, knocking the wind out of me. My lungs burned as I tried to suck in oxygen.

I'm sorry. He groaned as he rolled off me and onto his feet.

Not your fault, I replied as I sucked in a huge breath. *You caught me. It would've been worse if I'd hit the ground from the fall.*

The thrumming sensation in our bond flared, and his hands glowed as the lavender dragon huffed and whipped its tail at us again. Thorn raised his hands and caught it. Gripping the tail, he clenched his teeth and pulled hard on his magic. *Get out of the way in case I can't hold it for long.*

I climbed to my feet, ignoring the sharp pain in my ribs, and moved several feet back. The dragon whimpered as its body shrank. It was losing its strength, which meant Thorn wouldn't be struggling for much longer.

Glancing toward the magenta dragon, I noted Vlad, Theron, and Wyvern surrounding it with their daggers lifted. Saphira stood several feet away with her gun aimed at the dragon. The dragon hunkered down, blood pouring from one of its eyes.

Saphira had taken a shot. The dragon shook its head, whimpering as it flailed its legs and tail around to protect itself. If Saphira shot at it again, she'd have to aim close to Wyvern. She wouldn't chance hitting her mate.

I had a clear view of its nose, but I didn't want to chance Wyvern or Vlad getting in the way of a bullet, either.

I glanced at the lavender dragon. Its scales were fading to reveal a woman with long orange-red hair. It wouldn't be much longer until her dragon was completely gone, and she'd be permanently human.

I'm going to help the others, I informed Thorn, and took off with one target in mind.

Displeasure washed through our bond, but Thorn replied, *I'll be there in a moment.*

The magenta dragon shook its head from side to side and rolled around to keep Wyvern, Theron, and Vlad from reaching its face. Luckily for me, the eye nearer me was the bloody one, but it would sense me sneaking up on it.

I focused on moving swiftly but quietly. When I got within ten feet of the dragon, it sniffed, and I froze.

It jerked its head to the side so its good eye could see me while smoke trickled from its nose.

I had to move fast before he blasted me with fire. I lowered and tapped into my dragon, then ran toward it as quickly as I could. As soon as I was within striking distance, Thorn yelled, "Everly! No!"

The dragon opened its mouth, and flames encompassed me. My skin heated, and the fire swirled down my throat. Though it didn't feel as if I were being burned alive, the fire rubbed painfully against my skin. The closest sensation I could compare it to was when I was younger and a friend had gripped my arm with both hands and turned them in opposite directions. I hadn't expected it to be this painful—no wonder Thorn had yelled.

Gritting my teeth through the agony, I focused on putting one foot in front of the other. The closer I got to its mouth, the rawer my skin felt. The blast threatened to trip me backward, and I couldn't sense anything other than the flames crackling in my ears and the intense stench of brimstone.

When the roar of the fire and the scorching heat melded together, I had to trust I was at its mouth. I leapt, sweeping my dagger up, the flames burning under my arms, and swung down hard.

The flames vanished, and I was thankful for the fireproof dragon spray that we'd soaked our clothes in earlier. The wind rushed in the opposite direction, toward the dragon. Then there was an agonized scream.

When the air stilled and my hair blew out of my face, I found that I'd stabbed the dragon's tongue. I yanked the dagger out and swung again to make sure the jackass stayed down for the count. I wouldn't let any of my friends get hurt if I could help it.

Everly, move, please. Thorn's magic swirled through our connection. *I'm taking his dragon, and I don't want to risk affecting you.*

We both knew that likely wouldn't happen. He hadn't been able to remove my dragon when he'd tried to take it back, but I didn't want to take a chance. Not anymore. I wanted to remain a dragon shifter and be with my mate as an equal in all ways.

Stumbling back, I inhaled heavily, the pain still affecting me.

Saphira ran to me and threw her arms around me. I winced from the discomfort.

"What's that for?" I asked through gritted teeth.

"I couldn't shoot at him, and that dragon was getting its bearings." She dropped her arms. "If it weren't for you, one of the guys would've gotten hurt. But..." She paused and put a finger in my face. "Don't ever do that shit again, or you'll be hurting worse than a burn right now. I love you."

"I love you, too, and I wanted to make sure no one got hurt." I glanced at the former lavender dragon, now a girl passed out cold on the ground. Her breathing and heart rate were steady. Her skin was pale with freckles all over her body, so I was certain that was her natural skin tone and not from the trauma.

"That's so freaking crazy to see in person," Wyvern rasped as he joined Saphira.

We needed to get into the tunnel. The magenta dragon was already halfway back into its human form. The scales disappeared, revealing a naked middle-aged man. His eye was still bloody in human form, and my stomach roiled. But he'd attacked us. We'd had to protect ourselves.

I'll take Saphira and Wyvern into the tunnel, I informed Thorn. *Join us as soon as you can.* Vlad and Theron could keep an eye out until all three of them could come.

Sounds good, he answered, concentrating on his task.

I rushed over the slight rocky incline and went to the boulder that blocked the entrance to the tunnel. I reached around it, searching for a latch.

"Let me," Saphira said as she bent next to me. "I watched Vlad do it when we came to rescue you."

That hadn't been long ago, but it felt like ages. So much had changed between now and then, yet we were back here, right where Thorn's entire existence had started—at the royal château.

She dug her fingers into a small crack between the boulder and the one next to it and gritted her teeth. Something clicked, and when she removed her hand, her fingers were bleeding. She put them in her mouth before she dropped them. "There," she mumbled.

Wyvern growled and lifted the lid a little too roughly, as if to make the entrance pay for injuring his mate. I mashed my lips together, trying not to smile. That would only aggravate him further.

"Go on down." I gestured to the small makeshift ladder cut into the concrete. "I'll get the others."

Nodding, Saphira went down first, with Wyvern following right after.

I scanned the area to make sure no one else was approaching. Glancing at where Theron was standing, I saw the former magenta dragon in human form, lying very still on the ground.

The injuries he'd sustained had taken his life in human form.

Thorn's face was etched in agony. He knew that taking the man's dragon had led him to that fate, and his regret swirled into me.

We've got to go, I connected, afraid to speak out loud in case others in dragon form were close enough to hear us.

That was enough to snap Thorn out of his daze, and he waved Theron and Vlad toward me. They didn't hesitate.

I kept watch as Theron went down the ladder, but then Vlad pointed to me, then Thorn and the hole. He wanted to go down last, and I wouldn't argue. We'd already had the door open for far too long.

I lowered myself and jumped to the bottom. When I landed, my feet stung, but nothing like the burn still lingering from the dragon's fire. Thorn followed suit, jumping down after me, and a shiver ran along my spine.

I hated being down here. The area was just big enough to walk into upright, about ten feet wide and twelve feet tall, but the cobwebs throughout had me wanting to get out of there. I could hear the rats scurrying away from our feet.

Lovely.

There was no light in the direction we were going, and it was already dark here since the sun had gone down. But that wasn't a problem, as we were all dragons. None of us spoke until Vlad had climbed halfway down the ladder and shut the door. When it snapped closed, dirt trickled down into Vlad's and Thorn's hair.

Part of me relaxed, while another side tensed even more. This was the beginning of the end. We'd made it here, but the next stop was inside the château, where we had to face Drake.

It wasn't that I feared him but more that I couldn't stand the power he had over us. He was cruel, smart, and unpredictable, and he made me feel downright icky. The memory of his onion breath when he'd forced a kiss on me would haunt my nightmares forever, and I hated that he would always have that over me.

"How's everything going with the others?" Saphira whispered as she leaned against Wyvern's arm.

Vlad and Theron were the only two who could tell us, since their mates had stayed behind.

"They're holding on, but only because more people showed up to fight." Vlad's jaw twitched. "We need to move quickly. The new dragons are mostly untrained, and there've been some deaths on our side." He nodded toward the other end of the tunnel.

Theron ran a hand through his hair. "From what Hydra can guess, about fifty more showed up with weapons."

Surprise filtered through Thorn. "Every person helps."

How I wished we could've found more people and trained them, but we'd been on borrowed time. I was thankful more had come to fight alongside us. "That's because they believe in *you*."

No, they believe in us. Thorn took my hand and tugged me to the front of the group, squeezing past Saphira and Wyvern.

We led the way toward the other end at a rigorous pace. The stagnant, dank air had us moving more slowly than normal, even though we were supernatural.

"This is creepy as hell but an effective secret weapon," Wyvern mumbled.

"No one but the king knew about it, so it's safe to assume we've used it more than anyone," Thorn answered without breaking his stride. *When we get there, I need you to promise you won't run into danger if something happens to me.*

My breath caught. *Only if you make the same promise to me.* I looked at him, slowing slightly, raising an eyebrow. *As long as you make that promise, I might consider returning the favor.* I smiled sweetly.

He scowled. *That's different. He wants to take you as his wife.*

And he wants to kill you.

Death is better than the future he wants for you. His jaw clenched as his pupils slitted.

He had me there, but that didn't mean I would agree to his asinine request. *Doesn't matter. Life without you would be agonizing, so I'd rather keep you alive.* Especially a life where he was gone and I was Drake's *wife.* The thought had a cold settling deep into my bones.

The end of the tunnel approached, and with each step we took, Thorn oozed more frustration. He didn't like that I wasn't agreeing, but he shouldn't have expected anything else.

Drake is focused on both of us. I slowed as we reached the end. *And we're a team, right? As long as we work together, he can't touch us. So stop with the overprotective fated-mate act because I want to be the same way. As long as we trust each other to do what's best for ourselves and our people, we'll know we did our best.* I wanted to assure him that everything would work out, but I didn't know that. I'd had the same belief when it came to Mom and her illness, and I'd seen how that had ended.

Of course I trust you. He pivoted and pulled me into his arms. *I just don't want anything to happen to you, but you're right. If either of us made that promise, it would be a lie.*

You own me, forever and always. This almost felt like a goodbye, but I had to say it because the future was so damn uncertain.

His determination soared between us. *You know I feel the same way, but I won't say it. This is not how our story ends. I refuse to believe it.*

I heard Saphira and Wyvern kissing. We all knew what would happen next.

My skin sizzled from our touch, and Thorn kissed me. The kiss was full of promise...like he was forcing me to believe that everything would be okay.

I swept my tongue into his mouth, needing his minty taste to carry with me, and pulled away.

Vlad cleared his throat, and Theron, Saphira, Wyvern, Thorn, and I turned his way.

"Get your weapons ready." Vlad's entire body tensed. "There's no telling what's on the other side of that door."

The queen had confirmed that Drake was holed up in the royal bedroom. The windows had views of the front and the back of the house, which would make protecting him easy, but he didn't know about the secret passage in the wall.

"How many guards do you think he'll have there?" Theron held a dagger in one hand and a gun in another.

"Around five." Vlad held his weapons in his hands, too. "They'll be positioned everywhere, but we'll need to get him before other guards can get in the room. They'll be close by."

"All right." Wyvern held up his hands, ready to fight. "Let's get this done so we can save our people."

When Thorn noted we were ready to fight, he pushed the button...and the door slid open.

My heart dropped. Drake wasn't the only one surprised.

Thirty warriors turned toward us.

CHAPTER TWENTY-EIGHT

BOTH SIDES BLINKED at one another. We'd severely underestimated how many warriors Drake would have with him, but at least Uther, Jerry, and Gemma were part of the thirty. Hopefully, they wouldn't try to hurt us horribly...or at all. But a warning would've been nice.

The royal bedroom took up the entire side of the house, with three sections of windows that overlooked the backyard, the side yard, and the front. Five warriors were planted at each set of windows, leaving fifteen spread across the center of the room.

"Why didn't I know about that secret passageway?" Drake snarled as he rolled away from us across the gigantic gold-framed bed.

Move, Thorn commanded as he jumped into action, pushing two purple chairs out of our way. Vlad, Wyvern, and Theron were on his heels, springing into action.

Chaos ensued.

Ladon, Falkor, and Jessie hurried to surround Drake, their weapons at the ready. Falkor stood in front of Drake, not quite blocking him with his six-and-a-half-foot tall MMA fighter frame. His cobalt irises focused on us, and his pupils slitted, revealing his dragon.

"Warriors at the windows, stay put but fire at them if able. This could be a diversion. Everyone else, attack *him*." He gestured at my mate.

Nine warriors rushed us from all sides while Uther, Gemma, and Jerry paused near the dark cherrywood double doors.

Four warriors moved straight for Thorn, and the thrum of his magic took hold.

"Don't underestimate the others," Ladon shouted, and narrowed his ice-green eyes at my mate. He stood slightly behind Falkor and was smaller, but not by much.

"Do *not* severely harm the blonde," Jessie added, her short bleach-blonde bangs falling over her cinnamon-brown eyes.

One of the other warriors, a woman, hurried straight at me. She didn't pause as she swung a fist at my face. I ducked, and she hit only air. Grunting, she tried to correct her balance, but not before I slashed her neck with the dagger. Her eyes bulged as she clutched the wound, trying to stop the blood that oozed between her fingers.

My heart pinched in discomfort, but I didn't have time to acknowledge what I'd done.

I spun toward my mate in time to see him grip a warrior's arm. Thorn hadn't brought a gun, only a dagger, knowing he'd need to use his magic. Three other warriors attacked him from the front, back, and left. The one on his left sliced my mate's arm with a knife.

Thorn hissed as his dragon roared through our connection, and he released the man from his right hand, the magic sharply cutting off from inside. Whimpering, the warrior fell to the ground. I kicked him in the head as I jumped over his body to reach my mate. I aimed my gun and shot the warrior behind him in the chest.

The warrior fell back into the passageway from which we'd emerged, and I pivoted toward the warrior in front while Thorn spun around to fight the one who had cut his arm.

Another weapon fired, and Thorn dropped to the floor as a tranq dart whizzed over his head and hit the warrior I'd been about to face.

"Uther, Gemma, and Jerry!" Falkor shouted. "What the hell are you doing? Attack!"

Now that my opponent was down, I spun on my heels to find that the five warriors diagonal from us had turned in our direction, their guns raised. I clenched my teeth when I saw Uther, Gemma, and Jerry fire their weapons at the same five who were focused on us.

The other two warriors jerked toward the trio. They swung their weapons at them as the man on the outer edge screamed in anger or fear.

I fired my weapon at the screamer. My bullet landed right in the center of his eyebrows, and his body dropped.

As I prepared to take out the second one, sharp pain exploded in my right shoulder. I pushed through it, pulling the trigger, needing to help Uther and the others. All I managed to do was strike the second warrior's arm.

My shoulder felt as if it were covered with flames, and I glanced down at my injury. Luckily, it was a bullet wound, not a tranq. I'd be fine, but blood soaked my shirt.

"Do *not* hurt her," Drake screamed, and smacked Falkor in the back of the head. "I need her well so we can marry tomorrow during the coronation."

Falkor flinched, his body turning rigid. "She's killing warriors! I had to do something."

"Tranq them!" Drake spat.

Crazily enough, I was Drake's weakness...or rather, his obsession to have me was. Vlad rushed past me, focused on the warriors at the windows on the left, overlooking the front of the château, now that our warrior allies and I had eliminated the ones watching the backyard. Uther and the others raced to help him. We had thirteen warriors against our eight. Way better odds.

Falkor lifted a radio. "We need backup, *now*. In the king's chambers."

My heart dropped as Vlad said, "End this."

Out of the corner of my eye, I noticed Theron, Saphira, and Wyvern charging at the warriors at the windows past the bed.

We need to go for Jessie, Falkor, and Ladon, I connected with Thorn.

Just as I said that, all three of them lifted their tranq rifles at us.

Take cover under the mattress, Thorn connected.

Following him, I leapt to the side of the mattress and ducked, evading two darts flying over our heads by mere inches. If we hadn't moved, we'd have been knocked out cold in seconds.

"Shit, my gun is jammed," Jessie croaked, her fear leaking through.

"Stay with Drake," Falkor commanded as his footsteps stomped our way.

Then the bed dipped. The two of them were coming at us from both sides since the bed frame abutted the light gray wall.

Roll under the bed and hide. You're hurt. I'll take the two of them, Thorn connected, his own pain, stress, and anxiety swirling through the connection.

You are, too. You were stabbed, remember? Pretty much the same thing, I replied, refusing to budge. Since I was on the side further from Falkor, there was only one thing that made sense. *I'll take Ladon.*

Before he could argue, I jumped to my feet, Thorn's displeasure washing over me. Ladon was at the edge of the bed, and he startled back at my sudden appearance. I swung my dagger and stabbed him in the shoulder. Somehow, I hit the same area on him as the bullet had hit me, so we had almost identical injuries.

He grunted and fell backward as I heard Thorn make his move. As I leapt to the edge of the mattress, Ladon was getting back up. My dagger was still stuck in his shoulder, and I didn't have time to aim before shooting, so I reached up and gripped the bronze chandelier hanging over the bed. As soon as my body weight pulled on my shoulder, sharp, throbbing pain blossomed. My vision darkened at the edges, but I tapped into my dragon, using her strength to swing my feet into Ladon's chest. I made sure my foot hit the dagger protruding from his shoulder so it went deeper.

He stumbled backward, his feet tangling in the white comforter, and fell off the side in front of Jessie and Drake.

The fated-mate bond thrummed to life, informing me that Thorn was using his magic, which gave me some confidence.

I dropped onto the mattress, ready to take on Jessie and Ladon, when the sound of more guards approaching turned my blood cold.

Backup was here, and we hadn't secured Drake.

Grunts, gunfire, and punches echoed around me, but I couldn't lose focus. Not when so much was at stake. I dropped in front of Jessie, my gun aimed at her, but someone caught my legs. I crashed onto my stomach and looked down to see Ladon with his arms wrapped around me.

Drake laughed maniacally as Jessie swiped the gun from me and dragged me to my feet. She was stronger than me and easily forced my hands behind me, my shoulder smarting the entire time. A whimper escaped, despite my best efforts, and my vision blurred. *Jessie has me.*

I blinked, trying to clear my vision, and took in the room. Thorn had Falkor, his hands glowing brightly as the man tried to get away from him. Saphira and Wyvern had been tranqed. She was a lump on the ground, with Wyvern lying over her, protecting her from more darts. Theron had been detained by two warriors gripping his arms, while Vlad, Uther, and Gemma were facing the door. Jerry had been tranqed, along with the other five warriors they'd been fighting.

Releasing Falkor, Thorn turned to me, not worrying about the door. He growled, "Release my *mate*."

"Don't worry." Drake sneered. "She won't be your mate much longer." He pointed at Thorn. "Someone shoot him."

The bedroom doors burst open as Ladon clambered to his feet. Queen Mira entered the room with ten warriors following close behind her. Her striking baby blue eyes were devoid of the kindness that usually filled them, and her dark chocolate hair had been pulled haphazardly into a bun. She wore a long silk gown, but that was the only semblance of the queen I'd met not too long ago. Her gaze landed on Thorn as Ladon yanked the dagger from his shoulder, then lifted a gun with his uninjured arm. He stood just a foot away from me.

"Do *not* shoot him," Mira commanded, her jaw clenched and anger shining through.

Drake growled, "Get out of here. You have no business here."

"*I* am the *queen*, and you're still a *prince*." Queen Mira lifted her chin in challenge. "Until you're crowned, I'm in charge."

The ten warriors behind her charged into the room, two of them heading to Theron, their guns aimed at the men who'd detained him.

"Ladon, shoot him," Drake seethed. "Don't listen to the mumblings of a stupid *woman*."

That wouldn't happen. *Thorn, get ready.*

Everly, don't do— he started, but it was too late.

I leaned back, my shoulder searing in pain, and kicked Ladon in the side. Thorn roared as he vaulted over the mattress and landed right in front of Ladon, his magic churning as he ripped Ladon's dragon from his body.

Jessie released her hold on me, and I stumbled back and slammed into the wall. I hunched forward, ready to lunge at her as she attacked my mate...but something else happened.

Jessie turned her gun on Drake.

I inhaled sharply, trying to make sense of it. She was loyal to Drake. She was one with Ladon and Falkor. Why would she be helping us now? There had to be a catch.

"What are you doing?" Drake spat. "Take out the *abomination!*"

"No," she gritted. "He's not an abomination. *You* are. You killed the king, and he denounced you as the heir to the throne."

"You work for *me*." Drake smacked his chest, his face reddening. "Turn that gun on Thorn, or I'll make you pay."

Stepping forward, Uther straightened. "Your threats won't work on us any longer."

"What about your little girl?" Drake snarled, evilness etched all over his face and darkening his eyes.

Thorn dropped Ladon, and our connection went back to normal. "You won't harm her. She's hidden, and you won't ever find her."

Drake's nostrils flared even more. "It doesn't matter. I have others I'll take. People will *obey* me."

"Have you always been this way, and Arman and I were too blind to see who you really are?" Queen Mira's bottom lip quivered. "What have we done to instill so much hate in you? If anyone should be like this, it's Thorn, not you."

The hurt wafting from Thorn was worse than my bullet wound. I stumbled to him and took his hand, pushing my love toward him.

"Because I lived in his shadow," Drake hissed. "Everything you did was because of *him*. Even when I made you proud, there was sadness behind your eyes. I'm tired of it, and I deserve to *lead* and be the best king ever known!" Drake's chest heaved, and then he struck Jessie and reached for her gun.

The warrior ducked, countering the move, and when she rose again, she elbowed him in the nose. The pop of bone had Drake gripping his face, and Thorn released my hand, dodged Jessie, and launched himself on top of Drake.

Falling on his back, Drake moaned as Thorn straddled his waist and punched him in the face.

"You will *not* touch my *mate* ever again!" Thorn punched him in a rhythm. "You will *stop* calling her your *wife!*" And he jabbed again. "And *this* is for *kissing her.*" With each statement, Thorn hit Drake again and again. "And *this* is for looking at her *naked.*"

"Thorn, don't!" Queen Mira cried. She hurried to them and dropped to her knees. "Let him go."

The white-hot rage crackling through my mate was unwavering. All his anger and resentment was coming to a head, and Drake deserved every bit of it. Looking around, I noticed every warrior, along with Theron and Vlad, watching the scene unfold.

I cleared my throat. We needed everyone to get out of here and, more importantly, for the battle outside to end. "Someone tell the warriors outside to halt their attack! Drake has been captured and is no longer in charge."

One of the warriors who'd held Theron down glowered. "I don't have to listen to you."

Theron spun around, kicked the warrior in the face, and gritted, "Yes, you do."

"I'll handle it," Uther said.

I nodded, and he hurried out the door. I turned around and noticed how bloody Drake's face was. If Thorn kept it up, his brother would die.

Queen Mira continued to cry. She'd lost so much, and even though Drake was horrible, she didn't want to lose another son.

Knowing I was the only one who could get through to him, I squatted beside Thorn and touched his arm, hoping that it would be enough to make him pause. *There is a fate for him worse than death.*

He stilled, and his eyes turned to me. I sucked in a startled breath.

They weren't the eyes I was familiar with. They were dark, angry, and malicious...nothing like those of my mate...my husband.

Then I realized I couldn't just *try* to talk him into stopping. I had to succeed, or this might change him forever.

CHAPTER TWENTY-NINE

A COLD CHILL ran down my spine as the significance of this moment hit me. I pushed all my love and support toward Thorn, trying to break through to him the only way I knew how.

We shouldn't kill him.

His nostrils flared, and he shook his head. *That's not an option.* He turned to punch Drake in the face again, and instinct took over.

I leaned over Drake, blocking his face from Thorn's view with my own.

What are you doing? Thorn snarled, his chest heaving. He dropped his hand, and some of that anger faded into concern. *I could've hurt you.*

But I knew you wouldn't. I squeezed his arm softly, needing to take advantage of the moment. *If you kill him, it's the easy way out for him. You need to show our people that you have mercy but not forgiveness. That'll make you different from your grandfather and dad.*

Queen Mira sniffled but didn't say anything. I suspected she knew what I was doing, especially given the way I was protecting Drake.

What do you mean? The cold, distant part of him remained. He could snap in a second. *He deserves to die. After everything he did to you...to us...*

I know he does. I understood his reasoning, but that didn't make it right. *But he's out for the count and not attacking. Killing him would be no different from what he did to the injured. You'd be killing someone who can't protect himself. The warriors were different. They were attacking us.*

So we just...put him in prison and risk him escaping? Thorn's neck corded. *No fucking way.*

No, you take his dragon. With my free hand, I lifted his chin. *Then we use the story he and Peter gave the media about you kidnapping us. We blame them, find evidence that he has blackmailed and threatened people and killed your father, and expose my stepdad's fraud, landing them both in prison...human prison. Two birds, one stone...kind of. But it takes care of the accusation of you kidnapping us. There's no doubt Eva and Elliott will agree to correct that.*

He sucked in a breath, and his forehead creased.

What's a fate worse than death for Drake? I pressed. *He was determined to be the strongest dragon king imaginable and kill you because you're the rightful heir. That's been his whole goal. If we do this, he'll live as a human in human jail while you and I rule over our people. That's his own personal hell.*

There was silence for a moment, but when his irises lightened closer to their normal sky blue color, my lungs began working again. He was coming back to me.

For the record, I want to kill him. Thorn's jaw twitched. *I want him to die painfully, slowly, and to know it was by my hands. It scares the shit out of me that the desire is so strong. I'm not sure what to think of myself or if I deserve you.*

I know you want to. I do, too. I brushed the hair from his forehead and kissed the center of it. *He's an asshole and a complete waste of air. But we can't let him control us and make us into different people. That would give him power over us. Let's change it so he's miserable and hates himself for the rest of his very short existence. And this just proves that you* do *deserve me. You're this angry because of what he did to me, but you're listening to me when it's the last thing you want to do. If anything, I'm not worthy of you.*

He cupped my cheeks with both hands and kissed me. The all-consuming hate ebbed out of our bond as he connected, *I will always listen to you. You own me.* He pulled back, a twinkle in his now normal, breathtaking eyes. *And you're totally evil. You know that?*

I laughed, feeling completely carefree despite where we were. *Oh, I know. That's one reason you love me.* I straightened and glanced down at Drake.

His face was almost unrecognizable. One of his eyes was swollen shut, while the rest of his face was cut up and bloody. His white button-down shirt had blood spatter all over it, and there was nothing regal about him. He groaned in agony, and he turned his head and winced.

"Thorn?" Queen Mira's voice quivered.

Thorn and I knew what she was asking.

"I won't kill him, even though I *want* to." Thorn glanced at his cut-up knuckles. "But I will be taking his dragon and calling the police. My *mate* is right. He deserves to live out the rest of his life watching Everly and me lead and doing the opposite of what he intended."

"That's fair." The queen nodded and wiped the tears from her face. "Just as long as he lives."

"No," Drake groaned, his unswollen eye opening. "Kill me."

Thorn laughed humorlessly. *You were right, as always. He'd rather die.* Then he turned his head to Queen Mira and asked, "Where was that concern for me when I was six and hadn't done any intentional harm?"

My heart squeezed. "You gave the king his dragon back. It wasn't even a mistake since you didn't know what you were doing." I wouldn't allow her to accuse him of *any* wrongdoing, intended or otherwise, and I was glad Thorn was calling her out on her behavior.

Her mouth dropped open, and then she closed it, swallowing

hard. "It was a mistake. Losing you changed me in ways you'll never know."

That I could believe. Thorn was about to experience the same thing. The hurt emanating from him nearly shattered my heart, but now wasn't the time to dwell on it. It was time to step up. *Babe, we need to clean this mess up and check on the others.*

He tore his gaze from his mother and focused on me, our love flowing through the bond and soothing his pain a little.

He held his hands open, and the thrum vibrated through our bond as his palms glowed. He placed his hands on Drake's chest, and the sensation grew stronger, indicating he was pulling the magic from Drake's body.

A few of the warriors behind us gasped. Watching his hands glow had taken me off guard the first time, too, but not anymore. That was part of him, and eventually, no one would fear it.

Drake tried to push Thorn's hands away, but with the state he was in, he barely had the strength to move. Each time Drake did, he flinched, but with Thorn's magic pulling away his dragon, he must have gotten a second wind because he shifted onto his elbows and tried to yank his bottom half out from under Thorn.

My mate didn't budge an inch.

Trusting he had things under control, I stood and assessed the room. All eyes were on Drake and Thorn, but Uther had left to handle the fight outside.

"If anyone has reservations about following Thorn, you need to leave and find another place to live and work." One by one, I locked eyes with everyone in the room.

"What?" one of the men holding on to Theron asked. "You won't imprison us or threaten someone we love?"

The thrumming stopped, and Drake whimpered. Thorn stood and took the spot next to me, and I glanced over my shoulder to find Drake passed out.

Good.

"That isn't how my queen and I will rule." Thorn placed an arm around my waist as he addressed the room. "There will be laws that must be obeyed, but we will not blackmail or force anyone to work for us. However, if you maliciously break the rules or cause problems, we will lock you in prison without hesitation."

"But there will be repercussions if we leave," the same warrior insisted.

My throat constricted, and I leaned against Thorn for support. My shoulder ached from the bullet wound now that my adrenaline was wearing off, but it didn't compare to what all these people had gone through...what we *all* had been through due to Drake.

Thorn's hand tightened. *We need to take care of that. If the bullet is in there, it needs to be removed.*

I know. I'm a premed student, remember? I tried to tease, but the joke fell flat. The pain hadn't conveyed my humor at all. *Just reassure them, and let's get out of here.*

He nodded. "If you choose to leave your position as a warrior, there will be no repercussions. I want only people who are happy to protect my mate and me and who will find the position rewarding to stay on. There's no catch, but if you'll excuse me, I need to take care of my mate. She's injured and losing blood." He gestured at my shoulder, where my shirt was crimson.

"We'll handle it from here," Vlad assured Thorn. "And we'll find a room for Saphira and Wyvern until they wake."

For a moment, I expected the warriors to band together and prevent us from leaving, but they parted for us, and each bowed as we left.

***

I BLINKED A FEW TIMES, trying to believe what I saw in the mirror. It was ten minutes before the coronation, and two staff members had finished helping me into my dress, styled my hair, and done my makeup.

Like our wedding, it was a complete makeover. Unlike my

wedding dress, however, this dress was elegant but simple and far more my style. It was a flattering white, strapless dress with a sweetheart neckline and a gold wrap at my waist that blended with the gold-fitted skirt that brushed the marble tile. Silvery glitter dusted the gold, giving the fabric a regal sheen.

My blonde hair fell in gentle waves that complemented my features, and the makeup artists had used natural colors that brightened my eyes and complexion. They'd done an amazing job, including adding a slight red tint to my lips that I hadn't wanted, but I was glad I'd gone along with it. It added the right touch. I almost didn't recognize myself.

"You look gorgeous," Thorn murmured as he stepped behind me.

I smiled, my hand running over the ginormous marble sink in our royal bathroom. The very one that had been the king and queen's, then Drake's, before he was carted off to prison early that morning.

I turned from the mirror and scanned my mate. He almost didn't look like himself, either. He wore a fitted black suit with a white button-down shirt, a black vest, and a tie in the purple color of the dragon royal family. His normally messy hair was combed but not gelled into place, much to the hairdresser's chagrin. I wouldn't have liked it gelled, and I was glad he'd put his foot down.

In bed this morning, he and I had agreed that if we were going to do this, we'd do it with our own flair. We understood we had to look the part, but we hadn't been raised regal, and our reign would be about helping our people, not ruling over them. We couldn't lose the part of us that our people would relate to best.

"You don't look so bad yourself." I grinned, my body warming at his presence. "But seriously, this bathroom is so large, it's atrocious." I glanced at the marble tub behind him and the large rain shower to the right of it. The dual sink was as wide as the room, with more than seven feet between the two basins. To the right of the shower was a huge-ass walk-in closet where our clothes would soon be.

He waggled his brows. "We might not be too upset about it tonight when we get back to our room."

He picked me up and set my bottom on the marble counter, and my legs wrapped around him.

It'll be fun to make sure we violate every inch of this room and our new bedroom. His irises twinkled.

Warmth flared throughout my body. My dragon roared, not wanting to waste a minute before we got started. My human and logical side won out, but damn, it was hard...no pun intended.

A knock sounded on the bedroom door right before it opened. "Your *Majesties*," Elliott cackled. "Your fans await, and of course, Mindy, Eva, Sol, and I wanna escort you out in style."

Thorn tilted his head back and rolled his eyes. "You do realize you won't actually be escorting us outside, right?"

"Hey! Why not? My sister is gonna be royalty," he scoffed.

"Yes, Everly is." Mindy chuckled endearingly. "Not *you*."

I unwrapped my legs and realized the front of my skirt was wrinkled. I cringed. *I'm sorry.*

I'm not. His pupils slitted. *Anytime I have the opportunity to have your legs wrapped around me, they'd better be. I don't care if our clothes get wrinkled.*

My heart expanded. I loved him so damn much, it hurt.

He helped me off the counter, but when I started for the bedroom, he caught my hand.

Wait, he connected and tugged me toward him. *I want to give you this.* He reached into his suit pocket and pulled out the bracelet my mom had given me. I held my shaking arm out, and he fastened the bracelet around my wrist. "I figured we aren't in danger anymore, and since this is a special occasion, you might want to wear it."

My vision blurred. "It doesn't go with the dress." The white-gold bracelet with interchanging small hearts and diamonds and two dangling white-gold hearts—*Everly* engraved on one and *The love between a mother and daughter is forever* on the other—was more humble than dressy.

"It's perfect with your dress." He ran his finger across the hearts. "And fuck it if anyone disagrees. Their opinion doesn't matter."

A tear broke free, trickling down my face, and I truly understood, more than I'd ever thought possible, what he meant every time he told me these words... "You own me."

Hand in hand, we headed into the bedroom and outside to our people, ready to take the throne and crown that was rightfully ours.

THE CORONATION VIDEO played on repeat on the Dragonnet. Thorn, Saphira, Wyvern, Errol, Brenton, and I sat outside on the gray wooden terrace around a round glass table, a laptop open so we could scroll through the latest news as we ate breakfast. Thorn and I had our backs to the sunflower-yellow château, facing the massive back-yard where our wedding ceremony and coronation had taken place.

"This was the most attended coronation in dragon history." Errol mashed his lips together and smiled. "I'm so proud of you two."

Every time I saw the video, I got teary. More than five hundred people had crammed onto the château grounds to watch the cere-mony. When the news had spread that Thorn and I had taken Drake down and would ascend to the throne, people—especially the ones Thorn and I had helped—had shown up in hordes, driving all night, desperate to get here on time.

Wildflowers had lined the terrace where the ceremony took place. Errol had proclaimed us the new king and queen and crowned us with gold crowns designed in scales that matched our wedding bands. Then we'd stood and turned to our people, and the cries of joy still rang in my ears.

Most warriors had decided to stay on, but a few had left because Drake had forced them to be there. Not blaming them, Thorn and I had gladly seen them off. There were so many things Drake had done that couldn't be undone, but we wouldn't continue that legacy.

Speaking of Drake—he, Peter, Ladon, and Falkor were all in prison for numerous crimes and would be there for the foreseeable future. If the time came to release them, we'd cross that bridge when we got there, though none of them could threaten us anymore because they were no longer dragons.

The only downside of the situation was that Elliott and Eva had left. They'd even split up, each going to live with their fated mate's thunder. It made the most sense since their fated mates had loving, welcoming families, but they visited one week of every month, which was more than enough for us to get our fill of them.

Tyson had found his fated mate, too, one of Spike's thunder members. He'd wanted a fresh start and had left to live with her.

Though Theron, Hydra, Sol, and Eva had returned to their thunder, Wyvern had moved here with Saphira. Wyvern was the commander of the warriors, and Saphira had become my righthand woman. She was helping me locate all the shifters Thorn could heal. And of course, Brenton and Errol had taken positions as Thorn's and my chief advisors around finances and dragon affairs.

All the women we had protected had headed back to their thunders. As such, Jerry, Gemma, and Uther worked from their family homes, helping Wyvern, since Drake had forced them to relocate.

We decided to let Mira stay in what had been the guest house, the very one I'd been forced to stay in when I arrived. Thorn was slowly mending his relationship with his mother, though it would never be parental...more like close friends. I was glad he was trying; I never wanted him to have any regrets.

Cassidy and Vlad left to join Vlad's father's thunder. He'd lost twenty-one years with them, and now that Thorn wasn't in danger, it was time to mend their broken relationship. They didn't go long without visiting us.

"Well, that's one reason we're so busy." Saphira took a sip of her coffee while she scrolled through her notepad. "I'm scheduling a visit next week for a family that needs healing. What day works best for you two?"

I took a bite of eggs, and my stomach fluttered. I'd felt the same sensation last night, and it had caught me off guard. I swore I heard something softly beating in my stomach. I had to be imagining things.

But when Thorn's eyes bulged and he stared at my midsection, I knew I wasn't the only one hearing it.

Everly, when was the last time you had your period? Thorn glanced from my stomach to my eyes.

I pursed my lips. *Uh...over five weeks ago.* I dropped my fork, and it clunked loudly on my plate. I stared at him. *I'm never late.*

There was another flutter, followed by that fast, pounding rhythm. Like every time it fluttered, a heart worked harder...hard enough for us to hear what was growing in me.

He blew out a breath and smiled. *You're pregnant.* He jumped to his feet and lifted me from my chair, then turned toward the doors that led inside the château.

"Hey!" Saphira snapped. "Where are you two going? We're having a meeting."

"It can wait." He strode through the doors without pause and carried me upstairs.

The world passed in a blur as I locked eyes with him and murmured, "Where are you taking me?"

To our bedroom...to celebrate. He smiled. *Because we can finally be together without danger, and knowing our baby is coming makes me happier than I've ever been. I want to show you how much you own me.*

My body warmed, ready to show him the same thing.

He was right.

Nothing could get better than this.

ABOUT THE AUTHOR

Did you enjoy this book?
Please leave a review for it on Amazon.

Join Jen's newsletter to get exclusive content, enter giveaways, and receive free books and excerpts.

Join Jen's Newsletter here.

Follow Jen L. Grey on Facebook here.

Join Jen L. Grey's Facebook group here.

ALSO BY JEN L. GREY

Twisted Fate Trilogy

Destined Mate

Eclipsed Heart

The Marked Dragon Prince Trilogy

Ruthless Mate

Marked Dragon

Hidden Fate

Shadow City: Silver Wolf Trilogy

Broken Mate

Rising Darkness

Silver Moon

Shadow City: Royal Vampire Trilogy

Cursed Mate

Shadow Bitten

Demon Blood

Shadow City: Demon Wolf Trilogy

Ruined Mate

Shattered Curse

Fated Souls

Shadow City: Dark Angel Trilogy

Fallen Mate

Demon Marked

Dark Prince

Fatal Secrets

Shadow City: Silver Mate

Shattered Wolf

Fated Hearts

Ruthless Moon

The Wolf Born Trilogy

Hidden Mate

Blood Secrets

Awakened Magic

The Hidden King Trilogy

Dragon Mate

Dragon Heir

Dragon Queen

The Marked Wolf Trilogy

Moon Kissed

Chosen Wolf

Broken Curse

Wolf Moon Academy Trilogy

Shadow Mate

Blood Legacy

Rising Fate

The Royal Heir Trilogy

Wolves' Queen

Wolf Unleashed

Wolf's Claim

Bloodshed Academy Trilogy

Year One

Year Two

Year Three

The Half-Breed Prison Duology (Same World As Bloodshed Academy)

Hunted

Cursed

The Artifact Reaper Series

Reaper: The Beginning

Reaper of Earth

Reaper of Wings

Reaper of Flames

Reaper of Water

Stones of Amaria (Shared World)

Kingdom of Storms

Kingdom of Shadows

Kingdom of Ruins

Kingdom of Fire

The Pearson Prophecy

Dawning Ascent

Enlightened Ascent

Reigning Ascent

Stand Alones

Death's Angel

Rising Alpha

www.ingramcontent.com/pod-product-compliance
Lightning Source LLC
Chambersburg PA
CBHW020533310726
48979CB00014B/2320/J